American Star
&
Thrill!

Jackie Collins brings the wild and sexy world of super-stardom alive. Her phenomenally successful novels have made her as famous as the movers and shakers, power-brokers and superstars she writes about with an insider's knowledge. With 200 million copies of her books sold in more than forty countries, Jackie Collins is one of the world's top-selling writers. In a series of sensational best-sellers, she has blown the lid off Hollywood life and loves. 'It's all true,' she says. 'I write about real people in disguise. If anything, my characters are toned down – the real thing is much more bizarre.'

There have been many imitators, but only Jackie Collins can tell you what *really* goes on in the fastest lane of all. From Beverly Hills bedrooms to a raunchy prowl along the streets of Hollywood. From glittering rock parties and concerts to stretch limos and the mansions of the power-brokers – Jackie Collins chronicles the *real* truth.

Books by Jackie Collins

THE SANTANGELO NOVELS

Chances
Lucky
Lady Boss
Vendetta: Lucky's Revenge
Dangerous Kiss

Also by Jackie Collins

L.A. Connections
Hollywood Kids
American Star
Rock Star
Hollywood Husbands
Lovers & Gamblers
Hollywood Wives
The World is Full of Divorced Women
The Love Killers
Sinners
The Bitch
The Stud
The World is Full of Married Men
Lethal Seduction
Holywood Wives – The New Generation
Deadly Embrace
Hollywood Divorces

Jackie Collins

American Star
&
Thrill!

PAN BOOKS

American Star first published 1993 by William Heinemann.
First published by Pan Books 1993 in association with William Heinemann
Thrill first published 1998 by Macmillan.
First published by Pan Books 1998

This omnibus edition published 2005 by Pan Books
an imprint of Pan Macmillan Ltd
Pan Macmillan, 20 New Wharf Road, London N1 9RR
Basingstoke and Oxford
Associated companies throughout the world
www.panmacmillan.com

ISBN 0 330 44090 X

1 3 5 7 9 8 6 4 2

A CIP catalogue record for this book is available from
the British Library.

Printed and bound in Great Britain by
Mackays of Chatham plc, Chatham, Kent

American Star

In memory of my
husband Oscar

The shining light of my life.

PROLOGUE

December 1992

Today millions of fans across the world celebrate the thirty-fifth birthday of cult superstar Nick Angel, and the opening of his latest movie, Killer Blue.

A statement issued by Panther Studios disclosed that Nick will not be present at the Los Angeles première of Killer Blue *as expected.*

A personal spokesperson for Angel reported that the actor will spend his birthday in New York.

December, 1992
U.S.A. Today

Tuesday, December 15, 1992
New York

Mornings were always a bad time for Nick Angel. He lay in
bed, eyes closed, unwilling to surrender the peaceful darkness,
fighting the fact that he had to get up and face another day.
Especially this day. His birthday.

Thirty-five.

Nick Angel was thirty-five.

Jesus! The newspapers would have an orgasmic overdose on
this one. He was no longer the boy wonder. Age was creeping
up on him.

He lay very still. It was probably past noon, but the longer
he delayed getting up the better, for he knew that once he stirred
they'd be all over him. Honey – his live-in girlfriend. Harlan – his
so-called valet. And Teresa, his faithful karate champion assistant.

He heard a sudden movement in the room. A subtle rustle of
silk and the faint aroma of White Diamonds – Honey was a big
Liz Taylor fan. In fact Honey was a fan. Period.

So . . . why was he with her?

Good question. The problem was there were too many questions in his life and not enough answers.

Honey was on the prowl. Pretty blonde Honey with the
lethal body and vacant mind. He sensed her standing by the
bed staring down at him, willing him to wake up.

Too bad, sweetheart. Get lost. Not in the mood.

As soon as he was sure she'd left, he quickly rolled out of
bed and made it to the safety of his steel and glass high-tech
bathroom where he immediately locked the door.

Ah . . . Nick Angel in the morning. Not the man he once was, although still handsome in spite of ten pounds of excess flesh, bloodshot eyes, and an altogether dissipated demeanour.

He hated the way he looked. The extra weight he'd put on disgusted him. Had to stop drinking. Had to get his life together.

Nick Angel. Longish black hair. Indian green eyes. A pale skin, stubbled chin. At five feet ten inches he was tall without being overpowering. His handsomeness was not perfect. More brooding . . . mesmerizing. And in spite of being bloodshot his green eyes were hypnotic and watchful. His nose – once broken – gave him the dangerous edge he needed.

And now he was thirty-five.

Old.

Older than he'd ever thought he'd be.

But the world still loved him. His fans would continue to worship because he was Nick Angel and he belonged to them. They'd elevated him to a rare and crazy place where nobody could expect to remain sane.

It's too much, he thought bitterly, splashing cold water on his face. *The adulation, the never-ending attention. Crushing . . . stifling . . . suffocating . . . Too fucking much.*

He smiled grimly.

Welcome to the insane asylum.

Welcome to my life.

Reaching for the phone he buzzed the underground garage, connecting with one of his team of driver/bodyguards.

"I'm on my way down," he said, keeping his gravelly voice low. "Get out the Ferrari. No driver. And call the airport, tell them to have my plane ready, I'm taking it up."

"Right, Nick. Oh, an' happy birthday, man."

Screw this birthday crap. He knew he'd hear nothing else all day.

Finishing in the bathroom he dressed quickly in the trademark black he always wore. Pants, shirt, leather jacket and black tennis shoes. All he had to do now was make it out of the apartment before he was forced to endure more congratulations.

As soon as he hit the hall they came at him. Honey, all pearly teeth and rounded breasts encased in a pink angora sweater, her short skirt swishing sexily around her thighs.

Harlan – a crazed black man with wild hair extensions and subdued make-up.

2

And Teresa – who was six feet tall with a face like a man.

What a mismatched trio! But they were his. He owned them. He paid for every move they made.

"Gotta go," he said, edgily.

"Where?" Honey asked, thrusting angora clad tits in his direction.

"Where?" echoed Teresa, staring at him accusingly. "I should come with you."

"Yeah, where ya goin', man?" added Harlan, joining the chorus.

"I'll be back soon."

Maybe.

Maybe not.

Cleverly, he timed his words to coincide with the arrival of the elevator, and before they could nail him further he was out of there, downstairs, in his Ferrari, driving out of Manhattan as fast as he could.

It took him forty-five minutes to reach the private airstrip where he kept his two-engine Cessna plane. Several mechanics greeted him with birthday wishes.

Surprise, surprise. He'd known today was going to be a bummer.

He climbed aboard his plane, settled in the cockpit and guided the small aircraft down the runway until he was given clearance to take off into the unseasonably blue sky.

He sighed, a long heavy sigh. When did it all begin to get out of control?

Nick Angel.

Free at last.

But he had a solution. A plan he was about to put into action.

Colour me dead.

BOOK ONE

Chapter 1

Louisville, Kentucky 1969

"Do it!" the young girl gasped urgently, her breath coming in short frantic gasps. "Do it, *do* it!"

"I'm tryin'," Nick Angelo replied, heatedly. And indeed he was, but to his dismay the girl was so wet he kept slipping out.

Her voice was shrill and commanding. "Do it!" she insisted, wriggling back into position. "C'mon, Nicky. C'mon, c'mon, c'*monnnn!*"

Beginning to panic he jammed the point of entry yet again, and thank goodness managed to stay in place.

"*Uuuuuummm . . .*" The desperate shrillness faded from her voice and she began to sound pleased. "*Ooooooh . . .*" She continued to sigh sweetly as he pumped away.

Nick hung on, even though he was sweating and uncomfortable, but he hung on anyway because jamming himself inside this girl was the most important act in the entire world.

Vaguely he remembered one of his friends telling him sex was like riding a horse – mount up – get in the saddle – and take the trip.

Nobody had warned him it would be such a dangerous, hot, sticky journey.

And then it hit him. The most exciting, throbbing, out-of-control feeling he'd ever experienced. Holy cow! He was coming! And he was inside a real female – his hand and some dirty magazine had nothing to do with it.

The girl screamed out her satisfaction.

7

He felt like doing the same thing. But he was cool, a guy had to stay cool – even if it *was* his first time.

Nick Angelo was finally making out – and he couldn't think of a more mind-blowing way of celebrating his thirteenth birthday.

Evanston, Illinois 1973

"Please, Nick, *pleeease* . . . I can't take any more."

Maybe. Maybe not. But he'd been giving it to her for twenty minutes and she'd only now started to complain – although it was hardly a complaint, more an agonized cry of ecstasy.

"Ooh, Nicky, you're the best!"

Yeah? So he'd been told. Now if he could only teach them not to call him Nicky . . .

Making out was his specialty. It sure beat homework or any of that learning crap. And it certainly beat spending time at home watching his old man drink himself unconscious while his mother was out busting her ass working two jobs to keep the lazy slob in beer.

Family life. You could shove it. Just like he was shoving it up Susie or Jenny or whatever her name was.

One of these days he planned on taking off, getting out of this dump, and bringing his mother with him. But first he needed a job so he could score some bucks, then there'd be no holding him back.

Right now he was stuck in school because his mother thought education was important. Mary Angelo had this crazy fantasy that one day he'd get a scholarship to college.

Yeah, sure – a make-out college was the only place *he'd* get in.

Mary wasn't into reality – she was into dreams. At thirty-seven she looked ten years older. A bird-like woman – slight and nervous, with faded prettiness and wispy hair. She'd met Nick's father, Primo, on a blind date when she was sixteen and he was thirty. They'd gotten married exactly one week before Nick was born and Primo had hardly worked a day since. A carpenter by trade, he'd soon realized that picking up unemployment while sending his wife out to work was a far better deal than actually doing anything himself.

The Angelo family moved often, trudging from state to state, living in rented accommodations, always ready to be on the move whenever Primo felt that restless urge. And he felt it often.

Growing up, Nick couldn't remember being in the same town for longer than a few months at a time. As soon as he began to settle in they were on their way again. Eventually he gave up on any permanent relationships. New town. New girls to conquer. And on to the next. Now he'd gotten used to it.

"Can we go see a movie tomorrow?" Susie or Jenny or whatever her name was asked. "It'll be my treat."

"Nah." He shook his head as he got up, pulling on his pants. They were in the back office of a small car showroom – a venue he used often on account of the fact he sometimes ran errands for one of the salesmen, and in return he got to borrow the keys.

"Why not?" the girl asked. At eighteen she was two years older than him. She had short hair, freckles, and a well-developed chest. He'd picked her up the day before behind the counter of a Kentucky Fried Chicken outlet.

He tried to come up with a quick excuse. He excelled at sex. Hated to stick around. Past experience told him she wouldn't appreciate the truth. A screw is a screw – who needs it to be anything else?

"Gotta work," he said, brushing a hand through his unruly black hair.

"What do you do?" she asked, curiously.

"I'm an undertaker's assistant," he lied, straight-faced.

That shut her up.

He waited for her to adjust her clothing, even helped her up. Then he took her to the bus stop, left her there and walked the mile home.

Currently they were living in a run-down house with Mary's sister – his aunt Franny – a big woman with dyed yellow hair and a bleached moustache. It was only a small house, but as long as Primo had a television to watch and a plentiful supply of beer, he was satisfied.

Nick hoped Mary was home from work. If she was, there'd be a chance of something to eat. Franny never bothered to cook. She was on a diet of Reese's peanut-butter cups and diet soda – screw fixing meals.

Sure. Franny got fatter and everyone else starved to death.

9

Sex always made him hungry. Right now he'd kill for a hamburger, but he was broke as usual, so the only chance he had was working on Mary with his charm. Not that he'd have to do much work, his mother adored him, she put him before everyone, including Primo when she could get away with it, which wasn't often, for Primo demanded most of her attention when she wasn't working.

Nick's goal in life was to have as little to do with his father as possible. He hated the way Primo treated Mary. He couldn't stand listening to him bitch and complain about everything. And most of all he despised the way Primo sat on his big, fat can doing nothing.

The truth was that Primo scared him. He was a huge, overpowering man, and whenever he was in a bad mood Nick felt the back of his hand or the sting of his rough leather belt across his backside. Mary always tried to stop the beatings – protecting him as best she could – even if it meant getting beat herself. Primo didn't care who got in his way – he lashed out good.

Sometimes Nick wanted to kill him. Other times he accepted the beatings as a fact of life. The rage he felt was muted, buried. There was nothing he could do – not until he was older, then he'd get him and his mother out.

Halfway home it started to rain. Pulling up the collar of his old denim jacket he bent his head down and began jogging along the kerb, thinking about how great it would be to have wheels, imagining that one of these days he'd get himself a car – a gleaming red Cadillac with chrome wheels and a real fine radio.

Yeah . . . one of these days.

Primo was sitting on the steps outside Franny's house. Nick could see him as he approached. He tensed up, something was wrong. Why else would his old man have deserted his precious television and be sitting outside in the rain?

He approached warily. "What's up?" he asked, stopping and jogging in place.

Primo wiped the back of his hand across his nose and glared up at him, bloodshot eyes bulging. "Where've ya bin?" he demanded, slurring his words.

Nick felt the cold rain trickling down the back of his collar and he shivered – anticipating bad news. "Out with friends," he mumbled.

Primo heaved a mournful, beer-soaked sigh and hauled himself to his feet. His shirt was stuck to his body. His thick greying hair fell in greasy clumps on his prominent forehead. Raindrops continued to drip from the end of his nose.

"She's gone," he said, glumly. "Your goddamn mother went an' died on us."

Chapter 2

Bosewell, Kansas 1973

Lauren Roberts was sixteen when a man stopped her in the street and asked if she'd ever considered a modelling career. Lauren had laughed in his face. Who was this stranger? And why was he picking on her?

It turned out there was a film crew passing through town, an odd bunch of people. Lauren had been warned – along with everyone else in school – to have nothing to do with them.

When she got home she told her father.

Phil Roberts nodded sagely and said, "A pretty girl will always be bothered, but a wise girl soon learns to take no notice."

Lauren agreed. Pretty was one thing, but wise was better. Her father was smart. He'd always taught her that relying on her exceptional good looks to get by was a mistake. Being an A student was better. Getting good grades. Excelling at sports. Helping out with community service. And even though Bosewell was only a small town – population no more than six thousand people – there was always plenty of community service.

Lauren was certainly pretty. At five foot seven she was taller than most of the other girls in her class. She had long legs, a slender body, and her hair was thick and chestnut, falling beneath her shoulders, framing an oval-shaped face with expressive, long-lashed, tortoiseshell eyes, a straight nose and a wide mouth concealing a dazzling, heart-warming smile.

Lauren Roberts was one of the most popular girls in school, everyone liked her – even the teachers.

She was standing in the school yard with her best friend,

Meg, when Meg nudged her conspiratorially and whispered, "Here he comes. You'd better watch out!"

"He" was Stock Browning – Bosewell High's very own football star. Lately he'd been noticing Lauren in a big way.

Lauren frowned. "Shut up," she muttered, "he'll hear you."

"So what?" replied Meg, tossing her blonde curls. "I bet he's going to ask you out."

"No he's *not*."

"Bet he is."

Stock walked like a cowboy with a wide-legged rolling gait. His hair was white-blond and crew cut, and his eyes a teutonic blue. Big and tanned, he was well aware he could get anything or anyone he wanted. It helped that his father owned Brownings, the only department store in town.

"Hiya, Lauren," he drawled, stifling a strong desire to pat his crotch – snug in track suit pants.

It was the first time he'd called her by her name, even though they'd attended the same school for years.

I guess sixteen must be the magic number, she thought, skittishly.

"Hello, Stock," she responded, wondering, as she had many times before, where his parents had come up with his name.

"How 'bout you an' me taking in a movie?" he suggested, getting straight to the point.

Lauren considered his invitation. In a way she was flattered, after all, Stock Browning was looked on as the catch of the year. But then again she didn't – unlike most of the other girls in school – feel "that way" about him. He wasn't her type.

"Hmm . . ." she said, caught off guard and stalling.

He couldn't believe she was actually hesitating. "Is that a yes?" he asked.

"It's a when," she replied, carefully.

His blue eyes narrowed. "When what?"

"When did you have in mind?" she asked, trying to keep it light.

Goddamn it! Was she being difficult? Any other girl would be singing at the chance of a date with him. "Tonight. Tomorrow night. Whenever you like."

I'd like you to leave me alone, she decided. Even though she didn't have a boyfriend she was not interested in dating him. Absolutely not. He was too full of himself by far.

"Well?" He towered over her, and she couldn't help thinking of his big, sweaty body pressing down on hers if they ever did it. Not that she had any intention of doing it. Not until she was married to the man she loved – whoever he might be.

She continued to stall as she hated hurting anyone's feelings – even his. "I don't know, I've got a busy week," she demurred.

Now it was his turn to frown. A busy week! Was little Lauren Roberts actually turning down a date with him? Surely it wasn't possible?

"Call me when you make up your mind," he said brusquely, and stalked off.

Meg, hovering on the sidelines, giggled nervously. "You didn't say no, did you?"

Lauren nodded. "I said no."

"You *didn't*!" Meg clapped a hand over her mouth.

"I did."

They both burst out laughing and hugged each other.

"Holy cow!" exclaimed Meg. "I bet that's the first no *he's* ever had."

"Serves him right for ignoring us all these years," Lauren said, crisply.

"You're right," Meg agreed, although if Stock Browning had invited *her* out she would be boogeying down Main Street handing out flyers. "What are you going to do if he asks you again?" she asked, curiously.

Lauren shrugged. "I'll worry about it when it happens, and quite honestly, I don't think it will."

"It will," Meg said wisely.

"So I'll deal with it." Lauren felt that Stock Browning had occupied enough of their time. "Let's go get a malt."

Later that night she told her parents about the encounter, expecting them to agree that Stock was rich and spoilt and even though he was the son of the most affluent man in town she'd done the right thing in turning him down.

Jane and Phil Roberts had been married twenty-five years – the first ten childless. Just when they'd given up hope, along came Lauren. She had received nothing but their love and devotion – it would be hard to find a more united family. So it came as a shock to discover that no – her parents did not agree with her. It seemed they considered Stock a very nice boy with a bright future, and certainly a suitable candidate for their only daughter to go out with.

Lauren was crushed they felt that way. "I'm *not* dating him," she said stubbornly, before rushing up to her room.

Twenty minutes later her father knocked on her bedroom door. Phil Roberts was a pleasant looking man with sandy hair parted in the middle, a small moustache and a weak chin. "Lauren, dear," he said, soothingly. "We want the best for you, surely you know that?"

The best, don't you mean the richest?

"Yes, Daddy, I know."

Phil paced around her room, uncomfortable and ill at ease. "Spend an evening with the boy, give him a chance."

A chance at what? Her virginity?

"Okay, Daddy – maybe," she mumbled, noticing that tonight her father looked tired, and she didn't want to upset him.

"Good girl," Phil said, looking relieved.

Meg was right, it didn't take Stock long to ask again. A few days later he invited her to his cousin's twenty-first birthday party. "Black tie," he announced, grandly.

"I don't have a black tie," she dead-panned.

He didn't laugh. Bad sign.

"I'll pick you up at six-thirty," he said, patting his crotch – obviously a favourite habit.

Her parents were suitably pleased.

"We'll go to Brownings and I'll buy you a new dress," her mother said.

Lauren nodded. *Do we get a discount if I let him jump me?*

On the appointed evening Stock turned up washed and brushed – bristly blond crew cut, reddish tan, well-fitting white dinner jacket. Her parents were impressed. In fact she'd never seen her mother so giggly and girlish as she lined them up for a series of quick snapshots.

Lauren's new dress was sludge green. She hated it. "Made in New York," the saleslady had pronounced in hushed tones. After that her mother had refused to look at anything else.

Stock put his arm around her for the photographs. She felt the heat of his hand through the thin material of her dress and held her breath. The rumour was that Ellen-Sue Mathison had been forced to leave town because he'd gotten her pregnant. And Melissa Thomlinson swore he'd tried to rape her.

She shuddered.

"Are you cold?" Stock asked, solicitously.

"Oh, no, I'm just fine, thank you, Stock," replied her mother, twinkling gaily.

"Try this." Phil Roberts thrust a glass of champagne drowned in orange juice into his beefy hand. "One for the road. No harm, eh?"

Lauren was seeing her parents in a new light and she wasn't sure she liked it.

Stock drove a sleek Ford Thunderbird. He opened the door for her and helped her in, trying for a surreptitious peek up her skirt.

"Nice parents," he said, settling behind the wheel.

"Nice car," she responded, dully.

"It gets me there."

Not with me it doesn't.

Now that he had her he didn't know what to say, and she wasn't about to make it easy. She was here by default, and if he made one wrong move he'd find himself very, very sorry indeed.

Chapter 3

Evanston, Illinois 1973

Friday morning dawned bleak and icy. The rain beat down relentlessly, forming a muddy sludge on the ground.

Crammed into the back of a cab between Aunt Franny and his father, Nick felt the bile rise in his throat. They both smelt strongly of mothballs – due to the fact that they'd borrowed black clothes from the neighbours, one of whom, Mrs Rifkin, had magnanimously decided to accompany them to the funeral.

Mrs Rifkin sat in the front of the cab, chewing Chiclets and attempting to make conversation with the black driver who was more interested in breaking the speed limit and dumping them fast. He sensed a small tip, and nothing pissed him off more.

Franny extracted a half-melted peanut-butter cup from her worn purse, popped it into her mouth and said to Primo, "Well now . . . when do you think you'll be moving on?"

Great, Nick thought sourly, his mother wasn't even cold and this old bag was trying to get rid of them. So much for family attachments.

Primo opened his mouth to reply, and the foul aroma of bad teeth and stale beer wafted in the air jockeying with the mothballs for attention.

"What's your hurry, Fran?" Primo asked, letting out a not so discreet burp.

"Without Mary's pay-cheque I can't be lettin' you stay. Can't afford it," Franny stated, munching away.

"So you're throwin' us out? Is that it?" Primo said, nastily.

Franny smoothed down the folds of her skirt, rubbing a

newly discovered spot on the cheap material. She was damned if she was going to let her sister's lazy slob husband live off her. She hated the sight of his ugly face. "I plan on renting out your rooms," she announced. "The sooner the better. I – "

"Not to darkies I hope," interrupted a panicked Mrs Rifkin, forgetting who she was sitting next to.

The cab careered around a corner, throwing Nick up against his aunt's ample bosom. He wished he could throw up all over her, the old cow deserved it.

"An' how about Nick?" Primo asked, as if he wasn't sitting right there beside them.

"You'll take him with you," Franny replied, not even considering the idea of inviting him to stay on.

"He'll be better off with you," Primo insisted.

Franny rummaged for another chocolate. "What am I expected to do with a sixteen-year-old boy?" she said, in an exasperated voice.

Primo wasn't about to drop it. "At least he'll have a home."

Was his father actually thinking of him, or was it the thought of being free that urged him on?

"Yes. An' extra food t'buy. An' clothes, and all that other stuff young boys need," Franny said, indignantly. "No thank you. He's *your* son. He goes with *you*."

Case settled.

Nick leaned forward, trying to stop the despair that was rising up within him, a despair so great he could barely manage to breathe. One day his mother was there. The next – gone – just like that. Heart failure they said.

Heart failure at thirty-seven years of age? Desertion more like. She'd left him alone with Primo because she simply couldn't take any more.

When they got out of the taxi outside the cemetery Primo stood there fidgeting, until Franny realized he expected her to pay for the ride. She threw him a filthy look.

"Must've left my wallet home," Primo mumbled, sheepishly.

"Cheap monkey," she said sourly, counting out the exact fare. "You always were and you always will be."

The cab driver snatched the money and zoomed off, the wheels of his vehicle splashing them all with mud.

Mrs Rifkin was not pleased. She sprung open a faded umbrella, all the while muttering under her breath, "They shouldn't let 'em drive, that's what *I* say."

Nick shivered. How could his mother leave him alone with Primo?

Despair was replaced with anger. He wanted to shout and scream. If he could have gotten hold of her he would have shaken the life out of her.

Only it was too late wasn't it? She was already dead.

A thin man in a shiny grey slicker with a sinister hood announced he would be escorting them graveside. "Is this all of you?" he sniffed, sounding disappointed.

"Yeah," said Primo, belligerently. "Wanna make somethin' of it?"

The man ignored him.

"We haven't lived here long," Nick felt compelled to explain, as they trudged past endless rows of neatly lined up graves. "My mother didn't have time to make friends."

"Oh, dear," said the man, with about as much interest as a fish. He was into getting rid of this motley group as fast as possible.

"She was a wonderful woman though, really wonderful," Nick added, speaking too quickly, his words tripping over each other.

"I'm sure she was," said the man in the slicker.

Finally they arrived at a freshly dug plot of land where a cheap wooden coffin waited to be lowered into the ground.

My mother's in that box, Nick thought, suddenly losing it. *Oh, Jeez! My mother's in that box.*

And so the short ceremony began. And the rain pounded down. And Nick didn't know whether he was crying or not because his face was wet, so very, very wet . . .

Three days later they left. Franny was relieved to see them go. Just to make sure she packed them stale cheese sandwiches and a flask of lukewarm instant coffee. She stood outside her house waving them on their way, even though it was still raining and bitterly cold.

"Fat bitch!" mumbled Primo, as they drove away in the shabby old van he'd had for ten years.

"Where we goin', Dad?" Nick ventured.

"Don't ask no questions an' you won't hear no lies," Primo said grimly.

"I just thought – "

"*Don't* think," Primo interrupted, harshly. "Sit there an' keep

19

your big ugly mouth shut. Ain't it enough I gotta be responsible for you?"

There was a thickness in Nick's throat. Oh sure, he was used to leaving town, abandoning his friends and starting afresh every few months. But he was not used to being without his mother's protection. She'd always been the buffer between him and Primo, and now there was no one who cared.

"Soon as we get where we're goin' I'll look for a job," he said, staring at the windscreen wipers as they worked on the relentless rain, scratching against the windscreen with a dull scraping sound.

"Nah. Ya gotta stay in school," Primo said.

"I don't," he objected.

"That's where ya wrong. I made ya mother a promise."

"*What* promise?"

"Mind your business."

It was *his* life they were discussing, surely he was entitled to know? And since when did Primo care about keeping promises?

Primo slumped into silence, his bloodshot eyes fixed on the road ahead, his big hands clutching the steering wheel.

Nick's mind kept on drifting back to his mother being lowered into the ground, the rain soaking through the cheap wooden coffin. He was overcome with an unbearable sense of suffocation and loneliness.

Was she cold?

Was her body slowly beginning to rot?

Some kind of horrible wail began to beat and pound inside his head.

Why couldn't it have been Primo?

Why couldn't it have been his goddamn father?

They stopped for gas a couple of hours later. Nick got out and stretched his legs while Primo vanished into the men's room and didn't come out for twenty minutes. When he finally emerged he ignored his son and headed straight for the convenience store, where he purchased a pack of Camels and a six-pack of beer. Then he stationed himself by the pay phone and began making calls.

Nick knew better than to ask who he was phoning. He didn't care. It didn't matter what his father said, as soon as possible he would find a job, save his money and get the hell out.

He wandered outside and got back in the van. It stunk of

gas. Idly he rolled down the window and watched a blonde in a miniskirt and boots make a dash from her car to the ladies room, somewhat futilely holding a soggy magazine over her black roots.

Girls. They were all the same. He'd made out with enough of them to know exactly what they were like. In all his travels there hadn't been one girl he'd wanted that he hadn't had. It was hard to understand how some poor jerks agonized over getting laid because it was so easy – kind of like fishing. Put out the bait. Reel 'em in easy. Go for the kill. And then take off. Fast.

Nick Angelo could score with anyone. And he did – as frequently as possible – it gave him his only real sense of identity.

Primo lumbered out to the van, threw the six-pack – depleted by one can – into the middle of the seat, and started the engine.

"Uh . . . it's illegal to drive with alcohol in the vehicle," Nick muttered.

Primo wiped his nose with the back of his hand. "What're you, a cop?"

"Just pointing it out."

"Well, don't."

Yeah. Shut up. Sit still. Butt out. The story of his life.

Leaning back he closed his eyes, drifting into a sort of half sleep – until he was jolted awake when they almost skidded into the back of a massive truck parked on the side of the highway.

"Fuckin' drivers!" screamed Primo. "They don't give a crap where they dump it."

"Why don't *I* drive?" Nick suggested. It was beginning to get dark and Primo was already gulping down his third beer.

"Since when did *you* drive?" Primo sneered.

"I got taught driver's ed. in school. Took a test, got my licence."

"Don' remember that."

No, he wouldn't, would he? And even if he did he'd never have allowed him to use the van, but he'd taken it out on more than one occasion when Primo was slumped in a drunken stupor and he'd had no fear of getting caught.

The van skidded again. Primo grunted, finally deciding he'd had enough. Pulling over, he slid across to the passenger side, shoving Nick out into the icy rain.

Nick ran around the back and quickly jumped in the driver's seat. "Where we headin'?" he asked, gripping the steering wheel, anxious to get wherever they were going.

Primo finished his beer, crushing the can in his big hand and flinging it out the window. "Kansas," he said, burping loudly. "Some piss-assed town called Bosewell."

"Why there?"

"'Cause I got a wife there, that's why."

This was big news to Nick.

Chapter 4

Bosewell, Kansas 1973

What started out as a simple date seemed to be turning into a relationship, and everyone was pleased except Lauren. She'd fallen into some kind of dumb routine with Stock. Dinner and a movie on Friday night. Dancing and a party every Saturday. And two family brunches. This had been going on for six weeks.

"What's happening?" she wailed to Meg. "I used to be a free person, how did I get myself into this?"

"Has he tried anything yet?" Meg asked, lighting up a forbidden cigarette.

"No," she shook her head. "And stop pumping me all the time, you're like a district attorney!"

"No I'm not. I'm dying to find out the dirty details."

"Why?"

"C'mon, Laurie," Meg pleaded. "You *know* we share everything. He must've kissed you at least."

"Maybe," she said, mysteriously.

"Has he?" Meg pressed.

"Maybe," she repeated.

They were in Lauren's bedroom, and Meg began to bounce up and down on the bed, her face red with the frustration of not being able to get any good scoop out of her best friend. "Tell me, you rotten little B-word!"

She didn't particularly wish to confide in Meg – after all it wasn't that exciting – but now there seemed to be no choice. "Okay, so he's kissed me. Big deal. End of subject."

Meg's eyes gleamed. "Is he a good kisser?"

"He's got big teeth."

23

"What does *that* mean?"

"They get in the way. And besides," she sighed, "I *told* you, I don't feel anything for him."

Meg jumped off the bed. "Perhaps *I* should take him over. How's that for an idea?"

"Yes!"

"You don't mean it."

"I do! I do!"

Meg was exasperated. "You've got the hottest hunk in town panting all over you, and you're acting like it's no biggie."

"It's not."

"Then why don't you stop seeing him?"

She sighed again. "Because I can't. My parents like him. They like *his* parents. In fact, if you want to know the truth – my father's selling his dad some kind of big insurance thing."

Meg dragged on her cigarette like a veteran. "Oh, that's not so good."

"Don't I know it," she said glumly, trying to figure out exactly how it had happened. Their first date had been uneventful, Stock had behaved himself perfectly – he didn't even get drunk, while all around his football buddies were staggering zombies.

She'd had no reason to turn down his second invitation, especially with her parents urging her on. And then suddenly *her* father was selling *his* father insurance, and there was no way she could mess that up.

Before she knew it, everyone considered that she and Stock were a couple.

Now she was stuck. And she wasn't happy.

Mr Lucas, Bosewell High's history teacher droned on. Lauren attempted to concentrate but it was difficult – the man was dull – and getting anything out of his class was almost impossible, he had no idea how to fire his students' imaginations. They sat in front of him – twenty-four bored teenagers engaged in a variety of activities. Joey Pearson – the class clown – was busy writing dirty limericks and passing them around. Dawn Kovak – the school tramp – negotiated with one of the boys about what she might do to him during lunch hour. Meg sketched fashion designs beneath the cover of *World History*. And Lauren day-dreamed.

Her biggest day-dream was always about New York. When she was little her parents had taken her to see Audrey Hepburn in

Breakfast at Tiffany's and she'd never forgotten the thrill of seeing the big city on the movie screen.

New York . . . she'd definitely decided that one of these days she was going there just like Audrey Hepburn. And she'd have her own apartment, a fulfilling job and a cat. Oh, yes, she'd *definitely* have a cat. And of course a boyfriend. A *real* boyfriend. Not Stock Browning with his white crew cut and macho walk. A man more along the lines of Robert Redford or Paul Newman – she was quite partial to the dirty-blond look.

"Lauren!" Mr Lucas's waspish voice interrupted her reverie. "Kindly answer the question."

Question. What question? She quickly glanced at the blackboard and figured out what he'd been teaching, coming up with the correct answer just in time.

"You're amazing!" Meg whispered, stifling a giggle. "Even *I* could see you were somewhere in China!"

"New York," Lauren whispered back, "although I wouldn't mind visiting China one day."

"Fat chance!"

Meg and she viewed their futures differently. Meg saw herself married with kids living happily in Bosewell. Lauren knew there was a whole other world out there and she planned to explore it before settling down.

The bell sounded, signifying the end of class.

Stock was leaning on the lunch counter waiting for her. "I'll pick you up at six-thirty tonight," he said.

"You will?"

"Don't tell me you've forgotten."

"Forgotten what?"

"Dinner with my parents."

"Oh, yes," she said, listlessly.

"Don't go crazy with excitement."

What did he want from her? She was going wasn't she? Surely that was enough?

Bending down he pecked her on the cheek. He smelt of sweat and camphor. The sweat she could take, but the camphor almost made her gag. It was definitely time she had a chat with her father about the insurance he was selling Mr Browning. Was it a done deal? And if she stopped seeing Stock would it upset everything? She was sure that any moment he was going to make the big move, and she had no desire to star as the struggling victim trapped beneath his bulk in the cramped interior of his Ford Thunderbird.

On the way home she stopped at her father's small office – located on Main Street above the Blakely Brothers hardware store. The door was locked, the shade pulled down covering the glass. *Philip M. Roberts, Insurance*, was printed on the door. One day he'd hinted it would read *Philip M. Roberts and Daughter*. Lauren hadn't summoned up the courage to inform him she had no intention of going into the insurance business.

Disappointed he wasn't there, she carried on home.

Her mother was in the kitchen making a cake.

"Where's Dad?" she asked, sticking her finger in the mixing bowl and scooping out a taste of the creamy mixture.

"Stop that!" Jane Roberts scolded. She was a dark-haired woman with fine features and high cheekbones. It was easy to see where Lauren had inherited her good looks.

"Umm! Delicious!" Lauren stuck her finger in again.

"I said stop it," Jane repeated, sternly. "There'll be nothing left. This cake is for you to take to the Brownings tonight."

"No way!" she said, horrified. "I'm *not* taking them a cake, Mother."

"Then I'll have to ask Stock."

"No, mother, *no!* You can't embarrass me this way."

Jane stopped what she was doing and wiped her hands on her apron. "What's embarrassing about baking the Brownings a cake?"

Lauren hesitated. "Well, you know, it's sort of like . . . uh . . . sucking up."

Jane narrowed her eyes. "Sucking up?"

"You *know* what I mean."

"No. I'm afraid I don't." Jane glared at her only child with a *how dare you talk to me like that – wait until your father gets home* expression.

Uh oh. Mother was p.o.'d. Maybe she'd gone too far. "Okay, okay, I'll take the dumb cake," she mumbled, and rushed upstairs to her room.

It was quite obvious suck up was the name of the game, and right now there was nothing she could do about it.

Daphne Browning was a big woman with multiple chins and bright scarlet lips. She greeted Lauren graciously. "Your mother's *so* thoughtful. What a perfectly *lovely* gesture," she gushed.

"Of course my doctor forbids that *I* eat chocolate, but Benjamin simply adores it, don't you, darling?"

Benjamin Browning barely glanced up from his newspaper. He was a tall man, thick around the middle – with terse features, iron grey hair and matching bushy eyebrows. "Trying to diet," he grunted.

Stock prowled around the room, while Lauren settled herself stiffly on a damask chair in the very formal living room. A hovering maid whisked the cake away never to be seen again.

"When are we eating?" demanded Stock.

Daphne ignored him. "Tell me, dear," she said, scarlet lips quivering as she turned towards Lauren. "Is Stock your first boyfriend?"

Lauren could not believe she was being asked such a personal question. If she wasn't so polite she would have replied, "None of your business." Instead she began furiously petting Mrs Browning's Pekinese – a ferocious little dog who bared its teeth and growled viciously.

"What a cute puppy!" she exclaimed, trying to sound sincere. "How old is he?"

"She," corrected Mrs Browning.

"And her name is?"

"Princess Pink Pontoon."

"How unusual." She patted the dog again and the little rat snapped at her with its lethal teeth.

Stock guffawed. "It'll take your hand off if it can."

"Stock!" admonished Daphne. "Princess would *never* do that."

"Dinner is served," announced a black maid, appearing at the door.

Mr Browning put down his paper. "About bloody time," he said, irritably.

Dinner was a drag. This was one evening Lauren had no wish to repeat. Mrs Browning was a snob. Mr Browning was plain rude. And Stock was . . . well he was Stock.

On the drive home he got straight to the point. "They like you," he said.

"That's nice."

"Even though you're young."

What was *he* – all of eighteen? "I'm thrilled," she said, dryly. He missed her sarcasm. "They gave us permission."

"For what?" she asked, stifling a yawn.

"To get engaged."

Chapter 5

Aretha Mae Angelo opened the door of her trailer home and glared at Primo as if she'd seen him the day before. Actually it was seventeen years since he'd walked out on her, but she certainly wasn't about to let seventeen years stand in the way of a vigorous tongue-lashing.

Hunched in the van, Nick could hear every word as she tore into his father.

"What *you* want? Cheatin' slime. How come you sniffin' round here again? Y'ain't nothin' but a bum, so get outta here. Y'hear me? *Out.*"

She might be telling him to get lost, but Primo whined some kind of weak excuse, and before Nick could make out exactly what was happening the woman yelled more insults, dragged Primo inside the trailer and slammed the door shut.

Nick sat in the van and contemplated the last week. He was sixteen years old – nearly seventeen – and his life was over. Who cared about anything? He certainly didn't. His whole existence had been a lie.

Mary and Primo. His loving parents. Now Primo had informed him they weren't even legally married, because he'd still been married to this woman when he and Mary had exchanged their wedding vows.

Primo Angelo was a bigamist.

And if that was so, what did it make him?

He didn't care to think about it.

The rain had slowed to a drizzle but it was still icy cold. Nick huddled in the van, hungry and tired – empty of any emotion.

Some time later Primo emerged from the trailer followed by the woman. Yanking open the door of the van he thrust a dirty blanket at Nick. "You'll sleep out here," he said, gruffly. "No room inside."

The woman pressed forward trying to get a look at him.

Nick noticed she was dark-skinned, very dark-skinned. With a sudden jolt he realized she was black.

In the morning the rain had stopped. Asleep across the two front seats Nick was awakened by a faint scratching sound. For a moment he couldn't figure out where he was. He sat up, banging his head on the roof. His gut ached with hunger, and he felt an urgent need to pee.

Staring at him through the side window were two small black boys. One of them was scraping his fingernails against the window. As soon as they saw he was awake they ran away.

In the light of day he took in his surroundings. The van was parked in the middle of a sparsely populated trailer park. A few skinny dogs loped around a cluster of dilapidated looking trailers, while all around was mud, weeds and over to one side a massive garbage dump.

This place made Aunt Franny's run–down house in Evanston seem like a palace.

He got out of the van. Crouching on the ground a few feet away lurked the two black kids, still staring at him.

"Hey –" he said. "What's up?"

They didn't respond.

"Gotta take a piss."

One of the boys pointed to a ramshackle hut next to the garbage pile.

He made it to the hut and wished he hadn't, the stench was unbearable.

After doing what he had to do he hurried back to the van, his stomach rumbling uncontrollably. In his pocket he had exactly thirty-five cents. Not enough to do shit.

Leaning against the van he thought about his future and decided that things certainly couldn't get any worse. He was stuck in a strange town, waiting around in some crummy trailer park while his father re-acquainted himself with the woman he'd been married to for seventeen years and never told anyone.

One of the boys edged towards him, a handsome kid with bright eyes and dark chocolate skin. "What's your name, mister?" the boy asked, curiously.

"Nick. What's yours?"

"Harlan. I'se ten. How olds you?"

"Sixteen."

"What you doin' here?"

He shrugged. "Beats me."

After a while Primo emerged from the trailer clad only in his grubby underwear, scratching his bulging belly, a rare smile lighting up his unshaven face. Nick knew the look. It was his father's *I just got laid, aren't I a fine stud* look.

"Howdja sleep?" Primo asked, as if they'd spent the night in a fancy hotel.

"I didn't. I was too hungry," he muttered, angry with his father, and yet not sure how to express himself. What he'd really like to do was beat his stupid lying brains out.

"Doncha worry 'bout that," Primo said jovially, as if nothing was amiss. "Aretha Mae's one fine little cook." He clapped his hand on his son's shoulder. "C'mon, I wancha t'meet her."

Reluctantly he followed Primo into the trailer while the two boys hovered close behind.

Inside it was a crowded mess with clutter everywhere – clothes, magazines, old newspapers and junk piled high on every surface. In one corner was an unmade bed, and on the floor rested two mouldy sleeping bags.

Aretha Mae busied herself at a kerosene stove frying ham and potatoes in greasy bacon fat. She was a sinewy black woman with frizzy, dyed red hair and a wary look in her eyes.

"Sit yourself down, boy," she said to Nick over her shoulder. "You must be real hungry."

He squeezed on to a torn plastic covered bench next to a rickety table stacked with dirty dishes.

Aretha Mae dumped a plate of food in front of him, sweeping the used dishes to one side. "Eat," she commanded.

Primo chuckled, he saw a home in his future. "I knew you two would get along."

"Shut your mouth," Aretha Mae said. "We be talkin' 'bout who gets along later. Don't go thinkin' you're movin' in."

Nick was impressed by her nerve, although he half expected his father to smack her across the mouth.

Primo didn't. Primo laughed, a big-bellied laugh. "Still a feisty bitch," he said. "I like that in a woman. You haven't changed."

Aretha Mae threw him a stern look. "Don' use no bad language in front of my kids," she said, indicating the two silent boys by the door.

"Listen who's talkin'," Primo said, scratching his stomach. "I can remember when that's *all* you used."

"Things was different then," Aretha Mae said, primly. "Those was different times."

Primo continued to laugh and grabbed her ass. "They sure was."

She slapped his hand away and turned to Nick, busy wolfing down the greasy but delicious meal. "What your old man tell you 'bout me?" she demanded. "He tell you we was married? He tell you he ran out on me when I got pregnant? He tell you 'bout your half-sister he ain't never seen – let alone supported?"

Nick stopped eating. Sister? What kind of crap was coming his way now?

"I didn't know . . ." Primo whined. "You threw me out. I didn't know you was pregnant."

"Liar!" she snapped. "The baby in my belly was *why* you ran." She glared at him balefully. "An' then whaddaya do? Fix another woman so youse trapped anyhow. Dumb chickenshit!"

Primo wrapped his arms around her from behind, caressing her bony body. "C'mon, hon, I'm back," he crooned. "You always *knew* I'd be back, didn't'ja?"

Aretha Mae made a cross sound in the back of her throat. Not that cross. In fact it was becoming quite obvious she didn't mind having Primo's lumbering arms around her one little bit.

Nick thought of his hard-working mother lying in her grave and the greasy food turned in his stomach. He hated his father. He hated the whole stinking set-up.

Abruptly he stood up. "What sister?"

"She be away right now," Aretha Mae said, quickly. "She be visiting relatives in Kansas City."

"I got me a daughter," Primo marvelled. "I always wanted a girl."

"You got one all right," Aretha Mae said. "Oh, yessir me, you *really* got one."

Several days later they moved in after spending a few nights in Bosewell's only motel. Since there wasn't room for all of them in one trailer, Primo made a deal with the couple next door to take over their rat-infested storage dump – a place with no wheels and cardboard covering the window spaces. "It'll do for the kids t'sleep in," he convinced Aretha Mae. "Should clean up nice."

Nick spent three days hauling out junk, dodging rats, cockroaches and spiders while Harlan and his younger brother, Luke, helped out. They were jumpy little kids, petrified of their mother who ruled them with an acid tongue.

The two boys attended school every day. They walked the several miles, leaving the trailer park at six in the morning. Aretha Mae left shortly after that to go to her job as a maid to a rich family in Bosewell. This gave Primo plenty of time to himself, and although he promised Aretha Mae he'd start looking for a job he had no intention of doing so. The moment she left he settled in front of her small black-and-white portable television – a six-pack nearby. Nothing had changed for Primo. He knew his priorities and he stuck to them.

Nick hung around, he had nowhere to go.

After a couple of days Primo said, "Gotta get you back in school."

"I'd sooner get a job," he said, feeling restless and trapped. "Maybe –"

"I promised your ma," Primo interrupted, staring at the television. "Thought I told y'that."

"So what?"

Whack! Right across the mouth. It caught him by surprise cutting the side of his lip. He tasted blood and was filled with fury. There was no Mary to protect him now. School was in his future and there was nothing he could do about it, at least for now. As soon as he could he'd find a job, save his money and get out.

Nick Angelo planned to run, and nobody was going to stop him.

Chapter 6

"How exciting!" screamed Meg.

"Darling, I couldn't be more pleased for you," said her mother.

"This is great news," announced her father, like she'd just concluded a complicated insurance deal.

Idiot! She should have kept her mouth shut. All she'd done was tell them Stock had mentioned they should get engaged, and the next thing it was the town gossip. Now she was more trapped than ever in a relationship that totally confused her.

She was sixteen. She was too young. Oh sure, her mother had gotten married at seventeen – but that was a love match between two people who were crazy about each other, they'd told her the story enough times.

Her situation was different – she hardly even *knew* Stock – and what she *did* know she didn't much like.

"I'm not getting engaged," she informed her parents, panic-stricken at the thought.

Jane Roberts smiled and patted her daughter like she was an excitable puppy that needed calming. "Nerves, darling," she said. "Marriage is a big step. You'll have a long engagement, get to know each other. Stock's a nice boy from a fine family. Your father and I are very happy."

Oh, good, *they* were happy. What about her? Wasn't *she* the one supposed to be grinning uncontrollably and walking ten feet above the ground?

Love. From everything she'd seen and read it was a magical feeling and all *she* felt was sick.

In second grade she'd had a crush on Sammy Pilsner. She'd been eight years old and ecstatic. He'd made her shiver and shake whenever she saw him.

At twelve she'd fallen in love with one of her cousins –

Brad – a bony looking boy three years older than her. He and his family only visited at Christmas so she'd soon grown out of that.

At thirteen she'd had her first date. Disaster.

At fourteen her first kiss. Even worse.

And at fifteen she went steady for a satisfying six months with Sammy Pilsner.

Sammy didn't make her shiver and shake as much as he had when she was eight, but he was a good kisser and they got into many long lustful nights of heavy petting, although she never let him go all the way – she was too frightened of getting pregnant – even though he drove over fifty miles to a neighbouring town to buy rubbers, and tried to convince her they should do it.

Eventually Sammy's father got promoted at his job, and they moved to Chicago. She was a little bit heartbroken. She and Sammy corresponded for a few months, then his letters tapered off, and she realized she was free to see whoever she wanted. She dated several different boys. They all wanted one thing. If she hadn't given it to Sammy, why would she surrender it to a casual date?

One thing about Stock, he hadn't jumped her. Yet.

"I don't want to get engaged," she confided to Meg.

"Everyone's *soooo* jealous!" Meg squealed. "Has he given you a ring? When are you going to *do* it? You'll *have* to do it now you're engaged."

"But I'm not," Lauren protested.

Meg squinted at her. "Not what? Not engaged? Or not going to do it?"

"Not engaged, asshole."

"Nice talk from a virgin!"

"Asshole," Lauren repeated.

If her father ever heard her say that he'd kill her. Neither of her parents swore, at least not in front of her, although she'd once heard her father loudly groaning, "Christ! Christ!" when she was eleven and listening outside their bedroom door.

At least she knew what men said when they had sex. Although Sammy didn't. In the throes of passion, when she was doing something to him nice girls weren't supposed to do, Sammy Pilsner used to yell out, "Cowboys and Indians! This is an attack! Go for it! Go for it!"

Thinking of Sammy made her grin. His was the first and only penis she'd ever seen – she didn't count the time she'd walked in

34

on her father getting out of the shower. He'd gone red in the face and screamed at her to leave the room immediately. She was ten at the time. Shortly after, her mother had taken her to one side and told her to please knock when entering their bathroom.

Knock knock.

Who's there?

Daddy's penis.

I promise I won't look.

Sammy Pilsner was very proud of his penis, he wanted her to look all the time. In fact he wanted her to do a lot more than look.

She'd obliged, because at the time she thought she loved him, and at least you couldn't get pregnant that way.

She knew all about oral sex having read about it in *Playboy*. Her father kept copies of the magazine locked in a storage closet in the basement. She'd discovered his stash one day and over the course of the next few weeks had read them all. Each magazine was full of naked women, sexist cartoons and articles about all kinds of sexual activities. She didn't enjoy looking at it, but it certainly taught her a lot. Sammy Pilsner couldn't believe his luck!

But that was the past – now she had Stock to deal with.

A few days later he sidled up to her in lunch break and informed her that his parents had decided to throw a big engagement party for them.

She wanted to say, "But I never said we'd get engaged." Instead she found herself nodding and listlessly agreeing.

Maybe that's what Stock liked about her – her total lack of enthusiasm. As the football hero and son of the town's richest man, he'd had girls fawning all over him since sixth grade. Perhaps he found her cool attitude a refreshing change.

"Saturday night," he said, sliding his arm around her shoulders. "My mother's talking to yours."

Oh, great! She should put a stop to this now. Somehow it just seemed easier to go along with it. Like that girl in *The Graduate* she could take it all the way to church – and then some handsome hero would rush in to save her and she'd run off with him leaving Stock with his mouth open – probably patting his crotch to make sure she hadn't taken it with her!

One question. Who would the rescuing hero be? Sammy Pilsner? She didn't think so. Sammy was probably getting his penis licked by a cute little Chicago girl with long legs and a big mouth.

Idly she wondered if her mother ever did *that* to her father. The very thought made her shudder. No way. He probably didn't even let her *look* at it.

"I've got a big surprise for you," Stock said, surreptitiously checking out her bra strap through her sweater.

"What?" she asked, impatiently.

"Never you mind, you'll see."

Asshole.

On the way home from school she stopped by her father's office. Once more he'd closed up early. She rattled the handle just to make sure. Nobody home.

Downstairs she popped into the Blakely Brothers hardware store. The Blakely brothers were identical twins, both fat and fifty with jovial smiles and drooping bushy eyebrows. She had no idea how to tell them apart.

"Hi'ya, Mr Blakely," she said, cheerily. "How's your wife?"

He beamed. "If I had one she'd be fine."

Foiled again! One was married. One single. The rumour around town was that the single one was a homosexual.

She grinned. "Just testing. I knew it was you!"

"No, you didn't." He winked. "I hear you're engaged. That's very nice, Lauren."

Her father the blabbermouth. This was obviously no secret.

"Have you seen my dad? He seems to have left early again."

"Didn't notice him go."

She had a ton of homework. Perhaps it was just as well her father wasn't around, they would have started talking, she'd get home late, and then she'd have to work all through dinner.

She'd never told her father she knew about his secret stash of *Playboys*. She'd never told her mother either.

"Your mom ordered lightbulbs," Mr Blakely said. "Since your dad has left . . ." he trailed off.

"I'll take them," she volunteered.

He handed her a large brown supermarket bag piled high. When her mother ordered she did it in bulk imagining it saved her money.

The package wasn't heavy – merely cumbersome. Lauren slung her school bag over her shoulder and grasped the bag with both hands. "Bye, Mr Blakely."

"Goodbye, Lauren. You're marrying into a fine family. One of the best."

I'm not marrying into anything, Mr Blakely. I am merely getting engaged. Temporarily. Because I can't stand the fuss of wriggling out of it. Because I'm always trying to please people. Because I hate to hurt anyone's feelings.

Because I'm an idiot!

Crash! Some jerk ran right into her at the swing door, and her package fell to the ground, followed by the sound of breaking glass.

"Shit!" the jerk said. No "Sorry." No "Excuse me." Just a short, terse "Shit!"

She waited.

"You should look where you're goin'," he said, rudely.

She was outraged. "*I* should?"

"Yeah. *You* walked into *me*."

"I did no such thing."

"Sure you did."

"No. I didn't."

They stared at each other, two furious strangers.

He was skinny and not very tall, with jet black curly hair, a pale complexion, a slight indentation in the centre of his chin and intense green eyes. He wore a grubby white T-shirt under a battered denim jacket, indescribably filthy torn jeans and battered sneakers.

Against her better judgment she felt a shiver of excitement. "Aren't you going to help me pick everything up?" she asked, wondering who he was.

Nick returned her stare. Not bad. A bit square looking. Hardly his usual type. But he was horny, God, he was horny!

"Okay," he mumbled, bending to help her.

"What about the broken bulbs?" she asked, finding two smashed ones.

"Get the store to replace 'em, you're on their property," he said, trying to decide how long it would take to screw her. Small-town girl. Possibly a virgin. Definitely more than one date.

He leaned closer catching a whiff of her scent. She smelt like lemon soap, no cheap dime store perfume. And her hair – long and shiny – was some sort of chestnut colour. He checked out her body. Slim but definitely acceptable.

"I can't do that," she said, primly. "You'll have to pay for them."

He laughed. Not a very nice laugh. A sarcastic *who do you think you're talking to* laugh.

37

"Sweetheart, I got enough to buy one pack of smokes an' that's *it*."

"Am *I* supposed to pay for them?" she countered.

"No," he nodded over to the counter where Mr Blakely was busy with another customer. "I told you – go talk to old fatso. He'll give you back your money."

"Don't call Mr Blakely that," she whispered, furiously.

"He can't hear me."

"Maybe he can."

"What's he got – X-ray ears?"

Just as she was about to reply her father appeared, hurrying down the stairs that led from his office.

"Daddy!" she exclaimed, forgetting about the green-eyed stranger for a moment.

As soon as Nick heard the word "daddy" he was out of there. He'd learned at an early age to stay as far away from fathers as possible.

"Where have you been?" Lauren asked, grabbing her father's arm.

"Upstairs, working."

"But I went upstairs. The shade was down, the door locked."

"Nonsense. What's all this?" he indicated the mess on the floor.

Flustered, she looked around. The boy who'd so rudely crashed into her was gone. "Oh, I dropped Mom's lightbulbs."

Phil chuckled. "What's the woman doing – stocking up for the next three years?"

Lauren giggled, they were conspirators in her mother's excesses. "You know Mom," she said.

"Indeed I do," he replied. "By the way, Lauren, I haven't had a private moment to tell you how happy I am about your engagement. Stock is an upstanding boy with traditional values, his family is first class." A pause. "Your mother and I are very proud of you."

Shit! If a stranger could say it she could certainly think it.

I guess I'm engaged, she thought gloomily. *No way out. For now.*

Chapter 7

Aretha Mae arranged to get him into Bosewell High mid-term. "Cyndra goes there," she informed him.

"Who's Cyndra?"

"She be your sister, boy, an' don' go forgettin' it. Good-lookin' girl, that's her problem. An' I don' wan' it bein' yours, seein' as you all be sleepin' in together."

Wasn't it bad enough he had to squeeze in with Harlan and Luke?

He cadged a couple of bucks off his father and made his way into town. They'd stayed in some one-gas-station towns in their time, but Bosewell scored the prize. He explored Main Street, wandering into the hardware store where he bumped – literally – into a girl he considered making out with for a moment, but then her father appeared and he was out of there fast. She wasn't his type anyway, too clean-cut.

The waitress in the drugstore was more like it. Mid-twenties, big knockers and a slight squint.

He slid up to the counter and ordered coffee.

"Black?" she asked, hardly taking any notice of him.

He winked to get her attention. "With cream, sweetheart. Lots of it."

"You new in town?"

"How'd ja guess?"

"'Cause if you wasn't you wouldn't be tryin' to hit on me. You'd know Dave was my husband." She jerked her thumb at the short-order cook, a burly man about ten years older than her with muscles to spare.

Nick refused to give up. "He keep you happy?"

She raised a sarcastic eyebrow. "Does Mommy know you're out?"

39

They both burst out laughing at the same time.

"Louise," she said. "Welcome to Bosewell."

"Dave's a lucky guy."

"And you're a fresh kid. What you doin' here anyway? Passin' through on your way to reform school?"

"My old man moved us here."

She poured him a cup of coffee, adding a generous amount of cream. "An' what does *he* do?"

"Fucks up a lot."

Louise sighed, "Don't we all, dear. Don't we all."

"I gotta go to school," he said, gulping his coffee. "But I wanna work nights an' weekends, score some bucks. Got any ideas?"

"What do you think I am? An employment agency?" she said, smoothing down her gingham apron.

"Just askin'."

She softened. "Maybe Dave'll know of somethin'."

Her attention was taken by a group of High school kids who came crowding in making a lot of noise. She moved over to take their orders.

Nick checked them out. He was used to joining new schools halfway through the semester, it was always the same deal. The other kids regarded him with suspicion – usually there was some jerk who tried to start a fight, while most of the girls pretended they didn't notice him – although they did.

Every time he had to prove himself, every fuckin' time. It meant pounding the shit out of the school bully and screwing the prettiest girl. Somehow he always managed to do both.

He had one golden rule. Don't play fair. It worked good.

One of these days he'd be out of school once and for all, the routine was getting him down. Exactly how many times did he have to prove himself?

The group was asking Louise about him and staring over. A couple of the girls nudged each other. A big guy with a blond crew cut made a smart remark and they all laughed.

Instinctively he knew that this was the guy he'd have to deal with.

Tough shit, big guy. I'll give you a shot in the balls that'll take you all the way to Miami and back.

Louise returned and filled his cup.

He nodded towards Mister Crew Cut.

"Don' mess with him, honey," Louise warned. "His daddy owns most of this town."

40

"Yeah?"

"You'd better believe it." She brushed a strand of lank brown hair out of her squinty eyes. "Lemme go talk to Dave, his brother George runs the gas station. You know anythin' 'bout cars?"

"If it stops I can fix it. That good enough?"

"We'll see, hon, we'll see."

Back at the trailer it was the same old scene. Primo sat glued to the television, burping, swigging beer and picking at a bag of pretzels.

Aretha Mae stood in front of the kerosene stove, her shoulders slumped as she heated up two-day-old meatloaf – a gift from her employer, who allowed her the choice of throwing old food away or taking it home.

Harlan and Luke played outside, kicking around old tin cans and jumping in and out of the skeleton of what was once a car.

Nick strolled outside and joined them. "One of these days I'm gonna get me a Cadillac," he confided. "A goddamn red Cadillac with chrome bumpers an' leather seats."

"Can we ride in it?" Harlan asked, believing every word.

"Sure. Every day if you like."

The next morning he rode the bus to school with Aretha Mae. She told him where to get off and handed him a dollar.

"What's this for?" he asked, not wanting her charity.

"In case y'need it," she replied stoically, staring straight ahead.

He wondered what the going rate was for maids in Bosewell? Or maybe her employer piled her up with old food and clothes and considered that payment enough.

Bosewell High was a pale grey concrete building surrounded by green lawns on one side and an enormous parking lot on the other.

Clusters of students headed towards the imposing front entrance, most of them coming from the parking lot.

Nick felt the usual hollow feeling in the pit of his stomach. He tried to ignore it. Stay cool. No nerves.

Don't let the fuckers get you down.

Without having to ask he found registration and made himself official. The school secretary ran a disapproving eye over his grubby uniform of jeans, T-shirt and jacket.

"While we have no dress code here at Bosewell High, we do expect our students to look clean and well-groomed," she said.

"That means washed and pressed clothes at all times. And no torn jeans."

"Yes, ma'am." Hopefully he'd never have to see her again.

"Classroom number three, Mr Angelo. Your teacher will tell you what books you need."

"Thank you, ma'am."

Old cow. He could charm her if he wanted to.

Who wanted to?

Chapter 8

"Ohh . . . feast your eyes on *him!*" Meg nudged Lauren excitedly. "Now he's what I call *gorgeous!*"

Lauren glanced up from her desk, her mind elsewhere. "Who?" she asked, vaguely.

"*Him*. Standing by the door. He must be the new student. Dawn spotted him yesterday at the drugstore and she's in *love*."

"Dawn's in love every day."

"I know. But this one is – oh – I dunno – so sort of moody looking." Meg jumped up. "I'm going over to welcome him."

Lauren looked over at the door. And then she looked again. Meg was talking about the boy she'd run into at Blakely's hardware store. The one with the green eyes and smart mouth.

"Who is he?" she asked.

Too late. Meg was halfway across the classroom, while Dawn was fast approaching from the other direction.

Lauren sat tight. Let them make fools of themselves if they wanted to. He wasn't *that* great. Just different . . .

Meg was speaking to him now, eyes sparkling, cheeks flushed. Lauren watched her go for it. They were best friends, had been since elementary school, but sometimes Meg was too impulsive. She should have waited, let him come after her. Well-known fact. Boys liked to chase after girls, not the other way around.

Meg was pretty, with fluffy yellow hair and blue eyes. She was ten pounds overweight and on a permanent diet. Her two front teeth were crooked which sometimes gave her a rabbity look.

Dawn Kovak on the other hand was a tramp. She had dyed black hair, a prominent bosom, and wore too much make-up. She didn't look sixteen, she looked thirty.

Lauren observed them both in action, her best friend and the school dump – as Dawn was nicknamed.

43

He'd probably go for Dawn with her black hair and big bosom – they always did. Meg had virgin written all over her.

Surprisingly he chose Meg, allowing her to lead him to the only vacant desk, listening as she chattered on, giving her all his attention.

Lauren felt the smallest shiver of jealousy. Which was ridiculous really, because she certainly wanted nothing to do with him. She was engaged to Stock Browning. She was *very*, *very* busy thank you very much.

Hmm . . . maybe she should go over and greet him?

No need. Meg seemed to be doing a perfectly wonderful job of making him feel more than welcome.

She stopped watching and opened up her English Lit. book. Concentrating was not easy. She couldn't help glancing up to see what Meg was doing. Meg was heading back to her desk with a triumphant expression.

Just as she got back, their teacher entered the classroom.

"He's *fantastic*!" Meg whispered, sitting down, a silly smile lighting up her face. "*And* he's asked me out."

"He has?"

"Yep. Tonight."

"Where?"

"Who knows? I'm meeting him in front of the drugstore at eight."

"Your parents'll never let you out on a school night."

"I'll say I'm over at your place studying."

"Meg, you don't know anything about him, how can you go out with him?"

"Holy cow, Lauren, you sound like my mother."

"I do not!"

"Yes you do."

"Girls!" The high-pitched tones of Miss Potter – their English Lit. teacher – interrupted them. "Will you be joining us today?" she continued, sarcastically. "Or shall we set up a table for you two outside so that you may carry on your conversation uninterrupted?"

"Sorry, Miss Potter," they chorused, sounding like a couple of good little students.

Lauren couldn't resist one more quick glance over at the new boy. He caught her look and returned it.

Meg picked up her book trying to choke down a giggle. "I'm so excited!" she whispered. "He's really gorgeous!"

"You're crazy," Lauren muttered, and for one brief moment wished that *she* was the crazy one.

The chubby little blonde came on to him like gangbusters. He chose her over the dark one because he had a strong suspicion the dark one had nailed every guy in school, and while he was interested in getting laid, he was not interested in catching a dose of the clap – or even worse – crabs.

It was easy. As usual. Had something to do with his green eyes. He could fix them on a girl – just for a moment – and they had this sort of crazy, hypnotic effect.

Jeez! He was allowed to have *something* wasn't he? And God had given him the eyes.

He caught the girl he'd bumped into yesterday watching him from across the room. She didn't mean to, but he could see she couldn't help herself. Maybe after he was finished with the blonde he'd go for her, give her a cheap thrill. Maybe . . .

Bosewell High was going to be easy compared to some of the inner city dumps he'd been forced to attend. This school was strictly small-town, he could take his pick.

So far he hadn't spotted the beefy guy with the crew cut. The schlump was probably in a different grade, and that was good. If he played it smart perhaps he could avoid him altogether.

Deep down he knew this wasn't possible. Deep down he knew there was always one dumb asshole who'd go for his throat.

When school got out for the day he planned to return to the drugstore, find out if Louise had come up with a job for him, and then, if he was lucky, cadge a meal and hang around until it was time to meet Blondie.

The teacher noticed him and made him stand up and introduce himself to the class. *Jeez! What a drag!* He hated the way they all looked him over. Why didn't they ask for his rank and serial number while they were at it?

At lunch break he fell in behind the crowd and drifted down to the school cafeteria where he bought a cheese sandwich and a Coke, found a corner table and sat down.

Before long, Crew Cut made his entrance – trailed by an admiring group busy hanging on to his every word.

Nick munched his sandwich and surveyed the scene. Blondie waved at him from across the room. She was probably dying to talk to him again, but had decided to play it cool. Ha! He could even figure out how they thought.

And then the girl from the hardware store made her entrance, pausing in the doorway.

He knew she noticed him and half-hoped she'd come over, but she didn't.

And what was this? Crew Cut was on his feet, racing across the room, putting his arm around her and leading her over to a table. Shit! She was his girlfriend!

Immediately Nick wondered if she was gettable.

Yeah. Why not? He was always up for a challenge.

"The party's all set," Stock said.

"I know," Lauren replied. "My mother and your mother are like this." She held up two fingers to show exactly what they were like.

Stock smirked. "My mother likes bossing your mother around."

Lauren took offence. "What do you mean?"

He shrugged. "My mother likes bossing everyone, including me."

Just for a second Lauren felt sorry for him. It must be awful having a mother like Daphne, a huge, commanding woman with scarlet lips telling everyone what to do.

"Meg's got a date tonight," she found herself saying, anything to make conversation.

"Really?" He couldn't care less.

"With that new guy," she added.

"What new guy?"

"You know, the one that started school today."

"Yeah?" His lack of interest was quite apparent.

She gave up, there was only so much she could do.

Meg arrived at her house an hour before her date, barely able to conceal her excitement. She rushed up to Lauren's room making a mad dash for the mirror. "How do I look?" she demanded, fluffing out her newly-washed hair.

"Horrible," Lauren teased.

"Whaaat?"

"Only kidding."

"Don't do that," Meg wailed. "This is the first decent date I've had in months."

Lauren sat cross-legged on her bed. "How do you know he's decent?"

Meg was exasperated. "What's the *matter* with you?"

"What's the matter with *me*?" she retorted, sharply. "Take another look in the mirror. You're all excited over a guy you don't even know. He could be a sex maniac, a rapist, anything . . ."

"You're really weird," Meg said, shaking her head. "I mean, *really*."

"Thanks. All compliments gratefully accepted."

"Anybody would think *you* liked him."

She flushed, and jumped off the bed. "Don't be ridiculous."

"Forget it. *I* saw him first and he's mine. Anyway, you're engaged, or had you conveniently forgotten?"

Lauren pulled a face. "Would that I could."

"Nice talk," Meg said, adjusting the waistband of her new black skirt to make it shorter. "How do my legs look?"

"Like legs. What'll I tell your mother if she calls?"

"Tell her I'm in the bathroom. Anyway, she's not likely to."

"It could happen."

"You're a big help."

"Call me as soon as you get home. I want a full report."

Meg gave a jaunty wink. "You bet!"

"Hi." Meg felt suddenly shy as she approached Nick. He was leaning against the wall outside the drugstore, smoking a cigarette.

When he saw her coming he flicked the butt towards the kerb with an elaborate flourish. "Hi," he replied, taking her arm as if they'd been dating for months. "You look nice."

"Thanks," she giggled, nervously.

"I mean it," he replied "very nice." He'd scored a free hamburger off Louise, and a promise from Dave he could work at his brother's gas station Saturday nights. Things were looking up. Now all he had to do was get laid and perhaps he could get a good night's sleep, although it wasn't easy with Harlan and Luke coughing and farting the night away.

"Where are we going?" Meg asked, as he guided her along Main Street.

"Thought we'd catch a movie."

She'd already seen *The Poseidon Adventure* playing at The Bosewell, but so what? "Super," she said, eager to please.

Super. Hmm . . . Maybe he should have picked the sure thing with the black hair; this one was a baby.

When they reached the theatre he steered her away from the box office. "Buy your ticket, go inside, an' then let me in through the fire-escape door. Like I'm busted, y'know?" He gave her arm an encouraging squeeze. "Okay?"

Buy her own ticket? Usually on a date the boy paid. Lauren would *love* this. Still . . . it made life exciting. "Okay," she agreed.

He gave her a little shove. "It's easy, you'll see."

She purchased her ticket and entered the almost empty theatre. Then, when she was sure she wasn't being observed, she raced down the side aisle to the fire exit, opened the heavy door and let Nick in.

"Yeah!" he said, guiding her to the back row, which was conveniently empty.

The movie had already started. Putting his arm around her he settled back to watch. After a few minutes he moved closer. "I knew you and me would get along soon as I saw you," he said in a low voice. "It was like . . . y'know . . . uh . . . special."

"I know," she whispered back, thrilled they were thinking along the same lines.

"Sometimes these things happen," he said, massaging her back through her sweater.

"Right," she agreed, beginning to feel rather warm.

"Like it's meant t'be or somethin'," he added, his hand creeping around to the front, dangerously close to her left breast.

She opened her mouth to agree again and without warning his lips were on her, kissing insistently, his tongue probing.

She gasped for breath. This was all happening so fast. The last boy she'd dated had waited three whole weeks before trying anything. Now Nick's hand was definitely on her breast and she knew she should push him away, but at least she could enjoy it for a minute, couldn't she?

Nick circled her nipple through her sweater, his thumb and forefinger moving in circles.

She let out an involuntary groan as he slowly began to push her sweater up, fumbling in the dark for her bra clip.

"Don't," she managed, realizing she'd better put a stop to this now.

He didn't listen. He was too busy unhooking her bra.

Cupping her left breast he bent his head, licking her nipple with practised ease.

She tried to push his head away. "No!" she whispered, urgently.

"Yes!" he whispered back.

"Someone will see."

"It's empty in here."

"I don't want you to do this."

"Yes you do."

And it was true. She did. For a moment she relaxed, giving herself up to this glorious feeling sweeping over her. Was it so bad to feel so good?

He began to suck her nipple, at the same time reaching for her hand and jamming it on his penis – which somehow or other he'd managed to release.

Oh God! She'd never touched one before. Oh, dear! There was no way she should be doing this. Nice girls didn't do this – unless, of course, they wanted to be labelled easy or a tramp – like Dawn Kovak.

With a sudden burst of resolve she attempted to pull her hand away.

He was having none of it. "Hold it," he commanded. "It ain't gonna bite!"

"I can't," she said, desperately.

"Yes, you can." He groaned, helping her hand move up and down – faster . . . faster . . .

And then it happened. He spurted all over her. Hot, sticky, wet.

"Jeez!" he groaned again. "Ohhh . . . jeez!"

"My skirt!" Meg wailed, horrified. "You've done it all over my new skirt!"

He leaned his head back, closed his eyes and took a deep, satisfied breath.

Welcome to Bosewell. It had been one helluva day.

Chapter 9

Nick made the long trudge home thinking about Blondie. Nice tits. Too shy. Not for him. Jerk-off action was for boys Harlan's age.

Who was he kidding? Once in a while a jerk-off was better than nothing, and he knew if he'd tried to screw her she'd have bolted. As it was she was hysterical about her stupid skirt. What was it with girls and clothes?

Best not to see *that* one again, he thought. Better off to invest in a packet of rubbers and give the dark haired one a chance.

Girls, they were all the same. Easy. And he never cared if he saw any of them again. Once the sex was over he felt an emptiness, a void.

When he got back to the trailer the two boys were sitting on their pile of blankets flicking through well thumbed comic books.

"What's up?" he asked cheerfully, taking off his jacket.

"What's up with you?" Harlan retorted.

"Nothin' much." He nodded over at Luke. "How come he never speaks?"

"He jest don't," Harlan replied, suddenly sullen.

"Somethin' happen to him?" Nick asked, stripping off the rest of his clothes.

"Not your business."

"I'm only askin' 'cause I thought I might help."

"Not your business," Harlan repeated, fiercely.

Nick shrugged and settled himself down on his lumpy mattress, trying to find a comfortable spot. "No farting tonight," he said sternly, staring menacingly at the two boys.

Harlan stood up, pulled down his shorts, bent his rear end in Nick's direction and let one rip.

"Aw, god*damnit*!" Nick wrinkled his nose in disgust. "If I wasn't so beat I'd slap your skinny butt halfway across this trailer park."

Harlan burped. Luke laughed. At least he could do that.

Nick closed his eyes, and for some unknown reason began thinking about the other girl, old Crew Cut's girlfriend. No, he told himself sternly, mustn't look for trouble. The truth is they're all the same in the dark, and he'd never met a girl who could give him anything more than a hard-on.

In the morning he followed the two boys into the main trailer hoping to cadge breakfast. Aretha Mae handed out stale slices of bread smeared with congealed bacon fat. He grabbed one.

Primo snored loudly, sprawled across the rumpled bed.

Aretha Mae looked tired, her eyes sunken, her mouth pinched into a thin line. She clapped her hands together. "Out," she told the two younger boys. "Get movin' or you be late." She turned to Nick. "How 'bout I pay y'bus fare the rest a the week. After that you be on your own."

"Don't worry, I got a part-time job," he said quickly. "I'm workin' down at the gas station Saturday nights."

She was impressed that he didn't take after his idle father. "That's good," she said, wiping her hands on an old cloth. "That's real good."

He nodded. "Yeah."

Meg was late for class. She slipped into her seat and shuffled a few books around, attempting to look industrious.

"You didn't call," Lauren hissed. "I don't appreciate that kind of behaviour when I'm supposed to be your alibi."

"I had more important things to worry about," Meg hissed back.

"Like what?"

"Like a ruined skirt."

Mr Lucas coughed meaningfully and glared across the room at them.

Lauren returned her attention to her books. She'd had a miserable morning listening to her parents carry on about her engagement party. They were turning into a couple of social-climbing phonies right before her eyes – discussing what to wear, who would be there, how they should act.

"Today I'm going shopping for a new outfit," Jane had declared, enthusiastically. "And Lauren, dear – we'll buy you a pretty new dress too."

Lauren hated the word "pretty": it conjured up visions of pale pink ruffles. "I don't need a new dress," she'd said.

"What nonsense! We'll go shopping after school today. Bring Meg."

She'd been unable to wriggle out of it. This engagement thing was getting out of hand.

As soon as Mr Lucas signalled freedom she grabbed Meg. "Well?" she asked, breathlessly.

Meg shook her curls. "You were right. He's a sex maniac."

"He *is*?"

"Oh, yes."

"*Really*?"

"I'm not lying."

"What happened?"

"He's crazy about me."

"I'm sure. But what did you *do*?"

Meg sighed, ready to tell her story. Before she could, Nick put in his first appearance of the day, strolling by on his way to Math. Clinging on to his arm as if she owned him was Dawn Kovak.

He winked at Meg, greeting her with a cavalier, "Hey – How're ya doin'?"

"Fine," she managed, her cheeks burning with rage and humiliation.

"They're tenting the garden," Stock said, flexing his muscles.

"Isn't it too cold?" Lauren asked.

He smirked. "They've got those heater things."

"*Why* are they tenting the garden? Your house is so large, they could have everyone inside."

He proceeded to do a series of knee bends. "Beats me."

"Stock . . ." she began, tentatively.

"Yes?"

"Maybe we don't need a big party."

He continued doing knee bends. "Sure we do. Once we get rid of the old farts it'll be a blast."

"But everyone's making such a fuss. I'm not certain it's what I want. I –"

"Listen, hon," he interrupted, standing up straight. "We're talkin' a good time here. Relax, you'll love it."

"I will?" she said, unsurely.

"Course you will."

"Okay," she said, still not convinced, watching her mother pull into the driveway in the family station wagon. "I have to go. We're going shopping."

"Buy something sexy," he leered, unexpectedly pinching her on the ass.

She swatted his hand away. "Don't *do* that!"

He chuckled. "Why not? We're engaged. I'll soon be doin' a lot more than pinchin' your butt!"

Oh, no you won't, she thought, angrily. *I'm putting a stop to this as soon as I summon up the courage to tell my parents.*

"Okay, babe, see ya. I got football practice anyway." He swiped a kiss on her cheek and loped off.

"Lucky thing!" sighed Suzi Harden, coming up behind her.

Lucky thing indeed! Lauren didn't feel lucky. She felt like a cornered fieldmouse waiting for the trap to snap shut.

Sex with Stock was unthinkable. His big sweaty hands all over her. Crushed beneath his enormous bulk. No way!

"Where's Meg?" Suzi asked. "You two are usually always together."

"She didn't feel well – went home early."

And who could blame her? She was broken up over Nick's appearance with Dawn Kovak. One moment he was all over her, and the next he was consorting with "Anything Goes Kovak". Boys! Who could understand them? Who wanted to?

Her mother swerved the station wagon over to the kerb and she got in.

"Where is Meg?" Jane asked, adjusting her rear-view mirror. "I thought she was coming with us."

Maybe she should have a little card printed:

Meg is not coming.

Meg is humiliated and heartbroken.

All humans of the male species are sex-crazed animals.

Lauren shrugged. "She didn't feel up to it."

Jane looked concerned. "Is she sick? I hope not. We don't want *you* catching anything."

"She's sick of boys."

Jane laughed. "You girls!"

Ha Ha! Lauren thought sourly, catching a glimpse of Nick

53

Angelo – she knew his name – sauntering out of school with Dawn Kovak clinging to his arm. Obviously Dawn was now a permanent fixture.

He was real moody looking, a regular bad boy. She'd warned Meg, told her not to get involved, she should have listened.

Nick Angelo. Hmm . . . Meg had said he was a great kisser . . . So what?

One thing he'd learnt in life – if you're going to dump a girl, do it quickly. No excuses. No hanging around. One sharp cut and it's over.

Blondie was a mistake. Dawn was definitely more his speed.

"How come it took you so long to get here?" she'd asked, approaching him on the way into school.

"What's *that* supposed to mean?" he'd replied, checking her out.

She'd touched his cheek with a long red fingernail. "I've been waiting for a guy like you all my life."

Soul mates. She was even using his lines!

"So," he'd said, "here I am."

"So," she'd said, with a provocative wink, "I'm ready."

Dawn Kovak lived with her alcoholic mother on the wrong side of town. Not quite as bad as the trailer park, but getting there. She didn't have much going for her except her curvaceous figure and sultry looks, so she used them to full advantage. She might be the school screw, but at least her assets made her popular. During the day she filled him in about Bosewell. Small town. Small thinkers. No fun. No action. The nearest place where anything happened was fifty miles away – a town called Ripley – where there were bars and places to dance and a cool bikers' hang-out.

"You got a car?" was one of the first questions she asked.

"I can get hold of one," he'd replied, thinking of taking the van one night when Primo was out cold.

"You an' me – we'll make our own good times," she'd promised, seductively.

For now, Nick had thought, *while it suits me. Don't get too close, I'm only passing through.*

54

Chapter 10

When the Brownings did something they did it big. The garden was tented. A three-piece group played what was supposed to be dance music. The food was catered. And the tables set with fancy pink linen and fine silverware. After all, the Brownings were the richest family in town and once in a while they liked to show it.

Stock collected Lauren early and drove her straight to his house, proudly showing off the party preparations.

"When the old folks hit the sack we've got a disco all set up," he boasted. "And plenty of beer. I mean we're talking *plenty*."

He was telling her like she was a big beer drinker or something. "Great," she managed, tugging at the bodice of the pale yellow dress her mother had talked her into buying. She hated the dress: it made her look like a flower girl at somebody's wedding.

"Right now I have something *just* for you," he said, grabbing her hand and pulling her over to the corner of the garden.

Oh no! Was this the big moment? Was this the great attack?

"What?" she mumbled, praying he wasn't going to jump her – although it was highly unlikely in his parents' tented garden with sixty guests due any minute.

"This," he said, proudly pushing a small leather box into her reluctant hand.

She held it gingerly.

"Go on, open it," he said, encouraging her.

Easy for *him* to say. But when she opened it the net would tighten, for any fool knew it was an engagement ring.

"I always dreamt of going to New York," she blurted out, postponing the inevitable.

"We will," he assured her. "On our honeymoon if you like."

When was *that* going to be? Next week? Things were moving so fast she almost couldn't breathe.

"I figure we'll get married after I finish college," he said, as if reading her thoughts. "I know that sounds a long time – but when we're officially engaged it'll almost be like being married, won't it?"

Reprieve! Reprieve!

"Course, if you get pregnant we can do it earlier," he added.

Pregnant! Was he kidding? You had to have *sex* to get pregnant, and there was no way she was doing anything with him. *No way.*

With a feeling of relief she realized this was the answer to all her problems. No sex. No engagement. When she refused to put out he'd break the engagement. *He'd* break it off. *She'd* be the injured party, and her parents couldn't be mad at her. Whew!!! What an escape.

With renewed vigour she sprung the box open and stared at a heart-shaped sapphire surrounded by more than a dozen small baguettes. "Wow!" she exclaimed. "This is beautiful."

"I knew you'd like it," he said, smirking proudly. "My mother picked it out."

"How romantic," she said, dryly. As usual, her sarcasm was lost on him.

"Put it on," he urged. "See if it fits."

She did so – imagining the day she would give it back.

He took her hand, pressing it on his tuxedo-clad crotch. "Feel this," he said, with another proud smirk. "This is what you do to me."

She jerked her hand away. Their engagement was going to be shorter than anyone could possibly imagine.

Dawn Kovak was the girl of his wet dreams – ready, willing and always able. He knew her reputation – not that it came as any surprise because Joey Pearson had already filled him in. Joey was a good guy – funny, clever, a touch off-beat. They'd palled up instantly when it turned out they were both doing Saturday night shifts at the gas station.

"Look," he'd explained to Joey, "I won't be stayin' long. What do I care if she's screwed every guy in town? She's just the way I like 'em – experienced."

Joey had laughed. "Yeah, there's nothin' like a girl who knows what she's doin'."

Both of them had been recruited to park cars at the Brownings' party – anything to earn a few extra bucks.

A maroon Cadillac made its way up the circular driveway. Nick ran around to the driver's side and opened the door. A man got out. His wife was in the passenger seat. Meg emerged from the back and made a quick dash into the house.

"What happened with you an' her?" Joey asked. "Didn't you take her to the movies or somethin'?"

"Nothin' happened," Nick lied, easily. He wasn't about to tell tales. "My mistake. Picked the wrong girl. It was my first week in town, y'know how it is."

Yes. Joey knew how it was. His mother and he had arrived in Bosewell from Chicago a year ago. His father – a cop – had been killed in a bank hold-up, and his mother immediately decided they should move to the safety of a small town.

"When we first came here my ma said it was for my protection," Joey grimaced. "Like the minute I'm eighteen I'm outta here. It's back to Chicago for me. I'm gonna do stand-up."

Nick looked vague. "Stand-up?"

"Y'know, like tell jokes 'n stuff. Make people laugh."

"Sounds good t'me."

Joey searched through his pockets and produced a battered cigarette. He snapped it in two and handed Nick half. They shared a match.

"So . . ." Joey said, taking a deep drag. "I know what *I'm* doin' here. What brings *you* to this pisshole?"

Nick sucked on his half of the cigarette. "My old man," he said.

"What does *he* do?"

Nick laughed bitterly. "Fuck all."

"That's nice."

"Very nice. Like he was married to this woman . . . this black woman . . ." He paused, Joey didn't need to know this, nobody did. "Aw, shit. It's a bummer, it doesn't matter."

"Tell me about it," Joey urged.

Nick wasn't in the mood to reveal himself. "Some other time," he said, dropping the subject.

Joey shrugged. "I'm not goin' anywhere."

More cars arrived and they got busy.

"Y'know Stock Browning is the asshole of the world," Joey said, running back from parking a Buick. "The schmuck tried to beat me up once – I kicked him in the nuts an' got myself a knife."

Nick laughed. "I knew we'd get along."

"The funny thing is," Joey continued, "when I was goin' to school in Chicago I never got beat up once."

57

"Maybe 'cause your dad was a cop."

"Bullshit. There weren't any jerks like Stock Browning around."

"You really love the guy, doncha?"

"He's a prick. I'd sure like to know why Lauren's gettin' engaged to him. Dumb move."

"You ever take her out?"

"No way, man. She and Meg – it's virgin city."

"Maybe she's changed."

"Yeah," Joey said, disgustedly. "That can happen. Girls! Show 'em a wad of money an' it's legs in the air an' let's party!"

Another car entered the driveway and pulled up in front of the house.

"I'll toss ya for it," Nick said.

"What's the difference?" Joey replied. "We're splittin' all the tips anyway."

Nick nodded. "Right."

Meg was furious. "He's outside!" she complained to Lauren.

"Who?"

"Don't ask me who!" Meg snapped. "You *know* who. It's him. Nick. Isn't it enough that I have to see him at school? Now he's here, parking cars. I'm so humiliated. I arrived with my *parents*! How could you do this to me?"

"Calm down, Meg. I had no idea he'd be here."

"Oh, no, *sure*. You're too busy getting engaged to notice *anything* or anybody. How do you think I *feel*?"

"Meg," Lauren said, patiently. "Your date with him was three weeks ago. Forget it."

"Easy for you to say. Try putting yourself in my place." Her voice rose hysterically. "He practically *raped* me!"

Lauren looked concerned. "You didn't tell me that. You said he got your bra off and ruined your skirt. You certainly didn't tell me he tried to rape you. If he did, you should report him to the police."

"It's too late."

"If that's what happened, it's never too late."

Meg's face crumpled. "I hate him!" she cried out.

"So do I," agreed Lauren, ever the supportive friend. Although truthfully she couldn't say that she hated him, because she didn't even know him.

Of course, she knew he had green eyes; and black curly hair; and a great chin; and a James Dean slouch.

She also knew he was working part-time at the gas station, and that he and Joey Pearson were friends, and that most nights he saw Dawn Kovak.

She certainly found him intriguing, although she couldn't tell Meg, had to keep a tightly buttoned lip on *that* little piece of info.

"Are you enjoying the party?" she asked, moving the conversation along.

Meg narrowed her blue eyes and reached for a glass of watered-down punch. "Will you have to call your first-born Stock Junior?" she asked, in a mean voice.

"Not if it's a girl." Lauren smiled sweetly and moved over to join her parents who seemed to be having a perfectly fine time sucking up to the entire Browning clan.

Dawn was the uninvited guest – at least her name wasn't on the official list.

"Suprise!" she greeted Nick, arriving just before midnight in a car full of leather-clad friends who looked like they'd strayed out of *West Side Story*. "Stock told me to get here late."

This was not the rich kids' group. These were the tougher, older kids who smoked pot, drank alcohol, and blasted Joplin and Hendrix day and night.

Nick hadn't exactly fallen in with them – but thanks to Dawn he knew most of them, and they'd accepted him as a cool guy.

Behind the car were six or seven motorcycles. Dawn had recruited more friends from Ripley.

"Hiya, Nicky," she licked his ear, suggestively sticking her tongue deep. "Now the party can *really* get goin'. Dump this gig an' let's go inside."

"Yeah, go on, man," Joey encouraged. "There's only a few more cars. I'll take care of 'em."

"I don't wanna stick you –" Nick began.

"Go. We'll split the tips tomorrow."

Why not? If Dawn was invited he was entitled to tag along. He was certainly as good as any of these other creeps.

They blasted in noisy and out for a good time.

Stock greeted them surrounded by several of his football buddies all well on the road to oblivion.

"Hi'ya, sexy," Dawn said, provocative in an off-the-shoulder sweater and short tight skirt. She nuzzled in for a deep French kiss. "Takin' *you* outta circulation is a crime!"

Stock guffawed, winked and burped. "Let's get the disco goin' – you take care of it, Dawn."

"Sure thing, handsome – anything you want. An' I *mean* anything."

He stuck his tongue out, flipping it obscenely from side to side. "I've had *that*."

His friends roared. Dawn did too.

Nick headed for the bar. So Stock had screwed her. Big surprise.

He helped himself to a cold beer, swigging from the bottle and checking everything out. This was some set up, it must have cost big bucks – what with the tent, a full bar, dozens of tables and chairs – flowers and all that crap. There was even a dance floor, which Dawn was now dragging Stock on to as the disc jockey took over from the sedate three piece group, blasting everybody out of their seats with the Stones' raunchy rendition of "Satisfaction".

The last of the adults scurried towards the exit. Daphne and Benjamin Browning were long gone.

Nick helped himself to another beer.

"Oh, no!" Meg yelped. "He's here. What's he *doing* in here?"

Lauren was truly fed up with her friend; she'd done nothing but complain all night.

"I've got to go," Meg said, frantically.

Lauren was in no mood to stop her. "I'll see you tomorrow," she said, coolly.

"Are you staying?" Meg asked, surprised.

"It's my engagement party. Or had it slipped your mind?"

"I suppose *you* have to stay until the end. You don't mind if I go, do you?"

As a matter of fact she did mind, but there was no way she was begging Meg to stay. "No, that's okay."

"Thanks." Meg took off without a second thought.

Lauren sighed – so much for best friends. She wished she could say to Meg, "Stay. I need you." And she wished she could say to Stock, "Goodbye. I don't need you."

Her parents had enjoyed the evening. Phil Roberts had turned on the charm and talked up more prospective insurance to more clients than he could remember. Jane Roberts had declared herself belle of Bosewell, dancing with every old man in town.

Lauren had danced with Stock and all his buddies. She'd even had to dance with Benjamin Browning who'd held her too close and breathed whisky breath in her face. Now she was ready to call it quits, but Stock had other ideas. He was all set to let the good times begin.

He reeled off the dance floor fresh from Dawn, and grabbed Lauren. "C'mon, sugar, let's rock 'n roll," he said, leering drunkenly.

"I'm really tired," she said. "It's been a long night."

"Are you kidding?" he rolled his eyes. "The evening's just beginning."

"Do your parents know you've invited all these other people?" she asked, gesturing at the crowd.

"What do *you* think? I told them I was havin' a few more friends come by, they don't care. This is my party, I can do whatever I want."

"*Our* party," she corrected. "And *I* want to go home."

He shook his head, perplexed. "Sometimes you're a real pain. Have a glass of punch. Relax. Get with it."

"I had a glass of punch, thank you."

"So have another one. One of the guys spiked it. Now the party'll *really* swing." He attempted a kiss. She pulled away.

He laughed bitterly. "You're a helluva fiancée."

The Stones gave way to a raucous Rod Stewart. Lauren gave him a little shove towards the dance floor where all his cronies seemed to be having a great time. "Go dance with Dawn again. She loves it, I don't."

"If you're with me you'd better learn to love it," he slurred, beckoning Dawn.

What did he think this was, school? She'd learn to do exactly what she pleased and that was it.

Over by the door Nick caught the action. He didn't care about Dawn taking off — it didn't matter. Lauren was the girl that interested him, may as well admit it. And now was as good a time as any to do something about it.

Just as he was about to head towards her, a familiar voice said, "What in hell *you* doin' here, boy?"

It was Aretha Mae, a different looking Aretha Mae with her

61

frizzy red hair pinned back and a starched white maid's uniform covering her skinny body.

"I could ask you the same," he said, smartly.

She glared at him. "*I* work here," she said. "An' you better be gettin' your ass outta here." She balanced a tray of dirty glasses and marched back into the house.

Screw her. She wasn't his mother. He didn't have to listen to anything she said.

Lauren was still by herself. Seizing the opportunity he sauntered over, sitting down beside her. "How ya doin'?" he asked, casually.

She turned to look at him. They'd never been formally introduced, but what did that matter?

Oh, God! Meg would be furious if she talked to him.

"Uh, hi," she replied, trying to sound equally casual.

He nodded at Dawn and Stock on the dance floor. "They make quite a couple, huh?"

"Hmm," she said, non-committally.

"Isn't it supposed to be you up there with him?" he asked, helping himself to a cigarette from a box on the table.

He had a nerve. He knew perfectly well it was supposed to be her.

"How come *you're* not dancing with him?" he persisted. "Don't you like to dance?"

"Don't you?" she countered.

He gave her the benefit of his green-eyed stare. "Only if it's with somebody special."

She met his eyes for a moment, found them too dangerous and quickly broke the look. "I . . . I have to go," she said, getting up.

"Mr Football Hero's in no state to take you home," he said, also standing.

She wondered why her heart was beating so fast. "That's not your concern, is it?"

He kept on staring at her. "Maybe it could be."

"I beg your pardon?"

This girl wasn't reacting the way they usually reacted. A little warmth would be nice. "How come you're so uptight?" he asked, trying to throw her off balance.

"I'm not uptight," she answered defensively. "You're rude."

"Yeah?" he challenged. "What've I done?"

"Nothing – to me," she said, quickly.

"What's that mean?"

"You know."

"No, I don't. What?"

She wished she hadn't brought the subject up, but there was no stopping now. The words tumbled out. "The way you treated Meg. You took her out, jumped all over her, and then dropped her. How do you think she feels?"

Shit! That was the trouble with girls, they always confided in each other. "She told you about it, huh?"

"Meg's my best friend."

The truth, he decided, was the way to play it with this one. "And she's nice," he explained. "But not for me, so I . . . uh . . . didn't see her again. I thought I did her a favour."

Lauren faced up to him, fighting Meg's battle. "*That's* a favour?" she asked incredulously. "You don't lead someone on then dump them."

Time to change the subject. "Why are you getting engaged to this jerk anyway?"

Two bright red spots stung her cheeks. "You're the jerk. You don't even know him."

"C'mon, you know he's a jerk." He paused for a moment. "I suppose you're gonna tell me you're the happiest girl in the world."

"Just exactly who do you think you are?" she asked, angrily.

"Me? I'm just passing through, honey."

"And *don't* call me honey."

"Why?" he teased. "Does it turn you on?"

Their eyes met for a moment. He held the stare. Once more she broke it by walking away.

For some unknown reason her heart was still pounding as she hurried outside. Nick Angelo was dangerous and she knew it.

Chapter 11

Cyndra Angelo had been travelling on the bus for hours. She was tired and dirty. Her clothes were rumpled and uncomfortable. Her feet hurt and she was hungry. She peered out the window. It was raining. It was always raining.

She'd had to move seats three times. Every time the bus stopped and new passengers got on there was always some guy who chose to sit next to her. After a few minutes he moved too close, started to talk, and she was forced to shift seats again.

It wasn't as if she did anything to encourage them, they came on to her whether she wanted them to or not. Pigs!

Kansas City had been a nightmare. Staying with distant relatives of her mother's, she'd found the men in the family only too eager to put their hands all over her. It seemed that every male she met wanted to lure her into bed. What was it about her? What did she do to encourage them?

Nothing that she knew about.

She opened up her old tote bag, took out a compact with a broken mirror and studied her face. She wasn't white. She wasn't black. She was nothing.

It never occurred to her that she had the best of both worlds. That her skin was the most glorious olive – smooth and blemish-free. Her jet black hair was long and thick. Her eyes a deep rich brown. Her jawline strong and her cheekbones etched. She looked different from everybody else. The truth was that she was a very beautiful young girl indeed.

The bus stopped and two men got on. It didn't take long before one of them came sidling up the aisle and sat down beside her. "Hi'ya, sweetie," he drawled. "Where you headin'?"

"None of your business," she replied, turning her back to face the window.

"No need to be unfriendly," he complained.

She ignored him until he finally got the hint and moved away.

Maybe she was crazy for going home when she could've stayed in Kansas City and gotten herself a job.

Oh yeah . . . sure . . . some sensational job. Hooker, Call Girl, Stripper, Go-Go Dancer . . . There were a million and one opportunities for a girl like her. But Cyndra had bigger ideas. Somehow she was going to make something out of her life, and nobody was going to stop her.

She'd gone to Kansas City for an abortion. Paid for, she suspected, by the man who'd raped her. Of course, nobody would admit he'd raped her. Her mother had said it was her own fault, that she'd encouraged him.

She'd never done any such thing. She hated him, always had.

Mr Benjamin Browning. Big business man. Happily married family man. Big phoney son-of-a-bitch.

The Brownings. Her mother's employers. The fine, upstanding Brownings.

Oh yeah, she could tell the town a thing or two about the fine, upstanding Browning family. She'd had the unfortunate distinction of knowing them all her life.

When she was a little girl her mother used to take her to the house all the time and leave her in a back room while she worked. Sometimes Benjamin Browning would come to that back room and touch her. She was too young to understand what he was doing, but as she got older she began to dread going there.

When she was five she'd tried to tell her mother. Aretha Mae had slapped her sharply and said, "Don't you dare talk 'bout Mr Browning like that. I work for these people. Don't you *never* make up no bad things again."

So Cyndra had learned to shut up. At least her mother stopped taking her there – she put her into Kindergarten instead, dropping her off on the way to work.

School was another bad experience. She was jeered at because of her dark skin, and ostracized because her mother worked as a maid. Several times she was beaten up by the older kids. Eventually she'd learned to look after herself. Not quite well enough, it seemed.

Damn Benjamin Browning. Mister fine upstanding pillar of the community. Damn him and his money and everything about him.

She'd been away for a month. The abortion had turned out to be a frightening experience. It had taken place in the run-down house of a hatchet-faced woman and a grey-haired man with bony white hands, who'd called her Girlie and treated her as though she was a prostitute. For hours after she'd bled uncontrollably, until they'd had to rush her to the nearest hospital, dumping her on the front steps and abandoning her like a delivery of prime beef.

"What happened to you?" the doctor at the hospital had demanded. "We need names. You have to tell us who did this to you."

But she couldn't do that, so she kept quiet, just as she'd kept quiet her whole life.

Now she was on a bus coming home, and she didn't know if she was happy or sad.

"How old are you?" the doctor in Kansas City had asked.

"Twenty-one," she'd lied.

"I don't think so," he'd replied.

And he was right. She was sixteen. Sweet sixteen.

With a deep sigh she began day-dreaming. One of these days she was going to get out of Bosewell. One of these days the name Cyndra Angelo was going to mean something.

By the time the bus dropped her off the rain had almost stopped. The driver waved goodbye and she grabbed her bag and began the long trek to the trailer park. In a way she was pleased to be coming home. At least she had Harlan and Luke to look forward to. They were good kids and she genuinely loved them. She did not love Aretha Mae, although she grudgingly respected her for managing to survive on her own with three children to raise.

When Cyndra was six she'd asked who her father was.

"Never you mind," Aretha Mae had replied. "That be my business, not yours."

She knew he was white and that's all she knew. Harlan and Luke were the offspring of a black man called Jed who'd lived in the trailer for two years, then moved out one day when Aretha Mae was at work. Jed had never been seen or heard from again – which was just as well, for his interest in little Cyndra had been more than stepfatherly.

As she walked along the deserted pathway she started thinking about Benjamin Browning and what she would like to do to him. Kill him for starters. Maim him if that didn't work. String him up by his grungy old balls.

The truth was that she knew in her heart there was nothing she *could* do. It was her dirty secret and she was stuck with it.

She thought about how it had happened, and if there was anything she could have done to stop it.

No. Impossible. The man was an animal. Besides, he was over six feet tall and weighed at least two hundred pounds. Whereas she was only five feet five inches and one hundred and fifteen pounds. No contest.

It had happened on a Tuesday. Aretha Mae was sick with flu, so at her request Cyndra had taken time off from school to help out. The Brownings had another maid, but she was out sick too, so Cyndra found herself alone in the house. Mrs Browning was shopping, Stock was at school, and Mr Browning was at his office.

He came home early coughing and spluttering. "I feel lousy. There's this damn flu going around," he complained, loosening his tie. "Be a good girl and fix me a hot tea with lemon. I'll be upstairs."

She didn't like him, but she had no reason to be frightened of him. She was a big girl now, and he hadn't touched her since she was five.

She made the tea in the spacious kitchen, putting the china cup on a tray with a matching saucer next to it containing several slices of lemon. Then she carried the tray upstairs to the master bedroom.

He was in his bathroom. "Leave it on the bedside table and turn the bed down," he called out.

She did as he asked, touching the fine quality linen sheets, wondering what it must feel like to sleep between such luxury.

Mr Browning emerged from the bathroom clad in a terry cloth robe. It was a warm day and the window was open. Outside the gardener worked on the lawn.

"Close the window," Mr Browning said, clearing his throat.

She went over to the window and pulled it closed. Before she could turn around he grabbed her from behind and wrestled her on to the bed, pushing up her skirt and ripping off her cotton panties.

She was so startled she hardly had time to put up a struggle. "Stop!" she managed, trying to get away.

"Cunt, gimme that black cunt," he mumbled excitedly, thrusting himself roughly inside her.

She was too shocked to scream, it all seemed to happen so fast.

67

Mr Browning was enjoying himself. "C'mon, black bitch. Give it to me. Give it to me *good*," he grunted.

Frantically she struggled, still trying to push him off.

"That's what I like!" he crowed. "Keep on moving – I like it! I like it when you fight me."

He ripped into her, tearing at her insides, hurting her terribly. She thought she screamed but she wasn't sure. Whatever she did he had no intention of stopping, he was beyond control – until, with a long drawn out cry, he was finally finished.

He collapsed on top of her for a few moments – almost suffocating her. Then he got off, and she heard him go into the bathroom.

Drawing her legs up to her stomach she began to sob.

After a few minutes he came out of the bathroom fully clothed as if nothing had happened. "I'm not going to shower," he said in a conversational tone. "I want your smell on me all day." He walked to the door and stopped. "Oh, and by the way, Mrs Browning will be home soon, so you'd better stop that snivelling and get those sheets changed – they're covered in blood."

Six weeks later she'd realized she was pregnant. She had nowhere to turn except her mother, so she'd told her everything.

Aretha Mae had listened silently, her face clouding over with anger.

When she was finished her mother said harshly, "You're never done makin' up stories 'bout these people, are you?"

"It's the truth –" she began.

Aretha Mae slapped her across the face. "Shut up, you hear me, girl? I'll take care of it – but you must *never* talk 'bout this again. *Never.*"

Somehow Aretha Mae had come up with the extra money to send her to Kansas City for the abortion.

Now she was back, and she hoped Aretha Mae wasn't going to force her to continue school. It would be far better if she dropped out and got a job, they could certainly do with the extra money.

The rain had stopped, but the ground was still muddy. She wasn't frightened walking through the dark. There were no streetlights but she knew every inch of the trailer park – it was the only home she'd ever known.

When she arrived outside their trailer she was surprised to see lights on and hear the television blaring. It wasn't like her mother to stay up so late.

She opened the door and walked in.

A man was sprawled on the bed watching television. He had a can of beer in one hand and a stupid smile on his face. He was laughing at something Johnny Carson had just said.

Cyndra stopped abruptly. "Who're you?" she asked, alarmed.

Groggily he sat up. "Who am *I*? Who in hell're *you*?"

"Where's my mother?" she demanded. "Where's Aretha Mae?"

Primo's eyes focused on this beautiful slip of a girl. "Shee . . .it!" he exclaimed. "You must be my daughter. Come on over here an' say a big hello to your daddy."

Chapter 12

Since their engagement party Stock had been suitably deflated. He'd caught hell from his parents for inviting too many people, and allowing the party to get totally out of control. When Lauren left he'd been drunkenly reeling around the place with his so-called friends – who'd proceeded to wreck the place, smashing glasses and bottles, pulling down half the tent, generally causing chaos. Mr Browning was not amused.

"It wasn't my fault," Stock whined to Lauren. "You were there, why didn't you stop me from letting them all in?"

"Because I'm not your keeper," she said, crossly. "It's your own fault." And it *was* his fault. Who did he think she was – his mother?

They bickered on and off. Lauren was miserable and yet she didn't know what to do. Should she give him back his ring? She knew that's what she *should* do, but she didn't want to do it while he was having trouble with his parents. His father had cut his allowance. His mother was barely speaking to him. How could she turn against him too?

Stock did nothing but complain. She decided that as soon as his complaints stopped she would make her move. Meanwhile, she threw herself into a student production of *Cat on a Hot Tin Roof*. She'd landed the plum role of Maggie the Cat, which was exciting, and her husband, Brick, was played by one of the older boys, Dennis Rivers. Apart from being very good-looking, Dennis was a terrific actor. The rumour was that he liked boys instead of girls. Lauren couldn't care less who or what he liked, she felt privileged to be working with him.

Betty Harris was in charge of the drama group. They met after school at the old church hall once a week.

Betty was unlike the other teachers. A large, billowy woman

in her fifties, she had flushed cheeks and straw-coloured hair that never looked combed. She favoured loose, gypsy clothes and spoke in a breathy, excited voice encouraging her students to excel.

As far as Lauren was concerned drama group was the high point of her week.

"I hear you got engaged Lauren, dear," Betty Harris greeted her. She nodded.

"Too young," Betty said, shaking her head knowledgeably. "Much too young."

Lauren nodded again. At least *someone* understood.

When all of her students were assembled, Betty made an announcement. "I have a big surprise for everyone," she said, fluttering her hands. "You've often heard me mention my brother, Harrington Harris, the famous New York stage actor. Well, next week he's actually coming to visit us here in Bosewell."

An appreciative hum went around the room.

"So you will see that I am not actually making him up," Betty continued, her rosy cheeks glowing. "He will be with us very soon.' She paused, her protruding eyes darting around until they settled on someone at the back. "And on another note, before we start rehearsals today, I'd like to welcome a new student into our group. Will all of you please say hello to Nick Angelo."

Lauren turned around, startled. Lounging at the back of the room in his familiar outfit of jeans and dirty denim jacket was Nick.

Meg nudged her. "I just died!" she whispered. "If I can only keep him away from Dawn maybe I've got another chance."

"Do you still want one? I thought you hated him."

"I know," Meg agreed, "but who else *is* there? I mean, you've got to admit, he *is* gorgeous."

Yes, reluctantly Lauren had to admit it – in his own intense way, he certainly was.

Cyndra was shocked and angry to discover that while she'd been away her mother had allowed her long-time missing husband and his scummy son to move in. A husband Cyndra hadn't even known existed. And what's more, the man claimed he was her father. Her father for God's sake! A white trash piece of shit who made her sick just looking at him.

"I'm getting out of here," she threatened.

"Where you goin', girl?" Aretha Mae asked, her lip curling.

Cyndra was close to tears. "I'll get a job – find something, but I'm *not* stayin' here."

They argued back and forth until finally Cyndra realized it was useless. She had no money and nowhere to go. Once again she was trapped.

"You be sharin' the other trailer with your brothers," Aretha Mae said, glad to see her daughter, but sorry about the trouble she was bound to cause.

Reluctantly Cyndra moved into the battered old trailer next door. She put up a sheet dividing the already crowded trailer in two, and refused to speak to Nick. "Stay on your side," she warned him, "an' we won't have no trouble. Got it?"

He'd just looked at her, still trying to reconcile himself to the fact that he actually had a half-sister, and a black one at that.

"What've I done to you?" he asked one day. "It ain't my fault we're stuck here."

"You and your goddamn daddy," she replied, her brown eyes flashing. "He's nothing to me."

"Oh yeah – nothin' 'cept your dad."

"My dad your dumb ass," she fired back. "I hate both of you."

She was pretty but a real pain. He made no further attempt to speak to her.

Meanwhile he was doing okay at the gas station. Apart from Saturday nights he now came in on Saturday mornings too. He stashed away most of the money he made, handing a few bucks to Aretha Mae each week. When Primo found out he had a part-time job he soon had his hand out.

"Nothin' left," Nick said.

"What'n t'hell am *I* supposed t'do?" Primo complained.

"Whyn't you try getting a job?" Nick replied, standing up to his father for once.

Whack! Primo lashed out, his heavy hand swinging through the air. Nick was old enough and wise enough to know when it was coming and duck out of range.

Cyndra refused to walk with him in the mornings or even sit next to him on the bus. At school he noticed she was even more of a loner than he was, although on Saturday nights she hung out with the biker crowd from nearby Ripley.

Primo seemed to think they were living the great American

dream. Now that Cyndra had returned he tried to play the concerned father. "Don't want that girl runnin' around all times of night," he informed Aretha Mae.

"You've left it too late to be givin' her no orders," she said. "She ain't gonna take nothin' from you."

"She's my daughter," Primo roared. "An' *I* make the rules 'round here."

Aretha Mae shook her head wearily. She had Primo back after seventeen years, but the question was – did she really want him?

The scene from *Cat on a Hot Tin Roof* went extremely well. Lauren was glowing, she loved playing Maggie the Cat, especially with Dennis as Brick.

After class Betty Harris praised her. "Excellent, Lauren, dear. You really have talent."

She was delighted. "I do? You know one day I'd like to go to New York. Would I have a chance?"

"Acting is a tough business," Betty replied. She was wearing a voluminous caftan with multiple hanging gold necklaces, and every time she spoke the chains rattled against each other. "Too many actors chasing too few parts."

"But I'd love to give it a try," Lauren said, earnestly.

"A try would be good, dear, but don't depend on acting to make a living, it's far too treacherous a profession."

Stock met her after class, took her arm possessively, noticed Nick and said, "What's that creep doing here?"

Lauren jumped to his defence. "He's not a creep."

"Says who? Take a look at him – always in that stupid get up. Who does he think he is – James Dean?"

"Not everyone has to look like you," Lauren said, coolly.

"Not everyone *can* look like me," he boasted.

They went to the drugstore for a soda. *The Way We Were* was playing at the local cinema. Lauren wanted to see it, but Stock wasn't interested.

"I hate that sentimental crap," he jeered. "Give me Clint Eastwood any day."

She sighed. "You *promised* we could see it tonight."

"I got other ideas."

"Like what?"

"Going for a drive, talking about our future. It's about time."

"I guess so," she said hesitantly, taking a long deep breath. A drive was good; it would give her an opportunity to tell him she didn't think they had a future.

Stock drove like a rich kid showing off. His father had weakened and promised him a new car for Christmas, so he really let the Ford Thunderbird rip, zooming down Main Street as though he was competing in a drag race.

"Not so fast," she said, clutching the dashboard.

"Calm down."

She hated being told to "calm down" – like she was hysterical or something. "Where are we going?" she asked.

"Over to the old athletic field," he replied, taking one arm from the steering wheel and placing it around her shoulders.

The deserted field just outside town was a notorious necking spot. "No," she said quickly.

"Why not?"

"You know why."

"We're engaged. We can go anywhere."

"That's what I want to talk to you about."

"I thought *I* was the one wanted to talk."

"We should both talk," she said, seriously.

Against her better judgment she allowed him to drive to the edge of the old field, where he parked the car, dipped the headlights and immediately swooped.

"What are you *doing*?" she said, pushing him off.

"What I should've done a couple of months ago," he replied, his big hands roaming all over her.

She slapped his hands away. "C'mon, Stock, don't start this."

"What are you, Lauren? Some kind of ice queen?" he said, managing to clamp his lips down on hers.

She struggled free. "Will you stop it!"

He drew away from her clenching his fists. "Christ! When do I get to first base with you?"

"Never," she replied, heatedly. "This engagement thing's a big mistake. We weren't meant to be together."

He sat up straight. "What the hell do you mean by *that*?"

"I never should have said yes. I don't know why I did. My parents encouraged me . . . they like you . . . they like your family . . . they think we make a great match." She knew she was speaking too fast, but now she was on a roll and couldn't stop. "I'm not ready to be involved."

"You were involved with Sammy Pilsner," he said, slyly.

"What do you know about me and Sammy?" she snapped, her cheeks reddening.

"Nothing much. Just that he used to tell all the guys he was getting a blow-job from you."

She couldn't believe Sammy would have betrayed her. "I don't believe you," she said, fiercely.

"It's true isn't it? And if you did it to him – I want the same." And with that he launched himself upon her again.

She wasn't Meg about to let some oaf have his way with her. "If you don't stop I'm getting out of the car," she threatened, once more slapping his hands away.

"Go ahead," he replied, confidently. "It's a long walk home."

"You think that's going to stop me?"

"Aw, shit, you're behaving just like a dumb girl," he whined. "Anybody else would love being here with me."

He was nothing but a braggart and a bully. She glared at him furiously. "I'm *not* anybody else, it's about time you realized that."

Sensing her anger he rapidly changed tactics. "C'mon, Lauren," he wheedled. "I only wanna love you up a little." And it was hands all over her again.

Every time he launched an attack she felt incredibly vulnerable. He was so big and strong, it would be easy for him to overpower her. Right now she knew she had to make a move and make it fast. Hurriedly she groped for the door handle, sprung it open and bolted. "I'm out of here," she yelled. "You're nothing but a sex maniac!"

"And you're nothin' but a prick tease!" he yelled back.

"Get lost Stock Browning!" Burning with fury she set off down the road.

Stock suddenly realized she was serious. He started the engine, turned the car around and drove after her. Winding down the window he leaned out. "Get back in. Stop being stupid."

"I don't need this," she replied, marching along the bumpy country road.

He was contrite. "I won't touch you again. I swear I won't."

She stopped walking and whirled around to face him. "What do you swear on?" she demanded, not relishing the thought of a five-mile walk home.

"My father's life."

"Big deal."

"Okay, okay, I'll swear on my *own* life. Does that make

you happy? Now get back in the car." He threw open the passenger door and she climbed in. "I'll behave myself," he said, backing down all the way. "I'll wait until we're married. That's a promise."

You'll have a long wait, she thought. *A real long wait.*

Chapter 13

The school play was due to take place in December a few days before the Christmas break. Lauren was so immersed in her role that she decided to put the incident with Stock behind her and deal with him after Christmas. Her New Year resolution was to get rid of him once and for all.

Her parents were driving her crazy – all they wanted to talk about were wedding dates.

"I was married to your father when I was barely eighteen," her mother said.

"I'm only sixteen," she pointed out. "And I'm *not* getting married."

"Why not?" Jane and Phil chorused.

What was it with them? Were they trying to get rid of her? Or couldn't they wait to share in all the perks that being related to the Brownings would bring them?

Rehearsals became the most important thing in her life. The only interruption was the arrival of Betty's brother. Harrington Harris looked like a famous actor. Tall, in his early forties, he had a receding hairline, long sideburns to compensate, lecherous eyes and a disarming manner. Every girl in the class immediately fell in love, including Meg.

"Harrington's the most exciting man I've ever met," she confided to Lauren.

"Too old for me."

Meg winked. "Certainly *not* too old for me. *And* he's asked me out."

Here we go again, thought Lauren. "Maybe he's married," she said.

Meg was silent.

"Well, *is* he?"

"How do I know?"

Are you going out with him?"

"Of course I am. It's an adventure."

"And I suppose I'm your excuse?"

"Of course you're my excuse."

At least Meg finally seemed to have gotten over Nick, which meant that maybe she could talk to him now. It wasn't easy pretending she didn't notice him – even though they kept on exchanging long looks, and she was painfully aware of everything he did.

Meg set off for her date with Harrington Harris full of her usual enthusiasm. The following day her enthusiasm had turned to outrage. "He jumped me," she complained.

Lauren shook her head in wonderment. "What did you expect? A cup of coffee and an intellectual chat? Naturally he jumped you. Sex. That's all men want. Didn't your mother teach you that?"

Meg giggled, "As a matter of fact she did."

"So what did you do this time?"

"I told him I was a virgin. That frightened him off."

"At least you're learning."

A few days later Meg came down with the mumps. Twenty-four hours later so did Harrington Harris. Unfortunately, several other members of the cast caught the dreaded disease, including Dennis, much to Lauren's disappointment.

"What will we do about the play?" she asked Miss Harris.

Betty was as upset as she was. She surveyed her class of high school students searching their eager young faces for someone to replace Dennis, her eyes finally falling on Nick. He was such a handsome boy in an intense kind of way, and he certainly looked as if he might be able to handle it. Not that she had any idea if he could act or not, but she waved a script at him, and told him to get on stage and read with Lauren.

Sitting at the back of the class he jumped to attention. "I . . . I can't do this," he mumbled.

"Come along, dear," Betty said crisply. "You joined this group, I'm sure you're perfectly capable of giving it a try."

Reluctantly he got up and made his way to the stage where Lauren sat at a makeshift dressing table brushing her hair.

"This is the scene at the beginning of the play where Maggie and Brick have a confrontation," Betty explained. "You've watched the scene, Nick, you can do it."

He clutched the script tightly. Christ! He'd joined the group to get closer to Lauren, but he hadn't expected to get this close. What if he made a fool of himself?

He opened the script and stared blankly at the written words. It wasn't like he hadn't watched Dennis say them enough times, and if Dennis could do it so could he. Angry at himself for getting trapped he began to read.

Lauren turned around and responded to his lines, her eyes flashing.

Soon he relaxed and started to get into it. Hey – it wasn't as bad as he'd imagined. Suddenly he wasn't Nick any more, he was just an actor playing a role, and, jeez, it was a kick!

When the scene was finished he dropped the script to the floor and reality came flooding back.

Lauren was staring at him. She had the most beautiful eyes he'd ever seen. He turned to Betty Harris, anxious for her reaction.

"That was very good, dear," Betty said, beaming happily. "I'm impressed. Now all you have to do is learn the words."

Learn the words. Was she kidding? "Ah . . . yeah, yeah, sure," he assured her, sounding a lot more confident than he felt.

"Then there's no panic," Betty said, relieved. "Class, you can relax – we have our Brick."

Outside the old church hall it was cold and dark. Tiny white snowflakes were beginning to fall, silently hitting the ground. Nick emerged and leaned against the old bike Dave's brother had lent him. It certainly beat taking the bus. He waited patiently for Lauren. According to Aretha Mae, Stock and his parents were in Kansas City attending a family funeral, so there'd be no boyfriend lurking about.

She came out a few minutes later.

He stepped forward. "Hey . . . uh . . . I just wanted to say thanks," he said, kicking a pebble on the ground.

She stopped. "For what?"

"Y'know, for not letting me look like a jerk."

She held out her hand to catch a snowflake. "You handled it really well, you must have acted before."

He laughed. "Who, me? No way."

"Then you're a natural."

Now he was embarrassed. "Well, like I've seen a lotta movies, stuff like that."

"It's not easy the first time you have to get up in front of people. But honestly – you knew what you were doing."

He stamped his feet on the ground, warming up. "Thanks. That's a nice present."

"Present?"

"Yeah, it's my . . . uh . . . birthday today."

"Really?"

"Yep."

"How come you didn't tell anyone?"

"Hey . . . seventeen . . . s'no big deal."

"My parents always make sure *my* birthday's a big deal. I have a huge cake and friends over to the house and lots of presents. What did you get?"

"My family don't give presents."

She wondered about his family; there'd certainly been enough gossip about them in school. "Aren't you going to celebrate at all?" she asked, half-expecting Dawn to put in an appearance and drag him off.

He pulled up the collar of his denim jacket and stamped his feet again. "Nah, guess not."

"You *have* to do *something*," she said, prolonging the moment. "At least let me buy you a cup of coffee and a piece of cake."

He wasn't about to turn *this* invitation down. "Great," he said quickly, "let's go."

"I've got a car," she said. "Leave your bike here and we'll pick it up later."

"Do I get to drive?"

"It's the family station wagon," she said, apologetically. "Only I'm allowed to drive it."

He grinned. "What they gonna do, shoot you?"

"I guess they'll let me live," she said, smiling back.

Oh, God! Why was she doing this? She tried to tell herself she felt sorry for him, that nobody should be alone on their birthday. But it was more than that and she knew it. Nick Angelo was exciting, and she wanted some of that excitement.

They walked over to the car.

"Like one of these days I'm getting me a bright red Cadillac," he said. "Yeah, a Cadillac – that's the car for me."

"Why a Cadillac?"

"I dunno. It's just kinda . . . a cool car. An' it's made pretty good. It's American."

She smiled again. "You're very patriotic."

"You gotta be something, right?"

Their eyes met. "Right," she said.

The snow kept everyone home, and by the time they reached the drugstore it was almost empty. Nick guided her into a booth and slid across the other side. "What'll you have?"

"*I'm* buying," she reminded him.

"I'm driving so *I'm* buying," he countered.

She laughed. "No way. It's your birthday."

Louise came over, tapped her order pad and threw Nick a disapproving look. "What'll it be?" she asked, pen poised.

"I'm starving," Lauren said. "How about two cheeseburgers?"

"Yeah, an' let's go for a couple of chocolate malts along with that," Nick added, winking at Louise.

"And fries –" Lauren said.

"With ketchup –" he interrupted.

"And fried onions –"

"Yeah! Right!"

They both burst out laughing as Louise walked briskly to the kitchen.

"I like a girl who eats," he said, grinning.

"From what I hear you like all girls," she replied, immediately thinking – *Oh, no! Why did I say that? It makes me sound like a jealous idiot!*

"That's 'cause *I'm* not engaged," he said, staring pointedly at her ring.

She caught him looking and hurriedly slid her hands under the table. "Stock's very nice," she said, defensively.

"Very nice my ass."

"I don't know . . . maybe it's not going to work out the way everybody thinks." Why was she revealing herself to him?

He leant across the table. "Are you telling me you're *not* engaged?"

She hesitated for a moment, then plunged right in. "I'm just saying certain people have expectations. My parents think we make a great couple. But what I really want is to go to New York and give acting a try. When I'm older, of course."

"Sounds cool to me. You told him?"

"No," she said defensively. "I don't have to tell him. My future doesn't necessarily lie with Stock Browning."

He nailed her with an intense stare. "So take his ring off."

"I didn't *say* I was getting disengaged. I just said my future might not lie with him."

Louise marched over, slammed their order on the table and

81

threw Nick another sharp look as if to say, *What the hell you doing with her?*

Lauren took a bite of her cheeseburger. "Where's Dawn tonight?" Damn! She'd said it again. Why couldn't she keep quiet about Dawn?

He shrugged. "Who knows? I only see her when I feel like it."

She wanted to know more about him, but she didn't dare ask.

He wanted to know more about her, but he figured he shouldn't push it.

They ate in silence.

"I guess this turned out to be a pretty good birthday after all," he said at last.

She wondered why she felt so light-headed. "It did?"

"Yeah – like y'know – bein' with you, getting the part in the play, it kinda makes today special."

"That's if Dennis doesn't recover and come back," she reminded him.

"Whatever," he said casually, pretending it didn't matter, although by this time he was hooked and it did matter a great deal. "Y'know, this is my first birthday since my mother died. She never made me a cake or any of that birthday stuff – she was always too busy working. But sometimes she would like – y'know – slide me ten bucks."

"When did she die?" Lauren asked, softly.

"A few months ago, that's why we came here. Turns out my father married Aretha Mae seventeen years ago, then skipped town. He never got a divorce – so he an' my mother weren't legally married. She didn't know – nobody did. When she died, my aunt threw us out so we came here. We live over in the trailer park."

"What's it like?"

"Believe me, you never wanna know. I got this half-sister who refuses to speak to me, an' a couple of half-brothers – Harlan and Luke – they're okay. I share a trailer with 'em. My old man sits on his ass all day while Aretha Mae goes out to work. I'm stuck here until I get enough money to split."

"Where will you go?" she asked, widening her eyes.

"I dunno. New York. Maybe." He paused and grinned. "Wanna come?"

"My parents would *love* that."

He was suddenly serious. "They wouldn't have to know. We'd just take off . . . Ever thought of doing something like that?"

Why was she feeling so dizzy? "You're crazy, Nick. I don't even know you."

He looked at her very gravely. "One of these days you will. That's a promise."

Chapter 14

"Uh . . . the Christmas play is coming up," Nick mumbled, not quite sure whether to mention it or not.

Primo was lounging on the unmade bed, scratching his beer belly. "What?" he said, dragging his eyes away from *All In the Family* for a brief moment.

"I said it's the school play coming up," Nick repeated. "And . . . uh . . . one of the actors got the mumps, so I'm playing the lead." He hesitated for a moment. "I dunno . . . thought you might wanna come."

"*I* wanna come," piped up Harlan. "Me and Luke."

"No, you don't," said Aretha Mae, busy at the stove.

"Sure they do," Nick said. "I'll get 'em seats."

"Wanna go. Wanna take Luke," Harlan chanted.

"No," Aretha Mae said, sharply.

"Why not?" Nick asked.

"Because we don't belong with those people. We ain't gonna sit in no fancy theatre watchin' you make a damn fool of yourself."

"I don't make a fool of myself," he objected. "I'm good."

"Good?" Aretha Mae arched her eyebrows and curled her lip. "You be good for nothin', boy."

What was *she* bitching about? He gave her money every week, which was more than anybody else in the family did. How come she didn't pick on Primo? The lazy slob hadn't even attempted to get a job.

"I'm going into town," he said, like anybody cared.

He left the trailer, got on his bike and started the long ride. God, it was freezing. He didn't know why he was going into town anyway considering it was Sunday, and there was never anything to do. Everyone went to church in the morning and then retired into their houses never to be seen again. The drugstore was

84

closed. The gas station was closed. The movie house was closed. What was he planning? A fast ride up and down Main Street? Very exciting.

He decided that maybe he'd pay Dawn a visit seeing as they hadn't been together lately, and he was feeling decidedly horny. Since he'd been rehearsing for the play he hadn't seen much of anybody except Lauren. And there was no way he could make a move on her.

Ah, Lauren . . . He couldn't figure her out. One moment she was his best friend – the next cool and businesslike – as if the play was the only important thing. They met at rehearsal and went through their scenes. The moment they finished she hurried off to meet Stock who was always outside waiting to take her home.

He'd imagined things would be different after their one night together sharing hamburgers and a few home truths. But no. Everything was back to the way it was before.

He was mad that he'd opened up and told her about Aretha Mae and his father. It wasn't her business. She was just some rich girl, stuck up like all the rest.

When he reached Dawn's house, her mother told him she was away for the weekend. Great, now he didn't even have Dawn to take his mind off things.

"When's she comin' back?" he asked.

"Tomorrow," Mrs Novak replied, clutching a scarlet cardigan across her scraggy breasts. She was one of those rail-thin women with bulging eyes and a nervous tongue that kept on darting in and out, licking her dry thin lips. She smelt of whisky and stale cigarette smoke.

"Why don't you come in anyway and have a lemonade," she suggested.

Jeez, Nick thought, if she and Primo ever met they'd make the perfect couple. Fat and thin and both zonked out of their minds.

He declined Mrs Novak's invitation and got out of there fast.

"How are you feeling, Dennis?" Lauren asked over the phone.

Dennis told her he was depressed about not being able to appear in the play with her.

"Don't worry," she said, comfortingly. "We'll manage without you, but it won't be the same."

Liar, she thought to herself as soon as she hung up, *it'll be even better because Nick Angelo is playing your part.*

She felt disloyal and confused, and yet she was savvy enough to know that Nick meant trouble. She also knew she couldn't stop watching him at every opportunity, and she loved acting with him. But there was such a thing as self-preservation, and she was aware that it was essential to stay away from him, which wasn't easy, because every time they did the opening scene between Maggie and Brick she sensed a great surge of electricity between them.

Now it was almost time to perform the play on the stage with half the town watching. She shivered. Would everyone be able to spot the chemistry between them?

Stock was back in her life with a vengeance. Big and bossy and full of himself because he'd taken delivery of his new car – a super-fast Corvette. She stuck by his side whenever she could. It was safer than allowing Nick to get close.

"You don't have to come to the play if you don't want to," she told Stock.

"I'll be there," he said, confidently. "You're my girl – wouldn't miss it. I'm sittin' with my parents in the front row."

Oh great, that's all I need.

"I'm just saying you shouldn't feel obligated, I'm perfectly okay with the fact that you . . . you might be bored." She was almost stammering.

He didn't get it. "Is Dennis back yet?"

"Uh . . . no. That new guy's playing the role."

"That jerk, you mean," he said, sourly.

It seemed that both Stock and Nick were programmed to insult each other whenever they could.

Sometimes she felt as if she was going to explode. There was nobody she could confide in. Not her parents, and certainly not Meg who'd kill her if she knew she had these feelings for Nick.

Bury them, she told herself. *And Nick Angelo will go away. He's the kind of boy who comes to town, causes trouble and then takes off.*

There was plenty of activity in Bosewell at Christmas. First there was the play, followed by the school dance on New Year's Eve. Naturally, Stock had plans. "After the dance," he informed her, "Some of the guys have booked rooms over at the motel. We'll have a party."

"What kind of party?"

"Oh, you know, music, good times an' a few strong blasts . . . Relax, Lauren, you're such a square sometimes."

She hated being told to relax – it was so patronizing. "Remember what happened last time," she said, to her horror sounding just like her mother. "Your allowance was cut off and you told me I should've warned you about inviting all those extra people."

"This'll be different," he promised. "Oh – and ask your girlfriend, Meg, if she wants to go with Mack Ryan."

Mack was Stock's best friend. Bigger than Stock. Blonder than Stock. But not as rich.

"Why doesn't he ask her himself?"

"Maybe he doesn't want to, guys don't dig the idea of getting rejected."

Meg was delighted, she said yes immediately. *At least we'll be a foursome*, Lauren thought. Anything was better than being alone with Stock.

As the play drew nearer Betty insisted on more rehearsals. Lauren didn't mind, in fact she loved it.

Nick grabbed her arm one day on her way out. "Hey," he said. "Do I have to wait until my next birthday for you to talk to me like a human being?"

"I'm talking to you now," she said, trying to remain calm.

"Ha!" he laughed, bitterly. "You're back in the same old groove. You've got your rich boyfriend, your nice organized life, an' no time for me."

"We're working together," she said. "What gave you the impression it was more than that?"

He stared at her so intently she thought she might dissolve.

"You *know* it's more than that," he said.

"I . . . I have no idea what you're talking about."

"Yes, you do," he said. "Only you won't admit it."

She pulled free and rushed outside. To her relief Stock was waiting. Stock was always waiting.

The night of the play there was a blizzard. Betty Harris was in a bad mood because Harrington, whom she'd planned to show off, was still sequestered away with a bad case of the mumps.

Lauren was shaking. Why had she agreed to play the lead? Did she really want to stand up in front of the whole town in a skimpy silk slip and play Maggie the Cat, a sexual older woman? God, everybody would laugh her off stage.

Nick was nervous too – he couldn't figure out how he'd got conned into this.

87

Before going on they wished each other luck. "Break a leg," Lauren said.

He looked at her incredulously. "Break a leg?"

"That's what they say in the theatre for good luck."

"I always figured actors were a crazy bunch," he said, shaking his head.

She grinned. "I guess they are."

His throat was dry and he had a strong desire to run. "Well, anyway – we're gonna kill 'em. Right?"

"Right!"

Lauren made her entrance first. Nick waited in the wings, his heart thumping. When he made it to the stage he lost all fear and became the character.

Shit, he thought, *I can do this – I can really do this*. And he was right, because the play was a smash. Shocking and *risqué* for a small town like Bosewell, Betty had taken a risk putting it on – but the audience loved it anyway.

As they were taking their bows, Lauren spotted a scowling Stock sitting in the front row with his parents. She couldn't care less, she was too busy enjoying the applause.

After five curtain calls the elated cast mingled backstage. She looked around for Nick, found him and hurried over. "You were great," she said, warmly.

"So were you." He broke into a grin. "Hey – we both were."

Betty Harris approached them, beads and gold chains jangling. "We're a hit!" she gushed. "You were *all* wonderful. If only my brother were here to enjoy our triumph."

"I'm sorry he's still sick," Lauren said.

"His balls probably look like an elephant on a bad day," Nick muttered in her ear.

"What?" She couldn't believe what he'd just said.

"It's the mumps," he replied straight-faced. "Gets 'em every time!"

She choked back a giggle as a vivid picture of Harrington Harris with swollen elephant balls flashed before her eyes. Fortunately her parents appeared before she burst out laughing. She tried to introduce them to Nick, but he'd taken off.

A glowering Stock hovered behind them. "You never told me you were going to be up on stage half-naked for everyone to get an eyeful," he complained.

Wasn't he supposed to be congratulating her?

"You never asked," she replied.

"We'll see you later, dear," her mother said, wandering off with Phil in tow.

"How does it make *me* look?" Stock demanded. "You up there with that creep playing opposite you. You made a fool of me tonight, Lauren."

"I did not," she said, heatedly.

"Yes, you did," he argued.

She sighed. "Don't spoil it, Stock. This is a special night for me."

"It isn't for me."

"Then maybe you should go home."

"And what will *you* do?"

"I'll stay here and celebrate with the rest of the cast."

"Without me?"

"Yes, without you."

"You do that." He said, storming off.

Too bad. She wasn't exactly heartbroken.

Betty Harris had arranged dinner in one of the adjoining rooms for the cast. They were high with excitement, milling around congratulating each other. When they sat down Lauren found herself next to Nick.

"So . . . I guess that's it," he said, picking at a bread roll. "I won't get to see you until school starts next year."

She sipped a glass of water. "Next year sounds like forever. Vacation's only a few weeks, and we'll see each other at the New Year's dance. You are going, aren't you?"

"Nah . . . don't think so."

"Why not?"

"I can't get into all that organized crap where everybody's supposed to have a good time."

She bit her lip and tried not to say it, but out it came anyway. "Surely Dawn will want you to take her?"

He gave her a quizzical look. "I thought I told you, me and Dawn, we're not a couple."

"That's not what she says." *Oh God, Robert:. Shut up!*

"How come you're so concerned anyway? You've hardly talked to me lately."

"I'm talking to you now."

He stared at her. "Maybe I'd like t'do more than talk."

She looked away. She should have known he'd want to jump her, just like he'd done to Meg. Why were boys so interested in sex? Didn't feelings or getting to know someone ever come into it?

"Excuse me," she said, pushing her chair away from the table and getting up.

"Where are you going?"

"I've got a present for Betty in my car."

Leave me alone, Nick Angelo. I am not interested.

Oh yes you are, Roberts. Oh yes you are.

She hurried outside to the station wagon, opened the door and reached inside for the brightly wrapped gift.

"Hey –" He was right behind her.

She turned around, feeling weak and vulnerable.

Without saying a word he moved very close and kissed her.

It was not like any kiss she'd ever felt before. His lips were insistent and yet soft. His tongue was exploring, and yet not in a conquering way. Without thinking she began kissing him back.

"I've wanted to do this ever since I first saw you," he mumbled, pulling her in close.

She took a deep breath. "Blakely's hardware store. I was scrambling around on the floor –"

"Yeah, an' you looked pretty good that day."

She was about to say, "So did you," but before she could he kissed her again, and the second time was so incredible that she let herself fall into it and get lost. She'd kissed boys before – Sammy Pilsner, Stock, several boys she'd dated, but it had never been like this. Never.

He pushed his hands through her long hair. "You're so . . . I dunno . . . beautiful."

Nobody had ever called her beautiful before. Pretty – yes. Nice – naturally. Beautiful was something else. But even so . . . she mustn't get carried away. "We can't do this," she murmured, softly.

"I'm not forcin' you," he replied, pressing close.

She took another deep breath willing herself to make a move. "I have to go." Without waiting for a reply she turned around and rushed back inside.

For the rest of the evening she tried not to look in his direction or even think about him.

Betty Harris made a speech praising all her students, and when it was time to leave Nick was right behind her. "Can I drive you home?" he asked.

"No, I'm the one with the car, remember?" Lauren replied.

He grinned. "You're right."

"Good night, Nick," she said, politely.

"Good night, beautiful."

All the way back to the trailer park he thought about her. Then his mind started racing in different directions. The play had been such a triumph. He'd really got off on the feel of an audience watching him, studying his every move. On stage he wasn't some nothing kid, he was Brick, he was someone they responded to in a positive way.

And then his thoughts returned to Lauren. When he'd kissed her it had been like nothing he'd ever known. Oh sure, he'd had enough girls, but none of them had been like her – he'd never had that feeling of wanting to look after a girl, protect her, be with her all the time. This had nothing to do with scoring. This was different.

Was he in love?

Don't even think about it.

Maybe he could be an actor. The thought sneaked into his head unexpectedly.

Nah. He didn't stand a chance.

Or did he?

Chapter 15

Once Nick decided what he wanted to do he went all out. His first move was to visit Betty Harris and ask if she'd consider giving him private coaching.

"I can't pay you," he explained, "But one of these days I'll make it, an' then I'll pay you big."

Betty laughed. "If only I had a dime for every boy that thought he could be the next Marlon Brando or Montgomery Clift. You're no different, Nick. You're good, but you're no different."

"Hey – you don't understand," he said. "I'm not gonna be a nuclear scientist. I ain't got a chance of runnin' for President. I gotta go for *something*, an' I've decided this is it."

"Ah yes, but I *do* understand," Betty said, pacing around her small living room. "When I was young I had the same ambition. In fact I even went to New York."

He was surprised. "You did?"

"Yes. I made the rounds of auditions only to be told I was too tall, too short, too fat, too thin, too ugly, too pretty. Believe me, Nick, nobody knows what they want. They only know they want a carbon copy of somebody who's made it."

"So what did you do?"

"I got married," she said. "I married a man who liked to dress up in my clothes. He left me for another woman." She laughed, dryly. "Thank God it wasn't for another man!"

"Go on," he encouraged.

"I suppose I got older and certainly wiser. Every so often I landed bit parts here and there, until eventually I came back to Bosewell," she sighed, "and here I am, teaching the High school acting class. Teaching you all to do something you're never going to have a chance at."

"Everybody's got a chance, Betty."

She smiled, wryly. "Full of optimism. How old are you? Sixteen?"

"Seventeen."

"Well, Nick, I went to New York when I was twenty, came back when I was thirty. I'm now fifty. The last twenty years . . ." She trailed off, shaking her head, wondering where the time had gone.

"But your brother made it," he pointed out.

"It depends what you call making it," she said matter-of-factly. "In a town like Bosewell he's a star. But the truth is he's played three butlers on Broadway in the last six years, and that's the extent of his stardom. The last time he worked was advertising a cure for haemorrhoids on television."

"Harrington Harris?"

"Yes, the great Harrington Harris. But it makes everybody feel good when he comes back here. They *think* he's a star, and that's all that matters."

"Betty," he said earnestly, fixing her with his green eyes. "You gotta help me. I need to study, an' I have to do it with somebody who'll teach me things."

There was something about him that was so intensely sincere. Betty knew she shouldn't encourage the boy, but what did she have to lose? The winter was cold and lonely, and there were five weeks before school and acting class resumed. What else was she going to do with her time?

"Very well," she said. "You'll come over here three times a week at noon and we'll work from twelve until four. Be prepared to work hard and *never* call to tell me you have something else to do."

"I swear it," he said, excitedly. "I'll be here."

She smiled. "Good. It's a start."

Life at the trailer park was hard during the winter. The roofs of both trailers leaked, causing a rancid damp smell and numerous little puddles. It was almost like living outside.

Primo refused to do anything about it. "My arm hurts," he whined. "I ain't fixin' nothin'."

"You musta hurt it lifting a can of beer," Nick muttered, disgustedly.

"You're gettin' a real smart mouth," Primo slurred. "I could throw you out any time."

"I thought you promised my mother I had to graduate High school?"

"Don't be so sure," Primo grumbled.

Out of school, Luke and Harlan were bored. They ran into town every day and Aretha Mae couldn't stop them. One day Harlan came home beaten up.

"What happened to you?" Nick demanded.

"Nothin'," Harlan said, sulkily.

Nick turned to Luke. "What happened to him?"

Luke stared blankly.

"Jeez!" Nick exclaimed. "Open your mouth and talk, goddamnit!"

Luke ran out of the trailer, crying.

Aretha Mae stood in front of the sink stoically washing dishes. Primo snored in his usual position.

"Don't either of you give a shit?" Nick demanded.

"He better learn to defend hisself. This won't be the last time," Aretha Mae said.

Cyndra had gotten herself a job working down at the canning plant. She left early in the morning and arrived home late at night, barely acknowledging Nick's existence.

"You're a freakin' pain," he exploded one day. "When you gonna lighten up?"

"When you leave," she replied, brusquely.

"Don't hold your breath. I'm outta here on *my* time—not yours."

"Good," she said. "Make sure it's soon."

He kept himself busy. What with the work at the garage, and visiting Betty Harris three times a week, and trying to do a few repairs around the trailers, he never had a moment to himself.

Working with Betty was a kick. She chose plays she knew would interest him. He particularly loved *A Streetcar Named Desire*. Reading Stanley to her Blanche was a real blast. The good thing was that he'd finally found something he could absorb himself in and it was pretty exciting.

The honeymoon was over for Aretha Mae and Primo. Whenever she was home they'd taken to having long, vicious yelling matches. Primo beat up on her pretty good. Smack! That's all the bastard seemed to know.

Nick wished he could apologize for his father. He wanted to say, *Look it's not my fault. Throw us out. We'll go somewhere. Anywhere. We don't have to screw your life up, too.*

But now that she had him back, Aretha Mae had no intention of letting Primo go.

Christmas came and went. It was a dismal holiday. Aretha Mae brought home the remains of the Brownings' turkey and made a thick soup – that was the extent of their festivities. No tree. No presents. No nothing.

Nick didn't mind, he was more or less used to it, but he felt sorry for the kids – especially Harlan – it was useless trying to get through to Luke.

Occasionally he hung out with Joey who wanted to know if he was going to the New Year's dance.

"Haven't thought about it," he said.

"There's nothin' else to do," Joey said. "We gotta make plans."

"How do we get in?" Nick asked. "Don't we have to buy tickets?"

"Nah, it's a High school thing. Whyn't you take Dawn?"

He hadn't really thought about Dawn lately. He'd been so busy that the need to get laid hadn't arisen. "Yeah, I'll give her a call. Who'll you bring?"

Joey dragged on his cigarette and attempted to sound casual. "Maybe I'll ask your sister."

Nick looked surprised. "My sister?"

"Cyndra," Joey said. "I mean, it's not like I think she'd say yes or anything, but she always seems so . . . kinda – y'know – all by herself."

Nick made a face "Hey, if you wanna get your balls crushed, go ahead."

He had no feelings for Cyndra. Maybe as a brother he was supposed to feel protective, but what the hell – she was a bitch, he didn't care who she went out with.

"What do we wear to this thing?" he asked.

"Tux," Joey replied. "We'll take a ride to Ripley an' hire a couple of monkey suits."

They set off for Ripley the next afternoon. Joey had a second-hand motorcycle and they made it in a couple of hours. The rental place was crowded with manic people struggling to get themselves an outfit for New Year's Eve. Joey pushed his way to the front, grabbed a salesman and picked out two tuxedos.

"I feel like a jerk," Nick said, trying his on.

"You look like one," Joey guffawed. "But that's okay, so does everyone on New Year's."

He paraded in front of the mirror. The pants were too long, the jacket too big. "Have I really gotta wear it?"

Joey slapped him on the back. "Only for a night. You'll live."

They paid their money and left.

"I know a bar where they got naked girls," Joey said with a wink. "Bare tits an' ass."

They'd both acquired fake I.D.s so they swaggered into the bar full of confidence. Nobody stopped them. Nobody cared.

The place was jammed with construction workers busy watching the parade of half naked waitresses – girls who wore nothing but black stockings, garter belts, frilly aprons and phoney smiles.

Nick couldn't believe what he was seeing. He nudged Joey. "Ain't there some law against this?"

Joey sniggered. "Don't tell me you've never been in a topless bar before. They're the coming thing."

"Hey, hey, talkin' of comin'," Nick joked.

Joey laughed. "Let's have a little control here. You can look, not touch."

"Do they put out?"

"If you've got the bread."

He patted the top pocket of his denim jacket. "I got it," he said. "Yesterday was pay-day." He already had his eye on one girl – a pretty brunette with a sweet face who reminded him of Lauren. He hadn't seen her since the play, and sometimes he thought about her. But he tried not to – she wasn't exactly available. When the girl took their order he came on to her. "What're you doing later?" he asked.

She peeked at her watch. "I get off at three."

"I'm about ready to get off now," he joked. "How much?"

She tried to look insulted. "You think I'm a hooker?"

"Course not," he said. "How much?"

"Twenty."

"Twenty," he repeated. "What is it, mink lined?"

"Ten for you because you're cute."

"You got a room?"

"If you wanna go to my place it'll be an extra five."

He weighed up the possibilities. He'd never had to pay for it before, but somehow it seemed fitting, a New Year's present to himself, a girl he didn't have to sweet talk. "Okay," he agreed.

Her name was Candy and she lived in one room with two smelly cats roaming around, and a hamster in a cage.

"I don't usually bring people back here," Candy announced, shrugging off her coat. "But you seem like a nice guy. How old are you anyway?"

"Twenty-one," he lied. "How about you?"

"Twenty."

More like thirty, he thought. "You bin doin' this long?"

"Doing what?" she said, scrambling in her purse for a joint.

"A little action on the side."

"Oh. I don't really do this," she said vaguely, lighting up. "I needed extra money this week . . . and like I said, you're kinda cute."

Sure, he thought to himself.

She offered him a drag and began to undo the buttons on her blouse.

He drew deeply on the joint – it wasn't the first time he'd had marijuana – and watched her as she took her time removing her blouse. He'd already seen the goods on display in the bar, but it was more of a kick watching them revealed slowly just for him.

Underneath the blouse her small breasts were covered by a skimpy black bra. With a theatrical flourish she threw the blouse on the floor and unzipped her skirt, daintily stepping out of it. Quite obviously she hadn't bothered to wear panties. He felt that good old familiar stirring.

"What shall I leave on?" she asked.

He noticed she was chewing gum. "Your ear-rings," he replied.

She laughed, casually fingering her nipples. "Never heard *that* one before."

He stripped off his clothes. This girl was a challenge. She was a professional, and he wanted to see if he could make her feel as good as all his other conquests.

Candy plumped herself down on the bed and beckoned him over.

He made the trip across the room in record time and climbed aboard.

She took another drag of her joint and placed it in a chipped glass ashtray next to the bed.

"You're not really twenty-one," she said slyly. "Tell me the truth?"

No way was he admitting to seventeen. "Nah. Twenty-two," he lied, pumping away.

Candy had obviously expended all her energy down at the bar. She lay there like a corpse, chewing gum and looking blank as he gave her a little of the Angelo magic.

As soon as he was finished he couldn't wait to get away. Forget about pleasing her – this was the first and last time he'd ever pay for it. He left the money on the table and beat a hasty retreat.

Later Joey met him at the bar and they got on the bike and headed for home.

"What happened, man?" Joey wanted to know. "Gimme all the filthy details."

"You want details, pay for it yourself," he replied, shortly.

"What's the matter? You fall in love?" Joey teased.

He groaned. "Don't even mention the word."

Love. Was *that* the feeling he had for Lauren? He missed her and yet he was nervous about seeing her when school started because he didn't know what would happen. He was so used to being in control with girls. He got beat up enough at home, at least there was one part of his life where he had the upper hand.

Now he had this dumb feeling and it wouldn't go away.

Lauren Roberts. She was the only special girl he'd ever met and she belonged to somebody else.

The truth was it was about time he did something about it.

Chapter 16

Lauren spent a miserable Christmas. Over the holidays her mother's brother, Will, and his wife, Margo, came to visit from Philadelphia. This time they did not bring Brad – their nineteen-year-old son. Lauren's crush on him had been a long time ago and she didn't miss his presence.

The day after Christmas they spent at the Brownings' house. Stock gave her a cashmere sweater and two cookbooks – obviously chosen by his mother. She gave him a simple pewter money clip and a photo frame. And all day long she wondered what Nick Angelo was doing.

At night she lay in bed and thought about her future.

Only another two years and she'd be out of school. She was already campaigning for enrolment in an Eastern college. Her parents said Kansas City was as far as they'd let her go, but she had her mind set on New York.

Meg came by the house to find out about the New Year's dance. "What are you wearing?" As usual she was obsessed with clothes.

"I haven't thought about it," Lauren replied, vaguely. "Maybe that dress I wore to my engagement party."

Meg frowned. "You *can't* wear the same thing again."

"Yes I can," she said, stubbornly.

"What's the *matter* with you? You're so . . . sort of . . . different, lately."

Lauren wondered if she was different. All she ever thought about was Nick. On his birthday he'd seemed so sensitive and understanding, and the night of the play, when he'd kissed her, it was definitely something special. She couldn't believe he'd practically attacked Meg. The truth was that Meg had probably encouraged him and then backed off at the last moment, always a dangerous practice.

"I'm wearing black," Meg announced, dramatically.

"That's exciting," Lauren murmured. Frankly she couldn't care less.

The night of the New Year's dance there was thick snow on the ground. Lauren stared out of her window watching the snowflakes falling. She wondered if she could get out of going altogether.

No such luck. Stock called to announce he would be picking her up at seven. "Be ready," he said.

God, he was so overbearing. When had she ever kept him waiting? New Year resolution. Get out of this engagement once and for all. Stop thinking about it and do it.

For a Christmas present the Brownings had insisted she visit their store and pick out an outfit. She'd done so reluctantly, and only at her mother's insistence. She'd chosen a short, black off-the-shoulder dress. When her mother saw it she had a fit. "You can't possibly wear that, it's quite unsuitable."

"Why?"

Jane was perplexed. "It's too sophisticated. Besides, young girls don't wear black."

"This young girl kind of likes the idea."

Jane sighed. "I don't know what's the matter with you lately, you're so argumentative."

Hmmm. Had she and Meg been talking?

Stock arrived with a corsage of white orchids and an appreciative, "Wow! You look –" He was about to say sexy, but since Mr and Mrs Roberts were hovering in the front hall he changed it to "– sensational."

She smiled. For once he'd said the right thing.

Jane produced her camera. "Photo time!" she exclaimed, gaily.

Dutifully she posed for a picture with Stock, then kissed her parents, said, "See you later," and left the house. Usually there was a discussion about what time her curfew was, but since it was New Year's Eve and she was with Stock, it didn't seem to matter. All they were interested in was cementing the deal.

Mack Ryan was waiting in the car, and they set off to pick up Meg. When they arrived at her house she gave Lauren a filthy look. "You didn't tell me you bought a black dress. How *could* you? *I'm* wearing black," she muttered, furiously. "And you *knew* I was."

Lauren shrugged. Quite truthfully she'd forgotten. "It doesn't make any difference. We don't look alike."

"I wanted to stand out," Meg said, shaking her head petulantly. "Now we look like twins!"

"You do stand out," Lauren replied, thinking that her friend had put on a pound or two.

"No. *You* do," Meg said. "It's *always* you."

They got to the dance late, having stopped for champagne in the car. Lauren wasn't used to drinking – she hated the taste, but she'd decided this New Year was going to be different from any other. It was time she grew up.

When they arrived the dance was in full progress. Stock grabbed her by the arm cutting a swath through his cronies as he led her on to the dance floor. "You're looking hot tonight," he said. "I didn't want to say it in front of your parents, but boy – have you got a body!"

Was this the first time he'd noticed? She decided to respond in kind. "Boy, have you got a body, too!"

He wasn't sure quite how to take this, so he pretended he hadn't heard, and began to gyrate his hips to the strains of "Honky Tonk Woman' played by the local band. Not quite Mick Jagger – as a matter of fact not even close.

Lauren felt a little dizzy as she started to dance, her eyes continually searching the room.

What are you looking for, Roberts?

I'm looking for Nick Angelo. Want to make something out of it?

To Nick's surprise, Cyndra said yes when Joey asked her to the dance. "I hear you're going with Joey," he said.

She glared at him.

"One of these days you're gonna realize you're taking it out on the wrong person," he said, trying to fix his stupid bow tie.

"When that day comes I'll let you know," she replied, brushing back her long, dark hair.

"Gee, I'm holding my breath," he said, irritated by her pissy attitude.

They were interrupted by the sound of banging and screaming coming from the trailer next door. It was nothing new – ever since Christmas, Primo and Aretha Mae had been at each other's throats.

Cyndra glared at him with a spiteful expression as if it was his fault. "Maybe you won't be around here much longer."

"How many times I gotta tell you? This wasn't my choice."

"You belong to him, an' he ain't nothin' but dirt," she said, vengefully.

"Yeah . . . well, let me tell you this – you belong to him too."

Her eyes were full of fury. "I don't believe it."

"Are you telling me your ma lied to you, is that it?"

Her dark eyes continued to blaze brightly. "I don't believe that dumb ox is my father."

"He is. Get used to it."

Joey arrived to pick her up on his motorcycle.

Cyndra stood at the door of the trailer peering out with an angry expression. "It's snowing," she said. "How we gonna get anywhere on that dumb bike?"

Joey produced a rolled-up plastic raincoat, unrolled it with a flourish and threw it over her. "There you go. How's that for service?"

"Oh, this is classy," she grumbled. "A real classy date."

"What did you expect? A Kennedy?"

"Nothing," she said, curling her lip sourly. "Absolutely nothing."

Nick had been planning to ask Primo if he could borrow the van, but what with all that screaming coming from the trailer he decided to ride his bike over to Dawn's and see if they could borrow her mother's car.

He hated the rented tux: it was too big for him, and what the hell was he supposed to wear on his feet?

Fuck 'em. He'd wear his sneakers, and if anybody had anything to say about it he'd smash 'em in the mouth.

Harlan told him he looked nice. Luke stared at him like a zombie. It occurred to Nick that the kid should be getting some kind of professional help. Fat chance.

"What are you two doin' tonight?" he asked.

Silly question. What *could* they do? They had no way of getting into town unless they walked and the snow was pretty deep on the ground. They couldn't even slide into the other trailer and watch television on account of the fact that Aretha Mae and Primo were busy killing each other.

"Tell you what," he said, trying to cheer them up, "tomorrow I'll treat you both to the movies."

Harlan nodded, his face lighting up.

He set off for Dawn's on the bike. It was a long ride and by the time he got there he was soaked through.

Dawn greeted him wearing the tightest dress he'd ever seen. She did not believe in leaving anything to the imagination.

"Great date you are!" she said, shaking her head. "We've gotta get you dry before we can go anywhere."

"Can we borrow your mom's car?"

"It's all ours, handsome. She *was* gonna use it, but then she passed out. C'mon, get your clothes off, I'll try to dry 'em."

He followed her upstairs to her room and stripped off. Two large posters of Elvis Presley sneered down at him.

She ran an appreciative eye up and down his body. "Hmm . . . sure you wanna go to the dance? My mom won't surface until tomorrow."

"Hey, I didn't ride all the way into Ripley to hire a freakin' tux to sit at home."

She winked, suggestively. "Sitting wasn't what I had in mind."

"We can do that later, okay?"

"Whatever you want, big boy."

That was the thing about Dawn, she was much too obliging.

Lauren spotted him the moment he came in. In a way she hadn't expected him to turn up. In another way she'd hoped he would. And now here he was with Dawn hanging on to his arm like a leech.

She tried not to stare – she certainly didn't want him catching her. He looked great in his tuxedo – even if it was a little big. He'd obviously made an effort. Was it because of Dawn? *Bitch!*

Lauren immediately felt guilty. The trouble was that Dawn wasn't a bitch at all, she was a perfectly pleasant girl who just happened to be the school tramp. Lauren suspected Stock had slept with her. Not that he admitted it. Not that she cared.

Stock was having a fine time twirling her around the dance floor, full of himself as usual.

"Let's get a drink," she said breathlessly, breaking away.

He beamed, "That's more like it. How about going for the rest of the champagne out in my car?"

"I meant a soft drink."

"Excuse *me*."

She hated it when he tried to be sarcastic.

Over by the bar Nick handed Dawn a glass of watered-down punch. "Try this poison."

Her eyes scanned the room and she shook her head. "I dunno what *we're* doing here. We shoulda gone to Ripley." She threw him a sly look. "Or stayed home."

He had to agree with her, they didn't belong.

She swallowed a fake yawn. "We came, we saw, we got bored. Let's get the hell outta here, we can have more fun at my house. I'll show you mine if you show me yours!"

He wasn't prepared to leave until he'd seen Lauren, after all, she was the reason he'd hired a tuxedo and shown up.

"Hey – you told me you were such a hotshot dancer. How about showing 'em what a *real* dancer can do?"

Dawn was always up for a challenge. "Honey, I can beat any of 'em. Any time. Any way."

"What are we waitin' for?" He pulled her on to the crowded floor. Not that he was into dancing, but he could make the moves if he had to.

Dawn enjoyed showing off. She had her assets and she knew how to shake them – especially in her favourite tight dress.

A small crowd gathered as they put on a show.

And then he spotted Lauren. She was sitting at a table with Stock and a group of his friends, and naturally she looked sensational.

He knew he had to make a move. He didn't know what he was going to do or when he was going to do it, but he wasn't leaving until he did.

Chapter 17

"So?" Joey asked, leaning across the small table. "Do you like to dance?"

"No," Cyndra said, checking out the room with her dark moody eyes, wondering why Joey had invited her.

"How come?"

"How come what?" she snapped. "Just because I'm half-black I'm supposed to have rhythm?"

"I didn't say that."

"No, but you sure thought it. Is *that* why you asked me tonight? Black chick ain't got no morals – she'll be easy."

"Huh?"

"You heard me."

"I heard someone with a big hang-up."

"What?"

"A hang-up – like in chip on the shoulder shit."

She smoothed down the skirt of her green velvet dress – purchased at a second-hand shop – and tried to compose herself. She certainly hadn't dressed up and come out to get involved in a slanging match. "I don't have no chip," she said, controlling her temper.

"Maybe you should," he remarked. "It's a lousy deal – black mother, white dad, you can't figure out *what* colour you are."

Unexpectedly tears stung her eyes. He was right on, she wasn't one thing or the other and it hurt.

"*My* dad was Jewish," Joey continued. "A Jewish cop in Chicago married to a nice Irish Catholic girl. I never tell anyone I'm half-Jewish, s'not worth the aggravation."

"What aggravation?" she ventured.

"Y'know – the name calling, the dirty words. You know."

Yes. She knew all right. Mr Browning crying out in the

throes of his lust – "black cunt." Every man she ever met looking her over like she was there for the taking.

"You gotta learn to live with it," Joey said, wisely. "*I* did."

She sneaked a quick glance at him. He was kind of funny looking, tall and lanky with a shock of brown hair, a lopsided grin and crooked teeth. She didn't know why she'd accepted his invitation. Maybe because it was the first time anyone had asked her anywhere formal.

"Wanna dance?" He jerked his thumb towards the crowded floor.

She saw Nick out there breaking his butt with Dawn Kovak to the strains of "Sugar Sugar". "I . . . I don't think so."

He noticed her watching. "What've you got against him?" he asked.

She shifted uncomfortably. "Who?"

"Nick. What's he done to you?"

"He came here, that's what," she said, fiercely.

"It wasn't his choice." Joey said, taking a pack of Camels from his pocket and offering her one. "He's a cool guy. You should give him a chance."

She waved the package of cigarettes away. "You don't understand."

"Maybe one day you'll explain it to me. Sometimes it's good to talk – get it out in the open." He paused, realizing he was dealing with a touchy subject. "Whenever you like – I'm here. Okay?"

She narrowed her eyes and regarded him suspiciously. "What do you want from me?"

He shrugged. "Nothin', if that's all right with you."

"What time is it?" Meg asked, clinging on to Mack Ryan as if *they* were the engaged couple.

Stock consulted his expensive waterproof watch – a present from his parents. "Twenty-five minutes before midnight. Come five past an' we're on our way."

"You got it," said Mack, placing his hand on the back of Meg's neck and giving her a rub and a tickle. "This little lady an' I – we want some privacy."

Meg giggled. "We do?" she said, coquettishly.

Sure, Lauren thought. *And tomorrow this little lady is going to be complaining about how you nearly raped her.*

"Are we gonna *party* tonight!" Stock proclaimed.

Lauren took a hearty gulp of punch and immediately regretted it – the stuff tasted disgusting.

"C'mon," Stock urged, pulling her out of her chair. "They're playing my favourite."

His favourite turned out to be a soapy rendition of "Rocket Man". She hated it, especially when he began to get romantic, pulling her close, rubbing his crotch up against her leg and singing off key in her ear.

Tonight's the night, she thought gloomily. *He's going to make a move and when he does I'm giving him back his ring.*

About time too.

Across the dance floor Nick edged his way nearer to Lauren, guiding Dawn until she finally realized something was up and said, quite testily, "Where are we *going*? You're pushin' me around like I'm a vacuum cleaner!"

"We're gonna play excuse me."

"Huh?"

"Like I'll ask Lauren t'dance – an' you'll take care of Stock."

"I will?"

"Yeah. We gotta liven things up."

"That'll liven things up all right,' she said, getting the picture and not particularly liking it. If Nick thought he was about to score with Miss Thighs Together Roberts he had another think coming. Sweet little Lauren wouldn't give him a second glance. And Stock would punch his brains out if he made a move on his precious fiancée.

As soon as he'd manoeuvred them next to Lauren and Stock, he gave Dawn a little shove and an encouraging, "Go for it!"

Dawn smiled provocatively at Stock – after all she knew him well enough – they'd been secretly sleeping together on and off since eighth grade; his engagement had certainly made no difference to his sex life. "My turn," she said gaily, pulling him away from Lauren, throwing a perfunctory, "You don't mind, do you?" over her shoulder.

"Go ahead," Lauren said, one eye on Nick – who winked as if to say *how did you like the way I arranged this*?

Stock was easily led. Could he help it if girls found him irresistible? Dawn played her part, dragging him off to the middle of the dance floor, clinging on to him tightly.

"Hey –" Nick said, staring intently into Lauren's eyes. "Looks like you need someone to dance with."

She felt her heart begin to beat erratically. All of a sudden she could hardly breathe. "I guess so."

He took her in his arms pulling her in real close. "Tonight you're breakin' your engagement," he said, very quietly.

"I know," she found herself replying.

He held her even closer. "Just so long as you know."

"There's gonna be trouble," Joey said.

"What kind of trouble?' Cyndra asked.

"Big trouble," Joey replied, nodding towards the dance floor.

Cyndra had no idea what he was talking about, as far as she could see everybody seemed to be having a good time.

"You don't get it, do you?" he said.

She wondered what she was supposed to get.

"Stock Browning."

Browning. The very sound of that name made her shudder. Damn the whole disgusting Browning family, they were the worst kind of people.

"What about Stock?" she asked, trying to stay cool.

"Your brother's makin' a move on his girl."

She frowned. "How many times do I have to tell you? Nick's *not* my brother."

"Don't make no difference, he's gonna get his ass kicked."

"Good."

"You want him gettin' beat up?"

"I don't care."

"Yeah, well . . . I'll hav'ta get into it."

"Why?"

"'Cause he's my friend."

She studied the dance floor. Stock was gyrating with Dawn. Nick was way over the other side slow dancing with Lauren. "Nothing's going to happen," she said.

"I hope you're right."

"I usually am."

"What's Lauren doing with *him*?" Meg said, staring furiously across the dance floor.

"Y'know," Mack was not listening to a word she said, "I

always had eyes for you – even when I was going steady."

Meg was distracted. She was enjoying all the attention, but at the same time she didn't appreciate her best friend cosying up to Nick Angelo. "Where's Stock?" she demanded. "He should put a stop to this."

"You got the cutest little butt I've ever seen."

A compliment was a compliment. She forgot about Lauren for a minute. "I do?"

"Yeah. Cute butt. Cute face. I really dig you, Meg. Always did."

"Yes?"

"Let's go outside an' sit in the car for a minute."

"It's cold out there."

"We'll put on the heater, play the radio, finish up the champagne. C'mon . . . say yes . . . I wanna tell you about when I first noticed you."

How could she resist? "You won't . . . try anything?"

He looked suitably hurt. Girls were the most stupid creatures on Earth; did she really imagine it was conversation he was after?

"Who – *me*? I have too much respect for you, Meg. I surely do."

She allowed herself to be persuaded, after all he was pretty damn cute himself.

"Well . . . all right."

Ten minutes to touch down! With a great deal of effort he tried to keep his eyes off her plump, ripe breasts as he steered her outside.

As midnight approached a sense of anticipation hung over everyone. Excitement was definitely in the air.

The band blasted out a Beatles medley while Nick held Lauren very tight.

"This is a special night," he said, his voice low and warm. "The start of somethin' new."

"I know," she said, softly.

"This time in ten years we'll be old."

"Sort of."

"Very."

"I guess."

"But we'll be together."

He sounded so sure, and yet she knew this wasn't going to be easy. Stock she could deal with – but her parents would go crazy if she ever started dating Nick Angelo.

Don't be negative, Roberts.

Okay, okay. Take it easy. I'll try to be as positive as I can.

The Beatles medley ended, and the band blasted into their own noisy version of "Born To Be Wild".

Dawn grabbed Stock's hand as soon as he began backing off. "Where *you* goin' big boy? We was just getting into it." She licked her lips suggestively and wriggled her hips. "Don't flake on me now."

Stock felt altogether foggy. "Gotta find Lauren, it's almost midnight."

"Oh, yeah, midnight," Dawn sneered. "Big deal. I can show you a better time than little Miss Goody – *an'* you know it."

"Gotta find her," Stock repeated, slurring his words, his face red from too much Scotch surreptitiously sipped from his father's silver flask hidden deep in his pocket.

Dawn felt she'd done her part, she wasn't going to beg. Screw Nick Angelo – this wasn't how she'd planned on spending her New Year's.

Over by the edge of the dance floor Nick and Lauren were locked in each other's arms, oblivious to everyone around them. Stock spotted them and started over.

Joey stood up. "Here we go," he groaned, stubbing out his cigarette.

Cyndra toyed with her glass of watered-down punch. "Nothing's gonna happen."

The leader of the band grabbed his microphone. "Five minutes to midnight!" he roared, excitedly. "Five minutes to blast off! Are we ready?"

"Yeah," the crowd roared back, "we're ready!"

The band switched to "Crocodile Rock" – they were in an Elton John mood.

"Lauren –" Stock placed his hand on her shoulder and whined a plaintive "I didn't mean to dance with Dawn for so long. C'mon . . . it's time to go."

Lauren was startled, for a moment she'd forgotten about everyone and everything except Nick; Stock had ceased to exist. She turned to face him. "I . . . I don't want to go," she said quietly, her heart pounding.

"Why not?" he demanded, belligerently.

"Because I don't."

Stock began to get angry. Was she giving him a hard time on account of his dancing with Dawn? For a moment he stood there swaying, suddenly realizing that while he'd been busy, Lauren had been cosying up to Nick Angelo.

"What the hell you dancin' with *this* dumb prick for?" he demanded. "Take a look at him – he's wearing sneakers for crissake, can't even afford shoes."

She felt Nick stiffen, ready for battle. Quickly she touched his arm hoping to restrain him.

"Three minutes to midnight!' yelled the bandleader.

"You come with me where you belong," Stock said.

"No," she replied.

"You're my fiancée. Cut the shit an' do like I tell you."

Without saying a word she removed her engagement ring and handed it to him.

He was stunned. "What's this?" he said blankly, staring at the sparkling diamonds.

"It's over, Stock," she said, finally feeling in control.

"Over?" he said, incredulously. "It can't be over."

"It is," she replied calmly, experiencing an overwhelming sense of relief.

He raised his voice, his face becoming even redder. "Nothin's over until *I* say it is."

She stifled a hysterical giggle. Was it her imagination or did he look like a boiled lobster? "Don't yell at me," she managed, without breaking up.

"Two minutes!" from the bandstand.

"Shit!" from Stock.

Now people were beginning to notice something was going on and couldn't help watching.

Nick decided the time had come to join in. He put his arm around her waist. "Let's go," he said.

"*You* – fuckin' butt out," Stock shouted, enraged. "This has *nothing* t'do with you."

"You've got it wrong there," Nick replied, evenly. "It has *everything* to do with me."

"Fuck you!" Stock screamed.

"We're rollin' into countdown," the leader of the band yelled, his microphone outshouting everyone. "So let's all do it together. Countin' back from sixty. Fifty-nine. Fifty-eight. Fifty-seven –"

"Jesus!" Stock smacked his forehead with the palm of his hand and glared at Lauren. "Now I know why I couldn't get into your friggin' pants. This nigger-lovin' prick got there first!"

"How *dare* you talk to me like that," she said.

"I'll talk to you any way I want. You're nothing but a cheap tramp – I should've listened to my mother."

Nick stepped forward. "This asshole is askin' for it."

"No!" She tried to block him from getting to Stock.

"Nineteen. Eighteen. Seventeen –"

"Yeah, out the goddamn way," slurred Stock. "I'm teachin' this white trash punk a lesson."

"Don't!" She tried to stop them, she hadn't wanted it to come to this.

"– Eleven. Ten. Okay – Everybody together. Let's hear you all!"

The crowd launched into a raucous chant.

Joey fought his way through, hoping to stop the inevitable. Cyndra trailed behind him.

"– Five. Four. Three –"

Stock shoved Lauren roughly aside. Nick went to protect her, and before he realized it was coming, Stock hauled back and let one rip, taking him by surprise.

"– Two. One. HAPPY NEW YEARRR!!"

Nick didn't have a chance. He fell like a slab of concrete. Just before he lost consciousness he saw balloons. Hundreds and hundreds of pretty pink balloons floating through the air.

Chapter 18

He came to gradually, gasping for breath, his head aching like it was going to bust right open. Groaning he raised his hand to his face and touched sticky blood. Slowly he opened his eyes.

Lauren was sitting on the floor – his head cradled in her lap. They were in the corridor outside the gym. A few people stood around watching – waiting to see if he was dead, no doubt.

Mr Lucas, one of the school chaperones for the night, glared down at him. "That was disgusting behaviour, Angelo," he said sharply. "We don't condone fighting in this school."

"*He* didn't do anything, Mr Lucas," Lauren protested. "Stock hit *him*."

Mr Lucas ignored her. "Somebody better get him home," he said impatiently, puffed up with his own importance. "I have to go back inside."

Now the excitement was over the few onlookers drifted away. Only Joey remained, Cyndra hovering close behind him.

"Jesus, man, you all right?" Joey asked. "I was on my way over when that moron laid one on you."

Nick tried to think straight. He felt like shit. Gingerly he touched his throbbing nose. "I . . . I think it's broken."

"Then we'd better get you over to the Emergency Room," Joey said, taking charge.

"What Emergency Room?" Cyndra joined in. "This isn't Chicago, y'know. We've got two doctors in town and they're probably both out celebrating."

"Are you sure it's broken?" Lauren asked, filled with guilt.

He touched his nose again. "Yeah, I'm sure."

His face was covered in blood, some of it had dripped on to the skirt of Lauren's dress, leaving big wet stains.

"I didn't mean this to happen," she whispered, softly. "I'm really sorry."

He tried to make light of it. "Hey, a broken nose is worth it if it gets that asshole out of your life."

She considered his words. Yes. Stock was certainly gone, there was no doubt about *that*. "He is out of my life," she said, quietly. "Forever."

"Well," Joey said, "this is all very cosy, but what're we gonna do?"

"We could take him over to the hospital in Ripley," Cyndra suggested. "They've got an Emergency Room."

"How'll we get him there?" Joey said, scratching his chin. "It's snowing, freezing cold, an' it's New Year's Eve. How'll we do it? On the back of my bike?"

"I guess not," Cyndra said.

"He can't go to the trailer park," Lauren said, firmly. "It's too far. I'll call my father and ask him to pick us up. He can stay at my house tonight."

"Are you nuts?" Joey exclaimed. "Your parents will freak when you tell 'em you've finished with Stock."

"You're right," she said glumly, "but it's my fault he's hurt and I'll take responsibility."

Nick groaned, "I'd like t'kick that asshole in the balls."

"What makes you think he's got any?" Cyndra said, coolly.

He attempted a weak laugh. "So, it takes something like this for you to talk to me, huh?"

She shrugged. "Don't get carried away."

Lauren hurried off to call her parents. She stood at the pay phone, impatiently waiting for someone to answer. Then she remembered they'd gone to a party and probably weren't back, which was all the better to smuggle Nick into the house before they could object. She called the local taxi service and was lucky enough to get a cab.

By the time she got back Nick was on his feet.

"Listen – I can walk. Don't let's make a big deal out of this," he said, feeling embarrassed.

"Are you sure?"

"Yeah, I'm sure." He looked at Cyndra. "Tell 'em I won't be back tonight. Not that they give a shit."

"Like I'll be talking to them when I get home," she said, sarcastically.

Back at her house Lauren led Nick straight up to her room. "How are you feeling?" she asked, anxiously.

"Like a jerk. Your boyfriend took me by surprise. We should've taken it outside and I could've given as good as I got."

"Ex-boyfriend," she said matter-of-factly, pulling down the cover on her bed. "You'll sleep here."

He managed a weak grin. "With you?"

She smiled back. "Let's get serious."

He sat down on the side of her bed. "Okay okay, just asking."

She soaked a washcloth and gently cleaned the blood off his face. "Ouch!"

"Don't be a baby."

When she was finished he said, "Now what? Am I gonna roll between the sheets with all my clothes on?"

"I'll take care of everything," she assured him.

He grinned again. "Including undressing me?"

She shook her head, smiling. "One of these days . . . maybe. But right now you can do it yourself. You should get some sleep, we'll talk in the morning."

"Your dress is messed up. Hadn't you better change before your parents see it?"

He was right, her new black dress was stained with dark patches of blood. "I hated this dress anyway," she said, wryly. "Let's call it my farewell present from the Brownings."

"Hey, Lauren," he said, reaching for her hand. "It was worth it."

"Say that in the morning when you look in the mirror."

By the time her parents arrived home she'd made up a bed for herself on the couch, changed into her robe, and was waiting to greet them.

As they came through the front door she heard her father's angry voice. "Don't threaten me, Jane. Don't *ever* threaten me."

"I'm not threatening you," Jane replied in a strained voice. "But I can tell you this –" She spotted her daughter and abruptly stopped. "Lauren, what are you doing home so early?"

This was a new one. Home so early? It was one o'clock in the morning. "Uh . . . somebody got hurt at the dance."

"Not you?" Phil said, quickly.

"No, I'm fine," she replied.

"Who then?" Jane asked.

"It . . . it's, uh, Nick Angelo. Remember? He was in the school play with me."

"What happened to him?" Jane asked, totally uninterested.

"He was . . . he was in a fight. He didn't start the fight – but he got a broken nose and there was no way he could get home tonight what with the snow and everything, so I brought him here." She knew she was speaking too fast, but she couldn't stop. "Actually, he's asleep in my bed. It's all perfectly respectable, Mother. I'm sleeping on the couch."

Her father looked furious. "That boy is here – in your bed?"

"Yes, Daddy," she said, patiently. "But *I'm* not. I'm downstairs with you. Right?"

Phil and Jane exchanged horrified glances.

"I do wish you hadn't done this without asking us," Jane fretted. "I don't like strangers sleeping over. Who is he anyway?"

"I told you, Mother," she replied, patiently. "Nick Angelo. He was Brick in the play."

"Oh, him. Strange looking boy," Jane said. "Somebody told me he lives over in the trailer park. Is that true?"

"Does it make any difference?" Lauren challenged.

Jane frowned. Her daughter could be very stubborn, and she could see that this was one of those times. "Well, if you wish to sleep on the couch, I suppose there's nothing we can do about it. We'll see you in the morning."

Lauren gave them half an hour. She waited until they'd both used the bathroom and she heard their bedroom door close. After that there was the faint murmur of conversation, and eventually silence.

When the house was absolutely quiet she crept upstairs and looked in at Nick. He lay on his back, arms outstretched, eyes closed.

She stared down at him for a long moment.

Nick Angelo, you've changed my life, she thought. *And I am so very, very grateful!*

In the morning Lauren was up at six. She'd decided it was better to get Nick out of the house before he had to face her parents. If she moved quickly and quietly she could borrow the family station wagon and drive him over to the hospital in Ripley before they were awake.

She'd hardly slept at all. Everything was changing and so was she. She knew she had to be strong, ready to stand up to all the opposition she was bound to face. For so many years she'd been good little Lauren – hard-working little Lauren. Now she'd be labelled naughty little Lauren because she didn't wish to remain engaged to the richest boy in town.

Too bad. She could deal with it – the problem was, could they?

Upstairs in her room Nick sat on the side of her bed clad in his ruined tux. She entered the room, put a finger to her lips and whispered, "Shhh . . . We're leaving."

He nodded, relieved to be getting out of there.

She hurried into her closet and pulled on jeans, sweatshirt and a heavy duffle jacket. "Follow me," she whispered. He did as she asked and they crept downstairs.

In the kitchen she scribbled a note explaining why she'd taken the car and taped it to the refrigerator door.

Within minutes they were outside. "Whew!" she sighed, unlocking the car. "It's not easy acting like a criminal."

"I'll drive," he said.

"No," she replied, firmly. "Not this time."

"Did you get any sleep?" he asked, getting into the passenger side without a fight.

"No. Did you?"

Ruefully he touched his swollen nose. "What do *you* think?"

She eased the car away from the kerb. It had stopped snowing, and although the roads were wet and slushy they were driveable.

"I think we're both insane!" she exclaimed, perfectly happy.

"And you like it."

"I love it!" she replied recklessly. "I feel free for the first time in ages."

He looked at her intently. "Yeah?"

"Oh, yes. Stock was like a big dark cloud hovering over me."

"So why did you stay with him?"

"It seemed the easiest thing to do."

"Easy ain't always easy," he remarked, sagely.

She snuck a quick glance at him. "You look awful."

"Thanks!"

"How do you feel?"

"Like a tractor ran over my face. Apart from that – great."

"The doctor'll fix your nose."

"What doctor?"

"We're driving to Ripley."

"We are?"

"I owe you a new nose. It was my fault you got hit."

"Hey – any time, if it means sleeping in your bed." He grinned. "Loved the Snoopy sheets!"

"Don't make fun of me. My mother never throws anything out."

His nose continued to throb and he was in serious pain. So why did he feel like singing? After all, Lauren was only another girl – yeah – only the most beautiful girl in the world!

He studied her perfect profile. "What're your parents gonna say about everything?"

She grimaced. "I'll let you know."

He reached for the radio, tuning it to a rock station. If only they could stay in the car and keep on going. Was it too much to ask her to give up everything and run away with him?

They made it to Ripley in an hour and a half and drove straight to the Emergency Room. New Year's Eve had taken its toll – the place was crowded with survivors of various battles. There were bloody knife wounds, a shooting or two, a couple of beaten women and a large black man screaming obscenities. Lauren clung to Nick's arm as they took a seat.

"Hey – take it easy," he said, feeling somewhat queasy himself.

They waited nearly five hours before getting any attention, and then a harassed young doctor rushed him into an examining room and confirmed that yes his nose was indeed broken. He set it and covered it with bandages.

"I feel like I was in a war," Nick joked, as they left the hospital. Deep down he was wondering what he'd look like when the bandages came off. Hell, he'd always been happy with his appearance – now what? Another stroke against him?

"Don't worry," Lauren said, reading his mind. "You'll look fine."

Outside the snow had started up again with a vengeance. "Big cities," she said, shivering. "They frighten me."

He laughed. "This ain't no big city. This is Disneyland compared with New York or Chicago." He clapped his hands together. "Jeez! I'm freezing!"

"So am I. And starving!"

"Me too."

She glanced at her watch. "It's nearly three. My parents will murder me! We'd better start back."

"Not until we get something to eat."

Her parents were going to kill her anyway, what difference did another half hour make? "Okay," she said, wondering if she should phone them. No, she decided, save the big confrontation for later.

They left the station wagon in hospital parking and ran, slipping and sliding on the wet sidewalk, to a nearby hamburger joint.

A waitress approached their table. She had a cigarette hanging from the corner of her mouth and a jaded expression. "Yeah? What'll it be?"

"Double burger with everything on, a Coke and fries," Lauren ordered breathlessly. "Twice." She smiled at Nick. "Okay?"

He had twenty dollars in his pocket. "I'm buyin'," he said.

"No. *I* am," she insisted. "It's my fault we're here."

"Can't let you do that."

"Yes, you can."

"Two burgers or *what*?" The waitress was bored, she couldn't care less who was paying as long as the check got settled. Lauren nodded, and the waitress left.

Nick leaned across the table and kissed her.

"What's that for?" she asked, wide-eyed.

"Uh . . . I guess for bein' you."

She smiled. He decided she had the most beautiful smile in the world.

"Hey –" he blurted, unable to stop himself. "I think I . . ."

"Yes?" she asked, eagerly.

"Aw – Forget it."

Her eyes shone brightly, urging him to continue. "What?"

"Uh . . . like I think . . . uh . . . y'know – like I think I love you."

"Me too," she whispered softly, feeling as if she was going to melt with happiness. "Me too."

Chapter 19

At first Jane Roberts was pleased when she awoke and found that Lauren had left with Nick Angelo, she hadn't relished dealing with a stranger in the morning. Besides, she had other things on her mind, there was no time to worry about her stubborn daughter right now.

She frowned when she reached the kitchen and discovered Lauren's note. Phil was not going to be pleased to find that Lauren had taken the car without his permission, it was so unlike her.

She re-read her daughter's note.

> BORROWED CAR
> BACK SOON
> LOVE
> LAUREN

When Phil came downstairs he was furious. "We give that girl too much freedom," he grumbled. "How dare she presume she can drive out of here in my car."

"What'll Stock say?" Jane fretted. "I hope she's back in time for the New Year's lunch with the Brownings. We're expected there at one."

"She'll be back," Phil said, gruffly. "She's probably taken that boy home."

"I wonder who he was in a fight with."

"Who knows? Who cares?" replied Phil, opening the kitchen cupboard and reaching for a packet of cornflakes. "Whoever it was he was probably bigger. Lauren always protects the underdog."

"Yes," Jane said, "but it wasn't very nice of Stock to leave her alone."

Phil tipped the cornflakes into a dish and added milk. "We have to talk about us, Jane," he said.

Her face reddened. "We talked last night."

"Not enough."

"It was enough for me," she replied, her lips tightening into a thin line.

The phone interrupted what was about to be another fight. Phil picked up. "Yes?"

"Sorry, Mr Roberts, did I wake you?"

"No," he said tersely.

"It's Meg. Can I speak to Lauren?"

"She went out early."

"Where did she go?"

He ignored her question. "She'll call you when she gets back."

"Uh . . . thank you, Mr Roberts."

Shortly before noon Jane Roberts sat at her dressing table adding a touch of powder here, a dab of rouge there. She had a new cinnamon outfit with matching pumps. Over the top she'd decided to wear her fur coat. It was five years old, but perhaps when Lauren married into the Browning family and Phil's business started improving he would be able to buy her a new one.

Phil walked into the room and stood behind her tapping impatiently on his watch. "She's not back."

"Oh, dear," Jane said. "How can she do this to us?"

"It's snowing again," Phil said, moving over to the window and staring out. "I hope she hasn't had an accident."

"Lauren's an excellent driver."

"I know," Phil said, pacing up and down. "I don't understand where she can be."

"Nor do I," said Jane, more than slightly irritated that her daughter would choose today to mess things up.

The phone rang. "That'll be her," Phil said, grabbing the receiver.

It was not Lauren, it was Daphne Browning. "Phil," she said, in her commanding and slightly imperious voice, "let me speak to Jane."

"Certainly, Daphne." He covered the mouthpiece with his hand. "She wants to talk to you – don't mention Lauren."

Jane rushed to pick up. "Happy New Year, Daphne," she

gushed. "You left the Lawsons' party awfully early last night, but it was fun, wasn't it?"

Daphne was not into pleasantries. "I simply cannot believe your daughter's behaviour," she said, flatly.

Jane was startled. "I beg your pardon?"

"Lauren's behaviour," Daphne repeated, as if she was talking to an extremely backward child.

"What happened?"

"Surely you know?"

Jane took a stab in the dark. "About the fight?"

"Disgusting!" Daphne exclaimed. "You might think Lauren would have the decency to stay with her fiancé rather than go running off with that no-account boy from the wrong side of town."

Jane took a deep breath; she had known Lauren's engagement to Stock was too good to be true. "Are you still expecting us for lunch?" she said tentatively, knowing the answer before she asked.

"I don't believe there's any point, do you?" Daphne replied. A long, cold pause. "I'm extremely disappointed in Lauren. You should be, too."

"Lauren's always done the right thing," Jane said, finally coming to her daughter's defence.

"Certainly not this time."

"Well," Jane hesitated. "I'm sure whatever happened between them, Stock and Lauren will work it out."

"You're making very light of this," Daphne said, disapprovingly. "You *do* know she gave him back his ring?"

"Oh," said Jane, blankly.

"He doesn't care," said Daphne, her tone snappy and spiteful. "Not after the way she treated him."

"I have to go," Jane said, not wishing to prolong the conversation.

"Fine," sniffed Daphne, hanging up.

Phil walked back into the room, adjusting his tie. "We should leave," he said. "You'd better write Lauren a note telling her we've gone ahead."

"Too late," Jane said. "The engagement is off. We are no longer invited to lunch."

By noon the news was all over town that Lauren Roberts had broken off her engagement to Stock Browning. It was also common knowledge that Stock had smashed Nick Angelo in the face, and nobody seemed to know where Nick and Lauren were.

Joey was alarmed; he'd seen the electricity between the two of them and knew it meant trouble. Shortly before noon he rode over to pick up Cyndra.

"Did you hear anything from Nick?" she asked.

"No. Did you?"

"We don't have a phone in case you hadn't noticed."

Harlan was hanging around outside. "Nick was gonna take us to a movie," he said, sounding mournful.

"He got hurt," Cyndra explained. "He was in a fight."

"When's he coming back?"

"Later."

"He promised," Harlan said sadly. "Luke was lookin' forward to it."

"He'll take you another day," Cyndra said.

"Whyn't *you* take us?" Harlan asked, his eyes big.

"Some other time," she answered quickly. "Come on, Joey, let's go."

Cyndra didn't care to admit it, but she was pleased to see Joey. When he'd taken her home the night before he hadn't even tried for a kiss good-night. She felt safe with him. It made a welcome change to feel safe with a member of the opposite sex.

They rode into town on his bike and stopped by the drugstore. Joey settled her in a corner booth and went off to talk to some of his friends. When he came back he said, "Okay, so this is the story goin' around. Nick took a slug at Stock an' the big guy creamed him."

"But that's not true," Cyndra said, heatedly. "Nick didn't have a chance. Stock hit him when he wasn't looking."

"Yeah, *we* know it," Joey agreed. "But since he's on the missing list it's difficult to defend him. Oh, an' Meg says Lauren's not around either. She's been tryin' to call her all day."

They both thought about it for a minute.

"Hey –" Joey said at last, as if he'd had some kind of big revelation. "You don't think they ran off and did it, do you?"

Cyndra smiled, a sly smile. "Did *what*, Joey?"

He grinned back. "*You* know. What *we're* gonna do one of these days."

Oh, yeah? That's what *he* thought. "Don't bet on it," she said, sipping her Coke.

He threw up his hands. "Okay, okay. Only jokin'."

By late afternoon the light smattering of snow flakes had turned into a fierce storm.

"I'm calling the police," Phil Roberts said. "I'll give them the licence number and they'll track them down."

Jane looked dismayed. "How can she do this to us?" she asked. "Doesn't she know we're worried out of our minds?"

Phil shook his head as he marched across the room to the phone. "I'm calling the police," he repeated.

Jane nodded. There seemed to be no other answer.

Chapter 20

They sat in the hamburger place for two hours. They talked. They got to know each other. They gazed into each other's eyes. They held hands. They giggled. Neither of them had any idea of the time.

The two of them made a strange couple. Lauren all bundled up in her winter clothes, and Nick in his battered tuxedo, his nose bandaged, his dark hair falling on his forehead, his green eyes as intense as ever.

Eventually the waitress approached their table. "You can't sit here nursing a Coke forever," she said, sharply. "Either order somethin' else or leave."

Nick stood up. "We're outta here."

"Old bitch!" Lauren whispered.

"No bad language," he said, laughing.

"I'm not the little goody-goody everybody thinks I am."

"Yeah – like I've noticed."

He grabbed her hand and they ran outside. Now the snow was really coming down in icy blasts.

"I'd better phone home," Lauren said, feeling guilty.

"They'll only yell at you," he said. "Let's hit the road an' get back."

When they reached the station wagon it was piled high with snow. It was so cold that some of it had already turned to slabs of ice. Lauren got a shovel out of the trunk, and handed it to Nick who began trying to crack the ice.

"I'm gonna end up with no hands," he complained. "My fingers are frozen!"

"Can I help?"

"Yeah, get in the car an' start the engine. We'd better get goin' before it's dark."

The car didn't want to start. Lauren tried to no avail. She moved across the seat while Nick got behind the wheel. He gave it a couple of shots until the engine finally turned over and they set off.

The car began to skid and slide on the slippery roads. He tuned the radio to a news station. A weather warning announced blizzards, heavy snow falls and impassable roads.

"What now?" Lauren asked, helplessly.

"We can try an' make it."

"And if we get stuck?"

"I dunno."

"Maybe we should stay here," she said, tentatively.

"Then you're *really* gonna have to call home. You can't let 'em think you're never comin' back."

"Okay."

"There's a motel over by the gas station at the edge of town," he said. "Let's see if we can make it."

"Fine," she replied, thinking about how she would explain this to her parents.

By the time they reached the motel she was shivering with nerves. While Nick booked them in she hurried to a pay phone. Her father answered with a sharp, "Yes?"

"Daddy?" she ventured.

"Lauren," he replied, his voice harsh. "Where are you? Your mother and I are worried sick."

"I know. I'm sorry."

"You're *sorry*? We imagined you dead and buried under a snow drift, and you're calling to say you're sorry. Get home *right* now! Do you understand me? Right now!"

"Daddy, I can't, I'm in Ripley. The roads are closed."

There was an ominous silence. "Who are you with?"

"I . . . I'm with Nick. I took him to the hospital. You see it's my fault his nose is broken. I know I shouldn't have borrowed the car without asking you, but I didn't want to wake you. The Emergency Room was filled with people, we had to wait . . . I . . . I didn't realize it would take so long."

"Are you telling me you can't get home?"

"We thought we'd stay in a motel and drive back tomorrow."

"My daughter – in a motel? With that scum?"

"Nick's not scum," she said, defiantly. "He's a very nice person. It wasn't his fault Stock smashed him in the face, it was mine."

"You'd better speak to your mother."

Jane grabbed the phone. "Your behaviour is absolutely disgraceful," she said, in a low, tight voice.

"I'm sorry –" Lauren began.

"I don't wish to hear your excuses. If the roads are closed it's quite obvious you can't get home tonight. Since you are forced to stay in Ripley, promise me you'll stay in separate rooms and have nothing to do with that boy whatsoever. Can you promise me that, Lauren?"

There was no point in arguing. She crossed the fingers of her left hand and just to make sure her right hand too. "I promise, Mother."

"We'll deal with this tomorrow, young lady," Jane said, "and don't expect us to be lenient."

The motel room had fringed orange lampshades with scorch marks on. The faded yellow bedspread had seen better days. The blue rug was threadbare. But there was a television, and Nick found out there were soft drinks and a candy machine in the manager's office.

"It cost too much to get two rooms," he'd explained when she'd come back from the phone. "You don't mind sharin', do you?"

She didn't mind. She knew that when she got home it would all be over anyway – so why not make this a night to remember?

Once they were settled they both decided they were having a wonderful time. They'd stocked up with candy and potato chips, Cokes and 7-Ups, and now they sat cross-legged on the bed munching and watching an *I Love Lucy* re-run on television.

"This is great," Nick said, swigging Coke from the can.

"I can't believe we're here together," Lauren smiled, happily.

"Y'know," he said, "I always had you figured as a timid little small-town girl – frightened to make a move."

"Then why did you come after me?"

"'Cause I figured you were worth savin'."

"Thanks a *lot*!"

"You're welcome."

She began to laugh. "You look so silly with your nose all bandaged."

"Maybe I should rip 'em off. That doctor didn't seem to know what he was doin'."

"You were too handsome before."

"You thought I was handsome, huh?"

"Very."

"Not your type though?"

"Yes."

"Nope. You like 'em big an' beefy."

She reached for a pillow and threw it at him. "Will you *stop*."

"Only if you make me."

"I'll make you all right," she giggled, rolling on top of him, attempting to pin his arms to the bed.

With one swift move he reversed the situation and had her trapped beneath him. "Now you're my prisoner," he joked. "I can do anything I like."

"Go ahead," she whispered, suddenly serious. In her heart she knew that when they returned to the real world she would be forbidden to see him, and while she could she wanted to be as close to him as possible.

He was filled with mixed emotions. His body was urging him to go for it – but his head kept insisting he'd better hold back. Lauren Roberts wasn't just another one night conquest. She was pretty and sweet and talented and most of all special.

And yet he had a hard-on that could crack ice.

She gazed up at him, her eyes dreamy and inviting.

"Uh, y'know, maybe we shouldn't –" he began.

"Yes – we should," she said earnestly, reaching up to touch his face. "I'm ready, Nick. It's what I want. It's what we both want, isn't it?"

"Hey – only if you're sure –" he said, uncertainly.

"I'm *very* sure."

He started to kiss her, slowly at first, but as things began to heat up it was all he could do to control himself. For a girl who hadn't been around she could certainly kiss.

He reached under her sweatshirt, touching her breasts, groping for the clasp on her bra.

She helped him pull the sweatshirt over her head and went for the buttons on his shirt, tearing the material in her haste to get it off him.

He traced her breasts with the tips of his fingers – touching her softly, stroking her nipples until she began to make small gasping sounds.

Jeez! Her skin was like smooth satin, her hair long and silky fanning out over the sheets. And she smelt so clean and fresh. Most girls he'd slept with favoured heavy perfume and had cigarette breath. Dawn Kovak wore musk, he had to scrub to get her scent off him.

"Come on, Nick." Now she was leading *him*, reaching for his zipper, wriggling out of her jeans.

She had the longest legs he'd ever seen.

He peeled down her panties and tossed them on the floor, dipping his fingers, feeling her urgent need, and finally getting on top of her and carefully easing into the trip of a lifetime.

She opened up to him with no inhibitions. It was her first time but it didn't matter.

He broke through as gently as he could and took her all the way.

When they were both finished he held her in his arms – cradling her until she fell asleep, a smile on her face.

He'd made love a hundred times since the first time when he was thirteen – but never like this – never had feelings been part of it.

Lauren Roberts.

Lauren Angelo.

It sounded good.

He'd finally found a soul mate, and as far as he was concerned their lives were forever entwined.

Chapter 21

"You will *never* see him again," Phil Roberts thundered. "Do you understand me, Lauren? Do you?"

She understood him all right, and his harsh words came as no surprise – so why was her heart breaking into a thousand tiny pieces? Why was there a feeling of dread in the pit of her stomach? Why did she want to die?

She glanced over at her mother. Jane's mouth was set in a tightly compressed line. Lauren knew the expression – it meant *I'm not getting involved – don't ask me.*

"Daddy –" she began.

He held up his hand. "No! I do not wish to hear your excuses. What you did was unforgivable. Taking the car. Staying out all night."

"I called," she said, defiantly. "I explained the roads were closed. I *couldn't* get home."

"And as for the way you've treated Stock, it's beyond my comprehension."

"He's a jerk, Daddy. He called me a prick tease."

"Lauren!" gasped Jane.

"How dare you speak like that in front of your mother," Phil roared.

Lauren imagined herself as a stranger watching this dramatic family scene. Phil Roberts – red in the face, puffed up with self-righteous anger.

Jane Roberts – a faded beauty in a small town, her shoulders tense – standing by while her husband took charge.

And then there was Lauren. Sixteen years old and no longer a virgin. Sixteen years old and desperately, wildly, incredibly in love.

They couldn't stop her from seeing Nick. What were they

going to do – lock her in the house?

The moment she'd walked through the door they'd started on her.

Why did you break your engagement?

Nick Angelo is nothing but trash.

How can you do this to us?

What will people think?

Who cared what people thought? *She* certainly didn't. For once in her life she felt absolutely totally alive.

"Go to your room," her father said, harshly. "And stay there until we give you permission to come out."

Good. All she wanted was to be alone so she could think about Nick, re-live every wonderful, magical moment. The touch of him, the taste of him, the sheer thrill of being in his arms. She turned to go upstairs.

"We're very disappointed in you, Lauren." This from her mother.

Oh, go bake a cake! You have no idea who I am any more.

Her room was a mess, just the way she'd left it – her bed unmade, the sheets rumpled from Nick's overnight stay. She bent to sniff them, maybe catch his odour. Oh God! She had to see him again soon, she missed him already.

Her rock heroes – John Lennon and Emerson Burn – gazed down at her from above her bed. Once her idols, it now seemed silly to worship from afar. She unpinned the posters, rolled them up and put them in her closet. Then she stared at herself in the mirror, deciding that she looked exactly the same – no real change, except maybe the expression in her eyes. There was something new there – something intangible.

After making love she and Nick had slept in each other's arms all night as close as two people could be. And in the morning they'd made love again, and this time she'd enjoyed it even more. She'd cried out for him to fill her up, and then she'd cried out from sheer pleasure as her body jerked in response to his loving and she'd experienced a feeling so sensational, so amazing that she'd wanted to burst into happy tears.

"What was *that*?" she'd gasped.

"What?"

"That feeling I just had."

"You came," he'd told her.

"Came where?"

And he'd explained that making love wasn't only for the man's satisfaction.

"How do you know so much?" she'd asked, feeling a strong twinge of jealousy.

"'Cause I got taught by a whole bunch of older women. Now I can teach you."

She'd reached for him. "How about teaching me more?"

They didn't leave the motel until eleven in the morning. He drove slowly along the treacherous icy roads, while she snuggled next to him. By the time they reached Bosewell it was almost two thirty.

"I'll get off at the gas station," he'd said. "Unless you'd like me to come in an' face your parents with you. I don't mind."

"*I* do. It's better I handle them alone."

He'd pulled the car up across the street and jumped out. "I'll call you later."

She'd laughed and slid behind the wheel.

He'd come around and kissed her through the open window. "I . . . uh . . ."

She had a right to be demanding. "What? *Say* it?"

He'd attempted to make light of it. "I love ya."

"You too."

And she'd watched him run across the street – her hero in a blood-stained tux with a battered nose.

Now she was back to reality.

As soon as she reached the safety of her room she picked up the phone to call Meg and find out what had been going on in her absence. Before she'd finished dialling her father appeared at the door. "No phone privileges," he said, his face long and dour.

"But, Daddy –" she started to object.

"I said you will *not* use the phone," he repeated sternly, entering her room, pulling the phone from its jack and carrying it off under his arm.

They were angrier than she'd thought, probably because she'd broken up with Stock. It wasn't that they resented Nick, she rationalized, they didn't even know him. Maybe after a few weeks she could introduce him into their lives and they'd soon realize what a terrific guy he was.

The real truth was there was no way they could stop her from seeing him. School resumed in a couple of weeks and then she'd be with him every day whether her parents liked it or not.

Right now it was quite obvious they weren't going to let her out of the house. No car. No phone. No contact with friends. She was a prisoner. A prisoner with her thoughts.

Ah . . . but her thoughts were going to keep her very happy until she saw Nick again. Very happy indeed.

"You dumped on us," Harlan said accusingly, sitting on the steps outside the trailer, zinging pebbles at an empty can.

"Hey – couldn't help it. I had an accident. Take a look at my face," Nick said.

"You promised us a movie," Harlan said, glumly.

"I wasn't here," he explained, edging past him into the trailer. "I told you why."

Luke lay listlessly on top of the mattress he shared with Harlan.

"What's the matter with *him*?" Nick asked.

"I dunno," Harlan followed him in, shrugging. "He got sick."

"What's your ma say?"

"She ain't here."

He went over to Luke and placed his hand on his forehead. The kid was burning up.

"When did he get like this?"

"Dunno," Harlan said, sighing.

Nick stripped off his clothes realizing there was no way he could ever return the tuxedo. It was good that when Joey had checked out the clothes from the rental place he'd given a phoney address. "Where's Cyndra?" he asked, pulling on his jeans.

"Out with Joey." Harlan leaned against the door looking miserable.

"Tell you what," Nick said, cheerfully, "soon as Luke's better we'll go to that movie."

"You said that before."

"Yeah – but this time I ain't gonna be stuck in Ripley with a broken nose."

"You look funny," Harlan said, staring at him, his head on one side.

"Yeah, yeah, I know."

He wondered what Lauren was doing. After she'd dropped him at the gas station he'd worked for a couple of hours, but it was so quiet he'd finally made the trek home, picking up his bike from outside Dawn's without ringing her doorbell. Joey hadn't been at work, so he had no idea what the buzz around town was. He'd been planning on going back to the drugstore to see Louise and Dave, but now he didn't feel he should leave Luke.

"Anybody got a thermometer around here?" he asked.

Harlan gazed at him solemnly. "What that?"

"Forget it," he said, quickly. "Hang on, I'll ask Primo."

His father was in his usual position – stretched out like a sleeping rhino, snoring heavily. The television played loudly, and there were three cans of beer stacked in a row on the floor next to the bed. He wore a torn undershirt and dirty underpants. A half-eaten packet of potato chips spilled out on his chest.

Roughly Nick shook him until Primo came to, bleary-eyed and puce-faced. "Whassamatter? Wass goin' on?" he griped, burping loudly as he hoisted himself into a sitting position. His rheumy eyes focused on his son. "Wadda *you* wan'?"

"It's Luke," Nick said, trying to get through to him. "He's burnin' hot an' just lyin' there."

"Ain't my problem," Primo yawned, automatically reaching for a beer.

"It could be if anythin' happens to him," Nick said, hating his father even more if that was possible.

"Whyn't ya tell Aretha," Primo's attention was now taken by a bikini-clad blonde with jiggling tits cavorting across the television screen.

"She's at work," he said, shortly.

"Quit botherin' me. Throw a bucket a water over him – that'll cool him down 'til she gets back." Primo reached into his underpants and had a vigorous scratch. "An' don't tell her 'bout Luke 'til she done fixin' my supper."

For a moment Nick stood there trying to figure out what to do. Then he spotted the keys to the van on the table and swiped them on his way out. Fuck Primo. Fuck the fat pig.

By the time he got back to the other trailer Luke was breathing funnily.

He made a fast decision. "We're takin' him into town," he told Harlan. "Wrap him in a couple of blankets an' let's get movin'."

"Sit down, Aretha Mae," Benjamin Browning said.

Aretha Mae hovered in the doorway of his study, her expression wary and suspicious. "Why?"

Benjamin picked up a silver pen from his desk top and twirled it between his thick fingers. He did not relish the job Daphne had landed him with; the sooner it was done the better. "Because I say so," he said, irritably. "Come in. Close the door behind you and *sit down goddamnit.*"

She did as he requested, albeit reluctantly. Once she was seated he swivelled his leather desk chair at an angle so that he didn't have to look her in the eye.

"Yes?" Her voice betrayed her impatience.

"I am terminating your employment," he said, coldly.

She was startled. "What you sayin'?"

"I'm firing you. Your services are no longer required."

A nerve twitched beneath her left eye. "Oh, they ain't, huh?"

"Mrs Browning and I have decided you deserve six weeks severance pay on account of your years of service with us." He passed a signed cheque across the desk. "Mrs Browning has requested that you do not return to work after today. Is that clear?"

"Clear . . ." she muttered.

He thought she was accepting her termination without argument. Thank God for that.

"Well . . ." he said, willing her to go quietly. "That's all."

"That's all," she repeated his words, not moving.

"You may go," he said, dismissing her with a cursory wave.

Aretha Mae stood up, placed both hands on his desk and glared at him. "I ain't goin' nowhere y' son-of-a-bitch," she said, forcing him to make eye contact.

He'd known she would try to cause trouble. It was too much to expect for her to go quietly. Once . . . many years ago when she'd first come to work for them she'd been lovely. Young and vibrant with long legs, big breasts and a sassy smile – just like Cyndra – a juicy little piece – hot and sexy. Now – seventeen years later – she was a dried-up bitter old woman. Skinny and wild-eyed with sunken cheeks and dyed red hair. Even Daphne had aged better than her, and Daphne was ten years older. Not that he fucked his wife any more, but once a year on their anniversary he made her get down on her knees and give him a suck. He knew how much she hated it, and it gave him immense pleasure to watch his penis vanish into that scarlet slash of a mouth. Daphne didn't dare refuse him. Daphne would never give up the grand title of Mrs Browning.

"I'm firing you," he repeated. "Don't you understand English? You *have* to go."

"No such thing as Aretha Mae havin' t'do nothin'," she snapped, sitting back down. "No such thing, an' you know it."

He threw his silver pen down on the desk, full of exasperation. "I'll double your severance pay if that's what you're after. Three months' money and out of here today."

"Ain't goin'," she said, stubbornly.

Now he was getting really angry. "Why not?"

"'Cause three months down the line I ain't got no job, no money, no nothin'."

"You can find another job."

"In Bosewell? No shit? What other family got themselves a full-time maid?"

"There's always work in the paper factory or the canning plant."

She jumped up again. "No!" she said, forcefully. "I work here – an' this'n where I stay."

He was silent for a moment before saying, "What do you want?"

"Same money I'se gettin' now for the rest a my natural life. An' five thousand dollars in the bank for my Cyndra. Oh, yeah, an' a lawyer's letter t'say I gets it regular."

"That's blackmail."

"*Your* word – ain't mine."

"And if I refuse?"

"Then the whole town gets t'know who Cyndra's daddy is, an' the filthy things y'done t'her."

"What are you saying?"

"You *know* what I'se sayin'. Cyndra's *your* child."

Benjamin paled. "It's . . . it's not possible."

"That it is."

"How?"

"Remember when I first came t'work here?"

His throat was restricted. "Yes."

"You was chasin' me day an' night – soon as your wife left the house you was after me – an' I was sleepin' in that room down in the basement. Well, one night you came there, held your hand over my mouth, an' shoved your thing inside me even though I didn't want it."

"You wanted it," he said, angrily. "After the first time you were begging for it."

"You got me pregnant an' I didn't know what t'do. So I ended up marryin' the first man who'd have me – an' we moved t' the trailer park. Thing is – when I told him I was pregnant he ran out on me – an' all these years I bin alone. But I kept on workin' for you – an you kept on pokin' me 'till I wasn't young 'nuff for you no more."

"My wife and I supported you, and this is how you pay us back – by lying?"

She gave a hollow laugh. "Supported me – *sheeit*! I worked my black ass off for you an' your family, an' don' you forget it. Washin' your dirty underdrawers, cleanin' the shit in your johns, wipin' up all the mess."

"And now you're going to blackmail me with this far-fetched story?"

"I'm gonna get what's right for me an' that child a yours."

"She's not my child," he said, vehemently.

"Want me t'tell the town 'bout how you was screwin' me all those years? Want me to tell them how you raped your own daughter?"

"You wouldn't do that."

"Honey," she said, bitterly, "*I* ain't got nuttin' t'lose. How 'bout you?"

Chapter 22

Nick drove the van to the drugstore, parked in back, and entered through the kitchen, grabbing Louise as she passed by carrying an order of ham and eggs.

She stopped and let out a whistle. "Lookit you! Your damn face is one big mess."

"I need a doctor," he said, urgently.

"Seems like you should'a thought of that before."

"Not for me. Luke's sick – my kid brother. I got him in the van. Who can I take him to?"

"Gee . . ." She hesitated. "Doc Marshall's away, an' Doc Sheppard don't like bein' bothered at home."

"Where does he live?"

She placed her order on the counter and gave him her full attention. "What's wrong with the kid?"

"I dunno. He's hot, can't breathe good."

"Maybe I should take a look before you go waking up Doc Sheppard – he's an ornery old bastard." She untied her apron. "Hey – Dave –" she yelled, "I'm takin' a break; have Cheryl fill in."

Out in the van Luke was shivering uncontrollably. Harlan sat beside him looking miserable.

"Thought you said he was hot," Louise said accusingly, placing a hand on the child's forehead. "Oh, shit, yeah – he's hot all right."

"What do you think it is?" Nick asked.

"Dunno. But it ain't good." She climbed into the van. "Let's go – we'll wake up old Doc Sheppard. Hang a left, then take the second street on the right. An' Nick – put your foot down."

The bus ride took longer than ever. Aretha Mae sat by the

window gazing out. Usually she let her mind go blank – ridding herself of the cares of the day. But today she was filled with pent-up emotions – feelings she hadn't allowed to surface for seventeen years.

Benjamin Browning was Cyndra's father and she was glad she'd finally told him. Yes – glad to see the expression on his pompous white face when the full impact struck and he'd realized what he'd done.

Filthy pig. He was no good – only his money saved him from wallowing in the gutter.

With a deep sigh she recalled the day she'd started work at the Brownings. Her mother had answered an ad in the newspaper, and Mr Browning had agreed to pay her bus fare from Kansas City if she could start immediately. "My girl be there," her mother had assured him, delighted to be rid of one of seven daughters. Her mother had lied and said she was eighteen. The truth was she was barely fifteen and just out of school. "Work hard. Stay quiet. Don't get in no trouble." Those had been her mother's parting words.

Six months after she left home her mother was killed by a drunken driver. She had no father.

At first Aretha Mae liked working in a house with running water, indoor toilets, and unheard of luxuries like a refrigerator and TV. But Daphne Browning was not pleasant to work for. She'd recently given birth to Stock, and she had no intention of caring for the child unless he was clean and fresh at all times and never crying. Although she had all the housework to do, Aretha Mae soon found herself caring for the baby as well as attending to her other duties.

Benjamin Browning watched her like a tiger stalking its prey. She was aware of his lecherous eyes and roaming hands, but she managed to stay clear. He was in his early thirties then and quite good-looking. A self-made man with an abundance of energy and a canny mind. Daphne had pale skin, yellow hair and large breasts. They made love every night. Aretha Mae knew because she got to change the messy sheets.

The first night Benjamin came to her room he'd been out at a bachelor party. It was late, he was drunk, and she was asleep. He'd ripped the covers off her bed, placed a firm hand over her mouth, lifted her nightdress and thrust himself inside. She hadn't dared to complain. What good would it do? She had nowhere to run to.

When he was sure of her silence it became a weekly habit – sometimes twice or three times a week, depending on his mood.

After a while he stopped putting his hand over her mouth.

After a while – to her shame – she began looking forward to his nocturnal visits.

And then she got pregnant.

Aretha Mae was no fool – she knew if she mentioned it they'd throw her out, so she said nothing, merely bided her time, desperately taking hot baths, swigging gin when they were out, and hoping the baby growing in her belly would quietly go away.

Primo Angelo arrived in town at exactly the right time. He was a big handsome man with a cocksure swagger and a glint in his green eyes. A carpenter by trade he was doing work on the new school building. Aretha Mae did everything in her power to seduce him. She flattered him, babied him, told him he was the most handsome man she'd ever seen, and refused to sleep with him.

What was a man to do? He married her and they moved to the trailer park – although she did not give up her job at the Brownings.

Primo stopped working immediately. "I need my strength to make love to you," he told her. The man with the silver tongue and the lazy ass.

When she informed him she was pregnant he took off without so much as a fast goodbye. She was miserable for five minutes. Men – what could you expect? They were never faithful – never true.

When she had her baby everyone believed her vanished husband was the father. But she knew the truth, and she hugged it to herself like precious gold. One day the information would pay off.

Now – finally – that day had come.

The bus reached her stop and she climbed off, weary but triumphant. Benjamin Browning had agreed to her terms. He'd promised to arrange the papers with his lawyer, and soon – for the first time in her life – she'd be secure.

Doctor Sheppard lived in a large comfortable house with a big garden and a sign hanging over the front door that read: *COME*

ALL YE LITTLE SHEPHERDS AND GATHER HERE FOR SUSTENANCE AND COMFORT. Nick pounded on the door while Louise and Harlan stayed in the van with a steadily worsening Luke.

Nobody answered, so he pounded some more.

An upstairs window shot open and a white-haired old man in bright red pyjamas leaned out. "What's all that din?" he shouted in a crotchety voice.

"Somebody's sick. Can we come in?" Nick shouted back.

"Now?" replied Doctor Sheppard, his surprise evident.

"No, tomorrow morning, jerk," Nick muttered under his breath.

By this time Louise was beside him. "Doctor Sheppard," she yelled. "It's me. Louise. From the drugstore. Remember? You gave me that internal examination a couple of months ago. Said I had a lovely pelvis."

She'd succeeded in getting his attention. "I'll be right down," he croaked.

"Dirty old geezer," Louise said, disgustedly. "Stuck his finger up me like he was flippin' a pearl! Never again."

"You get the door open, I'll carry Luke inside," Nick said.

By the time he got back to the van Harlan was crying. "What's the matter, kid?" he asked.

"Is Luke gonna die?" Harlan worried, seeking assurance, tears rolling freely down his cheeks.

"No, he ain't gonna die," Nick assured him, gathering Luke up into his arms. "Don't think nothin' like that. You stay out here – he'll be fine."

He carried the small boy up to the house, not sure what was going to happen – he only knew it didn't look good.

Louise had the door open and was proceeding to charm Doctor Sheppard – a short man with hairy hands, a halo of white hair and big pop eyes. He was old and crusty and took a lot of charming.

"What's this?" he said, when Nick appeared with Luke in his arms.

"This child is sick," Louise said quickly. "Can you take a look at him, Doc? *Please.*"

"I'm off-duty," the miserable old man said.

"I know." Louise kept her voice soft and persuasive. "But I figured you'd do us this one favour – what with Doc Marshall bein' away an' all, an' you bein' the only doctor left in town."

She paused, giving him a seductive look. "I'm coming in to see you next week. I had those stomach cramps again, thought you could look me over."

Doctor Sheppard cheered up.

Louise continued to pour it on. "I guess I need another of those . . . uh . . . exams you're so good at giving. I felt so much better after the last time."

"Yes, yes," the old man said. "Bring the boy into the examining room."

She winked at Nick. He carried Luke into the examining room and laid him on the cold table.

The doctor bent down and peered at Luke. "This boy is black," he said, indignantly.

So? Nick wanted to say. *What the fuck does that matter?*

"We thought he was too sick to drive to Ripley," Louise said, quickly.

"That's where *black* people are supposed to go," Doctor Sheppard muttered bad-temperedly, rubbing his bulbous nose with the tip of his thumb. "I'm not supposed to look after coloureds."

"Hey –" Nick couldn't help himself. "It's nineteen seventy-four for God's sake, an' we ain't even in the South."

Doctor Sheppard turned to glare at him. "Who are you, young man? I've never seen you before."

"Thank God for that," Nick muttered, and then loud enough for the Doctor to hear, "I'm his brother."

Doctor Sheppard's bushy eyebrows shot up. "His brother?"

"Just take a look at the kid, will you?"

Ten minutes later they were out of there. "Nothing wrong with the boy," Doctor Sheppard had said. "All he needs is a good night's sleep and an aspirin."

Nick didn't believe him, but what could he do? "How about that other doctor he was talking about – the one in Ripley?" he asked Louise.

She shrugged. "I dunno. Never heard of him. I'm sorry, I gotta get back to work. Dave's gonna be pissed, y'know what he's like."

He dropped Louise off and began the drive to the trailer park. Maybe the old doctor was right – maybe all Luke needed was rest and an aspirin.

On the way home he spotted Aretha Mae trudging along the side of the road. He swerved over to the side.

"What you doin' with your father's van, boy?" Aretha Mae asked, sharply.

Quickly he explained about Luke. She jumped in the back, took one look at Luke and was as panicked as he was.

"I told him not to play out in the snow," she fretted, "I told him he was gonna catch cold. He's got somethin' bad, I know it."

"Yeah," Nick agreed. "That's why I took him to see Doctor Sheppard."

"That dumb old fool – he's no good," she said, shaking her head in disgust. "He won't treat us – whatever the law, says. We gotta take him to Ripley."

"The roads ain't clear yet. It took hours to get back earlier."

"We have t'go," Aretha Mae said, obstinately.

"What about Primo? He don't know I've taken the van."

"Too bad," she said.

"Okay," he shrugged. "Ripley it is."

He drove as fast as he could considering the conditions of the roads – even so, it was midnight by the time they reached Ripley.

Aretha Mae directed him to a house in a run-down neighbourhood, and when he got there she jumped out of the van and rang the bell.

An Indian woman in a sari answered the door. She didn't seem at all surprised to have patients arriving in the middle of the night.

"It's my child," Aretha Mae said. "He be real bad."

"Bring him in," the woman said, graciously. "I'll fetch my husband."

Doctor Singh Amroc was a slightly built Indian man, totally bald with a thin black moustache. After a cursory examination of Luke he said, "This boy has pneumonia. It's essential he's admitted to a hospital at once."

They all set off, crowding into the van, the doctor too.

On the way to the hospital Nick began thinking about Lauren. He hadn't called her, would she be mad? Girls were funny about things like phoning when you said you would – and yet he was sure that when he explained everything she'd understand.

He wondered if her parents had given her a hard time. He missed her already and couldn't wait to see her again.

At the hospital he sat in the waiting room with Harlan while the Doctor and Aretha Mae filled out the forms to get Luke admitted.

Harlan stared at his half-brother. "Thanks, Nick," he said, solemnly. "You're my best friend."

"Hey –" he shrugged, embarrassed, "it was nothing."

Primo's rumbling stomach awoke him. Bleary-eyed he groped for the large clock ticking away on the floor. It was late, very late, and where the hell was Aretha Mae?

He staggered to his feet, brushed a scurrying cockroach off the side of the bed and rolled outside, taking a piss in the nearby brush.

Then he lurched back inside, grabbed a can of beer and sat and brooded. After ten minutes he went outside again and kicked open the door of the kids' trailer. Nobody was around.

"Where *the fuck* is everybody?" he yelled. "Where *the fuck* is my dinner?"

Outside he noticed his van was missing. "Goddamn it!" he muttered, making his way back to the main trailer. The bitch had taken his van and the kids. The bitch would pay for being home late. *Nobody* treated him this way. *Nobody* kept Primo Angelo waiting and got away with it.

Luke had to stay in hospital.

"There ain't no way I'm leavin'," Aretha Mae said, her mouth set in a stubborn line. "No way at all."

"Hey – if you're stayin', we're stayin'," Nick said.

She shook her head. "No – you'd best get back. When Primo finds his van's missin' he'll be mad."

"I'm not goin' back without you and Luke."

"Yeah, me too, Ma," Harlan joined in.

"Suit yourself." She was too tired to argue.

"I know a cheap motel," Nick said. "We can all spend the night there."

"What'll we do about Primo?" Aretha Mae worried.

"I'll call Joey in the morning. He'll stop by the trailer an' tell him what's goin' on."

She nodded. "Good. Now you take Harlan to this motel while I stay here."

"Why don't we stay with you?"

"No," she shook her head. "Don't want Harlan comin' down sick, too. You go rest up."

Reluctantly he got up. "We'll be back first thing tomorrow."

"You got money, boy?"

"Well . . . dunno if I've got enough."

"Here." She rummaged in her purse and counted out fifteen dollars in worn bills.

"Thanks," he said, pocketing the money. "We'll get back here early."

They left the hospital and drove straight to the motel. The man in the manager's office recognized him. "You here again?" he said, winking lewdly. "Must've been a good one."

Nick ignored the comment. "We'll be stayin' one night," he said, paying in advance.

He took Harlan into the room, settled him in front of the television and hurried to the pay phone. For a moment he stood in the ice-cold booth wondering if he could phone Lauren at this late hour. No way. It was even too late to contact Joey – his mother would be seriously pissed. Shit! There was nothing left to do except go to bed. He'd call everyone in the morning.

Harlan awoke at six a.m. "I gotta bad feeling, my gut hurts," he whined.

"Hey –" Nick got out of bed and stretched. "Don't worry about it. Everything's gonna be fine."

Harlan shook his head. "No, it ain't, Nick. It ain't."

"Quit worryin' an' get dressed. We'll get to the hospital early."

Outside the wind was howling. Shivering, Nick pulled up the collar of his jacket, stuffed his hands in his pockets and ran over to the van. Harlan followed him and jumped in the passenger seat.

Five minutes later they were standing at the hospital reception. "Luke Angelo," Nick said.

The nurse consulted her admittance book. "Ward Five, fifth floor."

They took the elevator. At reception on the fifth floor Nick asked again, "We're here to see Luke Angelo."

The nurse glanced up. "Relative?" she enquired.

"Yeah – I'm like . . . uh . . . his brother."

"The doctor is with Mrs Angelo right now," the nurse said, all business. "Please take a seat."

"Uh, Luke . . . he's okay, right?"

"Take a seat."

They waited over ten minutes before Aretha Mae appeared, clutching her thin winter coat – a Brownings cast-off – around her.

Harlan ran down the corridor and clung to his mother's legs.

Nick knew it before she said a word. He got up and walked slowly towards her. His throat was dry and his stomach churning.

Aretha Mae shook her head, hopelessly. "He's gone," she said, her voice no more than a hoarse whisper. "My baby is dead."

Harlan let out a wail that could be heard from one side of the hospital to the other. It was a sound Nick would never forget.

Chapter 23

"Did Nick call?" Every morning Lauren asked the same question, and every morning her parents gave her the same stupid answer. "It doesn't matter whether he did or not. You are *never* seeing him again."

"I don't care," she replied, her heart beating fast. "I just need to know."

"It makes no difference," her father said, harshly.

"It makes a difference to me," she replied, wondering how she had ever imagined her father to be a kind and sensitive man.

"Then in that case he has *not* called you."

She didn't know whether they were telling the truth or not. She sat in her room and brooded. Did Nick consider her easy? Is sex all he'd wanted? *Oh, God, no! Please God, no!*

They'd been so close and now they seemed so far apart. She knew he didn't have a phone, so she couldn't call him. Not that her parents would let her get within ten feet of a telephone. They had her trapped in the house, guarding her as if she was a maximum security prisoner.

"What have I done that's so terrible?" she asked one day.

"You were engaged to one of the finest boys in town," her father replied, his face stony. "You should have taken into consideration that I was doing business with Stock's father before recklessly breaking off your engagement."

"I didn't realize it was a business arrangement," she muttered.

"You owed us the information," her father said.

She couldn't believe they were being so mean. "I've never done anything to upset you in my life," she said. "No alcohol, drugs or any of the things some of the kids at school get into. All I did was borrow the family car, and you're punishing me like I'm a criminal."

Together – the perfect team. "You have to learn the hard way, Lauren, or you won't learn at all."

"What will happen when school starts?" she asked. "You can't watch over me every day then."

"When the new semester commences we hope you'll have learnt your lesson," Phil said.

And what if I haven't? she wanted to reply. *What if the first time I see Nick we run off together?*

As if reading her mind her mother chimed in with, "If you see Nick Angelo at school, I want your solemn promise you'll have nothing to do with him."

She crossed her fingers behind her back, a habit she was getting used to. "Okay, Mother, if that makes you happy."

Yeah. Good little Lauren was learning to play the game their way – and it was their fault.

On her first day back she bumped into Meg on the way to history class.

"OhmiGod! OhmiGod!" Meg exclaimed excitedly. "I've been *desperate* to see you. I've called you *dozens* of times. I even came by your house and begged your mom. She wouldn't let me in. What *is* going *on?*"

"*You* tell *me*," Lauren said. "I've been held prisoner, cut off from everything."

Meg lowered her voice. "There's been rumours you were *pregnant* and had to have an abortion."

"Are you serious? Surely *you* know what happened?"

"You mean at the New Year's dance?"

"Right – when Stock hit Nick, broke his nose, and I drove him to the hospital in Ripley. I'm sure you heard we got stuck there overnight, the roads were closed and we couldn't get back. My parents were furious."

"Oh," Meg said, sounding disappointed, "is that all?"

"Isn't that enough?"

Meg wanted to know more. "What happened with you and Nick?"

"Nothing," Lauren lied. "I was punished for absolutely nothing."

"Nick Angelo is the worst. How come you drove him to the hospital? Stock's been so upset. Mack and I have tried to look after him, but he's like – heartbroken." Meg shook her head. "You treated him badly."

Lauren was incensed. "*I* treated *him* badly? How about the way *he* carried on?"

Meg continued as if she hadn't heard a word. "Throwing his ring at him and everything. *I* heard it was Nick tried to attack *him* and *that's* why Stock broke his nose – he was only defending himself."

"That's not true."

"Yes, it is. Nick Angelo is a real deadbeat. Look what he did to me."

Lauren attempted to remain calm. "What *did* he do to you, Meg?"

"Practically raped me."

She had a strong desire to smack her friend's smug face. "Oh, and I suppose you didn't provoke it?"

"What do you mean?"

"It seems to me that every time you go out with a boy the same thing happens."

Meg flushed. "It certainly doesn't."

"I thought you were my friend," Lauren said, sadly.

"And I thought you were a friend worth having," Meg replied, with a spiteful toss of her blonde curls.

Miserably Lauren sat in class, her eyes searching the room for Nick. He failed to appear.

Shortly before lunch break she spotted Joey in the corridor and hurried over. "Hi. Can we talk?"

He gave her a dirty look. "Oh, *you* resurfaced, huh?"

"What does *that* mean?"

"It would've been nice if you'd called Nick after all that happened."

"After *what* happened?"

"His little brother dying and all."

She was genuinely shocked. "*What?*"

He could see she wasn't acting. "You didn't hear?"

"I've been grounded since New Year's."

Joey felt uncomfortable. "I'm sorry. Nick told me you wouldn't talk to him."

She wondered how much Joey knew. "Why would I avoid him?" she asked, carefully.

"He called your house enough times. Your parents said you didn't want to speak to him."

"That was them talking – not me. Please, Joey, tell me what happened?"

"His half-brother got sick with pneumonia. Doc Sheppard refused to treat him, so they had to take him to another doctor in Ripley. The kid died in hospital there."

"Oh, God! That's so awful."

"Yeah."

"Where is Nick? I have to see him."

"He won't be back in school."

"Why not?"

"He was thrown out on account of your boyfriend."

"You mean expelled?"

"Yeah – the Browning family didn't want him around – they put on the pressure. Course it didn't help that he smashed up the sign in front of Doc Sheppard's house, and threatened to beat the shit outta the old fart."

"He did?"

"Yeah, Cyndra went with him. The old fuck called the Sheriff. Nick spent the night in the can. Cyndra wanted to join him – but I managed to persuade her it wasn't the coolest move in the world."

"Where is he now?" she asked, thinking about what he must have gone through.

"Workin' down at the garage full-time. Old man Browning tried to stop that too – but George wouldn't listen. If the Brownings had their way they'd run him out of town."

"Can you take me there?"

"Sure, but if we get caught there'll be big trouble."

"Don't tell *me* about trouble."

"Okay. Meet me in the parking lot in five minutes."

"I'll be there."

"An' don't mention it to your big-mouthed girlfriend either. She's real tight with Stock an' all his buddies."

"I understand."

She hurried to her locker and grabbed her purse and jacket. On her way downstairs she ran straight into Stock and a group of his ever-present cronies. Their eyes met. The group went silent.

"Uh . . . hi," she said, trying to make the most of an awkward situation.

Stock's jaw tightened, his right eye twitched, his hand strayed toward his crotch and he totally ignored her – pushing by as if she didn't exist.

Okay with me, she thought. *If that's the way you want it, Stock Browning, I can handle it.*

Joey was waiting out in the parking lot revving up the engine of his motorcycle. "Climb aboard," he instructed. "We'd better split before we get ourselves busted."

She jumped on the back of his bike and they took off. Whatever the consequences she didn't care. She was on her way to see Nick, and that's all that mattered.

Chapter 24

"Thanks, sweetie." The woman in the maroon Cadillac had enormous breasts stretching the confines of a tight pink sweater. She'd been in twice this week to gas up her car – not that she needed to, the second time he'd almost had an overflow at three gallons.

Nick strolled casually around the car. "Want me to check your oil an' water?" he asked.

"Why not, sweetie?"

While he was checking under the hood he noticed she was checking out her face in a flashy silver compact. The woman scrutinized. First the eyes – heavily mascaraed and outlined in black. Next the nose – powder, powder. And lastly the lips – full, sexy lips glossed and ready for action. She had long reddish hair and wore a fur coat which did not succeed in covering her outstanding sweater-clad breasts. She was old, at least thirty. Nick was an expert at figuring women's ages.

"Who is she?" he'd asked George, the first time she'd come in.

"Never seen her before," George had said, chewing tobacco. "Illinois plates – must be visiting."

"You got a johnnie here?" the woman asked, snapping shut her compact.

"A what?"

"Little girl's room."

He pointed.

She got out of the car.

She was tall – which was fortunate Nick thought, because with the pair she was carrying falling flat on her face was a distinct possibility. Her fur coat ended at the hip. Under it she wore a short skirt and thigh-high black patent leather boots.

"You from around here?" he asked, knowing she wasn't.

She ran her tongue across her front teeth. "Passing through on my way to civilization. Staying a week with my sister."

"Having fun?" He could have kicked himself. What kind of a dumb question was that. How could anyone have fun in Bosewell?

She looked him over slowly – seductive eyes raking him from top to bottom. "Nope," she said, sauntering off to the rest room.

George winked conspiratorially. "She's got the hots for you, boy. Better watch it! Didja get an eye-full of those gazumbas? Wouldn't mind a mouthful myself." George began to chuckle and wheeze.

A few weeks ago, Nick thought, this woman might have been a challenge. But now . . . who cared? All he was interested in was making money – plenty of money – and as soon as he'd saved five hundred bucks he was on his way out of this pisshole.

The woman had left her open purse on the front seat. He noticed her wallet poking out – crammed with bills. When she came back he pointed it out to her. "You shouldn't leave your purse open like that – it's askin' for trouble."

"Story of my life," she said, smiling laconically. "How was my oil?"

"Fine."

"I don't need anything?"

"You're perfect."

She handed him a credit card and he put it through the machine. Genevieve Rose. He'd already noticed the wedding ring – a fat band of diamonds.

"Where you from?" he asked, as she signed with a flourish.

"Chicago. Ever been there?"

"My friend has. His dad was a cop."

Another dumb remark. Jeez! What was the matter with him today?

"A cop, huh? The worst kind." She slipped him a five-buck tip and drove off without another word.

"Hey – she gave me a five," he told George.

"Frame it," George said. "It's the first an' last time you'll see a tip like that."

"Yeah." He went into the rest room and sniffed – her perfume lingered. He rinsed his face with cold water and noticed the mirror above the sink was still cracked, George said it wasn't worth having fixed. Peering at himself he gingerly touched his nose. It wasn't the same – it would never be the same – but it didn't look too bad. Not straight like before, slightly bent and rough looking. But somehow it gave his face more character and certainly made him appear older than seventeen. Betty Harris said his broken nose gave his face a strength it hadn't had before.

He wasn't sure.

"When you're famous you can always have it fixed," she'd said.

Famous! Holy shit! For her to say a thing like that was a compliment indeed.

Betty Harris had turned out to be the one constant presence he could trust. Now that he no longer had school to contend with he divided his time between work for money and work for pleasure. The long sessions with Betty Harris were pure pain mixed with intense pleasure. Acting satisfied him in a way nothing else had. Since he was thirteen he'd always had sex to get lost in, but after Lauren, mindless sex did not hold the same appeal, so now he took all of his pent-up energy and channelled it into the roles Betty allowed him to play. Hamlet was a particular favourite, and Stanley in *Streetcar*. Oh yeah, he could really let rip – pouring every emotion into the highly charged complex characters.

Betty was impressed. She praised him constantly, and her encouragement really helped. When he'd got himself thrown into jail for messing up the outside of Doctor Sheppard's house, Betty had put up his bail. He'd been charged with defacing property. If he'd had his way he'd have defaced the old white-haired gnome of a doctor from here to eternity. But for the old man Luke might still be alive.

After the initial shock Aretha Mae had reverted to her usual stoic self. Primo was unaffected – Luke hadn't meant anything to him. Cyndra was sad. And Harlan inconsolable. Night after night Nick listened to the kid sob himself to sleep. A few times Cyndra took Harlan into her bed and comforted him with stories and songs. Sometimes Nick joined in. The three of them formed a bond. For the first time since his mother died he really felt he had a family.

Primo had tried to cause trouble over him borrowing the van. For once Aretha Mae shut him up with an acid tongue-lashing he wouldn't forget in a hurry. Primo had slunk off like a beaten dog.

When they'd thrown him out of school he hadn't bothered telling his father. What was the point? George gave him a permanent job at the garage, and every buck he made he put away – stashing it under his mattress – watching the pile of bills grow larger every week.

As for Lauren – he'd shut her out of his mind. When he didn't hear from her . . . when there was never any message, he'd felt a deep sense of betrayal. He'd opened himself up to another human being and look where it had gotten him – exactly nowhere. Never again. Love – you could shove it.

Emerging from the rest room he bumped into George, who said, "You got a visitor. Use the office."

"Who?" he asked, but George was off doing something else.

He entered the small, crowded office and there she was – Lauren – perched on the edge of the old warped desk, looking as beautiful as ever.

"Hi," her soft voice was almost a whisper.

Jeez! Who needed this? "What're *you* doin' here?" he asked, roughly.

She got off the desk and came towards him. "I made Joey bring me."

"Good for him."

"I came as soon as I could."

"A few weeks late," he said coldly, "but I s'pose you were busy."

"My parents wouldn't let me out. I had no idea what happened." She moved closer. "Nick, I'm so sorry to hear about your brother. I didn't know. I thought I'd see you in school today and when I didn't . . ." She trailed off, shrugging helplessly. "You've got to forgive me – it wasn't my fault."

It sounded logical. Only why had both her parents sounded so sincere when they'd informed him she had no wish to speak to him and would he kindly stop bothering her? Still . . . parents . . . those fuckers could lie better than anyone.

He made one last effort to back away. "Hey – I'm cool, you don't havta feel sorry for me."

Her eyes filled with tears. "Sorry for you? Is that what you think?"

"Listen, it's –"

"I *love* you," she interrupted, her voice breaking. "I honestly love you."

Her words melted the ice, and suddenly she was in his arms, soft and sweet-smelling. There was no way he could resist her. There was no way he wanted to.

They talked for over an hour, clearing everything up, and by the time she left, they'd worked things out. Joey would be their liaison – he'd deliver notes and set up meetings.

"One of these days I'll talk my parents into you," Lauren

promised, "and then we can be together as much as we want."

Yeah, he thought, *don't bet on it*. Parents and him – not a good mix.

She kissed him before leaving. She wasn't even gone and he couldn't wait to see her again.

"Soon," she promised.

He wasn't so sure it would be as easy as she thought.

Chapter 25

And that's how they handled it – as carefully and secretly as possible. Of course, there's no such thing as a secret once more than two people know. Joey knew, and Cyndra. Harlan, of course, and George – who confided in Louise and Dave.

As the months passed and they grabbed furtive meetings here and there, Lauren began to show the strain of lying to her parents. She'd become an expert at inventing elaborate excuses that wouldn't rouse their suspicions, but still it was tough.

Nick felt it too. He didn't want to pressure her, but being with her in short sharp bursts was doing him no good. He wasn't a kid, and he was beginning to think he couldn't take one more evening of groping and fumbling – he needed more. He needed to be as close to her as two people can get.

As the weather improved and Spring took root he came up with the idea of bringing her to the trailer. Harlan was at school, Cyndra at work, and Primo never stirred.

The trailer was hardly the ideal place – but it was a lot better than the old abandoned car in the back of the gas station where they'd been forced to spend most of their time together.

He set it up, arranging for Joey to bring her to meet him at the gas station.

She was excited when he told her of his plans, and on the appointed day she warned her parents she was doing community service after school and would be home later than usual.

The day of their meeting dawned crisp and sunny. Lauren had settled into a stilted polite relationship with her parents. They thought she'd forgotten all about Nick Angelo – the bad boy who'd come to town and disrupted her life. Little did they know.

She left for school at the usual time, entered through the

front, avoided roll call and exited through the back. She knew she was living dangerously; skipping school was full of risks – the wrong word in the wrong place and she could be busted; then what?

The risk was worth it.

Fortunately she didn't run into anyone likely to question her. The close friendship she'd had with Meg was long over. Meg was part of Stock's group now, and Stock refused to speak to her.

How her life had changed over the last few months – and yet she was happier than she'd ever been.

Joey was revving up his bike in the parking lot ready to go. "Come on," he said. "Jump aboard an' let's get the fuck outta here."

At first it was awkward – the trailer being such a dump and all. Nick had tried to clean it up – shoving all the clothes into a corner, smoothing out the worn blanket on his mattress, but there wasn't much he could do to improve twelve square feet of space shared by three untidy people.

He could see Lauren was shocked by the shabby conditions, but she covered it well.

"Okay, so it's a pisshole," he said with a cocky grin. "But who promised you The White House?"

She pretended to look solemn. "I'll have to leave then."

"Yeah?"

"Maybe."

"Oh, really?"

"I think so."

"Come here."

"Why?"

"You know why."

He fell on the mattress, pulling her down beside him. They started to kiss, slowly at first – savouring each other's lips – and then faster until they both wanted it to be more.

He moved his hands under her sweater feeling her breasts. "I've missed you so much," he mumbled, working his way under her bra, trying to concentrate on something other than the feeling he was experiencing.

"You too," she managed.

He pulled her sweater over her head and unclipped her bra,

bending to kiss her breasts – his tongue moving slowly from nipple to nipple.

She sighed – a long drawn out sound.

It was too much. The moment of no return was upon them before either of them had time to stop and think, and even though she'd planned to ask him to wear a rubber – who cared? It didn't matter. Nothing mattered except the fusing of their two bodies.

He was more aggressive than the time before – entering her with a burst of energy – riding her like his life depended on it. And now that she knew what to expect she responded with a wildness and abandon she had not known she possessed.

Together they rocked the world – riding the roller-coaster until it peaked on the highest point of all – pausing for several mind-blowing seconds – before cruising smoothly all the way to stop.

"Oh . . . jeez!" he exclaimed. "That was the best ever."

"It was?"

"It was."

"Me too."

"C'mere, me too."

And she curled into his arms, wet and sticky, and fell into a blissful sleep.

When she awoke it was afternoon and he was lying on his back beside her, hands behind his neck. Slowly she traced the contours of his chest with her tongue – tentatively at first because she wasn't sure if he'd like it. He obviously loved it – so she really got into it – licking and sucking – teasing him with little love bites.

"Where'd you learn t'do this?" he asked, groaning.

"Hmm . . . wouldn't *you* like to know?"

"Yeah," he reached for her breasts but she brushed his hand away. "I think I would."

"Lie back and enjoy it," she said, leisurely travelling down his body until she reached his hard penis.

"Lauren –" he began. "You don't havta –"

"Yes I do," she whispered, teasing him with her tongue. "Because I want to."

By late afternoon they both knew they had to make a move. "You'd better get dressed," he said, wishing they could stay in bed forever.

"Uh . . . where's the bathroom?"

"I don't know how t'break this to you, but we ain't got one."

She thought he was joking and laughed.

159

"No, seriously – we don't."

"No bathroom?"

"Sorry."

"Where do you shower?"

"Down at the gas station. It's not exactly a shower – but I don't think you want the details."

She felt bad that she'd asked, she didn't want to embarrass him.

"Maybe we can come here every week," he said, getting up and pulling on his jeans. "Just you an' me – shut out the world."

"I can't take too many days off school."

"Yeah. An' I suppose George wouldn't be too happy if I ducked work on a regular basis."

"Nick," she stared at him, her face composed and serious, "What if I got –"

"Whoa – *no way*! I pulled out in time."

She was relieved. "You did?"

"Course I did. Wouldn't risk it."

"Thank goodness."

"Hey – you gotta learn to trust me – y'know that I . . . uh . . ."

"Say it!"

He grinned – "Love ya."

She smiled and softly touched his face. "Yes, I know."

"How was school today?"

"Huh?" Lauren tried to squeeze past her mother – who was standing in the front hall blocking the stairs.

"School?" Jane Roberts repeated.

If Lauren wasn't so intent on getting upstairs she would have noticed a tenseness in her mother's voice.

"Oh, the usual – boring math – dull history. And P.E. I *hate* P.E. In fact the showers were out of order – I feel all sweaty – maybe I'll take a shower now."

Jane did not budge. "Anything unusual happen?"

Warning bells rang in Lauren's head. Something had gone on at school that she didn't know about.

Gotta play it smart, Roberts. Wouldn't do to get busted.

"The thing is, Mother," she said quickly, "I wasn't going to worry you – but after P.E. I didn't feel so good. The nurse suggested I lay down for a while."

"Really?" Jane's tone did not warm up. Usually she would have been full of concern.

There was a short, uncomfortable silence. Since her mother didn't seem inclined to move, she decided to head for the kitchen. Jane followed her in – there was no escape.

Opening the ice-box she grabbed a carton of milk and turned around to find her mother staring at her with cold, accusing eyes.

She couldn't take it any more. "Is something wrong?"

"Why do you ask?"

She shrugged, reaching for a glass. "I don't know. You seem kind of . . . funny."

She wondered if she could make a dash past Jane and get upstairs without further questioning.

"Lauren," her mother said, in slow measured tones. "We've always brought you up to be a good girl. Truthful at all times."

Oh God, something was definitely up.

She tried to look innocent. "Yes, Mother?"

"You weren't at school today, were you?"

Now she had a choice. Did she continue to lie and take a chance? Or did she tell the truth?

Dear Mother, I spent the day in bed having sex with Nick Angelo. Did you, dear? How nice.

Gee, thanks, Mom, you're so understanding.

She bit her bottom lip – there was only one way to go. "I told you, I *was* at school, but I didn't feel good."

"The school secretary phoned to inform me you have probably been playing truant on and off for the last few months."

She managed to look amazed. "What?"

"Apparently you've been absent on several occasions with various excuses. A sore throat, a cold, a visit to the dentist. And all your excuse notes were supposedly signed by me. Miss Adams is no fool. Eventually she became suspicious – especially as this morning you were seen leaving on the back of a motorcycle."

Oh God, here it came. She was in deep trouble.

"We've always trusted you, Lauren, and now this. Your father is on his way home."

Naturally.

"It's *your* fault," she blurted out, her cheeks reddening. "You can't stop me from seeing Nick. We're in love."

"In love?" Jane laughed, derisively. "You're sixteen years old, what do *you* know about love?"

More than you think, she wanted to yell out. *More than you'll ever know.*

Words came tumbling out. "Don't you understand? Nick doesn't have anybody except me. I can't turn my back on him like everyone else. I can't do it."

"You'll do exactly what your father and I say you will."

Dread swept over her. This was no idle threat. Somehow she was going to have to deal with it.

Chapter 26

"We're outta here," Joey said.

"Huh?" Nick slid from under the Lincoln he was servicing. "Whatcha talkin' about?"

"I mean we're leavin' town, me and Cyndra."

"You don't have enough money," Nick said, wiping oil off his hands.

"Sure we do," Joey replied. "I bin workin' two jobs, remember? And Cyndra's bin doin' time at the factory. We've had it here."

Joey and Cyndra – the two people he was closest to were taking off. Wasn't it bad enough that he couldn't see Lauren any more?

"Anyway," Joey said, lighting up a butt, "we did some talkin' – an' we figured if you wanted to come with us it's okay."

"Where you plannin' on goin'?"

Joey shrugged. "Chicago. I got relatives there, friends, people who'd put us up until we find a place."

"You told your mother?"

Joey dragged on the butt, inhaling every last bit of smoke into his lungs. "Are you shittin' me? I'll leave her a note. She'll freak whatever I say."

"How about Cyndra?"

"She ain't tellin' nobody, only you." He dropped the butt on the ground crushing it underfoot. "We're goin' tomorrow."

Nick shook his head. "Jeez! Tomorrow! Like how about givin' me notice?"

"I know it's kinda sudden, but if we don't do it now we'll never make the move. You comin' with us or not?"

He was torn. Sure he wanted to go, but how could he leave Lauren? Even though he hadn't seen her for six weeks he still loved her. It wasn't her fault she'd gotten busted – it was his – he should have made certain they were more careful.

Things were a mess. They'd really blown it. Her parents had gone crazy. Phil Roberts had even turned up at the trailer. He'd listened when Phil had attempted to confront Primo – like the fat slob gave a shit. Some fucking joke.

"I want your assurance your son will have nothing more to do with my daughter," Phil Roberts had said, standing stiffly at the door.

"What in hell ya talkin' about? Get the fuck outta here," Primo had replied, a true gentleman.

Phil Roberts had retreated fast.

Nick unbuttoned his greasy overalls. "I dunno what t'say, Joey. I'm real tempted."

"Look . . . I understand it ain't easy."

"I can't run out on Lauren without seein' her."

"Whyn't you write her a letter? Tell her you'll be back for her when you got the bucks."

"Like when?"

"What am I? A fortune teller? Who knows? But you're sure not securin' any future for the two of you hangin' 'round here."

Joey was right. If he took off he could do anything he wanted – start a new life – anything – and when Lauren was eighteen she could tell her parents to screw off and they'd be together.

"Let me think about it," he said, peeling off his overalls.

"Don't think – do," Joey encouraged. "'Cause I ain't plannin' on endin' up here – an' neither is Cyndra. We're on our way, Nick – an' if you're smart you'll come with us."

He thought about it all day, and the more he thought, the more appealing the prospect became. Take off. Say goodbye to Primo, Bosewell, all the negative shit that plagued his life. Jeez – it was tempting.

Then he began thinking about Harlan. How could he dump the kid? Especially with Cyndra leaving too.

Hey man, what are you, a babysitter? Think about yourself for a change.

He needed to see Lauren but that wasn't possible. Writing her a letter seemed like a good idea. He could explain everything so she'd understand. That way she wouldn't think he'd run off without her.

After work he stopped by the drugstore. Louise greeted him, her usual cheery self. "What's up, Nick?"

"I need a big favour."

"What else is new?"

"Can you see Lauren gets a letter if I leave it with you?"

"You mean hand it to her when she comes in?"

"Yeah. Only not if she's with her mother."

"No problem."

"Lend me a pen an' paper, I gotta write it."

Louise was obliging as ever; she set him up with paper and pen and he hunched in a corner booth trying to figure out what to write.

Dear Lauren, I'm going, but I'll be back for you. It's dumb for me to hang around since we can't see each other anyway, so I'll keep in touch and you'll always know where I am.

It didn't exactly cut it. He tried again.

Dearest Lauren.

Too formal. And once more . . .

Lauren – I miss you so much that every night when I go to sleep all I can think about is you. I see your face. I feel your body. I smell you.

Nah, that sounded rude. He started again, and finally got the words right. Then he sealed it in an envelope, marked her name on it, adding a large PRIVATE! and URGENT! on the front. Now all he had to do was tell Joey he was going with them.

As he left the drugstore, Stock Browning drove up and got out of his car with a couple of his cronies. He swaggered past Nick, seeing this as a perfect opportunity to show off – his favourite sport. "Smell something, guys?" Stock said with a rude snigger. "Like an open trash can?"

His friends guffawed.

Nick had been waiting for this ever since his broken nose. "Hey, man," he countered. "How come y'always travel with bodyguards? Scared shitless you might run into me, huh?"

"Into *you*?" Stock smirked, showing off for his pals. "I squash white trash like you under my feet."

"Yeah – well they're sure big enough."

"What did you say, *jerk*?"

"You heard me, *asshole*."

Stock thought he'd be a big man in front of his friends. Since he'd creamed Nick once he figured it was easy. He turned towards him, his hefty right arm raised, ready to throw a punch.

This time Nick was ready – "Fuck you," he spat out, kneeing

Stock in the balls, following up with a sharp kick below his knee.

Stock let out a roar of pain.

Nick chopped him across the neck, and before anyone knew what was happening Stock was sprawled on the ground.

"Hey –" Nick said, prodding him with the tip of his sneaker. "I guess I owed you that." Turning his back he walked away.

Cyndra was in the trailer when he got home, busy cramming everything she owned into a small backpack.

"Joey told you, huh?" she said, rolling up her favourite sweater and squeezing it in.

"Yeah."

"What have you decided?"

"I'm gonna come."

She jumped up, threw her arms around his neck and kissed him. "I'm real happy, Nick."

"So am I."

They grinned at each other. It had taken time but they'd finally formed an alliance.

When Harlan came home he immediately knew something was up. "Where're you goin'?" he asked Cyndra, his big eyes accusing.

"Nowhere," she said, unable to look at him.

"We gotta tell him," Nick warned her in a low voice.

"Look – I love him as much as you do, but there's no way we can drag a kid along. I know my mom – she'll get used to me splittin' – but if we take Harlan, she'll send the cops after us."

"We can't just dump on him."

She stared at Nick, sour-faced. "If we tell him, he'll run straight to Aretha Mae."

"Not if he makes us a promise."

"What's goin' on?" Harlan asked, edging nearer.

"C'mere, kid," Nick said, patting the end of his mattress. "Howdja like to have this trailer all to yourself? You're gettin' older now, you can bring girls here, throw wild parties, huh?"

Harlan's eyes filled with tears. He'd known it was bad news. "You an' Cyndra goin' away, ain'tcha?"

"Yeah – we gotta go," Nick said, wrinkling his forehead. "But it ain't that bad."

Cyndra joined in. "Look – one of these days I'll come back for you. That's a promise."

Harlan shook his head. "No, you won't."

"Yes I *will*," she insisted. "Wanna bet?"

"I'll take the bet," Nick said. "An' if she don't – I will. How's that?"

Harlan was unconvinced. He wiped away his tears with the back of his hand and tried to pretend it didn't matter.

Nick felt bad – but what could he do? He'd made a decision and he intended to stick to it.

The next morning dawned exceptionally bright and clear. Since it was pay-day the plan was for everybody to go to work, pick up their pay-cheque and meet around six. Joey told his mother he would be away for the weekend. Cyndra told Aretha Mae the same thing. Unfortunately Primo overheard and launched himself into a sitting position. "Where you goin'?" he demanded, as if he had a right to know.

"None of your business," Cyndra replied sharply, hating the sight of him.

Aretha Mae sensed something going on. She pulled her daughter to one side and said in a hoarse whisper. "You got money comin'. Real money."

Cyndra was surprised. "I have?"

"Mr Browning – he came through."

"Why?" Cyndra asked, suspiciously.

"'Cause I told him he hadda do what's right."

"I thought you didn't believe me."

"Maybe I did – maybe I didn't. It don't matter – he owes you."

"How much money?" Cyndra asked, quickly.

"We'll talk about it next week," Aretha Mae said.

"Why not now?"

"Now's not the time."

On their way to work Cyndra told Nick about the conversation. "She knows," she said, nervously biting her thumb-nail. "That's why she's telling me 'bout this money now. Whyn't she tell me before?"

He shrugged. "Dunno. Why is old man Browning givin' you money anyway?"

"It's a long story," she said, clamming up.

He didn't push it; she'd tell him when she was ready.

Now that he'd made the decision to leave he was impatient, although he did want to take the time to say goodbye to Betty Harris, she'd been good to him and he owed her that.

*

Since leaving the Brownings, Aretha Mae had been working over at the canning plant. It was a tougher job than private service, but at least it was a job. She hadn't told Primo she'd quit the Brownings, it was none of his damn business. Taking Primo back had been a mistake. She'd thought she might enjoy having a man around again, but what did he give her? Pure nothing.

Benjamin Browning had kept his word – he'd had no choice really – he couldn't risk Aretha Mae revealing him for the pervert he was. She'd banked the five thousand dollars he'd handed over in cash. What a fine day that had been!

At first she hadn't planned on telling Cyndra about the money – it was there for an emergency. But that morning she'd had a funny feeling when Cyndra said goodbye. The girl was up to something – and that's why she'd mentioned the money. She didn't want her daughter doing anything foolish – like running off with Joey Pearson. A girl with Cyndra's looks could do far better than him.

On Fridays Aretha Mae worked a half-day. Lately she'd been meeting Harlan from school, taking him down Main Street and treating him to an ice-cream. They were both lonesome since Luke's death.

She thought of Luke often, and her heart was filled with sadness. Poor Luke . . . poor baby . . . he'd never had a chance.

Harlan was standing outside school when she arrived. She tried to take his hand but he pulled away from her.

"How ya doin', baby," she asked, thinking what a fine looking boy he was.

"Don' call me that, Mama." Harlan glanced around, making sure none of his school-mates had heard.

"Gonna buy you ice-cream," Aretha Mae promised.

Harlan's heart was heavy. He didn't want ice-cream – he wanted God to bring Luke back. And maybe at the same time God could persuade Cyndra and Nick to stay.

Betty Harris wasn't surprised. "I knew you'd be on your way one of these days," she said, inviting Nick into her living room. "I didn't realize it would be so soon."

"There's nothing for me to hang around here for," he explained, flopping down on her over-stuffed couch. "I gotta get away from my old man before I end up like him."

"What makes you think that would happen?" Betty asked.

"'Cause if I stay anywhere near him I ain't got no chance."

"And you imagine you'll have a chance in Chicago?"

"Why not? It's a big city."

"Big cities can sometimes be cruel places," she said, quietly. "You're young and good-looking. I'm sure you'll get plenty of offers – perhaps not always the ones you expect."

"I can take care of myself," he said, edgily.

"I know that." She sighed, thinking how vulnerable he was – in spite of his tough exterior. "I'll miss you, Nick. Teaching you has been a wonderful experience, you're really a talented boy. You have a natural ability to become whatever character you're portraying." She hesitated before giving him what she considered the ultimate compliment. "Sometimes you remind me of a young James Dean."

He laughed, slightly embarrassed. "Hey – let's not get carried away or maybe I won't go."

Betty Harris watched him, her expression serious. "If people see you, if you get the right opportunities . . . I shouldn't encourage you because acting is the most difficult profession in the world." She sighed again. "You *do* know that most actors are out of work most of their lives, don't you?"

"I gotta take the chance," he said, wishing she'd cut out the negative shit.

She nodded wisely. "Yes, that's the right attitude. Positive thinking. Wait here a minute."

She left the room and he got up and paced around. He loved being in Betty's living room, it was so warm and comfortable, a real home. There were photographs in silver frames and stacks of interesting books. God, how he wished he'd been encouraged to read as a child. He hadn't even known what a book was until his first day of school.

He picked up a picture of Betty in a white lace gown, her hair tumbling in soft curls around her youthful face.

"I was pretty, wasn't I?" she said, coming back into the room and startling him.

"You still are," he replied, gallantly.

"So young and so smart. There'll always be a woman to look after you."

"That's not what I want."

"I know." She smiled and handed him a padded envelope.

"What's in it?" he asked, weighing it from hand to hand.

"Something I want you to have," she said, earnestly.

"If it's money I can't take it."

"It's not."

"Can I open it?"

"Go ahead."

He tore the envelope open. It was Betty's precious signed copy of *A Streetcar Named Desire*.

"Betty – jeez – this is great."

"Good. I want you to have it."

He tucked the book under his arm. "Betty, I gotta tell you . . . you've been so good t'me, I'll always remember you."

"I'll remember you, too, Nick. Take care of yourself." Impulsively she stepped forward and hugged him. He hugged her back – tightly. Betty represented his last vestige of security and he was going to miss her and their intense sessions.

When he left her house he did so without a backward glance. It was time to move on. His new life was just beginning.

They met at six o'clock on Friday night – excited – maybe a little bit frightened – but none of them showed it.

Joey had the trip all planned. The last bus to Ripley – and then they'd hop a freight train all the way to Kansas City, and from there – Chicago.

The three of them stared at each other.

"This is it!" Joey said.

"Goodbye Bosewell," Cyndra said.

"I ain't comin' back 'til I've made it," Nick said confidently. "And I *will* make it. Then I'll come back for Lauren. Bet on it."

Chapter 27

Every morning Lauren awoke with the same blank feeling. As soon as she opened her eyes she felt a dull ache of despair, and there was nothing she could do about it.

She'd begun to hate her parents. Walking into the kitchen and having breakfast with them was an effort. Sitting at the table and listening to their inane conversation. Didn't they realize they were killing her inside? Didn't they realize they were mean-spirited and unrelenting and above all – wrong?

She thought about Nick all the time and in her heart she knew she had to see him. But how? That was the big question – how?

Every day her father took her to school, later on her mother met her, driving up in the family station wagon, giving her no chance to escape. This had been going on for six weeks – ever since she'd been caught.

"When are you going to trust me?" she asked one day.

"When your father and I feel that we can," her mother replied, with a pious expression.

There was no point in pursuing it. Trying to change their opinion of Nick was useless.

Today it was Monday, and Nick was on her mind more than ever. She walked over to her bedroom window and gazed out. The sun blazed hot and steady – unseasonably so. Downstairs she could hear her mother calling out, "Lauren! Breakfast is ready."

Soon she would have to sit in the car next to her father as he dropped her off at school. Delivered and collected. And she knew they checked with the school secretary every day to make sure she hadn't taken off.

Listlessly she wandered downstairs, ate the breakfast her mother had prepared – picking at the food with absolutely no appetite at all, and collected her books.

Phil Roberts appeared five minutes later. Was it her imagination or did the atmosphere between her parents seem tense? They hardly seemed to talk any more. She was sure she was responsible. It had to do with the fact that her father had not concluded the insurance deal with Benjamin Browning, therefore her mother had not received the social and financial boost she'd expected, and this had obviously put a strain on their relationship.

Too bad. It was nothing compared to what she was going through.

"It's hot today," Phil grumbled, struggling into his jacket and grabbing a slice of toast on his way through the kitchen.

"The weather report says it will be hotter than yesterday," Jane remarked.

Phil did not look in her direction. He walked into the hall and examined himself in the mirror, reaching up to pull out a strand of grey hair. "I'll be home late tonight," he called out, picking up his briefcase.

Jane did not respond. She slammed dishes into the sink and ran the water.

On the way to school Lauren decided to open up a conversation. "Daddy, can we talk?" she began, determined to get through to him.

"Not today, Lauren," he said, his eyes fixed on the road ahead. "I'm not in the mood."

"When *will* you be in the mood?"

"Stop bothering me."

Her life was breaking into little pieces and all her father could say was "Stop bothering me". Once she'd felt she could go to him with any problem, now there was a cold war between them. Didn't he care that he was driving her away?

When he dropped her off she didn't even bother saying goodbye.

Dawn Kovak lingered near the lockers. She and Dawn were not exactly close friends, but Dawn greeted her as if they were. "Did you hear what Nick did to Stock?" Dawn asked.

Lauren was immediately alert. "What?"

Dawn was determined to draw it out. "You mean you haven't heard?"

"No. Are you going to tell me or not?"

Dawn smoothed down her tight skirt. "No need to get edgy."

"I'm not edgy. If you have something to tell me, go ahead."

"Well, from what I hear, Nick knocked Stock on his ass." Dawn couldn't help giggling.

Lauren waited to hear more. "Are you sure?"

"It happened outside the drugstore. Stock was on his way in with a couple of guys, and Nick was on his way out. They got into some kinda beef and Nick creamed him. Funny, huh?"

Even though she was dying to hear all the details Lauren attempted to stay cool. "Is . . . is Nick all right?"

"To tell you the truth," Dawn replied matter-of-factly, "me and Nick – we don't see each other any more."

Lauren nodded. "Oh."

"Look," Dawn said, suddenly sympathetic, "I got the message about how he feels about you. I wouldn't interfere with that."

Lauren felt tears sting her eyelids. Nobody had spoken to her about Nick before, there wasn't anyone she could confide in. "My parents won't allow me to see him," she said, miserably. "I don't know what to do."

Dawn looked suitably concerned. "Yeah, Joey told me. Listen," she added jauntily, "parents are a pain – maybe they'll change their minds."

Lauren shook her head. "Not my parents." She paused for a moment. "I feel so bad about everything. It's my fault Nick got kicked out of school, I mean if it wasn't for me . . ." she trailed off.

"Don't sweat it – he's happy working down at the gas station, beats school any day. And it's *not* your fault. Stock's the one that had his parents do the dirty."

"I know you're right, but sometimes I wake up in the morning and all I want to do is run away."

Dawn nodded understandingly. "We all get that feeling."

"Really?"

"Sure – it's natural."

A couple of girls rushed past on their way to class. "C'mon, Lauren, you'll be late," one of them called out.

She hesitated for a moment. "What are you doing for lunch today?"

Dawn was surprised. "Who? Me?"

"I don't see anybody else standing here."

"What I normally do. Hang out. Why? You wanna eat with me?"

"I'd like it if we could talk some more," Lauren said.

Dawn seemed pleased. "So would I."

After dropping Lauren off, Phil drove straight to his office. Before going upstairs he stopped in at the hardware store and picked up the new kitchen scissors Jane had ordered.

Kitchen scissors, he thought grimly, *she's probably going to stab me to death.*

He collected them in the morning because he knew by the time he was ready to go home the last thing he'd be thinking about was picking up something for his wife.

Upstairs he unlocked his office door and entered. Eloise, his secretary, had not yet arrived. The place smelt stuffy and humid. He threw open the windows and settled behind his desk, thinking that perhaps he should have allowed Lauren to talk to him in the car. It wasn't right – this distance between them. If things were different at home maybe it would be easier for him to communicate with his daughter, but there was so much tension between him and Jane that he didn't seem to have the time to deal with anything else.

He considered calling Benjamin Browning. They'd been almost ready to conclude a business deal when Lauren had broken her engagement; after that he'd been unable to reach him.

The hell with it! Picking up the phone he dialled Benjamin's office before he changed his mind.

A secretary answered, cool and efficient. "Who may I say is calling?"

"Phil Roberts."

"Just one moment, Mr Roberts, I'll see if he's available." A beat of ten. "I'm sorry, Mr Roberts, Mr Browning is tied up in a meeting. May I take a message?"

"Yes, I've called several times. I need to speak to him as soon as possible. Can he return my call."

"I'll see Mr Browning receives the message. I'm sure he'll get back to you."

Yes, I'm sure he will, Phil thought, sourly.

Harlan told Aretha Mae he had a sore throat.

"Is it bad?" she asked.

"It feels real bad," Harlan lied.

"Where's your sister?" Her see-all eyes searched the empty trailer.

"She ain't back yet," Harlan said.

Aretha Mae fixed him with a steely stare, daring him to tell a fib. "Is she comin' back?"

He refused to meet her stare. "I dunno."

Aretha Mae screwed up her face, knowing perfectly well Cyndra wasn't coming back. She'd known it on Friday when the girl had come to her with some story about staying away for the weekend.

She started to poke around the trailer – all of Cyndra's favourite things were gone and Nick's too. So he'd run off as well. She wondered if she should tell Primo. No. She'd wait and see if he noticed his only son was missing – it would probably take him weeks – that's how much he cared.

In a way she didn't mind now she knew Nick was with Cyndra – at least he'd keep a watchful eye on her, and maybe the two of them together could forge a better life for themselves.

"It's okay," she told Harlan. "You can stay home."

He was delighted. He hadn't thought he'd get away with it. Harlan never told anybody about how bad school was, the names they called him – nigger and dirt poor and stinking bastard. He'd gotten used to it – he'd even gotten used to defending himself when they beat him up.

As soon as Aretha Mae left for work he sneaked into her trailer to see if he could scrounge some food. Primo was in his usual position, fast asleep with the television blaring. Harlan noticed his mouth was wide open and he couldn't help wondering if anything ever crawled in. Stifling a chuckle he crept inside the trailer, edged over to the small ice-box and peered inside. He spotted a leg of chicken – and without considering the consequences grabbed it and hurriedly slid out of the trailer before he was discovered.

Primo heard the door bang shut and woke up. He sat up, scratching his stomach. Even though it was early it was goddamn hot – he could feel the sticky sweat trickling down his body.

He got up, went to the door and stepped outside. A skinny mutt growled at him. Primo picked up a beer can and hurled it at the mangy animal.

Lately Primo found himself getting restless. He'd never liked staying in one place for long. Aretha Mae might be a good woman, but he was bored. After a while being with one woman always bored him. Maybe the time had come to move on – after all there was a whole country out there – and plenty of other women who'd be only too happy to take him in. He was still a fine-looking man. Yeah – fine looking *and* a stud. What more could any woman ask?

Continuing to scratch his belly he headed for the outhouse and relieved himself.

When he emerged he caught Harlan sitting on the steps of his trailer chewing a chicken leg. "What'ya starin' at, boy?"

Harlan lowered his eyes. "Nothin'."

"Don't give me that nothin' crap. How come ya ain't in school?"

Harlan didn't look up. "I ain't feelin' good," he muttered.

Aretha Mae and her chickenshit kids – they were always getting sick. Except Cyndra. His daughter. Now she was a real nice-looking girl. If she wasn't his own flesh and blood he would certainly consider bedding her down. She needed an experienced older man who could teach her a thing or two.

"Wanna take a ride?" he asked Harlan.

The boy's eyes widened. Primo had never spoken to him before, let alone offered him a ride. "Where to?" he asked, suspiciously.

"Into town, unless you gotta better idea."

"Nope."

"Okay – hop in the truck."

Primo wondered why he was being so generous allowing the kid to tag along.

Because there was nothing to do in Bosewell, that's why. It was a one-horse, hicksville town. No decent bar, no dancing girls, no nothing.

A new thought began nagging inside his head. If he decided to leave Bosewell, would he have to take Nick with him?

Nah, why should he? The boy was old enough and ugly enough to manage on his own. Besides, Aretha Mae seemed to have taken a shine to him – let *her* have the responsibility for a while.

Not that he was taking off today. Right now he was riding into town and stocking up with beer and pretzels. He'd leave the following weekend – right after Aretha Mae came home with her pay-cheque. There was nothing to stop him from borrowing it.

He'd leave in the middle of the night, that way he'd be a couple of hundred miles away before they realized he was gone.

Primo Angelo deserved a life too, and the sweet thing was – if there was nothing out there for him he could come back. Aretha Mae would always be waiting.

*

Eloise Hanson arrived at Phil Roberts' office at twelve noon exactly. She worked for him three afternoons a week – typing and filing – those were her duties. Not that there was much to file lately – business was grim.

Eloise was a small plump woman in her mid-thirties, with pink cheeks, a scrubbed complexion and gentle brown eyes. Widowed a year previously – her husband was killed in a freak accident at the canning plant – she'd needed extra money to support herself and her elderly mother.

At first the relationship between herself and Phil Roberts had been strictly businesslike, but as the months passed they'd formed a close bond that eventually turned into a love affair.

Both of them felt guilty.

Both of them hated the duplicity involved.

Both of them could not keep their hands off each other.

As soon as Eloise walked into the office, fanning herself and murmuring about the heat, Phil realized that work was over for the day. He took her hand and led her into his office. "No work today,' he said, squeezing her moist palm.

She blushed a little, knowing full well what he had in mind. "But there's letters to get out."

"Too bad."

She accepted his desire without question and slowly began unbuttoning her blouse.

Phil went to the outer door, pulled the shade down and locked it – hanging out the "Closed" sign.

Jane suspected the affair was still going on, even though he'd assured her it was absolutely over. He wasn't certain she believed him, but somehow he couldn't stop. Eloise was such a caring woman, so giving and kind. Most of all she was a tiger in bed – a woman without inhibitions. She made Phil feel like a real man in her arms.

Not that sex with his wife hadn't always been good – over the years they'd enjoyed a satisfactory relationship – satisfactory bordering on dull. Eloise was different – she brought out a passion in him he'd thought was extinguished. Eloise allowed him to re-live the excitement of his youth. After all, he was not even fifty, surely he was allowed this final fling?

Recently Jane had given him an ultimatum. "Fire her," she'd said, her tone allowing no argument.

"Why should I?" he'd replied, struggling to maintain control of his marriage. "She's an excellent secretary. And you know there's nothing between us any more."

"I couldn't care less," Jane had replied. "I do not want that bitch anywhere near you."

Jane never swore. To hear her say "bitch" was quite shocking.

Phil knew that firing Eloise was inevitable, but he kept on delaying the moment. Eloise was his escape, and without her – what exactly did he have?

Lauren and Dawn sat on the grass together sharing a tuna-fish sandwich.

"I know you went out with Nick," Lauren said, not anxious for the details, but unable to stop herself from finding out how serious it had been.

"It was before he started seeing you," Dawn explained. "As soon as you came into the picture it was over." She shrugged. "Look, I understand. I've met plenty of boys like Nick. I'm like a stop gap, you know? I'm there when they need me and then they move on. He loves you – he never loved me."

"Can I tell you something?" Lauren said, hesitantly.

"Go ahead," Dawn replied, biting into her sandwich.

"It's . . . it's embarrassing."

"Ha!" said Dawn. "Trust me. I've heard it all. *Nothin'* embarrasses me."

Lauren sighed – a long weary sigh. "It's just that my parents are very strict, and I haven't been allowed to see Nick in nearly two months, and the fact is – I don't know what to do."

"What is it?" Dawn asked. "You can tell me."

The words were difficult to say, but Lauren managed to get them out. "I . . . I think I'm pregnant."

Until she'd actually said it out loud she hadn't been prepared to believe it. Now that she'd voiced her suspicions she felt a great wave of relief.

"Damnit!" Dawn said. "How late are you?"

Lauren studied the grass. "Almost six weeks," she mumbled. "I daren't tell my parents. I . . . I have to see Nick. I have to tell him."

"Sounds like a good idea to me."

"How can I?"

"How *can't* you is more like it. If I was you I'd head straight over to the gas station and tell him. You shouldn't have to handle this alone."

"What if they find out?"

"You can't be any worse off than you are now, can you?"

Dawn had a point.

"I'll do it," she decided.

"Maybe the two of you can run off and get married," Dawn said, getting carried away. "*Very* romantic."

"That'll *really* thrill my parents."

"Stop worrying about them. Talk it over with Nick. The way I see it you've got two choices – marry him and have the baby, or get an abortion."

The word abortion petrified her. If there was a baby growing inside her she would never consider doing it any harm.

"Has this ever happened to you?" she asked.

"To tell you the truth, no. But I always take precautions. Didn't Nick wear a rubber?"

Lauren couldn't believe she was discussing anything as intimate as this with Dawn. "No . . . I, uh . . . he told me he . . . uh . . . pulled out."

"Oh, Jesus!" Dawn looked disgusted. "*Never* let 'em tell you that, it's the oldest line in the book. That and – let me just lay down next to you, I swear I won't put it in." She stood up and held out her hand. "Come on, get up, we gotta make plans. If you skip out of school now an' make it over to the gas station you can hear what he's got to say an' decide what you'll do. If you're lucky you'll be back before your mother gets here."

"You're right," Lauren said, drawing a deep breath. "It's the only answer, isn't it?"

"Sure – it's just as much *his* responsibility as yours. He's the asshole supposed to take precautions. An' don't worry, whatever you decide – I'm your friend, an' I'll help you if I can."

Lauren nodded gratefully, and felt sorry for all the bitchy things she and Meg had said about Dawn in the past. "Thanks," she said, squeezing her hand. "You've been great. I owe you one."

Chapter 28

Early Monday morning they made it into Chicago. Dirty, tired and hungry but totally elated.

"This is my kinda town, Chicago is," Joey sung, happily.

"Enough with the singin' – where we goin'?" Nick asked.

"Yeah, where?" Cyndra joined in. "I'm beat."

"Hey –" Joey said, "I got it all under control."

"I wish you'd get my stomach under control," Cyndra complained. "Travelling on that stinkin' freight train all night has made me starvin'."

"Okay, okay – I get the message. Let's go in here."

They entered a dingy looking café. Cyndra pulled a face while Joey ordered bacon and eggs, hot coffee and orange juice.

"Can we afford it?" she whispered. "Maybe we shouldn't be blowing our money like this."

"It's okay," Nick said. "We deserve a decent breakfast."

"This is the plan," Joey said, taking charge. "After we eat I'll make a few calls. Don't worry, we'll be sleeping in beds tonight."

"I hope so," Cyndra said, wearily. "'Cause I can't take another night sleeping rough." She went off to the rest room to wash up.

A rag-clad old tramp approached their table. "Gotta dime?" he wheezed.

"Buzz off!" Joey said, sharply.

Nick reached in his pocket and fumbled for loose change, handing the old man a quarter.

"What in hell're you doing? We might need that," Joey said, indignantly.

"It's like a superstition," Nick replied. "Never turn a beggar down."

"Oh – some superstition. They'll be following you like the freakin' Pied Piper!"

Cyndra returned from the ladies room having brushed her long dark hair and washed her face. "I feel better now," she said, ravenously attacking the runny eggs and greasy bacon.

"This'll havta last us until dinner," Joey warned, grabbing a piece of toast and mopping up his eggs. "Think I'll go make those calls now."

Fifteen minutes later he was back. "Friends," he said, sourly. "You can shove 'em."

"What happened?" Nick asked.

"Well, like, y'know, I had this best friend at school. He told me there's no way we can go to his house on account of he's havin' trouble with his dad – so strike him off."

Cyndra pressed forward. "Who else did you call?"

"This girl I used to go with, but when I told her there were three of us she cried off, so then I called my cousin."

"I thought we were forgetting about relatives."

"Don't sweat it. He changed his number – no new one."

"Is that it?" Nick asked. "These are the friends and relatives that were gonna put us up?"

"Hey – things change," Joey said. "We've got enough money for a hotel."

"Not for long," Nick said. "We've only got enough for three or four days – then we're out on the street."

"We'll get jobs," Joey argued.

"What jobs?" Cyndra asked.

"I'm gonna try out at a few comedy clubs," Joey said, cheerfully. "Face it – I'm young, I'm hot, I'm theirs!"

"I suppose I could do some waitressing," she said thoughtfully.

"And you can get a gig at a gas station, Nick," Joey said.

"Hey – if I wanted a job at a gas station I'd have stayed in Bosewell," Nick retorted, sharply.

"Stop bitchin'," Joey said. "We're here. We're outta Bosewell. Something good'll come along. Right now the most important thing is finding a cheap hotel for the night."

"I'm not sleeping on any park benches," Cyndra said, flatly.

"Nobody's askin' you to, sweetheart," Joey replied.

After an hour of traipsing the streets they checked into a fleabag hotel with flashing neon signs, vibrating beds and in-house porno movies. Joey and Cyndra registered as Mr and Mrs Pearson while Nick slipped around to the back alley. As soon as they reached their room they let him in through the fire escape.

"Some dump!" Cyndra complained, trying out the lumpy bed.

"You were expecting the Plaza?" Joey countered.

"Quit it," Nick said. "I'm not listenin' to you two fight all night long."

They began studying the newspaper, circling job opportunities. Joey found what he was looking for and got ready for action. He combed his hair, slicked it down with oil, put on his best jacket and said, "I'm visiting the Comedy Club. How old do I look?"

Cyndra leaned back, narrowing her eyes. "'Bout seventeen."

"You're full of it." He turned to Nick. "Whaddaya think?"

"Y'could pass for twenty."

"I'm growin' a beard, that'll do it."

Cyndra wrinkled her nose. "Ugh . . . I hate beards."

"You hate everything," Joey said.

"No, I don't," she argued.

Nick was getting edgy. "C'*mon* you two," he said.

"Listen to this." Cyndra pounced triumphantly, reading aloud from the paper. "'Beautiful young girls wanted for modelling jobs. Ability to travel abroad essential.' Sounds great," she jumped off the bed and paraded around the room. "I could be a model, couldn't I?"

"Sounds great," Joey mimicked. "They'll have you on a slow boat to China with a needle in your arm."

"Huh?"

"That's what they do to girls once they get hold of 'em. Ship 'em off to whorehouses in Bangkok."

"You and your imagination."

"I'm not kiddin'."

"I'm gonna take a walk," Nick said. "See you two later."

"Yeah, yeah," Joey said. "I'm doin' the same. Cyndra, you're on your own, so don't go signing with no modelling agency unless you check it with me first."

"Sure, Mr Bigshot," she said, sarcastically.

Joey grinned, he liked her sassiness. "You'd better believe it. We'll meet back here in a coupla hours."

Trudging around the streets of Chicago Nick felt his adrenalin begin to pump. Walking the streets was a kick – people-watching, getting the feel of the city. He passed a couple of Help Wanted signs and went inside only to find both positions filled. Who wanted to work in a hamburger joint or a barber shop anyway?

After a while he passed a restaurant/bar with the same old sign in the window. What the hell – he'd make a pretty good bartender. He ventured inside the dim interior and checked it out. The place was dingy – with low lights and a tired stripper gyrating to a gloomy sounding Glen Campbell on the jukebox. There were few customers.

He headed towards the bar where a gnarled old man with a Marine crew cut and bloodshot eyes stood guard.

"Yeah?" the man rasped. "What kin I getcha?"

"I'm interested in the job," he said.

The man snorted and turned away. "Round the back."

"What job is it?"

"Washin' dishes."

"That's not exactly what I had in mind."

"What *didja* have in mind?" the man said, picking up a glass and giving it a cursory polish with a grubby cloth.

"Your job."

"Ha ha, the kid's a comedian. Get your skinny ass around the back."

Nick decided he was better off repairing cars than washing dishes, but he was here anyway, so he made his way into the alley coming face to face with a large rat balanced on top of an overflowing garbage can. He dodged past it and entered through the back door into a filthy kitchen.

A very thin man in what once might have been a white apron sat on a stool, his legs propped on a counter top near the sink. He was smoking a cigarette, blowing lazy smoke rings towards the ceiling. On the stove a huge pan of fries sizzled in a sea of greasy black oil.

"Yeah?" the man said, looking down his long thin nose.

"I was wondering 'bout the job," Nick said.

"You wanna do some washin', jump right in," the man said, gesturing toward a chipped sink piled high with dirty dishes.

"How much?"

"Two fifty an hour – cash."

"That ain't enough."

"Whaddaya think I am – Rockefeller? You want the job or not?"

"How many hours a day?"

"A coupla hours lunchtime, two or three in the evenings."

Thirteen bucks a day if he was lucky, and he'd still have mornings and afternoons free to go on auditions. "Make it a straight three bucks an hour an' I'm yours."

"Don't go bargaining with me, kid. I can get a Mexi t'do it for half the price."

"Why don't you?"

The man blew smoke in his face. "Oh, you gotta smart mouth too, huh? Fuckin' Mexis break everything."

"Two seventy-five," Nick said.

"Jesus!" the man slapped his forehead. "Start now and you got the job — or shift your ass outta here. Take it or leave it."

He took it. It sure beat walking the streets.

Chapter 29

By the time Lauren reached the gas station she was hot and tired. The forecourt was deserted so she made her way to the office and tapped on the door.

George sat behind his desk going over some outstanding accounts. "Yes?" he called out.

"Excuse me," she said, putting her head around the door. "I'm looking for Nick Angelo."

"Nick don't work here no more," George said, gruffly.

"He doesn't?"

"Nah – he quit."

She was stunned. How could he quit his job just like that? She was about to ask more questions when the phone rang and George settled himself into a conversation.

She left the gas station, trying to decide what to do.

You've gone this far, Roberts. May as well go all the way. Take a bus over to his trailer and find out what's going on.

She was more nervous about telling Nick than facing up to her parents, but it had to be done. What would he say when she told him she was pregnant? Oh, God! Would he hate her? She couldn't stand it.

She hurried to the bus stop and waited ten minutes before the bus arrived. It was stiflingly hot and stuffy, and she was beginning to feel nauseous.

"Bad weather up ahead," the driver said, accepting her fare.

What was he talking about? It was a beautiful day, much too hot, but it certainly didn't look like rain.

"Thunderstorms," the driver said, nodding his head knowingly. "I can hear 'em miles away."

Settling into a window seat she looked outside – there wasn't a cloud in the sky.

As soon as the bus began to move she started thinking about her father. Phil Roberts had always taught her to be honest and true, so why couldn't she be honest with him? Because that's what she really wanted to do.

On impulse she jumped off at Main Street, deciding to visit him at work and make one last attempt to communicate.

By the time she reached the stairs leading to his office she'd made up her mind exactly what she would say. She'd tell him her life was over if she wasn't allowed to see Nick Angelo. And then she'd tell him about the baby.

The shade was down on his office door, and the "Closed" sign was displayed. Disappointed, she went downstairs to the hardware store and spoke to one of the Blakely brothers.

"When will my father be back?"

"He's upstairs, Lauren."

"He's not, the office is closed."

"I'm almost sure he's up there. Here – take the spare key, you can wait for him."

She took the key and went back upstairs. Her father was probably out having lunch. This break was good, it would give her time to compose herself. When he came back she'd be ready with a perfectly reasonable speech that he couldn't fail to understand and respond to.

She put the key in the lock and let herself into the small reception area. As soon as she stepped inside she knew she wasn't alone – there were strange muffled sounds coming from the inner office.

He's being robbed, was her immediate thought. Without thinking she opened the door and stood on the threshold.

Eloise, her father's secretary, was spread-eagled naked across the couch. Crouched above her, also naked, was her father.

Lauren's hand flew to her mouth and she gasped. Eloise let out a little screech of horror, and Phil Roberts turned his head around to meet his daughter's shocked stare.

"Lauren!" he said, rolling off Eloise and frantically grabbing for his pants. "Oh my God! This is not what you think. Lauren, what are you *doing* here?"

She turned around and ran from the room, stumbling down the stairs, trying not to cry. *This* was her father? *This* was upstanding Phil Roberts – the man she'd looked up to all her life?

He was a phoney. He was a nothing. And she'd never, ever forgive him.

Primo Angelo lumbered into the liquor store and bought four six-packs of beer. Harlan trailed behind him.

When he was finished in the store and the van was loaded he said, "I'm starvin', wanna grab a bite?"

Harlan could hardly believe his luck. "*Yessir*," he said, quickly. "I'se always hungry."

"Where can we find us a good 'burger?" Primo asked.

Harlan pointed down Main Street. "The drugstore."

Primo set off with Harlan loping behind.

Louise greeted them with a smile, a menu, and a crisp, "Hi there, folks," as they sat down at the counter.

Primo nodded. Nice looking piece of ass. Good tits too. "Coupla 'burgers," he said. "Make 'em plump an' juicy an' fast." He winked suggestively. "Just like you, honey."

The smile vanished from her face. "Cheeseburger, chilliburger, or plain?" she asked, curtly.

"Make it two cheeseburgers – well done," Primo said, undressing her with his eyes. He could see little slivers of sweat between her breasts and it began to excite him. He'd had it with Aretha Mae, she was old and dried up, he needed somebody younger, juicier – somebody like this hot-looking waitress with the big tits and sassy ass.

Louise stopped by the kitchen, gave the order to Dave, and went in the back room grumbling to herself. Some men had no manners. All they thought about was sex.

She removed her purse from the shelf and took out her lipstick and a hairbrush. Then she fluffed out her hair and teased her bangs, before applying more lipstick. Louise always liked to look her best, especially when dealing with sexist jerks. Just as she was putting everything away she noticed the letter Nick had left for her to give to Lauren lying on the bottom shelf.

Can't give it to her if she ain't been in, she thought.

Nick had marked it URGENT! and IMPORTANT! If Lauren didn't show up soon maybe she'd hand it to her friend Meg to pass on.

Louise propped the letter up so she wouldn't forget, and returned to the kitchen.

The school secretary phoned Jane Roberts at one o'clock. "Mrs

Roberts, I'm sorry to have to tell you this – but it seems Lauren is missing again. She was here this morning and now she appears to have left."

Jane's lips tightened. "You mean she's not in school?"

"I'm sorry, Mrs Roberts, but I must warn you if this behaviour continues . . . Well, I don't have to tell you the consequences."

"Thank you." Jane put down the phone and immediately dialled her husband's number. Nobody answered.

Why did Lauren have to put her through this? Wasn't it enough that Phil had been sleeping with his secretary? Wasn't it enough that she'd been humiliated by the Brownings' rejection?

Jane's perfect life was falling to pieces around her and she couldn't stand it.

She snatched up her car keys and rushed from the house.

Lauren ran down Main Street until she was away from her father's office and the whole sordid scene. She didn't stop running until she reached the bus stop.

Pictures of her father, bare-assed, pumping away on top of Eloise kept playing before her eyes.

Now it all became clear why her parents were always fighting. Her father was having an affair, and her mother probably suspected.

Oh, God! Was this the man who'd told her how to live her life? The man she'd respected and looked up to?

She wanted to cry, but tears wouldn't come. *Poor Mommy*, she thought miserably. *Poor me*.

There were so many thoughts crowding her head she thought it might crack wide open.

The bus trundled up and she leapt on. There was no doubt about where she was going now. She had to see Nick, he was the only person she could talk to. The only person in the world she could trust.

Two women got on the bus and sat across from her.

"I spoke to my sister this morning," said the first woman, a straggly blonde. "She told me they're having a big thunderstorm over in Ripley."

"Yes?" the other woman did not seem particularly interested. She was several months pregnant and looked exhausted.

"Heard a rumour we might be expecting a twister around these parts," said the straggly blonde.

"Not a chance." The pregnant woman shook her head. "It's beautiful here today – we're lucky."

Lauren tuned out. Her life was destroyed and these women were discussing the weather.

What was she going to do, that was the big question – *what was she going to do?*

Primo took a five-dollar bill from his pocket, rolled it into a tight cone and attempted to poke it down Louise's cleavage.

Forcefully she slapped his hand away, glaring at him. "What the hell you think *you're* doing?"

"Giving you one helluva tip."

"Hey, mister – you can take your tip and stick it up your –" She caught Harlan watching them. "Ah, forget it."

Primo got up and lumbered to the door. Harlan grabbed a few stray french fries from the basket on the counter and followed him out to the truck.

"You saw that bitch in there," Primo said sourly. "Women – mark what I say – they're all whores. You don't want nothin' t'do with any of 'em. Remember that." He sprung open a can of beer and took a couple of hearty swigs, then passed the can to the boy. "Try it," he commanded.

"Don't wanna," Harlan replied, kicking the asphalt.

"Try it!" Primo repeated. "Be a goddamn man."

Gingerly Harlan took the can and managed a few sips, almost choking.

Primo laughed, grabbing the can back.

He felt like action.

He felt like doing something.

He felt like getting laid.

"It's not your fault, Eloise," Phil Roberts kept on assuring her.

Eloise, dressed and pink-cheeked, sat on the office couch sobbing into a dainty lace handkerchief. "She'll tell your wife, I know she will."

"Not if I get to her first," Phil said, attempting to calm her. "I can explain what happened. Lauren's a good girl – she'll understand."

"What is there to understand?" Eloise raised her voice. "What we had together was special and now it's . . . it's dirty."

"It's not dirty," Phil objected.

"Yes, it is," Eloise insisted, continuing to sob. "Everything's ruined."

He didn't know how to cope with her. "Go home," he urged. "Let me take care of this. By tomorrow it'll all be forgotten."

Eloise shook her head. "Your wife will destroy my reputation."

Prudently, Phil had not told her that Jane already knew about their affair. "Go home, Eloise," he repeated, firmly. "I have to find Lauren."

I have to find her before she gets to Jane and opens up her mouth.

By the time the bus reached the stop nearest the trailer site it had started to rain – huge wet droplets. And yet the sun was still shining and the temperature remained muggy.

Lauren had visited Nick's trailer only once, but she was certain she could find her way from the bus stop. She walked quickly down the country lane trying not to think about her father any more. Nick would solve all her problems. Nick would make everything all right.

It was a strange day what with the heat and the rain – there seemed to be a stillness in the air, everything was so quiet. A van roared past her. She kept her head down and continued walking.

Eventually she spotted the trailer site up ahead and quickened her pace. A pack of dogs foraged by the overflowing piles of garbage. How could Nick live here? How could he put up with such a slum?

She recognized his trailer and hurried towards it. A big man was getting out of the van parked outside, a small black boy by his side.

The man noticed her. "Lookin' for someone?"

"Yes . . . Nick Angelo. Do you know if he's home?"

"Nick's my boy."

"I beg your pardon?"

"My boy, my son. Who're you?"

"Are you Mr Angelo?"

"Yeah – that's me all right. I'm the good-lookin' one in the family." He roared at his own humour, and patted her on the arm.

So this was Nick's father, this big untidy lout with a can of beer clutched in his right hand and a smarmy gap-toothed smile. Perhaps this wasn't the right time to be visiting.

"I . . . I don't want to disturb anyone," she said, unsurely. "Maybe I should come back another time."

"Disturb? What's to disturb? Come on in," Primo said, flinging open the door of the trailer.

Harlan attempted to attract her attention. "If you're lookin' for Nick —" he began.

Primo pushed him roughly aside. "Come in," he insisted. "Nick'll be here soon. You can wait, I'll enjoy the company."

Reluctantly she entered the cramped trailer and almost gagged – the stench of stale beer and sweat was overwhelming.

Harlan tried to follow them, but Primo shoved him out kicking the door shut. He gestured expansively, "Take a seat, anywhere'll do. Wanna beer?"

"No . . . no, thank you. Is Nick here?"

"The kid'll find him."

Primo checked her out. She was a pretty girl, a very pretty girl. More than likely Nick had been slipping her a slice of the old Angelo magic. Like father, like son. Yeah – the Angelo men – real studs.

Lauren felt extremely uncomfortable as she hovered nervously near the door wishing Nick would appear.

"Will'ya sit down," Primo insisted. "He'll be here soon. So —" he leered at her, "you two old friends, is that it?"

"We go to school together. That is we did – until Nick . . . uh . . . left."

Primo snapped to attention. "Whaddaya mean, left?"

She hesitated, it was more than likely Nick hadn't told his father about getting expelled. She corrected herself quickly. "Oh . . . I mean *when* he leaves . . . to go to his job, you know?"

"Yeah, yeah – his weekend job down at the gas station." Primo ran his tongue across his teeth. "Didja try there?"

"They told me he'd . . . quit." She knew as soon as she said it that she shouldn't have.

He squinted at her. "Whaddaya mean, quit?"

"Uh, for the day. He quit for the day."

"Oh." Primo sprang open another can of beer. "Wanna swig?"

"I really have to be going, Mr Angelo, my parents are expecting me."

He moved over to her, so close she could smell his foul breath. "Pretty girl like you, bet there's someone always waitin'."

Now she felt more than uneasy. His huge physical presence was threatening. Very carefully she began to edge towards the door.

With one fast move he blocked her. "Where ya goin'?"

"I . . . I told you, I must get home."

His voice turned to a lewd whisper. "You an' Nick doin' it? You an' my boy gettin' it on?"

Her stomach turned, and she tried to move. He lunged forward, grabbing her breast.

"Don't touch me! Don't you dare touch me!" she yelled, shrinking away from him.

Primo chuckled, "Hey – feisty little chickie, huh? If'n Nick's doin' it to ya, why can't I?"

Her eyes flashed angrily. "You'd better let me out of here or I'll scream," she said, trying not to panic.

"Who's gonna hear ya, girlie? Ya think there's anyone 'round here cares?"

Out of the corner of her eye she noticed a kitchen knife lying on the side of the sink. Slowly she backed towards it.

Primo was enjoying himself. "C'mon, chickie, loosen up. Ya fucked the boy, doncha wanna fuck the man?" he said, leering lecherously as he moved closer.

Her back was up against the sink. Carefully she manoeuvred one hand behind her groping for the knife. "I said let me out of here," she repeated in a low angry voice, managing to get a firm grip on the handle.

"When I'm ready," Primo replied, fiddling with his belt buckle. "When I'm *good* an' ready."

Outside the sky suddenly darkened and lightning flashed across the window followed by heavy peals of thunder.

She clutched the knife tightly. "You'd better let me go or –"

He guffawed. "Or *what*, Princess?"

The lightning flashed again, once more followed by huge cracked rumbles of thunder. Outside the sky turned even darker, and the light rain swelled to a heavy downpour.

Primo took no notice, so intent was he on getting what he wanted.

She decided that if this man touched her one more time she would stab him.

Outside Harlan started hammering on the door. "Lemme in," he shouted. "Lemme *in*!"

"Get lost," Primo shouted back, unzipping his fly. "Get the fuck outta here."

Harlan continued to yell and hammer on the door. He sounded desperate.

A strong wind howled eerily outside the trailer and the rain turned into pelting hailstones.

"C'mere, girlie," Primo said, pulling at her as she tried once again to dodge past him.

"Don't!" she warned.

He was in no mood to listen to her objections. He grabbed her – forcing his fleshy lips down on hers.

At school she'd learned self-defence and she put it to good use – bringing her knee up hard and sharp, catching him in the groin.

He let out a grunt of pain, but managed to hold on to her – bending her backwards until she could feel his disgusting hardness pressing up against her, and she knew she had to do something drastic. Gripping the knife behind her back she readied herself for action.

Primo pulled at her skirt, pushing it up and ripping at her panties. "C'mon, y'hot little bitch, you're gonna love this," he muttered, dropping his pants.

She lunged with the knife, blindly striking out as the trailer began to rock in the wind and there was a frighteningly loud roaring sound.

Tornado – the thought flashed through her mind. *Oh God, it's a tornado!*

Chapter 30

Jane Roberts was driving towards Main Street when the sky suddenly turned ominously black and from out of nowhere giant hailstones began pounding the windscreen of her car.

She pulled over to the side of the street, petrified, and waited for the ferocious rain to stop, prayed for it to subside – for Jane had lived in the Midwest all her life and she knew what this kind of weather could bring.

Louise peered out the wide front window of the drugstore and yelled to Dave, "Honey, you'd better c'mon out here right now an' get a load of this weather. It's raining hailstones bigger than golf balls."

Dave had hardly taken one step forward when in the distance they heard a thunderous roar – getting louder by the second.

"Shit!" Dave said, running to the window.

"What?" Louise asked, catching his note of alarm.

"Sounds like a twister to me. Jesus! Can you see it out there?"

Indeed she could. A writhing grey funnel of death and destruction. And it was heading in their direction.

Eloise was at the door of Phil's office, ready to leave when the sudden loud howling wind forced her to stand still. She turned to Phil. "What's that?" she asked, her voice quavering with fear.

He looked concerned. "I . . . I don't know. Put on the radio."

Eloise ran to the portable radio on her desk and switched it on. A country and western singer twanged about her man doing her wrong.

The howling wind was getting louder by the second, and

outside the sunshine vanished and the sky turned black.

"Find the news," Phil snapped.

"I'm trying," Eloise said, frantically searching for the right station.

"Try harder, I think we're in trouble."

Stock and Mack were in the middle of football practice on an open field, while Meg was nearby rehearsing a new routine with the cheerleading squad, when the physical ed. teacher spotted the tornado in the distance and began yelling – "Everybody inside! Everybody into the gym! Hurry! Go now! Hurry!"

Stock and Mack looked at each other. The sky was darkening, but they hadn't thought a little bit of rain would interfere with football practice.

Stock started to say, "What's his problem –" when Mack spotted the powerful cone bearing down on them.

"Holy shit!" he said, hoarsely. "We'd better move."

Mr Lucas ran out of the main building. "Inside!" he yelled. "Everyone get under cover. Do it!"

Mack dashed over and grabbed Meg by the hand. She wished it was Stock. "What's the matter?" she asked. "What's all the panic?"

"We gotta get inside," Mack said. "Can't you see? There's a tornado on the way."

Aretha Mae hurried to the side exit of the factory, looked outside and shuddered. There, only miles away and moving fast – she saw it – an enormous, howling, writhing funnel of grey dust bearing down in their direction, destroying everything it passed.

Aretha Mae had never been a religious woman, but now she crossed herself and fell to her knees. "Save Harlan, God," she whispered. "Please, God – save my little boy."

Chapter 31

"Mop the floor."

"I wasn't hired to mop the floor."

"Fuckin' *do* it. I got health inspectors up my ass."

Q.J. was the boss. Rat-faced, with long greasy hair, an aquiline nose and slit eyes. He wore a grubby white suit, cheap black shirt and bright green tie. He wasn't very tall and he walked with a limp and smoked thin cheroots. He hadn't reached forty yet, but was well on the way if he didn't get knocked off first. Q.J. had plenty of enemies.

Reluctantly Nick grabbed a mop and went to work. He'd only been there a few hours and was already thinking of quitting.

"Where'd ya find this bozo?" Q.J. demanded of Len, the so-called chef.

Len looked down his long thin nose. "He walked in off the street. I hired him on a temporary basis."

"Tell him I don' expect no lip."

"Yeah, yeah, I'll tell him."

They spoke about him as if he didn't exist. Surely they realized they were fortunate to get anyone to work in such a crummy place.

The tired-looking stripper he'd caught a glimpse of earlier strolled into the kitchen wearing nothing but a short kimono and a bright yellow hairband.

"Hi'ya, Q.J."

"Hi'ya, doll."

"Lousy business."

"It's that time of year."

She opened the big industrial ice-box, reached for the milk, drank from the carton and put it back.

"That's a filthy habit, Erna," Q.J. grumbled. "Some poor schnook's gonna get your spit in his coffee."

"They should be so lucky." Erna yawned, reaching inside her kimono for a vigorous scratch. "Who's the kid, Len?"

"We're tryin' him out," Len replied. "If he can break less than zero he's got himself a job."

"He's cute," Erna remarked, with a little wink in Nick's direction. "Put him out front – make him a busboy."

"Excuse *me*," Q.J. interjected. "*I'm* runnin' this place."

"Just a suggestion," Erna said, throwing Nick another wink. "Maybe the ladies wanna look at somethin' for a change."

"Shit," Q.J. said, shaking his head at Len. "Now I gotta listen to hirin' crap from your wife."

Len ignored him, he was busy pulling the innards from a dead chicken.

Nick wondered how Joey and Cyndra were doing. Before the night shift began he wanted to get back to the hotel and check in. He took a quick peek at his watch – it was almost six which meant he'd been cleaning up for three hours.

"What time you want me back?" he said, addressing himself to Len.

"Whaddaya mean – back?" demanded Q.J., stepping over a box of wilted lettuce stashed on the floor. "We're comin' up to busy. You'll stick around 'til we close."

"He told me a coupla hours lunchtime, an' two or three in the evenings," Nick said, nodding at Len.

Q.J. couldn't care less. "What can I tell ya? He lied."

"Do I still get paid by the hour?"

"Yeah, yeah," Q.J. said impatiently, shooting his cuffs, revealing over-size pearl and gold cufflinks.

Nick wondered if they were real. "When's pay-day?" he asked.

"Friday. Jesus! That's all I need – a fuckin' dishwasher with a mouth!"

"Leave him alone, Q.J. He's workin' hard." So spoke Erna – his new guardian angel. "This place looks almost clean – for once."

By the time he got out of there it was past one in the morning. If his figures held up he'd made himself over twenty bucks. But jeez he was tired – ready to drop, and now he couldn't remember where the dumb hotel was.

He walked the streets for an hour before giving up, diving into the subway and curling up on a bench outside the men's room.

He'd find the hotel in the morning, right now all he could think about was sleep.

Just before oblivion hit he thought about Lauren and he fell asleep with a smile on his face.

Hands awoke him. Frantic hands, insistent hands. He opened his eyes to find an elderly well-dressed man bending over him struggling with the zipper on his jeans.

"What the hell –" he began, shoving the man's hands away.

"I'll pay you," the man interrupted, a feverish gleam in his eyes. "I'll pay you good. Ten dollars to blow you – or if you'd sooner the other way round I'll –"

Nick leapt up, startling the man who cowered against the wall.

"I . . . I . . . can go to fifteen," the man offered, licking dry lips. "Even twenty . . ."

"Fuck you!" Nick snarled, running down the platform towards the stairs. "*Fuck you, pervert!*"

"No need to get –"

Nick made it up to the street and fresh air. He took a deep gulp. Shit! If this was the big city he'd better learn to watch out.

He glanced at his watch; it was past seven and the streets were already busy. Now that it was light it didn't take him long to find the hotel, sneak past the front desk and make his way upstairs to their room.

Cyndra and Joey were asleep. Nice. Like they'd really been worried about him. He gave Joey a hefty shove.

"Wassup?" Joey mumbled, opening one eye.

"I'm back, that's what's up."

Joey struggled to sit up. "Where were you, man?"

"Workin'. Where were *you*?"

Joey was impressed. "You got a job?"

"No big deal. Washin' dishes. I'll do it 'til I score somethin' else."

"Washin' dishes," Cyndra mumbled, surfacing from under the covers. "I didn't leave home t'do that."

"Yeah, well, *you're* not doin' it, are you? I am," Nick replied. "An' it's only 'til we connect."

"That'll be soon," Joey said confidently, leaping out of bed. "Real soon."

Unfortunately Nick discovered he was the only one who'd found work. Neither Cyndra nor Joey had been so lucky. Secretly he was proud of himself; he'd proved he could manage on his own and that was a big achievement – maybe he should have run from his father a long time ago.

Later, when he reported for work he felt more at home. The foraging rat by the garbage cans seemed like an old friend, and Len in his soiled apron even threw him a friendly wave, cigarette ash scattering everywhere.

Nick Angelo. Dishwasher. Some beginning.

But it was better than nothing.

Cyndra might be only seventeen but she knew the look – it was in most men's eyes as soon as they saw her.

This man was no different. This skinny little jerk with a bald spot, glasses and a nervous tic.

"How oldja?" he asked, picking his nose.

She was interviewing for a job as an usher in a movie theatre. How old did you have to be to direct people to their seats? She took a wild guess. "Twenty."

"Got references?"

"Nope."

He stopped digging for treasure and peered at her through his thick glasses. "No references, huh?"

Big deal. Try a smile. "This would be my first job," she said, politely.

The man stared at her breasts. "I'd hire ya – but the management needs references."

"How can I have references if I've never had a job?" she said reasonably, wishing she'd worn a heavier sweater.

The man pushed at his glasses. "Can't risk it."

This was her fifth interview of the day – probably her fiftieth for the week. She'd been out looking every day, and so had Joey. How come Nick walked in off the street and scored an immediate job? It wasn't fair.

She wondered if she wrote to the canning plant back in Bosewell if they'd mail her a reference.

To whom it may concern:

Cyndra Angelo worked her black ass off for several months making sure an extra peach didn't fall into the wrong can. She stood on an assembly line for ten hours a day and we paid her minimum wage. Oh yes, and every man in the place tried to fuck her.

No way. She'd left without giving notice. Gallagher – the foreman of her section – was probably still pissed off.

She left the cinema and hit the streets again. It was hot and her feet hurt. She sat down on a bench by the bus-stop and tried to figure out her next move.

Use your looks, a little voice whispered in her head. *Make 'em work for you.*

She remembered an interview a couple of days back. DANC-ING GIRLS NEEDED the ad had stated. She'd gone to a loft in the city and lined up with about twenty other girls while a shirtless man with a video camera had filmed the line. When he was finished he'd said, "Okay – now the nude shots. Anyone who don't wanna strip get out now."

She and three other girls had beat a hasty retreat. The rest had started to disrobe.

What would have happened if she'd stayed?

She shuddered, not wanting to know. No way was she parading around naked, it wasn't her style. And she did have style. Whatever happened to her, whatever the future held, she always had to believe in herself – otherwise she was finished.

"I gotta coupla friends – they both need jobs," Nick blurted out.

Tonight Q.J. was in a maroon velvet smoking jacket well worn at the elbows. As far as he was concerned Cary Grant better watch out. "Whatcha think this is? A fuckin' charity set up?" Q.J. said, pulling a face at Len as if to say *Who is this schmuck? And why is he workin' for me?*

Len pounded on a slab of rabbit shortly to be served up as Chicken Surprise. "Ya don't want conversation don' come in the kitchen. This kid never stops. He thinks he's an actor."

"An actor?" Q.J. managed to look amazed. "Only *I* would hire a fuckin' dishwasher who thinks he's a fuckin' actor."

As usual they were talking about him as if he didn't exist. That was okay. He was used to it by now. Two weeks working at Q.J.'s and he was used to anything. The place was a dump – but it had turned out to be a popular dump. It hadn't taken Nick long to find out that Q.J. was a reformed house burglar who'd spent so much time in jail that a couple of years previously he'd decided to give up his life of crime and open a restaurant/bar with his brother-in-law, Len – a former waiter at one of Chicago's more fashionable hotels. Erna – Q.J.'s sister, had declared herself in as head stripper. Every time she wasn't around Q.J. complained. "Ya gotta retire her, Len. When she takes 'em off half my customers get up an' leave!"

"*You* tell her," was Len's standard reply. "*I* havta sleep with her."

Q.J.'s clientele consisted of ex-cons, present cons and the more colourful element of Chicago's criminal population. Strictly small-time, but they all had money to spend, and Q.J. made sure everyone had a good time – in spite of Erna and her dance of the seven veils.

Q.J. was a genial host who did a touch of fencing on the side, and in spite of his tough talk he was a real easy touch. Which is why Nick decided to repeat his words.

"I gotta coupla friends – they both need jobs."

"Do I look like an employment agency?" Q.J. demanded, throwing his arms wide. "I gotta pay nine people a week – ten if ya wanna include the cleaner who don't clean shit. I am not –" he raised his voice for effect "– a fuckin' refuge for fuckin' teenage schmucks from the East."

"West," Nick corrected.

Q.J. threw him a filthy look. "Now I gotta stay outta my own kitchen on account of your mouth. What I do to deserve this?"

Len reached for his cigarette smouldering on the counter top. He took a puff, causing thick ash to drop on the pounded rabbit flesh. Neither Q.J. nor Len seemed bothered.

"Can I bring 'em in?" Nick asked, expertly stacking clean glasses ready to return to the bar.

"No," said Q.J.

"No," said Len.

"You'll like 'em both," said Nick.

Two nights later he arrived at six with Cyndra and Joey lurking behind him.

Q.J. took one look at Cyndra and rolled his eyes. "Too pretty," he said. "The broads'll hate her. Can't have a stripper better lookin' than the customers – they don't like it."

"I'm not a stripper," Cyndra said hotly, glaring at Nick.

Q.J. squinted in her direction. "What are ya, doll? A brain surgeon with tits?"

"A singer."

"A what?"

"You heard me."

Q.J. adjusted the collar of his striped shirt and loosened his cerise tie. The girl was a beauty – a little dark for his taste and dangerously young, but she had class. Maybe his customers would go for her if he had Erna dress her up in a tight red dress with plenty of cleavage. Yeah – maybe he'd be Mister Nice Guy and give her a chance.

"I gotta be crazy," he said, shaking his head. "One night. Ten bucks. If they don' like you, you're out."

"What about me?" Joey asked. "I'm a –"

"Save it, sonny. I did my good deed for the day."

Joey knew when to shut up.

Cyndra's singing debut was inauspicious. Dressed up by Erna in a tight revealing gown she hated, with teased hair and too much make-up, she stood in front of a boozy crowd and attempted to warble her version of Aretha Franklin's "Respect". A mistake. The only singing Cyndra had ever done was in private, and although her voice was pleasantly husky she had no idea how to use it.

After a few minutes the crowd became restless. "Get 'em off, sweetie," yelled one man, and others soon took up the chant.

Standing at the back of the room Q.J. chewed on a toothpick and scowled. He'd thought he might have made a discovery – but as usual he was wrong. The girl had faked him out – convincing him she could do something she wasn't capable of.

"You fuckin' her or what?" asked Petey the Frog, one of his regulars, his bug-eyes bulging.

"Nah – just givin' her a chance." Q.J. replied, smoothing down his velvet smoking jacket.

"C'mon, ya gotta be fuckin' her," Petey the Frog said, slurping his drink.

"Too young," Q.J. said shortly, walking away.

Cyndra finished to desultory applause and a few more raucous cries of "Get 'em off!" She ran from the small stage.

"I quit!" she told an amazed Q.J.

"You quit?" he managed. "You fuckin' quit? I'm firin' ya, doll."

She glared at him. "You can't fire someone who already quit."

"And I ain't payin' ya, either," Q.J. added, red in the face.

"Oh yes you are," she said, fiercely. "I performed. You'll pay. It's not my fault your customers are a bunch of stupid apes."

Q.J. had never come across a girl like Cyndra before. She was a young one – but she had guts and he couldn't help admiring her. It was a shame she had no talent.

His first wife had been like that – Sassy Sarah everyone had called her. She'd run off with their electrician while he'd been languishing in jail. His second wife had chosen the plumber. He'd been single now for eight years and that's the way he planned to stay.

He paid Cyndra her ten bucks. She didn't seem particularly grateful. "I don't havta do this," he informed her.

"Yes you do," she replied, walking out into the night.

Q.J. did not appreciate her attitude, a little ass kissing would have been nice.

"Don't bring in no more of your friends," he warned Nick.

"You shoulda let her practise or somethin'," Nick said.

Q.J. shook his head at Len. "What the fuck's goin' on here? I gotta dishwasher lippin' off, an' a broad that can't sing shit givin' me a hard time. Do I deserve this?"

"That's life," Len said, dipping his finger into a bowl of cream.

"Shit!" said Q.J. "*Shit!*"

"Listen –" Nick began.

"One more word outta you an' you're fired," Q.J. said, gruffly.

Erna entered the kitchen beaming. "Big hit, huh?"

"With all due respect," Q.J. said to his sister, "You wouldn't know a big hit if it landed on ya ass an' bit you!"

By the time Nick finished work and got back to the hotel Cyndra and Joey were waiting outside with their bags packed. It was two in the morning.

"What's up?" he asked, dreading the answer.

"We got thrown out," Joey said, stamping his feet against the cold night air.

"How come?"

"'Cause we owe 'em."

"But I gave you the money to pay."

Joey looked sheepish. "I kinda lost it in a street hustle."

"Jerk!" muttered Cyndra.

"Hey – this place cost too much anyway," Joey said, quickly. "Tomorrow we'll get us a one-room apartment – it'll be cheaper."

Nick was angry. He was still the only one working – and now Joey was taking his hard-earned money and blowing it on street con games for dumb tourists. Maybe it was time to split up.

"I'm cold," Cyndra said, sounding like a little girl. "Where'll we sleep?"

She was his sister, he couldn't desert her.

"C'mon," he said, "we'll find you a nice comfortable park bench, cover you with newspapers an' you'll sleep like a baby."

She recovered her edge. "Gee, I can't wait."

Joey snapped his fingers. "Whaddaya want? The penthouse at the Ritz Carlton?"

She looked at him as if he was a lowly worm. "Yes," she said. "And one of these days that's exactly what I'll get."

"Sure," Nick agreed. "But tonight it's the park, so let's hit it."

They picked up their belongings and set off.

As they trudged towards the park he began thinking about Lauren and how much he missed her. By this time she'd have read his letter, and maybe if he got a post office box and wrote again, care of Louise, she'd reply.

The first thing they had to do was find somewhere to live. Joey was right: the hotel – cheap as it was – had been too expensive – they should have moved weeks ago.

An icy wind blasted them as they turned the corner. Joey stopped to gather a stack of old newspapers sticking out of a garbage can – disturbing a mangey cat. It ran off down the street screeching. Two drunken old tramps staggered by. A couple of junkies huddled in a doorway busy shooting up.

Cyndra clung to Nick's arm, shivering. "I'm frightened," she whispered.

"Don't worry," he said, trying to reassure her, "we'll be all right."

She clung tighter. "Promise?"

"Hey listen, kiddo – as long as y'hang out with me I'll never let you down. Okay?"

"Yes, Nick."

He may have sounded full of confidence, but it was a cold hard world out there and sometimes he was frightened, too.

Chapter 32

It all seemed to happen at once – one moment she was fighting off
Primo, and then everything became a horrifying deadly blur. First
the howling wind, followed by a thunderous roar as the tornado
bore down on them, catching the trailer in its path, scooping it
into the air and carrying it along for several hundred yards as if
it were made of papier mâché.

Lauren could hardly remember anything as she was hurled
from the door to the ground outside and knocked unconscious.
When she came to, the tornado was off in the distance, sweeping
a path of destruction, ripping up everything as it headed for the
centre of town.

Lying on the ground, she groaned, lifted her hand and felt blood
on her cheek. She tried to sit up, overcome with an overwhelming
sense of despair as she attempted to remember exactly what had
happened.

Primo . . . grabbing her . . . tearing at her clothes . . . the knife.

Oh, God, the knife! Had she killed him?

Panic stricken she staggered to her feet forcing herself to
think clearly. All she could remember was the power of the
tornado descending, and being propelled from the door as if
by some magic hand as the trailer was lifted up and swept
away.

Somehow she'd been saved. Why?

She looked around the trailer site – it was more or less
obliterated, everything gone. Even the trees had been plucked
from their roots.

Living in the Midwest she'd heard about tornadoes all her life,
but she'd never experienced one. Now the reality was upon her
and she saw for herself the devastation it could cause.

In the distance she could still see the wreathing grey funnel twisting on its way, its awesome destructive power demolishing everything it encountered.

There was no more rain, just an eerie stillness, and a deathly silence.

She tried to force herself to move, but her legs felt weak and could hardly hold her weight. Somewhere a dog barked mournfully.

I've got to get home, she thought. *They'll be so worried about me.*

She began to walk. Back towards town. Back to the house she hoped was still standing.

The tornado swept down Main Street like a lethal weapon, cutting its deadly path with incredible strength. Everything in its way was sucked up into its white-grey funnel. Trees, people, animals, cars – it was not selective.

Picking up strength as it travelled on its way it hit Main Street at its peak, propelled by winds of up to two hundred and fifty miles an hour.

The plate glass windows of the drugstore caved in, sending great shards of glass smashing to the ground.

Louise held tightly on to Dave, fervently praying.

He dragged her out into the street as the ceiling collapsed and falling debris crashed around them. Protecting her as best he could he threw her to the ground and lay on top of her – both of them trembling with fear. A sheet of glass sliced through his leg, cutting it off below the knee.

Louise let out a long, anguished scream as the blood from Dave's injury pumped all over her.

The tornado continued on its way, demolishing the Blakely Brothers hardware store, above which Phil Roberts and Eloise clung together in his office. They hardly knew what hit them. The very last words Phil Roberts heard was Eloise screaming, "I never meant to do it, God. Forgive me for my sins. Please forgive me!"

And then there was nothing.

Jane Roberts' car with her inside was swept up into the wind funnel and carried along for almost a mile. She died of shock.

The car, containing her body, was recovered twenty-four hours later – miraculously, it was still perfectly intact.

Bosewell High School suffered a direct hit. As the students raced into the gym, the tornado sucked the roof off the building, pelting everyone with flying glass and jagged chunks of concrete. Crashing debris hit a gas main causing a major fire.

Meg managed to grab hold of Stock as he hung on to the climbing rails, the only part of the gym that remained. She held on for dear life, trying to ignore his hysterical sobs and keep a clear head.

Mack had vanished – sucked away in the awesome cone of dust.

"Help me!" Stock sobbed, hysterically. "Somebody help me!"

"I'm here," Meg cried, soothingly. "Don't worry, I'll look after you, I'm here."

Aretha Mae watched the factory vanish before her very eyes. She stood in the middle of the destruction completely unharmed and continued to pray.

By the time the tornado left Bosewell fourteen people were dead, over a hundred and fifty injured. More than sixty buildings were damaged or destroyed and the small town declared a disaster area.

In the big story nobody bothered to mention Bosewell – for the killer tornado cut a path of death and destruction throughout the Midwest, making the small town of Bosewell only a minor victim.

By the time the story hit the major news services, Bosewell was hardly mentioned.

BOOK TWO

Chapter 33

Chicago, 1979

Nick lay back in bed his eyes following the naked redhead prowling around his tiny one-room apartment. Her name was DeVille and she was a natural redhead.

He liked watching her in his home, it sure beat observing her gyrate on stage while dozens of horny old men got off ogling her considerable charms. She was, at twenty-six, an older woman, but only by four years, which fazed neither of them.

DeVille had a sweep of long hair, pale aquamarine eyes, pouty lips, voluptuous breasts and a sunny disposition. She'd been living with him for almost six months.

"Can I fetch you anything, sweet thing?" she asked, prancing around his apartment, all curves.

"Yeah." He leaned back in bed putting one arm behind his head. "Get over here."

DeVille did not argue, she never argued. Sometimes he wished she would. He'd heard of easy, but she was ridiculous.

She approached the bed and stood beside him. He reached up and touched one perfect size thirty-six tit – no silicone – DeVille was all natural, the only phoney thing about her was her name.

Rolling her extended nipple between his fingers he made a suggestion she was not about to turn down.

DeVille was pleased. Her last lover had been twenty years older than her and a grouch. Nick was a real treat.

"My, oh my!" she exclaimed, pulling the sheet off him and widening her eyes. "What big . . . *thighs* you have."

"All the better to grab your ass!" He pulled her on top of him and they both laughed as she straddled him with her long white legs. DeVille liked being on top. He didn't mind, he knew it was her one power play.

They started to make frantic love – DeVille was a screamer – their neighbours did nothing but complain.

When they were finished he rolled out of bed and strolled into the cramped bathroom.

"How about I make pancakes?" DeVille called out.

"I ain't hungry," he said, quickly. The one thing she couldn't do was cook.

He noticed a spider crawling along the side of the tub. Picking it up by one of its legs he carefully placed it on the window-sill and watched it dart to safety across the fire-escape.

"I'll make coffee then," she sang out.

At least she could do that. He stepped into the rusty tub and turned the knob to activate the wall shower – as usual, getting nothing but a trickle of lukewarm water.

He had a hangover. The night before had been a long one, plenty of action and he hadn't gotten home until three in the morning.

Who'd have thought Q.J.'s would become *the* place? And who'd have thought he'd become the manager?

Yeah, some success story. From dishwasher to manager. And all it had taken was five years. Wow!

"What shall we do today?" DeVille asked, popping her head around the bathroom door.

"I'm easy."

"Maybe we could catch a movie – there's a new Paul Newman."

Yeah – Paul Newman. That meant he'd definitely get laid again. "Sure," he said, easily.

By the time he emerged from the bathroom, DeVille was dressed. On Sundays she liked to play at being ordinary. She'd put on jeans, a sweater, and braided her long red hair. Looking at her today nobody would guess she performed one of the horniest acts in town.

"Oh – I forgot to tell you. This letter came for you yesterday," she said, handing him an envelope.

He studied the writing on the front – it was from Cyndra. "How many times I gotta tell you? When I get mail I want it right away," he said, irritated.

"I told you – I forgot."

The envelope looked in bad shape. "What did you do, steam it open?"

"As if I would!"

"As if you wouldn't."

DeVille had a jealous streak he didn't appreciate.

"Is it from your sister?" she said, peering over his shoulder.

"You *did* open it," he accused.

"No, I did not. Her name's on the back, big deal."

It was a stupid thought, but one of these days he still hoped he might receive a letter from Lauren. Yeah – a real stupid thought. Lauren was his past, long gone. He'd written her many times and never gotten a reply. After a while he'd given up, it was obvious she didn't care about him.

But that didn't mean he couldn't think about her once in a while, did it? He imagined her still in Bosewell, married with kids, happy, never giving him a second thought – she probably didn't even remember his name.

He opened Cyndra's letter. She'd left Chicago with Joey over four years ago. The two of them had taken off when the winter got too cold and neither of them could keep a job. They'd tried to persuade him to go with them, but by that time he was settled at Q.J.'s doing everything from taking over the bar to running errands for Q.J.

Cyndra had stayed in New York with Joey for a couple of years, until eventually she'd met some sharp-shooter called Reece Webster, who'd lured her out to California with a few phoney promises. She was still with him. From what Nick could gather the guy was married, but on the brink of leaving his wife. He'd been on the brink for the last two years.

He scanned her letter.

Dear Nick:

Well, things are good in Los Angeles, you'd really love it here. It's hot all the time and there's these great palm trees everywhere – but I guess I've told you that enough times – right?

Why don't you come visit me? I've got plenty of room if you don't mind sleeping on a sofa-bed. Reece is never here at weekends so we could have fun and you know how much I miss you.

As far as my career . . . well, I'm taking singing lessons – ha ha! Aren't you glad? I'm also meeting lots of people Reece says can help me.

I haven't heard from Joey in a while. I think he's driving

*a cab. You know Joey, always waiting for the big break.
Aren't we all – ha ha!*

*I'm serious, Nick – please think about coming out here
even if it's only for a long weekend.*

I love you and I miss you lots.

As always,
Your sister,
Cyndra

She wasn't the world's greatest letter writer, but at least
she bothered to write.

"You ever been to California?" he asked DeVille, folding the
letter and putting it in his pocket.

"Once," she replied. "When I was eighteen. There was this
rich guy with his own private plane. He flew me and three other
girls to a party in Vegas. We put on a show *they* didn't forget in
a hurry!"

"What kind of show?"

"Stripping, parading the goods, what else?"

"Did you ever do any hooking?"

Her mouth tightened. "Why are you asking me that?"

"I'm throwing it into the conversation."

"Throw it out again, Nick," she said, glaring at him. "I take
my clothes off, and that's *all* I do."

"Yeah, yeah, I'm sorry. I don't know why I said that."

"Nor do I." She marched into the bathroom slamming the
door behind her.

She'd sulk for five minutes and then come out. DeVille never
stayed angry for long.

Q.J. had this theory about women. He considered them all
hookers under the skin. Sometimes he'd give Nick the benefit of
his wisdom. "You gotta look at it like this – when they marry a
guy, what the hell ya think they're doin'? They're havin' sex for
money, right? So the husband screws her one night, an' buys her
a dress the next day. The poor schmuck pays for everything. Why
don't he leave a hundred buckerooneys on the bedside table an'
call it quits?"

Q.J. was a true cynic. Maybe that was the way to be. Nick
had no intention of ever getting married. Every time DeVille so
much as hinted he'd laughed, not taking her seriously.

Once again his thoughts drifted back to Lauren. He couldn't
help thinking about her – she hovered at the back of his mind –
a distant memory he couldn't forget. He'd hoped that over the

years Joey or Cyndra would go back to Bosewell for a visit – but neither of them seemed inclined. As far as he knew Joey had never contacted his mother, and Cyndra had no urge to get in touch with Aretha Mae, although she occasionally mentioned Harlan. They both felt guilty about leaving the kid. "When I make it I'll go get him," Cyndra said.

Yeah. Sure.

Once in a while he thought of calling Louise at the drugstore – just to find out what was going on in town. But something always stopped him. The truth was he really didn't want to know.

Over the years he'd worked hard, helping to make Q.J.'s the successful place it was today. Five years ago it was a hang-out for petty con artists and their one-night stands, offering nothing but bad food and a couple of tired strippers. When disco got really big he'd started badgering Q.J. about dumping the strippers and bringing in a disc jockey.

"Are you outta your fuckin' skull?" Q.J. had said. "My customers get off on the girls – anyhow, we ain't got no space for dancin'."

"Make it," he'd urged. "You gotta get into this disco thing before it's over."

"I hire a fuckin' dishwasher an' all of a sudden he's tellin' me what to do."

"I ain't a dishwasher no more."

"What are you then?"

"Your assistant."

"If you say so."

Q.J. was too cheap to hire a disc jockey, and too nervous to risk losing customers by firing the strippers, so he'd compromised by making Nick the disc jockey, and persuading Erna to stop stripping – putting her in charge of two new girls he hired. Business had picked up immediately.

Nick was triumphant. "I told ya," he'd said.

"Yeah, yeah, you told me," Q.J. had replied. "Like I didn't already know."

Nick really got into the music. It was a kick hanging out at the record stores listening to all the new sounds and picking out the latest hits.

The sound system Q.J. elected to put in was shit, but he quickly learned how to work the room – mixing the old with the new – a little bit of Elvis, followed by Al Green, throw in some

Bobby Womack, then calm them down with Dionne Warwick and Smokey Robinson.

When he wasn't working the turntables he was behind the bar.

The resident bartender didn't like it. "Get that ratty kid away from me," he'd complained, "or I'm outta here."

There was nothing Q.J. liked better than a threat. Plus he could get away with paying Nick half the money he was paying the old man. "So quit," he'd said.

The bartender did, and Nick had found himself in charge of the bar, too.

"We gotta hire somebody else," he'd complained. "I can't play records *and* run the bar."

"Jesus Christ, you're gonna break me," Q.J. complained.

"No," he'd corrected. "I'm gonna make you."

Erna was his biggest supporter. Even Len got into the spirit of things by hiring an assistant chef who could actually cook. Q.J.'s really took off.

Not that anybody had ever thanked him. He didn't need thanks – a steady job was enough.

He considered the situation. He'd walked in off the street five years ago with exactly nothing, and now he was the son Q.J. never had. Not bad. Not good. He'd come to Chicago hoping to be an actor and done nothing about it. He was twenty-two years old – if he didn't start soon he never would. While he stayed at Q.J.'s there was no time for anything else – not even acting class. He'd managed to save a couple of thousand dollars over the years, and now California beckoned. The letter from Cyndra was a sign. If he didn't make a move he'd be stuck at Q.J.'s forever, wearing cerise shirts and shooting his cufflinks just like Q.J. himself. A frightening thought!

DeVille bounced out of the bathroom. She was pretty, sexy and amiable.

It was over. Six months was his limit. Besides, he couldn't take her with him; excess baggage was never a good idea.

"Are we going to the movie?" she asked.

"Sure."

God, she had a great mouth.

It would be tough kissing it goodbye.

Chapter 34

Philadelphia, 1979

"Excuse me, Miss Roberts."

"Yes, Mr Larden?"

"I notice that it's raining outside, and I wondered if I might offer you a lift home."

"That's very nice of you, Mr Larden, but my cousin is meeting me."

"Oh." Mr Larden stared at her. He was a man of medium height in his thirties with thinning hair and a drooping mouth. He was also a married man with two children, one dog and several hamsters. He was her boss.

"Are you sure, Miss Roberts?" he asked, hopefully.

"Yes, I'm sure, Mr Larden."

They played this game all the time. He pretended to be the concerned boss always looking out for his secretary's welfare. She pretended that he really did want to give her a lift out of the kindness of his heart because it was raining outside. They both knew this was a lie. He wanted to get her into bed any way he could.

Lauren had worked for him as his personal secretary for two years now, and she knew she had to leave or go completely crazy.

"Well," he said, collecting his briefcase. "I'll see you tomorrow, then."

"Yes, Mr Larden."

She waited until he'd left before picking up the phone. "Brad," she said, in a low voice. "I can't see you tonight."

"What do you mean you can't see me?" he spluttered.

217

"It's difficult to explain now. Let's talk tomorrow." She put the phone down quickly before he could argue.

Bradford Deene, her cousin. Good old Brad. Without him she probably couldn't have gotten through the last five years. But their relationship was sick, it had to stop, and she was the one who was going to end it.

Five years ago she'd arrived in Philadelphia a shivering wreck. Her mother's brother, Will, along with his wife, Margo, had met her at the airport.

"We're so sorry, dear, so very, very sorry," Margo had said, but she hadn't shed a tear.

Will seemed more sincere. "Your mother was a wonderful woman – always a good sister to me. We shall miss her."

The Deenes had taken her to their house on Roosevelt Boulevard. It was a nice house, but it certainly wasn't home. Brad, her nineteen-year-old cousin, was away at college and they allowed her to stay in his room. At night she overheard them whispering. Margo first – "What are we going to do with her? We can't keep her here."

Then Will. "Lauren is my sister's daughter, Margo. She has no other relatives. We *have* to take her in, after all, she's only sixteen."

"I know, I know. But for how long?"

Jane and Phil Roberts had both perished in the deadly tornado that had practically totalled Bosewell. Lauren remembered very little of the nightmare. She'd arrived in Philadelphia still numb with shock. And shortly after arriving she'd had to tell Margo she was pregnant.

Her aunt had gone completely crazy. "How did this happen? Were you raped?" she'd demanded.

"It just . . . happened . . ."

"Was it that boy you were engaged to? Stock? Because if it was we can force him to marry you."

"No, it wasn't Stock."

"Who was it then?"

"It doesn't matter."

"Your poor parents . . . they'd be so . . . so . . . disappointed in you."

"I want to have the baby," Lauren had said, quietly.

Margo had shaken her head. "Absolutely out of the question. It's enough that *you're* here – we cannot look after a baby, too."

"There *is* no choice in this matter," her uncle had said. "You'll have to have an abortion."

She remembered the termination as if it were yesterday. Margo had taken her to a male gynaecologist – a bald man with sleepy eyes and rubber-gloved hands.

"What have you been up to, young lady?" he'd said with a jovial wink as she lay on the cold hard examining table, feeling naked and vulnerable beneath the paper garment the nurse instructed her to wear.

"Come along, put your legs in the stirrups, dear."

He'd probed and poked until she could stand it no more.

"I don't want to lose my baby," she'd whispered.

"It's nothing," he'd said. "Don't worry about it. Next time you open your legs be a little more careful, that's all."

Then they'd given her an injection, and she remembered nothing much at all except the harsh feel of cold steel between her legs.

After that there was no more baby, no more Nick.

At the time she'd thought about him every second of the day, but now she'd forced herself to stop. Nick Angelo had left her, run out of town without so much as a goodbye, and she'd never heard from him again – not even after the tragedy.

In a way she hated him. He'd used her for his own selfish reasons and then dumped her – leaving her pregnant and alone. She was shocked that he'd left. No note, no word, no nothing. She hardened her heart towards him, but for some inexplicable reason she still didn't want to lose his baby.

Margo and Will insisted she go back to school. She did so reluctantly because she'd had no choice.

One night Margo and Will had called her into their living room and given her the bad news. "Your father's estate left nothing. Death taxes took what little there was. He was heavily in debt."

"I'm sorry, Lauren," Margo added. "There's no money to send you to college. You must understand that we can't afford it. We've worked hard all our lives to allow Bradford all the advantages he's had, and now we're entitled to enjoy what's left."

"I don't want to go to college," she'd said. "As soon as I graduate High school I'll find a job."

"You could always try for a scholarship," Will ventured, feeling guilty. "After all, you're a smart girl."

They didn't understand that she meant it when she said she had no wish to attend college.

For several years she'd had nightmares about the tornado. In her mind she could see it sweeping down on the trailer – and sometimes in her dreams the tornado would turn into Primo. He would be part of it – leering at her . . . touching her . . . saying lewd things – until he forced her to raise the knife and strike out.

She'd killed Primo.

Or had she?

The uncertainty drove her crazy.

As soon as she graduated High school she'd taken a job at the local bank and started saving money. The moment she had enough she planned to move out of the Deene household.

Since coming home from college Brad was always around. He was good-looking with curly brown hair and a ready smile. He was taller than Nick, more muscular. She still compared every man she met to Nick, it was a habit she couldn't break.

By the time she was nineteen she'd saved enough money to move out. She had good secretarial skills and immediately got a job at Larden and Scopers, Attorneys at Law. Mr Larden himself had interviewed her and informed her she was perfect – exactly what he was looking for.

Her life was simple until Brad complicated it. He'd dropped by her small apartment one night, stayed too long and drunk too much. Then he'd confessed he thought he loved her, and somehow or other they'd ended up in bed even though they'd both known it was wrong. She'd tried to make it one time only but he wouldn't let her. He'd talked her into it, and once in she couldn't get out. Besides, it felt good to be with someone who cared.

Their affair had been going on for several months and she was suffocated with guilt. She wanted out. All she had to do was tell him.

She left the office and took the bus to her small apartment, running the last few hundred yards to her building, getting soaked.

Brad was inside, sitting on *her* couch, his feet up on *her* table watching *her* television.

"I told you I couldn't see you," she said, removing her raincoat.

"You didn't mean it," he replied.

"I want my key back," she said, clicking off the TV.

He frowned. "What's with you lately?"

"Brad, you know this isn't right. It has to end."

"No way, baby," he settled back, totally at ease.

The way he said "baby" made her stomach turn. She knew for sure she wasn't the only girl he was sleeping with.

"Please," she said. "I want it to be over."

He held out his arms. "Come over here."

"No, Brad."

"Are we playing hard to get?"

He wouldn't leave and she couldn't make him.

"What if I told your parents," she threatened.

"You wouldn't do that."

"I might."

"They'd blame you."

"Do you think I care? They never wanted me to come and live with them anyway."

He considered her threat. He wouldn't put it past her. "What is it, the wrong time of the month?" he asked, clicking the television back on.

She had a plan. If he wouldn't go, she would.

A week later at the office Christmas party, a drunken Mr Larden grabbed her in his office, trapping her up against his desk.

She knew exactly how to deal with men who tried to force her to do something she didn't want to do. She grabbed a letter opener and stabbed him in the arm.

Mr Larden yelled out his surprise and pain. "Are you *insane*?" he shouted.

"Try taking no for an answer," she said, making it to the door.

"You're fired," he said.

"Good."

By the time Christmas arrived she had every detail of her departure planned. On Christmas Day she went to Margo and Will's for lunch – they'd been a lot nicer to her since she'd moved out and they weren't obliged to support her. Brad was there with a girl called Jennie. The two of them spent the entire day giggling and necking.

"I think they might get engaged," Margo confided in the kitchen.

"That's nice," Lauren said. If he'd brought his girlfriend to make her jealous it wasn't working.

Sitting at the dining table she noticed Brad's hand creep under the table and up Jennie's thigh.

"You know," Margo said, turning to Lauren, obviously unaware of her son's furtive adventure, "you're perfectly welcome to bring a date here. Are you seeing anyone?"

Lauren shook her head. "No."

"A pretty girl like you," Will said, cheerfully. "You should have dozens of boyfriends."

"She's probably hiding them from us," Brad said, laughing confidently as his fingers played with the elastic on the brief panties guarding his girlfriend's moist crotch.

Lauren sighed. He was good in bed and he knew it. He played her like an expert, touching everything in just the right way.

Later that night when he'd gotten rid of Jennie, he arrived unannounced at her apartment. She allowed him to make love to her for the last time, only he didn't know it was the last time – he was under the misguided impression she was going to be available for him whenever he felt like it.

As soon as he left she hurried to the shower, washing him away forever. Then she packed, and early the next morning she took a cab to the bus station and boarded a Greyhound bus bound for New York.

She left no forwarding address. As far as she was concerned she'd been in mourning long enough.

Lauren Roberts was about to start a new life.

Chapter 35

Several things convinced Nick it was time to move on, not the least being the Carmello Rose incident. Carmello was a short grizzly man in his fifties with a beak nose, dark skin and a raspy, menacing voice. He was a rumoured Chicago hit man who visited Q.J.'s from time to time, always with several nubile young girls in tow, always with an eye to pick up more.

This particular night he arrived with only one woman – a tall redhead in her late thirties with large breasts and a sour expression.

"Fuck!" Q.J. said, agitatedly. "That broad's his wife."

"So," Nick asked "what's the big deal?"

"You'd better make sure nobody says nothin' 'bout none of the other skirts he's bin hangin' out with – 'cause if his wife finds out she'll blow his shrivelled ass to Cuba an' back. She's a wild woman."

"You worry too much," Nick said, calmly. "I'll take care of Mr Rose myself."

And why not? Carmello Rose was known for leaving hundred-dollar tips.

When he got near the table and took a closer look he had a feeling he'd seen this woman somewhere before. She was wearing a dangerously low-cut black cocktail dress, and he couldn't help his eyes from straying down her generous cleavage.

Carmello caught him catching a peek and fixed him with a frog-eyed stare that said all right to look, but no touching.

"What can I get you, Mr Rose?" Nick asked.

Carmello ordered a bottle of champagne.

"I just found out it's his wife's birthday," Q.J. said, agitatedly, stalking Nick behind the bar. "Get Len to arrange a cake."

"What does his wife do?" Nick asked.

"What does she *do*? What the fuck you *think* she does – looks after him."

"Then how come he's always hangin' out with other women?"

Q.J. looked testy. "We don't know nothin' 'bout that, do we? Take him a bottle of the best – my compliments."

"How come *you're* not going over?"

"'Cause Carmello frightens the crap outta me. Is that a good enough reason? Ya just gotta look sideways at his old lady an' he has a freakin' fit."

"Y'know, I got a feeling I've seen her somewhere before."

"Jesus, Nick, ain'tcha got enough broads of your own? This one's too old for you, anyway."

"Who's interested? I just wanna recall where I seen her."

Q.J. shook his head. "Forget it."

He took the champagne to the table informing them it was from Q.J. "On account of it bein' Mrs Rose's birthday an' all," he said, with a smile.

Carmello grunted.

"Thanks, sweetie," Mrs Rose said.

Was it his imagination or did she throw him a wink? He took another peek at her impressive breasts and it suddenly came to him. She was the woman whose car he'd gassed up in Bosewell a few years ago. The one in the sweater with the attitude. Who could ever forget those tits!

"How's your sister?" he asked, pouring her a glass of champagne.

She ran her tongue across her front teeth and darted a nervous glance at Carmello. "Huh?" she said, blankly.

Carmello snapped to attention. "Whadda *you* know about her sister?"

"She lives in Bosewell, right? I used to live there too."

Obviously he'd made no impression on her. She had no idea what he was talking about.

"Hey – I gassed your car a coupla times. You were visiting your sister, remember?"

Carmello threw her a filthy look. "You know this guy?"

"No, I certainly don't," she snapped, three large, diamond rings flashing on her fingers.

"He sure seems to remember you."

"Everyone remembers me," she said, defiantly.

"Hey, listen, no big deal," Nick said quickly, sensing trouble. "I musta made a mistake," he added, pouring more champagne into Carmello's glass before walking away.

Five minutes later he was in the stockroom when Carmello entered, kicking the door shut behind him. Before he could say a word Carmello took out a gun and shoved it in his stomach.

He lost his legs, it was like they weren't even there. "*Jesus!* What the hell you *doin'?*" he mumbled, panic-stricken as his life flashed before his eyes.

"Ya wanna know what *I'm* doin'," Carmello snarled gruffly, jabbing him with the gun. "What the fuck was *you* doin' with my wife?"

His throat was so dry he could barely speak. "I gassed her car, nothin' else."

"You gassed her car, huh? That it?"

He was breaking out in a cold sweat. "I swear. I was a kid – I promise you." Jesus! He needed to pee in the worst way.

Carmello shoved the gun into his stomach even harder. "Swear a little louder, ya dumb punk. Get down on your knees and fuckin' swear."

"It's the truth – God help me it's the truth."

"Turn around an' get down on your knees, fuckhead."

Maybe Carmello was going to shoot him, maybe he wasn't. He'd never know, because at that moment Q.J. opened the door and walked in on them. "Everything all right?" he asked calmly, like he didn't know anything was going on, although of course he did.

Reluctantly Carmello put his gun away. "Sure, sure. The kid an' me – we was talkin'."

And that was that. Crisis over. But Nick knew the time had come to get out.

Two days later he visited Q.J. in his office.

"I quit," he said.

"You *what?*"

"You heard me."

"Sure I heard you, but I don't believe what I'm hearin'."

"I've been in Chicago long enough."

Q.J. glared at him. "Yeah. Long enough to learn everythin' I know, is that the deal? You're gonna open your own place. I shoulda known it." He got up, marching angrily around the room. "I took you in, treated you good, now you're gonna stab me in the heart."

"That's not it," Nick said. "I'm plannin' on takin' a trip to California."

Q.J. rubbed together nicotine stained fingers. "What for?"

"For a chance."

"*I* gave you a chance. Ain't that enough?"

"I always had this thing 'bout gettin' into acting. If I don't try it now I never will."

Q.J. snorted his disgust. "Act. Schmact. You're in the bar business, that's where you belong."

"When I get settled I'll call, let you know how I'm doing."

"Who gives a shit? All I care about is you stayin' here. You're my manager, you take care of things. How about showin' some appreciation?"

"When I came to work here I never said it was a lifetime thing," he explained, hoping Q.J. would understand.

"Jesus!" Q.J. rolled his eyes. "You can't trust nobody no more."

"I'll stay 'til you find a replacement."

Q.J. was steaming. "I don't need nobody else. Don't worry 'bout a thing – you ungrateful little prick. Shift your ass outta here, see if I give a shit."

He knew Q.J. didn't mean it. "How about I stay around for two weeks?" he suggested.

"Do what you want," snapped Q.J.

Later Erna grabbed hold of him. "There's a rumour you're going to Hollywood," she said, thrilled at the thought.

"Yeah, I'm gonna give it a shot."

She nudged him slyly. "Like me to come with you?"

"Uh – I don't think Len would appreciate it."

She giggled. "Perhaps you're right," she said, tugging at an escaping bra strap. "I had a chance to go there once. I coulda been a famous starlet." She winked, knowingly. "Course, it meant sleeping with a fat old producer, so I stayed here, married Len, and now look at me."

"You're happy, aren't you?"

"I'm married to Len, that doesn't make me ecstatic."

"He seems like a nice guy."

"He's no Q.J."

Erna had confirmed his suspicions – she definitely had a crush on her brother.

When DeVille heard the news of his imminent departure she flew into a fury because he hadn't told her himself. Usually she left the club before him, but this particular night she stayed, joining the table of a customer – something she never did.

Nick realized this meant trouble. If he was smart he'd have taken off without telling anybody.

At closing time, DeVille dumped the customer and left with him, hanging on to his arm. She was drunk and angry – not a happy combination.

"Y'know something, Nicky," she slurred in his ear, well aware that he hated being called Nicky.

"What?" he said, steering her unsteady body into a cab.

"You're a son-of-a-bitch, that's what you are." She nodded, reassuring herself. "Yeah, a son-of-a-bitch."

"Hey, listen, I *was* gonna tell you," he said, defending himself. "But I had to tell Q.J. first. I owed him that."

"You owed him that," she mimicked. "And what do you owe me?"

He raised an eyebrow. "Y' think I owe you somethin'?"

"Bastard," she spat.

The cab driver – a weary veteran – glanced warily in his rear-view mirror.

"Goddamn bastard," DeVille said, hauling back in an attempt to slap him. "We live together – doesn't that mean *anything* to you?"

The cab swerved over to the side of the street and the driver turned around. "I don't want no trouble," he said. "Out. Both of you."

"It's all right, man," Nick said, gripping DeVille firmly by the wrist. "There ain't gonna be no trouble. Keep driving."

"The last couple hadda fight in my cab wrecked it," the driver muttered, sourly.

"I said keep driving," Nick repeated. "I'll take care of you good."

Still muttering under his breath the driver set off.

DeVille began to cry. Her anger he could take, but crying always got to him.

"Hey," he said, trying to comfort her. "I'm only going for a month or two."

"You're lying," she cried, leaning all over him, getting mascara on his one and only jacket.

"Maybe I'll send for you."

"Now you're *really* lying," she sobbed.

DeVille was no fool; they both knew it was over.

As soon as they reached his apartment she began to pack, hurling her things into a suitcase, well recovered from her crying jag. "I thought you were different," she yelled. "But no way – you're just like every other guy – selfish, self-centred, all you care about is your precious dick."

She looked good when she was angry and somehow or other they ended up in bed. DeVille thought if she was the best she'd ever been he might take her with him. It was quite an experience. At four o'clock in the morning their neighbours couldn't take the moaning and groaning any longer and called the police. They ended up hysterical with laughter.

In the morning they parted company. DeVille was sober and tense and, in a funny sort of way, dignified.

When she left he almost missed her – only almost.

"You're a scumbag, you know that? No loyalty." Q.J. was on a kick and he didn't intend to stop.

"Leave the kid alone," Erna said, coming to Nick's defence.

Q.J. glared angrily at his sister. "Did I ask for your input?"

"No, but –"

"I treat him like a son," Q.J. interrupted. "Grooming him, y'know what I mean?"

"Grooming him for what?" Erna asked, sharply. "To be in the bar business all his life like us? Who wants that?"

They were at it again, talking about him as if he didn't exist.

Len entered into the conversation. "He'll be back," he said, nodding wisely. "It's too hot in California."

Q.J. didn't seem so sure. "Ya think?" he said.

"No," said Erna, spitefully. "He won't be back. Why would he?"

On his last night Q.J. relented and threw him a big farewell party after the bar closed. For the first time he wondered if he was making the right move. Everybody was so warm and friendly. The waitresses, strippers, Erna, Len – even Q.J. In a way, this was his family now – the family he'd never had.

DeVille put on a show – and what a show it was! Enough bumping and grinding to turn on a priest! Maybe she wanted him to know exactly what he was leaving behind. He knew all right, but he still couldn't help himself.

Q.J. clapped him around the shoulders. "Ya know somethin', Nick, if y'ever wanna come back, y'got your job waitin'. I ain't never said that to nobody who worked for me before. Consider yourself honoured."

"I consider myself honoured," he said, grinning.

"In the meantime," Q.J. continued, "when ya get to LA I want ya t'look up my ex-partner."

"Who's your ex-partner?"

"Some guy used to be known as Manny the Menace, now he's strictly legit. Call him Mr Manfred and don't go mentioning his nickname – it drives him beserko."

"What does he do?"

"Runs a car service. Respectable. Just like me."

Nick burst out laughing. "Whoever said *you* were respectable?"

"Very funny." Q.J. smoothed an imaginary crease in his pin-stripe pants which did not go with his bright red jacket and green polka-dot tie.

"You're sure this guy is straight?" Nick asked, thinking that tonight Q.J. looked like a waiter in a whorehouse.

"Would I lie to you?"

"Yes."

"Go see him, Nick. He'll give you a job. All ya gotta say is I'm callin' in the favour he owes me. Q.J.'s collectin' – that's what ya tell him. He'll know what you mean."

"Shouldn't you contact him first?"

"We don't speak."

"So why would he want to –"

"Trust me." Q.J. scribbled on a piece of paper and handed it over. "Here's his number. Do like I say and phone him soon as y'get there."

"Thanks," he said, shoving the paper in his pocket. It was certainly better than arriving in LA cold.

Erna hugged him, covering him in her cloying scent. "Don't forget about us now, you hear me?"

"How –" he grinned, "could I ever forget *you*?"

'Not much chance of that," she giggled, coyly.

Len was his usual stoic self. They shook hands. "You'll be back," Len said, knowingly.

"Maybe – one of these days."

Now he was really beginning to regret his decision to leave. He had no idea what Los Angeles was like. He had no friends there, no job, just Cyndra, and he hadn't even warned her he was coming, figuring a surprise would be good.

In the morning Q.J. was on the missing list. "He don't like goodbyes," Erna explained, as she and Len drove him to the airport. "Gotta see you off in style," she added, with a saucy wink.

They couldn't park so they dropped him off kerbside. He grabbed his carry-on bag from the trunk and stood on the sidewalk waving to them as they drove away in Len's two-toned gold Chevrolet with the dented front fender.

As soon as they were gone he felt alone, but only for a moment. Then he picked up his bag, turned and strode purposefully towards the airline desk.

Chapter 36

The Greyhound bus delivered Lauren into New York at noon. She waved goodbye to the driver, collected her suitcase and stood alone in the middle of the busy bus station.

Before she could take two steps a scruffy looking man stinking of cheap aftershave approached her. His long greasy hair hung in strands around his face, and a cigarette dangled from the corner of his chapped lips.

"Hi'ya, lovely. Lookin' for a place t' stay?"

She was no naïve little country bumpkin getting off the bus in New York ready to be picked off by some lurking pimp.

"I have somewhere, thank you," she said, giving him a withering look.

"Just askin'. Can't do more than that, pretty chick like you."

She hurried away, only to be accosted a few yards later by a dark-skinned man in a filthy white suit who sidled up behind her.

"Wanna be a model?" he offered, speaking out of the corner of his mouth.

She kept walking.

"Wanna be a model an' make a lotta bucks?" he said, keeping pace with her.

She ignored him.

"Wanna fuck me?"

She stopped, turned to look at him, and said in a very loud voice, "Leave me alone or I'll call a cop. Got it, pervert?"

He slunk off.

Outside the bus station she found a cab, got in and gave the driver the address of the Barbizon Hotel for Girls.

"How many times you get hit on in there?" the driver asked, shoving his foot on the gas and zooming away from the kerb – missing another cab by mere inches.

"Enough," she replied, gazing out of the window at the dirty sidewalks, scurrying crowds and snarled traffic.

It was like a dream. Here she was, finally in New York, and she was free, she had nobody to answer to except herself.

She'd booked a room at the Barbizon before leaving Philadelphia. She'd also been buying the New York papers and circling job opportunities, setting up several appointments by phone.

After she'd unpacked and settled in, she took a walk over to Fifth Avenue. Oh yes, it was just like *Breakfast at Tiffany's*. The same wide street, the same expensive stores. She found herself outside Tiffany's staring into the windows like a tourist. She stifled a giggle – all she needed now was a cat and she was all set!

The next day she awoke early. It was autumn and the weather was brisk. She dressed carefully in a simple dark blue dress, adding low-heeled shoes and her mother's pearls. Over the top she belted a navy trench coat. She pulled her thick chestnut hair back securing it with a barrette, and wore very little make-up. The plainer the better, she thought. But there was no disguising the fact that at twenty-one Lauren was a natural beauty with her perfect oval face, unusual tortoiseshell colour eyes and dazzling smile.

Before doing anything else she opened a bank account and deposited her four-thousand-dollar savings. Then she set off on the first of three interviews.

The first one was with a law firm housed in a tall chrome and glass building on Park Avenue. There she was interrogated by an attractive black woman, who asked her a series of probing questions, and made her fill out a personality analysis form. After that she had to sit in a room and produce a sample of her typing.

The woman timed her. "Excellent!" she exclaimed. "Where can we reach you?"

Her next interview was with a firm of accountants on Lexington Avenue. The building was not so nice, although it was near Bloomingdale's and she'd certainly heard plenty about Bloomingdale's. The man who interviewed her was a junior partner. He was friendly and didn't seem on the make. He read through her references twice and asked if she could start the following week. She told him she'd have to let him know.

Her third interview was with a modelling agency on Madison Avenue called Samm's. They'd advertised for a booker. Lauren had no idea what a booker did – but working at a modelling agency might be fun, and she could certainly do with a little fun in her life.

A harassed girl in a purple jumpsuit told her that she'd made a mistake and better come back the next day because there was nobody to see her.

"I can't come back tomorrow," she said. "My appointment was for today. I have two other jobs under consideration and I have to make a decision."

The girl looked at her like she was nuts. "So don't come back," she said. "Take one of the other jobs, I should care."

"I'd like to make a choice," Lauren said, reasonably. "Why can't somebody see me today?"

"They're all over at the big photo shoot for Flash Cosmetics. Is that a good enough reason for you?"

She nodded, went downstairs, found a phone booth, and looked up Flash Cosmetics. Then she called their main office. "Can you tell me where the ad. photo session is taking place?" she asked. "This is Lauren from Samm's."

"Sure, just a moment," said a voice on the other end of the phone. Two minutes later she had the information – and the address of a photographer's studio on Sixty-fourth Street.

She walked to the studio. It only took her fifteen minutes and when she arrived she informed the girl at reception that she had something to deliver from Samm's. The girl told her to go to the studio in back.

She made her way down a narrow corridor which led into a large, brightly-lit studio jammed with people.

The first person she noticed was a short, flamboyant man hovering behind a camera set-up, while several other people stood around watching. In front of the camera languished the most startling looking girl Lauren had ever seen. She was an exceptionally tall blonde with masses of curly hair, huge blue eyes, pouty lips and a low-cut, slinky, silver sequin gown. Lauren recognized her as Nature, the current darling of the fashion magazines.

"Get yer finger out, Antonio," Nature screamed. She had a voice like a fishwife and a cockney accent that could sharpen knives. "I'm freezing me balls off."

"Close your legs, darling, maybe that will help," murmured a thin, fortyish, redhead standing to one side.

Lauren hovered on the periphery.

Nature struck a pose.

Antonio started shooting. "*Bellissima*, darling, *bellissima!* You are the most fantastic woman in the world!"

The more he flattered her the more Nature loved it. She postured and preened, making intimate contact with the camera, her glossy lips quivering with emotion. Her big blue eyes mesmerizing.

Antonio shot several rolls of film before calling for a break. Everybody clapped. Nature threw her head back and laughed, sounding like a demented parrot. "Me bleedin' feet are killin' me," she roared, collapsing into a chair while make-up and hair rushed forward to attend to her every need.

"Excuse me," Lauren tapped one of the camera assistants on the arm. "Can you tell me who the executives from Samm's are?"

"Over there." He jerked his thumb in the direction of the redheaded woman.

Tentatively Lauren approached her. The woman was in the process of lighting up a long, thin cigarillo.

"Uh . . . excuse me," she said. "My name's Lauren Roberts. I had an appointment today with someone at Samm's, but the girl told me everyone was here."

The woman dragged on her cigarette and stared at her. "Too short, too heavy, too eager."

Lauren frowned — at five feet seven she'd never been called short — and as for heavy . . . no way. This woman was definitely peculiar. "I beg your pardon?" she said, hotly.

"You'll never make it, darling. You don't have the attitude."

"I'll never make what?"

"A model. Isn't that what you want to be? Isn't that what they all want to be? Although, I must say, it's *très* original, following me to the studio."

She stood her ground. "I didn't follow you anywhere. And nobody's ever called me heavy before."

"For a real person you're not the least bit heavy. For a would-be model you're grossly overweight."

"We had an appointment," Lauren said. "Someone was supposed to interview me about the booker's job. I went to your office and the girl said there was nobody to see me."

"So you decided to come here?"

She couldn't stop herself from staring at the woman's blood-red, inch-long nails — talons her mother would've called them. "Yes."

"In that case you get full marks for using your head. Can you type?"

"I sent in my résumé."

"Can you type?" the woman repeated, impatiently.

Don't get aggravated, Roberts, stay cool. "Yes, I can type."

"Can you answer phones?"

She couldn't keep the sarcasm out of her voice. "It sounds like a really challenging job."

The woman was unfazed. "Oh, don't worry, dear, it's challenging all right. I'll try you out. Be at the office at nine o'clock tomorrow."

"*If* I decide to take the job, I can start Monday."

The woman looked at her like she wasn't quite sure she'd heard correctly. "If you *decide* to take the job? My God, little Miss Independent, aren't we?"

"I have two other job offers I'm looking into."

"And what would you do if I said this offer was only open now, this very moment, and if you turn it down, don't bother coming back."

There was a brief silence, broken by Nature screaming, "Get yer bleedin' arses in gear – I'm ready ter shoot."

Lauren took a moment to consider the possibilities. She could accept the job with the law firm, but she already knew what that would be like – boring, boring, boring. Or she could say yes to the position with the accountancy firm – another laugh a minute. Her third alternative was to take the job with this bossy, redheaded woman. It could prove to be interesting.

"Well?" the woman said, abruptly. "Are you joining us or not?"

"What's the salary?"

"Not enough," the woman replied, brusquely.

"I need to make a decent salary. I have to get an apartment and afford to eat."

"You can share an apartment and starve. Builds character. Let me know when you make up your mind. You have exactly five minutes to think about it. After that, my dear girl, this job opportunity is over."

Chapter 37

Reece Webster had her exactly where he wanted her – pinned beneath him – waiting for the big moment – almost begging. He knew he gave her good loving, the best she'd ever had, so he could afford to keep her hanging.

He paused mid-thrust. "What's your name, little lady?" he demanded.

"Cyndra," she gasped.

He prolonged the moment. "Cyndra what?"

"Don't torture me, Reece."

"Cyndra *what*?"

"Cyndra Webster."

He laughed, and let her feel him move inside her. "Who owns you now?"

She moaned, almost there. "You do."

"An' who's gonna love you 'til you drop?"

"You are."

Now he heated up the action, giving her his best shot. "And who am I?"

"You're . . . my . . . husband."

"Damn right, baby. Damn right!" He let rip and she came on cue. What a stud! Nobody did it like he did.

Cyndra shuddered and rolled away from him, curling her beautiful body into a tight little ball. Some guys might be offended by her immediate withdrawal, but not Reece Webster – he was a man – a real man – and he could take it. In fact, it was a relief – women who wanted to cuddle and talk after sex gave him that *let's get outta here* feeling.

The good news was he'd finally had the smarts to shed his first wife, a going nowhere blonde, and two days later he'd turned around and married his little darkie songbird –

Cyndra. Now *this* was a girl destined to go places, and *he*, Reece Webster, was going right along with her. Cyndra Angelo was an investment – his. He'd married her to protect himself.

Reece Webster was five feet ten inches tall, with sandy hair, a thin blond moustache, slit eyes and a penchant for wearing flashy cowboy clothes, even though he'd been born in Brooklyn thirty-eight years ago. He was sixteen years older than Cyndra, but as far as he was concerned this was a good thing. It meant she didn't know as much as he did. He could mould her any way he wanted, and that's exactly what he was doing.

They'd met in New York at a club where her boyfriend was working as a temporary bouncer. Joey hadn't stood a chance once Reece Webster moved in.

After introducing himself as a personal manager he'd asked her what she did.

"I'm plannin' to be a professional singer," she'd said, very full of herself.

"Then you just met the man who's gonna make you a star," he'd replied, equally confident.

Corniest line in the world, but it worked every time.

At first his interest had been purely sexual. A quick lay and on to the next. But she wasn't interested in accompanying him to his apartment. She had no desire for a quickie – not even when he'd told her he produced records and had something to do with the rise of John Travolta's career. Both lies of course – but who was listening?

Usually he didn't like them so young – but there was something special about Cyndra, so he'd continued the pursuit, reeling her in carefully. The key word was career. He'd hired a studio for a couple of hours and paid for her to cut a demo. She'd had no idea what she was doing – but there was a voice there somewhere – and he'd decided that if he could bring it out they'd be rolling in dollar bills.

"I'm goin' back to Hollywood," he'd told her casually one day. "Yeah . . . Hollywood's the place a girl like you could really score."

"Well –" she'd hesitated. "One of these days Joey and I –"

"Forget about Joey. He's a loser. Hang out with him an' you'll end up like him. On the other hand – come with me an' I'll do somethin' 'bout that singin' career of yours."

And so it came to pass that she finally dumped Joey, and drove with Reece across country in his shocking pink 1969 Cadillac, consummating their relationship in a Holiday Inn somewhere near Galveston.

Once they'd settled in LA Reece had arranged singing lessons for her. He wasn't disappointed, she was a natural.

Now, two years later, all his hard work and well invested money was hopefully beginning to pay dividends. He'd managed to interest a couple of record companies in her – and they were both considering meeting with her and maybe cutting a demo.

In the meantime he'd married her. Reece knew a lifetime meal ticket when it stared him in the face.

Curled up in a ball, knees hugging her chest – Cyndra couldn't figure out why she didn't feel any different. She was married for God's sake. Married! And yet she still felt the same.

Well, I've only been married one day, she reasoned, *maybe I'll feel different tomorrow.*

She thought about Aretha Mae and wondered what she'd have to say about this. For the first time since leaving Bosewell, she almost considered going home. Just for a visit of course – a very short visit. She'd ride up in Reece's big old Cadillac and Harlan would come running to greet them. God, he must be a big boy now – sixteen. Aretha Mae would cook up some of her special fried chicken and greasy fries. What a treat!

The only problem was she'd never told Reece about her poor beginnings. He thought she came from a nice middle-class family. As far as he knew, her mother was a housewife and her father made his living as a car salesman. She didn't have the nerve to tell him the truth. The fact was she was ashamed of where she came from.

Reece Webster had entered her life at exactly the right time – just when she and Joey were beginning to fight non-stop. New York was tough; she'd had seven different jobs and it was getting her down. If she'd had to serve one more plate of beans and hash she knew she'd go nuts.

When Reece Webster first came on to her she'd thought he was just another on-the-make hustler. "You haven't even heard me sing," she'd said scornfully, when he announced he'd make her a star.

"I don't have to," he'd replied. "With your looks all you gotta do is open your mouth an' every guy in the place will do the fandango. Get it?"

Yes, she got it. He didn't have to tell her about men and their reaction to her.

Joey had been furious when she'd informed him she was leaving; they'd argued non-stop. "What do you know about this guy?" he'd said.

"Enough," she'd replied.

"You're making a big mistake."

Maybe she was and maybe she wasn't, but she had to take the chance. It was time to leave, so she'd packed up and taken off in spite of Joey's objections.

In Los Angeles Reece had set her up in what she considered total luxury. A nice apartment on Fountain Avenue, no roaches or rats, and a palm tree outside her window. A palm tree! She thought she was in heaven.

Reece vacillated between staying with her, or spending time with his wife who lived in Tarzana. For two years he'd threatened to get a divorce, now he'd done it, and they'd jumped in his Cadillac, driven to Vegas and gotten married.

"Just you wait," Reece had said. "When you're rich an' famous we'll do it again. An' this time the world will come. You'll see, honey, you'll see."

The first thing that hit Nick when he stepped off the plane in Los Angeles was the sunshine – dazzling, blinding sunshine. And his next impression was one of a laid-back, casual friendliness, the like of which was not evident on the streets of Chicago.

Out on the sidewalk, with the sun beating down, he hailed a cab and gave the driver Cyndra's address.

On the ride in he took in the scenery. Wide streets, tall, dusty palm trees, and a proliferation of gas stations, fast food chains and used car lots. Pedestrians were sparse on the street, but cars were everywhere.

As they got closer into town the greenery overwhelmed him. Every garden seemed to be filled with exotic plants, and every street lined with trees.

He couldn't help feeling excited. After all, this was the real thing, he was in Los Angeles for crissake. Hollywood. Land of the movies. Jeez! If he was lucky he might even bump into Dustin Hoffman or Al Pacino walking down the fucking street!

The cab pulled up in front of Cyndra's apartment house – a three-storey pink stucco building. He jumped out and checked the row of buzzers by the main door. Sure enough one of them was marked with her name, so he pressed and waited.

Five minutes later when she still hadn't replied he realized he should have called.

A well-preserved woman in tennis whites and running shoes. walked up to the door balancing two bags of groceries.

"Hi," he said.

"Hi," she replied, groping for her key.

He went to help her with the grocery bags. "Can I give you a hand?"

She flashed a row of perfect white teeth. "Why not?"

Hmm . . . in Chicago she'd have told him to get lost. People were obviously more trusting in LA.

He balanced her grocery bags in one arm, picked up his bag with the other, and followed her in as she opened the gate.

The first thing he saw was a swimming pool. Holy shit! Cyndra must be rolling in it.

Around the swimming pool there were several apartments.

"You wouldn't happen to know where Cyndra Angelo lives?" he asked.

"Are you a friend of hers?"

"I'm her brother."

"Apartment three, across the other side."

He handed her groceries over. "Thanks."

She smiled again. "You're welcome. Have a nice day."

"I plan to, but thanks anyway."

He went over to Cyndra's apartment – knocked just to make sure, and when nobody answered, placed his bag against her front door and tried to decide what to do. Since this was his first day in LA and there was nobody out by the pool he decided to take a swim. Stripping down to his shorts he leaped in, splashing around like a fish. Goddamn it! This was luxury!

He spent the afternoon on a lounger catching some rays and waiting for his sister. By six o'clock it was obvious she was going to be late. Other people were arriving home from work and entering their apartments. A couple of them gave him strange looks.

He knew he'd better make a move before someone became suspicious. With a few deft strokes he used his credit card to spring her lock. Nobody was around to notice as he slid inside. Mental note – make sure Cyndra got herself a decent lock.

Once inside he looked around. Little sis was living pretty good. He opened the refrigerator and uncovered a dish of cold spaghetti. It looked inviting so he ate it, then he drank from a carton of milk and began roaming around the small apartment. He didn't mean to be nosy, but he couldn't help checking out the bathroom cabinets and opening up the closet. There was definitely a man in residence – some asshole who favoured cowboy boots and ten gallon hats.

On top of the Sony stereo in the living room was a framed picture of Cyndra with an older guy. He picked it up and studied it.

So this was the notorious Reece Webster. The man looked old enough to be her father – skinny and blondish with a thin mouth, droopy moustache and shifty eyes. Cyndra looked sensational in a sexy tank top and shorts. Little Cyndra was all grown up.

He lit a cigarette and settled in front of the television. After a few minutes he dozed off.

When he awoke it was way past midnight and the cigarette had burnt a hole in the arm of the couch. There was still no sign of Cyndra, so he grabbed a blanket from the bedroom, curled up on the couch and went back to sleep.

Cyndra didn't want to go home. She'd fallen in love with Las Vegas.

"This place is the best," she told a dumbfounded Reece.

"This place is a pisshole, honey," he replied, amazed that anyone could actually like Vegas.

"Then why did you bring me here?"

"Because this damn pisshole is gonna make us a whole lotta money."

"How come?"

"You're gonna be a star here, baby. I feel it."

She wanted to believe him. She basked in his enthusiasm. "I am?"

"Sure you are. Tomorrow I've set up appointments for you to meet the talent scouts from a couple of the big hotels. You're gonna impress the custom-made pants off 'em."

"How'll I do that?"

"By lookin' sexy an' singin' for 'em, sugar."

"Why? When we've got those record companies waiting to cut demos with me back in LA?"

"Good business," Reece said, very sure of himself. "Never put it all in one place. When we go in an' see these guys, you listen – don't talk."

That night he took her around all the best hotels. The Sands.

Desert Inn. Tropicana. Cyndra was thrilled; she'd never seen anything like the lavish hotels with their multi-coloured fountains, oversize sculptures and enormous colourful casinos filled with middle America losing their hard-earned money.

"Consider this little tour an educational trip,' Reece said, as he swaggered from hotel to hotel in his cowboy boots and ten gallon hat masquerading as a Texas millionaire. He jerked his thumb at a girl singer in the lounge of The Golden Nugget. "You see her? She can't sing for shit, but she sure puts in a pretty appearance."

"Why are you telling *me*?" Cyndra asked.

"'Cause, Mrs Webster, not only do you look good, but you can sing too. An' we're gonna use everything we got to make you bigger and better than anyone else."

Reece made her feel she could achieve anything. "Can we stay a couple of extra days?" she begged, "Can we? *Please*. After all, it *is* our honeymoon."

He tilted his hat. "What'll you give me if I say yes?"

She smiled. "I'll make it simple. Anything you want, Reece. Anything at all."

Nick awoke in the morning uncomfortable and hot. There was no Cyndra around – she must have taken off somewhere. He should've called to let her know he was coming. Shit! Too late now.

He helped himself to a banana, made a cup of instant coffee and then sauntered outside to the pool.

An athletic looking girl in a one-piece swimsuit swam lengths, her brown arms and legs flashing through the inviting blue water.

"Hey," he called out. "Any chance you know where Cyndra Angelo is?"

The girl took no notice of him as she pounded the water, hardly coming up for breath. He squatted down beside the pool waiting for her to surface.

After a few minutes she swam to the shallow end and climbed out, shaking herself like a shaggy dog. The girl wasn't pretty in a conventional way, more interesting looking – with a pert face, snub nose and bright blue eyes. She was five feet three with a sensational compact body and very short red hair.

"Excuse me," he said. "I'm trying to find Cyndra Angelo."

"Who're you?"

"Her brother."

"*You're* her brother?" she said disbelievingly, grabbing a towel and drying herself. "Cyndra never mentioned she had a brother."

"I flew in from Chicago – figured I'd surprise her – I guess it wasn't such a good idea."

"What did you do, break into her apartment?" she said knowingly, towelling a bronzed thigh.

"Technically, yeah, but I know she'd want me to make myself at home."

"Tell *that* to the Super."

"Is he around?"

"I wouldn't dig him up if I were you, he'll throw you out."

"So you can't help me?"

"Come to think of it – I did see Cyndra walking out of here carrying a bag on . . . let's see – maybe it was Thursday. She's probably away for a long weekend."

"Today's Tuesday, I'll wait."

The girl threw him a suspicious look. "Are you sure her boyfriend's going to like that?"

"Who is this boyfriend?"

She laughed. "He's okay – if you like watered down cowboys." She finished drying herself and walked towards her apartment across the other side of the pool. "See ya," she called over her shoulder.

She certainly had a body.

"Yeah – see ya. Uh . . . what's your name?"

She turned around at her apartment door. "Annie Broderick. Oh, and by the way, if you rip her off, I *can* identify you to the police. And I will."

He stared at her quizzically. "Do I look like I'd do a thing like that?"

"No. You look like an actor. Worst kind." She entered her apartment slamming the door behind her.

She couldn't have said anything nicer if she'd tried. An actor, huh? Some compliment. He hadn't performed in so long he wondered if he still remembered how.

By noon he was bored; sitting around waiting was not his style. Out of curiosity he picked up the phone and called the number Q.J. had given him.

"Manfred Glamour Limousines," a woman's voice said.

Glamour Limousines – was she kidding? "Let me speak to Mr Manfred," he said quickly, before he changed his mind.

"Who's calling?"

"Tell him . . . uh . . . tell him it's a friend of Q.J.'s."

Her voice rose. "Q.J.'s?"

"Yeah – he'll know who you mean."

There was a long wait. A very long wait. So long that he almost hung up. Then a gruff voice snapped, "Who's this?"

"You don't know me," he explained, speaking fast. "But your ex-partner said I should give you a call when I got to LA. Q.J. mentioned you might have a job for me."

"Who the fuck are ya?"

"Nick Angelo. I ran Q.J.'s bar in Chicago."

"And what ya got in mind t'do for me?"

"Anything you want if it's legit."

"I don't fuckin' believe this," Manny grumbled. "You pick up a phone, mention that putz to whom I don't speak no more, and ya really think I'll give ya a job?"

"Hey – listen, if it's a problem, forget it. Q.J. insisted I call. He told me to say Q.J.'s collecting – for that favour you owe him. But if it means nothing to you . . ."

A weary sigh. "Come in and see me."

"When?"

"Be here in an hour."

"Where's here?"

"Sunset past La Brea. You can't miss it." Manny hung up without so much as a goodbye.

Nick decided to go for it. After all, he had nothing to lose.

Chapter 38

"Don't you ever date?" Nature asked, studying her face in a large magnifying mirror she'd extracted from her enormous purse.

"Not if I can help it," Lauren replied.

"Not if you can 'elp it," Nature shrieked, in her sharp cockney tones. "Cor blimey – that's a funny one. Me – I can't get through the day if I don't 'ave a fella waitin' for me at the end of it."

"You're you and I'm me," Lauren said, sensibly.

"Bleedin' right," Nature agreed, searching for imagined blemishes on her perfect peaches-and-cream skin.

Lauren had been working at Samm's for three months. It was certainly different. Definitely not boring. In fact she was so busy she never had time to think about anything except work. A booker, she'd soon found out, did everything for the band of models who trudged in and out of the place like a constant parade of dazzling beauty. They were all gorgeous, but every one, it seemed, had a screwed-up personal life.

Nature, Samm's most famous client, was the most screwed-up of all. She'd taken to dropping by and sitting on Lauren's desk so they could chat. Nature had confided she was fed up with people who brown-nosed her to death.

"You're like a real person," she'd told Lauren. "I can talk to you, you're so sort of normal."

That's nice, Lauren wanted to say, *but I have work to do*.

The phone at Samm's never stopped. Along with Nature, the agency handled three of the other top models in New York – Selina, Gypsy and Bett Smith. At the agency they were known as the Big Four. Selina was a willowy blonde with cat eyes. Gypsy was Eurasian, exotically beautiful. And Bett Smith was an all-American blonde with a cute snub nose and just enough freckles.

245

Samm herself had turned out to be the woman Lauren had encountered at the first photo session she'd crashed. Samm Mason, former top model – now a very successful agent.

In the late fifties Samm had been one of the top models in the country. When she retired she'd opened her own agency, and over the years built it into a formidable rival to Eileen Ford and the Casablanca Agency. Samm was tough, but it worked for her. She ran a tight operation, protected her girls and expected everybody in her employ to do the same. "I know how easy it is to get treated like a piece of shit in this business," she'd often tell her employees. "That's not going to happen to any of my girls. Not while they work for me."

Lauren palled up with an American-born Chinese girl called Pia who'd worked at the agency for several years as Samm's personal assistant. Without Pia to help her through the early days she might have given up. It was certainly nothing like working in a law office – the modelling world was chaos. People on the phone day and night screaming for this girl or that girl. The models yelling that they didn't want to go to Alaska, they would prefer to do the shoot in the Bahamas. Boyfriends calling up, men trying to track them down, clients complaining. In fact, the phones never stopped for one reason or another. Lauren's job was to see that everybody arrived in the right place at the right time. She was also expected to keep everyone happy. She soon became adept.

After a few weeks Pia had said, "You're doing okay, Samm's really pleased. Are you having fun?"

Fun was not exactly the best way to describe her first couple of months in New York. She'd hardly had time to think, let alone have fun, there was always something going on. Early on Samm had asked if she minded working weekends. Like an idiot she'd said she didn't mind. But still, she had nothing else to occupy her time, and it meant making extra money.

She'd moved from the hotel to a one-room apartment in the Village. It wasn't the perfect location. Upstairs an angry woman practised the piano at all hours. And downstairs a young boy who claimed he was a performance artist turned tricks.

The good thing about being in New York was there was never time to feel lonely, she was always busy doing something.

"So," Nature said, leaning across her desk. "Last night I met this tall geezer, sort of a Euro-trash type. He was 'anging out at one of the discos. Bleedin' hell, he came on so strong even

I couldn't fight him off – an' that's sayin' somethin'!" Nature snorted with laughter. "Bloody Italians – they've got their hands all over you before you so much as find out their name. Good job I know 'ow to fight back. Kick 'em in the cobblers an' run. Me mum taught me that."

"Did you go out with him?" Lauren enquired, thinking that a kick in the balls from Nature was enough to kill any normal man. Nature was over six feet tall and extremely well-built – not skinny like her main rival, Selina.

"Out with 'im? *In* with 'im is more likely," Nature chortled. "He dragged me back to 'is hotel and we 'ad a party."

"What kind of party?"

"What kind of party do you think? Some grass, plenty of rock 'n roll – although 'e wanted to play Julio Iglesias. I put a stop to that *dead* quick, I can tell you."

Lauren finished typing a sheet of paper and handed it over. "Here's your instructions for the Acapulco shoot. You leave on Thursday. I've arranged a car and driver to pick you up at your apartment and you'll be back the following Tuesday in time to be in the studio Wednesday morning for the *Cosmopolitan* cover session."

Nature grabbed the piece of paper barely looking at it. "Acapulco," she snorted. "It's so bleedin' hot."

"Have you been there before?"

"About ten times."

Lauren sighed – sometimes she envied the models and the exotic trips they all seemed to take for granted. "It must be absolutely marvellous," she said, wistfully.

Nature made a face. "If you like sunshine and a bunch of dark geezers runnin' about all over the place. Personally, if I 'ad me choice, I'd be back in London with me mum 'aving a nice cuppa tea."

"How long is it since you've been home?"

"Must be a year now. Samm promised I can take a few weeks off at Christmas."

"Do you need her permission?"

Nature chortled. "Don't knock it when it's all happenin'. Samm got me where I am today. I listen to what she 'as to say, she's a smart old bird. Which reminds me, I gotta see 'er. Is she by 'erself?"

"Let me buzz her."

"Thanks, darlin'. You're such a sweetie."

Samm was available. Nature marched into her office leaving Lauren with the ever-ringing phones. There were two other bookers, but neither of them paid as much attention as she did. She hadn't intended on making herself indispensable, but deep down she knew everyone depended on her. It was a big responsibility – but at least she felt needed.

The rest of the day passed quickly – everything happening at the usual breakneck speed. By the time she was ready to leave she was wiped out.

Pia caught her by the door. "It's Samm's birthday next week; the girls want to throw her a surprise party. She'll hate it. What'll I do?"

"If she'll hate it, tell them no."

Pip tapped long red fingernails on the side of her fake Chanel purse. "Have you ever tried telling those spoilt bitches no?"

"You can do it."

"It's Samm's big one," Pia worried. "I suppose we *should* have a party. Can you make arrangements for food and music, flowers and whatever else you think we need? Selina's offered the use of her boyfriend's apartment."

"Which boyfriend?"

"Haven't you heard? She's in love again."

It was a well-known fact that the models changed boyfriends as often as they changed their panties. Men were one of the perks of the business.

"Who's she in love with now?" Lauren asked.

"That English rock star, Emerson Burn," Pia giggled. "When Nature finds out she'll kill her – she thinks anything British is automatically hers."

Lauren tried to remain cool. In a way it was all too much – one minute she was sitting in Philadelphia slogging away at a job she hated with a boss who was always chasing her – not to mention her affair with Brad. Now she was in New York mixing with models and rock stars. Emerson Burn was famous. And she was going to meet him. Emerson Burn! It wasn't so long ago that she'd had his poster on her wall hanging next to John Lennon.

Calm down, Roberts, he's only a person. And from the sound of his publicity not a very nice one.

"Can I depend on you to handle it?" Pia asked, already on her way out. "I'd do it myself but you're so good at everything – so organized."

I'm not so organized, she wanted to scream. *I'm twenty-one years old and I'd like to have a life too.*

"Sure," she said. "Leave the numbers on my desk and I'll get started tomorrow."

"Gee!" Pia peered at her watch. "It's past seven, my guy's gonna kill me. We're seeing *Manhattan*. I'm crazy about Woody Allen. Can you check all the lights are off and lock up?"

Thanks a lot, Pia. Why don't I collect your pay-cheque too?

She took the subway home, ignoring an elderly flasher in the requisite grubby raincoat.

Two giggly girls sitting opposite her screamed with laughter when the flasher turned his attention on them. "Get it blown up an' frame it!" one of them yelled, making a rude gesture.

The flasher slunk off down the train searching for more docile victims.

Lauren stopped at the corner market near her apartment and bought a can of beans and a loaf of fresh bread. *Another gourmet dinner coming up*, she thought, wryly.

Since arriving in New York she hadn't been out once. Her routine was work and home – it didn't deviate. A couple of guys had asked her for a date – one a photographer who'd dropped by the office to see Samm, and the other an assistant to Samm's accountant. She'd declined both offers. Who needed the hassle of a man? She certainly didn't.

Nick Angelo.

Every so often his name popped into her head for no reason at all, and she found herself wondering where he was and what he was doing, and most of all – was he happy?

Who cared? Nick Angelo was her past. She didn't give a damn if she never saw him again.

Chapter 39

Manny Manfred was without doubt the fattest man Nick had ever seen. Manny wasn't just fat, he was gargantuan – with beady eyes, layers of jowls and chins and dyed yellow hair sporting inch-long black roots. He sat in a specially made naugahyde chair behind a cluttered desk, sucking 7-Up through a straw and tossing handfuls of cashew nuts into his greedy little mouth. He was not what Nick had expected. Q.J. and Manny together must have been the sight of the century!

"I'm Nick."

"So what?"

"You told me to come by."

"Oh, yeah, Q.J. sent ya."

"That's right."

"Whaddaya want?"

"A job. Part-time. I need to be free to go on auditions if they come up."

"What auditions?"

"I'm an actor."

"Says who?"

"Says me."

Manny shifted his enormous bulk and sighed. "Can ya drive?"

"Yes."

"Can ya drive good?"

"Yes."

"Ya gotta clean licence?"

"You bet."

"See Luigi. Tell him I said t'put you on the airport run."

"Is that it?"

"Whaddaya want – a kiss an' a cuddle? Scram."

He scrammed. Saw Luigi – a bullet-headed man with a broken

front tooth and a sour expression – got a short lecture on the dos and don'ts of driving a limo, and was told to report back at eight p.m. It was as easy as that.

It wasn't so easy getting back into Cyndra's apartment. The Super pounced on him just as he was using his credit card on her door. The Super was a ferocious looking man with shoulder length dreadlocks, two gold teeth and a take-no-prisoners attitude. He clamped his burly hand on Nick's shoulder. "What you up to, mon?"

He attempted to explain.

The Super was having none of it. He threw him out.

Nick realized he was lucky to get away without the Dreadlock King calling the police.

He hung around outside the building until Annie Broderick emerged. She looked different in clothes. A track suit covered her curvy body, and a baseball cap hid her short red hair.

"Remember me?" he said.

"No," she said.

"Sure you do," he said, laying on the irresistible green-eyed stare.

"What do you want?" she asked, unimpressed.

"Your help."

She walked over to an old brown Packard and opened the door. "Why?"

He spread the charm waiting for the usual reaction. "'Cause you know me. We're friends."

She seemed surprised. "We are?"

"Sure we are," he said, persuasively.

Annie had wasted enough time. "Now, listen," she said, sharply. "Cyndra's brother – or whoever you are – stop bugging me. I may look like an easy touch – but trust me – no way."

"I'm not after your money," he said, quite affronted.

"That's good, 'cause I don't have any."

"All I want to do is leave a note for Cyndra. Tell her where she can reach me."

"Who's stopping you?"

"The Super's on my case. I can't even get my bag outta her apartment – I need to explain."

"Explain to me. I'll pass it on," she said, waiting expectantly. He didn't say a word.

"Well?" she was getting impatient. "Where shall I say you'll be?"

"I don't have a place."

Now this is where she was supposed to feel sorry for him and offer the use of her couch.

"You don't have a place," she repeated, blankly. "Too bad."

So much for the old Angelo charm. This female had a cold heart.

"No – but I got a job," he said quickly, as if that might change her mind.

"Good for you." She glanced meaningfully at her watch. "I'm late for class."

Maybe she was a dyke – anything was possible. "Just tell her I was here and I'll be calling her. Okay?"

Annie nodded and took off.

He spent the rest of the day wandering around Hollywood – checking out the star's names embedded in the sidewalk, mooching through a small shop filled with stills and photos from movies, and finally ending up at Farmer's Market on Fairfax where he ordered corn-beef and cabbage from one of the many open-air counters offering all different kinds of traditional fare.

He thought about what he was going to do next. Money was no problem: he'd left Chicago with twelve hundred bucks in his pocket – not bad considering he spent as he earnt. If he wanted he could rent an apartment and get himself settled – although it made more sense to wait for Cyndra to get back and camp out on her couch for a few weeks until he got the feel of the city and decided whether he wanted to stay or not.

Renting a car was definitely a priority. He'd soon realized that in LA the buses ran slow and did not cover the city. There was no subway – so a car was a necessity. He looked up rentals in the yellow pages and arranged himself a month-long deal on an old Buick.

Behind the wheel of the car he felt a lot more secure. At least he had a place he belonged – somewhere to call home.

"Ya ain't plannin' on wearin' what ya got on?" Luigi demanded, squinting at Nick with a disgusted expression.

"What's wrong with what I got on?"

"Ya gotta be fuckin' kiddin'." Luigi ran his hand over his bullet-head. "Ya look like a bum."

They glared at each other. This was not an auspicious start.

"I don't have anything else," Nick said. "I lost my bag."

"There's a closet in there." Luigi indicated the back room.

"Find somethin' that fits you. And for crissakes move, you're on the airport run."

"Who am I meeting?"

"Mr Evans. He's a businessman. Ya hold up the card with his name on, ya escort him out to the limo, ya shut the privacy glass, an' you drive him anywhere he wants to go. Oh, an' remember t' drive nice an' smooth. Mr Evans don't like no sudden stops."

"Sure."

"An' another thing – no talkin' unless he speaks first. Them's the rules of the game. These people pay good money for a limo, they don't want no conversation."

Ha! Like he was looking for a meaningful communication with a total stranger. What kind of schmuck did Luigi take him for?

He searched through the closet in the back room and found a pair of black pants, a dark jacket and a none-too-clean white shirt. The clothes didn't fit properly but what the hell – he'd be sitting behind the wheel of a car, anyway.

There were a couple of other drivers back there smoking and playing cards. Neither of them took any notice of him.

Luigi thrust a form at him. "Fill it out," he ordered.

He put down Cyndra's address and lied about his driving experience, writing that he'd driven for a limo company in Chicago. That information took the edge off Luigi's scowl.

Idly, he wondered what favour Manny owed Q.J. One of these days he intended to find out.

Luigi gave him a silver limousine to drive. It was shined and polished pretty good, but once he got in he realized the limo had seen better days. The back, where the passengers sat, was all spruced up with a single rose in a glass vase, a fresh bowl of fruit and side compartments stocked with booze. But in front the leather covering the seat was cracked, and there were plastic strips peeling off the side windows. So much for Glamour Limousines. The car reminded him of a gorgeous girl with the clap.

"You know the way to the airport?" Luigi scowled.

He had no idea how to get there but he nodded anyway. As soon as he left the garage he parked the limo on a side street and studied a map he'd found in the glove compartment. No big deal. LA was all straight roads going in different directions like one big board-game. He clicked the radio on and zoomed out to the airport listening to Jimi Hendrix at full volume.

He reached L.A.X. twenty minutes early and had no idea

where to park. Traffic cops were everywhere – yelling and shouting – making sure all the vehicles kept moving.

Rolling down his window, he waved ten bucks at a porter and asked where he could put the car.

The porter grabbed the money and obligingly told him where to leave it so he wouldn't get a ticket.

His passenger arrived on a flight from Switzerland. Mr Evans was a swarthy man with patent-leather hair and wrap-around black shades. Kind of strange at ten o'clock at night, but Nick was getting used to the foibles of people who lived in Los Angeles.

Mr Evans had no luggage except a snake-skin briefcase that he clutched firmly to his side, snarling ungratefully when Nick attempted to take it.

"Only trying to help," Nick said with a shrug, accompanying the man to the limo.

Mr Evans lived in a high-rise on Wilshire. Nick dropped him off and waited for a tip, a word of thanks – anything.

Mr Evans was not into pleasantries. He walked into his building without a backward glance.

"Screw you, too, buddy," Nick muttered, deciding that maybe the life of a limo driver was not for him.

Back at Glamour Limousines, Luigi sat in his office picking his nose while speaking on the phone. "I'm gonna hump your juicy ass off, sweetie. I'm gonna –" He stopped abruptly when Nick entered. "What the fuck *you* want?" he asked, covering the mouthpiece.

"I brought the car back. Thought you'd like to know I delivered your passenger safely."

"Whaddaya want – a medal?" Luigi was like a lesser version of Manny – they'd obviously both graduated from the same charm school.

"Same time tomorrow?" Nick asked, wondering what kind of woman Luigi had panting on the other end of the phone.

"Yeah," Luigi snapped, anxious to get back to his sweetie.

"I'll be here."

Maybe.

If nothing better comes along.

He got in his rented Buick and cruised down Hollywood Boulevard, finally stopping at a motel where he booked a room for the night.

"Wanna hooker?" the desk clerk enquired, reluctantly shifting his attention from a well-thumbed porno magazine.

"Not tonight."

The clerk regarded him suspiciously. "Why doncha?"

He didn't bother replying.

Lying on a lumpy bed watching Johnny Carson do his mono-
logue he wondered if he'd made the right move leaving Chicago.
He'd left a good job at Q.J.'s, a great-looking woman – and for
what? A fleabag motel and a shit job servicing other people.

He'd give it a couple of weeks and if things didn't improve
he was on a plane out of there.

Chapter 40

Emerson Burn had a mane of hair better than any girl. Lauren couldn't help staring. She'd been a fan for so many years, loved his music, and now she was in his presence. It didn't seem possible. His thick, shaggy, honey-coloured hair fell way below his shoulders. His eyes were a dreamy grey shadowed by long curling lashes. His nose aquiline and his lips surprisingly full for a man.

You're staring, Roberts.

I can't help it!

Lauren wasn't alone with him. Also present were his manager, his publicist, his personal assistant and Selina, who – clad in a leopard-skin catsuit – prowled his apartment as if she owned it. Selina was incredibly thin and almost as tall as Nature. She had straight white-blonde hair that hung to her waist and incredible cat eyes set in a classically beautiful face. She kept fixing her eyes on Emerson as if to say *This is mine and I don't want anybody touching it.*

"So," said Emerson, standing up and stretching. "I guess that's it."

Even though he was in his late thirties he was still in great shape. He wore skin-tight black leather pants on his long skinny legs, scuffed boots and a white shirt with some kind of ridiculous frill down the front. Ridiculous or not, on him it worked.

Lauren, busy making notes on an oversized pad, realized he hadn't looked at her once. And why should he? She was only the hired help.

Selina floated over to Emerson and kissed him full on the mouth, making sure everyone noticed the little bit of tongue play she indulged in. "You're such a sport, letting us use your apartment," she sighed. "Samm's going to be absolutely amazed."

"S'long as we 'ave fun, darlin'," he replied, putting his arm around her, pressing her in the small of her back and guiding her in for another kiss.

They kissed as if nobody else was in the room – in fact their smooching session went on for so long that Lauren thought they were going to leave the meeting and rush off into the bedroom. Nobody else seemed to take any notice. She imagined they'd seen it all before.

When the kiss was finished so was Emerson. "Bye, everyone," he called, striding to the door.

His entourage leapt to their feet and followed him.

"Later, strong man," Selina whispered, blowing him more kisses.

As soon as he was gone Selina stopped being the ethereal little flower and turned into the tough balls-breaker she really was. "Are we all organized, Laura? I don't expect any fuck-ups."

"Yes, Serina," Lauren replied, sarcastically. "Everything's under control."

"It better be," Selina said threateningly, as if Lauren was her personal slave. "And," she spun around, "if Samm finds out about the party before it happens I'm holding you personally responsible."

Lauren decided that out of all of the girls Selina was the worst bitch.

Back at the office Samm gave her a blast. "And exactly where have you been all morning?"

"I had to go to the dentist," she lied.

"Not good enough," Samm said, curtly. "Make dental appointments on your own time, not when you're supposed to be working."

"I don't have any personal time," Lauren explained. "You've got me working weekends and I'm here late every night. I had a toothache – what was I supposed to do?"

"Hmm . . . I suppose you had no choice," Samm said, giving in. She frowned. "I hate to say it, but this place is chaos without you."

"You managed very well before I came along," Lauren pointed out.

"Yes, well, that was then and this is now. Let's get back to work." Samm tapped her painted nails on her desk top. The polish looked like the high gloss finish on a car.

Lauren sat down and prepared to take notes.

"First I want you to send a bottle of champagne to Antonio,"

Samm said. "He had a vile time on the Selina shoot. I'm really going to have to talk to that girl before she trips over her own ego. Oh – and then call Flash Cosmetics, they need Nature in the studio on the same day she has that big *Vogue* shoot. Contact Nature and tell her she'll have to start earlier. Ignore her screaming. After that talk to *Swimwear Magazine*, they need all the girls on the tenth. I've told them it's impossible to get anybody out to the Virgin Islands before the twelfth – but they're insisting. You deal with it, Lauren, you're so good with people."

"Consider it all taken care of," she said, getting up.

As soon as she reached her desk Pia was beside her whispering, "Everything okay?"

"All systems go."

Pia looked relieved. "You're so good at this!"

Yes, Pia. I should be doing your job and making your salary.

At lunchtime several of the girls stopped by the office with a cake and faked Samm out.

"God, I hate birthdays," Samm said, reluctantly blowing out the candles. "Who told you all?"

Nobody owned up.

"At least she thinks it's over and done with now," Pia murmured. "Boy, will she be surprised!"

"How are you getting her up to Emerson's apartment?" Lauren asked. It was the one detail she hadn't been in charge of.

"Selina's taking her. She's told Samm that she and Emerson have a surprise they want to tell her personally."

"Did Samm fall for it?"

"Absolutely. She thinks they're planning marriage, and she's all set to talk them out of it."

Later, Nature managed to corner her at her desk. She was all blonde hair, blue eyes and glowing Acapulco tan. "I can't believe Selina "as bagged Emerson Burn," she complained. "She's not "is type, too bloody skinny. He likes a bird with a bit of meat on "er bones – me fer instance!"

"Do you know him?" Lauren asked.

Nature licked her lips. "No, but I intend to."

Lauren sensed trouble ahead.

As soon as she could she left the office and raced over to Emerson Burn's apartment to check on all the arrangements. She was wearing a pleated skirt and plain blue sweater, her hair pulled back in a thick braid. There was obviously not going to be time for her to get back to her apartment and change into something more festive. So what? Nobody cared how she looked, as long as she stayed in the background and did her job.

Selina was already there, floating around the apartment issuing orders. Emerson's four servants hovered in the background with surly expressions. They did not appreciate every single one of his girlfriends coming in and trying to take over.

"Thank God you're here," exclaimed Selina. "Do go and talk to the caterers. Check that they know what they're doing. Oh, and Laura, you did make sure everyone was told to be here promptly at eight o'clock?"

"All taken care of." She paused. "By the way, my name is Lauren not Laura."

"Whatever." Selina waved a beautifully manicured hand in the air.

Bitch! Lauren thought as she hurried into the kitchen to confer with the caterers.

Various members of Emerson's entourage skulked around unhappy because he'd thrown open his apartment for Samm's surprise party.

After she was done with the caterers she viewed the flower arrangements, checked out the guest list with a burly guard at the door, and finally found a moment to spend alone.

Locking herself in the guest bathroom she gazed at her reflection in the mirror. Was this how she planned to spend her life? Arranging parties for other people to have a good time? She'd wanted to become a famous New York stage actress. Now she was this unimportant little gofer doing things for other people. Lauren Roberts – invisible.

Somebody tried the door of the bathroom. She ignored them, they could wait.

Whoever it was hammered on the door again.

Angrily she flung it open and came face-to-face with Emerson Burn.

"Who're you?" he demanded.

"Lauren," she replied, curbing a strong desire to reach out and touch his shaggy mane of honey-coloured curls. "From Samm's Agency. I'm organizing the party – remember? We did meet."

He shook his golden hair and took her arm. "Follow me, I want you to "ear something."

"Pardon?"

"Don't argue," he said, grabbing her arm and leading her down a plushly carpeted corridor into the back part of the apartment where he'd built a state of the art recording studio. "Sit down an' 'ave a listen to this."

Exactly who did he think he was bossing around?

"Mr Burn," she said, "I have no time to listen. I'm trying to organize a party for you – I have to see everything runs the way it's supposed to."

"This is *my* bloody apartment. *I'm* paying for the bleedin' party, so sit down an' shut up."

He sounded like Nature. Maybe the two of them *did* belong together, after all they shared the same accent.

She sat stiffly on a chair while he marched over to a control panel and pressed a couple of buttons. Suddenly the room was flooded with sound.

She recognized his voice immediately – that sexy, cocksure rasp. She'd been thirteen when he'd burst on to the scene and taken America by storm with his most famous single "Dog Days and Wild Women".

The song playing was a love song, not the romantic kind, but a driving, hard love song called "Viper Woman".

"Listen to this and tell me what you think," Emerson said, pacing up and down his studio.

She studied his leather-clad legs. "Does it matter what *I* think?"

"Yeah, you're the public," he said, speaking quite slowly as if she was an idiot. "You're the girl in the street. You won't kiss my ass – you'll tell me the truth." He turned up the volume, almost blasting her out of the room.

The lyrics hammered her senses.

She loves me for my money
She loves me for my power
She even goddamn loves me for my big fat car
She's a Viper Woman
Loves to rock 'n roll
She's a Viper Woman
She only got one goal
Oh yeah!
Money money
Sex and honey
She got her eye on it all
Money money
Sex and honey
This bitch is pretty damn cool!

The record certainly wasn't vintage Emerson Burn.

He turned the volume down and stared at her. "Well?"

"It's . . . it's okay," she said, standing up and smoothing down her skirt.

"Okay." He repeated okay like it was a dirty word. "What are you – deaf?" Then he raised his voice. "It's my new single for crissake. It's a fuckin' *hit*!"

Hmm . . . obviously he didn't care to hear the truth. Maybe she should lie and say it was the best thing she'd ever heard.

Oh, the hell with it, why should she?

"I don't like it," she said. "I don't appreciate you calling women bitches. If it's a love song why isn't it more loving?"

"Who *the fuck* do you think you are?" he exploded. "'Viper Woman's' one of the best things I've ever recorded."

"Who the hell do you think *you* are?" she blazed back. "I'm not some burned-out groupie who's going to tell you it's wonderful if I don't think so. You asked for my opinion and you got it."

"Get the fuck outta my sight," he snarled. "You don't know shit."

She was furious, but there was nothing she could do. A party was about to take place and she had to make sure everything ran smoothly.

With as much dignity as she could muster she left the room.

"I knew this was going to be a good day."

Lauren turned around and faced Jimmy Cassady, the photographer who'd asked her out a few weeks earlier.

"Hi," she said, glad to encounter a friendly face.

"Hi," he replied, with a smile.

She groped for conversation. "Do you think Samm was surprised?"

"Surprised?" he laughed. "More like pissed."

"I guess it's not much fun being forty."

"Forty?" He laughed even louder. "You think Samm's forty? The woman is fifty."

"What?" Lauren was amazed. "She doesn't look it."

"She doesn't even look forty," Jimmy said. "Samm's a phenomenon. Have you seen pictures of her when she was modelling?"

"No."

"Dynamite!"

Lauren's eyes darted around the crowded party. Most of the guests had arrived on time and when Samm put in an appearance with Selina on one side and Emerson on the other they'd all screamed "**SURPRISE!**" right on cue. And now everything was going so well she thought she might sneak out.

"What's *your* story?" Jimmy asked, lighting a cigarette.

She turned to look at him. He was in his early thirties, short and wiry with a pointed face and hair that was thinning on top and long in the back. He wore it in a pony-tail. He also wore John Lennon eye glasses and tight blue jeans. The jeans immediately reminded her of Nick.

Sternly she put Nick Angelo out of her head.

"I don't have a story," she said, deciding she could exit through the kitchen without anyone noticing.

"Everyone has a story," he replied, confidently. "And I'm interested in finding out yours."

She shrugged. "Small-town girl, came to New York, got a job. That's it."

"There's a lot more to you than that. I could tell the moment I asked you out."

"Not used to getting turned down, huh?"

He drew on his cigarette and regarded her with a contemplative expression. "You're not married, are you?" He looked pointedly at her left hand, bereft of rings.

"No, I'm not married," she said, defensively.

"Going steady? I don't notice a guy with you."

"I'm not seeing anyone."

"Then why can't we go out?"

Good question, but she owed him no explanation. "Has it occurred to you that I might not want to?" she said, hoping to put an end to the conversation.

He refused to be put off. "Is it just me or does everyone get the big no?"

"I'm leaving," she said, and then added, "Everything's going nicely, they don't need me any more."

He took the hint. "You organized this event?"

"Right," she began a slow edge towards the kitchen.

He followed her. "You did a pretty fine job, but you'd better not leave."

"Why?"

He gestured over to the corner. "Because Selina is just about to kill Nature. Take a look."

Lauren looked. Nature was all over Emerson Burn, who lounged on a couch, his leather-clad legs stretched out before him.

Her shrieking laugh could be heard all the way across the room.

Selina hovered behind him clad in a floating chiffon dress, her cat eyes signalling immediate danger.

"It's not my problem," Lauren said.

"How come?" Jimmy asked. "You're known around the office as the solver of all problems."

"I am?"

He grinned. "Yeah – have you any idea what they call you behind your back?"

She wished he'd leave her alone. "I'm sure you can't wait to tell me."

He seemed amused. "Miss E."

Now she was really irritated. "Miss E? What's that supposed to mean?"

He laughed. "Miss Efficiency."

"Oh, thanks a lot," she said, not exactly thrilled with the title.

He pressed on. "It's true isn't it? You do everything for everybody. You've made yourself indispensable. How long have you been there – three months? The other bookers must love you. I bet even Pia's getting nervous about her job."

How come he knew so much about her? "What are you talking about?"

He stubbed his cigarette in a nearby ashtray. "I'm talking about you. You're the ideal personal assistant – and don't think it's escaped Samm's notice, because nothing escapes Madam."

"I'm not after anyone's job," Lauren said. "I'm perfectly happy doing what I'm doing."

He stared at her from behind his John Lennon specs. "Yes?"

"Yes," she replied defiantly, preparing to take off.

"Oh, shit!" he exclaimed.

"What?"

"Take a look at them now."

She glanced over at Selina, Nature and Emerson in time to observe Selina slowly and deliberately pour a full glass of champagne over Emerson's head.

"Leave 'em to it," Jimmy said, putting a restraining hand on her arm just in case she was about to take care of that problem too. "They'll work it out between 'em."

Emerson Burn was now on his feet, stoned and swaying, champagne dripping down his face. "Yer stupid bleedin' cow," he shouted. "You've ruined me bleedin' hair."

"Yeah," Nature joined in. "Look what you've done."

"Stay out of it, bimbo," yelled Selina.

"What'd you call me?" Nature yelled back.

And before anyone could stop them they were at each other like a couple of wildcats, tearing at hair, chiffon, ear-rings – anything they could get their hands on.

Emerson prevented anyone from getting near them. "Let 'em at it," he shouted, happily. "This is the best part of the bleedin' party."

"Come on," said Jimmy, taking Lauren's arm. "I'm escorting you out of here."

Before she could argue he steered her to the door and they slipped away into the night.

Chapter 41

Cyndra stormed around her apartment raging in disbelief. "Someone's been in here. I don't believe it! Look, Reece, *look*, there's cigarette butts in the ashtrays and a burn hole on the arm of the couch."

"Even better," Reece shouted from the bedroom, where he was investigating further. "Instead of taking *our* stuff they've left a bag here."

"What?" she said, marching into the bedroom to see what he was talking about. Sure enough, there was somebody's bag full of clothes. She began searching through it.

"I don't understand," Reece said, scratching his chin.

"*I* do," Cyndra said, pulling out a pair of worn jeans. "This is Nick's stuff."

"Who's Nick?"

"I told you about him – he's my brother."

Screw it! Reece thought. *Relatives! That's all I need.* "How'd he get in? An' where is he?" Reece demanded.

"Knowing Nick, he broke in. Is there a note or something?"

"That's a helluva thing, breakin' into a person's apartment," Reece grumbled.

"Oh, like *you* wouldn't."

He chewed on his lip. "How long is it since you've seen this brother of yours?"

"Going on four years."

Reece's imagination began running wild. Cyndra, his little darkie beauty, probably had a brother who was over six feet tall and black as his patent-leather shoes. What's more, it was likely that he'd want to beat the shit out of him. "You gotta be careful of relatives," he cautioned.

She turned on him angrily. "Nick's my brother. I love him."

265

"Well," Reece said, hoping the brother would not put in a return appearance, "There's nothing we can do about it. I'll store his bag in the closet and we'll see if he contacts you. One thing, honey – if he does – I've had experience – don't get too cosy with relatives, 'cause they come to stay and then you can never get rid of 'em."

"Thanks, I'll take your advice," she said, sarcastically. "I'll throw my own brother out on the street and hope he doesn't bug me again."

If they'd been married longer Reece might have smacked her – he didn't appreciate sassy women. But he knew that the moment you hit a woman you had to have her in a position where she couldn't leave, and since they'd only just gotten married, she might take off on him, and then where would he be, what with the money he'd laid out on singing lessons, clothes and all the rest.

"I'm going to a meeting,' he said, adjusting the tilt of his stetson.

She didn't reply. She was too busy thinking about where Nick might be.

The second night of working for Glamour Limousines Nick landed the airport run again. This time his passenger was an anorexic woman producer with cropped hair and a bad-tempered attitude. Julia something or other. She sat in the back of his limo snorting coke and talking non-stop on a portable phone.

When they reached Bel Air he got lost in the winding hills, and she screamed at him, calling him a dumb fuck and a stupid prick. He almost stopped the car and threw her out, but wisdom prevailed.

When they reached her house she changed moods and invited him in.

"What for?" he asked.

She had desperate eyes and bad breath. "A fuck."

"Sorry – got another job."

Sweet revenge. Not that he'd have fucked her with somebody else's dick.

So far he was not having a wonderful time in LA.

That night he stayed at the motel again, and in the morning he called Cyndra.

"Nick!" she exclaimed, excitedly. "I've been waiting for your call, I *knew* you were here. I went through your bag and

266

unpacked it. Naturally I had to wash all your clothes, you filthy hog. Nothing's changed, huh?"

"Where've you been?" he demanded. "I came all this way and you weren't even home."

"Where are you?"

"In some crappy motel on Hollywood Boulevard."

"Get over here fast! You'll stay with me and Reece. Hurry up, I'll make you breakfast."

"Since when did you cook?"

"This is California. I take it from the freezer, put it in the toaster and call it waffles. You'll *love* my cooking!"

He made it over to her apartment as fast as possible, parking his car on the street.

She greeted him at the door, almost jumping up and down with excitement. Throwing her arms around him she hugged him tightly and dragged him inside.

"It *was* you, wasn't it? You broke into my apartment."

He grinned. "What could I do? You weren't around, so I spent the night here, an' when I came back the next day the Super wouldn't let me in."

"Don't mess with Rasta," she giggled. "He's a wild man."

They went into the tiny kitchen where she poured him coffee and toasted her famous frozen waffles.

"So where were you?" he asked again.

"Guess?" she said, grinning happily.

He hated playing games. "I can't guess."

She took a deep breath. "I got married."

Oh great. "You did?"

"Yes – me and Reece got married in Las Vegas." She looked at him with a half-guilty, half-delighted expression – seeking his approval. "Oh, Nick, I hope you like him. He's helping me with my career – he really cares about me."

"Good. 'Cause if he didn't I'd have to kill him," Nick said, making it sound like a joke.

"He does, you'll see. I mean, when you first meet him you might think he's a tiny bit older than me, and y'know, like maybe his cowboy clothes are kinda silly, but he's gonna help me make it big."

"If you say so."

Her marriage had taken him by surprise. He'd imagined them sharing an apartment and hanging out together just like Chicago. Now she had a husband and there was no way he could stay.

He tried to find out more. "What does this character do?"

"Personal manager," she said, proudly.

"Who does he manage?"

"Who do you think? *Me*, of course!"

Of course. "So how does he make money?"

She waved her hands vaguely in the air. "I don't know, he has an office he goes to. We don't discuss money. He always has enough."

Sometimes his sister was extremely naïve, how could she not know what her husband did?

"You'll stay here," she said. "The couch turns into a bed – you'll be very comfortable."

It was different now, he was certainly glad to see her, but he didn't plan on moving in. "No, it won't work out – not with you bein' newly married an' all."

She couldn't hide her disappointment. "You've *got* to stay here, Nick."

How could he resist her big brown eyes? "Maybe just for tonight, but then I'll find my own place."

"You can listen to my tapes," she said, proudly. "They're professional. I'm a real singer now."

"Yeah?" He remembered her singing debut at Q.J.'s – a total disaster.

"I've been taking lessons," she said. "Reece has a record company interested in cutting a demo with me. Oh yes, and when we were in Vegas I met a couple of the talent bookers at the big hotels, and they might hire me to sing in one of the lounges."

"Sounds great."

"And it's all because of Reece."

"I'm glad you're happy."

"So what made you come to LA? I thought everything was going so well in Chicago."

Yeah – going so well – all the way to nowhere.

"I finally decided I hadda give acting a shot. You know it's what I've always wanted to do."

"This is the right place. Maybe Reece can be your manager, too."

Sure. Bring him in on a family package.

When Reece arrived home he and Nick sized each other up, circling warily.

Nick thought Reece looked like a dumb asshole with his fringed suede jacket, stupid cowboy hat and droopy moustache. Not good enough for Cyndra by a long way. And too old.

Reece was relieved to discover that Nick was white. All day long his imagination had been running riot – Cyndra's brother had been getting bigger and blacker as the day progressed. Now here was this skinny white kid, and he didn't feel threatened at all.

"What do you do, Nick?" he asked, going for the friendly brother-in-law approach.

"I was running a bar in Chicago, but I came out here to get into acting."

Reece couldn't help himself. "Yeah – you and every other schmuck in town."

"Excuse me?" Nick said, holding his temper in check because he didn't want to upset his sister.

"Oh . . . no offence. I mean kids come to Hollywood all the time tryin' to make it. Everyone wants to be a star."

"Oh, I'll make it," Nick said, confidently.

"That's nice," Reece replied. "Y'see, with me behind her, your sister's gonna be a big star."

"Is that why you married her?" he asked, hitting pay dirt.

Reece glared at him. "I married her 'cause I love her."

"That's nice," Nick replied, giving him a long hard stare. "Because if anyone ever hurts my sister, they're dead."

Reece couldn't wait to corner Cyndra in the kitchen. "How long is he gonna stay?" he asked, agitatedly.

"Only for the night," she said, not catching his concern. "I'm trying to persuade him to hang around longer. Why don't *you* talk to him?"

"Sure," he said, although he had no intention of doing so. The sooner the brother was out of their way the better.

The next morning Nick sat at the kitchen table studying the newspaper, circling apartment possibilities. "I fancy gettin' a place at the beach," he said.

"That's easy," Cyndra replied. "I've heard the rent is lower in Venice, we could look around later today."

"Good idea," he said, folding the newspaper.

Later, when they were driving along Santa Monica, he asked her if she ever heard from Joey.

She brushed back her long black hair. "I wish I did – I wrote him several times, he never bothered to reply. The last time I called, someone said he'd moved and left no forwarding address."

"Sounds like Joey."

269

She nodded, wistfully. "Sometimes I miss him. We shared so much together."

Nick felt the same way. "Yeah, we did, didn't we?" he said, thinking of the good old days when the three of them had faced the world alone – hitching rides, sleeping on park benches, sharing a motel room.

The first apartment they looked at was a rat-hole with broken windows, stained carpets and barely hidden roach motels. As soon as they got outside, Cyndra said, "Ugh, if that's the kind of places available I still say you should stay with us. Reece wouldn't mind. He likes you."

Sure, Nick thought. *Like a rat loves a cobra.*

"Will you think about it? Please?"

He promised he would, but of course he wouldn't. One night with Reece Webster was one night too many.

The second apartment they saw was better. Unfortunately, the rent was too high so they moved on. The next three were hopeless. On their sixth try they found a pleasant if somewhat run-down house on the beach in Venice divided into one room apartments.

The landlady – a slovenly woman in a grubby orange robe and fluffy carpet slippers – showed them the front-room apartment overlooking the beach. It was a large, sunny room with a small kitchenette.

"No bathroom?" Nick asked.

"You share with the other apartment in front," the landlady said, a cigarette dangling from the corner of her mouth.

"I dunno –"

"The tenant is never here – she travels all the time, so you more or less got it all to yourself."

He looked at Cyndra. "What d'you think?"

"It certainly beats anything else we've seen."

"You superstitious?" the landlady asked, picking tobacco from her teeth.

Nick noticed a hole in one of her slippers. "Why?" he asked, trying not to stare.

"'Cause a guy died in here last week. Hung himself." She hoisted an escaping bra strap. "I'm up-front about it – don't wanna fool you. If you're into that karma thing, you may not wanna live here."

He shook his head. "Karma thing? Shit, the rent is right an' it's on the beach – I'll take it."

Cyndra squeezed his hand. "Reece and I will help you fix it up. If we all come here next weekend with a bucketful of paint we can make it look terrific."

"You got yourself a job. And you –" he said, turning to the landlady, "got yourself a tenant."

After leaving a deposit he drove Cyndra back to Hollywood. She talked all the way about old times and the future and her career. Finally she just threw it into the conversation. "Did you ever hear from Lauren? Remember – that girl you liked in High school?"

As if he was going to forget. Was she crazy? He would *never* forget Lauren.

"Nope. I guess she dumped me," he replied, making it sound casual. "I wrote her a lot – she never replied."

"She probably married that big jerk she was engaged to," Cyndra said, rolling down the window. "Strick – wasn't that his name?"

"Stock," he corrected.

"Oh, yeah, Stock." She giggled. "Dumb oaf! Hey – remember that New Year's Eve when he broke your nose?"

"What a prick!"

"And then a few weeks later you beat *him* up."

"Those were the good times," he said, dryly.

"Would you ever go back?" she asked, wide-eyed.

"Would you?" he countered.

She hesitated. "Only if I was a star. A real big star. I'd be driven into town for a visit in a fancy limo – and I'd show 'em *all* who I was – every damn one of them." Now she was warming to her subject. "I'd be wearin' one of those big fox fur coats like Diana Ross, an' some kinda slinky sequinned dress. And I'd have a car load of presents for Aretha Mae and Harlan."

"Do you miss him?" Nick asked, pulling up at a stop light.

Her expression was wistful. "Sometimes I feel bad about leavin' him behind – kinda guilty."

"Yeah, I know what you mean. But we couldn't have taken him."

"I know."

"Hey – maybe we'll *both* make it big an' we can go back together. How's that?"

She nodded enthusiastically. "Yeah! We'll show that damn town a thing or two."

As he was dropping her off at her apartment they bumped into Annie Broderick getting into her car.

"I see you two found each other," Annie said. "Is he really your brother?"

Cyndra nodded happily, clinging to his arm. "Absolutely. Didn't you believe him?"

"You aren't exactly the same colour," Annie said, bluntly.

"We share the same father, not the same mother," Cyndra explained matter-of-factly.

"I was only looking out for your interests," Annie said, pushing her hand through her short red hair. "Didn't want some stranger breaking into your apartment."

"You looked after her interests all right," Nick said. "I almost had to sleep in my car."

"At least you've got a car. Think yourself lucky."

"Thanks, Annie," Cyndra said quickly – defusing the situation.

"What's *her* problem?" Nick asked, as soon as she left.

"It's tough being a single girl alone in LA."

"No boyfriend?"

"She's into her career."

"What does she do anyway? She said something about going to class the other night."

Cyndra looked amused. "What do you *think* she does? What do you think *everyone* does in LA? She's an actress of course."

"So – how do you get into this class of hers? Do you have to pay?"

"Dunno – never been. Talk to Annie about it."

"Maybe I will."

A few weeks later Nick had settled into the LA routine. He had his job at Glamour Limousines. He had his apartment at the beach. He'd even started to work out a little and eat healthier foods, and he spoke to Cyndra on the phone every couple of days.

All she could talk about was the deals Reece was about to make on her behalf. He didn't trust Reece. The guy had con artist written all over him – he'd seen enough cheap hustlers in Q.J.'s to recognize that combination of smarmy charm and bullshit a mile away. Still . . . it wasn't his business, Cyndra seemed happy enough.

One day he asked her for Annie Broderick's number.

"Why? Are you plannin' on taking her out?" Cyndra asked.

He hadn't considered it, but it wasn't such a bad idea if he wanted to find out more about her acting class. Plus he was feeling horny, oh was he feeling horny! Of course, Annie Broderick was not his usual type, too gamine looking and short – but he had to admit she did have a sensational body – and it had been too long between pit stops. He was even starting to miss DeVille.

Cyndra gave him Annie's number. He waited a day and called. "I'd like to buy you lunch," he said, expecting an immediate yes.

"Why?" she asked, suspiciously.

Oh, shit, he was going to have to work for it. "'Cause I kinda think we got off on a downer, an' I don't have many friends here."

She was silent.

He was prepared to work – but not that hard. "Hey – big deal – you wanna have lunch or not?"

She was not exactly filled with enthusiasm. "Maybe."

Didn't she realize this was Nick Angelo calling? "Maybe. What's that supposed to mean?"

"Well . . . can you come to where I work?"

"Tell me where –"

"The Body Beautiful on Santa Monica."

"Are you kidding me? What's the Body Beautiful?"

"It's a health club."

Glamour Limousines. The Body Beautiful. They sure loved to foster illusions in LA. "Okay," he said.

"I get a break at noon."

"I'll be there."

The Body Beautiful was a big white building on Santa Monica. The place was alive with people hurrying in and out, all wearing shorts, tank tops, cut-outs, tights, every kind of variation on work-out gear.

"Can I help you?" asked a California blonde, perched behind the reception desk, her perky breasts covered by a white Body Beautiful T-shirt.

"I'm looking for Annie Broderick," he said, checking out her attributes.

She caught him looking, fluttered long fake lashes and smiled. "Oh . . . you must be Nick."

He was surprised Annie had mentioned him – maybe she liked him better than she'd let on.

"Is she around?"

"She's getting changed. She'll be with you in a minute." The girl's smile brightened. "I understand you're new in town."

"Sort of."

"How did you meet Annie?"

"She lives in the same building as my sister," he said, noticing that she wasn't wearing a bra.

"Hmm . . ." she eyed him hungrily. "I wish *I* did."

He knew a come-on when it hit him in the face. "What's *your* name?" he asked, going along for the ride.

Annie cut him off at the pass by appearing at the reception desk. "Let's go," she said briskly, taking his arm and leading him out of the building.

"Where are we going?" he asked, thinking she looked healthy and glowing and really quite attractive – even if she wasn't his type.

"There's a health food place across the street. Have you ever tried a turkey burger?"

"Is that like a hamburger without the taste?"

She smiled. "Come on – you'll love it."

"I will?"

"Yes, you will," she said, firmly.

They crossed the street, entered the restaurant and sat at a window table. Annie immediately ordered two health burgers. "Turkey, soya and seasonings. It's the most delicious thing you've ever tasted," she assured him.

"I'm drooling!"

"You're funny."

They exchanged smiles.

"So," he said. "You work at a health club, eat healthy foods and exercise in the pool. What are you in training for – the Olympics?"

She tapped her fingers on the table. "I don't know if I told you or not, but I'm really an actress. That's why I have to stay in great shape."

"Isn't being a good actress enough?"

"Producers expect you to have a Raquel Welch body."

"In case you have to do a nude scene, huh?"

"Maybe."

"Would you?"

"If it was an integral part of the story."

He burst out laughing. "Come *on* – that's like me saying I read *Playboy* for the articles."

274

She couldn't help laughing too. The waitress delivered their turkey burgers to the table. Nick looked at his suspiciously.

"Go ahead, taste it," Annie encouraged.

"Can I have ketchup?"

"You can have anything you like."

"Anything?" he teased.

"Within reason," she replied, beckoning the waitress. "Susie, bring us a couple of glasses of the big A, oh, and a bottle of ketchup."

"You come here all the time, huh?"

"It's convenient." She paused for a moment. "Uh, Nick, I'm sorry I might have seemed a little tense with you when we first met, but I had no idea who you were. And it seemed kind of strange – you know, Cyndra being, well . . ." She hesitated, then blurted it out. "Black."

"Yeah – I see your point."

The waitress brought the ketchup and two large glasses of deep brown liquid.

He picked up his glass. "What's this?"

"Pure apple juice," she explained. "No preservatives. Drink up – you'll enjoy it."

"Jeez! I've *really* gotta get used to you."

"Maybe you'll have a chance," she said, casually.

Was he finally getting through? "Cyndra told me you go to acting class," he said, smothering his burger in ketchup.

"That's right."

He took a bite – it wasn't half bad. "Howdja get into that?"

She sipped her apple juice. "If you're not working you have to study, it's important to keep on learning."

"What kind of class is it?"

Her eyes shone with enthusiasm. "It's an actors' workshop. We do all kinds of interesting things. Scenes from plays and movies. Improvisation. A lot of working actors go there."

"Yeah?" he said, taking a gulp of apple juice. "Sounds interesting."

"It is."

He studied her pertly pretty face. "Have you ever had a professional job? Like in a movie or on television?"

She looked pleased that he'd asked. "As a matter of fact I've been in three commercials."

He was impressed. "I guess you've got an agent then?"

"How come all these questions, Nick?"

He decided to confide in her. "Why do you think? Listen, I had a great job in Chicago running a bar – I was the king of my own little kingdom. But ever since High school I've had a thing about acting."

"You can't just do it. You have to be good."

"Oh, I'm good," he boasted.

"Glad to hear it, because one thing you need is plenty of confidence." She sighed. "It helps when you get rejected twenty times a day."

He had no intention of getting rejected. Once he got through the door – whoever's door it was – he was going to make such an impression they'd never let him go.

"I'd like to come to class with you – I could sit in back and watch."

"I don't see why not. You're allowed to observe two sessions, after that you have to pay – that's if Miss Byron accepts you."

"Who's Miss Byron?"

"Joy Byron – the best acting coach in town."

If she was the best he wanted her. "When can I come?"

"How about tonight?"

"No, nights are out. I got this gig driving for a limo company."

"I had a friend who sold a script to a producer while he was driving him to Santa Barbara."

"Really?"

"It can happen. You have to find out exactly who you've got in the car and go for the pitch. That's what my friend says. It certainly worked for him. His point is if they can afford to hire a limousine they must be someone."

He remembered Luigi and his ferocious scowl. "I got strict orders not to talk to the paying customers."

"You don't look like a man who follows orders."

She was right, it was about time he found out who he was driving and did something about it.

"I'll let you in on a little secret about this town," Annie confided, her bright eyes meeting his. "I've been here three years, and if there's any way you can make a connection, go for it. Don't let anything stand in your way."

He leaned across the table and took her hand which was surprisingly small and soft. "Thanks, I like good advice."

They finished lunch, and as they were parting company she suggested he might want to come to class with her on the following Saturday.

"Sounds good," he said. "I'll pick you up."

"Okay. I'll see you at four."

That night, when Luigi assigned him Mr Evans again, he was not exactly thrilled. This Evans guy was a deadbeat, no connections to be had there.

It turned out to be the same routine as before. The same bad-tempered face, the same briefcase clutched to his side, the same non-tip. Nick had a good mind to tell Luigi he didn't want to drive him again. He'd talked to the other drivers and found out that most customers handed out cash tips on top of the percentage added to the bill. No chance with this tight-wad.

"That Evans guy is a real cheapo," he complained to Luigi when he dropped the limo back. "Do me a favour an' stop assigning me to him."

"Am I hearin' right?" Luigi demanded, eyes bulging. "Mr Manfred gives ya a job outta the kindness of his fuckin' heart – an' now you're mouthin' off an' tellin' me who ya will an' who ya won't drive."

"I'm entitled to an opinion," he said, stubbornly.

"You're entitled t'suck my nuts if I tell ya to," Luigi steamed.

"I guess I'll pass on that tempting offer."

Luigi made a rude gesture. "In your eyes, punk."

The next night when he reported for work Luigi greeted him with a knowing sneer. "Mr Manfred wants ta see ya."

"What about?"

"Do I strike ya as a fuckin' information centre?"

Manny Manfred greeted him looking fatter than ever. It didn't seem possible, but could he have gained another twenty pounds?

"How's it goin', Nick?"

Surprise. The fat man remembered his name.

"Okay," he said, carefully.

"An' the actin' thing? Any auditions yet?"

"I'm lookin' into it."

"That's the way ta do it," Manny said, reaching into a bowl of jelly beans, grabbing a handful, and promptly stuffing them into his surprisingly small pink mouth.

Nick noticed he was wearing a Rolex – the heavy gold watch gleamed as it caught the light.

"I talked to Q.J.," Manny said, munching away.

"You did?"

"He likes ya."

"I know."

"He trusts ya."

"I should hope so. I worked for him nearly four years."

Manny spat out a red jelly bean. It landed with a disgusting blob of spit on his huge knee. He brushed it to the floor.

"Loyalty an' trust – them's the things ya can't buy."

"Right." Nick waited for the pitch he knew was on its way.

"So . . ." Manny said, not disappointing him, "I gotta proposition."

"Yeah?"

"Ya look like a smart kid."

Jeez! Compliments! From the fat man himself.

Big fucking deal.

"I can handle myself," he said, carefully.

"That's what I like t'hear," Manny said, beaming. "Soon as Luigi told me ya was complainin' I knew ya wasn't satisfied sittin' behind the wheel of a car – drivin' some rich motherfucker ya knows you're better than."

"It's a job."

"An' so's what I got in mind for ya."

"Is it legal?"

"Are you bothered?"

"Whyn't you tell me about it?"

Chapter 42

Lauren had been out with Jimmy Cassady several times – four dates exactly – the last two ending with a chaste kiss on her front doorstep. Now they were on their fifth date and she knew that tonight he expected more. Not that he actually came out and said so – he wasn't that obvious – but she picked up little signs here and there, and after a quiet dinner in a romantic Italian restaurant he hailed a cab, and instead of giving the driver her address he gave him his.

"I want you to hear the new Joni Mitchell album," he said, putting his arm around her.

"I'd love to," she replied.

Well, Roberts, she thought. *What are you going to do?*

I don't know.

You'd better decide.

I can't.

Why?

Good question. Why couldn't she decide?

The answer came out of nowhere.

Because I still love Nick Angelo.

"You're quiet tonight," Jimmy said, taking her hand in his. "Something I said?"

She shivered, trying to block the memory of Nick from her mind. "No, I'm tired. I had a tough day."

"Too tired to listen to Joni Mitchell?"

He was asking one question with his mouth and another with his eyes.

"I can't think of anything I'd rather do," she replied, while voices continued to scream inside her head.

All he wants is a quick lay – that's what they all want.

You sound like your mother.

279

I'll sound like her if I want!

"We're here," he said, paying the driver and helping her from the cab.

She followed him into the elevator – filled with trepidation. Jimmy Cassady seemed like a genuinely nice guy.

Sure, they all do until they get what they want, and then they dump you, run out on you, leave you alone and pregnant. Leave you . . . leave you . . . leave you . . .

"What are you thinking?" he asked, squeezing her hand.

"Nothing," she said, banishing Nick from her thoughts and concentrating on Jimmy. What did she know about him? Not that much. He'd told her he'd come to New York from Missouri seven years ago and started out as a photographer's assistant – moving out on his own four years later. For the past three years he'd been building his reputation as one of the most innovative photographers around with his stark black and white images.

In the course of talking to some of the girls she'd discovered nothing about his personal life. Usually the models gave chapter and verse on every photographer they'd worked with – including graphic details of size, sexual preferences and how many times they liked to do it a night. There were no reports on Jimmy – except from Nature, who'd worked with him once and then announced, wide-eyed with surprise, "Well, 'e's gotter be gay, ain't 'e? 'Cause 'e 'din't even hit on me once!"

After their fourth date, when he'd dropped her outside her apartment with only a kiss, she'd thought that maybe Nature was right. But tonight she knew it wasn't so; he had that look in his eyes and she was well aware he was all set to make the big move.

His apartment wasn't an apartment at all – it was loft space, divided into compartments by six-foot stucco walls that ended long before the soaring ceilings. His furniture was minimal modern – everything either black, white or stainless steel. Stark, like his photographs.

"This place is amazing," she exclaimed, wandering around taking in every detail. "Did you design it yourself?"

He laughed. "No professional decorator could come up with this. Besides, I happen to like it."

"So do I," she said, exploring further. "But you have to admit – it *is* different."

"That's *why* I like it," he said, following her into the compact stainless steel kitchen. He moved closer. "That's why I like you," he added, unexpectedly pinning her up against the cold steel of the refrigerator door and kissing her on the mouth. No, *Would you like a drink? Can I give you a tour?* He didn't even bother putting on the Joni Mitchell album he'd been talking about all night.

Just the kiss.

Hard and sensual. Not like his usual goodnight peck. This was definitely the real thing.

She gasped for breath, but he didn't stop.

For a moment she resisted, her body rigid – not allowing him to get too close.

He persevered, and slowly she felt herself begin to respond – a warmth sweeping up her body – a tidal wave of desire so long repressed that it took her by surprise – rendering her helpless to resist.

After a few minutes his hands moved down to her breasts – touching – feeling – stroking.

She began a half-hearted objection. "Jimmy . . . I don't know –"

"I do," he said surely, hands creeping down the neckline of her dress, moving around to the back and unsnapping her bra.

And all the while his lips remained on hers, his insistent tongue exploring her mouth, his warm breath all over her.

She threw her head back and surrendered as he exposed her breasts and his lips travelled slowly down to the tips of her nipples.

Gently he pushed both her breasts together, tongueing her nipples simultaneously as his hands worked the zipper on her dress and it fell to the floor.

She closed her eyes trying not to think of Nick, trying to forget him once and for all. This was all happening so fast, and yet she felt powerless to stop him.

"You smell so good," he whispered.

It didn't matter any more, nothing mattered. She'd reached the point of no return, he could do whatever he liked.

He picked her up and carried her to the bedroom, placing her gently in the middle of his large water-bed.

She lay back and opened up her soul to him. There was no choice any more, she'd been lonely too long.

And Nick Angelo was never coming back.

"I'm getting married," Lauren said, nervously clenching her fists.

Samm glanced up from a contract she was studying and

raised her oversized horn-rimmed glasses. "What did you say?"

"Married," she replied, as if this wasn't a major announcement.

Now she had Samm's full attention.

"I don't believe it!" the older woman said, placing her glasses on the desk.

"It's true," she managed, sounding a lot calmer than she felt.

Samm reached for one of her long thin cigarillos, her blood red nails lethal weapons. "And may I ask to whom?"

"Jimmy Cassady."

"*My* Jimmy Cassady?" Samm was very possessive of all the photographers who worked with her girls – she considered every one of them belonged to her.

Lauren nodded. "I guess so."

Samm was silent for a moment while she digested this unexpected information. Then she said, "Isn't this rather . . . sudden?"

Lauren felt like a school kid standing in front of the principal. Why was she putting herself through this? She didn't owe Samm an explanation. "We've been seeing each other for six weeks," she said. *And sleeping together for three* – she wanted to add, but didn't. Her sex life was her business.

Samm picked up a thin gold pen and tapped it on her lacquered desk top. "Six weeks is not a long time to get to know someone."

"Long enough for me," she replied, thinking that she certainly didn't need a lecture from Samm.

"Don't you think –" Samm began.

"Congratulations would be nice," Lauren snapped, shattering her "good little Lauren" image once and for all. "Oh, and I'm giving you two weeks notice – Jimmy wants me to work with him."

Samm was too wise to say another word – Lauren was obviously under Jimmy Cassady's influence and nothing she said would make any difference. Men! They'd caused her more problems over the years than she cared to think about. Usually it was the models who got hooked by a glamorous playboy or some fast-talking would-be manager. She certainly hadn't expected Lauren to get swept away.

Samm might be sceptical, but the girls in the office thought it was sensational news. Pia seemed especially pleased for her. And when Nature heard, she made a special trip to the office, shrieking, "This is bleedin' smashing! So, 'e's not a fag after all!"

Trust Nature to come right out with it.

From the moment they'd slept together Jimmy had started talking about marriage. He wanted to do it immediately. "What's the point of waiting?" he'd demanded.

The point of waiting, she'd thought, *is to decide whether we're making a mistake*. Samm was right – six weeks was not a lot of time to get to know somebody. But the more she got to know Jimmy, the more special she decided he was, and certainly different from the other men she'd come across in New York.

Even so, at first she'd said no.

"Why not?" Jimmy persisted.

She could think of no good reason.

He'd pressed until she'd finally changed her mind. Jimmy was attractive, serious about his work, a good lover, and he genuinely seemed to care for her. Besides, she was swept up in the excitement of his desire. And the thought of belonging to someone and being safe was too tempting to resist.

She didn't love him – whatever love was. But maybe that would come in time.

Once she'd said yes, they both agreed they should do it as soon as possible. For one rash moment she'd considered calling her aunt and uncle in Philadelphia, but then she'd changed her mind. Who needed Brad knowing? Besides, both she and Jimmy wanted the ceremony to be as simple as possible.

"What about your family?" she'd asked.

"We lost touch," he'd said, vaguely.

"How come?"

He'd raised an eyebrow. "Am *I* questioning *you*?"

Soul mates.

Pia announced she wanted to throw her a wedding shower, but she was soon overruled by Nature, who decided a proper bachelor-girl bash was more in order. "You deserve it," Nature announced cheerfully. "You work ever so hard lookin' after us all, now it's our turn to do something for you."

In a way Lauren wished she hadn't told anybody. Maybe it would have been better if they'd just done it quietly with no fuss.

Too late now, Nature had plans.

Lauren protested, but Nature – as usual – refused to listen. "Be at me apartment next Saturday at six o'clock. And don't expect to get home until three in the morning – that's if you're lucky!"

There was no point in fighting Nature, she was like a great

big Mack truck – the safest thing to do was climb aboard and enjoy the ride.

As the days passed Lauren realized leaving Samm's was going to be a wrench – she'd made so many good friends there. But Jimmy assured her it would be fun for her to help him out at his studio, and it didn't seem like such a bad idea.

Meanwhile there was so much to do. They had to take blood tests, get a wedding licence – and finally she went shopping with Pia, searching for the perfect outfit which Samm insisted on paying for.

By the night of the wedding shower she was a wreck. Nature herself was in top form – screaming and yelling all over the place. She'd ordered a convoy of limos for the night, and following behind the limos she surprised everyone with six leather-jacketed bikers sitting astride their Harleys.

"Ain't it nice 'aving an escort," Nature joked, winking conspiratorially at the convoy of guys. "Muscles an' black leather – me favourite combination!"

First they went to an Italian restaurant where everyone presented Lauren with their gifts. She managed to put a good face on it, opening the presents one by one and dutifully exclaiming that each gift was exactly what she wanted.

Nature presented her with a huge black vibrator, which elicited much mirth around the table.

When she was finished with her gifts, one of the better-looking bikers swaggered into the restaurant, hit a button on a tape machine, and proceeded to do a raunchy strip to the Stones "Satisfaction". He was merely the appetizer, because from there they all piled back into the limos and headed for a male strip club.

Lauren watched in fascinated amazement as the guys at the club proudly presented their assets – thrusting them into the eager audience's faces.

"Too many dicks," Pia said, solemnly.

"Don't you mean assholes," Lauren murmured, longing to get out of there.

Nature was in her element – hooting and hollering at the guys to take it off. Sticking ten dollar bills down their skimpy G-strings – loving every minute.

At last it was over, and they dropped her back at her apartment. She fell thankfully into bed. As far as she was concerned the evening had been a nightmare. Still . . . they'd meant well, and she was lucky to have people who cared about her.

The next day she gave up her apartment and moved all her things over to Jimmy's place. That night they ate dinner by candle-light and made love. For the first time since leaving Bosewell Lauren felt she finally belonged somewhere, and she knew that her decision to marry Jimmy was the right one. She fell asleep in his arms, happy and content.

The day before the wedding Pia picked her up and took her over to her place. "You can't stay with your future husband the night before the wedding," she scolded. "It's big bad luck."

In the morning Nature arrived, breezing through Pia's apartment, bossily taking over. "'Ere," she said, removing a large sapphire ring from her finger. "You'll wear this. It covers borrowed, blue *and* new. Now all we've got to worry about is getting you something old."

Pia produced a pair of exquisite filigree ear-rings. "These were my great-grandmother's," she said, handing them over. "I'd be honoured if you wore them."

Lauren put on the oyster satin suit Samm had bought her, Pia's ear-rings and the sapphire ring.

Nature peered at her critically. "I wish you'd let *me* fix your 'air."

"I like it just the way it is."

"Yeah, all neat and understated," Nature replied. "Unlike me," she added, fluffing out her blonde curls.

"You look beautiful, Lauren," Pia whispered.

They set off in a stretch white limousine – Nature's choice. "Shut your eyes and pretend you're a rock star," she giggled.

By the time they arrived at City Hall Lauren's stomach was doing somersaults. The driver helped her out of the car and she entered the building, flanked by her friends.

They bumped into Samm by the elevator. "How are you feeling?" Samm asked, chic as ever in a scarlet Chanel suit.

"Nervous," she replied.

"It doesn't show. You look lovely."

"Thanks." Her throat felt dry as she clutched her corsage of white orchids and wished that everything was over and done with.

Pia and Nature ushered her into a side room to await the arrival of the bridegroom. Jimmy was coming alone. When she'd asked him who his best man was, he'd replied he didn't want one. "I travel alone," he'd said.

Fine with her. Maybe that's why they got along so well.

She couldn't sit still. She got up, pacing nervously up and

down the small room, her mind racing this way and that. A few minutes seemed like an eternity.

Nature kept checking her watch. "'E's bleedin' late, ain't 'e," she finally said in an exasperated voice.

"Maybe it's the traffic," Pia said, giving her a warning look.

"Yeah, well, bleedin' traffic or not, 'e's late. S'not nice to be late for your own wedding."

After fifteen minutes, Pia slipped out of the room, found a pay phone and called Jimmy's apartment. There was no reply.

Nature cornered her in the corridor. "What the 'ell's going on? Where *is* the scummy bastard?"

Pia shook her head. "I have no idea."

"You wait downstairs," Nature said, "while I keep 'er busy here."

Another twenty minutes passed and Jimmy still hadn't shown up. Pia called Samm out of the main room and Nature joined them in the corridor for a conference.

"Looks like 'e's dumped her," Nature said. "What a low-life!"

"Has somebody called his apartment?" Samm asked.

"Yes, I did," Pia said. "There's no answer."

Samm shook her head, she'd had a feeling about Jimmy Cassady.

"What shall we do?" Pia asked.

"Fuck 'im!" Nature said, cavalier as usual. "Men! They're all no bleedin' good."

By the time an hour had elapsed it was obvious Jimmy wasn't coming. Lauren took the news stoically, although she was breaking up inside.

Pia, Nature and Samm accompanied her back to his apartment. There was a note pinned to the refrigerator door.

Sorry! he'd scrawled. *Gone on assignment to Africa. Be back in a few months. You can stay at the apartment until you find somewhere.*

Lauren read the note twice before handing it to the others.

"Bastard!" exclaimed Nature, scanning it quickly.

"Oh, dear," said Pia.

Samm was more eloquent. "That lousy son-of-a-bitch!" she said, forcefully. "I never trusted him."

Lauren felt totally blank. Another rejection. It didn't matter. Nothing mattered. One thing she knew. She would never trust another man again. Never. Of that she was sure.

Chapter 43

The proposition was this – Manny wanted him to take the limo across the border into Tijuana, pick up a passenger at the Tijuana Sunset Hotel and then drive back into the US. It sounded simple enough.

"That's it?" Nick asked, warily.

"Easy, huh?" Manny leaned back in his oversized chair, double chins wobbling.

"Sure," he replied. "Depending on what the passenger's carrying."

"Let's make it none of your business," Manny said, rubbing his chin. "That way you don't know from nothin'."

Nick decided he wouldn't trust Manny with a nun, but he sensed an opportunity to make money, and since his stash from Chicago was fast running out he investigated further. "How much?"

Manny shot him a knowing wink. "More than you're making now."

"Listen," he said, "I don't know what I'm bringing in, but I ain't crossin' the border for less than two grand."

"That's a lotta money."

"The way I'm hearin', it's a lotta risk."

"Okay, okay," Manny said, grudgingly.

The fat man had agreed too readily. Nick immediately wished he'd asked for more. "When's this supposed to take place?" he asked.

"Sometime next week. Things are bein' set up now."

"Who's the passenger?"

"A school kid."

"A school kid?"

"Yeah – wanna make something outta it?"

Nick knew he was stepping on to dangerous territory. There was no way Manny's activities were legal. He took a beat. Did he really want to get involved?

Yeah – for two grand he *really* wanted to get involved.

"I got somebody for ya t'meet," Manny said.

"Who?"

"A special broad, so keep her outta your dirty mind."

Oh. Like he was going to hit on a girl that had anything to do with Manny. Big chance.

Manny hit a buzzer and the door opened.

"Say hello to Suga," Manny said, presenting her as if she was the Queen of England. "Suga an' me – we bin together five years. Married for two," he added, proudly. "Happy as a coupla sandbugs."

Suga was twenty-three, looked sixteen, and acted as if she was twelve. Her choice of dress was black rubber, barely making it to the top of her chubby thighs, worn with lace-up white boots and as much fake gold jewellery as she could manage without falling down. She was top heavy, short, her flesh was rosy and her hair shoulder-length spikes of dyed blonde with inch-long black roots. She smoked non-stop, chewed gum, and bit her nails.

Stationing herself next to her husband she stared balefully at Nick. She had small beady eyes surrounded by too much make-up and mean little lips curved in a perpetual sneer.

"Suga's a classy broad," Manny said. "Helps me with a lotta things."

Yeah, Nick thought. *I bet she does.*

"I figured you two should meet," Manny continued, touching his wife on the thigh, "on account a it's Suga you'll be collectin' in Tijuana."

Jesus Christ, what was he getting into? "You said it was a school kid."

"Don't worry – she'll be dressed like one."

"You're putting me on?"

Suga spoke up, her voice a shrill squeak. "Screw you," she said, chewing gum like an angry cow.

This was going to be some trip.

Joy Byron's acting class was held in a disused warehouse on the wrong side of Wilshire. Joy Byron herself was an elderly English woman with a voice like a hack-saw. She wore a long flowered dress on her bony body and carried a parasol, giving her a somewhat eccentric Mad Woman of Chaillot look.

Nick would never admit it to anyone, but he was dead nervous. "So, uh, like what do I do?" he asked, trying to sound cool.

"Nothing," Annie said. "You're merely an observer. Will you relax?"

"Okay, okay," he said, wondering why he was putting himself through this.

She grabbed his hand. "Come on, I'll take you over to meet her."

Reluctantly he allowed himself to be led across the room.

"Miss Byron," Annie said. "This is a friend of mine. Is it okay for him to sit in?"

Joy Byron turned around and studied him. "And what is your name, young man?" she asked, in imperious tones.

"Nick," he mumbled.

"Do we have a surname?"

"Nick Angelo."

"Lose the 'O'." She gestured theatrically. "Nick Angel, I can see it on marquees now."

"Yeah?"

"But of course." She turned to speak to another student and Annie pulled him away. "She likes you."

"How do you know?"

"I can tell."

He grinned. "Yeah, well, I'm not just anybody."

"That's what I like about you, Nick – no ego. Come on, we'll grab a seat over here."

His eyes darted around the large musty room. There were a bunch of guys in T-shirts and jeans doing their best Brando imitations, and lots of pretty girls who seemed to take themselves much too seriously. Actors. Just like him.

When everybody was settled Joy Byron stood at the front and addressed her class. "Today we shall speak about motivation," she said. Long dramatic pause. "When I worked with Olivier, Gielgud, in fact *all* the English greats, one of their first thoughts before going on stage was motivation, motivation, what exactly *is* my motivation."

Nick could see this was going to be different from drama classes with Betty Harris way back in Bosewell. And he was right. Joy Byron revelled in lecturing her students on what she thought they should know, talking a great deal about her fabulously successful career in England.

"Was she some kind of big star over there?" he whispered to Annie.

Annie nodded, eyes shining. "She's a great teacher."

"How come she gave it up?"

"I don't know."

Halfway through the class Joy summoned two of her students to the front and instructed them to improvise a scene about anger. Nick watched carefully as the two young actors went to work.

They were good.

He was better.

After they were finished Joy stood up again, gave a long harsh critique and then invited the class to comment. Some of the students couldn't wait to pick the two actors to pieces, while a few of them were quite flattering.

"You have to take the good with the bad," Annie murmured. "Everybody has their say. Believe me – it can be brutal up there."

He couldn't make up his mind whether to get involved in this shit. Acting in Bosewell was one thing, but this was Hollywood and who needed criticism?

On his way out Joy Byron stopped him, laying a dainty blue-veined hand on his arm.

"You've got the look, dear boy," she said, in her gravelly English voice.

"I have?" he replied, carefully.

"Oh, yes. I always recognize it," Joy said. "You've got the look."

He took a deep breath, inhaling her scent of musty roses mixed with mothballs. "Yeah, well, uh . . . glad to hear it."

She fixed him with watery eyes. "On your next visit you'll perform something for me."

"I haven't joined the class yet."

"Ah, yes, but sometimes I accept students without fees. We'll see. Next time come prepared."

"What did she say?" Annie wanted to know as soon as they were outside. When he told her she got really excited. "My God, you never even did anything and you made an impression on her."

"Maybe she's horny," he joked.

Annie was unamused. "That's not funny," she said, sternly. "Joy Byron is a true professional."

He took her arm. "Hey – there's something I've been meaning to ask – do you have a permanent guy in your life?"

"Why?" she asked, suspiciously.

"I thought you'd help me out. Like if you don't have a boyfriend you'd come by my place on Saturday night."

There was a long pause before she answered. "Nick," she said hesitantly, "I'm not looking to get involved with anybody."

"Hey – who's asking? All I want you to do is read with me. I have to prepare something, don't I?"

"Oh," she was embarrassed at having gotten the wrong impression, "I'd be happy to."

Saturday night his landlady was having her usual weekend party. He ignored the hangers-on lingering outside and steered Annie straight through to his apartment. The smell of marijuana was overwhelming. "Don't breathe too deeply," he joked. "One lungful and you're stoned for the rest of the week!"

She walked over to the large windows overlooking the beach. "How did you find this place?"

"Cyndra helped me."

"Nice view."

"Yeah, I was lucky."

The landlady's stereo blasting reggae almost blew them out of the room.

"This is the down side," he explained. "She throws a party every Saturday. You gotta be in the mood." He opened his refrigerator and inspected the contents. "How about a drink? I got rootbeer or Coke. Take your choice."

"Both bad for you," Annie said. "I'll have plain water."

"Don't you do *anything* that's bad for you?" he teased, reaching for a glass.

"Not if I can help it," she said, primly.

He found his precious signed copy of *Streetcar*, and flipped it open to a scene he particularly liked, handing it to Annie. "How about I read Joy a scene from this?"

"Hmm," she flicked through the pages. "You want to do it with me?" she asked, settling on the couch.

"Do I want to do *what* with you?" he replied, still teasing.

Her cheeks were flushed. "Nick, get serious."

He moved in on her knowing he shouldn't. "I *am* serious," he said, sliding his arm around her shoulders and pulling her close.

She was vulnerable and jumpy as he began to kiss her. Feebly she tried to push him away.

"Relax," he coaxed, well aware he had her nailed. "You gotta have *some* fun in life," he added, pressing his lips down on hers.

Just as he was getting somewhere they were interrupted by a loud knock on the door. Annie seized the moment to wriggle out of his grasp and jump guiltily to her feet.

"Ignore it," he said. "It's probably someone looking for the john."

"You'd better see who it is," she said, glad of the distraction.

"Jeez, just when we were gettin' comfortable, huh?" he said, walking over to the door and flinging it open.

Standing there was DeVille carrying a suitcase.

"Hi, honey," she said. "I'm here."

Chapter 44

Pia wanted Lauren to stay with her, but Nature insisted she'd be more comfortable at her place. Frankly, Lauren couldn't care less where she went – Jimmy's behaviour had left her without any feelings. It didn't matter, nothing mattered. She packed up her things and moved into Nature's huge white apartment without an argument.

Nature was delighted. She led Lauren into the guest bedroom announcing proudly, "This is where me Mum stays. You'll like it. It's ever so cosy."

Lauren decided it was a good place to hide. Maybe she'd stay forever – who needed the real world?

Nature yelled at her assistant to cancel all her appointments for the rest of the week.

"You can't do that," Lauren protested. "You have the *Vogue* shoot, and the Antonio session for *Harper's*. You're booked solid."

"I can bleedin' do what I want," Nature replied, tartly. "I'm not a bloody work machine. I understand what you're goin' through – the truth is it 'appened to me once."

"What happened to you?"

"Course, it was when I was young an' innocent – ha ha!" Nature threw herself down on the bed, ready to talk. "There was this geezer I was seeing before I was a model – a right layabout. I worked in a 'airdressing salon, and this bloke used to come in all the time. He seemed ever so nice. And sexy – wow! Anyway, the truth is 'e dumped me – just like that. Ran off with me best friend an' married her. I bet 'e's sorry now – she's a fat old cow an' I'm a big star – well sort of. I never forgave 'im."

"I had no idea," Lauren murmured, sympathetically.

"I'm not gonna bloody advertise it, am I? After that I got meself discovered an' flown to New York. Never looked back.

Course me Mum's not thrilled – but *I* am. It's great gettin' away from the family. Where's your family anyway?"

"I don't have anybody," Lauren said, admitting it for the first time. "My mother and father are both dead."

"Oh, sorry, luv."

"That's all right."

Nature jumped up. "Well, listen, you're welcome to stay as long as you want."

And that's exactly what she did. For two weeks she hid away in the guest room, huddled under blankets watching television day and night, until Pia visited one day, marched into the room and said, "Okay, enough. Time to get back to work. Samm says your job is waiting."

"No." She shook her head. "Too many bad memories."

"You can't force her," Nature said, entering the room.

"Staying here doing nothing certainly won't help her," Pia said sharply, not appreciating Nature's interference.

Lauren spoke up, after all it was her they were discussing. "Pia's right. It's time I found an apartment and another job."

"Jobs aren't so easy to find," Pia warned. "If you're smart you'll come back to Samm's."

"I've got it!" Nature shrieked, joining in as usual. "I've bleedin' got it!"

"What?" Lauren asked.

"You'll work for *me!* You can be my new assistant. It'll be a lot more fun than sitting in an office picking up the bleedin' phone all day."

"I don't know," she said, unsurely.

Nature was on a roll. "So now you don't 'ave to move out. It'll be nice 'aving you 'ere permanently – someone to talk to when I get 'ome."

"Yes, very nice," Pia interjected. "Don't do it, Lauren. You'll be on call twenty-four hours a day."

"Well?" Nature questioned, flashing her big blue eyes.

Lauren shrugged; she had nothing else in mind. "Why not?"

Pia sighed, "You'll regret it."

"No, she bleedin' won't," snapped Nature.

And that was that.

Sometimes Lauren thought it was the best decision she'd ever made and sometimes she thought it was the worst. Working for

Nature filled her days, and living in the same apartment filled her nights. If she'd thought she had no life working at Samm's, she certainly had none at all working for Nature, although it was never boring.

Nature did not lead a dull life. As her personal assistant she was expected to do everything from collecting the dry cleaning to watering the plants. She soon delegated the duties she had no wish to do to the maid, and concentrated on getting Nature's life as organized as possible – which was not easy, because Nature was a true gypsy and had thrived on chaos for years.

"You're fantastic!" Nature said one day. "'Ow did I ever manage without you?"

"Beats me," she replied dryly, thinking was this her lot in life – to be the girl nobody could manage without?

Nature had aspirations to act. "Can't be a model forever," she confided. "I gotta grab all the opportunities I can."

"You're twenty-two," Lauren pointed out. "What's your hurry?"

"I won't look like this for long. Once the lines start 'appening, an' I get a bit of sag here and there, it'll be over."

"You're crazy," Lauren said. "You've got another twenty years of looking great."

Nature shook her head. "Twenty years? You must be jokin'! All those little sixteen-year-olds sneakin' up behind, sniffing at me heels – wanting what *I* got. This modelling lark ain't easy."

Lauren realized it was true – modelling was not easy, and the most successful girls worked hard to keep themselves at the top. Nature never allowed herself to gain an extra pound – every day – no matter how early she had to get up – she worked out for a solid hour, pushing her strength to the limit.

Emerson Burn arrived back in town from a world tour. Nature read about it in the *New York Post* and immediately hatched a plot. She had Lauren call his apartment.

"Tell 'im I wanna 'ave a dinner party for him."

"When?"

"Any night he likes. Now that 'e's dumped that stupid Selina cow I'm in with a chance."

Lauren called and spoke to his personal assistant who rudely informed her Mr Burn's social calendar was full.

She waited a day and phoned again saying it was Candice Bergen. This time she was put right through.

Emerson Burn sounded like a male version of Nature. "'Allo?"

"Emerson Burn?" Lauren asked, just to make sure.

"Candy Bergen?" he countered.

"No, this is Lauren Roberts – Nature's assistant. She'd like to invite you to dinner next week."

He sounded disappointed. "I thought you was Candy Bergen."

"Your secretary must have gotten your calls mixed up."

"Okay . . . dinner with Nature. She's on."

"What night?"

"Tuesday – eight o'clock. But only if she'll cook."

Lauren choked back laughter. Nature in the kitchen – that was a good one. "Do you have any special requests?"

"Yeah – tell 'er I want roast beef, Yorkshire pud and roast potatoes."

When Lauren informed Nature of his request she panicked. "Oh Gawd! I can't bleedin' cook. Can you?"

"Don't worry, we'll hire a caterer."

"I don't *want* a bleedin' caterer," Nature wailed. "This has gotta taste like a 'ome-cooked meal. Look – find a cooking school and learn – then I'll pretend I made it. 'Ow's that?"

Lauren laughed. "It's different."

And that's how she found herself attending a cooking class learning how to make roast beef and Yorkshire pudding. She learned fast.

The night of Nature's date with Emerson she prepared the meal, gave strict instructions how to serve it, and retreated to her bedroom in the back of the apartment.

At three a.m. she awoke, walked quietly out of her room preparing to turn the lights off in the living room, and discovered Nature and Emerson asleep on the white bear skin rug, naked and wrapped in each other's arms.

For a moment she stood quite still staring at them. Then she felt too much like an intruder and hurried back to her room, closed the door and attempted to sleep.

It was impossible. She knew the time had come to move on. No more hiding behind Nature. She had to resume living.

Chapter 45

On the morning of the Tijuana run Nick awoke at seven. He wasn't into getting up early, but today he was on edge and found it impossible to sleep.

DeVille lay quietly beside him. DeVille with her pale red hair and glorious white body. He hadn't sent for her, but she'd arrived anyway, and since she was standing on his doorstep he'd taken her in. He'd tried to explain to Annie, who'd pretended it didn't matter, grabbed her purse and run out of his apartment like she'd had a rocket up her ass.

He couldn't make up his mind whether she was angry with him or not. Probably she was. Women were like that – overly sensitive.

For a couple of days he'd lost himself in sex. It was so good it should be illegal – especially with DeVille, who knew everything he liked and made sure he was the happiest man on the block.

"I can get my own apartment if you want," she'd offered, not really meaning it.

"That's a good idea," he'd replied, not really meaning it either, and they'd fallen back into bed.

Now she'd been at his place for five days and he knew it was time for her to go – only he hadn't gotten around to mentioning it.

Tomorrow I'll do it, he thought. Give her fifty bucks and ease her out gently by telling her that living together was not a good idea on account of his career.

What career?

The career he was going to have after Joy Byron saw him perform and found him an agent – who in turn would secure him his first professional acting job.

Confidence, you had to have confidence – and he was brimming with it.

By eight o'clock he'd taken a run on the beach, eaten a healthy breakfast of bran and chopped bananas and got himself mentally ready for his first phone call of the day. He called Annie. She was suitably cold.

"Hey, listen," he said. "Remember I was supposed to work on some kinda scene for Joy Byron?"

"Yes?" she said in her *who gives a damn* voice.

"You promised to help me out. I haven't had a lot of time this week –"

"I can imagine," she interrupted.

"I've found the scene I want to do. I thought that I'd drop by tomorrow and read through it with you."

"I'm working tomorrow," she said, coolly.

"I'd really like to rehearse before I do it for Joy," he said, hoping to persuade her.

"Miss Byron," she corrected. "Nobody calls her Joy."

"You *will* read with me, won't you, Annie?"

"Did I say I would?"

Time to turn on the charm, not so easy over the phone – he did better in person. "Are you pissed at me?"

"Should I be?"

He shrugged, "I dunno." A short pause. "Hey – about DeVille arriving on my doorstep – she's an old girlfriend from Chicago who blew into town with nowhere to stay. She'll be moving on soon." He glanced over at DeVille – still asleep on his bed. DeVille wasn't moving anywhere.

There was a long awkward silence, finally broken by Annie. "I bumped into Cyndra yesterday," she said. "She'd like to hear from you."

"I've been meaning to call her."

"What are you waiting for? She *is* your sister."

"I'll call her tomorrow. I'm driving to Mexico today."

"Mexico?"

"Yeah, I'm picking up a passenger. Somebody's kid's getting out of boarding school."

"Boarding school – in Mexico?"

"You think I'm making it up?"

"I'm never sure what you make up and what's the truth."

He got off the subject. "So . . . can I see you tomorrow?"

There was another long pause before she finally said, "Okay, I guess so. Come by at five, we'll go to class together."

"I'll be there," he said, hanging up and deciding that after scoring the two grand he was going to tell Manny goodbye. One trip was enough. Soon he'd have an acting job and wouldn't need this crap.

Manny had told him to go out and buy a chauffeur's uniform. He'd done so reluctantly. Jeez! There was nothing worse than dressing up in a uniform, feeling like somebody's lackey.

The uniform hung in his closet. He took it out, looked at it, put it away and went back to bed.

DeVille groaned in her sleep as he snuggled up behind her, letting her know he was awake. Tomorrow he really would tell her to leave. May as well make the best of this last opportunity.

"I finally heard from your brother," Annie remarked, rubbing suntan oil on her legs.

"What's he up to?" Cyndra asked, turning on her lounger beside the pool. "I call him all the time – he's never home."

"That's because his girlfriend came in from Chicago."

Cyndra sat up. "*What* girlfriend?"

"Some tall showgirl type with long red hair."

"Jealous?"

"Who, *me*?"

"Come *on*, Annie. I *know* you like him."

"Well . . . I must admit I thought there might be something between us, but that was before I found out he was the Don Juan of the out-of-work actors."

Cyndra nodded knowingly. "Nick's always been like that. Back in High school he could have any girl he wanted."

"You should have warned me."

"I didn't think you were planning on getting involved."

"*You're* the one who gave him my phone number."

"I had a feeling you two might be good together."

"Listen, the *last* thing I need in my life is a guy who can't keep it in his pants."

Cyndra laughed. "Okay, okay, I get the message." She glanced up as Reece emerged from their apartment wearing a pair of striped madras shorts with several heavy gold chains swinging around his neck.

"Hi, Reece." Annie greeted him with a desultory wave. "Another hard day's work?"

"Don't look like *you're* exactly bustin' *your* ass," he said, throwing her a dirty look before settling down on the lounger next to Cyndra.

"Reece likes to work on his tan," Cyndra said, quickly.

"You don't have to explain nothin' to her," Reece snapped.

"I wasn't explaining."

Annie jumped up before they got into a fight. Lately she'd heard a lot of yelling coming from their apartment. "What's happening with that demo record you were supposed to do?" she asked.

"These things take time," Cyndra said.

Annie nodded. "I guess they do. See you guys later."

Luigi managed to ignore Nick when he arrived to collect the car. Nick ignored him back as he made his way through to Manny's office.

"The uniform suits ya," Manny wheezed, looking him up and down. "Now, make sure ya got this right. Ya drive across the border, pick up Suga from the hotel, an' drive straight back to LA. If they stop ya at the border ya don't know from nothing. Ya was hired to pick up a school kid." He sucked on his cigar. "Who was ya hired by?"

"Prince Limos," Nick said, reciting his part.

"Yeah – no mention of Glamour. Ya got the address I gave you?"

"All set."

"Did Luigi put new plates on the car?"

"They're on."

"Okay, you're ready."

Yeah, Nick thought. *As long as I don't get busted.*

What was he bringing back? He hoped it wasn't drugs.

Who was he kidding? Sure, it was drugs. What else could it be?

On the drive to San Diego he played Rolling Stones tapes non-stop, making the trip in record time. He was ahead of schedule, so he parked the car in an underground garage and sat in a Burt Reynolds movie killing time. After that it was all the way to Tijuana.

Once there he parked outside the hotel, slid inside and searched the lobby looking for Suga.

He couldn't see her. *Shit!* Manny had said she'd be standing right in front.

Yeah, sure.

Just as he was about to approach the desk an apparition snuck up behind him and tapped him on the arm. It was Suga, looking twelve. Scrubbed of make-up, her hair in braids, a school cap on her head and in full uniform she resembled a truculent tomboy.

"Are you blind?" she hissed from the corner of her sulky mouth. "I bin standin' here forever."

He did a double take – the transformation was quite remarkable.

"Pick up my goddamn suitcase," she commanded, marching outside.

He followed her, carrying the case which weighed a ton. Maybe he should spring it open before they crossed the border and check out the contents. For all he knew he could be carrying a goddamn body, it was heavy enough.

Suga stood next to the limo stamping her feet impatiently.

He sprung the trunk open, loaded the suitcase, then got into the driver's seat.

"Bust your ass outta here," Suga squeaked, jumping in the back. "I hate these runs – they make me wet my pants."

"How many times you made this trip?" he asked, sliding the car away from the kerb.

"Too many," she replied, popping bubble gum.

They drove in silence for a while until he couldn't contain himself any longer. "What's in the suitcase?"

"Did Manny say you could ask questions?" she snapped. "Whyn't ya just drive. You're making your money – what do you care?"

He eased the limousine along the crowded streets. Now he was getting nervous. Two grand was one thing, but it wasn't worth getting busted.

Yeah, well two thousand dollars is a lot of bucks, he reasoned. It would take months of real work at Glamour Limousines to score that kind of money – especially with clients like cheapskate Evans. Although right now, as he headed towards the border, Mr Evans seemed like a dream passenger.

Suga didn't care for his Rolling Stones tapes. "Turn that crap off," she whined. "I hate Mick Jagger."

He saw no reason to take her crap. "Anybody ever told you to shut up?"

"Oh," she said, sarcastically. "*You're* gonna tell me. Big fat chance."

"How much older than you is Manny?"

"Mind your fuckin' business."

"Why'd you marry him?"

"Get fucked."

So much for conversation with little Miss Charm.

There was a long line of cars at the border. It was getting dark and he was more nervous by the minute.

Suga sat in the back, chewing gum, perfectly calm.

By this time he imagined the suitcase was filled with cocaine. They'd throw him in jail for fifty years if he was caught. Never again. This was *it*.

By the time they reached the guard, he was sweating through his clothes.

The guard leaned down and looked through the window. "Do you have any fruits, vegetables or plants?" he asked, peering into the back of the car.

"No, just one juvenile delinquent I'm delivering to her parents," Nick said, pleasantly. Jeez, he actually sounded cool!

"Okay," the Guard said, walking away.

Okay? Did that mean they could go?

Apparently it did. He put his window up and drove the car out of there.

"Faster!' Suga urged from the back.

"I gotta stop an' take a piss."

"No!" she yelled. "Get away from the fuckin' border."

By the time they reached San Diego he was high. It was so easy, like nothing. Christ, he could make this trip twice a day if he had to. He checked out the rear-view mirror. Suga was busy wriggling out of her schoolgirl clothes and struggling into a short skirt and tight sweater.

"Hey –" he said. "Now you can tell me. What's in the case?"

"Two hundred and fifty thousand buckeroonies in cash," she said, casually. "Wanna take it an' run off together, Nick?"

"Are you shittin' me?"

She hitched her skirt down. "Would I do that?"

"No drugs?"

"You think I'd have anything to do with drugs?" she sniffed, indignantly. "What *I* need is to find me a guy with enough balls to split. Manny would track us, but we'd have the money, wouldn't we? We could vanish good."

Two hundred and fifty thousand dollars! Holy shit! What if he dumped *her* and took off by himself?

For a moment he thought about it. But only for a moment.

He had no desire to spend the rest of his life running from Manny Manfred.

"Well?" Suga challenged. "You got the balls or not?"

The little bitch was testing him so she could report back to Manny. "Whyn't you shut up," he said.

"Dumb prick," she muttered. "I meant it, you know."

He never found out if she was putting him on or not, because as soon as they got back to the garage she jumped out of the car and vanished.

Luigi opened the trunk, removed the suitcase and brought it to Manny's office.

"When do I get paid?" Nick asked, following him.

"Don't sweat it. Nobody's leaving town," Luigi said.

I made a mistake, he thought. *I should have gotten the money up front. Now they're gonna screw me.*

"I made the run, I took the risk. I want my money."

"Later," Luigi threw over his shoulder.

He followed him all the way into Manny's office where Luigi put the suitcase down. "I want my money," he repeated.

"Yeah, Nick, sure," Manny said, producing a thick bankroll and peeling off several hundred dollar bills. "Here ya go, ya did a nice job."

He didn't trust the fat man. Standing in front of his desk he counted the bills. "There's only one thousand here,' he said, when he was through.

"That's right," Manny answered, reaching for a handful of cashews. "A thousand for the first run, two grand for the second."

"No – we had a deal – two grand for this run."

"Tell ya what I'll do," Manny said magnanimously, crunching on the nuts. "I'll split the difference. Ya get fifteen hundred for this run, an' two an' a half for the next. How's that?"

Nick was angry. "Who the fuck d'you think you're dealing with?"

Manny's voice hardened. "Some punk kid who's lucky to have a job."

"I want my two thousand, Manny, or you'll regret it."

Manny's beady little eyes froze. "*I'll* regret it? You're *threatening* me?"

"I know what's in the suitcase."

"Howdja know that?"

Suga might be a pain in the ass but he wasn't about to put her away. "Do I get my two grand?"

303

Manny wheezed with laughter. "You're okay, kid. Q.J. said ya was." He peeled off several more bills and handed them over. "Ya can work for me any time."

Yeah, like he wanted to. Snatching the money he walked out.

"See ya tomorrow," Luigi called after him. "Mr Evans is comin' back t' town. Nine p.m. L.A.X. Don't be late."

Fuck Mr Evans.

Fuck Glamour Limousines.

He had his two grand – this was the last they'd see of him.

Chapter 46

"You can't leave," Nature shrieked.

"I have to," Lauren said.

"But why?" Nature demanded, petulantly. She was so used to getting her own way that she didn't understand the word no.

Nature was involved in a full-fledged affair with Emerson Burn. It was not peaceful – another reason why Lauren had decided to move on. Their screaming fights were legendary. Even worse, their passionate reconciliations.

Valiantly she tried to explain. "I feel like I'm living in your shadow. It's time I got my life back on track."

Nature pouted. "We're having fun, ain't we?"

"Yes, but it's not enough for me."

Reluctantly Nature accepted defeat. "What will you do? Work for Samm again?"

She shook her head. "I was thinking of starting my own business – kind of a . . . you know, like a Girl Friday."

"Girl Friday, what's that?" Nature asked, hooting with laughter.

"Someone who does everything. I'll put myself out for hire and people will pay me by the hour. I can even work for you occasionally."

"That's nice."

"Actually, I've been speaking to Pia and she's going to be leaving Samm's."

Nature raised a sceptical eyebrow. "Pia's quitting? Samm'll have a freaking fit."

Lauren hadn't planned on confiding in Nature, but now she couldn't stop herself. "We've already talked about going into business together. We'd call ourselves Help Unlimited."

Nature nodded. "Sounds good to me – but only if I can get you back any time."

Lauren grinned. "Pay my hourly rate and I'm all yours!"

Help Unlimited was an instant hit. Word travelled fast, and before they knew it Lauren and Pia were inundated with clients. In fact, so many, that after the first three months they had to hire two helpers. It was a hectic existence. One day Lauren found herself watering house plants in a Park Avenue duplex and the next organizing a fantastic midnight dinner for thirty on top of the Empire State building!

Pia had met a man she was crazy about. His name was Howard Liberty, and he was an executive with Liberty & Charles – one of the most prestigious advertising agencies in New York. Howard was short and sandy-haired with a pleasing personality. Lauren liked him immediately.

"Good, because we're talking marriage," Pia admitted, excitedly.

Nature's affair with Emerson Burn continued on its erratic course. Once in a while he used their services, but Lauren always made sure Pia dealt with him; somehow she never felt comfortable in his presence.

Every so often someone tried to fix her up even though they knew she wasn't open to a new relationship. She'd erected a wall around her emotional life and it was there to stay. All her energy was directed towards creating a successful business.

"What are you gonna do – stay celibate?" Nature demanded.

"I don't have to jump in and out of bed to be happy," she replied, calmly. "I'm building a business."

"You're *really* strange," Nature said, shaking her head. "No way *I* could go without sex."

Big surprise!

Pia and Howard fixed a wedding date.

"I hope this doesn't mean you'll be leaving the business," Lauren worried.

"No way!" Pia replied, adamantly. "I certainly don't plan on sitting home having babies."

"Good!" Lauren said, relieved.

One Monday morning Nature called at six a.m. Lauren groped for the phone in her sleep.

"It's me!" Nature screeched. "I'm in Vegas. I bleedin' got hitched, didn't I?"

"Hitched?"

"Married, of course! Me an' Emerson finally did it."

"Oh, no," Lauren mumbled.

"What do you mean, *oh no*? 'Ang out the flags. I'm bleedin' Mrs Emerson Burn, ain't I?!"

Lauren couldn't think of a worse combination. The two of them together were much too volatile – they'd kill each other. She struggled to sit up. "Why did you do it?"

"Oh, this is nice," Nature said. "You're the first person I call, an' all I get is negative shit. We're in *love*, Lauren. In love!"

"Do the press know?"

"Not yet."

"When they find out they'll be all over you."

"Emerson's calling 'is manager. I expect he'll arrange a press conference. Can you fly out here to be with me? I'll pay."

"You don't have to pay. If you want me, I'm there."

"We're flying back to LA this afternoon. Emerson's a bleedin' maniac at the tables – there's no controlling 'im. Gotta get 'im outta 'ere quick. Tell you what, why don't you meet us at 'is LA house tomorrow? Oh, an' do me a big favour."

"Name it."

"Call Samm, an' tell her. If I call 'er, she'll only scream at me."

Samm took the news stoically. It wasn't the first time one of her girls had run off and married a rock star, and it wouldn't be the last.

Pia wasn't thrilled when Lauren informed her she was flying to LA. "You know I'm getting married next week. I need you here," she said.

"I'll be back," Lauren assured her. "All the arrangements are in place – everything will go smoothly – and I promise you I'll be here."

"*Why* do you have to go?" Pia complained.

"Because Nature is my friend," Lauren said.

"Ha!" Pia exclaimed. "Nature likes you because you do things for her."

Trust Pia to be cynical.

"Thanks a lot."

Pia sighed. "What will you do? Sit by the pool watching them fight while I run the business all by myself?"

"Come on, Pia", she said, persuasively. "I've never been to LA. I'll only stay a few days."

By the time she'd organized her departure, Nature and Emerson's marriage had hit the airwaves in a big way. Even though Nature had said there were no press present,

307

photographs of them began appearing everywhere – Nature in a short white mini dress lovingly feeding Emerson wedding cake. Emerson in black leather, his mane of shaggy hair falling way below his shoulders. Nature grinning. Emerson scowling.

They looked happy.

They looked stoned.

Lauren sat on the American flight studying the *New York Post*. A picture of Nature and Emerson dominated the front page.

"Rock stars," sniffed a blue-haired woman in the next seat. "They're all degenerates, you know."

Lauren ignored the woman and closed her eyes. She was *en route* to LA. It was a long way from Bosewell.

Disembarking from the plane she felt like a movie star. A uniformed driver greeted her at the gate and accompanied her to the luggage carousel where she pointed out her one small suitcase.

He looked surprised. "That it?"

"That's it," she replied, sure it must be a disappointment for him having to meet a nobody like her. But he seemed quite cheerful as she followed him outside to the limo.

Everything in Los Angeles seemed bigger and better. The sky was bluer, the trees greener, and the limousine she climbed into was longer and more luxurious than any limo she'd ever seen. It was white with black windows, and inside there were little fairy lights dotted all around the sides.

"Ever been to LA before?" the driver asked, as they cruised along the freeway.

"Never," she replied, settling back into the luxurious leather upholstery.

"It's a trip," he said, peering at her through the rear-view mirror. "I've been out here ten years now. Came from Chicago. Name's Tucker."

"And you like it better here?" she asked, politely.

"LA life is easy."

"How long have you worked for Emerson Burn?"

"Six months. He's a good guy. Sometimes I get to travel with him."

"I guess his marriage surprised you."

Tucker laughed. "When it comes to rock 'n rollers, *nothing* surprises me."

Emerson lived in a mansion high in the hills of Bel Air. A guard waved Tucker through, and the huge gates closed behind them as the limo snaked its way up a long, winding driveway. At the top of the hill was the largest house Lauren had ever seen.

As soon as the limousine drew up to the front door Nature came running out, wearing a red polka-dot bikini and little else. "You're here!" she screamed, happily. "About bleedin' time." They hugged, warmly. "Come on in," Nature said, pulling her through the massive front door. "Welcome to me ever so humble home."

The house was a palace. High vaulted ceilings, old masters on the wall and heavy over-stuffed furniture. "Course," Nature said matter-of-factly, dragging Lauren through a domed ceiling hallway towards the pool in the back. "S'not exactly my taste, but I'll soon get 'im to change everything."

"It doesn't look like his taste, either," Lauren remarked, taking it all in.

"Some queen decorator did it," Nature said offhandedly. "Probably wanted to give 'im one." She laughed at the thought. "C'mon outside an' congratulate the bridegroom."

Emerson Burn rested on a lounger beside an enormous blue pool wearing nothing but a brief black Speedo bikini.

Lauren's eyes travelled to the bulge. Either he used padding, or everything you saw up on stage was the real thing.

His shaggy mane was bunched into a pony-tail emerging from a black baseball cap. Ominous black shades covered his eyes. On either side of him were small tables. One held a phone, a tall jug of apple juice, two bottles of Stolichnaya vodka and several glasses. The other table was piled high with scripts.

Nature bounced over. "You remember Lauren, don't you, darling?"

Emerson removed his shades and stared at her with his dreamy grey eyes.

Lauren stared back, wondering if he used mascara on his long curling lashes. "Uh . . . congratulations,' she mumbled.

"Thanks," he said, putting his shades back on and lifting his chin to catch more sun.

"Come back inside," Nature giggled. "I'll give you the grand tour."

By the time Nature had dragged her all around the huge mansion she was exhausted. "Can I take a shower?" she asked hopefully.

"Yeah, 'ave a sleep, too, 'cause tonight we're gonna party!"

"I didn't come here to party," she objected. "I came to help you out."

"Don't need any help, luv – Emerson's got sixty thousand people working for 'im. I'm entitled to 'ave a friend visit, ain't I? I just got married, for God's sake." She paused by a mirror in the hallway attracted by her own reflection. "Hmm . . . I'm gettin' fat," she remarked, pinching her curvaceous waistline.

"No, you're not," Lauren said, firmly. "How can you say that?"

"It creeps up on you, luv," Nature replied, frowning as she turned this way and that – inspecting her body. "Oh, by the way, what did Samm say?"

"She wasn't exactly ecstatic."

"I *bet* the old bag wasn't. Did you tell 'er to cancel all me bookings for the next month?"

"No, I thought we'd discuss it first."

"There's nothing to discuss."

"Just because you're married doesn't mean you should give up your career."

"Who's giving it up? But I ain't workin' me bleedin' arse off when I can stick with Em." She lowered her voice to a confidential whisper. "'E can't be trusted, y'know. 'Ave you any idea what happens on these tours? Rock stars got dumb little groupies crawlin' all over 'em like bleedin' fungus. I'm gonna travel with 'im, protect me interests."

"You won't be very popular if you cancel your bookings."

"This ain't a popularity contest," Nature retorted, flinging open a door and leading Lauren into a large sunny room overlooking the pool. "'Ere's your room."

"Oh my God! It's bigger than my apartment!"

"Everything's bigger and better in California," Nature announced. "You'll soon get used to it. How long can you stay?"

"Three days."

"You 'ave t' stay at least a week."

"I can't run out on Pia."

"She'll manage."

"Three days, Nature."

"Four days."

"Okay, deal."

Nature smiled, knowingly. "By that time you'll be beggin' to stay longer. 'Ave a lie down – someone will wake you at six."

Lauren took a shower in the marble bathroom and then lay in the middle of the king-size bed. Within minutes she was asleep.

When she awoke it was late in the afternoon. She wandered over to the window and observed Emerson Burn in the pool. He was swimming lengths as if his life depended on it. Anything to keep in shape.

Her first Hollywood party and everyone was dressed to overkill. The mansion, owned by a record tycoon, was bigger and better than Emerson Burn's. Servants abounded.

"'Ave a gander over there," Nature said, nudging Lauren sharply in the ribs. "It's Jack bleedin' Nicholson, ain't it? Wanna meet him?"

"No," Lauren said, horrified at the thought.

Nature giggled. "When you're out with me you can meet anyone you want – who do you fancy?"

"I fancy sitting in a corner by myself."

"You're 'aving fun, ain'tcha?"

"You know my idea of fun. I prefer to watch."

"Very kinky!"

"Do me a favour – go off with your husband and enjoy yourself. I'm perfectly happy."

Nature didn't need much encouragement. "Okey-doke – I'll check you later."

Looking around, Lauren couldn't get over the fact that there were more waiters than guests. She requested a club soda from one with a blond crew cut, and found a corner for herself, trying to remember everything she saw to tell Pia.

Not only was Jack Nicholson present, but she recognized a whole slew of other famous faces. A smiling Burt Reynolds, a gorgeous Angie Dickinson, a strutting Rod Stewart and a dignified looking Gregory Peck.

The little girl in her said, *Why didn't I bring my autograph book?* The big girl said, *I don't want to be here. Let me out!*

Everybody kissed each other, only their lips never touched. Conversation seemed transient. The women wore jewels the like of which she'd never seen.

Nature revelled in it. Lauren watched her as she fluttered from person to person – blonde, big and luscious. Emerson didn't follow her around, he sat at the bar and everybody came over to pay homage. He was a rock star. It was his due.

Lauren found it easy to blend into the background. Although at one time she'd been the prettiest girl in Bosewell, she certainly didn't impress anybody in Hollywood. Not that she was trying. In fact, as usual she'd played her looks down – her hair was neatly drawn back, and she wore no make-up and her simple outfit blended into the background. Nature often screamed at her about the way she dressed, and Pia was into giving lectures claiming she didn't make the most of herself. "I'm perfectly happy the way I am," she'd told them both.

By midnight she was ready to leave, but Nature was still going strong and Emerson showed no signs of moving. The house had its own discotheque – a mirrored room with flashing strobe lights, black granite floors and a disc jockey stand complete with a wasted looking disc jockey.

Lauren managed to grab hold of Nature as she fluttered by on her way to dance. "I'm falling asleep," she whispered. "Do you mind if I go?"

"Don't worry," Nature screeched. "We'll be out of 'ere soon."

"Maybe I can take the car and send it back for you?"

"Do what you want," Nature replied vaguely, continuing on her way.

Tucker was outside talking to a group of drivers.

"They're not ready," Lauren said, "but I am."

Tucker nodded. "I'll bring the car around."

Sitting in the back of the luxurious limo she closed her eyes all the way back to Emerson's mansion. When she arrived she couldn't wait to fall into bed.

Sometime before dawn she was awakened by a screaming fight between Nature and Emerson.

What else was new?

Chapter 47

The next few months passed quickly. Nick had his apartment, a stash of money from the Tijuana job, and Joy Byron's class to keep him busy. Joy Byron had turned out to be the teacher of his dreams. She didn't criticize, she nurtured – carefully watching every move he made. The other students in the class couldn't wait to pick everyone's performance to pieces. Fuck 'em. As long as Joy thought he was good, that's all that mattered.

"I've decided to give you extra coaching," Joy announced one day, her watery eyes darting around the room.

"Can I afford it?" he asked, half-jokingly.

"Probably not," she replied, crisply. "But you'll pay me back . . . one day."

He began visiting her run-down house way up in the Hollywood Hills on a regular basis, and in her dusty living room he got to do anything he wanted. Joy Byron had bookshelves piled high with every play ever written – it was better than a trip to the library. She allowed him to indulge himself – reading with him, giving pertinent advice and teaching him about diction, posture, timing, make-up and the best lighting and camera angles.

"This information is invaluable," she said. "You, my dear boy, are going to be big."

He wasn't intimidated by her. "Hey – *I* know that," he replied, cockily.

"Good," she said, unfazed by his sureness. "Confidence is everything."

When she came on to him he was taken aback, the woman had to be at least sixty-five. He quickly made up a fiancée, a true love, waiting patiently for him in his home town.

Joy did not believe him, but she backed off anyway, remarking that she had plenty of lovers and certainly didn't need the likes of him.

He wondered if it would make any difference to their student/teacher relationship. It didn't.

Annie was not pleased. The only time he ever saw her was in class and she'd taken to ignoring him.

"What's the matter?" he asked one day. "You're treatin' me like I got a bad case of BO."

"You used me," she said, turning on him full of pent-up anger. "All you wanted was an introduction to Joy, and now you're her pet project nobody hears from you. I don't appreciate being used, Nick."

"Hey – what's wrong with me gettin' everything I can out of this?"

Annie refused to be placated. "You're kissing her ass."

It didn't take long to realize most of the other students felt the same way. Well fuck 'em – if they didn't like it that was their problem; he fully intended to learn everything he needed to know.

Joy announced she was putting on a student production of *On the Waterfront*. Naturally she gave Nick the coveted Marlon Brando role. This did not go down well with the rest of the class who resented him even more.

So far Joy had advised him not to seek out an agent or manager. "Many important people come to my shows," she informed him. "I'll find you the right agent. Follow my guidance, dear boy, and we can't fail."

That was okay with him; he had no desire to traipse around agents' offices getting a series of turn-downs.

DeVille was still living in his apartment – somehow she'd never gotten around to moving out. He didn't mind. It meant he didn't have to go looking for sex – she was always ready and available. Occasionally he asked her to read with him. She wasn't half bad and soon started dropping hints about maybe accompanying him to class.

That, he didn't need. He was having trouble enough – he could just imagine what would happen if he showed up with DeVille on his arm.

As for Manny Manfred and Glamour Limousines, he'd never gone back. As long as he had enough money who needed to work for a living?

Cyndra called to complain she never saw him. "I'm going

to be playing Vegas," she said, full of enthusiasm. "Reece has me booked to sing at one of the best hotels. Will you fly out?"

He assured her he would, but he still hadn't gotten around to it, he was too busy putting all his energy into preparing for his upcoming role.

In between rehearsals he continued to spend most of his time at Joy's house. The night before the big event she came on to him stronger than ever.

"I bring people luck, Nick," she announced grandly, her bony hand hovering dangerously near the top of his thigh.

"Yeah?" he said warily, backing off as usual.

Her watery eyes bored into his. "If I told you about some of the men I've slept with, famous men . . . powerful men. They all claim I bring something . . . *special* into their lives."

By this time her hands were all over him.

He knew there was no way he could get it up and yet he couldn't risk disappointing her. "Hey – listen, Joy, you're a very attractive woman," he lied, speaking fast while desperately removing her hand from his leg. "But like I said – I got this fiancée, an' we promised we'd never cheat on each other."

Joy muttered something lethal under her breath and threw him out.

He drove back to his apartment hoping he hadn't made a mistake.

Hell, no – gotta have some principles.

When he arrived home DeVille was sitting in a chair facing the door dressed for business. Next to her were two packed suitcases.

"Going somewhere?" he asked, throwing off his jacket.

She smiled, a trifle sheepishly. "I'm finally moving out. Remember, we discussed it a couple of months ago?"

He threw open the fridge and surveyed the meagre contents. DeVille was a lousy housekeeper. "Hey, I didn't ask you to go," he said, reaching for a can of beer.

She pushed back her pale red hair. "I know, Nick, but I've stayed long enough."

"Where's your next stop?"

She lowered her eyes, almost afraid to tell him. "I met this guy."

Funny, but he wasn't at all jealous. "Yeah? What guy?"

"A producer."

He snapped the can open. "A *real* producer? Or some Hollywood phoney?"

315

"He's asked me to live with him."

"How come you never mentioned him before?"

"It didn't seem necessary."

Nick wasn't used to being walked out on, but so what – there was no way he was begging her to stay. If she wanted to get conned by some would-be producer it was her problem.

That night he slept restlessly. He had a hunch that starting tomorrow everything was going to be different.

"Come over here, darlin'," Reece said, patting the empty seat beside him.

Cyndra hesitated. She had no intention of sitting with Reece at the small round table in the cocktail lounge of the busy downtown casino. The night before she'd joined him and two of his so-called "friends". As soon as she'd sat down he'd got up and vanished for over an hour. The men had started making suggestive remarks and trying to grope her. She'd soon put them straight. When Reece had returned he'd been furious.

"Those were important guys," he'd told her. "*Real* important. What's the *matter*? You dumber than you look?"

His words had stung like a slap. How dare he talk to her in such a way – he never had before. But since they'd been in Vegas he'd changed, and it wasn't for the better. First of all there was the matter of the hotel where she was to perform. Reece had assured her it was going to be one of the big ones.

"Which one?" she'd asked, imagining her debut was to be at The Sands or Desert Inn.

"It's a surprise," he'd said mysteriously, not looking her in the eye.

Some surprise. A downtown dump full of hookers and hustlers with only a pianist to back her – a surly Puerto Rican who could barely talk English and was usually half-drunk.

"What happened?" she'd asked, furiously.

"We gotta get you more experience before we hit the big time," Reece explained. "This is a fine start, honey."

Reece talked a good game. First the demo recordings which failed to take place. Now Vegas and this crummy place.

Cyndra told herself she shouldn't blame him – at least he was trying. But he'd made such big promises and look where they'd got her.

When they'd returned to their motel room she'd refused to

speak to him. Now he was sitting in the audience like nothing had happened, expecting her to join him.

Well screw him, he could think again.

She narrowed her eyes and checked out the table. At least he was alone.

Hmm . . . he probably wanted to apologize.

Hmm . . . maybe she'd give him a second chance.

There was a buzz about performing for an audience – a buzz he'd never felt before. Better than sex – almost orgasmic in a way. Jeez! This was it. Give him a steady diet of applause and he'd be a happy man.

Joy hovered at the side of the stage encouraging, criticizing, whispering in his ear every time he came off. Do this. Do that. More gestures. Use your voice.

Fuck you, lady, I'm flying! I don't need your help.

And the audience loved him. They fucking loved him! Marlon move over – Nick Angelo is here to stay!

By the end of the show he was on fire – adrenalin pumping through his veins like pure heroin.

Joy was pleased. She had a big smirk on her face, especially when half the audience came piling backstage to congratulate her.

He wished he knew who was important and who wasn't – it wouldn't do to waste his charm on the wrong person. He looked to Joy for guidance. She was deluged by people.

"Not bad," Annie said grudgingly, passing by with a group. "We're going to the Hamlet on Sunset. Want to join us?"

Hamburger Hamlet was not exactly what he had in mind to celebrate his triumph. Plus Annie was really beginning to piss him off. Why couldn't she tell him he was fantastic; what was with this "not bad" shit? She was such a downer.

"Maybe," he mumbled. *If nothing better comes along.*

Joy beckoned him. "Nick, come over here – I want you to meet someone."

The someone turned out to be Ardmore Castle – a small-time agent well-known for his penchant for good-looking young actors.

"Hello . . . Nick." Ardmore had anxious eyes, plump jowls and a hungry expression. He was chasing fifty.

Joy moved away. Nick nodded, scanning the room. Ardmore Castle's reputation preceded him. Maybe Joy figured if *she*

317

couldn't have him then Ardmore was in with a chance.

The agent fixed him with a lecherous stare. "I enjoyed your performance."

"Uh . . . thanks."

"Very macho."

"Yeah, well, it's written that way."

"You brought something special to it."

Major eye contact. Jeez! Where was Joy when he needed her?

Ardmore cleared his throat. "Perhaps you'd care to join me at my house later. I'm having a few friends drop by."

"Gee . . . sounds great, but I got a date."

"Bring him," Ardmore said, boldly.

"It's a her," he responded, quickly.

Ardmore realized he was getting a brush. He pursed his lips. "Suit yourself."

"I intend to."

"*Very* bold. For an unknown."

Joy descended, accompanied by a hatchet-faced middle-aged woman in a man's pin-stripe jacket and black pants. The woman brushed past Ardmore as if he didn't exist.

"Hello, Frances dear," Ardmore said, determined to be acknowledged.

She blew cigarette smoke in his face, barely nodding in his direction.

Joy grabbed Nick's arm in a proprietary way. "Nick, dear – meet Frances Cavendish, the casting director." She said casting director in meaningful tones. He got the message.

Frances didn't bother with pleasantries. She was a strong-jawed woman with a stern demeanour. She was also fast-talking and to the point. "My office. Tomorrow. Noon," she said, flicking a business card at him. "Might have something for you."

Deftly Joy plucked the card from his hand. "We'll be there, Frances dear," she said, smiling sweetly.

"Don't need you, Joy. I'm sure Nick can walk and talk on his own."

What was this little scene? He felt uncomfortably like a piece of meat lying on a slab while the dogs sniffed around deciding who'd get lucky.

Ardmore expressed his disapproval. "You need an agent," he said. "Someone who'll protect your interests."

"Yes," Frances said, dryly. "Someone who'll allow you to keep your pants on."

Nick took a deep breath, snatched Frances Cavendish's card back from Joy and mumbled, "I'm outta here."

"Where are you going?" Joy asked, hands fluttering.

"Gotta get some fresh air. See ya."

And he was gone before any of them could object.

Chapter 48

Nature took on the role of tour guide, deciding that Lauren had to see everything there was to see in Los Angeles.

"Can we take a break?" Lauren begged, after they'd been to Disneyland, Universal City and Magic Mountain all in one day.

Nature looked surprised – "What for? You're only here a few days – we gotta do everything we can – besides, I've never been to any of these places myself. It's a kick!"

While they were exploring, Emerson lay out by the pool working on his suntan and reading scripts.

"He's looking for a movie for us to do together," Nature confided.

Sure, Lauren thought.

Every day around noon his entourage arrived at the house and stayed until he threw them out – usually not until two or three in the morning. They laughed at his jokes, assured him he was the best thing since Elvis and freebied all over the house.

The pack was led by his manager, Sidney Fishbourne – a lanky man in his forties with shoulder-length frizzy black hair. Sidney was usually accompanied by April – a thirty-year-old married redhead he referred to as his executive assistant, although everyone knew she was his mistress.

The rest of the entourage consisted of Emerson's clothes designer, his make-up artist, his hair-stylist and his personal publicist.

The group spent most of their time discussing Emerson's image for his upcoming world tour.

"You gotta get wilder," Sidney insisted. "Break a few guitars, throw stuff around the stage, get the girls screaming."

"No fuckin' way," Emerson said adamantly. "I'm not doin' all that sixties shit again."

"He should be involved in a cause," his publicist said, twirling her worry-beads. "Perhaps something to do with nuclear power – or the environment."

"It's all in the clothes," his designer insisted. "No more black leather. I think suits."

"Suits are old," Sidney snapped. "We gotta start appealing to a younger audience."

His designer persevered. "Sophistication is very in."

"Who gives a shit," Emerson said flatly, and that was the end of the suit discussion.

Nature complained to Lauren that she felt left out. "All we ever talk about is 'im – what about *me*?" she demanded. "I'm famous, too."

"You married a rock star," Lauren pointed out. "His first interest is obviously going to be himself, especially with a world tour coming up."

"It's not that I'm jealous or anything," Nature continued, "but I'm hardly the bleedin' girl next door. I *should* get more attention, don't you think?"

"It depends," Lauren said, carefully. "Do you really *want* attention from that bunch of ass kissers?"

Nature giggled. "You're right as usual. Who cares about them?"

"What you *should* do is get back to work. You're not the type to sit at Emerson's feet. Show him you're independent – that's why he married you, isn't it?"

"Hmm . . ." Nature wasn't entirely convinced. "I dunno."

"Well *I* do," Lauren said, forcefully. "*Never* give everything up for a man."

It didn't take long before Nature and Emerson were embroiled in another of their famous fights. This one was triggered off by April, who innocently remarked she'd seen Selina, Nature's arch rival, on television discussing her first movie role.

"Ha!" Nature said, spitefully. "What's *she* playing – dumb cunt of the year?"

They were all sitting in the breakfast room picking at an array of salads and fruit plates. Emerson was into losing a few pounds which meant no real food allowed.

"C'mon, luv," Emerson said, mildly. "Selina's never done anything to you."

That was all Nature had to hear. She exploded in a jealous rage, lashing out at everyone.

"Got the rag on, 'ave we?" sneered Emerson, furious with her display of temper in front of everyone.

"Fuck you!" Nature screamed, picking up her plate of Caesar salad and flinging it in his face. "Go back to Selina if that's who you really want!" And with that she stormed from the room.

Lauren was embarrassed for both of them – Emerson with small pieces of oil-covered lettuce stuck to his face and hair – and Nature, who'd made a jealous fool of herself in front of everyone.

Emerson glared at his entourage. "Get the fuck out," he commanded. "Show's over for today."

Obediently they all filed out. Lauren started to follow. "*You* don't 'ave t'go," Emerson called after her.

She pretended not to hear and hurried upstairs to her room where she called the airline and booked a flight back to New York the following morning. She'd kept her promise and stayed four days. It was more than enough.

Later that afternoon she ventured down to the pool. She'd seen Emerson leave in the limo, and Nature had not returned from her lunchtime exit.

Lying out in the sun with nobody around was wonderfully peaceful. No rock music blaring. No Nature shrieking. No entourage clinking glasses and making inane conversation.

She closed her eyes and allowed her mind to drift – thinking about Bosewell and her parents. Meg, Stock – all the old crowd. And finally Nick.

Oh, God, she didn't want to think about Nick. She tried to keep him out of her thoughts as much as possible – it wasn't worth re-living memories so bitter-sweet and painful.

Nick Angelo with his black hair, green eyes and killer smile.

Nick – whom she'd given herself to totally.

Nick – who'd taken off without so much as a goodbye, leaving her pregnant and alone.

She opened her eyes forcing him from her thoughts. Standing over her, straddling the end of her lounger, was Emerson.

"What are you doing?" she asked, startled.

"Watching you," he replied, and she smelt the liquor on his breath.

She attempted to move her legs so she could get into a sitting position, but moving meant touching his crotch – and, oh no, she could see his hard-on – the brief bikini bottom he wore did nothing to hide it.

Stay calm, she warned herself. *Stay in control and nothing will happen.*

"Is Nature back?" she asked, trying to sound casual as she quickly pulled up the top of her swimsuit.

"I want you t'suck my cock," Emerson announced, swaying drunkenly.

Voices screamed inside her head. *Don't react! Don't panic! Stay cool!*

There was a long moment of silence. Neither of them moved. She noticed the small, spiky, black hairs on the insides of his thighs and the tiny spot of moisture staining his bikini briefs.

"Emerson, don't do anything you'll regret later," she said, trying to keep her voice even.

"Who says I'll regret it?" he slurred.

Where were the servants and Tucker? If she screamed would they hear? Would they care?

Damn Nature for putting her in this position.

She remembered Bosewell and Primo and that fateful day five years ago.

I think I killed a man.

No. The tornado killed him.

She'd never know the truth.

Her mind began to race, formulating a plan of action. If she raised one knee sharply and unexpectedly she'd catch him right on target, probably giving her enough time to run. But where would she run to? Surely if there was no one in the house she'd be putting herself in an even more vulnerable position?

Emerson stuck his fingers in the top of his briefs and began pulling them down.

Perfect! As soon as they were down far enough he'd immobilize himself and she'd make her move.

She made one more attempt to warn him off. "Don't do this, Emerson. Please don't. You're drunk. You're not thinking straight."

He looked surprised. "C'mon, Lauren, y'know you've been dyin' t'suck my dick ever since you got here."

They moved together like clumsy ballet partners. He pulled his pants down. She brought her knee up. He fell to one side, cursing. She struggled to her feet and started running towards the house. A count of three and he was behind her, kicking his bikini away from his ankles, running naked.

She sprinted swiftly across the marble terrace, hardly daring to glance behind because she knew he was close.

He caught her by the steps to the house, slammed her from behind, and they both fell to the ground.

"Gotcha!" he yelled triumphantly, like they were in the middle of a fun game. Then he pinioned her arms behind her head and rolled on top of her. "Now I'm gonna fuck you like you never bin fucked before," he rasped, gripping both her arms with one hand, while attempting to roll the top of her swimsuit down with the other.

"Don't you have enough girls," she gasped, turning her head. "Girls who want to be with you. Understand me, Emerson – I don't."

"Try to believe it, baby," he said, ripping at her swimsuit, rolling it down around her waist and grabbing her breasts. "You'll want me so much you'll be beggin' for it. You hear me? *Beggin'* for it."

He tore at the crotch of her swimsuit, pushing it to one side, doing his best to enter her.

"You son-of-a-bitch!" she screamed, suddenly losing all control. "LEAVE ME THE FUCK ALONE!" If she'd had a knife she would have stabbed him, just like she'd stabbed Primo.

Now he was really enjoying himself. He had her where he wanted and there was no way she could escape. "Temper, temper!" he mocked. "Mustn't use dirty words. Mummy wouldn't like it."

She felt the tip of his penis about to force an entry and she was filled with despair.

Suddenly a new voice filled the air. "You dirty low-life, scumbag *rat!*" It was Nature's unmistakable shriek. "You lying, cheating, mother-fuckin' *pig!*"

Emerson's hard-on deflated.

Lauren seized the moment and rolled out from under him, pulling up her swimsuit, fighting back angry tears.

"And as for you," Nature turned on her, blue eyes blazing. "I thought you was me bleedin' friend – but you're just like all the rest of the slags – couldn't wait t'get your hands on me old man."

"Now wait a minute –"

"Get outta me house," Nature shouted, her cheeks red with anger. "I *never* want to speak to you again."

Emerson began to rock with laughter. He had no intention of coming to her defence.

What a couple. The truth was they deserved each other.

She ran into the house without looking back.

Chapter 49

"Are you straight?" Frances Cavendish asked as if it was the most normal question in the world.

"Want me to pull down my pants an' prove it?" Nick replied, damned if she was going to embarrass him.

Frances leaned back behind her desk and adjusted the *diamanté* studded glasses covering her flinty eyes. "Go ahead," she drawled, challenging him.

"Don't bet me, lady," he warned, still trying to figure her out.

Frances laughed – a big bawdy laugh. "The kid's got attitude. I like it."

He didn't appreciate her talking down to him. "The *kid* is a hell of an actor. What I need from you, lady, is a job."

Coolly Frances appraised him, dragging on her cigarette. "What's your professional experience?"

"I done a lot of stuff," he mumbled.

Frances' expression said she didn't believe him. "Do you have a résumé? A tape? Photographs?"

"Uh . . ." He trailed off. She wasn't going to do anything for him. He'd made the trip to her fancy office for nothing. Frances Cavendish, casting agent. She must have known he had no experience. The old broad probably got off on humiliating people.

Frances continued to drag on her cigarette and squinted at him. "Are you fucking Joy Byron?"

"Now wait a minute –"

"No. *You* wait a minute," she said, sharply. "You slouch in here in your tight jeans with your bad-ass scowl expecting exactly what?"

"You asked me to come," he fired back.

"Did I?" She took off her glasses and studied him further.

He felt her gaze penetrating beneath his clothes. She wanted a fuck. That's what they all wanted. And if he wasn't giving it to Joy — who at least treated him like a human being — he certainly wasn't giving it to this one. He turned, making his way towards the door; there was no point in hanging around.

Frances stopped him at the threshold, her voice strong and commanding. "I'm sending you on an audition."

He threw her a look. "Yeah?"

"It's a small role — but juicy."

"I got all the juice y'want."

"I'm sure you have," she said coolly, putting her glasses back on. "Conditions."

"What?" he asked, suspiciously.

"Take my advice and get rid of Joy — she'll hang around your neck like a cement block. Oh yes, and stay away from agents like Ardmore Castle. If you get the part I'll recommend a legitimate agent to take care of you."

He felt obliged to defend Joy, after all she'd been good to him. "Joy's a great teacher," he said, quickly.

Frances was having none of it. "Joy's an old hack living in the past. Drop her now, Nick, before it's too late."

"You're a hard lady."

"I'm honest — an almost impossible attribute to come by in this town."

He wondered what she wanted. Then decided he had nothing to lose by asking. "So . . . uh . . . what am I gonna owe you?"

"Occasional escort services. When I need you. Get yourself a tuxedo — you already have the attitude." She paused, inhaling deeply, heavy smoke drifting from her nostrils. "Escort duties end at the door. Which is more than you can say for Joy or Ardmore. Do we have a deal?"

This was some straight-talking old broad. "What's the part?"

"Small-time hood with a heart of mush. It's a minor role — but showy. I'm sending you over to meet the director and producers. If they ask about experience — lie. Tell them you've done stock, off-Broadway and commercials. If they ask for photos refer them back to me. I'll make an appointment for you to have photographs taken later this week. You'll pay me back when you get your first cheque."

He couldn't figure her out. "Why are you doin' all this?"

"Because when you make it you'll owe me. I like that. Write

down your number. I'll call you tomorrow and give you their reaction."

He was apprehensive. "You mean I'm goin' on an audition *now?*"

She stubbed her cigarette out in a full ashtray, immediately reaching for a fresh package. "Unless you'd prefer to wait a day or two."

He didn't hesitate. "Lady – I'm ready."

"That's *exactly* what I thought."

"You'll do things my way, or you're gonna find yourself doing nothin' at all." So spoke Reece.

Cyndra felt a shiver of fear. This was not the man she'd married – the laid-back cowboy with the big promises. This was someone else – a stranger. "You'd better stop getting on my case or I'm likely to walk," she said sharply, challenging him.

He caught her with a slap around the face, taking her by surprise. "Get it into your head – you're my wife," he said, harshly. "*My wife,* do you understand me? I fucking married you – that means you belong to me, and you'll do anything I tell you to do."

Her hand flew to her face stinging from his slap. "I don't belong to *anybody!*" she yelled.

"That's where you're wrong," he yelled back. "And if you don't believe me, maybe you'll believe this."

To her horror he pulled a gun from his belt and waved it in her direction.

She backed into a corner of their motel room, her eyes wide with fear. "Reece . . . Reece, what are you doing?"

"What the hell you think?" he replied.

"Where did you get a gun?"

He strutted around the room. "I always had it. Never know when it might come in useful. Man's gotta protect himself."

She took a deep breath and tried to stay in control.

"Put it away . . . put it away now."

"I got your attention, huh?" he smiled slyly, pleased with himself. "So maybe you'd care to give some of that attention to my friends 'stead of making me look like a jerk."

Her mouth was dry; she couldn't believe what was happening. Within the last few minutes her life had crumbled around her. Wasn't it enough that she'd had to escape from Bosewell? Did she have to escape from this man, too?

"Listen to me *good*, bitch," Reece said, enjoying her attention. "I found you bumming around New York – now you're singin' in Vegas, so don't ever forget it's *me* got you here. An' if I expect you to be nice to my friends, then you'll do it. Understand?" As he spoke he waved his gun in the air.

"Yes, Reece," she whispered.

"Say it louder," he commanded.

"*Yes!*"

"*That's* what I like to hear." He stuck the gun back in his belt. "Tomorrow night mebbe I'll have a coupla guys join us after the show, an' you'll be nice to 'em, honey. You'll do whatever I tells you t'do."

She nodded blankly.

Later, when he was asleep, she thought about creeping from the room and running. But where could she run to? If she took off she knew Reece would come after her.

With a feeling of deep despair she realized there was no escape. Once more she was trapped. It was a bad feeling.

Nick did exactly what Frances had told him to do. He lied. When they asked him about his experience, he made up a travelling stock company he'd performed in, then mentioned a few commercials and several original off-Broadway plays. In fact, he lied pretty good.

There were two producers in the room. A tall, nervy man who sat in the background, staring. And a middle-aged woman with great legs that she kept on crossing and uncrossing. The director was Italian/American, short, with swarthy features and a shock of greasy brown hair.

Nick checked them out. Three assholes all in a row. Fuck it. He wasn't nervous – although the casting assistant was really pissing him off – when they read together she didn't know acting from shit. But still, the three assholes seemed to like him – in fact they made him read through the scene twice.

When he'd arrived the girl in reception had handed him several pages of dialogue. He'd had half an hour to study them. He'd also had half an hour to study the other actors waiting to go in. Talk about a cattle call – you could feel and smell the competition.

He remembered Frances' words – "small-time hood with a heart of mush" – and that's who he became. Not Nick Angelo

– an actor chasing a role – just a small-time hood with a heart of mush. Some fucking description!

He finished reading the second time and waited for their reaction.

"Good seeing ya, Nick," said the director, dismissing him as though they were old friends.

"Thank you," said the woman producer, crossing her legs again, while eyeing him contemplatively.

The tall man said nothing.

Before he could think about it he was out of there.

He stopped at the reception desk and spoke to the girl. "How long before I get to hear?" he asked.

She looked amused. "New at this?"

"Nah . . . well, yeah, I guess. I'm new in town. I was, uh . . . workin' in Chicago an' New York."

"Oh, you're a New York actor," she said, a little bit impressed. "Don't worry, you'll soon get to know the routine. Sometimes these auditions go on for months. They see you, like you, then they see fifty other guys. After that maybe they'll call you back. You never know."

"So it's like a long wait?"

She shrugged. "Face it. This town is a crap shoot."

She was using his dialogue! He wondered if she ever got to listen in on the producers' conversation after the actors left the room.

"Hey, what's your name?" he asked, going for the friendly approach. "And when do you wanna have dinner?"

"Marilyn," she replied, still smiling. "*Married* Marilyn," she added, holding up her hand to display a wedding ring. "But thanks for asking anyway."

Outside in the parking lot he contemplated driving back to Frances' office and giving her a report.

Nah. Instinct told him he should wait until he heard from her. But now he was high from the audition and there was no way he could sit around waiting for the phone to ring. He decided to pay Annie a visit.

She was vacuuming when he arrived and didn't look thrilled to see him. "Oh, the big star is here," she said, continuing to vacuum.

He pulled the plug from the outlet. "What is this crap with you?"

She sighed. "How many times have we had this conversation?

329

Like last night – why didn't you join us at Hamburger Hamlet? What *did* you do, take off with Ardmore Castle?"

"You calling me a fag, Annie?" he said, feigning indignation.

"I'm not calling you anything, but you . . ." She shook her head. "Oh – I don't know, Nick, you confuse me."

"I went home – alone."

"That's nice."

"I met this casting director – Frances Cavendish. I dropped by and saw her today and she sent me on an audition."

"What audition?"

"Small part in a movie."

"Did you get it?"

"Dunno."

"Did you read?"

He grinned. "I was great!"

"Mister Modest."

"Listen – if *I* don't sing 'em – who will?"

She pushed the vacuum over to a corner closet and stored it. "Are you coming to Joy's class tomorrow night?"

He wandered around her small apartment. "I kinda figured I might drive to Vegas, see Cyndra. Beats sitting around waiting for the call to tell me I didn't get the part. This is like difficult shit."

"Nobody ever said it was easy."

"Whaddaya think? Should I go to Vegas?"

"Cyndra would love to see you."

"How long's the drive?"

"Five, six hours, I'm not sure."

"Wanna come?"

She shook her head but he could tell she was tempted.

"C'mon – live dangerously – throw a few things in a bag, it'll be fun," he said, encouragingly.

Annie began to relate a list of excuses.

Nick shot them all down.

An hour later they were on their way.

Chapter 50

Back in New York Lauren refused to talk about her LA trip.

"What happened?" Pia was anxious to know.

"Nothing," she replied, quickly. "Exactly nothing."

"Why aren't you telling me anything?" Pia complained. "And how come if Nature calls you don't want to speak to her? *Something* must have gone on."

Lauren's only desire was to forget about LA, and with that in mind she threw herself back to work. In her spare time – of which there was little – she began attending a self-defence class, studying French, and also taking a gourmet cooking class. These activities left her no time for a social life, and if anyone tried to fix her up they got a blank "No thanks".

Shortly after getting back, Lauren attended Pia and Howard's wedding in the garden of his uncle Oliver's house in the Hamptons. Oliver Liberty was one of the founders of Liberty & Charles. He was a distinguished looking man in his late fifties, with a dry sense of humour – the complete opposite of his wife, Opal, a vacuous blonde he'd married on the rebound after an expensive divorce from his first wife of thirty-one years.

It was a beautiful wedding. Lauren sat back and day-dreamed about how it might have been if things had been different with Jimmy. She even allowed her mind to drift back to Nick. So many years ago . . . but when she thought about him it still hurt and she shut off the thoughts abruptly.

Oliver Liberty strolled over and sat down beside her after dinner. "I hear you and Pia are building quite a business," he said, one eye on his flashy wife who was cavorting on the dance floor in a too-tight red dress.

"We're doing okay," she replied, adding with a smile, "I'm sure you can't wait to steer all your clients in our direction."

He nodded. "Always thinking ahead. That's what I like – a smart woman."

If that's what he liked how come he'd married the blonde – who, according to Pia, had an IQ of zero?

"So . . . will we be getting your clients?"

He smiled. "I'm sure, Lauren, you always get exactly what you want."

Shortly after Pia moved out the calls started. The first one came at two o'clock in the morning. Lauren groped for the phone in her sleep mumbling a groggy, "Hello."

"I wanna talk to you," a familiar voice said.

She knew immediately it was Emerson Burn. For a moment she held her breath before quietly replacing the receiver.

He called back within seconds. "Don't 'ang up on me," he complained. "That's not nice."

"What do you want?" she asked, amazed at his nerve.

"It's about time we got together," he said, confidently.

"Are you crazy?" she said, struggling to sit up.

"Seems like a normal request to me."

"Have you forgotten what happened in LA?"

"Nothin' happened."

"That was because Nature came back."

"What are you gettin' so uptight about? So I came on to you. Big deal. Most girls would give their left tit to 'ave me come on t'them."

"I don't *believe* this. You tried to rape me, and the only reason you didn't get away with it was because your wife came home. *Your wife* – remember her? She used to be my best friend – now she no longer talks to me thanks to you. You're an asshole, you know that?" She slammed the phone down.

It rang again immediately.

She took the receiver off the hook and buried it under her pillow.

The next day three dozen red roses arrived at the apartment with a note. The note read, *Sorry! E.* She dropped the flowers off at a nearby hospital.

A few days later while lunching with Samm she casually enquired about Nature.

"Did you two fall out?" Samm asked, raising an elegant eyebrow as she picked at her tomato and lettuce salad.

"You know what Nature's like better than anyone," she replied cagily, sipping a glass of water.

"That's true," Samm replied, with a weary sigh. "The girl can be absolutely impossible. I don't know what she sees in that mangy rock star, he looks like he's in desperate need of a shower – several in fact. Those leather pants stick to his body like tacky tape – and I *do* mean tacky."

"So they're still very much together?"

"About as close as two enormous egos *can* be," Samm said dryly, before adding, "You *do* know she's been bad-mouthing you all over town."

Lauren sighed – this was all she needed to hear. "She has?"

"I wouldn't worry – nobody takes her seriously."

Emerson called again the following week. "Changed your mind?" he asked casually, like they chatted every day.

"About what?"

"Gettin' together."

The man was in ego overdrive. "I have a news flash," she replied, sharply. "You've finally met the one person who doesn't want to go out with you."

He was not to be put off. "If you're worried about Nature she's in LA."

"I thought she came with you on every trip to hold your hand."

"Nah, can't 'ave her trailin' me, can I? S'not good for the image. Come on, we'll hit a few clubs, 'ave us a time."

"You know what, Emerson?"

"*What*, babe?"

"Stop calling me."

It seemed inconceivable that Emerson Burn had decided to pursue her. Did he honestly think that a near-rape was prelude to a romantic relationship?

Three months after getting married Pia announced she was pregnant. "Howard and I talked it over, and we want you to be godmother."

"I'd be honoured," Lauren replied, thinking how lucky Pia was to be married to the man she loved *and* pregnant.

Help Unlimited was doing so well that they'd finally rented proper office space. Pia decided to keep working until a month before the baby was due. "I'm not the sitting-at-home type," she explained. They now employed six people which gave Lauren the luxury of choosing the jobs she wished to do. Since she'd taken the cooking course, small dinner parties were her forte. She enjoyed organizing incredible meals, and it also kept her busy most nights – which suited her fine.

Sometimes, late at night, lying in bed, a wave of unbearable loneliness swept over her. But she'd decided it was better to be lonely than to suffer another broken heart.

Now that Pia had moved out of the apartment they'd shared, she decided to re-decorate. It wasn't the most luxurious place in the world, but it was comfortable and cosy and she was happy there. Weekends she liked nothing better than strolling along Eighth Avenue exploring the antique shops and picking out special things.

One Saturday afternoon she was walking across Park and turning on Madison when she noticed a long white limousine crawling along the kerb behind her.

She quickened her step, but the limousine kept pace, and when she stopped at a street corner the door of the car was flung open and Emerson Burn leaped out.

Emerson – the leather-clad rock star with the mane of golden hair – grabbed her arm and spun her around to face him. "You bin avoiding me," he said, accusingly.

Was he so dumb he really thought she was ever going to talk to him again?

"What now?" she said, attempting to shake his arm off.

His grip tightened. "Get in the car an' I'll tell you."

"Forget it."

"I ain't forgettin' it, darlin'," he said, loudly. "*That's* the friggin' point."

Two girls spotted him and froze as if they'd just seen Jesus.

Emerson's bodyguard jumped out of the car. "Time ta split, Em," he said, watchful eyes raking the street.

Emerson ignored him.

The girls clutched on to each other and braced themselves for the rush.

"You ain't bein' fair t'me," Emerson complained, holding tight. "I wanna explain. I was drunk. I had a problem."

"Now look –" she began.

The girls sprung into action – sprinting towards him with purposeful looks in their eyes. The bodyguard saw them coming. So did Emerson. "Oh, shit!" he exclaimed. "Here comes trouble."

Lauren felt a thump in the small of her back and was rudely shoved aside as one of the girls moved in on him.

"I'm insane about everything you do!" the girl yelled hysterically, pulling at his jacket. "I love you! I *really, really* love you!"

Before Lauren could think about what to do the bodyguard bundled Emerson into the limo – somehow pushing her in behind him. The car immediately took off.

"Well,' Emerson said. "That settles it. You're trapped, darlin', an' there ain't nothin' you can do about it."

Chapter 51

"I've never done anything like this before," Annie said, throwing Nick a sideways glance.

He laughed. "Anybody would think we were planning on robbing a freakin' bank!"

"You know what I mean, taking off like this – it's . . ." she looked at him questioningly, "I guess it's fun."

"*Now* you're beginning to learn."

They'd been driving for several hours. The freeway ride was long and boring, but the thought of seeing Las Vegas for the first time excited both of them.

"Hey, how much money you got on you?" he asked, realizing he hadn't come prepared.

"About fifty dollars. Why?"

"'Cause we're gonna blow it, that's why."

"Oh no, not with my money," she said, indignantly.

Grinning, he steered the old Chevrolet on to an off ramp. "C'mon, Annie, you gotta take *some* chances in life."

"It's my rent money," she objected.

"So we'll double it. How's that?"

She glanced over at him. "You know, Nick, you're really strange."

"Oh, so now I'm strange. What's *this* leading up to?"

"Can I be honest with you?" she asked, earnestly.

"You can be whatever you like," he replied, pulling into a Chevron station.

"It's just that sometimes it seems you're coming on to me, and then other times you act as if you're my brother."

Oh, shit – the last thing he needed was Annie developing a crush on him. But then again, why not? DeVille was long gone and he was bored with the endless stream of one-night stands he could have any time he wanted.

"Are you interested in me or not?" she asked, putting it firmly on the line.

He stalled for time. "Is this a proposition?" he said lightly, winding down his window.

"I . . . I need to know."

"Hey, I'm here with you, we're driving to Vegas."

"Is that your idea of a commitment?"

Commitment! The very word gave him nightmares. What was it with women and commitments? Why couldn't they take it day by day?

The gas station attendant leaned into his window – saving him a reply. "What'll it be?" the old man asked, scratching his grizzled beard.

"Fill her up," Nick said. "An' check the oil an' water while you're at it."

"Well?" Annie demanded, not letting him off the hook.

He took his time before replying. "We're goin' on a trip," he said, carefully. "Whyn't we take it nice an' easy and maybe we'll find out."

Reece Webster sat back in the smoky atmosphere of the small casino bar and watched Cyndra sing. She was good. She was *really* good. So how come she wasn't getting anywhere? The record labels hadn't liked the deal he'd proposed, and the bigger hotels had said she needed experience. Experience goddamn it! He was giving her experience, and what kind of thanks was he getting? Exactly nothing. Cyndra had no appreciation of the things he did for her.

Well, what did he expect? Women were all takers and Cyndra was no exception.

He hoped he hadn't wasted his time marrying her – he'd been so sure she was going to be his ride to the big time – now all he did was pay the bills. The money she made at the casino didn't even cover his expenses. Some dud investment. He'd put two years into singing lessons and grooming and it simply wasn't paying off.

His narrow eyes raked the room. Several men were watching Cyndra with that look on their faces. Reece knew the look well. It was the *I wanna fuck your brains out* look.

He studied her dress. Not sexy enough. She needed more

cleavage and maybe a deep slit in the skirt. She had great tits and long legs. He'd have to deal with that. He'd have to pay for it, too.

Cyndra was beginning to remind him of his first wife. That bitch had dragged him down like a lead weight; all she'd been capable of was grabbing everything he had. Now Cyndra was falling into the same category, and it was about time he did something about collecting on his investment.

The other night he'd overheard a couple of guys talking while Cyndra was on stage. "I wouldn't mind a piece of that," one of them had said.

"Yeah, with gravy all over it!" the other one replied.

Reece had sidled over. "Wanna meet the little lady?" he'd offered. "'Cause if you do, I'm the man can arrange it."

Both men had nodded eagerly, so Reece had negotiated a deal. The problem was he'd forgotten to tell Cyndra, and when he'd sat her down with the two guys and they'd come on to her she'd insulted them both. The men were real riled up – and who could blame them? Much to his chagrin he'd had to return their money.

So what the hell was wrong with a little light hooking on the side? The truth was, convincing Cyndra was a bitch. Except that today he'd asserted himself – put the fear of God into her. *That's* what women expected – a little fear in their lives. They had to know who the boss was; they *needed* to know.

Sipping his malt whisky he scoped out likely prospects, focusing on a stocky man sitting alone at a corner table watching Cyndra like he'd just discovered candy for the first time. The man was middle-aged with a florid complexion. A brightly-coloured Hawaiian shirt and open sandals on his feet announced tourist.

Casually Reece wandered over. "Howdy," he said, tipping his cowboy hat.

The man looked up. "Do I know you?"

"No," Reece said, "but I got a strong suspicion you'd like to."

"Get your homo ass away from me," the man said, his florid face reddening even more.

"You got it wrong," Reece replied, scowling. "I ain't that way. I came over here t'do you a favour."

"What favour?" the man asked, suspiciously.

Reece gestured towards Cyndra. "Y'see that little lady standing up there? She's what I got in mind for you, but if insults is what I get – then we got no more conversation." He turned to go.

"Wait a minute," the man said.

Reece stopped. "You interested or not?"

The man glanced around furtively. "I'm interested," he said, lowering his voice. "How much will it cost me?"

"Did you win or did you lose? 'Cause if you lost you can't afford this baby."

"I won at craps."

"Then you're a lucky son of a gun, 'cause she's gonna cost you two hundred and fifty big ones."

The man licked his lips and thought quickly. His flabby wife was upstairs sleeping off the effects of winning at the slots. His snotty teenage son was out chasing girls. This was the opportunity of a lifetime and he didn't want to blow it. But two hundred and fifty bucks was an awful lot of money – he could buy a second television for that much money. "I . . . I don't know," he said, hesitantly.

"You don't know," Reece repeated, as if he couldn't believe what he was hearing. "You got a chance for a piece a that and *you don't know*?"

Sweat beaded the man's thick neck. "Is she good?" he asked, hoarsely. "Is she worth it?"

Reece tilted his cowboy hat even further back on his head. "Are you shittin' me? Does Kentucky give fried chicken? Does Cadillac give the smoothest ride goin'? Man, this little lady is the best *you* ever had."

They came upon Las Vegas like a shimmering jewel sitting in the middle of the desert. It was dark and they'd been driving for hours without any light at all. Now, in the distance they saw the flat city spread out before them and it was a startling sight.

"It's incredible!" Annie gasped.

Nick grinned. "I told you – you gotta get out an' do things. No good sittin' on your ass all day expecting . . . I dunno –" he looked at her quizzically. "What *do* you expect, Annie?"

She shrugged. "I work hard, go to class . . . one of these days I'll get a break."

"Yeah, I guess that's what we all think." He pulled the car over to the side of the road, sliding his arm around her shoulders. "I'm glad you came."

"So am I."

They were silent for a while staring at the mirage ahead – at least that's what it looked like in the middle of the barren desert. Finally he broke the silence. "I never asked you before – where's your family?"

"They're in Florida where I grew up. I left three years ago and took the bus out to LA." She snuggled closer. "What about you? Cyndra's never talked about your family. Where are your parents? Do you have any other brothers or sisters?"

He drew away from her on the pretext of reaching for a cigarette. "No sad stories," he said, shaking loose a Camel. "Cyndra and me – we got a father in common, a real charmer. Neither of us has seen him in years."

"You don't speak to him?"

"Nope."

"That's a shame. Family is all we really have."

"Yeah, well, you ain't met mine," he said flippantly.

"What about your mother?"

He struck a match and lit up. "She died when I was sixteen. Left me."

"She didn't leave you, Nick," Annie said, softly. "Dying is not exactly making a choice."

He didn't need to dredge up any more memories, it was painful enough without having to talk about it.

"Hey, can we quit this conversation? Let's appreciate what we got in front of us. Take a look at that view!"

"It's beautiful," she murmured.

"Yeah," he said, starting the car. "Let's go get us a piece of it."

"This is my friend," Reece said.

Cyndra nodded, not looking anywhere near the man in the Hawaiian shirt.

"My *good* friend," Reece added, in case she hadn't quite gotten the message.

"Uh huh," she said, dully.

The man nudged Reece. "When we gettin' out of here?" he asked, perspiration beading his forehead. "It's not good for me to be seen with you people. Where we going anyway?"

"Close by," Reece replied, reassuringly.

"You're not like those con people I seen on TV," the man said, anxiously. "They lure you to a room with a girl, take your money and beat up on you."

Reece tipped his cowboy hat. "Do I look like a con man?"

he said, his lip curling. "Does she look like a con woman? Don't worry, partner – *you* are about to have the dream trip of your life."

Cyndra caught snatches of the conversation. She knew what Reece expected, he'd made that very clear, but she still couldn't believe it.

"Okay, hon," Reece said, all nice and friendly. "Let's go so you an' this fine gentleman can get to know each other better."

"I'm warning you," she hissed under her breath, just loud enough for him to hear. "I'm not doing this."

His hand strayed towards his belt. "Co-operate, hon. I told you this mornin' – I bin carryin' you too long; it's about time you gave something back."

The three of them walked out of the casino into the parking lot where the humid night-time air enveloped them like a heavy cloud. She wondered what Reece would do when she refused to go through with this. He'd probably blow her head off – he was crazy enough. But still, he wouldn't be in the room watching them, and once he left she'd tell the guy the position she was in – appeal to his better nature. He looked like a family man, although he sure didn't smell like one. He stunk of beer and pretzels. She shuddered – his smell reminded her of Primo.

They rode to the motel room in Reece's shocking pink Cadillac. By the time they got there the man was sweating even more profusely.

"Take my licence number," Reece suggested, sensing that this dude could back off at any moment. "It'll make you feel more secure."

"No, no, I trust you," the man said, although he didn't. "How'm I gonna get back?"

"I'll stay around," Reece said. "Whistle when you're done an' I'll drive you."

Cyndra got out of the car and stood stiffly beside it.

"Get your cute little butt to the room, honey," Reece said, coaxingly. "An' don't forget t'leave the door open for our friend." He waited until she was out of sight and then snapped his fingers; it was time for business. "Gotta have cash," he said. "No cash, no pussy."

The word pussy turned the man on. Feverishly he counted out several large bills.

Reece checked it through twice. When he was satisfied he said, "Room eight, near the pool." Then he winked. "Do the double loop for me, partner, compliments of the house."

When Cyndra reached their room she thought about locking the door and keeping everyone out. Unfortunately she knew it wouldn't work – if she didn't let the man in Reece would only kick the door down.

She was pretty, she was young, she had talent – why hadn't her career taken off? If it had, everything would be all right. Reece was doing this to punish her. *How about divorcing him?* a little voice whispered in her ear. *How about getting out while I still can?* But she knew it was hopeless, he'd let her go unless she paid back every cent he'd spent on her.

There was a knock on the door. Swallowing hard, she smoothed down her dress, walked over and threw it open.

The man barged past her into the room, his Hawaiian shirt sticking to his chest. "Let's do this quick," he blurted. "I'm about ready – so hurry it up."

"I'll fix you a drink," she said, stalling for time. "There's a Coke machine down the hall and we got a bottle of Scotch or vodka. What'll it be?"

"Nothing," he said, already fumbling with the buttons on his fly.

She noticed the gleam of a wedding ring on his finger. "Does your wife know you're doing this?" she asked, sharply.

He stopped short. "What's my wife got to do with anything?"

"I . . . I just wondered, that's all."

His eyes darted around the room, settling on the bed. "I do it the conventional way," he announced. "Whyn't you lie back and take your clothes off?"

"I'm not a conventional girl," she replied quickly, continuing to stall.

"I don't got all night," he said, glancing at his watch.

"If you'd sooner forget it . . ." she ventured.

He jumped to attention at that. "I paid good money for you."

"How much?"

"What's it to you?"

His words infuriated her. "It's *me* you're supposed to fuck, isn't it?"

He reached over, pinching her left nipple through her dress. "I'm not used to women talkin' dirty."

She shrunk away. She was no hooker and she wasn't about to act like one. If Reece wanted to blow her head off, then so be it. "There's been a mistake," she said, her voice a dull monotone.

His eyes began to bug. "What mistake?"

342

Still with the flat voice. "I don't do this sort of thing."

"But I was told —"

"I don't care *what* you were told. Zip up your pants and get out of here. Go home to your wife."

Without any warning he burst into tears. "I knew I shouldn't a come here," he sobbed. "I knew it was a bad thing to do."

Cyndra was taken aback, she'd expected a violent reaction, not this. "Look," she said, showing some compassion. "I'll get Reece to drive you back to the casino. He doesn't have to know nothing happened."

The man continued to sob.

"We'll tell him it was the greatest. That way we'll both come out of this okay — you'll look like a real stud and I won't get my head bashed in." Gently she began steering him to the door. "This'll work out, you'll see. We'll —"

With a sudden spurt of anger he threw her arm off and choked out a frustrated, "What about my money?"

"I can't help you with that."

"I paid good money for you. I want it back."

"You'll have to ask Reece, and if you ask him he's gonna know."

The man seemed to have recovered from his crying jag. Now he was red-faced and angry. "I want my money," he said, stubbornly.

"I told you — I don't have it."

"Then you'd better get it, you cheap little hooker."

"He's got a gun," she said, in a flat voice. "He could blow both our heads off. Whyn't you do us both a favour an' go quietly?"

"This was a set-up all along," the man said, bitterly. "I seen you people on television, you had no intention of putting out."

"Listen, mister, you're the one started to whine like a baby."

"You black bitch — if I'm not getting my money, I'll sure get my money's worth." Unexpectedly he grabbed her, his wet lips slobbering all over her neck.

She shoved him off, but he came at her again.

Suddenly she was back in the Browning house in Bosewell and he was Mr Browning — grabbing her — forcing her to do things. Every bad memory flooded over her.

"I . . . won't . . . do . . . this,' she screamed, kicking out.

"You'll do it unless I get my money back," he said, roughly squeezing her breasts.

Was money all anybody cared about? Mr Browning's words

hung in the air – *black cunt* . . . *black bitch* . . . She could hear his voice, his insults. It was like it had all happened yesterday.

They fell back on the bed and her screams became louder. Somebody knocked on the dividing wall yelling a terse, "Shut up!"

The door flew open and Reece marched in. "What in hell-fire's goin' on here?" he demanded, narrow eyes pinning Cyndra accusingly.

"He . . . he . . . tried to attack me," she gasped.

"Damn whore," the man muttered. "The bitch wouldn't give me nothin'."

"I left you two to have a good time," Reece said patiently, tapping one of his pointy-toed cowboy boots on the frayed carpet. "An' all you're doin' is fighting. "*Course* she's gonna give you any sweet thing you want." He threw her a warning look. "Get it together, hon, or you *know* what'll happen."

"Screw you, Reece," she spat. "You can't treat me like this."

His hand hovered near his belt. "Oh, I can't, huh?"

The man decided the time had come to get back to his hotel room and his flabby wife. "I want my money," he said, making one last attempt to claim what was his.

"No refunds," Reece snapped.

"You had no right to pull this on me," Cyndra said, tears stinging her eyes. "I'll divorce you, that's what I'll do."

Reece stood dangerously still. "Honey, you'll *do* what *I say* you'll do."

"Why don't I take my money and leave," the man suggested, not liking the way this was going.

"Shut your mouth an' stay out of this," Reece said, not even looking in his direction. This was between him and Cyndra, and she had to learn a lesson.

"Maybe what I *should* do is call the cops," the man threatened. "You stole from me."

Reece jumped to attention, pulling back his jacket and revealing his gun stuck casually into his belt. "You ain't going nowhere, partner."

"Aw, Jesus!" the man groaned, the colour draining from his face. "Aw, sweet Jesus!"

Reece turned his attention back to Cyndra. "You – get your clothes off. I hear one more scream outta this room an' you *know* what'll happen."

The man began a slow edge towards the door.

Cyndra stared at Reece, a deep rage burning inside her. "You know what, Reece – you're nothing but a dumb pimp," she said, the words spilling out. "In fact, that's all you're capable of – pimping. How does it feel to be pimp of the year? Pimp of the fucking century?' Her voice rose. "How does it feel to know you CAN'T DO ANYTHING ELSE?"

The person next door hammered on the wall again.

"You callin' *me* a pimp?" Reece yelled. "Well, what does that make you? A whore, honey. A drippin' bloodsuckin' whore."

"Oh, I ain't no whore, mister. Don't you get it? *I ain't no whore*!" She leaped off the bed furious.

Removing the gun from his belt Reece waved it in her face.

"Don't threaten me," she yelled, hysterically. "You can't control my life. You can't control *me*." She lunged at him grabbing for the gun.

The man reached the door, sweat coursing down his face. These two were crazy. And he was equally crazy to have been tempted.

His hand clutched the door-knob as Cyndra and Reece struggled for possession of the gun. His hand was so slick with sweat he couldn't get it open.

And then a shot rang out. One lone shot.

The bullet ricocheted against the wall and hit the man in the back of his head. He fell to the ground without a sound. There was a long moment of frozen silence.

"Oh, *shit*," Reece said, panic-stricken. "Look what you done, you crazy bitch – you shot the dumb motherfucker. You killed him, you stupid cunt. You gone and goddamn killed him!"

Chapter 52

"I'm not as bad as you think," Emerson said.

"How do you know *what* I think?" Lauren replied, sliding along the leather seat as far away from him as she could get.

"It's not exactly difficult figuring you out."

"Figure this out, Emerson. I'd like to get out of this car, and I'd like to get out now."

He shrugged. "Okay, I'll admit it – I was bombed outta my skull – I gave you a hard time – so I'm sorry – I'll make it up to you."

She shook her head. "What does it take to get you to understand that I don't want anything to do with you?"

He began to laugh. "That's what I like about you. You're dif.erent from the rest of 'em. You can even string two words together."

"So can Nature," she snapped.

"*You* try living with Nature," he said, gloomily. "It's a bloody nightmare. Anyway – we split – didn't she tell you?"

Lauren leaned forward and tapped on the smoky black glass separating them from the driver.

"Whattaya doin'," he asked, lounging back and stretching out his long, leather-clad legs.

"Telling your driver to stop the car."

He looked amused. "I thought I told you – you're my prisoner."

"This is kidnapping."

He shrugged. "So arrest me."

She sat back trying to decide what to do. In spite of everything there was no denying that he was a very charismatic figure, and if she really wanted to face up to it she *was* attracted to him in spite of what had happened. Besides, what did she have to lose? Exactly nothing. Nature wasn't talking to her anyway.

"Okay," she said, with a weary sigh.

"Okay what?"

"I'll have lunch with you. Impress me. Dazzle me with your charm. Show me that you're really just like the boy next door."

He chortled with laughter. "Babe, I 'aven't been like the boy next door in twenty years."

"Make an effort."

"For you – anything."

He took her to a small Italian restaurant on Third Street. The jovial owner ushered them to a table in the back, treating Emerson like a king, while his bodyguard stayed at the front of the restaurant scanning the sidewalk for trouble.

"Champagne, caviar, what'll it be?" Emerson asked, tossing back his mane of hair.

She glanced at her watch. "It's three o'clock in the afternoon."

He couldn't have cared less. "So?"

"So I'll have a small green salad and some pasta. Then I have to go. Besides, this place doesn't have champagne and caviar."

"Wanna bet? I can get anything I want any time I want," he boasted.

"And if you don't get it you take it. Story of your life, right, Mr Burn?"

"What's with this Mr Burn crap?"

"I'm giving you a little respect, you should try it some time."

He leaned across the table staring directly into her eyes. "You're beautiful, y'know that? You got somethin' I really get off on."

She hit him with a little light sarcasm. "Gee, you certainly have a way with words."

He didn't seem to mind. "It's me upbringin'," he said, cheerfully.

"Where was that?"

"Elephant an' Castle – or asshole as we liked to call it back in the good old days. Sorta Brooklyn with a cockney accent."

"You and Nature have a lot in common – including a country."

He laughed, derisively. "Me and Nature 'ave exactly nothing in common."

"You married her."

"Big friggin' deal. I 'ad a hangover at the time."

"Is that your excuse for everything?"

"Oh – now you're gonna give me the "you drink too much" speech."

"I really don't care what you do."

347

"You're wrong."

"About what?"

"About not caring. From the first time I saw you I knew we had something goin'. You were like this little mouse runnin' around organizing that party for Samm up at my apartment – remember? I noticed you immediately 'cause you seemed different – you still are – that's what I like about you."

"I'll tell you what you like about me," she said, crisply. "You like the fact you can't have me, because you're so used to having every girl that breathes, and now finally somebody says no. *That's* the only thing you like about me."

"Wrong."

"I don't think so."

"Whyn't we put it to the test?"

"How?"

"Sleep with me an' see if I'm still around tomorrow."

"Very funny."

"Glad I got you laughin'."

After lunch he decided he had to buy some books so they stopped at Doubleday's on Fifth Avenue. Two minutes after leaving the limo word was on the street and he was mobbed. He grabbed her hand and ran her back to the limo. As soon as they were inside, the car took off.

"Home. Mine," she said, breathlessly.

"Deal," he replied. "I'll pick you up at ten."

"I'm asleep at ten."

"Tonight's different. Be dressed and ready to hit the town."

"I didn't say I'd go out with you."

"You didn't say you wouldn't. Just remember, I could have kept you prisoner for the rest of the day, but I'm letting you go. Now you owe me."

"Exactly nothing."

"Do you always 'ave to 'ave the last word?"

"Yes."

Upstairs in her apartment she found herself unable to settle down. This was crazy. Emerson Burn was a dilettante rock star. She wanted nothing to do with him. Or did she?

How come you had lunch with him, Roberts?

Why shouldn't I?

Do you find him attractive?

Yes, as a matter of fact I do.

The phone rang and she grabbed it, ready to tell Emerson

348

she was definitely not going out with him that night or any other night for that matter.

"Hi," Pia said, brightly. "What are you doing?"

"I just walked in. Why?"

"Howard and I want to take you to dinner."

"I don't like the sound of your voice."

"What's wrong with my voice?"

"Whenever you use that tone there's always some single guy you think is perfect for me."

"I resent that," Pia said, indignantly. "As a matter of fact, we're dining with Howard's uncle, and we thought it would be nice if you made up the foursome."

"Where's his wife?"

"At their house in the Hamptons."

"Hmm . . ."

"Lauren. We're talking about Howard's *old married* uncle – he's hardly likely to jump all over you."

"He's a man, isn't he?"

"Oh, *please!*"

"Okay, I'll come."

Pia was so used to getting a no that this was a surprise. "We'll pick you up at eight," she said quickly, before Lauren changed her mind.

Hmm . . . dinner with Howard's uncle. At least it got her out of the house, and when Emerson arrived and found nobody home maybe he'd take the hint and leave her alone.

Or then again – maybe not.

349

Chapter 53

She didn't know how long she'd been sitting there, she only knew that Reece had gone and left her. Left her with a dead man lying on the floor.

She crouched on the bed, hugging her knees to her chest, her eyes wide with fear, while the man's body lay in a huddle behind the door.

"*I* didn't shoot him, *you* did it," she'd screamed at Reece when it had happened, breaking away from him, her body trembling.

"Oh no no *no* – baby, I don't take the rap on this one," Reece had said, frantically stuffing his clothes in a suitcase and running for the door.

"You . . . can't . . . leave . . . me," she'd said, the words sticking in her throat.

"Just watch me, honey," he'd said, throwing the gun at her.

And then he was gone.

At first she'd thought about calling the police. In fact, she wouldn't have been surprised if they'd turned up, because the people next door must have heard the gun shot. But nothing happened. Absolutely nothing. So she stayed on the bed too frightened to move, knowing she should have followed Reece and taken off. But how could she? He had the car and all their money – she was left with nothing.

So she sat in the middle of the bed, tears rolling down her cheeks, clutching on to the gun – her only protection.

Her life was over and there was nothing she could do about it.

"This is just like I've seen it on television!" Annie exclaimed. "Look at all these lights!"

"Yeah, this is really something," Nick agreed, pulling into

the parking lot of a downtown hotel.

"Where are we going?" she asked. "Shouldn't we find Cyndra?"

"First we're gonna gamble. That's what you're supposed t'do in Vegas."

"Nick –"

"Try an' enjoy yourself, Annie," he said, teasingly. "Today's your day for takin' chances. Bring it t'the edge – you never know – you might enjoy it." He got out of the car, grabbed her by the hand and they ran across the parking lot into the hotel lobby.

"Holy shit!" Nick exclaimed, taking in the banks of slot machines all in constant use. A grin spread over his face. "Y'know, I always wanted to do this." He groped in his pocket for change, coming up with several quarters. "C'mon, pick a machine – we're gonna win big time!"

"We are?" she asked, unsurely.

"You bet your ass we are!"

They played the slots for two hours straight, ending up ten dollars ahead. By this time Nick had the fever – he was all set to carry on, but Annie was ready to quit. "We'd better go find Cyndra," she worried. "It's one o'clock. What will they say when we turn up in the middle of the night?"

"They won't care. Tomorrow night we'll catch Cyndra sing, then we'll drive back to LA."

"I can't take off work again tomorrow," Annie objected.

"You'll call in sick. Big deal."

She sighed. "You're making me as bad as you are."

"Hey – that can only be an improvement, right?"

"Thanks a lot!"

Armed with directions they drove to the motel where Cyndra and Reece were staying. It was not the most glamorous place in the world – just a few rooms located around a small pool.

"I bet they're asleep," Annie said, accusingly. "I told you we should have come earlier."

"I bet they're not," he retorted, confidently. "Nobody sleeps in Vegas."

They parked the car, found the room and knocked a few times getting no answer.

"I gotta stop making a habit of this," he grumbled. "I'll spring the lock – no problem."

"You can't do that," Annie said, alarmed.

"Yeah, *right*," he said, working his magic on the lock and pushing the door open.

The first thing they saw was Cyndra sitting in the middle of the bed holding a gun. The second was the body slumped on the floor behind the door.

"Oh my God!" Annie gasped.

Cyndra stared at them blankly while Nick edged his way towards her. "Take it easy," he said, speaking fast. "Take it real easy." Gently he removed the gun from her hands. "What happened?"

She covered her face with her hands and began to sob. "Oh, Nick . . . Nick . . ."

He put his arms around her, cradling her to him.

"C'mon, baby, you can tell me."

Slowly she began to choke out her story. "Reece wanted me to sleep with this . . . man. He brought him to our room . . . and then . . . then the guy wanted his money back because I wouldn't do it, and . . . and . . . Reece took out his gun . . . we were fighting . . . and . . . it went off. It was an accident, Nick, it really was."

"Where's Reece?"

"He ran."

"And left you like this?"

"What's going to happen, Nick? Nobody's gonna believe me. The cops won't understand."

Cyndra was right, she wouldn't stand a chance.

He went over to the man, staring down at his immobile body, hoping this was all a big mistake and that the guy would breathe – move – *something*.

No such luck.

"I'll phone the police," Annie said, pale and shaken.

"No," he said, quickly. "This don't look so good." He turned back to his sister. "You're *sure* you didn't know him?"

She shook her head. "Reece picked him up in the casino; I never saw him before."

"So there's no connection between the two of you?"

"Not unless we were seen leaving together."

He bent down, gingerly groping inside the man's jacket for his wallet. It was imitation leather and contained five hundred dollars cash, a couple of credit cards and a driver's licence made out to George Baer.

"We gotta get him out of here – an' fast," he muttered, thinking aloud. "Yeah, that's what we gotta do."

Annie asserted herself. "No. What we must do is call the police."

"Will you shut up about the cops," he said, glaring at her. "Cyndra's in trouble, we gotta help her."

"I can't be an accessory," Annie said, stiffly.

"I'm asking you a favour."

"It's too big a favour."

He pinned her with his green eyes. "I'm worth it, aren't I?"

She hesitated. "I . . . I don't know."

"Do it for me, Annie," he said, persuasively. "Nobody has to know what happened here tonight."

"*I'll* know," she said, vehemently. "And I can't live with it."

She was getting on his nerves. Fuck her if she didn't want to co-operate. "If that's the way you feel you'd better take a walk."

"Don't you understand," she said, her eyes filling with tears. "This is wrong."

"Cyndra's my sister – she needs me, so get off my fuckin' case."

"I'm not leaving," Annie said, stubbornly.

"If you're staying you're helping, an' that makes you part of it."

"What are you going to do?"

"I'll deal with it, okay?" he replied, tired of her questions.

He coaxed Cyndra off the bed and told her to pack her things. Then he stripped the blanket from the bed and began the arduous task of trying to roll the man's body into it. No easy job. There was blood everywhere and Annie's accusing eyes nailed him every move he made. Sweat enveloped him. His mouth was dry and his heart pounding. Shit! He didn't even know if he was doing the right thing, but if he was to get Cyndra out of this mess there seemed to be no other alternative.

Finally he had the body wrapped in the blanket. The next move was to get it out of the stinking motel room and into the trunk of the car. He stood back and took a beat.

"Nick, I'm really frightened," Cyndra said, clinging to his arm.

"Don't be," he said, sounding more confident than he felt. "It's almost taken care of. I'm gonna drive the body out to the desert and bury it. You two'll stay here until I get back."

"No," she said, sharply. "I can't let you do this alone. I'm coming with you."

"If you're going so am I," Annie said, quickly joining in.

The two of them were beginning to drive him crazy, but it was probably safer to take them with him. "Okay, okay," he said, reluctantly. He went outside and took a look around. When he was sure it was all clear, he backed his car up as close as he could get. Then, still keeping a wary eye out, he dragged the body out of the room and somehow or other bundled it into the trunk.

By the time they set off everyone was tense and on edge.

"We're taking this nice and easy," he said, trying to keep them both calm. "If we get pulled over for anything – anything at all – stay cool, right?"

He drove carefully out of town through the gaudy neon-lit streets until they reached the quieter outskirts, and then eventually the desert. Then he drove another half hour before pulling over to the side of the road, lugging the man's body from the trunk, dragging him across the sand for what seemed like an eternity – and then digging a makeshift shallow grave using his hands.

When he was finished he rolled up the blood-soaked blanket and carried it back to the car. "We'll bury this somewhere else," he said, throwing it in the trunk. "Don't want any connection between the body and the hotel room."

"What about the gun?" Cyndra asked, anxiously.

"I'll get rid of it on the way back to LA."

"This is a nightmare," Annie said, shaking her head. "I wish I'd never met either of you."

"Well, sweetheart – you did, an' now you're part of it, so shut up," he said roughly, not in the mood to listen to any more of her complaints.

Within minutes they were on their way back to LA.

Chapter 54

"I made a mistake," Oliver Liberty said.

"Excuse me?" Lauren replied.

They were sitting in an exclusive New York club, sipping brandies while Pia and Howard clung together on the small dance floor. The sound of Frank Sinatra singing "In the Wee Small Hours of the Morning' flooded the darkly panelled room.

Oliver puffed on a long thin cigar – it suited his aquiline features. "I said I made a mistake," he repeated.

"About what?" she asked, politely.

"When my wife left me I was very angry. We'd been together for over thirty years until one day she decided she'd had enough. She became an overnight feminist, and suddenly I was the enemy."

"That's not good."

"An understatement, my dear."

"So you met Opal –"

"And foolishly married her."

Lauren wasn't sure she wanted to hear this. Sitting in a nightclub listening to Howard's uncle tell her all about his failing marriage was not her idea of heaven. But then again she'd had a nice enough time. They'd been to an expensive French restaurant, talked about everything from politics to the latest fashions and although he might not be the youngest man in the world, he certainly had an abundance of charm.

"Are you sure you should be telling me this?" she asked.

"I can talk to you," he said, nodding as if to reassure himself. "You have a certain quality."

"What quality is that?" she asked, lightly.

"Something in your eyes. An understanding. And let us not forget, you're also a very beautiful woman."

This certainly seemed to be her week for compliments. "I'm flattered," she said, "but I'm no psychiatrist."

"I didn't say you were," he replied, nodding towards the dance floor. "Shall we?"

"Okay," she said, getting up.

He stubbed out his cigar, took her hand and led her on to the crowded floor. For a moment he held her at a discreet distance, and then without warning pulled her into his embrace. "I've already spoken to my lawyers," he said.

"About what?" she asked, inhaling his expensive aftershave.

"A divorce."

"Why are you telling me?"

"Because you're easy to talk to, and I want to see you again. That's if you don't mind being in the company of an older man." He smiled when he said it, taking the curse off his words.

She thought about saying *I have no intention of getting involved*, but it seemed presumptuous to assume anything at this early stage, so instead she murmured, "I'd like that."

"So would I," he replied. "How about tomorrow night?"

Outside the club Oliver's Japanese chauffeur and sleek black Rolls waited patiently.

"Not bad, huh?" Pia whispered, climbing in the back while Oliver and Howard discussed business on the sidewalk. "Do you like him?"

"He's married," Lauren whispered back. "Stop trying to fix me up."

"Ah, but he's getting a divorce."

"Pia, he's old enough to be my father, maybe even my grandfather."

"So what?"

"Do me a favour – quit trying to match-make."

They dropped Howard and Pia off first, and then the Rolls proceeded to Lauren's apartment. On the street she spotted Emerson's limousine parked outside her building. The last thing she was in the mood for was another confrontation. Turning to Oliver she said, "Do you have a guest room?"

He looked at her, quizzically. "A guest room?"

"There's somebody I want to avoid, and uh . . . it seems to me if I went home with you it would save me a problem."

"Certainly," he said, only too happy to oblige.

Oliver's apartment was sumptuous by anybody's standards. Located in a stately old building overlooking Central Park the

356

ceilings were high, the rooms large, and the view incredible. He led her into the living room and offered her a drink.

She shook her head. "I have to work tomorrow. Would you mind if I went straight to my room?"

"Not at all," he said, leading her down a spacious corridor into a guest bedroom. "Can I get you something to sleep in?"

"Maybe an old shirt?"

"I'll be right back."

She explored the tastefully decorated room obviously designed by a woman – certainly not his current wife – perhaps a decorator?

Picking up a silver frame she studied the photograph of a younger Oliver and a woman who was obviously his previous wife. They made a handsome couple.

Oliver returned and handed her a plastic wrapped toothbrush, a tube of toothpaste, a silk shirt and a hairbrush. "All settled?" he asked, smiling.

She smiled back. "Thank you, I've got everything I need – you must have done this before."

"No, Lauren," he replied, seriously. "I can assure you I haven't." He hesitated at the door. "Tell me, my dear, exactly *who* are you avoiding?"

She shook her head. "Nobody important."

The next morning she was dressed and ready to leave by eight thirty. A housekeeper greeted her in the hallway.

"Mr Liberty has already left. He asked me to tell you that his driver is downstairs waiting to take you wherever you wish to go."

She felt a tinge of disappointment – she'd hoped to see him, but apparently he was an earlier riser than she.

Taking advantage of his car she had the driver drop her at her apartment where she quickly changed clothes. No messages from Emerson. She felt relieved – or did she? Too confusing, she couldn't make up her mind.

At the office Pia bombarded her with questions. "What do you think of him? I told you he's getting a divorce, didn't I? Hmm . . . he *is* attractive, isn't he?"

Lauren shook her head. "*Stop* fixing me up."

"I'm not fixing you up – I'm trying to marry you off! One day you'll be old and shrivelled – what then?"

"I'm sure I'll be very happy, thank you."

Pia pulled a face. "You know what, Lauren – you're a hopeless case. Oh, and by the way – Emerson Burn called you three times this morning. What does *he* want?"

"If I knew I'd tell you."

"*Sure* you would."

"I would."

"Oh yes, and pigs will wear tutus and fly down Fifth Avenue!"

"Very funny."

"You don't need a rock star, Lauren. You need Oliver. He's stable, rich and crazy about you."

"I'll tell his wife."

"Ex-wife."

"Not yet."

"Sooner than you think."

"Yeah?"

"Yeah."

Chapter 55

Back in LA Nick found two messages from Frances Cavendish. Good sign? Bad sign? He didn't know. He'd brought Cyndra and Annie back to his place because he'd figured it wasn't safe for either of them to go to their own apartments, but now they were getting on his nerves. Cyndra wandered around in a daze, and Annie complained hotly because he hadn't dropped her home.

"We gotta get our stories straight before anybody goes anywhere," he said. "I'll call Frances Cavendish back – then we'll talk."

Annie glared at him. He ignored her.

"Where have you been?" Frances said, testily.

"Out of town."

"In future leave a number where I can reach you."

Who the fuck did she think she was talking to? "Yes, *ma'am*," he said, biting back a sharper retort.

"They like you, sonny," she drawled, calming down. "They like you a lot."

"What does that mean?" he asked, suspiciously.

"They want to see you again. In fact they might even test you."

"Is that good or bad?"

She made an exasperated sound in the back of her throat. "How long have you been in this business, Nick? A test costs them money – if they're paying of course it's good."

He wound the phone cord around his wrist, snapping it back and forth. "When do I get to do this?"

"Today, be at my office at ten." She hung up before he could reply.

Well, why not? She knew he'd be there. He was an actor after all, and when a casting agent says jump it's all systems go.

Annie had stationed herself by the door. "I want to go home," she said, daring him to say no. "I want to go home now."

"Okay, okay. But Cyndra stays here. And listen carefully, if Reece shows up, you know nothin'. You never went to Vegas, you've been with a girlfriend for the last twenty-four hours. Got it?"

She continued to glare at him. "Yes."

"And don't go making any phone calls you might regret. Whatever happened in Vegas – it's history."

"If you say so," she said, tightly.

"What's that mean?"

"I've never had to bury a body before."

"I said forget about it, Annie, it never happened."

"Maybe *you* can pretend it never happened. I can't."

"Okay – I'll take you home." He glanced over at his sister. She sat by the window staring out. "Cyndra, you stay here. Don't answer the door or phone. I'll get back soon as I can."

She nodded, dully.

Annie gave him the silent treatment on the drive to her apartment. Her attitude was shit, but there was nothing he could do about it.

"Call you later," he promised, dropping her off on the street.

She didn't say a word as she marched inside. He had a strong suspicion she was going to cause trouble.

Regrettably there was nothing he could do about it.

The woman producer had eyes for him. No mistaking that hungry look.

The tall man hated him. Probably a closet queen with a yen he didn't want to let loose.

The director was into pleasing everyone.

"I don't think we need to test him," the woman said. "Do you, Joel?"

The tall man shrugged. "Whatever."

"I'm happy," the director said.

Nick sat in the room listening to them talk about him as if he wasn't there.

"Shall we have him read again?" asked one of the casting people.

"Not necessary," said the woman, tapping her foot impatiently.

"The camera'll love him," said the director, running a hand through his greasy brown hair. "He's got the eyes."

"I'd like to see his body," the woman said, crossing her legs, silk stockings crackling.

He wasn't sure but he thought he caught a glimpse of suspenders.

"Would you mind removing your shirt?" said one of the casting people.

Where was Frances when he needed her? Nobody had warned him he'd have to strip off.

"There's a scene in the movie where he's in bed with the hero's girlfriend," explained the director. "Can't have you looking better than the star."

They all laughed.

He stood up and awkwardly removed his shirt.

"Fine," said the woman.

"No competition," said the director.

"We'll get back to you," said the tall man.

Getting out of there was a pleasure.

Outside he sat in his car trying to re-live the events of the last twenty-four hours. He'd buried a body for crissakes. He'd buried a fucking body in the Nevada desert, and that made him an accessory to murder. Jesus. Maybe Annie was right. Maybe they should have called the police and let Cyndra explain.

No way. She wouldn't have stood a chance.

The woman producer strode out of the building and got into a cream coloured sports Mercedes. She wore large mirrored sunglasses and a knowing smile.

Nick wondered who she was fucking. The tall man for sure. The director – maybe.

He hadn't liked removing his shirt in there, it was demeaning. He was an actor, not a stripper.

The woman drove off and he followed her for a while. Her Mercedes sped down Sunset. He drew alongside her at a stop light and said, "Hi." She looked at him as if she'd never seen him before in her life.

"Nick Angel," he said, dropping the O, just as Joy had advised.

"Do I know you?" she said, adjusting her huge mirrored shades. Bitch!

He gunned the light and drove straight home. Cyndra was gone. This wasn't his day.

His landlady was sunning herself outside. "You're two days late on the rent," she reminded, as he rushed past.

"You'll get it."

"I'd better or you're out."

Money was a problem. He'd almost blown the Tijuana stash and there was nothing coming in. If he paid his rent there'd be hardly anything left.

"Did you see my sister leave?"

"Your sister," his landlady sneered. "No, I didn't see your *sister*."

He jumped back in his car and headed for Annie's.

"We're going to the police," Annie said. She was dressed and ready for action, a silent Cyndra by her side.

He'd arrived just in time, they were almost out the door.

"You can't do that," he said.

"Oh, yes, we can."

He appealed to Cyndra. "I helped you out – you go to the cops now an' it'll be me who gets it. Don't kid yourself – we'll all be in deep shit. Is that what you want?"

"I don't know . . ." she said, unsurely. "Annie says it's the right thing to do, otherwise this'll always be hanging over us."

"Fuck!" he muttered angrily, turning on Annie.

She backed away.

"Don't you understand?" he said, angrily. "It's *too goddamn late*. We're in this together an' we'd better learn to trust one another, so stop this runnin' to the cops shit. I can't take it every time I leave the house."

"But –" Annie began.

"But nothing – you do this again an' so help me I'll –"

"You'll what?" she asked, defiantly.

He'd almost raised his arm to her. He'd wanted to strike out – just like Primo, just like his father. Oh, God! There was no way he'd ever allow himself to become like that fucking loser. He slumped into a chair. "Don't do this to us, Annie. You gotta let it go."

Her eyes filled with tears. "I'm trying."

"Try harder."

She nodded, acquiescing.

They were safe – for now – but who knew how long it would be before she spilled it all? Annie was dangerous. But he had a solution, and the sooner he put it into action the better.

Chapter 56

Emerson dropped out of sight and Oliver moved in. Lauren had never been courted before and it was strangely seductive. Oliver sent her flowers every day, called at noon without fail, always checked out his plans with her, and never so much as attempted a good-night kiss.

After three weeks of this courtly treatment she was beginning to wonder what was wrong with her.

"He adores you!" Pia confided, perching on the side of her desk. "He told Howard."

"That's nice," Lauren replied, busily organizing a pile of papers.

"Stop being so cool and in control," Pia said, hardly able to hide her exasperation. "What do *you* think of *him*?"

"He's a very charming man."

"You're so non-committal."

"What do you *want* me to say?"

"Have you slept with him?"

"Pia – if I had, you'd be the last to know."

"Why?"

"Because since you've become a married woman you do nothing but gossip."

Pia's eyes gleamed. "Is he sensational in bed? Older men are supposed to have fantastic technique," she giggled, slyly. "I hear they give great head."

"I wouldn't know."

"What are you waiting for?"

Good question. What *was* she waiting for?

Actually she was waiting for Oliver to make a move. The fact that he hadn't intrigued her. Was there something wrong with her? Did she turn him off? It was about time she found out.

363

Later that week they went to the opening of a Broadway show and the following party. Oliver seemed to know everyone. The musical comedy actress who starred in the show; a slew of New York socialites whom he jokingly called night runners; a famous senator and his equally famous model girlfriend. Lauren guessed that he probably even knew Emerson Burn – crazy Emerson who'd flashed into her life and vanished just as quickly. A good thing – because he was definitely trouble. She'd read that he'd left on a world tour.

On the ride home they discussed the evening. Oliver enjoyed filling her in on everyone – he had interesting stories and was not shy about telling them. According to him the musical comedy actress liked other women; the senator wore red sequinned stockings to bed; and the model only slept with men worth over ten million dollars.

"How do you know all this?" she asked, studying his distinguished profile.

"I'm in advertising. It's my business to know everything."

"Then who's going to be the new Marcella girl? I hear they want Nature and she's holding out for too much money."

Oliver frowned; he hated it when somebody knew something before he was prepared to tell them. "Who told you that?"

"Samm."

"If she was worth it, I'd recommend they pay her."

"You don't think she is?"

"Too many covers in too short a time," he said, brusquely. "Her face is overly familiar."

"Is it your account?"

"Between us?"

"No. I'm taking an announcement in *Ad Weekly*."

"Very amusing, Lauren."

"Well?" she pressed. "*Is* it your account?"

"It wasn't, but it will be."

"Really?"

"They're coming in to see what we have to offer tomorrow."

"And what *do* you have to offer?"

"A surprise."

She grinned. "I love surprises."

"Good."

The car drew up outside her building. She'd never asked him before, but the time seemed right. "Would you like to come up for a drink, Oliver?"

He shook his head. "I didn't want to bother you with this before, but my charming wife has detectives following me. Apparently she feels she'll get even more of my money if she can prove I'm sleeping around."

"I asked you up for a drink, nothing else."

"My dear, *I* know that. But I would never put you in a compromising position."

Thoughtful as well. He was turning out to be the perfect man.

"Tomorrow night – I'll pick you up at eight," he said.

"Not possible, I'm catering a dinner."

"Have someone else do it."

"No."

"Why not?"

She hated it when he tried to tell her what to do. "Because I want to do it myself."

He went to say something, then changed his mind. Lauren had that determined look, he knew better than to argue.

Chapter 57

Things happened fast. "You've got the part," Frances told him over the phone. "Shooting begins in two weeks. I've made an appointment for you to see an agent friend – she'll handle the deal. And I've booked you a photo session with another friend of mine. The session's gratis – all you have to pay for are the prints."

"Hey, Frances – this is great. I –"

Frances was a fast talker. "Saturday night. Escort duties. You're taking me to an industry party – wear a suit."

He started to say something but she cut him off again.

"I'm putting you on to my assistant, she'll give you the details. Oh, and Nick, don't forget who got you started."

"Frances, I –" She was gone.

He had a role in a fucking movie. He was about to get an agent. He was going to be a star! Things were definitely moving in the right direction.

His new agent was a short, middle-aged woman called Meena Caron. She had dark, bobbed hair and thick "no nonsense" glasses. She was with a large important agency, which was reassuring.

"It's two days work," she said, all business. "You'll be shooting in New York. They'll fly you in the day before – tourist – only above the title gets first."

"What does that mean?"

"Above the title?"

"Yeah."

She looked at him quizzically. "You *are* new to the business, aren't you."

"Gotta learn sometime," he said, cheerfully.

Meena tapped a silver Cartier pen on her desk top. "*Stars* get their name above the title. The star of your movie is Charlie

366

Geary. He's young, red-hot and a real-life pain. Stay away from him – he'll do his best to get you fired. And don't try to screw the leading lady – that's Charlie's privilege."

Oh, yeah?

"Who's the girl?"

"Carlysle Mann. Very pretty. Very crazy."

"I never went for crazy."

Meena didn't crack a smile. "As soon as you get your photos bring them in. There's a pilot at NBC you could be right for. You *can* act, can't you?"

"Frances wouldn't've sent me to you if I couldn't."

Meena stood up – she was finished with him. "Frances has her own reasons for doing things. You look good. I'm sure she's taking you on the party circuit."

He didn't answer. It was none of her goddamn business. Maybe he should have opted to go with Ardmore Castle instead of this storm trooper.

The photographer Frances set him up with was a tall gawky woman who worked fast, shrieking directions at her harassed assistant. Didn't Frances ever deal with men?

She circled him like a predatory animal. "Stop trying so hard," she kept on telling him. "For God's sake attempt to look natural. Dump the put-on scowl, it's so phoney."

He hated her too. He was used to women falling all over him. The agent and the photographer didn't appear to give a fast fuck.

After the session he figured he should go home – check up on Cyndra. But then again Joy was probably wondering where he'd vanished to, and he didn't want her mad at him. Christ, this was like walking a tightrope without a net. Surrounded by women and he wasn't even getting laid.

Joy greeted him frostily.

He told her about the movie.

"Bit part," she said, screwing up her nose in disgust. "You should have held out for better."

"At least it's a job. My first professional one."

"Crap movie. Crap director."

Why couldn't she be pleased for him instead of criticizing everything? "Gotta start somewhere," he said easily, refusing to let her get to him.

"Ha!" she sniffed.

He told her about Meena Caron.

367

"Second rate."

"She's with a big agency," he pointed out.

"You'll get lost. You should have signed with Ardmore."

"I don't like Ardmore."

She narrowed her eyes. "Who said you have to like people? It's what they can do for you that counts."

Maybe. Maybe not. But right now Joy was bringing him down, so he got out of there fast and stopped by to see Annie at the health club. She was suitably cool.

"My movie's shooting in New York," he said. "Maybe Cyndra can stay with you while I'm away."

"*Your* movie," she sneered.

He'd had it with her attitude. "Yeah. *My* fuckin' movie. Two days work – it's more than you're doin'."

She looked hurt. "Thanks, Nick. Remind me that I can't get a job. Remind me that every time I go on an interview all they want is a six foot blonde with big tits."

He did his best to soften her up. "Two days, Annie. I can't leave her alone."

"Why not?" she said, bitterly. "I'm here to do anything you want. Right?"

Slowly Cyndra recovered and tried to think positively. After all it wasn't her fault, *she* hadn't shot the man, Reece had. It was *his* gun, *his* responsibility.

Damn Reece Webster. He'd gone. Vanished. Good riddance.

"I'm moving back to my apartment," she told Nick.

"You can't do that," he said, trying to reason with her.

Cyndra had a strong stubborn streak. "Why not?" she asked, tilting her chin, preparing for a fight.

"'Cause you're not ready."

She sighed, brushing a hand through her long dark hair. "Stop worrying about me, Nick. I won't go to the cops, and nor will Annie."

"An' what'll you do if Reece comes back?"

"He won't."

"You don't know for sure."

"Look – if he does, I'll tell him the guy got up an' walked away."

Was she stupid or what? "The man was dead, Cyndra, fuckin' *dead*."

"Reece doesn't know that. He ran out of there so fast he

doesn't know anything. Go off and do your movie, it's a great break for you. It'd be nice if *one* of us made it."

He couldn't argue with that.

Frances worked a room good. She knew everyone and everyone knew her. Nick trailed behind, feeling out of place and inadequate in his rented suit. He was in a freakin' mansion for crissake – the like of which he'd never seen. It made the Browning house back in Bosewell resemble a shack.

Frances ordered a drink and made him carry it. She didn't bother introducing him to anyone – not that anyone seemed interested in meeting him – they looked right through him as if he didn't exist. As the evening progressed so did his sense of aggravation. He felt invisible, unimportant – it wasn't a feeling he enjoyed.

Dinner was seated, and he was not seated next to Frances. He found himself between a fat woman in a maroon cocktail dress and an older man in an ill-fitting tuxedo. He didn't have to be a genius to figure out it was the worst table in the room.

The fat woman talked to a vivacious blonde on her other side. The older man morosely sipped his drink.

Frances was across the room at a table filled with familiar faces. Everyone at her table was laughing and talking. Shit! How did he get stuck in these situations?

He gave conversation a shot, asking the man what he did.

"Banking," was the cold reply.

"You work in a bank or you own it?" he said, going for the flippant approach.

The man was unamused.

After a while he got up and made his way outside to the bar. Two waiters were sneaking a smoke. "Anybody know who's giving this party?" he asked.

"Some studio exec," said one of the waiters.

"That's his daughter," said the other waiter, gesturing across the well-kept gardens, where a young blonde was entwined around a guy with long hair. They were making their own entertainment.

"At least someone's having a good time," he mumbled.

It took forever before Frances was ready to be escorted home. He got behind the wheel of her old Mercedes and gunned the engine.

"Did you enjoy yourself?" she asked, puffing on a cigarette.

Was she kidding?

He stared unseeingly at the road ahead. "I had a lousy time."

She couldn't have cared less. "Really?"

"Those people don't wanna know you unless you're important."

"That's Hollywood, dear," she said, matter-of-factly. "Make the most of it – when you're famous they'll be crawling all over you."

He liked the sound of her words. Glancing at her quizzically he said, "You really think I'm gonna be famous, Frances?"

She blew smoke in his face and regarded him with her flinty grey eyes. "Yes, Nick, as a matter of fact I think you're going to be very famous indeed."

Chapter 58

"I'm finally divorced," Oliver announced over the phone. "Tonight we're celebrating."

Lauren was at work. Cradling the receiver under her chin she doodled on a yellow legal pad. "How did it happen so fast?" she asked.

"We made a deal. My ex-wife loves deals."

She drew a circle enclosing it with a square. "Congratulations, Oliver."

"Thank you, my dear."

"Where are we going?"

"We're staying home. My chauffeur will pick you up at seven." A slight pause. "Oh, and Lauren . . . bring a toothbrush."

Was this his way of telling her they were finally going to consummate their relationship? Hardly romantic, but Oliver was nothing if not to the point.

She went home early, washed her hair, took a leisurely bath, rubbed perfumed cream into her skin and thought about the evening ahead. She liked Oliver – he was entertaining. He had panache and style, wore great suits, always got the best table in restaurants. He was a good dancer, charming and witty.

But I don't love him.

So what? Who do you think's going to come rushing into your life? There are no Prince Charmings left.

But I don't love him.

Get real. He's the man for you.

He's old enough to be my grandfather.

It doesn't matter.

She dressed carefully, still thinking about what lay ahead. She'd slept with three men. Nick – who'd gotten her pregnant and dumped her. Brad – her bad seed cousin. And Jimmy – who'd taken off the day of their supposed wedding.

Some trio.

Except Nick is special.

Bullshit. Nick Angelo is nothing but a loser.

I loved him.

No you didn't.

I still love him.

For God's sake!

Oliver's apartment was filled with white orchids; his favourite jazz pianist – Erroll Garner – played background music on the stereo – the lights were low and Oliver was in a very good mood indeed. He greeted her with compliments and a glass of champagne, while the butler served small wedges of toast loaded with caviar from a silver tray.

"I don't like caviar," she said, wrinkling her nose.

Oliver looked amused. "It's an acquired taste. Acquire it, my dear, you'll soon grow to adore it."

They ate in the dining room with candles lighting the table and Erroll Garner giving way to the smooth sound of Ella Fitzgerald.

Lauren picked at her food and gulped two glasses of wine, wondering if she should encourage him.

A little late, Roberts. You've encouraged him for three months. Why stop now?

After dinner he dismissed his servants and led her into the darkly panelled library where they sat in front of a burning wood fire sipping brandies.

"I don't usually drink –" she began.

"I know," he interrupted, removing the glass from her hand and leaning over to kiss her.

This was not the first time they'd kissed, but it was certainly the most intense. She was glad she'd had the champagne and the wine at dinner and now the brandy.

God! She was nervous.

He moved slowly, kissing her for a long time before suggesting they go into the bedroom.

Her affair with Jimmy had taken place over a year ago – she hadn't been with anyone since, and yet she did not feel that incredible rush of excitement. Instead she felt apprehensive – as if she was about to embark on a trip she might regret.

The bedroom was alive with red roses, the seductive scent of them filling the air. Oliver touched her lightly on the cheek. "Do you want to undress in the bathroom? There's a robe in there for you."

She hadn't planned on undressing herself, but that was apparently what he expected.

Shutting the bathroom door she stared at herself in the mirror. Little Lauren Roberts. High school prude. About to embark on a sexual adventure with a man who was older than her father. Oh, God!

For a moment she flashed on to the memory of Phil Roberts that fateful day in Bosewell. Her father and his . . . woman. Her father and that cheap tramp.

And then she saw Primo, leering at her with his wild eyes. She could almost feel his beer gut pushing up against her, and his filthy laugh began ringing in her head.

You killed him, Lauren.

I'm not sure . . .

Oh yes, Lauren, you killed him all right.

She removed her clothes and put on the silk robe Oliver had so thoughtfully provided. The material was soft and sensuous. She pulled it around her protectively.

He was waiting under the covers with the lights off. A single candle lit the room. The scent of the roses was overwhelming.

Standing next to the bed she slipped the robe from her shoulders, allowing it to fall to the floor.

"You're so beautiful," Oliver murmured, holding the covers open.

She dived for safety.

Slowly he began stroking her naked body – apparently in no hurry – content to touch and caress her, until she felt herself longing for more.

Tentatively she stretched her hand beneath the sheet, reaching for him. To her surprise and disappointment he was not hard.

"Don't worry, it'll happen," he murmured, unconcernedly. "Lie back, my darling, before anything else I plan to make you feel wonderful."

His head began to move down her body, his tongue tracing little patterns on her breasts and stomach as he descended, until finally his head was between her legs and his fingers started prying her apart – all the better for his tongue to gain entry.

She gasped. This was a first and she was unprepared and wary of what to expect.

"Relax, my sweet, relax and enjoy," he said soothingly, his tongue flicking in and out with practised ease.

"Oh . . . my . . . God," she whispered. This was so intimate, so private, and yet – she had to admit – so breathtakingly enjoyable.

She threw her head and arms back and did as he requested, allowing herself to fall into the beauty of the moment.

He held her open with his thumbs – all the better to penetrate as far as he could.

Was this what Pia had been talking about when she'd said older men gave great head? Was this it? – because if it was Oliver certainly knew what he was doing.

Before long she began to feel little shock waves of pleasure. They started in her toes and travelled up her entire body – causing her to moan softly. Shivering uncontrollably she threw her legs wide.

He devoured her with a passion until she climaxed with a long drawn out cry of ecstasy.

Oliver surfaced, a smile on his face. "I can't think of a better time to ask you." He paused for a moment. "My beautiful Lauren, will you do me the honour of becoming my wife?"

"Let me see the ring," Pia said for the hundredth time – at least it seemed to Lauren it was the hundredth time.

She held out her hand while Pia admired the four-carat emerald surrounded with baguette diamonds.

"Gorgeous!" Pia sighed.

Lauren patted her friend's evergrowing stomach. "Gorgeous!" she said, enviously.

"Seriously, Lauren, I'm so happy for you."

When I'm thirty he'll be almost seventy, Lauren thought. *When I'm fifty he'll be dead.*

"Is he okay about you continuing to work?" Pia asked.

"About as okay as Howard is with you."

"That's encouraging. Howard begs me daily to give it up."

Lauren looked perplexed. "Why is it that men are always so threatened by working women?"

"Because it means we have our own money," Pia said, wisely. "And with our own money comes independence. Samm is my shining example."

"Samm is a lonely old spinster."

"But a beautiful one. *And* she doesn't have to wash anyone's socks."

"Pia, you have a maid."

Pia giggled. "I'm only joking. I *love* washing Howard's socks!"

Lauren knew that was something she'd never have to do. It was quite obvious Oliver had no plans to change his lifestyle. He was very comfortable, a man of habit. He had his live-in housekeeper, two daily maids, a butler when he entertained, and his trusty Japanese chauffeur. At the office he had a slew of assistants who obviously adored him.

They planned on getting married in the Bahamas where Oliver kept a bank account and a house. "You'll love it there," he'd assured her. "It's very peaceful and the people are delightful."

Their target date was six weeks.

Since that night nothing much had changed. Oliver was totally into pleasuring her, and when she tried to reverse the situation he always had the same answer. "Give me the joy of making you happy now – when we're married it'll be different."

She didn't fight it, there was no hurry – after all she was marrying the man – she had the rest of her life to make him the happiest man alive.

Chapter 59

Working on a movie was a new experience and Nick immediately knew he was going to love it. He'd arrived in New York to be met at the airport by a car and driver – not a limo, only a sedan, but it sure beat taking the subway. They had him staying at a small hotel near Times Square where most of the crew were, and upon arrival he found a typed call sheet giving him instructions for the next day.

In the meantime, he had to meet with Waldo, the men's costumer. They spent the afternoon shopping in the Village for a suitable outfit. Actually he could have used his own clothes, because they ended up purchasing tight jeans, black shirt and leather jacket.

"Do I get to keep the clothes?" he joked. "They'll blend right into my closet!"

"Only if it's in your contract," Waldo replied, fussing with the leather jacket.

"My agent's got the contract."

"Then it's probably too late." Waldo stood back and surveyed him. "Steal 'em," he said, archly. "They'll never notice."

Nick laughed. "*Now* you're talkin'!"

"I'm surprised you got this role," Waldo remarked, pursing his lips.

"How's that?"

"Our macho young *star* is hardly going to be thrilled when he sees you."

"Oh, you mean Charlie?"

"Do you know him?"

"Nah, never met him, but we'll get along."

"Don't be so sure."

"C'mon, Waldo, believe me – I get along with everyone."

376

How wrong he was. Charlie Geary was the jerk everybody said he was. A former television star, Charlie had hit the movies in a big way with two box office bonanzas. He was shorter than Nick with a baby face, a shock of reddish hair and a bad cocaine habit. The moment he saw Nick he was on the director's case.

"What the fuck you hire him for? *I'm* supposed to be the star of this movie."

"We gotta have someone who looks halfway decent," the director replied. "In the movie he's in bed with your girlfriend – why else would she hop in the sack with him?"

Charlie's baby face creased into a sour expression. "Do I give a fuck? Do I care? Fire him."

"Too late," the director said.

"Don't fucking tell *me* it's too late," Charlie replied, his eyes popping. "Because I'll tell you it's never too late for me to walk."

The director conferred with his producers. The producers, who'd had enough of Charlie Geary and his enormous ego said they weren't firing anyone.

Their first scene together took place in a bar. Charlie Geary was at a table with his cronies and Nick had to enter the shot, exchange insults with Charlie, and walk off camera.

Although Charlie only had a few lines, he managed to blow them every time. The director kept calling "Cut" and going for another take.

Nick had his lines down pat. He loved the feeling on the set, the family atmosphere, the way everybody fussed around him. Plus it was a real blast being in front of a camera.

Make the most of it, he told himself. *You're only here for two days.*

Because of Charlie the scene took all day, continuing into overtime. The director was pissed, the producers more so as they worked into the night.

Waldo took Nick to one side. "You'd better plan on being here an extra day," he said. "They'll never get to your scene with Carlysle by tomorrow."

"Hey – I'm here for as long as they want me," Nick replied. "I could really get used to this."

Back at his hotel he tried calling the number he had for Joey.

"Joey moved outta here a year ago," a female voice said. "I took over the apartment from him."

"You got any idea where he went?"

"Yeah, there's a number somewhere."

"Can you find it?"

She did not sound enthusiastic. "I dunno."

He went into persuasive overdrive. "I'd really appreciate it if you could."

"You visiting or what?"

"I'm shooting a movie here."

Her voice perked up. "Oh, you're an actor?"

"You got it."

"Well, um . . . you here alone?"

"Find me the number an' we'll talk."

Her voice heated up considerably. "Whyn't you come over and I'll give it to you personally."

"Because I need to call him now."

"I like actors."

Oh, shit! Why did he always get lumbered with the maniacs? "So I'll send you an autographed picture. Be a sweetheart an' get me the number."

She finally delivered and he called Joey. A stoned woman answered.

"Joey around?" he asked.

"Who wants him?"

"An old friend."

"He owe you?"

"No, I told you – I'm an old friend."

She snorted, derisively. "Sure, same old story. It's always an old friend, an' he always ends up gettin' his brains beat out. I told you, mister, he ain't here."

"Tell him it's Nick – Nick Angelo. Okay?"

"Wait a minute." She kept him on hold for a while, then she got back on the phone and gave him the address of a club. "You'll find Joey there."

This was like playing tag. Find Joey in the big city. Christ!

The club she sent him to was a dump. Nude photos displayed outside proclaimed, "*SEVEN BEAUTIFUL GIRLS – TOTALLY NAKED.*" An Indian bouncer slumped wearily on a canvas folding chair picking his nose. It cost ten bucks to get inside, and once there he was immediately pounced on by a topless waitress with droopy tits who offered him a complimentary glass of champagne and the choice of a hostess to sit with him.

He declined both offers. "I'm lookin' for Joey."

She lost interest in him and jerked a finger towards the bar.

He walked over. It was not difficult finding Joey – he was the only customer. Nick tapped him on the shoulder. "Joey?"

Joey spun around. "What the fu – Jesus! *Nick?*"

"Yeah, it's me."

Joey almost fell off the bar stool. They hugged awkwardly and grinned at each other.

"How're you doing, man?" Nick asked, thinking that Joey did not look good at all. He was skinny and pale, with dark circles under his sunken eyes and a nervous facial tic. "Don't even tell me – you look like shit."

Joey managed a weak grin. "Thanks. S'good to see you, too." He dragged on his cigarette. "How come you're here? I heard you were livin' in LA."

"Can you believe it – I'm in a movie."

"A movie, huh? You're finally doin' that acting thing."

"Yeah, well, I stayed in Chicago for a while – then moved to LA, found myself an agent, went on this audition and got lucky. It's only a small role, but at least I'm workin'."

Joey snapped his fingers at the girl behind the bar. She bounced over wearing nothing but a short sequinned miniskirt and long fake eyelashes. "Get my movie star friend a beer – an' don't water it down."

"Anything you want, Joey," she said, squinting at Nick. "Movie star, huh? What you bin in?"

"Never mind," Joey said, waving her away.

The girl moved off and Joey gestured around the dingy club. "Classy joint, huh? My place of work. I come on between strippers – the crowd really gets off on me. I'm doing stand-up like I always wanted."

Yeah, and from the looks of you that's not all you're doing.

"That's great, Joey."

"Don't give me polite crap. This gig is about as great as a rattlesnake up your ass. I'm doin' a shit job in a shit place, but it's all I got right now." He stubbed out his cigarette, immediately reaching for another. "So," he added, rubbing his bloodshot eyes. "What's happening with Cyndra? You seen her?"

"She married that Reece Webster guy – who incidentally turned out to be creep of the century. He's not around any more."

"What's she doing?"

"She was singing in a Vegas hotel. Small stuff, she'll do okay."

"We kinda lost touch."

"Looks like you lost touch with everyone."

Joey laughed, ruefully. "It's always that way, huh?"

"Did you ever make it back to Bosewell?" Nick asked.

"No. Did you?"

"Nope."

"I guess once we got outta there – that was it."

The topless bar-girl delivered his beer in a cracked glass. "Enjoy," she said, holding out her hand for money.

"Put it on my tab," said Joey, irritated.

"Your tab's overd –"

"I said put it on my fuckin' tab," he snarled.

She flounced off.

"You look like you could do with a break," Nick said. "How about flyin' to LA an' staying with me for a while?"

"Oh, yeah – an' give up my job?"

"There's plenty of comedy clubs in LA."

"I can't afford to take the chance."

"Why? You got such a wonderful life here?"

"Nah, I'm living with this girl."

"Somebody special?"

"If I told you, you wouldn't believe me."

"Try it."

"She's a hooker."

"Okay, so I believe you."

They both laughed.

"Seriously. She's the proverbial hooker with a heart of gold. I met her at a party. She likes having me around. I like being around. She pays the rent an' I give her what I can. It works out okay."

"Hey, Joey," shrieked a blowsy blonde. "Get your ass up on stage. *Now.*"

Joey shrugged, stubbed out his cigarette. "My boss. Charming lady. Hang around, Nick, catch the act."

"I'd love to, but I got an early call tomorrow. Whyn't you come by the set? Here, I'll give you the address." He scribbled on a piece of paper and handed it over. "Drop by tomorrow an' we'll talk about you coming to LA."

"Yeah, maybe."

When he got back to the hotel he called Cyndra. "Everything okay?"

"Everything's fine."

"No sign of Reece?"

"No."

"Is Annie behaving herself?"

"I told you, Nick, everything's fine. Stop worrying."

He cleared his throat, ready to give her the big news. "Guess who I saw tonight?"

"Who?"

"Joey."

There was a long silence. "How is he?" she finally asked.

"Not in great shape. I'm trying to talk him into flying back to LA with me."

"Not on my account. I've had it with men."

"Listen – the three of us went through some hard times together. Be nice to hang out, huh?"

She answered a touch too fast. "I told you, Nick, don't drag him back because of me. I'm not interested."

"I get the message."

She changed moods. "How did the filming go today?"

"It's a trip."

"What's Charlie Geary like?"

"A stoned prick."

"Really?"

"Wouldn't kid you."

"Y'know, Nick, I've been thinking. Tomorrow I'm going to contact the record company Reece was dealing with and see if they're still interested in me."

"Sounds like a good idea."

"You think so?"

"What's to lose?"

"That's how I feel," she said, glad to have his confirmation.

"I'll call you tomorrow," he said. "Take care, little sis."

"'Bye, Nick."

Running into Charlie Geary early in the morning in the make-up room was not a pleasant sight. The famous actor was wasted; he looked worse than Joey.

"Boy, did I have a night last night!" Charlie boasted. "Even though I say it myself I gotta cock that never quits. I had this little pussy creamin' herself all over me – I mean she was comin' an' com –"

"Shut up, Charlie," the make-up girl said, wearily.

"Don't tell *me* to shut up, sweetheart. You wanna stay on this film you'll suck my dick if I tell you to."

Nick sat down in the second chair. Charlie stretched and burped in his direction. "So – where'd they dig you up from?"

"I been around," Nick said.

"Yeah?" Charlie yawned, throwing his arms up and back, almost hitting the make-up girl in the face. "Couldn't tell it from your performance. You really fucked up yesterday – I hate working with amateurs."

He was not about to take this little asshole's shit. "You got a short memory – it wasn't me that fucked up, it was you."

"Don't bother with him," the make-up girl murmured, moving past. "He's not worth it."

"What didja say, cunt?" Charlie demanded, almost falling off his chair.

"Why don't you leave the girl alone?" Nick said.

"Why don't you get fucked."

Fortunately an assistant entered, summoning Charlie to the set. He got out of the chair unsteady on his feet and lurched to the door.

"He's stoned," the make-up girl said.

"No kiddin'?" Nick replied.

Later, on the set, Charlie played the same game – screwing up his lines, forgetting cues, generally messing up.

Nick noticed the two producers conferring in a corner. The woman wore a bright scarlet suit, her long legs in matching tights and very high heels. The tall man had assumed a permanently grim expression, while the director ran around looking frantic.

After the lunch break Charlie failed to appear at all. The A.D. said she couldn't get him out of his trailer. Forming a group, the two producers and the director stormed off to personally escort him to the set. They returned with no Charlie.

"Tell you what, Nick," the director said. "We'll shoot your close-ups. Charlie's not feeling good – he may not be able to do the rest of the scene this afternoon."

As little as Nick knew about production, he realized this did not bode well for the shoot. But screw it – he wasn't complaining – close-ups sounded good to him.

Joey did not show, so at the end of the day he called him again. This time Joey picked up the phone himself.

"Where were you?" Nick asked.

"Hadda meetin'."

"You couldn't've come by after?"

"Hey, man, what's the problem?" Joey said, belligerently. "We don't see each other for a few years – you come back inta my life an' I'm supposed t'jump?"

"Forget it. I'll see ya."

"C'mon, Nick, don't go gettin' pissed. I'll be there tomorrow. Right now I got a lot on my mind."

"Anythin' I can help out with?"

"Nah. Just small problems."

"See you tomorrow."

"Bet on it."

Nick settled back to study his script. Tomorrow he had his big scene with Carlysle Mann – and he didn't want to blow it. This filming shit was seductive.

He fell asleep with the script clutched tightly in his hands.

The next morning he was sitting in make-up at seven a.m. calm as can be, when the A.D. entered looking flustered.

"They need to see you at once," she said.

"Who needs to see me?" he asked, patiently.

"The producers."

"Yeah?"

Oh, shit. This is it. Charlie Geary's getting his way and I'm about to be canned.

"He's nearly through," the make-up girl said, blending dark pancake on his neck.

Yeah, sweetheart, you can say that again.

"There's a crisis," the A.D. said. "They need him immediately."

"Better let you go," the make-up girl said.

He got out of the chair and followed the A.D., silently rehearsing his objections.

It didn't matter what he said, he was out and he knew it.

Chapter 60

Lauren was frantic, suddenly there seemed so much to do before she left for the Bahamas. Pia was not much help – seven months pregnant, she waddled around with a smile on her face, arriving late and leaving early. Lauren didn't blame her, but still it left most of the responsibilities of the business to her.

"I wish Howard and I were coming with you," Pia said with a wistful sigh, obviously expecting Lauren to say, "Why don't you?" But she'd decided it was going be her and Oliver – nobody else. She'd experienced one wedding where everybody stood around waiting and the bridegroom didn't show up, and she did not plan on doing it again.

"Who'll run the business while I'm away?" she worried.

"*I* will," said Pia.

"You're hardly here any more."

"Don't obsess. I'll be around all the time while you're away."

Lauren knew that the business only survived because of her personal touch. She'd gained such a good reputation, especially with her dinner parties. Lately, all Pia took care of was the financial side.

She had one more dinner to organize before leaving for the Bahamas. This was at the house of Quentin and Jessie George. Quentin was the managing editor of *Satisfaction*, the avant garde magazine of the moment, and Jessie was a social whirlwind. She'd catered dinner parties for them before and it was always an enjoyable experience. The Georges put together an eclectic group of guests, mixing politics and fashion, rock 'n roll and movies. Jessie was a delightful character – a woman of indeterminate age, not conventionally pretty, but loaded with style.

The night before the dinner Lauren visited their brownstone

to go over the final details. Jessie had heard about her upcoming marriage and couldn't wait to complain.

"I suppose we'll be losing you," she lamented. "You won't want to do this any more."

"I didn't say that," Lauren objected.

"Ah, but Oliver will never let you."

"Oliver's not going to control what I do and what I don't do."

Jessie nodded, knowingly. "Darling, when you're married you'll see."

"Jessie, when I'm married I'll see nothing. I'll carry on exactly the way I please."

"Hmm," Jessie said. "That's what I thought when I married Quentin, and look at me now."

"It seems to me you have a fantastic life."

"Some would say so." Jessie waved her bracelet-adorned arms in the air. "Now, let's get down to business. I have a brilliant idea for hors-d'œuvres – imagine scooped out melon balls filled with golden caviar – doesn't it sound divine?"

Oliver was very much involved with the Marcella girl campaign. Marcella was a very successful, large make-up manufacturing corporation in Italy who were all set to take a large chunk out of the American market. They planned to rival Revlon and Estée Lauder. Now that Oliver's firm had landed the account, the search was on for the perfect girl. So far they'd tested and photographed at least thirty candidates.

Lauren viewed the photos and watched the video tapes with Oliver. He was extremely critical – as far as he was concerned this one was too glamorous, this one too old, this one too young and so on.

"Your expectations are too high," she said. "I can see at least seven or eight of them who'd be great."

"No," he said, shaking his head. "None of them have it. The Marcella girl has to have a special quality that appeals to the public, something that makes women say, "I want to look exactly like her – and if I wear Marcella make-up I can." She has to have a certain ordinariness, combined with that magical something else."

"I've no idea what you're getting at."

"It's a quality. Grace Kelly had it. Marilyn didn't. Ingrid Bergman had it."

"Who's Ingrid Bergman?"

"Never mind." He stared at her closely. "You have it."

"I have what?"

"The quality I'm talking about."

"Is that good or bad?"

"If you were in the running for the Marcella girl it would be good."

She walked over to his desk and helped herself to an apple from a bowl of fruit. "Fortunately, Oliver, I'm not."

He frowned, looking at her intently. "But you could be."

"You *are* joking."

"No," he said, very seriously, "I'm not."

She laughed. "Oliver, I am *not* a model, I do not want to be a model, I am perfectly happy doing what I'm doing, so kindly forget it."

"Will you do something for me before we leave?"

She sighed. "What?"

"Will you let my people organize a photo session with you?"

She crunched her apple. "Now why would I do a thing like that?"

"Because it would be very helpful if I could show them exactly who I'm looking for."

She flopped into an armchair. "You're so funny."

"Then humour me."

"I don't have time."

"Do I ask for much, Lauren? Wouldn't you enjoy having your hair done and your make-up and wearing beautiful clothes? It could be fun."

"It might be your idea of fun, but believe me, I have better things to do."

"Please, Lauren – for me? As a wedding present. Think of the money you'll save."

"Oliver –"

"Yes?"

She weakened. "Well, as long as you promise not to take it seriously."

"You have my solemn promise."

Humouring Oliver turned out to be more enjoyable than she'd thought. To go into a studio and be totally made over by professionals was an interesting experience. Pia thought it was a hoot and insisted on accompanying her. They giggled like a couple of schoolgirls as the make-up artist and hairdresser went to work.

"At least you'll have some incredible photographs to show your grandchildren," Pia said, perching behind her on a high stool.

"*What* grandchildren?" Lauren exclaimed. "I haven't even got any children yet – let's not get carried away."

"You *are* going to have some, aren't you?" Pia asked, anxiously. "I need a playmate for mine," she added, patting her huge belly.

"I guess so," Lauren agreed. "But give me time to enjoy my marriage first."

"You got fab 'air, darlin'," said the English hairdresser, his cockney accent reminding her of Emerson. "The colour needs livening up a bit, an' you're in desperate need of a cut – apart from that you're perfect!"

"I've always had long hair," she said, alarmed.

"Yeah, but it's just 'angin' there, ain't it? Let me work it over – leave it to me."

"Don't take off too much," she said, when he started wielding his scissors.

"Trust me, darlin', you'll be thankin' me."

She shut her eyes and hoped he knew what he was doing. The make-up artist was next. He came at her with a pair of tweezers, plucking at her eyebrows, squinting at the shape of her face.

"I don't like to wear much make-up," she ventured.

"Nor do I," he said, tartly. "What we have to do here is the illusion of no make-up at all while I create *the* most incredible face."

And so they transformed her. Lauren Roberts – small-town beauty – was turned into Lauren, face of the moment. The hairdresser had added ever so subtle light streaks into her chestnut hair, and the cut had given it more body and shape, so that although it still fell below her shoulders, it was fuller and more flattering.

The make-up artist had worked on her face with a palette of natural colours – playing with browns and beiges, bringing out her eyes in a way they had not been emphasized before.

"My God!" Pia said, genuinely amazed. "You look fantastic!"

"Oh, thanks a lot," Lauren said, pretending to frown. "Was I such a dog before?"

"You know what I mean. You've always been pretty, but my God, now you're absolutely stunning!"

Next it was the photographer's turn. Antonio worked fast

with a minimum of fuss and the maximum of assistants. He knew exactly what he wanted, and even though Lauren had never been in front of a camera before, she fell into the poses easily, having watched Nature so many times. It was a kick. There was great music playing, she was clad in beautiful designer clothes. When it was all over she confided to Pia that she'd actually enjoyed it.

"Who wouldn't?" Pia said, shaking her head in amazement. "You really *do* look incredible."

"I wish you'd stop saying that. God knows what I must have looked like before."

"I can't wait to see the photos," Pia said.

"And I can't wait to wash this make-up off."

Later, Oliver asked her how she'd enjoyed the session.

"It was okay," she said, laughing. "Never again, though. You can only talk me into it once."

The next morning was a different kind of frantic. She left early for the market accompanied by a couple of her young, college student assistants. They picked out fresh fruit and vegetables, and then stopped to buy flowers. Jessie and Quentin were very particular and that's exactly the way she liked it.

"Have Oliver come to the dinner," Jessie urged, when she arrived at their house.

"No way," she objected. "I don't want him sitting there while I'm working."

"But I adore Oliver – he's so droll," Jessie said. "At least have him drop by to pick you up."

She called Oliver at his office. "Do you want to come by later and pick me up from the Georges' dinner party?"

"I'd like that," he said.

"Jessie particularly requested you. How well do you know her?"

"We had a hot and steamy affair once."

She almost believed him. "Oliver – *did* you?"

He laughed. "No, my dear. I am not the hot and steamy affair type."

"You could have fooled me."

"Ah," he promised. "Wait until our honeymoon."

From four o'clock on she commandeered the Georges' kitchen. It was the kind of kitchen she liked, large and spacious, with all modern conveniences. The menu she'd planned was one of Jessie's favourites. Cold vichyssoise followed by rib-sticking chicken casserole with creamy mashed potatoes, lightly sautéd carrots and creamed spinach, all accompanied by a healthful chopped salad.

"I love it when you serve those kind of meals,' Jessie confided. "It makes people feel comfortable and relaxed, and when they're in that kind of mood the conversation *really* sparkles. Oh dear, Lauren, what am I going to do when Oliver takes you away from all this?"

"I'll still keep the business," she said. "I'll cook occasionally."

"Shall we bet on this?" Jessie suggested.

Lauren grinned. "Only if it's cash."

Later Oliver called her at the Georges'. "Remember how you said the other day you loved surprises?"

"Did I say that?"

"Yes. Well, I have a surprise for you."

"What is it?"

"If I told you it wouldn't be a surprise. When I come by later I'll bring it."

"Does it have four legs?" she asked, remembering her recent request for a puppy.

"Be patient, my dear. I'll show you later."

Chapter 61

Carlysle Mann was pretty beyond belief. She had one of those etched faces with alabaster skin, huge blue eyes, a snub nose and a beguiling overbite. She was petite, with baby-fine blonde hair curling around her face, and a perfect figure.

For the first time in his life Nick felt intimidated meeting somebody. He'd seen her in a couple of movies, but actually meeting her was something else.

"Hi," he said, almost shyly.

"Congrats," she replied, pretty blue eyes gazing into his. "This is some great break for you."

Yeah, congratulations were definitely in order. He had not been canned. Instead he had gotten the chance of a lifetime. While Charlie Geary was being rushed off to a drug rehab centre, he, Nick Angelo – excuse me, Nick Angel – had been presented with the big break. He'd been given the lead in the movie, and it was a career-making role – that of a young hood who reforms, finds true love, and ends up as the hero.

"You've got the look," the woman producer had said, crossing and uncrossing her elegant legs.

Yeah, I've got the look all right, he'd wanted to say. *A look you didn't even recognize when I pulled alongside you in my car in LA.*

"We're giving you this chance," the director had said, "in the hope you'll deliver."

"We've spoken to your agent," the tall man had added. "You'll probably want to give her a call."

Want to give her a call? Holy shit! He couldn't believe this was happening. Charlie was dumped and he was in.

"I can do it," he'd blurted. "I've studied the script – I can do this good."

"That's exactly why you're getting this opportunity," the woman had said.

The truth was they didn't have much choice. Charlie Geary was out of action and they couldn't afford to shut down production while they waited to negotiate for another star. They were prepared to take a chance on Nick.

The next few days were crazy time. His main worry was Cyndra and Annie. Could he trust them alone in LA? Would they be all right without him? Or would Annie go running to the cops, ruining everything. It was a chance he had to take.

He called them both. Annie sounded sulky as usual. She didn't even rustle up any enthusiasm when he told her about his lucky break.

"Tell you what," he suggested. "Give me a few days, then maybe you'll fly to New York for a weekend. I'll spring for your ticket and room. I talked to my agent, I'm making okay money."

"I don't think so," she said coolly.

"C'mon," he persuaded. "You want to see New York, don't you? You've never been here."

"I'll let you know."

Cyndra was genuinely thrilled. "You'll be sensational Nick," she assured him.

"I'll do my best. Can't do more than that."

His agent had been suitably businesslike. "It's an excellent opportunity for you to show them how good you are. Of course, you're still very inexperienced. It may not work out – don't get your hopes up."

"How come they went with me?" he asked.

She told him the truth. "This is not a big budget movie. If they wait for a replacement for Charlie it'll hold them up and cost them money they can't afford. You're there, and as far as they're concerned you seem capable of doing the job. Carlysle's name will carry the film. Oh, and Nick – remember what I told you – don't screw her – it'll get in the way of your performance."

"You told me not to screw her before because it would get in the way of Charlie Geary. Now he ain't around."

"Nick, you're new to this business – *don't* screw her."

Frances expressed the same sentiments. "Save everything you've got. Getting laid takes time and energy. Put all that sexual juice into your performance."

Once he met Carlysle he knew exactly where all his sexual

391

juice was going. They'd hit it off immediately. He asked around and found out her story. She'd been a child star since the age of eight, now she was twenty-two, recently divorced from a rock and roll drummer, and very career orientated. She had a mother who usually accompanied her on shoots, but so far had not arrived in New York.

"Watch out for the mother," Waldo warned. "The woman is a complete nightmare."

"Why are you telling *me*?" he asked.

"Because we all know what's about to happen between you two," Waldo replied, with an evil chuckle.

Nick laughed. "How about fillin' *me* in?"

Their second day on the set Carlysle invited him out. "I have to go to this dinner party tomorrow night," she said. "My mother was coming with me, but since she's not here . . . Will you take me?"

She gazed up at him with her big blue eyes and he wasn't about to say no.

"Yeah, sure. Should we go from the set?"

"No, I'll have to go home and change first. Pick me up at my apartment."

"I thought you lived in LA."

"I do. I've got a house in LA and an apartment here."

Wow! This girl really had it all together. "What time?" he asked.

"The dinner starts at seven-thirty, but they probably won't sit down to eat until nine. Get me at eight-thirty and we'll make a late entrance."

"Uh, what do I wear?"

She smiled. "Whatever you like. I'm sure you look fine in anything."

Cyndra was determined the incident in Vegas was not going to drag her down. She'd come so far and she was not allowing it to pull her under. It was unfortunate, but it was her past – just like Mr Browning, her abortion, and all the other bad things she'd gone through.

Annie, on the other hand, kept on insisting they had to do something about it. If Nick knew he'd throw a fit.

"You'd better shut up about this," Cyndra warned her. "'Cause the only thing you can do is get us all into big trouble."

"You agreed with me at first," Annie reminded her.

"I was upset then. I wasn't thinking clearly. Understand, Annie, Nick is right, it's *our* secret, and if none of us blow it we'll keep it that way."

"How can you forget what happened?" Annie demanded. "That poor man – what about his family? Don't you *care*?"

"Stop giving me that poor man crap," Cyndra said, angrily. "He was in a motel room with me, wasn't he? He thought I was a hooker. You should have heard the names he called me."

"He didn't deserve to die for it."

"It was an *accident*, Annie. Reece didn't shoot him purposely, it was just one of those things. Like when you get on a plane you don't expect it to crash. When you go for a ride in a car you don't expect it to be totalled. These things happen."

"I still think –" Annie began.

"Will you shut up," Cyndra said, finally losing her temper, her dark eyes blazing. "Shut up about it, Annie."

She went through her apartment and packed all of Reece's clothes into two suitcases, stacking them in a closet by the front door. Nick had suggested that as he was going to be in New York for at least six weeks she should give up her apartment and move into his. Since she didn't have any money it struck her as an excellent idea. He'd also left her his rented car to drive, so at least she was mobile.

Searching through Reece's papers she found the name of the producer he'd been dealing with at Reno Records. Marik Lee. She called him on the phone and asked if she could drop by.

"Where's your manager?" Marik asked, sounding guarded.

"You mean Reece Webster?"

"That's the guy."

"He's no longer my manager."

"Good," he said.

"Good?" she questioned. "How come?"

"Drop by and we'll discuss it."

She didn't need a second invitation. Within the hour she was at his office – dressed to make an impression in a tight red dress which showed off her figure and flattered her glowing skin. Her hair, dark and lustrous, fell almost to her waist.

Marik Lee did a double take when she walked in. "*You're* Cyndra?" he said, standing up.

She nodded, checking him out. He was black, a little overweight, and kind of homely looking, but he had nice eyes and a big friendly smile. "Why do you sound so surprised?" she asked, sitting in a chair across from his desk and crossing her legs.

His eyes wandered. "I had no idea you were so . . . so . . . pretty."

"Thank you," she said demurely, accepting the compliment.

"Now tell me," he continued. "That guy you were hitched up with — that uh — Reece Webster. He definitely out the picture?"

"Yes," she replied. "Very definitely."

"Between you and me he was a bad case. We don't like to get involved in those situations."

"What situations?"

"Y'know what I'm saying. He talked about you like you were a slab of meat, like you'd do anything he wanted. We expect our talent to be able to talk for themselves."

She sat up very straight. "Oh, I can talk for myself all right."

He looked at her appreciatively. "Yeah, I can see that."

She thought about Nick in New York about to get his big chance. She wasn't planning on playing the little sister role — dragging along behind. She had every intention of making it just as big as he.

"Mr Lee," she said, boldly.

"Call me Marik."

"Marik. Tell me the truth — do Reno Records and I have a future together, or am I wasting my time?"

Nick was in the wardrobe trailer trying on different clothes.

"They're very happy with the dailies," Waldo confided, *sotto voce*.

"Dailies?" he said, zipping up a pair of tight black jeans.

"Oh, Nick, *please*. Surely you know what I'm talking about? The dailies are the scenes from the previous day. My friend is the projectionist — I get a full report."

He was pleased. "So they like me?"

"Yes, they certainly do. Why do you think they hired you in place of Charlie? They took one look at your close-ups and realized they had something with you. According to my friend the camera simply loves you." He reached for a pair of cowboy boots. "Try these, please."

Nick sat down grabbing the boots. "Yeah, well — I always knew I could do this," he said, pulling on the left boot.

"You can do it all right, although of course, there's no such thing as a sure thing. You might have what it takes and the audience can still hate you."

"No way they'll hate me," he said, confidently. "I'm putting everything I've got into this performance. They're gonna respond. You'll see – they're gonna respond big time."

"I'm sure they will," Waldo said, selecting a denim jacket from the rack. "And what are we wearing tonight when we take little Miss Madam out?"

He pulled on the other boot and stood up. "How come my date with Carlysle is public knowledge?"

"This is a film set, Nick. If you fart in the privacy of your dressing room everyone knows about it."

"Great!"

"Just be careful with little Madam. She appears to be angelic, but watch out."

He grinned. "Hey – Waldo – this may come as a big shock to you, but when it comes to women I know my way around the block an' back again."

"Actresses are not women," Waldo murmured. "Oh dear me, no."

Nick burst out laughing. "You're a character, you know that?"

"You have been warned," Waldo said, primly. "Nobody can say you haven't been warned."

"Thanks, but I guess I'll take a chance."

Waldo rolled his eyes.

"Hi," Carlysle said, greeting him at her apartment door wearing nothing but a welcoming smile and a skimpy bath towel wrapped sarong style around her body.

"Uh . . . hi," he said, standing on the threshold.

"Come on in," she said. "As you can see, I'm not quite ready."

Oh, he could see all right!

She led him into a comfortable living room and waved him in the direction of a small bar. "Fix yourself a drink. I'll be quick – I promise."

"Take your time," he said, checking the place out.

"Ooops!" Her towel slipped and she quickly hitched it up, but not before he caught a glimpse of her large, rosy, disturbingly erect nipples.

She noticed him looking and giggled, her blue eyes widening. "Isn't it stupid the way we all try to hide ourselves? Wouldn't it be better to walk around without anything on? After all, we weren't born fully dressed, were we?"

"Works for me," he said, opening the ice-box behind the bar and extracting a beer.

"Good," said Carlysle, dropping the towel.

Instant erection. He didn't even have time to think about it.

"Why don't you take your clothes off, too?" she said, with an innocent little smile.

"Hey –" he began.

"You're not shy, are you?" she teased.

No, baby, I'm not shy, but I am used to being the instigator and this is a different trip.

He shrugged off his jacket and began unbuttoning his shirt.

Carlysle was not a patient girl. She ran towards him and went right for his zipper, pulling down his pants and underwear. Before he knew what was happening she had him in her mouth giving him one of the finest blow jobs known to man! He came in record time because it was so unexpected and so good, and the truth was he hadn't gotten laid in a while and he was beyond horny.

"Ah . . . Jesus!" he groaned. "That was . . ."

"Yes?" she asked breathlessly, still on her knees.

"Pretty . . . damn . . . good."

"Good? Surely you mean sensational?"

"That, too. C'mere," he said, reaching for her breasts.

She jumped to her feet, skipping out of his range. "Later," she said, in a little girl voice. "Gotta get dressed. It wouldn't do to be late for the party, would it now?"

Chapter 62

The guests had all arrived, the hors-d'œuvres had been served and Lauren began her own private countdown to dinner. Her two assistants, Hilary and Karen, knew her well, anticipating her every request. Actually, the truth was she'd trained them so efficiently they could probably do it without her. Which was good, because when she and Oliver were married she'd have to delegate a lot more. Oliver had already told her he wanted her to travel with him, and why not – she was dying to see Europe. He took six weeks' vacation every year, travelling through Italy, France and England. Help Unlimited would just have to manage without her for a few weeks.

Jessie popped into the kitchen. "Almost ready," she said, beaming in her severe, man's-style velvet suit. "The melon and caviar was a riot!"

"We're all set when you are," Lauren said, adjusting the flame under her sautéd carrots.

"Spectacular!" exclaimed Jessie.

One of the things Lauren liked about catering dinners for the Georges was their unbridled enthusiasm. Quentin – whenever he appeared – was exactly like his wife. The two of them enjoyed life and it was infectious.

"Who's out there tonight?" Lauren asked Hilary, who'd been busy serving hors-d'œuvres.

Hilary recited a list of celebrities – including a controversial black politician, an avant-garde dress designer, a famous ball player and two movie stars. Jessie sure loved to mix people up.

Lauren decided Oliver would be happy when he dropped by. He enjoyed hanging out with celebrities. She didn't. If she was lucky she wouldn't have to emerge from the kitchen all night long.

"Did you like it?" Carlysle giggled, holding tightly on to his arm in the back of her limo. "Was it the best – the very *very* best you've ever had?"

He grinned, lazily. "The best."

She squeezed his arm. "Don't lie to me, or I'll have to do it again – right now – in the car."

He laughed. "Sure."

Her blue eyes sparkled. "You think I wouldn't?"

"I'm positive you would."

"Want me to?" she asked, stroking his thigh.

He felt himself getting hard again. "What about the driver?" he said.

She pressed a button and the black privacy glass slid up. "Oh, he's not getting any – he's *definitely* not on my list."

Before he could question her about what list that might be, she was on him again – going for his zipper with practised hands – springing him free – and bending her blonde curls.

He gave himself up to the moment, pressing the top of her head, forcing himself into her mouth as deep as she could take him.

This time he lasted longer, and when he came it was an explosion. "*Shit!*" he exclaimed, falling back on the leather seat. "Holy *shit!*"

She laughed, triumphantly. "I'm good, huh?"

"You're great."

"The greatest?"

What was it with this girl? All she wanted to hear was how great she was. "Yes," he said.

"The greatest you've ever had?"

He reached for her breasts again, but she slapped his hands away. "We're here," she said. "Didn't you notice the car stop?"

"Sweetheart," he sighed, "I didn't notice anything but you."

He'd said the right thing. Carlysle beamed like a cat who'd just devoured a saucer full of cream – and in a way she had.

"Later I'm gonna fuck you," he said.

"Later I'm going to let you," she replied.

Grinning, they alighted from the limo and entered the house.

The vichyssoise was served. The guests were happy. In the

kitchen Lauren concentrated on the mashed potatoes, making sure they had just the right combination of cream, butter and milk. Cooking was therapeutic. She really enjoyed creating a meal and watching as all the empty plates came back into the kitchen.

"Carlysle Mann just arrived," Hilary said. "She's *sooo* pretty."

"You're pretty, too," Lauren said, crisply. "You're equally as pretty as any movie star."

"No way!"

"Yes, you are."

"She's got fantastic skin," Hilary said, enviously.

"Talking of skin – did you see the guy she's with?" Karen said, joining in.

"Cute," they both said in unison. "Very *veree* cute." They burst out giggling.

Oh, to be young again, Lauren thought. Hilary and Karen were so bright-eyed and full of life. She was only six years older than them, but sometimes she felt like a staid old lady. "Come on, girls, concentrate," she said. "Let's get this meal on the road."

Carlysle's hand began creeping up his leg again. Shit! She was actually doing it in front of all these people. And important people, too. He glanced around the table and couldn't believe he was sitting amongst them.

"Hey – stop that," he whispered.

"Why?" she whispered back.

"'Cause somebody's gonna see."

"So what?" she replied.

"So what? You're crazy – you know that?"

She leaned very close and nibbled on his earlobe. "If I had my way I'd give you a blow job right under the table now."

This girl was not bluffing. "You would too, wouldn't you?"

"Ooops! I dropped my napkin – excuse me." She started to dive under the table.

He grabbed her arm, stopping her. "Don't you dare!" he warned.

"So, Carlysle sweetie," said Jessie, turning in their direction. "How's your new film going?"

"We only just started," said Carlysle, abandoning her under-the-table plan. "I guess you heard about Charlie? He had a kind of . . . uh, virus."

"I'm so sorry. Is he in the hospital?"

"Not exactly. Well, sort of – yeah, I guess you could say he is."

"I always thought you two made such an adorable couple," Jessie said.

"Uh . . . thanks."

Jessie turned away to talk to the politician on her other side. Nick nudged Carlysle. "I didn't know you and Charlie were a couple."

"We weren't," she said, shortly.

"Then why'd she say that?"

"We went on a few dates – that's not exactly being a couple."

He imagined her on her knees in front of Charlie and he wasn't too thrilled. But still, he hardly knew her, he couldn't start acting possessive at this stage.

Soon she began trying to unzip his jeans again, her hands working feverishly.

"Give me a break!" he objected, catching a look from the dress designer on his other side who had orange hair and an attitude.

Carlysle giggled. "Stop acting like a prude."

This girl was a wild one.

Oliver arrived at the dessert stage.

"The dinner was simply divine," Jessie informed him. "You're marrying the best cook in the world."

Oliver was amused. "I'm not marrying Lauren for her cooking, Jessie, dear."

"I'm sure you're not."

He put his head around the kitchen door. Lauren was busy organizing desserts. She'd baked two *tartes tatins*, and a batch of double chocolate brownies.

"You're busy," he said.

"Very astute," she said.

"Jessie wants you to come out and join the party."

"I can't do that. Anyway, I'm not dressed."

"You're more beautiful than any of the guests."

"You're such a smooth talker, Oliver."

"Which is *exactly* why I'm where I am today."

She ladled whipped cream into a cut glass dish. "Oliver, please – I'm trying to get this together."

He nodded, understandingly. "Very well, I'll go and sit down and wait patiently. When you're ready I'll take you home."

What about my surprise? she wanted to say. She'd been looking forward to a puppy all night, but then again he couldn't have brought it to the Georges' house. Maybe he had it waiting at home.

Everybody carried on about the delicious desserts. Jessie had squeezed Oliver in between Quentin and a vivacious book editor with teased black hair. Suddenly she stood up, tapping the side of her champagne glass. "Listen, everyone, I have an announcement," she said, beaming around the table.

Nick felt Carlysle's hand slide inside his zipper. This was wild, but he couldn't help being aroused.

"I know you've all enjoyed the excellent food tonight, and I'm bringing our chef out to allow you to thank her personally. You may also congratulate her, because she and Oliver Liberty are engaged. You all know Oliver, but I don't think you've met his lovely fiancée." Jessie beckoned a waiter. "Have Lauren come out," she said.

In the kitchen Lauren was mortified. "I'm not going out there," she said, backing into a corner. "What does she think this is – a show?"

Karen gave her a little shove. "You have to, she's waiting."

"Oh, no!" Lauren groaned.

"Oh, yes!" Karen and Hilary chorused, enjoying every minute. They loved working for Lauren, and they were delighted to see her get the kind of attention she deserved.

Reluctantly she allowed herself to be propelled to the dining-room doorway. If there was one thing she hated it was being the centre of attention.

"Ah, Lauren, dear, there you are." Jessie raised her champagne glass. "Here's to you."

There was an enthusiastic round of applause from the guests.

She felt like a total fool. Her eyes scanned the dinner table, checking out the guests. She looked once, twice and couldn't believe her eyes. Nick Angelo was there. *Her* Nick was actually at this dinner.

No, it couldn't be.

Yes, it was.

She looked again. He was older, more handsome than ever, skinnier. His eyes were still deep green and intense. His hair that incredible jet black. Oh, God! She wanted to die. The only good thing was the fact that he hadn't seen her. He was all over the girl sitting beside him, who happened to be Carlysle Mann, the movie star.

Desperately Lauren tried to breathe, to recover her composure. *Move slowly. Get out before he spots me. Get the hell out!*

As she turned to bolt from the room he looked up and their eyes met. He was as startled as she was. They gazed at each other in disbelief before she broke the stare and rushed back into the kitchen. She didn't hesitate, grabbing her coat and purse she ran for the back door.

"Where are you going?" Hilary asked, startled.

"I don't feel good. I have to get out of here," she mumbled. "Tell Oliver I had to go."

"One of us should come with you," Hilary insisted.

"No – I have to get out now," she said, flinging open the door and racing out of the apartment before anyone could stop her.

"What's the matter?" Carlysle said. "What happened?"

His hard-on had deflated. "Nothing," he said, brushing her hand away as he surreptitiously tried to zip up his pants.

"What do you mean, nothing?" she said, her chin tilting belligerently.

He got up from the table. "'Scuse me, I gotta take a piss."

"I'll come with you," she volunteered. "You'd be surprised what we can get up to in the john."

"Hey – Carlysle, I'm not surprised at anything you do. Stay here. I'll be back."

Outside the dining room he grabbed a hovering waiter. "Where's the kitchen?"

"Through there, sir. Can I get you something?"

"Nah, it's okay," he said, hurrying into the kitchen.

She wasn't there. He stopped a pretty girl in a striped apron. "Where's Lauren?"

"She left," Hilary said, quite intrigued by this intense looking guy. "She didn't feel good."

"Where can I contact her?"

"Do you need to have a party catered? We have a very comprehensive service. Here – let me give you one of our cards."

She handed him a card and he stared at it. Help Unlimited was printed in the middle with an address and phone number. In neat script on either side were two names – Lauren Roberts and Pia Liberty.

"You can contact us any time," Hilary said, wishing he'd flirt with her. "During business hours, of course."

"Oh, I will," Nick said, pocketing the card. "Bet on it."

Chapter 63

The couple entwined on the bed made love fast and furiously until they climaxed with a series of grunts and moans.

"Oh, baby, baby, that was freakin' sensational!" said Marik.

Cyndra rolled away from him, flushed and surprised at her own boldness, yet at the same time strangely exhilarated. Marik had only been in her life a week, and she already had him in her power.

"Was it good for you too, baby?" he asked, sitting up and reaching for a cigarette.

"You *know* it was good for me," she replied, coming out with all the right words. "You're an amazing lover, Marik. The best."

They'd been to dinner at a cosy Italian restaurant, following an afternoon in the studio where she'd finally cut a demo record. Marik had liked what he'd heard. When they were finished in the studio he'd said, "We're goin' out to celebrate, 'cause when the big boss hears your sound – you're gonna be signin' your life away!"

She'd glowed with delight. "Really?"

"Yeah, babe. Really."

Cyndra liked Marik, he seemed nice enough. But more than that, she wanted something from him, and she was beginning to learn that if you wanted something you had to offer a prize in return. Her way of doing this was to get him into bed where she knew she had the power.

"Do you really like my voice?" she asked again, anxious to hear him repeat the compliment.

"Hey, baby, how many times I gotta tell you? You sound *good!* A little raw in places – nothing I can't fix when we record your first single."

She'd been waiting to hear those words from somebody legitimate all her life. She moved closer to him, brushing her breasts against his chest. "What happens next?"

"Anything you want," he said, puffing on his cigarette with a blissful smile.

"I want a contract."

"Baby, as far as I'm concerned – you got it."

"I want to start making money."

"I'm the man to do it for you."

"And I need somewhere to live. I moved out of my apartment. Right now I'm staying at my brother's."

"Oh, wow, you're in a bad way, huh?"

"I had to get away from Reece. Now I plan to start fresh."

"You will, baby. When the big boss hears your voice and takes a look at you, we're goin' all the way."

"That's exactly what I needed to hear."

He laughed. "Come back here, and I'll show you *exactly* what *I* need."

Marik was true to his word. Within a week she was installed in a new apartment, she'd signed a contract with Reno Records, and finally met the big boss. His name was Gordon D. Hayworth, and he was a powerful looking black man in his forties.

Gordon D. Hayworth was handsome – he was also married. As soon as Cyndra stepped into his office she'd noticed the family pictures on his desk. One wife – very beautiful. And two young children. The perfect American family.

"You've got some voice," he told her. "It's not strong – more soulful and sexy – but I like that."

"You do?" she asked, widening her eyes.

"Yes, I do," he replied. "We'll find the right single for you to record and see what happens."

"Really?"

He looked at her very seriously. "It's what you want, Cyndra, isn't it?"

"It's what I've always wanted, ever since I was a little girl."

"You must've been a cute little girl," he said, smiling.

She wondered how cute he would've thought she was when Mr Browning was raping her, when she was having the abortion, and all the other bad things that had happened to her.

"Yes, I was very cute," she said, smiling back.

405

"We're happy to have you with us, Cyndra," he said, standing up and walking around his desk to pat her on the shoulder in a fatherly fashion.

"I'm happy, too," she said.

"We'll be seeing lots of each other."

I hope so, she thought.

He continued to smile as he escorted her to the door.

She walked out of his office and realized for the first time in her life she'd met a man she knew she could fall in love with.

"I'm flying to New York to see Nick," Annie said.

"That's nice," Cyndra replied. "It'll be a break for you."

Annie frowned. "I have to be honest with you. I'm going there to tell him I can't keep quiet any longer."

Cyndra turned on her, her eyes flashing angrily. "*No*, Annie. How many times must I tell you? It's not just Nick you'll hurt – it's me. And now my career is about to take off, you mustn't do this."

"I have to," Annie said, stubbornly. "I can't live with myself and keep this secret."

"Screw you!" Cyndra exploded. "I'll deny it ever happened. Let them go out and search for the body. You'll look like a fool 'cause I'll deny everything. You're not dragging me down, girl, so don't you try it. I'll tell them you're crazy, I'll tell them you've always been crazy."

"You can say what you like," Annie said, refusing to look her in the eye. "But I'm going to the police when I get back."

As soon as she was alone Cyndra called Nick. "Annie's gonna blow it," she said. "You'd better be prepared to do something about her."

"I know what I have to do," he said.

"Good, 'cause otherwise we've both had it."

406

Chapter 64

"What happened?" Oliver said, standing on her doorstep trying to conceal his anger.

"I didn't feel well. I had to get out of there."

He tapped his foot impatiently. "May I come in?"

She wasn't in the mood to deal with him. "I still don't feel good, Oliver."

He walked past her into the living room. "Why didn't you tell me? I could have driven you, my car was downstairs."

She trailed behind him. "I needed some air. I walked halfway home."

He looked at her as if he didn't quite believe what he was hearing. "You left me there and walked home? You left me looking like a fool, Lauren."

"No, I didn't," she said, refusing to admit she might be wrong. "Nobody knew I'd gone."

"I'm sure they did."

"Please, Oliver, I'm not in the mood for a fight. I told you, I don't feel well."

"Do you need a doctor?"

"No, I'll be all right. It was just the pressure of cooking dinner, and their kitchen was so hot, and I just . . ." She trailed off and sighed. "Oliver, don't you ever feel that you're about to explode?"

"No," he said, in an irritated voice. "And if I did I would tell you."

"Thanks," she said, listlessly.

"Sometimes, Lauren, I don't understand you."

He could say that again. Perhaps she should enlighten him before it was too late.

"There's a lot about me you don't know. Maybe we should think about this marriage thing."

Now he was really aggravated. "I don't have to think about it, and nor do you."

"If I told you about my past you might change your mind."

"Oh, now you're going to tell me you have a hidden past, is that it?"

"It hasn't all been exactly *Little House on the Prairie*."

"Listen, my dear, everyone has secrets. I have no need to hear yours. I love you, that's enough for me."

She was determined to be heard whether he liked it or not. "When my parents were killed I went to live in Philadelphia with my aunt and uncle. I had an affair with my cousin."

"Am I supposed to be upset about that?"

"Then I came to New York, met Jimmy and slept with him."

Oliver frowned; he was not enjoying this. "Lauren, how old are you?"

"Twenty-four."

"You're twenty-four years old and you've had affairs with two men. You wouldn't be normal if you hadn't." His tone softened. "You know, darling, I hardly imagined you were a virgin."

"There was somebody else – somebody I knew when I was very young."

"Who was that?" he asked, patiently.

"A boy in High school."

"What about him?"

"Oh, nothing . . ." She trailed off. There was no point in telling him about Nick. "Please, Oliver, I really need to be alone. We'll talk tomorrow. Go home."

"I was going to give you your surprise," he said, refusing to budge.

"Give it to me tomorrow."

His lips formed a thin tight line. "Very well," he said, obviously not at all pleased. "Get a good night's rest." He pecked her on the cheek and left.

As soon as he was gone she paced around her apartment a nervous wreck. God! She was so confused. She didn't know what to do or what to think. She'd never imagined running into Nick. As far as she was concerned he was out of her life forever. And yet there he was, sitting at the dinner party with that Carlysle person, and every feeling she'd ever had for him came flooding back over her. She'd loved him so very much, she would have given her life for him.

Seeing him again had unnerved her. Her memories of him were so vivid. And he'd looked so good, so great, so fantastic.

Get real. Nick Angelo is your past.

It doesn't have to be that way.

Yes, it does.

Had he seen her? Had he recognized her? Their eyes had met for an instant and yes – she knew without a doubt he'd recognized her.

If only she could tell somebody, but there was nobody to confide in. Who would understand about her and Nick? They'd say it was a teenage crush, a stupid little affair. But it wasn't. She'd lived for him and he'd crushed her.

Nick Angelo – why was she getting in such a state? He was a son-of-a-bitch. He'd dumped her like all the others. He'd set the pattern.

Well, she'd show him. She was marrying Oliver Liberty, a man of substance. And when she was Mrs Liberty he couldn't touch her ever again.

The next morning she woke up and fervently wished it had all been a dream. She showered, brushed her teeth, put on her make-up, dressed and went into the office.

As soon as she walked in Pia was on her case. "Nick Angelo called," she said. "He sounded anxious to reach you. Who is he?"

Her stomach did a somersault. "Nobody important – tear the message up."

On her desk there were a dozen red roses from Oliver and a note asking her to meet him for lunch. She knew he must be feeling anxious; they were supposed to leave for the Bahamas in two days and her behaviour had obviously unsettled him.

"Uh, Pia . . . do me a favour," she said, staring at the roses.

"Yes?"

"If Nick Angelo calls again, say I've left town. In fact, you can tell him I'm about to be married and don't give him any other information."

"Who is he?" Pia asked, curiously.

"Oh . . . just somebody I knew a long time ago in High school."

"He's got a great voice," Pia said. "Kind of sexy."

"That's nice," she replied, wishing Pia would get off the subject.

Oliver was waiting when she arrived at the restaurant. "Feeling better today?" he asked, solicitous as ever.

"Much better, thank you," she said, sliding in beside him.

"Good. Because I have your surprise."

"Does it bark and eat plenty of food?"

"No, my dear, it is not a puppy, you know how I feel about puppies. I refuse to have them peeing all over my Persian rugs."

"Then I'm very disappointed, Oliver."

"You won't be," he said, groping for a large envelope on the banquette seating. "Take a look," he said, handing it to her.

"What is it?"

"Open it and you'll see."

She opened the envelope and pulled out a large poster. Staring at her was her own image. Above the photograph in bold lettering were the words: THE NEW MARCELLA GIRL!

"What's this?" she asked.

"You can see what it is. It's your photograph from the session."

"I know, but why does it say The New Marcella Girl?"

"Because, my darling, that's exactly who you're going to be."

Carlysle tried every way she knew how, but she could not get any further action out of Nick that night. Unbeknown to her he was in a state of shock because he couldn't believe he'd run into Lauren after all those years. It was all he could do to escort Carlysle home.

"Aren't you coming up?" she asked, as he helped her from the limo.

"Nah, early call," he explained.

"So've I," she pointed out. "We could go in to the studio together."

"I got a headache," he said.

"*You've* got a headache?" she laughed, hysterically. "Isn't that supposed to be *my* line?"

She went for his zipper again. He slapped her hand away.

"What happened?" she demanded. "I thought we were having a good time."

"We were. It's nothing personal."

"God, you're behaving really strangely."

He was behaving strangely? Had she ever thought about her own behaviour?

"Look, I'll see you on the set tomorrow," he said.

She marched into her apartment building without a backward glance. Her driver took him back to his hotel.

He couldn't get over seeing Lauren. What exactly was she doing in New York? And who was the old guy she was engaged to?

How could she be engaged to a man old enough to be her grandfather? And how come she hadn't acknowledged him? She must have busted her ass to get out of there so fast.

He had so many questions and he needed answers. It wasn't that he was going to forgive her for not answering his letters, but it would be nice to find out why.

At the hotel there was a message from Annie. He returned her call.

"I'm coming in," she announced.

"Oh . . . that's great," he said, thinking it wasn't so great. The last thing he needed was Annie.

"I'll be arriving tomorrow at four. Will you meet me?"

"I'm on the set," he said. "But I'll arrange to have someone there."

"We have to talk," she said.

Oh, Christ! Cyndra was right, this didn't sound good.

First thing in the morning he called Help Unlimited.

A female voice said, "Pia Liberty. Can I help you?"

"Yeah, let me talk to Lauren."

"She's not in yet."

"I need to get in touch with her like immediately."

"I'll see she gets the message."

"Maybe you can give me her home number."

"No, I'm sorry."

"We're friends from way back."

"I'm sure you are, but we never divulge personal numbers. Why don't you call again at ten?"

He took off for the studio. Carlysle greeted him with a scowl; she was obviously unused to not getting her own way.

He studied his script, conferred with the director and tried to throw himself into character, but it was difficult holding his concentration. As soon as he got a break he rushed to the phone. "Is Lauren in yet?"

"I'm sorry, you've missed her. She's left town. She's getting married, you know."

"Is this Pia?"

"Good memory."

"Listen, Pia, I *have* to talk to her. It's very important."

"I gave her your message. Maybe she'll call you."

"You don't understand. We really go back a long way."

"She said she'd contact you."

"She did?"

"Yes."

He hung up the phone feeling depressed. What was he chasing her for anyway? She'd dumped him. What more could he have done than written her a hundred times without receiving one single reply.

The truth was – if he wanted to face up to it – Lauren Roberts had never wanted him. It had all been a game for her. Nick Angelo – the jerk from the wrong side of the tracks – and pretty little Lauren Roberts, who'd amused herself at his expense.

Well screw her. Let her go off and marry some rich old man. What did he care?

But deep down he did care. And although he'd never admit it, seeing her again had stirred up every painful memory of the love he'd once had for her.

He wanted Lauren to be his past. Somehow he knew it wasn't possible.

Chapter 65

Annie had her own agenda – he knew it as soon as she arrived direct from the airport and came straight to the set. In New York she looked very Californian with her deep suntan, athletic body and brightly coloured clothes.

"Who's she?" Carlysle demanded, the moment Annie hit the set.

"A friend," Nick replied.

Carlysle smiled a secret smile. "I bet she doesn't give head like I do."

Waldo, hovering on the sidelines, raised his eyebrows and tut tutted.

"She's not my girlfriend," Nick explained to Carlysle.

"You haven't fucked her?" Carlysle questioned.

"No."

"But she wants you to."

"Why do you say that?"

"Take a look at her, Nick, she's mooning after you like a baby who wants to suck mama's tit," Carlysle giggled, wickedly. "Only it's not your tit she wants to suck."

"Has anybody ever told you you've got sex on the mind?"

"Something wrong with that?"

One thing about Carlysle, she wasn't a clinger. She didn't give a damn who he was sleeping with – which was just as well because he didn't plan on answering to anyone.

He introduced Annie to the director, which pleased her. Later she sat in his chair and watched while they shot a restaurant scene. When it was done she reluctantly admitted he was good.

"Thanks," he said.

"Joy would be proud of you. Aren't you glad I took you to her class?"

Was this her subtle way of telling him that if she hadn't taken

413

him to Joy Byron's class none of this would have happened?

Filming finished shortly before seven, and they rode back to his hotel in a cab.

"I booked you a room," he said. "It's one floor up from me. Oh, and they need to know how long you're staying."

"That depends on you," she said, in an edgy voice.

Shit! Why did it depend on him?

"What d'you mean?" he asked.

She stared straight at him. "How long do *you* want me to stay?"

Carlysle was right. Annie was waiting for him to make a move, and unfortunately the only way he could stop her from opening up her mouth to the cops was to make her his girlfriend.

They ate Chinese food in a nearby restaurant, talked about the movie and LA and Cyndra's record deal. Then they got down to the real reason she'd come to New York.

"I suppose Cyndra warned you," she said, sipping Chinese tea. "I'm sorry to do this to you, Nick – but it's too big a burden for me to carry any longer."

"Yeah," he said, thinking about how to handle her. "I understand."

She was surprised. "You do?"

"I know how difficult it must be for you, Annie. You're all alone – you've got nobody to talk to – you're trying to get connected and acting jobs aren't easy. Yeah, I understand." He moved right along, talking about Joy and the class and her job at the health club.

She was confused. She'd expected him to try and talk her out of going to the police and she'd had all her arguments ready. But no, he'd gone completely in the opposite direction and it wasn't what she'd expected.

On the walk back to the hotel he put his arm around her, held her hand and told her how pretty she looked. By the time he got her to his room on the pretext of rehearsing the next day's scene, she was all his. But still he proceeded carefully, and when he started to undress her she was more than ready.

He took it slowly – pacing himself – going at her speed, which was slow. She did have a terrific body – compact and muscled, not really his type – he liked his women on the more voluptuous side.

When they finally made it he was shocked to discover she

was a virgin. "You must be the only virgin left in Hollywood," he joked, trying not to hurt her as he went for the final thrust.

"Don't joke about it, Nick," she gasped. "I believe in waiting."

He broke through and felt her gush. Then he proceeded to make her very happy indeed.

By the time he was finished he knew the cops would be the last place she'd go.

Annie stayed a week. The moment she left he resumed service with Carlysle, whose only comment was why hadn't the three of them got it on.

"You're somethin' else," he said, shaking his head.

With Annie safely back in LA they proceeded to have sex whenever and wherever they could. It became a standing joke that if either of them were needed on the set they had to be prised apart first. Their on screen love scenes were sizzling, especially when Carlysle did things to him under the sheets that nobody knew about except the two of them.

He got to see the dailies and knew it was working for him. Carlysle and he had great chemistry.

Most nights they went out. Carlysle was invited everywhere, and there was always a party or opening. She really got off on public sex – the more dangerous the better. They'd done some form of sexual activity everywhere from the first night of a Broadway show to the toniest restaurant. And he never made a limo trip without Carlysle giving him one of her famous blow jobs.

"Don't you ever get tired?" he asked, only half-jokingly.

"I've got the rest of my life to get tired. Live for the moment, Nick – we won't be around forever."

If she carried on at this pace she'd wear out his dick! And then where would he be?

The female producer started paying more attention to him. He figured her to be in her early forties, but extremely well-preserved. One day she informed him she had a script she'd like him to read and invited him up to her hotel suite.

"Can *I* come, too?" Carlysle begged.

"No," he said firmly.

"She wants to fuck you," Carlysle said.

"According to you everyone wants to fuck me."

"When this movie comes out they will. You can take odds on it."

Carlysle, as usual, was right. The producer poured him a vodka on the rocks and sat opposite him, crossing and uncrossing her long elegant legs while he attempted to read the script. She'd already informed him it was under wraps and could not leave her hands.

Twenty pages in and she dropped her skirt, revealing a black lace garter belt, stockings and a black bush. She obviously did not believe in panties.

He remembered the stop light where she'd ignored him and he fucked her good.

Afterwards she asked him what he thought of the script.

"Not bad," he said, confidently. "But the fuck was great."

Carlysle wanted details. She savoured every juicy one, and it so turned her on that they made out in an alley behind the latest hot disco where they were attending a party.

Meanwhile he called Annie every other day. She sounded fine. He was relieved; at least he had her under control.

One day he received a distraught call from Joey's hooker girlfriend.

"Those bastards beat Joey up good," she said. "He's in the hospital."

As soon as he finished work he rushed over to visit. Joey lay in a public ward with bandaged limbs and a pulped face. His eyes were mere slits and his lips swollen to twice their size.

"This is really nice," Nick said, cheerfully. "Can't leave you alone for a minute. How'd it happen?"

"Got inna fight," Joey mumbled.

"What with – a meat truck?"

Joey tried to raise his arm. "Don' make me laugh."

Later he talked to Joey's girlfriend again and found out the true story. According to her Joey owed big drug money on account of a heroin habit he wasn't about to quit.

"I'll take care of it," Nick promised, and he went to Carlysle and asked to borrow money so he could help Joey out. "I wanna put him into some kinda clinic – get him straight," he explained. "It costs, an' I don't have that kinda bucks. This'll be a loan – I'll even pay interest."

Carlysle was unconcerned. "My mother handles all my money," she said, blithely dismissing his problem. "I can't touch it."

You could if you wanted to, bitch.

He went to his producer. She asked questions. Satisfied with

416

his answers she agreed to the loan in exchange for an option agreement making him available for her next film.

In Los Angeles Meena Caron objected bitterly. "I'm hearing excellent reports, Nick. It would be suicide to tie you up now."

"Gotta help a friend," he explained, and signed the agreement.

Before the movie was over the word was out. There was a new hot property on the horizon. And his name was Nick Angel.

Chapter 66

"Do you, Lauren Roberts, take this man, Oliver Liberty, to be your lawfully wedded husband?"

She hesitated for only a second. "I do," she said, breathlessly.

"Do you, Oliver Liberty, take this woman, Lauren Roberts, to be your lawfully wedded wife?"

He turned to look at her, his eyes full of pride. "I do."

They stood on the terrace of his house in the Bahamas overlooking a glorious never-ending white beach and a bluer-than-blue ocean. The setting was idyllic. Lauren wore a simple white dress and flowers in her hair. Their witnesses were Oliver's housekeeper and her husband – a friendly black couple who did nothing but beam happily.

When she said, "I do," Lauren felt a shudder of apprehension. She was giving her life to another human being. She was joining with Oliver and things would never be quite the same.

It's what you want, isn't it, Roberts?

No.

Don't think that way.

What I want is Nick Angelo.

Oh, for God's sake.

Oliver bent to kiss her and she quickly shut out the images of her past.

Later that night they dined quietly, just the two of them on the terrace overlooking the sea.

"So, my darling," he said, clasping her hand. "How do you feel?"

She wasn't sure how she felt. "Light-headed, I guess."

"That's good, because I feel I'm the luckiest man in the world," he said, clinking his champagne glass with hers.

She sipped her champagne, and listened to the soothing sound of the surf.

I'm Mrs Oliver Liberty.
He's forty years older than you.
I don't care.
You've married a father figure.
That's not true.

After dinner Oliver retired to his study to make a few phone calls. "It'll give you time to relax," he said.

Why would she require time to relax on her wedding night?

She wandered around the house, finally settling in the master bedroom. It was a light and airy room with another picturesque view. Decorated in earth tones, there was an intricate white lace cover on the bed and piles of luxurious cushions. She wondered who'd decorated it. Wife number one or wife number two? She decided it was wife number one – far too tasteful for wife number two.

In the pale beige limestone bathroom she took a shower and slipped into the sheer white nightgown she'd purchased especially for her wedding night. By the time she returned to the bedroom Oliver was lying on the bed in silk pyjamas perusing a stack of mail.

"Don't you ever stop?" she asked, standing silhouetted in the doorway.

"I believe in taking advantage of every moment. This is correspondence I didn't have time to deal with before I left."

She moved over to the bed. "Was it absolutely necessary to bring it on our honeymoon?"

He must have noticed her tone of annoyance, because he pushed the mail to one side. "I'm sorry," he said, reaching for her hand. "You, my darling," he continued, looking at her for the first time, "are absolutely ravishing."

Will you ravish me tonight, Oliver?
Will you ravish me until I can't breathe?

"Thank you," she murmured.

"Come over here," he said, pulling her down on to the bed.

This was the first night of their married life and she wanted it to be memorable. So far their sex life had not progressed very far. Oliver kept on telling her that when they were married things would be different, and she was ready for the change. She needed a man to take her on a passionate trip. Only Nick had managed to satisfy her every need, and she craved that same satisfaction.

Oliver began to kiss and caress her. She responded with a passion she'd kept hidden from him before.

"Oliver, tonight should be memorable . . ." she murmured, voicing her thoughts.

"Isn't our lovemaking always memorable?" he asked, smoothly.

No, it's not, she wanted to reply. *We've never made love properly. All you've done is make love to me with your tongue.*

She demonstrated with actions what she wanted to do to him. As she began to bend her head, he stopped her abruptly.

"What are you doing?"

"I'm going to make you very happy."

"No, Lauren, I don't like you to do that."

"But you do it to me all the time. In fact, that's all you do."

"Because you deserve it."

Deserve it? What kind of comment is that?

"Oliver, let me do this to you. You know you'll love it."

"No, Lauren, I will not love it. I refuse to see you in that position."

"I only want to please you," she said.

"I know, my darling, but that doesn't please me. It's an act I associate with sex for sale. It's demeaning and I don't expect you to do it."

She was shocked by his words. Surely, when two people were married, nothing was demeaning if it was something they both desired? But if that's the way he wanted it, so be it.

They kissed and caressed some more. His hands fondled her breasts, stroking her gently. Then his head began travelling down her body, heading for what he considered to be his proper destination.

Some women might be wild with joy at the thought of a man who gave them non-stop oral sex, but she'd had enough. Especially as he wouldn't allow her to do it to him.

"No, Oliver," she said, moving. "I want you to make love to me properly."

"But, my darling, you enjoy every second of what I do to you."

"Tonight it should be different," she said, reaching to feel his hardness – disappointed to discover he was only semi-erect.

"Lauren, my darling," he said, drawing away.

"Yes?"

"I have no desire to disappoint you."

"Why would you disappoint me?"

"Because I'm not twenty-five."

She couldn't help being sarcastic. "Oh, really? And I thought you were."

"Don't be flippant. When I was a young man I made love all night long. When I got to be older I realized there were other pleasures that could give a woman more joy than anything else."

"What are you saying?"

"I'm not sure I can satisfy you in the way you expect."

"Why can't we try?"

"It's simply that . . ." He hesitated. "Well . . . since I had my pacemaker –"

"Pacemaker?" she said, alarmed.

"Surely I mentioned it? About two years ago I had a heart irregularity, nothing serious. My doctors decided a pacemaker would solve the problem."

"You never told me, Oliver."

"I probably didn't think it was that important."

"Of course it's important. We're married. I should know everything about you."

"Why – would it have made a difference?"

"No . . ." Her mind was racing. A pacemaker. Did that mean he was sick? If they made love could he suddenly die? Oh God, what had she gotten herself into?

He stepped off the bed and walked over to the window. "I'm sorry, my dear. You're right, I should have told you."

She tried to make it better for him. "Well, you didn't and now I know. But we can still make love, can't we?"

"Yes."

"Then come back to bed. I'm not demanding. All I want is to be close to you."

They stayed in the Bahamas for ten days, during which time Lauren realized she'd married a man who was not prepared to consummate their marriage in the normal way. The truth was he wanted to make love to her his way or not at all. And although his way was very pleasant, it was hardly the same as being joined together with another person.

Oliver was also obsessed with business. She'd thought that once he was away from the office he'd be able to relax.

She'd imagined long walks on the beach, swimming, snorkelling, maybe taking a boat out. She did all of those things by herself, because Oliver spent most of his time on the phone.

Occasionally the subject of the Marcella girl came up. When he'd first suggested the idea she'd said a very resounding no. However, he wasn't prepared to take no for an answer. Every other day he asked if she'd changed her mind.

"I told you, Oliver, I'm not a model, nor do I want to be."

"I understand," he replied. "But this is hardly a modelling assignment. You'll be spokesperson for Marcella. You'll also make a lot of money, become well-known and enjoy every minute of it."

She disagreed. The idea of making money was appealing, but she had no wish to become well-known.

Pia called from New York. "Well? Are you going to do it or not?"

"Not," she said, firmly.

"You're blowing an opportunity if you don't," Pia said. "What have you got to lose? Oh, and by the way, take a look in yesterday's *New York News*. There's a photo of that Nick Angel guy – the one who called you. You didn't tell me he was an actor. And you certainly didn't tell me he was gorgeous."

When Lauren hung up she immediately searched for yesterday's New York papers. Sure enough, on page five of the *News* there was a picture of Nick with Carlysle Mann. She studied the picture, then read the copy:

Carlysle Mann, out on the town with her new co-star, Nick Angel. Carlysle and Nick are shooting Night City *on location in New York. Word has it that Nick lights up the screen – especially in the sex scenes – of which there are many. Ladies look out . . . he could be your new Saturday night rave . . .*

Nick was actually in a movie! She could hardly believe it. Nick Angel – whatever happened to Angelo? God! He was a professional actor. He'd done what they'd both talked and dreamed about.

She stared at his picture again, and hated Carlysle – which was stupid, because she didn't even know her. Then she read the copy through three times, folded the paper and put it in a drawer.

Later that day she approached Oliver. As usual, he was on the phone.

"Hang up," she said, standing in front of him.

He covered the mouthpiece. "What's the matter?"

"Hang up. I have to talk to you."

He excused himself and put the phone down. "I hope this is important," he said, irritably.

"It is."

"Well?"

"I'm accepting."

"You're accepting what?"

"I'll be the Marcella girl."

He perked up. "Really?"

"Yes, Oliver. And I want Samm to be my agent. She'll negotiate my price."

He laughed. "*She'll* negotiate your price?"

"I'm expensive," Lauren said. "But if you want me you'll pay."

Back in New York Pia waddled around looking like she was going to drop the kid any moment. Lauren realized that if she was going to embark on this Marcella girl campaign, then it was time to think seriously about Help Unlimited.

"What do you want to do?" she asked Pia. "You're having a baby, you've got the responsibility of Howard. Maybe we should dissolve the business."

"I *like* having the business," Pia said. "Although I suppose you're right. I won't have the time to spend there. And if you get the Marcella job, nor will you."

It was sad, but they decided the best thing to do was to close it down.

Lauren met with Samm, who was quite amused by the turn of events. "Do you realize how many of my models will want to scratch your eyes out, darling?" she said. "They'll say you used your influence with the boss."

"No, Samm – he used *his* influence with *me*. But I want a killer deal, otherwise I'm not doing it."

Samm nodded. "I like killer deals. Are you giving me permission to walk in and make the deal of the century?"

Lauren smiled. "That's *exactly* what I'm doing."

"And can I stroll casually away if they don't care to accept it?"

"I wouldn't expect you to do anything else."

"Lauren – you're my kind of girl."

Oliver came home that night with raised eyebrows. "Are you insane? You're asking for more money than a top model."

"Sweetheart, this was your idea, not mine. If Marcella would like me to represent them, then this is what they'll have to pay."

He shook his head. "I didn't realize I'd married a tough business woman."

"It wasn't my idea to be the Marcella girl, kindly remember that."

"I've talked with the client," Oliver said. "They have my recommendation. I've also given them several other suggestions. The final decision is theirs."

"Good," Lauren said. "Because I don't care either way."

Although deep down she did. Deep down she knew that she wanted to be somebody. Just like Nick Angel was going to be somebody. She didn't want to be left behind. She wanted to be just as important as he.

Chapter 67

"You need a publicist," Frances said.

"What for? I'm getting plenty of publicity. Carlysle and I are all over the columns."

"You need somebody to shape an image for you. Give you a profile – a very high profile."

"Forget it. I don't have the money."

"What did you do with the money you got for the option agreement you so foolishly signed against Meena's advice?"

He shrugged. "I had a friend in trouble. That was the deal."

"How sweet," Frances said, dragging deeply on her cigarette. "He has a kind heart."

"I always thought it was cool to help out friends," he said, throwing himself on her couch. "Isn't that the way it's supposed to work?"

"You really are a genuinely nice person," said Frances, sounding surprised.

"So I guess you've got a publicist you want to recommend," he said, reaching for a cigarette, deciding it was his turn to blow smoke in her face.

"You have to admit," Frances replied, "you *do* like my recommendations. Your new photographs are excellent and Meena is doing well for you. Of course, she could do better if you hadn't tied yourself up to that ridiculous option deal."

"Hey," he shrugged. "What's so ridiculous about signing for another movie? A couple of months ago I couldn't have gotten arrested. Why the big fuss?"

"Learn to understand this business," Frances said, sternly. "From all reports, when *Night City* comes out you're going to be hot. When you're hot is the time to act. But since you've tied yourself up for another film, Meena cannot do anything for you."

"Yeah, Frances, but I'm not a total jerk. I don't have to do the film immediately. There's a clause in there that says I can do something else if they're not ready by a certain date. It's cool."

"So now you've decided to be your own lawyer?"

"Hey, I've been meaning to talk to you about that. Can you recommend a good lawyer?"

"There's a cocktail party tomorrow night," Frances said. "You'll take me. There'll be several top lawyers there. You can quietly audition them."

"I don't know if I can make tomorrow night."

She looked at him sharply. "Nick, I don't expect you to forget our deal so early on in our relationship."

"Okay – I'll make it," he said.

He'd only gotten back to Los Angeles the day before after nearly two months shooting in New York, and although he'd spoken to Annie on the phone he hadn't seen her. He'd promised to take her out the next night for a welcome home dinner. Now that Frances required his company he'd just have to switch nights on her.

Frances wrote down the name and phone number of a publicist and handed him the paper. "Go see her," she said.

"Another woman?"

Frances narrowed her flinty eyes. "What's the matter? Don't you like dealing with women? Believe me, dear, they'll look after you much better than men."

Like she was telling him something new.

Marik, Cyndra had decided, was too nice for his own good. He treated her like a princess. Initially she'd lured him into bed – although he didn't take much luring – to get him under her power. Now she had him where she wanted him and more besides, because not only was he producing her single, but he was also her attentive and caring companion. The trouble was she didn't want a companion. She was perfectly happy making it on her own. Being married to Reece was enough companionship to last her a lifetime.

Marik was a California boy. He wanted her to meet his mother and sisters. She said no until she ran out of excuses and then she accompanied him one sunny Sunday afternoon. His family lived in the valley and they were all equally as nice as Marik.

Unfortunately, he was in love with her. She liked him, but she certainly didn't love him.

Gordon Hayworth was another matter. Every time she saw him she experienced exquisite little chills running up and down her spine, and a nervous stomach that drove her crazy. He dropped by the recording studio when she was making the demo and she spied him talking to Marik through the glass. She wanted to stop everything and go over just to be near him.

Casually she asked around. Usually the secretaries had the scam on everyone, but Gordon had no scandal attached. He was married to a beautiful ex-model and never came on to anyone else.

Gordon Hayworth had a presence and dignity she'd never observed in a man before. And she wanted him almost as much as she wanted a big career.

Marik was excited. The song he'd found for her was called "Child Baby", and it was written by a couple of up-and-coming songwriters. He'd put together a backing ensemble that really complimented her voice, and the arrangement was killer.

"Reno Records is behind you all the way, baby," he told her. "When this little old record hits the airwaves people gonna find out about you big time!"

The next weekend Marik wanted to take her to Palm Springs. He was so anxious to please that she didn't want to disappoint him, even though she'd sooner not have gone.

They drove down on a Friday night in his white Corvette and stayed at a small hotel surrounded by a backdrop of magnificent mountains.

"What was the story with you and that Reece guy?" Marik asked as he unpacked his overnight bag.

"Why?" she said carefully, unfolding her clothes.

"'Cause I'm interested. He said you were married. True or false?"

"No, we weren't married," she said, quickly. "We lived together for a while. I was young and stupid – I didn't know any better."

She didn't care to tell him the truth. If he'd known she was married to Reece it may have affected their business relationship, not to mention their personal one.

Later that night they sat outside in the bubbling Jacuzzi gazing up at the stars.

"This is oh so very, very nice," Marik said, stretching his legs.

"Yes, it's really pretty," she replied.

"No, baby – *you're* really pretty."

She threw her head back, her long hair trailing in the bubbling water. "So, tell me, Marik, how long have you been with Reno Records?"

"I've kinda been around Reno for five years."

"Where were you before that?"

"I put in time at a couple of the big companies. Produced some damn good artists. Then Gordon came along and offered me this job. It was a chance to do bigger and better." He laughed. "Gordon kinda stole me away."

"I expect he's good at that," she said.

His hand touched her leg. "Yeah, Gordon's a powerful personality. He's sure heavy on charisma."

"Why don't you tell me about him, he seems like an interesting guy."

"He had a small record company in New York, sold it for mucho bucks and moved out to LA about ten years ago. Then he started Reno, and the rest is a big success story."

"Is he married?" she asked, knowing full well that he was.

"Yeah."

"Who's his wife?"

"She was a top model – gave it all up when they married – Gordon didn't want his wife working."

"Are they happy?"

"Very happy." His hand snaked up her leg. "Hey, baby – what's with all the questions?"

"I should know who I'm working for."

"Stick with me, girl, and you don't have to know nothin'!"

He held open his arms and she moved into his bubbly softness. California was so health conscious, she wondered if Marik had ever thought about attending a gym. He should firm up his pecs, work on those stomach muscles. She didn't want to hurt his feelings by asking.

He was a good kisser so she leaned back and let him do his business. Marik was taking her all the way to stardom – why fight it?

Bridget Hale, Nick's new publicist, reminded him of a thinner, less cheerful Meena – what did these women have – a club? At least she seemed to know what she was doing; she'd already set him two interviews for later in the week – one with a news service for a piece that would run throughout the country, and one with a popular entertainment weekly magazine. He'd done a few interviews on the set and found it to be kind of a kick talking about himself.

Bridget trained him in the ways of the world. "We have to make up an interesting background for you," she said. "I don't know where you're from and I don't particularly care. We'll start from zero."

"I'm from the Midwest," he said.

"No, I don't think so. Something foreign will do. Your father was in the CIA – you were raised in China. Let me work on it."

"You gotta be kidding."

"Another point to remember – never tell them your age – let them guess. The more mysterious you are the better. Hollywood loves a loner."

"How come?"

"Because when you're on the cover of *Time* we don't want some nosy journalist visiting your home town and checking with all your old friends. If we can maintain it, mystery is the best, remember that."

"So what *do* I say when they ask me?"

"That you don't believe in pasts, only futures."

He laughed. "Sounds good to me."

"Frances and Meena are very high on you," she said. "And their praise does not come easily."

"They haven't seen me on film yet."

"Frances and Meena hear everything first. If you're good in this movie then they're aware of it."

He knew he should visit Joy, but he also knew she'd do nothing but bitterly criticize everything he'd done, and he wasn't in the mood for that. While he was prepared to acknowledge her help for introducing him to Frances, he was not prepared to listen to her negative comments. He wanted to feel good about himself. He was finally on the road and the main thing was to enjoy it.

He'd gotten Joey out of the hospital in New York and now he was safely stashed in a drug rehab clinic somewhere in the middle of the country. As soon as Joey was through with his treatment he'd arranged for him to come straight to LA.

In the meantime there was Annie to deal with.

They had dinner at a little restaurant near the Santa Monica Pier, and talked about what they'd both been doing. Towards the end of dinner she leaned across the table and fixed him with

429

a penetrating stare. "Nick, am I going to move in with you?" she asked. "Is that what we're planning?"

He hadn't been planning anything of the sort, but it was obviously what she expected. He stalled for time, finally saying, "Uh, you mean you'd give up your apartment?"

She nodded. "If we're going to be together it seems only sensible. Why waste money paying rent on two places?"

The last person he'd lived with had been DeVille. Towards the end he'd felt beyond claustrophobic. "Are you sure it's what you want?" he asked, hoping she'd say no, but knowing she'd say yes.

"Very sure," she said firmly, just as he'd predicted.

He knew if he backed away she was going to start with the *I'm going to the cops* crap again. He couldn't afford to take the risk.

"If that's what you want, you should move in."

"Are you sure, Nick?"

He took her hand and squeezed it. "Yeah, course I'm sure."

What a lie. He liked Annie as a friend. He didn't love her, and the last thing he wanted was to live with her.

Trailing Frances around another industry party was the same old story. However, he felt a little more secure. He'd starred in a movie and a couple of people seemed to know who he was even though the movie hadn't come out yet.

He felt even more secure when he bumped into Carlysle. He'd missed the on-the-edge excitement of being with her. This was a different Carlysle from the girl he'd known in New York. She wore a neat little dress with a Peter Pan collar and a sweet angelic smile.

"This is my mother," she said, introducing him to an untidy looking woman who practically ignored him. "Mommy, this is Nick Angel – he starred in *Night City* with me. Remember? I told you about him."

"Oh," Mommy said. "So you're Nick. I hear you've done a good job."

"I'm hoping," he said.

Carlysle did not make a pass at him. Carlysle was a different person when she was with Mommy.

After the cocktail party Frances took him to dinner. "So, you did fuck her," she said, studying the menu.

"Who?"

"Carlysle. It was all over New York."

He grinned. "I had no choice."

"A word of advice," Frances said, sipping a J&B on the rocks. "Never let your cock interfere with your career."

"I'll remember that, Frances," he said, trying to keep a straight face.

A week later Annie moved in. He hated having to share his closet. She hated the fact that the bathroom was down the hall. "I'll look for something better," he promised, although he was fond of his little place by the beach.

Six weeks later he was invited to view a rough cut of the movie. Annie and Cyndra accompanied him. He sat in the theatre sweating, wondering what it was going to be like seeing himself on the screen. He'd attended a couple of day's rushes, but that was it. Meena, Frances and Bridget were in the audience. Having them there made him extra nervous. He nodded at his two producers – the woman didn't even crack a smile. Carlysle was there with her mother, looking demure.

Cyndra squeezed his hand. "This is so exciting!" she whispered.

"Yeah, almost as exciting as your record debut. When's it coming out?"

She grinned. "Two weeks. I can hardly stand it!"

"We'll celebrate," he said.

"You *bet* we will."

He wished something would come along for Annie; he knew she must be feeling left out, working at the health club watching their careers take off while she never got a break. It couldn't be much fun.

When the lights dimmed, he slid down in his seat barely able to watch the screen. Carlysle got star billing. He got an, *INTRODUCING NICK ANGEL AS PETE.*

Jesus! That was his name up on the screen. He'd actually made it – he was in a fucking movie!

The film was fast paced, gritty and surprisingly good. At the end of the screening there was a burst of spontaneous applause. Bridget was smiling – unusual for her.

Frances came up to him. "I like the film, I like you in it."

"Lunch, tomorrow," Meena said on her way out. "It's about time you met the head of the agency."

Cyndra was more excited than anybody. "Oh God, Nick, this is so great! You're fantastic, you really are!"

431

Annie was more controlled. Naturally. It wasn't in her nature to get excited about anything.

The three of them went to a restaurant on the Strip where they celebrated with double Margueritas and huge steaks.

Later, at home alone with Annie, he felt like making love, but not with her – she failed to turn him on. He was only with her because he had to be – it was a sad thought.

But tomorrow was another day and he'd figure out something – maybe.

He lay awake for a long while thinking about the movie, wondering what would happen next.

Eventually he fell asleep with a smile on his face.

Chapter 68

Lorenzo Marcella was the quintessential Italian man. Tall, exquisitely dressed in the finest Armani had to offer, proudly handsome in an aristocratic way. His dirty-blond hair was longish and lightly touched with silver at the temples. His jewellery was discreet and solid gold. His car was a black Masarati – not exactly ideal for Manhattan – but he would not dream of letting down the image. He was forty-two years old and the only heir to the family fortune. While he waited to inherit he'd been sent to America to spearhead the Marcella girl launch.

Lorenzo had no idea Lauren was married to the head of the powerful advertising agency Liberty & Charles – the very agency who were handling the Marcella account. And even if he had it wouldn't have made any difference. "This is the girl we use," he announced, picking out Lauren's photo from a select group.

"She's expensive," Oliver said, trying to curb his amusement, for he'd known there was no contest.

"How expensive?" Lorenzo demanded.

"Very," Oliver replied, straight-faced.

"Does she represent any other product?"

"No," said Howard, sitting in on the meeting with several other Liberty & Charles executives.

Lorenzo studied Lauren's photographs one more time. "Then we sign her to an exclusive Marcella contract. I don't mind what she costs. She is the girl."

"Good," said Oliver. "I think you've made the perfect choice."

Lorenzo flashed a movie star smile. "But of course!"

"Well, my dear," Samm said, her cat eyes gleaming. "You *are* the new Marcella girl – it's a done deal."

"You got my price?" Lauren asked.

"Yes, this was a record breaker and I am very happy indeed. Of course, as I mentioned before, most of my models will want to kill me. They'll blame me for not getting *them* the job. You're going to be a star."

Lauren laughed. It didn't seem possible. "I'll be in a lot of magazines, and my face will be around, but that hardly makes me a star, Samm."

"Just you wait," Samm said, nodding wisely. "Hollywood will come chasing after you. Didn't you once tell me you wanted to be an actress?"

"That was a long time ago."

"Well, sweetie, you're hardly ancient. How old are you now?"

"I'll soon be twenty-five."

"An old hag," Samm laughed. "I'd like to see Jimmy Cassady's face when he picks up the first magazine with you on the cover."

"Being the Marcella girl does not mean I'll be on any covers."

"Oh," Samm said, acidly. "If they want you in *Vogue* you'll turn them down?"

"Yes, I told you – I'm doing this for the money."

"I'm sure Oliver can look after you very nicely indeed."

"Yes, he can – but I prefer to be independent."

"You *do* know that Nature was up for this job, don't you?"

"How is she?"

"Living in LA with a producer."

"What happened to Emerson?" Lauren asked, trying to sound casual.

"According to Nature, he sent her a telegram from Japan announcing he was ending the marriage. By that time she'd moved in with her producer so she didn't much care. Don't you read the gossip columns?"

"Actually, I don't."

"Smart girl. Who needs to fill one's mind with trivia."

Oliver, who'd been so enthusiastic at the idea of her being the Marcella girl, was now not so pleased. "Perhaps I've created a monster," he said.

"Don't be silly, Oliver."

"I know what's going to happen. I'll never see you."

"Representing Marcella will not take all my time. I've read the contract carefully. Two photo sessions a year, six public appearances and one commercial."

He shook his head. "You have no idea how much of your time they'll require."

"You were the one that got me into this in the first place."

She was confused. She hadn't wanted a career in the public eye, but now it seemed that's exactly what she was about to have. All she'd really wanted was to marry Oliver and live a happy, fulfilled life. Only this was not to be; her husband could never fulfill her. Oliver could not make love the way she expected, and whenever she raised the subject he dismissed it as though it wasn't important.

Did he really think she was going to want nothing but oral sex from him their entire married life? If the truth were known, he'd tricked her into marriage. He should have told her about the pacemaker.

Meeting Lorenzo Marcella was an experience. The only Italian man she'd ever come in contact with before was Antonio the photographer, and he was gay. Lorenzo was the complete opposite. He kissed her hand, gazed into her eyes, inundated her with white orchids and told her she was the most beautiful woman who'd ever breathed.

"You *are* my Marcella girl," he said. "You will make every woman in the world want to be you. And every man want to be with you."

She backed off; his avid attention made her edgy. "I'll do my best," she said.

"Ah, but your best is going to make me a very happy man," Lorenzo crooned, continuing to gaze into her eyes.

They were at a luncheon in her honour – arranged so she could meet the other executives from Marcella.

"Did you tell them we're married?" she whispered to Oliver.

"No," he shook his head. "I imagine they'll find out soon enough."

"But he's coming on to me."

"Take no notice, my dear. Italian men come on to every woman. Whether they be six or sixty – it doesn't make any difference to them."

Obviously, Lorenzo's outrageous flirting did not bother Oliver, so she went along with it.

Lorenzo had many plans and he was not shy about revealing them. "I will have a wonderful party to present you to the press. It will not be another boring press conference. It will be a fantasy ball – and you will make a divine entrance in the middle of the party."

"I will?"

"Yes, *bellissima*! You shall introduce Marcella Cosmetics to the world as only you can. Everyone will fall in love with you – just as I have."

"You have?"

Lorenzo flashed his dazzling smile. "But of course!"

Chapter 69

The next few months proved challenging and exciting for both Cyndra and Nick. Neither of them could really comprehend what was happening to them.

"It's like a dream come true," Cyndra said. "Can you believe it, Nick – you and me? My record's taking off and your movie's like a big hit. It's incredible."

It was incredible. If he wasn't stuck with Annie he might have enjoyed it a lot more. He was so tired of faking his emotions – pretending to be someone he wasn't.

And Annie smothered him. Because her own career had failed to go anywhere, she leeched on to his – voicing her opinion on everything. This was exactly what he didn't need. It was enough he had Frances giving him advice, Meena handling his career, and Bridget guiding him through the maze of hungry press.

He also had his producer friend anxious for him to start her next movie. He'd read the script. It was not exactly what he wanted to do. Meena said they'd try to get him out of the contract.

"How?" he'd asked.

"With the right lawyer we can do anything," she'd replied, confidently.

Night City had launched his career. It was one of those low budget films the critics loved and the public flocked to. His reviews were excellent and suddenly he was an actor people were talking about. He'd followed Bridget's advice and made up a past for himself, not revealing too much.

"Try not to smile in interviews," she'd told him. "Cultivate that moody look. Women love it."

He did as she asked. Especially with the reporter from *Satisfaction*. They ran a cover story on him that blew his mind. He was on the cover of a fucking magazine and everybody in the world was going to see it!

In the meantime, Cyndra's record was getting plenty of air play. Gordon Hayworth had financed a trip for her and Marik to visit some of the most influential disc jockeys in the country. Marik loved the idea of travelling with her, but she wasn't so thrilled. She would have preferred that it was Gordon accompanying her.

Shortly after she got back Nick took her for a long drive. It had been a while since they'd been alone and had a chance to talk privately. He drove his rented car to Paradise Cove and parked. It was a beautiful September day and they got out and strolled along the beach.

"So," he said, stopping to flip pebbles in the sea. "How you feelin', kid?"

"Sensational! What about you?"

"The agency is trying to get me out of that contract. They have another film for me to do. This time it's a big movie with an important director."

"Is it what you want, Nick?"

"Yeah, I'm doing all the things I always dreamt of."

"So am I," she said. "Thanks to you."

"Why me?"

"Because you're stuck with Annie. You've saved us both."

He shrugged. "Annie's a nice girl."

Cyndra pinned him with her eyes. "But she's not the girl for you, is she?"

"You can talk. Marik's not the guy for you – but sometimes we do stuff to make things work."

"How do you know Marik's not for me?"

"I see it in your eyes."

"Oh, thanks a lot, Nick. Am I that obvious?"

"Hey – I'm your brother. I should be able to read you, huh?"

She stopped walking and flopped down on the sand, hugging her knees to her chest. "Wait until *that* little item hits the press."

He zoomed another pebble and watched it skim across the smooth ocean. "What, that I'm your brother?"

"Somebody's bound to find out."

"Y'know, I've been thinking," he said, squatting on the sand beside her.

"What?"

"Now that we're both getting all this publicity, maybe it's time to go back to Bosewell."

"Really, Nick? Y'know, sometimes I wake up in the middle of the night and I get all these guilty feelings about leaving Harlan."

He nodded. "I know what you mean."

She rushed on. "I always thought I'd send for him, but it was never the right time. It would be nice to go back and let them see how well we're doing – although I'll catch hell from Aretha Mae."

He frowned. "God knows why I'd want to see Primo."

"'Cause you wouldn't let me go by myself."

"You really think we should do it?"

"Definitely."

"Okay – so this is the plan," he said, jumping up.

"What?"

He reached out his hands and pulled her to her feet. "Now that I'm in a position to buy a car, I'm gonna get me the biggest, reddest Cadillac you've ever seen. And I'll take delivery in Kansas, then we'll drive to Bosewell. How'd'ja like *that* image?"

She began to laugh. "With fifty copies of *Satisfaction* on the back seat so you can hand them out. Right?"

He grinned. "Hey – Bosewell's a small town – maybe they haven't heard."

"But we'll tell 'em, huh?"

"If we're goin' back we gotta do it big time."

"Right on, Nick. When shall we do this?"

"How about next weekend."

"Just the two of us?"

He nodded. "Just the two of us."

They flew to Kansas and took a cab directly to the car showroom. When Nick saw his gleaming red Cadillac it was one of the happiest moments of his life. He'd always dreamt about it, but he'd never actually thought the day would come.

The car dealer in Kansas handed him the keys with a shiteating grin. "Enjoy. This little baby's gonna give you plenty of pleasure."

Nick tried to stay cool – had to keep his image – he was getting good at it.

"Uh . . . thanks."

"Finest car on the market."

"I know."

"Liked you in *Night City*."

"Thanks."

He finally got rid of the salesman. Then he sat behind the wheel of the Cadillac with Cyndra beside him and let out a whoop of joy. "Holy shit! I got it! It's all mine! It's all fuckin' mine!"

"I know," Cyndra said, bouncing up and down on the seat. "It's so fantastic."

"Hey – get a load of the radio, look at the chrome, feel the leather. I *love* this freakin' car. I goddamn *love* it!"

She leant across the seat and hugged him. He started the engine and switched on the radio.

"It's my record!" Cyndra screamed. "They're playing my record!"

"Shit!" he said, grinning. "This day belongs to us!"

Their plan was to drive to Bosewell, visit Aretha Mae and Harlan, take a walk around town and then drive back to LA. Nick had estimated it would take them a couple of days, but they'd both decided they needed the break.

When he and Cyndra had first talked about visiting Bosewell he'd hoped that Joey might come with them. He'd called him up and asked. Joey had said no.

He wasn't about to argue and Cyndra was hardly disappointed. "Joey's a loser," she'd said. "He always was and he always will be."

When Joey had gotten out of the drug rehab clinic he'd run straight back to New York. Nick had decided he'd done all he could.

Later that day they arrived in Ripley. Nick had booked them the biggest suite in the best hotel. They ordered room service and recalled old times. Then they drove around the city, and Nick detoured past the spot where the motel he'd spent his first night with Lauren was situated. The motel had been replaced with a gas station. So much for memories.

Cyndra stared out at the grimy streets. Maybe it wasn't such a good idea coming back. She was starting to remember all the bad things. What if she came face to face with Mr Browning? Would she talk to him?

Hell, yes! She had nothing to be scared of now.

Early Saturday morning they set off for Bosewell. In the back seat of the car were stacks of Cyndra's single and piles of *Satisfaction* with Nick on the cover.

"We should've found out if *Night City* played there yet," Cyndra said, snapping open a can of 7-Up.

"Don't worry, I already did," he said, laughing. "I had somebody call – it was on a month ago."

"Where's our first stop?" she asked, sipping from the can.

"The trailer park, where else? Then we'll go to the drugstore and drive up and down Main Street."

She giggled. "Handing out records and magazines!"

"Right on!"

Suddenly she felt anxious. "Oh, Nick, I hope we've made the right move. It feels so strange being back, doesn't it?"

He glanced out of the window. "It sure does. Small-town people stuck in a one-gas-station town. I bet nothing's changed."

"You're probably right."

He'd gone to the bank before he'd left and withdrawn a thousand dollars in cash. He planned on making an extravagant gesture and handing it to Primo. Let the asshole see what a big man his son had become.

Here, Dad, thought you might need some money.

Fuck you, Dad. Make the most of it because I'm never coming back.

He drove straight to the trailer park. They were both startled to discover it no longer existed. In its place there was now only wild brush, overgrown grass and huge mountains of abandoned garbage.

They looked at each other in surprise. "Probably moved them somewhere," Nick said. "We'd better drive into town – see what we can find out."

She squeezed his arm. "Nervous?"

"Yeah. How about you?"

She nodded.

They started the drive towards town. When they reached Main Street they both realized it did not look the same. The buildings were different. Everything was different. It was almost as if they were visiting an alien place.

"What the hell happened around here?" Nick said. "I don't recognize anything."

"I guess they've done a lot of improvements," Cyndra said. "Look how built-up everything is."

He drove slowly down the street. "Christ! Where's the freakin' drugstore?"

"Look over there," she said, pointing. "Isn't that where Blakely's

441

hardware store used to be — now it's like one of those mini shopping malls."

He pulled the car into a parking space and they got out in front of a book store and a fast food place — both new stores.

"Do you see anybody you know?" he asked.

She shook her head.

"Some triumphant return, huh?"

"How are we going to find anybody?"

"We'll ask."

They walked into the book store and up to the counter.

"Can I help you?" said a woman with frizzy grey hair.

"Yeah, as a matter of fact, you can," Nick said.

Standing on a ladder behind the woman was a girl stacking books on a shelf. She took one look and did a double take. "Oh, my goodness!" she said, almost falling off the ladder. "Aren't you . . . aren't you Nick Angel?"

"Uh . . . yeah."

"I saw *Night City*," she said, excitedly. "I saw it three times!"

"I guess you enjoyed it."

She could hardly speak. "Oh, I did! I did!"

The woman was looking at him with a new respect.

"How long's this store been here?" he asked.

"Five years," she said. "Although I've only been working here for two. Can I find you a particular book? We have a very large selection."

"There was a hardware store here before. Uh . . . Blakely's hardware. Have the Blakely brothers still got a place in town?"

The woman shrugged. "I don't know — never heard of them."

The girl stepped forward, clutching a raggedy piece of paper. Her hand was shaking. "Can I have your autograph?" she asked, staring at him as if he was Clint Eastwood.

He and Cyndra exchanged glances. "Yeah, sure," he said, self-consciously scribbling his name.

She took the scrap of paper and gazed at it in awe.

They walked out of the book store and stood on the sidewalk. "This is what I think we should do," he said.

"What?"

"Go see George at the gas station. He'll know everything."

"You're right."

They got back in the Cadillac and drove to the gas station — a familiar sight at last. There didn't seem to be anybody around, so

Nick got out of the car and walked into the office. Sitting behind the desk, speaking on the phone, was Dave.

"Hey," Nick said, in a loud voice. "I got a red Cadillac outside needs a lot of attention. Anyone around here care?"

Dave didn't look up – he waved his hand as if to say *Don't bother me, can't you see I'm on the phone?*

"Where's George?" Nick said, speaking even louder. "Tell the old bastard to haul his lazy butt out here."

Dave covered the mouthpiece of the phone and glanced up. "'Scuse me?"

Nick burst out laughing. "You fuckin' old fart."

Dave's mouth dropped open. "Holy cow! Nick! It's you, ain't it?"

"You bet your ass it is." He beckoned Cyndra into the office. "You remember my sister, Cyndra. You've probably heard her record on the radio."

"Sure have," Dave said, beaming widely. "Everyone's heard it. You two are famous around here."

"We are?" Nick said, getting off at the thought.

"I saw your movie. Haven't gotten so lucky with Louise in a long time."

Nick walked around the familiar office remembering old times. "Oh, Jesus, it's good to see your ugly face," he said. "We went to the trailer park – it's gone. We drove down Main Street – everything's different. Where's the drugstore? Where's Blakely's? We come back and nothing's the same."

Dave nodded. "Since the tornado there's been a lot of changes."

"What tornado?" Cyndra asked.

Dave rubbed his chin. "You weren't here when it happened?"

Cyndra looked concerned. "When what happened?"

"The big tornado of 1974. The whole town was darn near wiped out."

Cyndra stepped forward. "What are you talking about?"

"Gone. Everything gone. People killed, devastation. You must've read about it."

"Oh, Jesus," Nick said. "We didn't read anything. We didn't know – we were in Chicago."

Dave shook his head. "I'm sorry I had to be the one to tell you."

"What about my mother?" Cyndra asked, clasping her hands tightly together. "Do you know where Aretha Mae is?"

"Plenty of people left town," Dave said. "There weren't any jobs here – not until we started to rebuild."

"How about Louise?" Nick asked. "Is she okay?"

"She's doing good," Dave said. "Fact is, we've managed to have us a few kids. They keep her busy."

"Hey, at least there's some good news," Nick said.

"You can say that again," Dave said, reaching for his crutches behind the rickety old desk.

Nick glanced down and saw that half of Dave's leg was missing. "Oh, jeez – what happened?"

"The tornado," Dave said, matter-of-factly. "Cut my damn leg in half. One of these days I'm gonna get myself a false limb. Can't afford it now – what with the kids an' all. But I manage – doesn't bother me that much."

"How am I going to find my mother and Harlan?" Cyndra worried. "I have to find them."

Dave propelled himself around the table. "I don't know what to tell you. Maybe Louise knows – she's always in on everybody's business."

"Where is she?" Nick asked.

"Stop by the house," Dave suggested. "She's at home with the kids. It'll give her a thrill to see you. We watched your movie together. Couldn't darn believe it was you up on the screen."

"Are the Brownings still in town?" Cyndra asked.

"Yep. You know what they say – when the poor get poorer the rich get richer. He built another store; he's got two places now. They're still living in that big house. The tornado never touched them."

"Give Louise a call and tell her we're coming," Nick said.

Dave shrugged. "I would if we had a phone. Things been tough around here these last few years. Ring the doorbell and say hello – she'll be real glad to set eyes on you."

"Where's George? I'd like to say hello before we go."

"George fell victim to the big C. Died last year."

"I'm sorry, Dave. That's too bad."

"Yes, we were all sorry to see him go. He left me this piece of property, makes life a little easier."

"I'm sure it does."

Outside the gas station they sat in the Cadillac and stared at each other.

"Shit!" Nick said. "Nothing but bad news. I don't fucking believe it."

"We have to find Aretha Mae and Harlan," Cyndra said,

clasping her hands together. "They must think we deserted them."

"We didn't desert them. We had no idea what happened."

"I only hope they're all right."

"Primo would've taken care of them."

"Get serious, Nick. Your old man probably ran the moment it happened."

"Yeah, you're right. But don't worry, we won't leave until we find 'em."

Louise was not the same sharp-tongued woman they'd once known. She looked twenty years older and thirty pounds heavier. She stared at Nick with saucer eyes, as if she was a fan. "OhmiGod! OhmiGod!" she kept repeating, wiping her hands on a grubby apron. A couple of whining toddlers crawled on the floor of the untidy living room and a baby cried lustily in its crib. The place was run-down and a mess. So was Louise.

"Let me make you a cup of coffee," she said, after she'd gotten over her initial shock. "I can still do that."

"I'm sorry about Dave," Nick said, shaking his head. "I never knew. We took off to Chicago – and that was the last we heard of Bosewell."

"You're lucky to have missed it. A lot of people lost everything. Fortunately, there weren't too many died, but it was an unbelievable scene, like someone dropped a big fat bomb on us."

"Who got killed?" he asked.

"Remember that girl you liked – Lauren Roberts?"

"Lauren's okay," he said, quickly. "I just saw her in New York."

"No – not her, but both her parents. Her mother was carried away in her car – literally swept up into the air. It was terrible. And her father was in his office when the entire block got wiped out. He was killed instantly. So was his secretary."

Nick suddenly realized that Lauren had probably never received any of his letters. "Uh . . . Louise – do you remember if you handed Lauren that note I gave you the night I left town? I know it's dumb to ask after all that's gone on, but did she ever get it?"

Louise shook her head. "You've got to be joking. The drugstore was completely destroyed – nothing left except rubble. Me an' Dave – we're lucky to be alive."

"It must've been tough for you."

"It was tough for everyone," she said. "Especially Lauren. We all felt so bad for her, she took such a big loss."

445

"I'm trying to find my mother and brother," Cyndra said. "They lived at the trailer park."

"That was all gone, too," Louise said. "But I heard Aretha Mae went back to work for the Brownings." She shrugged. "Look, I wish I could tell you more. It was one big nightmare for everyone."

"What about Betty Harris – is she still in town?" Nick asked.

"You mean that acting teacher?"

"Yeah."

"If I recall she moved to New York – even though the houses on that side of town weren't touched. People got nervous it could happen again. Trouble is, with three kids I don't get around much any more. I used to know everything. Now I'm trapped in the house all day."

"Mommy! Mommy!" One of the toddlers dragged on her apron strings, his chocolate covered face crinkling into tears. "I'm hungry!"

"I gotta feed 'em," she said, apologetically. "It's been a treat to see you both. You here for long?"

"Just long enough to find Aretha Mae and Harlan."

"Try the Brownings. I'm sure they can tell you where she is."

"Thanks, Louise." He leaned forward and kissed her warmly on the cheek.

She blushed. "You were always a nice kid, Nick. You deserve every bit of your success."

The Browning mansion looked the same as ever, although after living in LA it was not the palace they'd both once thought it was.

"Is it okay to walk up to the front door and ring the bell?" Cyndra asked, unsurely.

"What do you wanna do – go around the back?"

"I don't know, Nick . . . this is so strange . . ."

"What is it with you and the Browning family? Just because your mother worked for them –"

"It's more than that."

"Wanna tell me about it?"

"Not now. Maybe on the drive back to LA."

They rang the bell and waited.

The door was opened by a plump blonde in tennis shorts with heavy thighs and a dissatisfied twist to her mouth. She stared at them, they stared at her, and then her mouth fell open and she said, "Nick Angelo," in reverent tones.

He didn't recognize her. "Do I know you?" he said, politely.

"Do you know me?" she laughed, gaily. "I was your first girlfriend in Bosewell. I'm Meg."

"Meg?"

"Remember *The Poseidon Adventure*? When you made me sneak you in the back without paying?"

He recognized her. It was Lauren's ex best girlfriend, Meg.

"What are you *doing* here?" she asked, looking flushed.

"What are *you* doing here?" he countered.

She sucked in her cheeks and stood up straighter. "I'm Mrs Browning. Stock and I got married five years ago."

"You did?"

She nodded. "Nick, we're all so excited by your success. The whole town is talking about it ever since your movie played here. And Cyndra dear, nobody can believe you're doing so well. Oh, I'm so rude leaving you standing on the doorstep. Do come in."

"We're trying to find out what happened to Cyndra's mother,' he said, following her inside the house. "We heard she was working for the Brownings again."

Meg looked blank. "Cyndra's mother?"

"Aretha Mae," Cyndra said.

"Oh, yes, of course, she's your mother. Well, as far as I know, Aretha Mae went to live in Ripley – it must have been a year or so ago."

"Do you have an address for her?" Cyndra asked.

"No," Meg said. "I have no idea where she went." She turned to Nick again – far more interested in speaking to him. "You look wonderful," she gushed. "We saw *Night City* twice. Stock loved it. He's such a fan of Carlysle Mann. Is she nice? What's Hollywood like? We're both so *proud* to be your friends – we always knew you'd do it."

He couldn't believe the crap that was coming out of her mouth. Stock had hated his guts. And so had she. What a couple of major phonies.

"Is Benjamin Browning here?" Cyndra asked.

"He's in the breakfast room. Do you wish to see him?"

"Yes, maybe he can help me with the information we need."

"This is so exciting," Meg said, leading them through the hall, tugging at the back of her shorts, failing to hide ripples of cellulite.

"So you married Stock?" Nick said, thinking to himself, *So you married the asshole. Well, somebody had to get stuck with him – it may as well be you.*

"We have two adorable children," Meg announced, proudly. "Miffy and JoJo."

"We only just heard about the tornado," Nick said. "Must've been a tough time here."

"It was terrible. You have no idea – the destruction was tragic."

"I heard about Lauren's parents."

"Yes, it was a terrible tragedy. She was devastated. Went to live with her aunt and uncle in Philadelphia. We lost touch a long time ago. I have no idea where she is now."

"You two were such good friends."

"We were children," Meg said. "Babies."

They all trouped into the breakfast room. Benjamin was sitting at the table drinking coffee and reading a newspaper. He looked up, startled. Cyndra was satisfied to see that he was older, greyer and fatter.

"Remember me, Mr Browning," she said, standing in front of him, hands on her hips. "Or should I call you Benjamin?"

He stumbled to his feet. She noticed he'd grown a thin Hitler-like moustache.

He stared at her, his mouth twitching. "What are *you* doing here?" he said.

"Looking for my mother. I thought you might · be able to help me."

His shifty eyes darted this way and that, searching for an escape.

"You were always very close to my mother, weren't you?" Cyndra continued, watching him squirm.

He cleared his throat and shot a filthy look at Meg for letting them into his house. "Aretha Mae moved to Ripley," he said.

"Do you have an address for her?"

"I'll get it," he said.

"I recall coming to this house so many times," Cyndra called after him, as he left the room. "I have so many fine memories, Mr Browning . . . Benjamin, don't you?"

Meg, oblivious to the tension, said, "Stock is playing tennis, but I know he'd adore to see you both. Can you come back later? We could all go out and have a drink – wouldn't that be nice?"

"We gotta get back to LA," Nick said. "We only came to see Cyndra's mother and my dad."

"Oh yes, your father," Meg said.

"What about him?"

She looked embarrassed. "I really don't want to be the one to tell you."

"Tell me what?"

"He's . . . he's dead."

Nick felt absolutely nothing. He knew he should be upset, but the news didn't affect him. "How did it happen?" he asked, blankly.

"The tornado," Meg replied. "I'm so sorry."

Mr Browning returned with Aretha Mae's address written on a piece of paper.

"Why did she leave?" Cyndra wanted to know.

"I have no idea," he replied, his face an impassive mask.

"She wasn't hurt in the tornado?"

"No. Her trailer was destroyed, which is why Mrs Browning and I took her in out of the kindness of our hearts."

"What a prince you are," Cyndra said, sarcastically. "And did you take Harlan, my brother, in too?"

"He came here for a while and then went to Ripley. Your mother followed him."

"Thank you so much . . . Benjamin. C'mon, Nick, let's go."

They sat in the Cadillac and contemplated the latest information.

"Are you upset about Primo?" she asked, squeezing his hand.

"I guess I'm supposed to be . . ."

"It doesn't matter if you're not. You don't have to feel guilty."

She was right. Primo had never given a shit about him – why should he care?

But still . . . Primo *was* his father . . .

"So many changes here," Cyndra murmured. "And we knew nothing."

"You know what this means," Nick said, starting the car. "Lauren never got my letters. She must've thought I ran out on her."

"It was a long time ago."

"You don't understand. *I* was mad at *her*. I thought *she* didn't care. A few months ago I saw her in New York."

"You never told me."

"I was at a dinner party with Carlysle. Lauren was catering it. She was engaged to this old rich guy – one of the guests. I tried to contact her the next day, but I was told she'd gone off to get married."

"Did you speak?"

"No, we made eye contact, an' you know what? It was like time stood still."

"Really?"

"I always loved her, and I guess I always will."

"Don't go getting romantic on me, Nick. I can't stand it."

"There'll never be another girl like Lauren."

"Listen to you – it's pure soap opera."

"Fuck you, Cyndra. I've got to find Lauren and explain what happened."

"Didn't you tell me she got married?"

"It doesn't matter – I have to see her."

"I wouldn't mention this to Annie if I were you. She might not appreciate it."

"Annie has nothing to do with this."

"I know, but be careful. Annie could rock our future."

"Don't worry, Cyndra, I'm more aware of it than you."

"I'm sorry, Nick."

"About what?"

"Vegas. What happened there."

"It's nothing. Everything's gonna work out just fine. Now let's go find Aretha Mae and Harlan."

Chapter 70

Apparently it did not concern Oliver one little bit that Lorenzo Marcella was launching a kamikaze attack on his wife.

"I'm going to tell him we're married," she informed Oliver.

"Do whatever you wish, my dear, but I can assure you – it won't make any difference to the attention he pays you. Italian men are incorrigible."

"Don't you care?"

"Naturally I care. However, I trust you. You know how to handle yourself."

She didn't understand him. He refused to make love to her, and now a much younger, attractive Italian was all over her and it didn't appear to bother him. As a matter of fact, the more time she spent with Lorenzo the more she enjoyed his company. He was outrageously phoney, but his charm was addictive. His latest plan was for her to come to Italy and visit the big Marcella factory.

"This will be important," he announced.

"Can my husband come, too?" she asked.

They were in his office on Park Avenue, only it looked more like a luxurious apartment. Sheepskin rugs on the floor, an enormous white desk, oversized couches and leopard skin throws.

"You mention this husband all the time," Lorenzo said. "And yet I have never seen him. Who is he? Tell me and I will have him killed." He smiled.

She smiled back. "You know my husband, Lorenzo."

"I do?"

"I thought somebody would have told you by now."

"Told me what?"

"My husband is Oliver Liberty."

Lorenzo looked at her with a quizzical expression. "You are not serious?"

"Yes."

"I do not believe you."

"Why would I lie?"

"He's too old for you."

"That's rather a presumptuous thing to say."

"You are young, beautiful, vital. Oliver is – how do you say in English? Ah yes, he is over the mountain."

"You don't have to be young in years to be vital. Oliver has a tremendous amount of energy – probably more than you and me put together."

"Ah, well," Lorenzo said, sighing. "I will simply have to steal you away from him."

She laughed. "You're incorrigible."

"But you like it."

She had to admit that she did. Lorenzo made her smile. He made her feel young and light-hearted. Living with Oliver had turned into all business.

Pia gave birth to a baby girl, a golden child they named Rosemarie. Lauren was appointed godmother. She loved going over to Pia's apartment and cradling the baby in her arms; all her maternal instincts sprung to life. The thought occurred to her – if Oliver never made love to her, how was she going to get pregnant?

As the months passed she found herself drawing away from him. If he didn't want to make love to her properly, she didn't want him to touch her at all. Whenever she tried to discuss it he walked away as if it didn't matter.

You made a mistake, Roberts.

I'm getting good at that.

One Saturday afternoon she went by herself to see *Night City*. She sat in the dark movie theatre and watched Nick up on the screen. He was so good. His intensity worked for the camera. When he was in bed with Carlysle Mann she closed her eyes – she couldn't bear to watch.

Their affair was long ago and far away – and yet it seemed like yesterday. Maybe she should have taken his call the day after the Georges' dinner party. Instead of speaking to him she'd run off to the Bahamas and married Oliver. Foolish girl. She should have listened to what he had to say.

Too late now. Nick Angelo was a movie star, and she was about to be launched upon an unsuspecting public.

"Lorenzo wants us to go to Italy," she told Oliver.

"I can't go anywhere," he replied. "I'm in the middle of landing an important client."

"What client?"

"Riviera Champagne."

"Surely you can get away for a few days?"

"No," he said, abruptly. "The owner is coming to town. It's a personal thing. Only *I* can talk him into switching his account to Liberty & Charles."

"Can't Howard handle it?"

"Howard is *not* me, Lauren. I'm training him, but it will take time and experience before he can pull an account from another agency the way I do."

"Do you mind if I go with Lorenzo?"

"What is this trip for?"

"He wants me to meet the other Marcella executives and visit the factory. He feels that if the campaign works in America they'll want me to spearhead the whole European campaign. I've spoken to Samm, she likes the idea and so do I. Of course, it will mean more money."

"Are you asking me what I think?"

"Yes."

"Then you should go – it's important."

"You wouldn't mind?"

"Of course not."

Screw Oliver. He honestly didn't care. He was sending her to Europe with an eligible, devastatingly attractive Italian lech.

"It's settled then," she said.

The next morning she had coffee with Pia in her apartment.

"You're going to Rome with Lorenzo?" Pia said, almost spilling her coffee.

"Oliver seems to think there's nothing wrong with it."

Pia leapt up. "Ha! Howard wouldn't let me exchange a handshake with Lorenzo Marcella! Those Italian men are lethal – especially when they look like him."

"Why?" Lauren asked, casually. "Do you think he's attractive?"

"What a ridiculous question. The guy is devastating – he looks like a movie star."

It wasn't his looks that attracted Lauren, it was his attitude.

"When do your ads start appearing?" Pia asked.

"They'll be in the Christmas magazines, which means they'll hit the stands at the end of November."

"Wow, that's exciting."

"Can I see the baby?" Lauren asked.

"She's sleeping."

"Why don't we wake her?"

Pia grinned. "Why not?"

The private jet was the most luxurious form of travel Lauren had ever imagined.

"It's nothing," Lorenzo said, with a sweeping wave of his hand.

His idea of nothing was a state of the art cabin fitted out with full stereo equipment, a kitchen, a marble bathroom and a bedroom in the back. The interior of the plane was decorated as though it was a penthouse apartment. It was the company plane, but Lorenzo had full use of it whenever he wanted.

"I'm sorry your husband was unable to accompany us," he said, strapping himself into the seat next to her, not meaning a word he said.

"I'm sure you are."

"No, really, *bellissima*. I would never pay attention to another man's wife."

He could have fooled her. "Have you ever been married?" she asked.

"No, my princess, I have yet to meet the woman of my dreams. Besides, we have one life to live – why confine oneself to the same meal every day?"

She wrinkled her nose. "You're beginning to sound like a chauvinist."

"What is a chauvinist?" he asked, innocently.

"You know what I mean – comparing a woman to a meal. That's hardly very nice."

Watching her closely he said, "You are the most beautiful woman in the universe. I love it when you speak. The way your mouth moves, the way your lips quiver. Everything about you is so . . . so tempting."

"You're full of it, Lorenzo."

It was her first trip to Europe and she couldn't help being excited.

Lorenzo was amused. "I have crossed the Atlantic so many times that I have lost count," he boasted.

454

"Lucky you," she replied, fastening her seatbelt and tensing for take-off. Every time she flew it made her nervous.

Lorenzo seemed totally at ease. He took her hand and turned it palm up.

"Ah . . . you, too, will be very lucky," he said, studying her palm. "I see it here."

"What, Lorenzo?"

"Did I not tell you that my grandmother was a gypsy? I read palms, I can foresee the future."

"And what do you see in my future?"

"You will be very famous, and very rich. Ah – you notice this broken line here – it means you will have a divorce."

"Lorenzo," she scolded, pulling her hand away.

"No, no, my princess, I am not joking." He took her hand again. "Maybe lots of little bambinos – two, three, ah yes, four." He frowned. "I see something else," he said, peering closely.

"What?" she asked, alarmed.

"I see they are not American babies – they are half-Italian."

She began to laugh. "You're bad, you know that?"

"Ah, yes, I've been told many times. But I am not bad where it matters."

"And where's that?"

"In the bedroom."

He had seductive eyes, a thin nose and carved cheekbones. She liked looking at him, and so did the two stewardesses who paid him avid attention.

After take-off they sipped champagne, ate a delicious meal, and then Lorenzo watched a movie while she fell asleep.

He woke her gently when they were preparing to land. "Ah, *bellissima*, you were exhausted. Twenty minutes and we will be in my home country."

She struggled awake and went into the bathroom to repair her make-up and brush her hair. What had her life become? Here she was on a plane with a very attractive Italian while her husband had elected to stay behind in America. She knew she was going to be tempted. It was inevitable.

Let's see how you handle this one, Roberts.

I can do what I want.

There was a welcoming committee waiting to greet them. A small child in a long white dress rushed to present her with a bouquet of roses. She accepted it gracefully, although several of the thorns stuck into her flesh. A television crew captured every moment.

Lorenzo introduced her to several people at once. They shook her hand and kissed her on both cheeks. She was overwhelmed by all the attention.

Lorenzo rushed her out of the airport into a limo which sped through the streets of Rome as if it was competing in a race. She hardly had a chance to view the sights. The limo deposited her at the Villa Marcella, where the guest suite was bigger than the apartment she'd lived in when she was single in New York.

"Tonight you will rest," Lorenzo said. "And tomorrow there will be a big reception gala in your honour." He put both hands on her shoulders and placed a tender kiss on each cheek. "I have things to do now. Anything you want, just ring. Tomorrow, *bellissima*."

The next few days were magical. Rome was the most beautiful city she'd ever seen. Lorenzo arranged a tour for her and she saw everything from the incredible ruins of the Coliseum to the Appian Way and all the fine buildings and monuments in between. She particularly loved the narrow cobblestone streets and colourful kerbside cafés.

She met Lorenzo's family. His father was an older version of him and his mother was a frighteningly chic blonde woman. Everybody treated her like a queen. She visited the factory and met many of the employees. Her picture was everywhere.

"They love you," Lorenzo smiled. "They have named you the innocent American girl."

"I'm not so innocent," she said.

"You have that special quality Grace Kelly possessed. It's very appealing to Europeans."

She'd expected him to make a pass, but Oliver was obviously right – Italian men flirted a lot, but took it no further.

On their last night in Rome he invited her to dinner at an open-air restaurant located near the bottom of the Spanish Steps. She'd expected it to be the usual group of people, but it turned out to be just the two of them.

"Tonight we enjoy the typical Italian meal," he said. "No champagne, no caviar. We have pasta, a little fish, plenty of vino – we relax."

He amused her with stories about his past and she found herself having a wonderful time. Later he invited her back to his apartment. "You will see the best view in Rome," he boasted. "Or maybe you'd prefer to go to a disco?"

"No, I'd like to see your apartment."

She knew she was treading on dangerous territory. She'd drunk too much wine and the city was a seductive siren, luring her to misbehave.

He held her captive with his eyes. "Are you sure, Lauren? I don't want to force you to do anything you do not wish."

"All I'm doing is coming back to your apartment."

He smiled. "Yes, *bellissima*, that is all." Although they both knew this was not the case.

His apartment did indeed have the best views in Rome and was furnished most luxuriously.

"Now is the time for champagne," he said. "To finish the evening."

He poured them both a glass, put Billie Holiday on the stereo and held open his arms. "Good Morning Heartache" serenaded her and for a moment she thought about Nick. Then she closed her eyes and allowed Lorenzo to sweep her into his arms. They danced together slowly, their bodies pressed closely against each other.

I wonder what Oliver is doing now?

Ha! Working. What else.

You never loved him, Roberts, why did you marry him?

That's my business.

Lorenzo's fingers pressed through the thin material of her dress. When he started to lower her zipper she didn't stop him. He peeled the dress from her shoulders and expertly unclipped her bra.

She knew she was about to be unfaithful to her husband, but somehow she couldn't stop herself.

457

Chapter 71

Aretha Mae stared at Cyndra as if she'd seen a ghost.

"Mama?" Cyndra said softly, shocked at how thin and wasted her mother looked. "Mama, it's me, Cyndra."

Aretha Mae shook her head in disbelief.

"Can we come in?" Cyndra asked, standing at the door.

"Oh, girl, lookit you," Aretha Mae said, speaking in a low shaky voice. "You so pretty."

Cyndra's face lit up. "Yes, Mama, you think so? You really think so?"

"I should be spanking your ass," Aretha Mae said, recovering her composure. She peered at Nick. "And what you have to say for yourself?"

Christ!. This was just like being a kid again. "It took us a while to find you," he mumbled.

"I would've left you an address if I'd known where you run off to," she said, tartly – the same old Aretha Mae.

They followed her into the small room she called home. The place was cluttered with stacks of newspapers and magazines. On the mantel were two old photos of Luke, surrounded by several burnt-out candle stumps.

"What are you doing now, Mama?" Cyndra asked, running her finger along the mantel and finding thick dust.

"Don't work no more," Aretha Mae said, fiddling with the glasses hanging on a string around her neck. "Don't have to. Got me some money, 'nough to manage on."

"Is Harlan here?" Nick said, anxious to see him and get the hell out.

"What you wanna know 'bout him for?" Aretha Mae said, suspiciously.

"Is he okay, Mama?" Cyndra asked. "The tornado happened

458

after we left. We knew nothing about it – we only heard today. Were you all right?"

"'Bout as all right as a person can be when their home gets destroyed," Aretha Mae snapped.

Cyndra sat down on the worn old couch. "If I'd known I would've come back."

Aretha Mae pursed her lips. "You did right, girl, gettin' out."

"I'm a singer now," Cyndra said, proudly. "I got a record; they're playing it on the radio. And Nick's in a movie."

Aretha Mae shook her head from side to side, her expression blank. "Don't get out much," she muttered, her voice weak again.

"Maybe Harlan knows?" Cyndra said, hopefully. "Where is he?"

"I don't see your brother no more," Aretha Mae said, sharply.

"Isn't that why you moved to Ripley – to be close to him?"

Aretha Mae stared accusingly at them both. "Who told you those lies?" she demanded.

"Mr Browning," Cyndra said, frightened by her mother's strange behaviour.

"You saw that cracker?" Aretha Mae sneered. "Why'd you see him?"

"We had to track you somehow."

"Why'd you go near him?" Aretha Mae asked, narrowing her eyes. "You shouldn't've done that."

"'Cause I had to find you."

"You found me, girl. Here I am."

"We heard about Primo," Nick said.

Aretha Mae began to cough, the harsh sounds racking her thin body.

Cyndra jumped to her feet. "Are you all right? Mama? You sound terrible."

"I feel fine."

"Have you seen a doctor about your cough?"

"Doctors! Ha!" Aretha Mae shrieked with crazy laughter.

"You should see one. You're too thin."

Aretha Mae frowned. "Don't go tellin' *me* what to do, girl."

Cyndra tried to put her arms around her mother. "I'm sorry I left you. I always meant to write. I know I didn't, but that doesn't mean we can't be close now, does it?"

Aretha Mae darted across the room to escape her daughter's embrace. "You always saw things your way, Cyndra. It always had to be your way or nothin'."

"That's not true," Cyndra objected.

"Oh yes it is."

"No, it's not."

"Where're you living?"

"We live in California. Los Angeles."

"That Hollywood place – fulla sex an' drugs an' all those bad things I read 'bout," Aretha Mae said, churlishly.

Cyndra laughed. "It's not full of sex and drugs. Maybe you'll visit me one day. I'd like that."

"*I* wouldn't."

"So tell us about Harlan. Is he working?"

"You don' want nothin' t'do with him."

"Why not?"

"He got himself in trouble."

"Maybe we can help," Nick suggested.

"You don' wanna help him, oh dear me, no."

"That's our choice."

Aretha Mae glared at him. "You don' wanna help no pansy boy."

"What?"

"Pansy boy. Sells himself down on Oakley Street. Gets in a car with anybody he does. He ain't my son no more. Luke's my son – the only one I care about – him and Jesus."

"Jesus?" Cyndra said, glancing quickly at Nick.

"Yes, girl, Jesus. An' you better learn to repent your ways. Otherwise, Jesus gonna shut you out, an' your fancy black ass gonna burn in hell."

"Mama, I never did anything wrong."

"Oh, yes, you did wrong, girl," Aretha Mae said, her eyes burning feverishly. "Oh, yes, you led Mr Browning on. You led him into Satan's bedroom."

"I didn't," Cyndra said, her eyes filling with tears. "You know I didn't."

Aretha Mae sat down in an old chair, wrapped her arms across her chest, and rocked back and forth. "Deny all you want, but Jesus knows, Jesus sees."

Nick took Cyndra's arm. "We gotta get goin'."

"Don't *say* that, Mama," Cyndra said, pushing his hand off. "Don't say that to me."

Aretha Mae cackled. "An' the guilty shall burn in hell. An' the fire'll take out their eyes. An' a girl like you – a temptress – will be the devil's playmate. You done things no decent person can forgive."

Cyndra was frantic. "What are you *talking* about? I didn't

460

do anything. Benjamin Browning *raped* me – you know it."

A strange smile snaked around the corners of Aretha Mae's downturned mouth. "You sinned, girl. Mr Browning – he be your daddy. And you let him sin with you." Her voice rose. "You gonna burn in hell. Oh, yes you are."

"He's not my father," Cyndra screamed, angrily.

"He be your daddy for sure, girl. When you got rid of that baby – you murdered your own brother. You killed Luke, didn't you?" She leapt up. "You killed Luke, you little whore!"

Nick grabbed Cyndra's arm again and physically dragged her out of the room. She was sobbing hysterically. He pulled her down the stairs and into the street.

"What's she talking about?" Cyndra yelled. "Nick, help me, tell me what she's saying? What's she trying to do to me?"

"Can't you see she's crazy. God knows what happened here."

"I have to see Harlan."

"Okay, okay – we'll find him."

"When?" she demanded.

"Now," he replied, pushing her into the car.

They drove to Oakley Street, parked the Cadillac and sat in it and waited. After a while Nick left her in the car and went into a nearby bar to find out what the action was.

"You can get anything you want on Oakley Street," the barman told him. "Only ya gotta watch out – it can look like a girl, it can talk like a girl, but you're likely to find a big old surprise swingin' between their legs."

"Transvestites, sweetie," crooned a fat woman sitting at the bar downing a vodka surprise. "This street is crawling with them. Now, why don't you sit down with me, buy me a drink and I'll tell you everything you ever wanted to know."

"Thanks, another time," he said, hurrying back to the car. Cyndra had been crying.

"You don't wanna take any notice of Aretha Mae," he said, trying to comfort her.

Her voice was shaky. "She said Benjamin Browning was my father. Do you know what that means?"

"She doesn't know what she's talking about."

"Oh, yes, she does. She's telling the truth. I'm sure of it."

"Hey," he said, flippantly. "Look on the bright side – Benjamin's your father you can claim half his money when he drops."

"Be serious, Nick. You don't seem to understand. When I was sixteen Benjamin raped me, and my mother did nothing. He made me pregnant, and I had to have an abortion. You remember when you came to live at the trailer? I was in Kansas – getting rid of my own father's baby."

Nick decided this trip was a horrible mistake. They'd have been better off leaving Bosewell in their past where it belonged. Now all of this bad stuff was happening and he didn't like it.

By dusk the transvestites began to hit the street in full drag. Several of them cruised past the car in pairs, bending down to peer in the window.

"We're looking for Harlan," Cyndra said, talking to them in a friendly voice. "Do you know him?"

"What's wrong with me?" lisped a beefy six footer in a long blonde wig and transparent white mini dress.

"You're lovely," Nick said. "But we want Harlan."

"If the bitch puts in an appearance I'll send her over," the man said, patting his wig.

"I've got a big feeling we're not gonna like this," Nick said.

"Whatever – he's still my brother," Cyndra said, fiercely. "If Aretha Mae's telling the truth – you're not."

He was hurt. "Hey, Cyndra, we'll always be brother and sister. It doesn't matter who your father is."

"I know, I know," she said, sorry for what she'd said.

They sat in the car for a long while, watching the parade from the window.

"How will we recognize him?" she asked. "What if he's all dressed up? We left a little boy behind – now he's a man."

"I hate to point this out," Nick said, "But black faces aren't exactly heavy on the street."

"You're right."

Around nine o'clock Cyndra thought she spotted him.

"Are you sure?" Nick said, peering into the darkness.

"I don't know, but like you said, black faces aren't exactly common."

"Okay, whyn't I go see." He got out of the car and approached what appeared to be a black woman in a scarlet dress, feather boa and long black wig. "Harlan?" he questioned, edging close so as to get a better look.

"Don't you mean Harletta?" the creature shrieked.

"Harlan, it's me – it's Nick."

The creature put a finger to its chin. "Do I know you? Have I *had* you?"

"Harlan, for Christ's sake, it's Nick. Cyndra's in the car. Come talk to us."

The creature backed further into the shadows. "Harletta never goes anywhere unless she's paid handsomely."

He fumbled in his pocket and produced several bills which he shoved at the creature. "Get in the goddamn car!"

"Oooh!" Harlan shrieked. "I love it when you talk rough."

And so that's how they found Harlan. A drugged-out street hustler. An embittered young man who'd had no chance to be anything else. They'd taken him back to their hotel and counsel--led him for hours, but he apparently had no desire to change his lifestyle. He laughed at them.

"Come back to LA with us," Cyndra pleaded.

"My friends are here," Harlan replied, roaming restlessly around the hotel suite.

"Your friends are street people," Nick pointed out. "Hookers and hustlers. What kind of friends are those?"

"At least they're here when I need them," Harlan sniffed, suddenly pulling off his wig and throwing it petulantly across the room. "You two ran off an' left me. You don't know what it was like after you'd gone. There was no money, no place to live. Aretha Mae had to take charity from that Benjamin Browning pig."

"Did he touch you? Did he do anything to you?" Cyndra asked.

"What do you think?" Harlan replied, his grotesquely painted lips twisting contemptuously.

"I'll kill that bastard one of these days,' Cyndra said, staring blankly ahead. "I'll blow his fucking head off."

"Calm down," Nick said.

"He deserves it."

"Oh yes," Harlan agreed. "An' I'll watch. Front row seats, please," he added, archly.

They couldn't persuade Harlan to leave with them. But he did accept their money and after hours of discussion he reluctantly promised to keep in touch. Not that either of them believed him. "We'll be lucky if we ever see him again," Nick said.

Finally they got in the red Cadillac and made the long drive home to Los Angeles.

The moment he arrived back Nick sold the car.

"I don't understand you," Annie complained. "Why would you do that? You've dreamt about owning a Cadillac all your life."

"There's a lot of things you don't understand about me, Annie," he said.

"Maybe we should try spending more time together," she suggested.

Wasn't it enough they were living in the same apartment? What did she want from him?

He went out that night by himself and called Carlysle from a phone booth. "Are you with your mother?" he asked.

"She's out of town," Carlysle replied. "Why? Want to party?"

"Yes."

"Come on over."

When he arrived at her house he found she was not alone. There was another girl there, an exotic Indonesian model. The three of them ended up in the jacuzzi playing games he'd never played in school.

He lost himself in a round of hedonistic pleasures. He needed the release. By the time he left Carlysle's house he felt better.

The next day Meena informed him they'd gotten him out of his contract for the movie with the woman producer and arranged a deal for him to star in *Life* – a big budget movie about a young killer and his father.

"This is an excellent break, Nick," Meena said, briskly. "Top director, first-class production – and here's the best news – I've doubled your money."

He wasn't as elated as he should have been. He had Lauren on his mind and somehow or other he knew he had to see her.

He went home and told Annie that he had to go to New York for a couple of days.

"Can I come with you?" she asked, hopefully.

"No. It's business." He kissed her on the cheek. "See you in a couple of days."

At the airport he made out a cheque for six thousand dollars and sent it to Dave. It was all the money he had in his account. But he was lucky, there was more coming in.

He made the evening flight. Soon he would get to see Lauren, one way or another. He didn't know what he'd say to her. He only knew that he had to resolve the situation. And the sooner the better.

Chapter 72

Lauren was filled with guilt because she'd slept with Lorenzo and hadn't meant to. It had only happened once – the last night she was in Rome – and she had no excuse. The experience was memorable – which didn't please her because she would have preferred to have forgotten it.

Maybe I take after my father, she thought, miserably. *Why should I feel guilty – he obviously never did.*

Upon their return to America, Lorenzo behaved like a perfect gentleman. She told him she regretted it had happened, it would never happen again, and would he please never refer to it.

"I respect your wishes," he'd said. "But when you get rid of your husband, I will be waiting."

Oliver suspected nothing. "How was your trip?" he'd asked.

"I wish you'd been with me," she'd said.

"Next time," he'd promised. "In fact, I was thinking that in the summer we might cruise the Riviera on a yacht."

"That would be nice, Oliver. Can you get the time away?"

"I'll make time."

She'd already done the photographs for the Marcella girl campaign, and now it was time to shoot the commercial. Digging down into her past she drew on her acting experience, relaxed and had fun in front of the camera. It was quite an elaborate commercial and took a week to shoot.

Lorenzo visited the set every day, still behaving like a perfect gentleman. He did nothing more than flirt with his eyes – but, oh, those Italian eyes! She remembered their one night together in Rome and her body screamed out for more. It was only her mind that kept her from doing anything about it.

You're a married woman, Lauren.

You don't have to keep on reminding me.

465

She enjoyed making the commercial, being the centre of attention. It made her feel special – like she really mattered in the scheme of things.

It seemed that now Oliver possessed her he paid less and less attention to her. Work, as usual, came first.

She decided that if he could put work first, so could she. Over lunch with Samm she told her that if any other good modelling jobs came along she was prepared to do them.

"I thought you weren't interested in modelling," Samm remarked, sipping a glass of white wine.

She picked at a salad. "I've changed my mind."

"You won't be able to represent other products, but you can certainly do photographic work," Samm said, thoughtfully. "I'll see what I can get you."

"Get me the cover of *Vogue*," Lauren said, with a persuasive smile. "You know you can do anything."

Samm waved at a fashion editor, leant back and also smiled. "My, my – aren't *we* getting ambitious."

"Why not? It's about time."

"By the way," Samm said. "Did you hear about Jimmy Cassady?"

"What about him?" Lauren asked, coolly. As far as she was concerned he was ancient history – even hearing his name failed to bother her.

"He emerged from the closet."

"Huh?"

"Gay, my sweet. Positively festive in fact!"

So there was the answer to that little mystery.

Most weekends she spent with Pia, Howard and the baby. Sometimes they stayed in town – other times they drove to Oliver's large estate in the Hamptons where he spent most of his time in his study on the phone – relaxing was not for him.

Sunbathing on the beach one day, Pia said, "Do you realize you have three homes now? The apartment in New York, the house in the Bahamas and this place."

"They're Oliver's homes," Lauren said, enjoying the hot sun. "I never chose any of them."

"If you feel that way you should sell them and buy something else. Be nice to start fresh, wouldn't it?"

Lauren reached for the suntan oil. "I'm sure Oliver would let me do exactly what I like. He probably wouldn't even notice."

"Hmm," Pia said. "Do I detect a note of dissatisfaction?"

She rubbed the greasy oil over her legs. "You detect a note

of 'I've married a man who never stops working'."

"Ah," Pia said, wisely. "That's *why* you have three houses."

"Very quick."

Pia looked thoughtful. "I think Howard's following in Oliver's footsteps," she said, pensively. "He didn't come home last night until nine o'clock. Maybe he's got a mistress."

"Howard?" Lauren started to laugh. "I can't imagine Howard with a mistress."

"Why?" Pia said, quite affronted. "Don't you think he's sexy?"

"To you he's sexy – to other women he's your husband."

"Sometimes I wish we'd kept the business," Pia said, wistfully. "I love Rosemarie and looking after her, but playing mommy is not my life."

"Get a job," Lauren suggested, lying back.

"I don't want to go that far. Being my own boss is one thing, but working for somebody else – no, that's not for me. Unless you'd like me as your personal assistant – I'd be very efficient."

"I'm not busy enough for an assistant," Lauren murmured, closing her eyes.

"You will be. Wait until the ads start appearing. And Samm tells me you want to start doing other work."

"I wouldn't mind."

"Nature's turned to acting, you know."

"Really?"

"Yes, she's living with this producer guy and he's put her in his movie. She's the new discovery on the block."

"That'll make her happy."

"And I read in one of the columns that Emerson Burn gets back from his world tour this week."

"You're a regular little gossip monger."

Pia sighed, enviously. "You certainly have some interesting exes. And when you came to work at Samm's we all thought you were so quiet."

"Emerson's not an ex."

"Is Nick Angel?" Pia asked, curiously. "You never speak about him. He sure was anxious to talk to you, though."

"I went out with Nick in High school," she said casually, like it really meant nothing.

"Wow! High school – was he gorgeous then?"

"Yes," she said, very quietly. "He was."

467

As soon as Nick arrived in New York he called Help Unlimited. The operator told him the number was no longer in service.

"Shit!" he said, slamming down the phone. He thought for a moment, then called Carlysle in LA.

"Oh, boy!" she exclaimed. "That was *some* good time! I didn't realize you were so adventurous."

"Yeah, well, that makes two of us."

"Can you come over now? My friend's still here."

"I'm in New York."

"Shame."

"I need a favour."

"What?"

"You remember that dinner party you took me to when we were shooting *Night City*?"

"We went to so many places."

"The hostess had on all those crazy bracelets."

"You mean Jessie George."

"That's the one. What's her number?"

Carlysle giggled. "Oooh, Nick, isn't she a little old for you?"

"I need to ask her something."

"Wait a sec, I'll get my book."

She gave him the number and he hung up and dialled. All he had to say was, "Nick Angel," and Jessie knew exactly who he was.

"Nick, how nice to speak to you," she said. "I so enjoyed *Night City*. Memorable performance."

"Thanks."

"What can I do for you?"

"Do you have the number of Help Unlimited?"

"Unfortunately they're not in business any more."

"They're not?"

"No. I'm sad myself. But I do have another caterer I can recommend."

"Remember that girl . . . the one who did all the cooking?"

"Do you mean Lauren?"

"Who was that guy she was about to marry?"

"Oliver Liberty. They got married in the Bahamas."

"What does he do?"

"Oliver owns the biggest ad agency in New York – Liberty & Charles."

"Can you give me his home number?"

"Certainly. By the way, I'm having a dinner party tomorrow night. I'd love you to come."

"Well, uh, I don't know . . . I'm only here for a few hours. Gotta get back to LA."

"What a shame – Oliver and Lauren will be here."

"Maybe I don't have to get back so fast," he said, quickly.

"Eight o'clock. Casual. I'm putting you on my list."

So, Lauren had actually gone ahead and married the guy. This wasn't good news. But then again all he wanted to do was apologize; it wasn't like they were going to fall into each other's arms. A long time had passed. They were both different people now.

Yeah, sure. And what else was new?

Odile Hayworth was the most exquisite woman Cyndra had ever seen and she hated her on sight. Gordon belonged to Odile. Odile belonged to Gordon. It was patently obvious.

Marik had arranged a cosy dinner for four at a French restaurant and Cyndra was loathing every minute of it. Odile was uncommonly pretty, with amber eyes, fashionably short black hair and a wide smile. She was also at least thirty-five.

Old, Cyndra thought. *Surely he needs someone younger?*

"Marik tells me you used to be a model," Cyndra said politely, not that she cared.

"I was a model all right – until Gordon came along and rescued me," Odile replied, squeezing her husband's hand. He squeezed hers back.

How sweet, Cyndra thought.

"I saw her across the room at a crowded party," Gordon said. "Took one look and knew my life was over."

They all laughed.

"Hmm," Odile said, pretending to sound cross. "Your life was only just beginning, *and* you know it."

He smiled. "She's right. Before Odile I was a womanizer. After I met her I repented."

"Oh, yes, did you repent," smiled Odile. "Before you met me you were a *dog!*"

Marik took Cyndra's hand in his. "I kind of feel the same way myself."

This was news to her. She knew he liked her a lot, but he'd never expressed any serious intentions.

"It looks like you two are pretty cosy already," Odile said. "Do I hear moving in together noises?"

Gordon sipped a glass of brandy. "We like to see our artists happy. And I have some news, Cyndra, that should make you very happy indeed."

"Yes?"

"Your record broke the top forty."

She was wild with excitement. "It *did*?"

"True."

"Oh, this is so great!" She turned to Marik. "Did you know about this?"

He grinned, sheepishly. "Yeah, I knew, but Gordon's the boss – he wanted to tell you himself."

"I needed some good news in my life."

"Baby, you're gonna get all the good news you can handle," Marik said.

Later they made love. She thought about Gordon at home with his pretty wife and his two little children. He'd never so much as second glanced her. She was a recording artist – *his* recording artist – and that was all she meant to him. One of these days he'd look at her in a different fashion. One of these days he'd want her as much as she wanted him.

Cyndra knew there was no such thing as an ungettable man.

Later that night Nick dropped by to catch Joey's act. The club had not improved in his absence, nor had the lack-lustre hostesses.

Joey was funny – he had genuine talent – a talent he was pissing away in this joint.

"You promised you were comin' out to stay with me," Nick said.

"Hey, man, you're like a nursemaid," Joey complained. "Stop checkin' up on me."

"Tell you what – you come to LA an' I'll try to get you a role in my new movie."

Joey's lip curled. "Oh, big star now. You can get me a role, huh?"

"Maybe. But not if you're sitting on your ass in New York."

"I ain't sitting on my ass, man. I'm workin' for a living."

Nick took a good look at Joey. He wasn't an expert, but he could've sworn his friend was back on drugs.

"I'm sending you a ticket,' he said.

"I can buy my own ticket."

"Hey, listen – I got more money than you. Take advantage of it while you can."

"Fuck you," said Joey, grinning.

"Likewise," Nick replied.

He called Meena when he got back to the hotel. "I need a favour."

"Just tell me one thing," she said, sounding annoyed.

"What?"

"Who said you could fly to New York without telling me?"

"Am I supposed to check in?"

"No, but you *are* supposed to be in costume fittings tomorrow morning at nine a.m. sharp."

"I'll be back in forty-eight hours."

"In future, tell me."

"Yes, Mommy."

"Hilarious, Nick," Meena said, dryly. "What's the favour?"

"I got this talented friend. I'd like him to have a part in the movie."

She couldn't control her amusement. "Who do you think you are – Burt Reynolds?"

"At least get him in for a reading."

"What part did you have in mind?"

"He'd be good as the jail snitch."

"They've got someone they like."

"Make 'em see him, Meena, he's good."

"Very well, Nick, I'll try and arrange it. By the way, what *are* you doing in New York?"

"My publicist taught me one thing."

"What's that?"

"Always keep 'em guessing!"

In the morning he took a brisk walk through Central Park. A couple of girls recognized him, clutched on to each other and fell into fits of hysterical giggles.

Back at the hotel he called Jessie and told her he was definitely coming to her dinner.

"I'm delighted," she said. "Will you be bringing a date?"

"No, I'll be alone." He paused for a moment. "Uh, Jessie?"

"Yes?"

"Put Lauren next to me."

"You mean Oliver's wife?"

"Yeah, yeah. You see, Lauren and I . . . we, uh . . . we knew each other a long time ago."

"I wasn't aware of that."

471

"We lost touch, so it would be nice to catch up on old times. No big thing – but if you can seat her next to me I'd appreciate it."

"Of course, Nick. I look forward to seeing you."

Jessie put the phone down thoughtfully. Far be it from her to read anything into it, but it did seem rather odd that at first Nick had called to get Oliver's number and now he was requesting that Oliver's wife be seated beside him.

Oh well, it wasn't for Jessie to question, it was just for her to do. She had an interesting group planned, and Nick Angel would make it even more so.

If her instincts were correct it was going to be quite an evening.

Chapter 73

Lauren had been back from her trip to Rome for five weeks when she realized something was wrong. She'd been feeling queasy for a few days, and when she checked her calendar she realized she was late. This was unusual because she was never late.

One big thought loomed at the centre of her mind – was she pregnant?

Once she'd started to think about it she couldn't stop. She went to the gym and vigorously worked out. Then she came home and sat in a hot bath for an hour. She wanted a baby, and yet it wasn't possible because Oliver had never made love to her. So, if she *was* pregnant, how was she going to explain it?

I will not have an abortion, she thought. *I will not kill another baby.*

What are you going to do now, Roberts?

I don't know.

See where your little jaunt in Rome got you?

Shut up! Shut the fuck up!

There was only one answer: she had to get Oliver to make love to her properly.

He arrived home from the office early for a change.

"Can we talk?" she asked, handing him a martini.

He seemed distracted. "If we're going to the Georges' tonight, I have several calls to make before we leave."

"Oliver," she said, evenly. "I'm requesting a conversation. Is that too much to ask?"

"Of course not. I am merely pointing out I must make these calls before we go. Can our talk wait until later?"

"You're always tired when we come home."

"I won't be tired," he promised. "I'll make time for you."

Oh, how generous! The truth was he was beginning to get on her nerves.

She wondered if she could cancel the Georges. If they didn't go she'd have Oliver to herself and then who knew what could happen.

You have to get it up before you can get it in, Roberts.

I told you – shut the fuck up!

The thought of calling Jessie and cancelling out at this late hour was not one she relished. Jessie would throw a fit, especially as they hadn't seen her in a while.

With a sigh she realized they'd have to go.

She put on a simple black dress, brushed her hair and applied a careful make-up. Then she stood back and surveyed her image. Since she'd been doing the Marcella girl campaign there was a certain glow about her. Oliver called it the glow of success.

She wondered if it was the glow of having great sex with Lorenzo.

Once.

Once was not enough.

She was too guilty to do it twice.

Walking into the Georges' apartment she felt as if she should head straight for the kitchen and start cooking.

Jessie had gathered together her usual interesting mix, it would not be a dull evening.

She lifted a drink from a passing waiter, and spoke briefly to one of Oliver's competitors from a rival agency.

"Congratulations," the man said, standing too close. "I've seen the Marcella ads – they're very sleek. Trust Oliver to find the face of the year and marry it."

"I'm glad you like them," she said, surreptitiously backing off. "You have excellent taste."

He chortled. "So does Oliver."

She had her back to the door, but she sensed somebody important entering. Turning around she was startled to see Emerson Burn. His mane of hair was longer and wilder and he had acquired an even deeper suntan. Pale beige leather pants emphasized his long legs and he wore a stylish fringed jacket. The girl with him looked about twelve.

It didn't take long before he made his way over to her. "How you doin', luv?" he said, like they'd spoken the day before. "I 'ear you got married."

"I hear *you* got divorced," she responded, coolly.

He didn't seem too concerned. "It was bound to 'appen. Nature drove me bleedin' bonkers. Crazy bird."

Lauren indicated the young girl hovering by the door. "Is that your daughter you're with – or a date?"

"Ha, ha, still a comedian."

"You always bring out my sense of humour, Emerson."

"That's not exactly what you bring out in me." He pointed at Oliver across the room. "Is that the old geezer?"

"Don't call Oliver an old geezer."

"He ain't exactly in the first flush of youth." he said, scrutinizing her. "You're lookin' pretty good. Marriage must agree with you."

"You should know. *How* many times have you done it now?"

"Enough to know better."

Lorenzo swept down on them. Lorenzo in his impeccably tailored suit with his charming accent. He kissed her on both cheeks. "Ah, *bellissima*, every other woman in the room pales beside you."

"Cor, blimey," Emerson said. "I've 'eard a load of cobblers in me time, but this takes the cake."

"Emerson, meet Lorenzo Marcella."

"It is my pleasure," Lorenzo said, proffering a manicured hand. "I listen to your music – it brings me much delight."

"What do you do, Lorenzo?" Emerson asked.

"He owns Marcella Cosmetics," Lauren said, quickly. "It's an Italian firm whose products are just about to hit the American market."

"Em," Emerson's petite young girlfriend marched determinedly over with a frown on her face and a plaintive whine in her voice. "You left me standing over there by the door. I don't know anybody here. How can you do that to me?"

"Shush, love, there's grown-ups present."

"Yes," Lorenzo said, ignoring the interruption. "Lauren is the Marcella girl. Starting next month you will see her face everywhere."

"Well," Emerson said cheerfully, "it's a pretty enough face."

Shortly before dinner she began to feel queasy. She hurried into the bathroom, soaked a towel with cold water and held it to her forehead.

I'm pregnant.

How do you know?

Because I do.

Then it's your own fault.

Oh God! How was she going to explain it to Oliver?

Sweetheart, I know we've never had proper sex, but something miraculous has happened. We've had an immaculate conception.

It didn't sound too convincing.

When she emerged from the bathroom everyone was seated. She entered the dining room and slid into her empty seat. Lorenzo was on her left. "Are you feeling all right?" he asked, solicitously.

"Fine, thank you."

She turned to see who was seated on her other side and could not believe it.

"Hi, Lauren," said a familiar voice. "It's been a long time."

Nick.

Nick Angelo.

Her past swept over her rendering her speechless.

Their eyes met and locked together. For a moment she couldn't catch her breath. She felt her heart pounding in her chest and she didn't know what to do. There was no escape. She had to face up to him – it was inevitable.

"Hello, Nick," she said, weakly. "This is a surprise."

"I guess we're destined to meet at Jessie's parties, huh?" he said.

"It seems that way," she replied, trying to sound as casual as him.

Oh, God! His eyes were the same piercing green. His hair jet black and curly. He still had the indentation in the middle of his chin which drove her totally crazy.

"It's good to see you," he said, thinking that she looked more beautiful than ever.

"You too," she murmured.

They talked all the way through dinner. She never turned to her other side and Lorenzo was not pleased.

They started off with surface talk, gradually getting more personal, until eventually he mentioned his trip back to Bosewell and that he'd heard about her parents and how sorry he was.

She nodded. "It was a frightening time."

"You do know I wrote you," he said, staring at her intently.

"No, I didn't know that."

"Yeah, many times. I guess there was nowhere for the letters to go. I also wrote you a long letter when I left town explaining why I had to leave."

"Where did you send it?"

"I left it with Louise at the drugstore. She said she never had a chance to give it to you, but I didn't know that until I went back." He continued staring into her eyes. "How're you doing?"

"Fine," she said, not knowing how she was managing to talk at all.

"So you got married," he said.

"Yes. That's my husband at the other table," she said, pointing Oliver out.

He took a good look. "I don't mean to be rude or anything, but isn't he too old for you?"

"You *are* being rude," she said, trying to breathe evenly.

He grinned. "Yeah, well, remember me? I was never Mister Polite."

She couldn't help smiling back. Yes, she remembered him, she remembered him only too well. For a moment she got lost in his green eyes and it was all over. "I thought you didn't care," she murmured, softly.

"I thought the same about you."

She broke the stare and grabbed her glass of wine. Her hand was shaking and she wished it wasn't, but there was nothing she could do about it. "It was a long time ago – we were both very young."

"Yeah," he agreed. "Little kids."

"Not that little."

He leaned closer. "You're so . . . goddamn . . . beautiful."

She gulped more wine. "Nick . . . I . . ."

"Yes?"

"Oh . . . nothing." Desperately she tried to change the subject. "Who else did you see in Bosewell?" She held her breath, waiting for him to tell her his father was dead.

How did he die, Lauren?

You killed him.

"Saw your old friend, Meg. Guess what?"

"What?" she asked, breathlessly.

"She married that asshole Stock Browning."

"No! Really?"

"Are you surprised?"

"Well . . . I guess they do make a perfect couple."

"Jeez! What a pompous prick he was. And you were engaged to him."

"Only by default," she said, quickly.

"Don't use big words on me."

She picked up her wine glass again. "Remember the night he broke your nose?"

"Oh, yeah," he said, ruefully. "Like I'm gonna forget that.

477

You took me home with you and your parents were really thrilled."

"And in the morning we drove to Ripley."

He fixed her with another long stare. "Now *that* was memorable."

"Very," she said, returning his look.

He shook his head. "Jesus, Lauren – it seems like such a long time ago."

She turned the stem of the wine glass in her hands. "I thought about you a lot, Nick. Where did you go?"

"Chicago. Got a job in a club, ended up doing everything – barman, disc jockey, you name it I did it. Then I moved to LA."

"It must have been exciting."

"Hey, anything was exciting after Bosewell." He hesitated for a moment, then added, "Missing you wasn't."

"Did you think about me?" she asked, softly.

"Every single day."

"Me, too."

"There's something I need to say –" he began.

"Lauren." Lorenzo had had enough. He jabbed her sharply in the ribs. "Introduce me to your friend."

She was shaken back to reality. "Oh, uh, this is Nick . . . Nick Angelo."

He cleared his throat. "It's Angel now."

"Of course. How could I forget." She began to giggle hysterically. "Angel. What kind of name is that?"

He grinned. "Hey – it's my professional name, don't make fun of it."

"Oh, well," she said, still giggling, "in that case – Lorenzo, meet Nick Angel, we used to go to High school together."

"We used to do a lot of things together," Nick said, catching her with his eyes.

They exchanged intimate smiles.

I love you, Nick. Nothing's changed.

Get real, Roberts. You're a married woman carrying another man's baby.

Lorenzo did not appreciate this situation one little bit. He sensed competition and reacted fiercely. The husband was one thing – easy to deal with. But this man was a threat, and Lorenzo did not like threats.

"Recently Lauren and I were in Rome together," he said,

snaking a possessive arm across her shoulders. "Ah, such a romantic city! Have you been there . . . Rick?"

"It's Nick," Lauren said quickly, moving so that she dislodged his arm.

"Whatever," Lorenzo said, disdainfully.

"No," Nick said. "But I may make a movie there next year." He was lying – but screw this Italian prick who quite obviously had big eyes for Lauren.

"Gina Lollabrigida is a very good friend of mine," Lorenzo said, adjusting a perfect silk cuff.

Nick looked at him blankly. "Gina who?"

"Gina is one of the biggest movie stars in Italy. And a great beauty."

"This'll be a contemporary film," Nick said, winking at Lauren.

She pushed her chair away from the table and stood up. She was feeling queasy again.

"You look pale, *bellissima*," Lorenzo said, leaping to his feet.

"No . . . no, I'm fine. I'll be right back," she said, glancing over at the other table. Oliver was making conversation with Emerson Burn. Good. She had enough to handle with Nick and Lorenzo surrounding her, she didn't need any more complications.

The guest bathroom was occupied, so she made her way down the corridor to Jessie's bedroom where she sat on the edge of the bed and attempted to think straight. It was all too much. Oliver, Emerson, Lorenzo . . . and Nick.

The only person she really cared about was Nick. In fact, she loved him just as much as she always had. He was in her heart and in her soul, but she was trapped in an impossible situation, and there was nothing she could do about it.

"What's going on, Lauren?" Nick walked in, startling her.

"Uh . . . nothing."

"Can I see you?" he asked, urgently.

"You are seeing me."

His green eyes captured her attention. "You know what I mean."

She knew exactly what he meant.

He walked over and stood very close, pulling her to her feet.

She was melting inside. Falling . . . falling . . . And when he began to kiss her it was like time stood perfectly still and nothing else mattered. They kissed feverishly.

His hands touched her face. "Oh God, Lauren, I missed you so much."

She managed to push him away, fighting for her life, desperately trying to gain control of the situation. "Nick, you're forgetting something. I'm married. *Very* married."

"Get a divorce."

"It's not that easy."

"We'll make it easy."

"No ... I ... I can't."

He kissed her again, forcing her to be silent.

She closed her eyes and she was sixteen again, and there was no more pain. She was safe with Nick; she'd always been safe with him.

He held her tightly and she felt his urgent desire pressing against her. She knew she should break their embrace, but she didn't have the strength nor the inclination.

"I love you, Lauren." He whispered the words she was waiting to hear. "I've always loved you."

She wasn't sixteen any more. She was a grown woman and she could do what she liked.

How do you know he's not lying to you? It's easy for him to say he wrote you. But remember – he left you pregnant, and now you're pregnant again.

"Nick ... I ..."

It was too late to protest. She was just as caught up in the passion of the moment as he was.

They fell back on the bed locked in a dangerous embrace.

His hands began exploring her body beneath her clothes and she lost all sense of time and place.

"I love you, Lauren," he kept on repeating like a mantra. "I love you – love you –"

"Excuse *me*," a woman's voice interrupted them.

Guiltily they broke apart.

Jessie hurried over to her dressing table pretending she hadn't noticed what they were up to. "Lauren, Oliver is looking for you," she said casually, picking up her silver hairbrush. "Oh, and Nick, why don't you stay here for a few moments?"

Lauren felt her cheeks burning. She adjusted her dress and fluffed her hair. Real life was back with a vengeance.

"Call me, I'm at the Plaza," Nick said in a low voice. "I'll wait for your call."

She nodded, knowing she wouldn't call.

It was too late to go back.

Nick Angelo was her past. It had to stay that way.

BOOK THREE
1988

Chapter 74

The crowds went crazy. Totally berserk. Nick could hear them before he left the safety of his limo, screaming his name, yelling hysterically. Annie sat beside him, impassive as usual. He took another swig of Scotch from the leaded glass in his hands, put it on the carpet of the limo and said to his bodyguard, "Okay, let's go."

Igor, an enormous bald black man, said, "Yes, boss," in a feathery little voice that did not quite match his looks.

They had a routine. Igor left the limousine first and met up with his other two bodyguards who followed in a back-up car. Then the three of them formed a shield around Nick, and Annie trailed behind as they made a rush for the entrance of the theatre.

It was the première of Nick's new movie, *Hoodlum*. On each side of the red carpet press and paparazzi lined up, thrusting cameras at him, screaming his name. They were almost as bad as the fans.

He'd learnt how to handle it. Stare straight ahead – don't look to the left or right – just keep walking, never stop.

Stardom.

It was a pisser.

The crowds tonight were unruly. They began trying to break through the barriers, struggling with the police holding them back.

He quickened his step, holding on to Annie's hand, dragging her along behind him. After all, she was his wife, it wouldn't do to lose her.

The crowd began to chant. "NICK! NICK! WE LOVE YOU! WE LOVE YOU!"

Yeah, it was all very nice, but sometimes he felt like such a phoney. Who was this person they'd created? This icon. Was it really him? Was it really Nick Angelo?

They made the lobby of the theatre, where he was greeted by his agent, Freddie Leon. Meena Caron no longer handled his career, he was now looked after by Freddie, the head of a rival company to Meena's – I.A.A. – International Artists Agents.

Freddie was a poker-faced man in his early forties, with cordial features and a quick bland smile. His nickname was The Snake, because he could slither in and out of any deal. Nobody ever called him The Snake to his face.

Since Nick had been with him – which was over four years, now – Freddie had guided his career to superstardom status.

Freddie gave Annie a quick peck on the cheek and then ignored her. She was Mrs Angel. She deserved an acknowledgement, but that was about it. Stars' wives had to know how to stay in the background, look attractive and keep quiet.

Annie was not good at it. Her anger bubbled beneath the surface like a volcano about to erupt.

Freddie put his arm around Nick's shoulders and they walked into the theatre together – the superagent and the superstar. The celebrity-filled audience turned to look. These two men were Hollywood royalty.

Mrs Freddie Leon waved to Annie and they exchanged empty kisses on the cheek.

Everybody was smiling except Nick. Bridget, his original publicist had taught him well. Moody was best. Moody worked every time.

Bridget was no longer his publicist. He was now represented by Ian Gem, a wiry PR dynamo with flat red hair that looked like a wig, although it was all his own.

Nick sat down in his reserved seat with Freddie on one side and Annie on the other. He wished he'd brought his drink in with him, but that would have caused Ian to throw a fit. It wouldn't do to be seen drinking in public.

Why the hell not? He could do what the fuck he liked.

Carlysle Mann walked down the aisle and waved at him. She was with her new husband – a studio head with a tired expression and crinkle-cut hair. Christ! Living with Carlysle was enough to make anybody exhausted.

He and Annie rarely exchanged words any more. Nearly seven years of a loveless marriage and they were growing more apart every day. The more famous he became the more hostile Annie was. She would never forgive him for the career she'd never had.

He'd married Annie for two reasons: One – the anonymous body buried somewhere in the Las Vegas desert; Two – the fact that she was pregnant. He had a daughter now – the one light of his life. She was called Lissa.

The audience settled into their seats, twisting and turning, greeting him if they could, waving, blowing air kisses, generally brown-nosing. These were the same people who'd once ignored him. Fuck 'em. He could play the Hollywood game as well as anyone.

He'd seen the movie at least fifty times. One of the enjoyable things about making movies was the editing process. He'd gotten into that on his third movie, and now with every film he made, he liked to sit in with the editors – viewing the film frame by frame, shaping it to make it exactly what he wanted.

He knew he was only allowed to do this because he had the power. Last week he'd told Freddie that he wanted to direct.

"Whatever you want," Freddie had replied, totally unfazed.

Being a superstar meant never having aspirations you couldn't achieve.

The lights began to dim. Nick hunched his shoulders and slid down in his seat. It was all so unreal, this movie stardom shit. He'd done nothing to deserve it, and yet he was now at a place where the atmosphere was so heady he could hardly breathe.

Nick Angel – superstar. How had it all happened?

He tried to think – clear his mind. Every day there was so much going on – so many demands on his time. He never had a moment alone. Sitting in the darkened theatre was a pleasure – no one to bother him – no fucking leeches clinging on to his every word.

Annie fidgeted beside him. Annie who'd turned into the definitive Hollywood wife. She gave great charity – yes, Annie was extremely generous with his money.

This was the first time she'd seen *Hoodlum*. She hadn't gone to any of the previews or special sneak screenings that gauged early audience reaction. No. Annie had told him she didn't care to sit through his latest movie more than once. Bitch! If she could find an opportunity to put him down she did.

According to Annie he'd sold out, become a movie star instead of the fine actor he could have been. *Bullshit*. What was wrong with making six million bucks a movie? He noticed she had no trouble spending it.

They'd moved three times in the past seven years. First the modest little house above Sunset with a breathtaking view of the city. Then the larger house in fashionable Pacific Palisades. And finally the Bel Air mansion.

Who needed a fucking mansion? He certainly didn't.

Annie was into decorating. She'd surrounded herself with a bunch of gay interior designers and they all had a high old time spending, spending, spending.

His name appeared on the screen and there was a ripple of applause. Hey – he didn't have to turn in a performance, they loved him anyway.

He wasn't quite sure how it had happened – he only knew it had happened fast. From modest success to cult superstardom. Three easy steps. Meena Caron had taken him the first two levels – Freddie Leon had whisked him into the stratosphere.

The movie started and his image filled the screen. His co-star was a moody blonde with downturned lips and smoky eyes. They'd had an affair. It was one of the perks of being a superstar – you got to fuck whoever you wanted – and leading ladies were up for grabs.

Freddie could get to do the same thing if he wanted, but Freddie never availed himself. He'd once told Nick that the high he got from a great deal was far more satisfying than any transient fuck.

Lucky Freddie. He had his power base agency, an attractive intelligent wife who'd been his college sweetheart, and a couple of well-behaved teenage kids. He had it all.

Nick did not consider himself so lucky – although some might say he was the luckiest man in the world. How many red-blooded males would love to be in his position? He was a star. He could have any woman he wanted. People laughed at his jokes. He got the best tables in restaurants. He was fêted wherever he went. He was adored, worshipped and loved.

But it wasn't enough. He didn't have Lauren.

He often thought about the last time he'd seen her. It was in New York at Jessie George's dinner party. When they were together it was like no time had passed. They'd ended up in the bedroom, about to renew their relationship when Jessie had interrupted them.

Lauren had promised to call. He'd never heard from her again. Five long gut-wrenching days he'd sat in his hotel room waiting before he was forced to fly back to LA to start the new movie.

When he'd got back he'd tried to contact her, but she'd refused to take his calls.

Soon after their meeting in New York, photographs of her had started appearing in all the magazines. He'd been prepared to forget her, but it wasn't possible. There she was staring out at him – that beautiful, incredible face. The Marcella Girl.

Over the years she hadn't gone away. As his star had risen so had hers. She was probably the most famous model in America now. And he was probably the most famous movie star.

But it wasn't enough. Not by a long way.

When he'd returned to LA after the New York trip Annie had been waiting as usual. He'd been considering having a talk with her, saying it wasn't working out. But he was sure if he did, she'd run straight to the police. She had him where she wanted him – and she knew it.

Annie had greeted him with unexpected news. "We're having a baby."

What did he have to lose? Lauren was married, and obviously didn't want anything to do with him, so he'd married Annie because he didn't like the idea of his baby growing up with no father.

Bridget and Meena had thrown a fit. According to them marriage was a career killer. They'd made him keep it secret for two months, until one day Annie had blurted it out to a reporter – by accident, she'd said, but nobody believed her.

After that she'd started getting the attention she thought she deserved. Mrs Nick Angel got a lot more kudos than plain Annie Broderick.

Joey had finally made his way out to the coast and Nick kept his promise and got him a part in his movie. Joey had taken to California immediately, and Nick was so pleased that he'd made it a habit to put Joey in every movie he made. Eventually Joey had overdosed on his minor success. Three years after coming to live in LA he was found dead in his girlfriend's apartment with an empty vial of crack beside him.

Nick had not blamed himself. He'd done everything he could for his friend – but drugs won. Joey's death was inevitable.

Sitting in his seat Nick began getting that old restless feeling. Watching his face on the screen drove him crazy. Sometimes he wished it had never happened. Hadn't he been happier in Chicago running the bar for Q.J. and living with DeVille? No pressure then. Now there was so much fucking pressure he sometimes thought he'd explode.

He got up.

"Where are you going?" Annie hissed.

"Gotta take a leak."

He walked outside, grabbed an usher and handed him a hundred-dollar bill. "Do me a favour, run to the liquor store and buy me a quart of Scotch. Keep the change."

"Yes, sir," said the young guy, fully impressed.

He paced around the lobby until the usher returned, then he took the bottle into the john and took a few solid swigs. The strong liquor burned a hole in his stomach. He hadn't eaten all day, had to keep the gaunt look, had to keep the Nick Angel image.

Peering in the mirror he wondered why it had happened to him. Oh yeah, sure he looked okay, but he was certainly no Redford or Newman.

Shit! The trouble was he had everything, and yet he knew for a fact it could all vanish tomorrow.

Why wasn't he happy?

Because he was living with a woman he didn't love, and it made him feel empty inside.

He swigged enough Scotch to give him the strength to go back to his seat.

As soon as he sat down Annie smelt the liquor on his breath. "Couldn't you wait?" she said, in an angry whisper.

Screw you, he wanted to say. *Get out of my life. Go to the police if you want. I've paid for burying that body a million times.*

And yet at the back of his mind he knew she could ruin everything if she exposed him.

Cyndra was unconcerned, but Cyndra lived in her own world; she thought nobody could touch them.

After the movie there was the obligatory party. He didn't mingle – he didn't have to. He sat at a table with Freddie, while people trouped over to pay their respects.

"Sometimes I feel like the Godfather," Freddie joked, loving every minute of his silent authority.

"You've got the power," Nick said, gulping a glass of Scotch.

"So've you," Freddie replied, sticking to Perrier.

Nick got along with Freddie because Freddie didn't give a damn about anything except the deal. There was something likeable about his steely single-mindedness.

Freddie's wife, Diana, engaged Annie in light conversation. They weren't exactly bosom buddies, but Annie was about as friendly with Diana as she was with anybody.

Annie was no social butterfly. Women didn't warm to her because she was too critical and outspoken. She was also bitter and a bitch. She and Cyndra had stopped speaking long ago. Cyndra knew that Annie had forced him into marriage, even though he tried to deny it. "Listen, I made her pregnant," he'd explained. "I wanted to be a father to my baby." Cyndra wasn't having it.

He had to admit that he loved his little girl; Lissa was quite a character. The only time he was really at peace were the afternoons he spent with her – teaching her to swim in the pool, running around the garden with her, watching her play with her toys.

Annie always managed to spoil their times together. She'd appear at just the wrong moment and summon Lissa in for a piano lesson or a dancing class.

"Leave the kid alone," he'd say.

"I want her to have all the advantages I never had. Don't try and stop her progress."

"Fuck you, Annie."

It had become his lament. *Fuck you, Annie.*

Hoodlum was well-received. The critics loved it. Right now he could do no wrong. Each movie he did received more and more praise.

The brooding intensity of Angel's performance propels this movie to new heights read one glowing review.

Angel scores again! A dark performance filled with pain and bitterness as only Angel can portray it, read another.

He'd thought about taking a break, maybe visiting Hawaii with Lissa and the nanny.

Annie soon put a stop to that. "She has to go to summer school," she said. "I want her to learn Spanish."

"She's six years old," he objected. "Give her a chance to have some fun."

Annie glared at him. "You control your career. At least let me control what happens to our child."

Over the next few months he met with the writer and director of his upcoming movie, *Miami Connection*. It was the kind of role he hadn't tackled before and he liked it a lot. A young cop who gets caught up in a drug scam, is coerced by the villains, and eventually turns the tables.

The search was on for a suitable co-star. The director wanted a star. Freddie, who had very good instincts, suggested they go with somebody new.

"Let's discover somebody," Freddie said, enthusiastically. "I'm in the mood to make a new star!"

Carlysle Mann phoned Nick and told him she wanted the part.

"It's not up to me," he said.

"You're full of shit," she said.

Ah, Carlysle . . . still as sweet as ever.

A few days later he was having lunch in the private dining room at the I.A.A. offices when Freddie picked up a magazine and threw it across the table.

"Take a look at this girl," he said. "She's the top model in the country. I've been asked to represent her. What do you think? Should we bring her out for a screen test?"

Before Nick looked at the magazine he knew who it was.

Lauren.

"Yeah," he said. "I'll test with her myself. Fly her out."

Chapter 75

Lauren sat behind the desk in her Park Avenue office. The room was light and bright, furnished with sleek bird's-eye maple furniture and comfortable beige couches. On the walls were framed covers of all the top fashion and women's magazines featuring her. The Lauren Roberts image dominated. Sexy. Sweet. Thoughtful. Provocative. She could be anything the photographer required – hence her enormous success. A block of *Vogue* covers took pride of place. She'd asked Samm for one cover. She'd got it and gone on to be their favourite cover girl for the last seven years.

Concluding a meeting she stood up, walked around her desk and shook hands with the two men and one woman she'd been meeting with. "I like your ideas," she said. "Put everything in writing and I'll give you my decision."

"As soon as possible I hope," said one of the men, his bull neck flushed with the thought of success.

"It's your move," Lauren replied, smiling.

"I think we can lay out a deal that'll please you."

"Good. I'll look forward to it." She ushered them from her office and closed the door. "No way," she said, turning to Pia, who sat unobtrusively in the corner.

"How come?"

"'Cause they're a nickel-and-dime operation. I knew it was a waste of time meeting with them."

"They're offering you a lot of money for one simple exercise video."

"What do you want to bet it's all deferred payments? I'd sooner deal with legitimate people and make less money."

"In that case why did you agree to see them?"

Lauren grinned. "To test out my gut instinct. Trust me, it's still working."

Her secretary buzzed. "Mr Liberty on line two."

"I'll take it." She picked up the phone. "Oliver, what can I do for you?"

It struck Pia that she talked to her husband as if they were working colleagues rather than man and wife.

"Okay," Lauren said, rather irritably. "I know. I'll be there." She put down the phone and glanced at the Art Deco Cartier clock on her desk. "Oliver's getting panicky. I promised I'd go to the Raleigh cocktail party. Damn! I'm late, aren't I? Do you think I have time to go home and change?"

"You look great," Pia said, and marvelled at exactly how great Lauren looked. She was staggeringly beautiful, although it was no longer the innocent somewhat naïve beauty she'd once possessed. Lauren was sleek, almost feline with her long thick chestnut hair streaked with blonde, unusual tortoiseshell eyes and full sensuous lips.

At thirty she was more stunning than she'd ever been. Glossy, slick – but still with that faint vulnerability – Lauren was the face of the decade.

Sometimes Pia thought she envied her. Other times she knew she didn't. Lauren had everything, and yet she had nothing. She had an empty marriage, no children, a business empire and great fame, but she was always chasing more. She wanted to be tops at everything she did. It wasn't enough that she was one of the most sought after models in the world. That she had lent her name to a very successful clothing line, and co-authored a beauty book. Now she was looking into an acting career.

"Why don't you take some time off and enjoy your success?" Pia said to her one day. "You're always in such a hurry to conquer new mountains."

"I love working," Lauren had replied. "Working is my life!"

No wonder she and Oliver got along. Twin personalities.

Outside her Park Avenue office Lauren got into her car. She had her own limo and driver – preferring not to share Oliver's. Their schedules were never in sync so they needed separate cars.

She told her driver where to go, and reached for the day's newspapers stacked neatly on the seat opposite her. Lauren did not believe in wasting time; car journeys allowed her the perfect opportunity to scan the newspapers.

She went through the *New York Post* in record time, perused the *Wall Street Journal*, glanced at *Newsday* and stopped at a column piece in *The News*. It was a short gossip item about Nick. He'd been spotted out and about with his latest leading lady. Nothing new about that.

Hmm, she thought – *if Nick Angel had screwed every woman he was linked with he'd be dead.*

She put the paper down and frowned. She wished she could stop thinking about him. She wished that he would vanish. But this was not to be. Nick Angel was a superstar. He was everywhere she went.

She thought about the last time she'd seen him in Jessie George's New York apartment and shivered. Every so often she re-lived that night in her head. Being in the same room with Emerson, Lorenzo and Oliver was unnerving enough – but when she'd seen Nick everything had changed. At first it had been so good to see him, so wonderful – and she'd gotten carried away with the moment. But it was only for a moment, because reality soon reminded her that she was a married woman. And not only that, she was pregnant – or at least she'd thought so at the time.

A week later she'd gotten her period. It had all been a false alarm.

"Probably the European trip threw you off schedule," her gynaecologist had told her. "It often happens."

If there wasn't Oliver to consider she would have been a free person. She'd thought about calling Nick and seeing him again, but she didn't have his number in LA, although it would have been easy enough to find if she'd really wanted to. But did she?

She woke up one morning a few months later and realized that yes, she did. Maybe if she divorced Oliver there'd be a chance for her and Nick to be together after all.

She'd decided to use her connections, find out where he was and call him.

Before she had a chance, the papers were full of the news. Nick Angel had gotten secretly married.

With a dull feeling of hopelessness she'd known it was too late for her to do anything.

Lauren arrived at the cocktail party late. Oliver glowered at her. "It was important for me that you were here earlier," he snapped.

"I'm sorry," she replied coolly, not really sorry at all. "I was in a meeting. Surely you understand better than anyone that business comes first?"

She knew why he wanted her there. People were impressed when they found out she was his wife.

After the cocktail party there was a boring dinner with business people. She excused herself and left early, much to Oliver's chagrin.

Back at the apartment there were several messages on her private answering machine. Two were from Lorenzo.

Ah, sweet faithful Lorenzo. He'd never given up hope, even though he was now a married man. He'd wed a beautiful eighteen-year-old Italian girl, but he still lusted after Lauren.

She called him first. "What can I do for you, Lorenzo?"

He laughed. "You know what I would like you to do for me, *bellissima*."

"Cut it out, Lorenzo. It's late, I'm tired and I'm not in the mood for your phoney Italian bullshit."

"Ah, such a lady. Whatever happened to the sweet innocent girl I used to know?"

"She grew up."

"I was thinking," he said. "Would you entertain the idea of adding a line of cosmetics to your fragrance line?"

Lorenzo sure knew how to make a girl interested.

"It's a great idea – when did you come up with it?"

"Your fragrance has been so successful the other directors and I thought it might be a good idea if we started a limited line. We would call it The Lauren Roberts Collection. You like that?"

"I like it," she said, enthusiastically. "Can you stop by my office, say at noon tomorrow, and we'll discuss it?"

"But of course," he replied, pleased because he had her full attention.

She hung up the phone and smiled. The more she achieved the better she liked it. Three years ago Marcella had financed her with her own scent collection. It had been an enormous success. To branch into make-up would be an interesting challenge.

Being a model had never been enough for Lauren. She felt that her beauty was a gift and that taking advantage of it and forging a good professional career was an excellent way to handle her gift. Her business acumen she'd developed. In a way it was much more important to her than merely looking good. She wasn't going to be a model forever. She was thirty now and she had to protect her future.

There were several more messages on her answering machine.

The only call she decided to return was the one from Samm. It was past eleven, but Samm was a night person.

"I'm not waking you, am I?" she asked.

"Not at all," Samm replied. "I was hoping you'd get back to me tonight."

"What's up?"

"Can you fly to Los Angeles tomorrow?"

She laughed incredulously. "No, Samm, I cannot fly to Los Angeles tomorrow. What are you talking about?"

"I'm talking about that big chance you've been waiting for."

"I've had plenty of big chances," Lauren replied. "And I'm not waiting for anything."

"Short memory," Samm said, crisply. "For the last eighteen months you've been badgering me about a film career."

"And you've told me it's not something I should pursue. You said models do not make good actresses – all they make is fools of themselves."

"Yes, Lauren, but when you talk I listen. You're very smart."

"Thanks, Samm. Coming from you I guess that's a compliment."

"Without your knowledge I've been speaking to Freddie Leon. Do you know who he is?"

"Oh, come on, I took the straw out of my hair a long time ago."

"Anyway, I thought if you were going to have representation in LA it should be the best. As you know, Freddie handles only a very few select clients, and they're all top stars."

"So?"

"So, he's interested in representing *you*. He wants you to fly to LA tomorrow to test for the new Nick Angel movie." There was a long silence. "Lauren – are you there?"

"Yes, I'm here."

"Will you do it?"

She took a deep breath. "Yes, I'll do it."

Chapter 76

"How many times must I tell you, Marik? I have no desire to get married."

"But, baby, baby, we're so good together."

"I know," Cyndra relented – but only a little. Marik was the sweetest man she'd ever met and she didn't want to hurt his feelings. "I don't see us married," she said.

Actually she did see them married, but it was impossible. Somewhere out there was a man called Reece Webster, and she had no idea where. All she knew was that she was legally married to him, and there was nothing she could do about it.

Or maybe there was. Lately she'd been considering confiding in Gordon. He was an important and powerful man and now she was his important and powerful recording star. If she went to him in strict confidence maybe he could help her.

Of course, she wouldn't tell him anything about the shooting, that was privileged information. She would just tell him she was once married to this guy who'd run out on her, and how could she get a divorce.

Over the years Gordon and she had forged a good friendship. There'd been one little glitch three years ago when she'd come right out and confessed her feelings for him. He'd sat her down and talked to her like a father.

"Cyndra," he'd said. "When you find what *I* have, you never want to risk losing it. You're a beautiful and fine woman, and I love you in my own way. But Odile is my life, and nothing will ever change that."

Strangely enough she'd understood exactly what he was saying and accepted it. Since that time they'd been best friends.

Marik and she were still an item. It was better to be with

one guy than fight off the lines of men that came sniffing around after she became a star.

Stardom. Nick hated it. She loved it. What a trip! She'd had eight hit singles, three mega albums and was even now contemplating the offer of her own television series.

One night she and Nick had started laughing about it.

"Maybe there was something in the water at Bosewell High," he'd joked. "It's crazy that we've all made it so big. You, me and Lauren."

"What about the rest of them?" she'd asked.

"Yeah, well, you had to drink the water and *then* get out fast," he'd explained, laughing. "That's the way it works."

A year ago she'd persuaded Aretha Mae to come and live with her. The old woman was very sickly and stayed in her room all day muttering to herself.

"Are you out of your mind?" Nick had said. "What do you want her around for?"

"Because she brought me up. Because she busted her ass so I could go to school and have food on the table. And I couldn't live with myself if I didn't care for her now."

Marik also thought she was nuts. "I hate the way that batty old lady looks at me," he complained.

"What do you mean, looks at you? She never comes out of her room."

"She spies on me from her window."

"Big deal. It shouldn't bother you."

"She's loco – and you know it."

"Yeah, but she's also my mother."

Neither she nor Nick had achieved any success with Harlan. He'd never contacted them. They weren't even sure if they had the right address any more, but they both regularly sent money.

"One of these days," Cyndra said, "I'm gonna ride into town in a big old limo with an entourage and a couple of strong bodyguards. Then I'm gonna find Harlan, throw him in the back of my car, and bring him back here."

Nick had no doubt that one day Cyndra would do it. She was strong-willed enough.

Every couple of weeks she and Nick spoke on the phone.

"Why don't you ever come by the house?" he asked.

"You know why. I try to avoid that wife of yours – she's such a bad-tempered witch."

"Lissa misses you."

"Really?"

"You know she likes seeing you."

"So bring her over to my house one day. Maybe she'll lure Aretha Mae out of her room."

He changed the subject. "Lauren's coming to town."

"How do you know?"

"Because she's testing for my new movie."

"I'm proud of you, Nick. How did you fix that?"

"Freddie's thinking of representing her. He suggested it."

"Oh, and you didn't exactly fight it?"

He laughed. "Nope. I guess not."

"You'd better not let Annie find out," Cyndra warned. "She'll slice your balls up and lay 'em out for the fans."

"You got a graphic way with words."

"How long is it since you've seen Lauren?"

"I look at her every day. All I have to do is pick up a magazine."

"You're not exactly out of the limelight yourself, Nick. Anyway, she's still married, isn't she?"

"Yeah."

"Then you're both perfectly safe."

"Gee, thanks. That's just what I wanted to hear."

Freddie was totally unaware that Nick and Lauren were already acquainted. He sent one of his minions to meet her at the airport, and then visited her when she was installed in a bungalow at the Beverly Hills Hotel.

He called Nick later. "I'm not usually impressed," he said, "but I have just met the most beautiful woman I've ever seen. And sweet, too. And sharp. And intelligent."

"You met Lauren, huh?"

"What's with the Lauren bit?"

"Neither of us advertise the fact, but we went to High school together."

"You're kidding?"

"No, I'm not kidding."

"Then how come you didn't nail her? She's gorgeous. And you know me, Nick, I do not get enthusiastic about anybody."

This was true. Freddie rarely noticed or commented on women. Sexual chemistry was not his thing.

"Uh . . . do me a favour," Nick added. "Keep this information to yourself. I'm not sure Lauren wants people knowing. And I certainly don't think it's a good idea to spread it around."

"Why? What's the big secret about going to High school with someone?"

Nick sighed. "We did more than go to High school."

"You *did* nail her?"

It was so unlike Freddie to talk like one of the guys that he was quite shocked.

"Hey, Freddie," he said, edgily. "Maybe she nailed me. What's the difference? I don't answer questions like that."

Freddie didn't seem to notice his aggravation. "She's *really* beautiful, Nick."

"I know."

After he hung up he was unreasonably pissed off. What the fuck was Freddie getting interested for? Before he had a chance to think about it further, Annie buzzed him on the intercom.

"Dinner's ready," she said.

They had a cook who usually attended to such menial tasks as cooking, but recently Annie had been attending a gourmet cooking class, and now, three nights a week, they were treated to her culinary concoctions.

He went downstairs, sat at the dining-room table and toyed with a plateful of pumpkin ravioli.

"Don't you like it?" she asked, accusingly.

"It's bitter," he replied, pushing it around the plate.

"God, I can never do anything right, can I?"

"You asked for my opinion."

"You're at home now, Nick," she said, angrily. "You're not on show for the fans. You don't have to make a fuss about everything – I'm not waiting on you hand and foot, so don't expect me to."

"Annie, you know what?"

She turned on him, eyes blazing. "What?"

"Aw, shit . . . forget it."

That night he couldn't sleep. He lay in bed imagining Lauren ensconced in the Beverly Hills Hotel. What was she thinking? Was she looking forward to seeing him as much as he was looking forward to seeing her?

Annie came to bed wearing her peach peignoir. It signalled sex.

Christ! Occasionally he did it with his wife. He had to, didn't he? He never would have thought that sex would become a chore, but it was.

The next morning he was up early and out of the house

before Annie awoke. Lauren was going to be testing with him. He didn't want to keep her waiting.

The studio limo picked her up at seven. She wore jeans, sweat-shirt, a baseball cap, no make-up and huge shades.

"Morning, Ms Roberts," her driver greeted her, checking her out in the rear-view mirror. He was young and good-looking, standard Hollywood fare. "It's a clear day today. No smog."

"That's nice," she said.

"Unusual," he said.

Damn, he wanted conversation and she wasn't in the mood. Once she would have humoured him, been polite, chatted all the way to the studio even though she didn't want to. Now she was a different Lauren, no longer into pleasing everyone. She pressed the privacy glass cutting him off mid-sentence.

Pia had wanted to come with her, but she'd said no, this was one trip she had to make by herself. This trip was a test. She was all grown up and she wasn't about to turn to mush when she saw Nick again.

Arriving at the studio she was hustled straight through to make-up. "I have my own ideas," she said to the make-up artist.

"Fine with me," the girl said. "I'll do whatever you want."

"I see this character as tough looking – yet with a vulnerable streak. Smoky eyes, natural eyebrows, not much lipstick."

"Sounds good," the girl said.

Lauren had studied the script on the plane. As usual, the female role was somewhat passive, but if she got the part she had lots of ideas.

"I heard a rumour that Nick Angel is coming in to test with you himself," the girl said, in reverent tones.

Lauren wasn't surprised. She'd known he'd be around. Well, she was prepared. They were both married now – they were even.

"He's a nice guy," the make-up girl volunteered. "His wife's a real pain, though. She doesn't visit the set often, but when she does – oh boy, run for the hills. You'd think she was royalty."

"Is she an actress?" Lauren asked.

"From what I hear she tried to be and never made it."

"Oh," Lauren said. She'd seen pictures of Nick with his wife. She wasn't the woman she'd imagined he'd marry.

I am not tingling with anticipation, she told herself, sternly.

When I see him I will not fall to pieces like I did last time. I'm a different person now. I've finally grown up. It's been a long time.

Yes, Roberts?

Yes.

They met on the set, so there was no time to get personal as they were surrounded by people.

"Hey, congratulations on all your success," Nick said, a polite but friendly stranger. "It's really great to see you again."

"You, too, Nick. You're amazing. I can't believe your career."

He smiled. "I know – it's good, huh?"

She smiled back. "Very good."

He peered at her closely. "Now – let me see – there's something different about you."

She grimaced. "Yeah, wrinkles – I'm older."

"You – *never*."

"Thank you."

The director came over to introduce himself, and ask her if she was comfortable with the scene. She assured him she was.

"I've studied the script. I understand this character."

"Good," said the director, moving off to confer with his lighting cameraman.

"Freddie Leon's very high on you," Nick said, impressed with the way she handled herself. "He thinks you could be big."

"I'm glad I have the opportunity to test for this movie. You know I always loved acting."

He nodded, remembering Betty and their acting class in Bosewell. "This sure takes me back. Remember *Cat on a Hot Tin Roof*?"

She smiled. "How could I ever forget it?"

"You were the actress then," he admitted. "I was the amateur."

"And now it's the other way around."

"Hey, don't knock it – you're just as famous as I am."

She nodded. "It's funny, isn't it?"

"Yeah – Cyndra and I were talking the other night. We decided there must have been something in the water at Bosewell High."

"In that case . . ."

"I know what you're gonna say –" he interrupted, laughing. "So what happened with Stock an' Meg and all the rest of 'em?

501

The scam is this – you had to drink the water, *then* get out of town."

They were both quiet for a moment before she continued the conversation. "Congratulations, Nick," she said. "I haven't seen you since you got married. I understand you have a child."

"Yeah, Lissa – she's a little beauty."

For one painful moment Lauren thought about the baby she'd aborted. Nick's baby. She'd never told him. She'd never told him about what happened between her and his father, either. It was better that way.

The director returned and asked if they were ready.

"Let's do it," Nick said. "Let's make it as good as old times." He looked at her. "Right, Lauren?"

She took a deep breath. "Right, Nick."

He made sure the scene went smoothly, filling her in on camera angles, lighting and the best way to play to the camera. "It's different than working in the theatre," he explained. "You play it down instead of up. The camera catches everything."

He obviously hadn't seen her commercials; she knew exactly what she was doing.

When they played the scene, he gave it to her – wanting her to get the role. They were finished before lunch. "Okay," he said, "I'm buying."

"No, Freddie Leon is," she replied, quickly. "He's sending a car for me."

Nick felt a stab of uncontrollable jealousy. What the fuck was Freddie up to? "Am I invited?" he asked lightly, walking her back to her dressing room.

She shrugged. "I don't know – you'd better ask Freddie."

"Hey – I don't have to ask, he's my agent." He paused for a moment. "You don't *mind* if I come, do you?"

She stopped at the door to her dressing room. "Not at all."

"I'll have someone call Freddie – tell him I'll bring you to the restaurant. Why don't I meet you here in fifteen minutes?"

As soon as he left she rushed to the mirror, staring at her reflection.

Nothing had changed. Absolutely nothing. She was still as hooked as she'd ever been.

Tough luck, Roberts.

Screw you.

Freddie dominated lunch. He was charming, funny and completely unlike himself. They ate at Le Dôme on Sunset, sitting at a round table in the back room. Nick settled back and watched Lauren in action. She was different, he decided. More sophisticated, stylish, and definitely more worldly. But underneath the gloss he knew there was still the same sweet Lauren he'd fallen in love with.

"You know," Freddie said, with his new charming smile. "This lunch was for me to persuade Lauren to become an I.A.A. client. I guess I can't do that with you sitting in on the meeting, Nick."

"You're doing a pretty good job," he replied, determined to stick around.

Lauren sipped a glass of Perrier, well aware of the interaction between the two men. "It's so good to see you again, Nick," she said, as if they were nothing more than polite strangers. "And meeting you, Freddie, is a pleasure."

He wanted to touch her so badly he didn't know how he controlled himself. And he wanted to smash his best friend, Freddie Leon, in the face.

Eventually Freddie left the table to go to the john.

He waited until he was out of sight and leaned across the table. "Can we have dinner tonight?"

She kept her voice even. "I'm planning on taking the late flight back to New York."

"You just got here," he pointed out.

"I know, but I have an important meeting tomorrow morning. Marcella has offered me a deal to start my own cosmetic line."

"Oh, like you're not busy enough?"

She was immediately defensive. "How do you know how busy I am?"

"I read the papers. You're always in the New York columns doing this and that."

"I read the papers, too, Nick," she replied, staring straight at him. "You're always in the paper, screwing this and that."

He laughed. "Nice talk."

"How's your marriage?" she couldn't help asking.

"How's yours?" he countered.

Their eyes met and there was a long moment of silent intimacy.

Freddie bounced back to the table. "Lauren," he said. "I know you're not making any decisions today, but I'll be in New York next week, so why don't we have dinner and talk about it then?"

Why don't we have dinner and talk about it then? Nick couldn't believe what he was hearing. This was Freddie – faithful Freddie. Freddie Leon with a definite hard-on.

"I'd like that," Lauren said. "Do you get to New York often?"

"Only when it's important," Freddie replied, homing in on her.

"Are you taking Diana?" Nick interjected.

Freddie shot him an annoyed look. "No."

"Who's Diana?" Lauren asked.

"Freddie's wife," Nick replied. "Terrific woman. They've got a couple of great kids. You should meet the family."

Freddie continued to glare at him. Lauren looked from one to the other. She knew exactly what was going on and it amused her.

Freddie signed the cheque, and they got up to leave.

"I'll drop Lauren back at her hotel," Freddie said.

"That's okay," Nick said. "I'll take care of her."

"As a matter of fact," Lauren said, "I'm not going to my hotel. I thought I'd stop by Neiman's and do some shopping – I never get time in New York."

"My offices are right there," Freddie said. "Maybe you'd like to come up and meet some of the other agents."

"Not today. Perhaps next time."

"Yeah, stop hustling her, Freddie," Nick said. "She hasn't signed with you yet."

"She will. Won't you, Lauren?"

She smiled her dazzling smile. "I'll have to see."

Lauren walked around Neiman Marcus in a daze. She hadn't seen Nick in seven years, and yet he had this incredible effect on her. She was still the same stupid wreck.

What kind of hold did he have over her?

What kind of a hold did she want him to have?

She sighed. They were both married. It was an impossible situation.

She wandered around the store – tried on a Donna Karan jacket, picked out a couple of Armanis, and charged it all to her American Express. Shopping was not her thing, but it was better than going back to her hotel and sitting there until she had to leave for the airport.

"Hey –"

She turned around, startled. It was Nick. "What are you doing here?" she asked, her heart immediately starting to pound uncontrollably.

"I'm taking my fucking life in my hands," he said.

"What do you mean?"

"I don't travel anywhere without bodyguards. I'll get mobbed in here."

She laughed. "Oh, come on, nobody's taking any notice of you. This is Beverly Hills, they're used to movie stars."

A saleswoman rushed up to him. "Can I have your autograph for my daughter," she gushed. "She loves you. She sees everything you do."

He shot Lauren a triumphant look.

"And you're the Marcella Girl, aren't you?" the woman continued, turning to Lauren. "My daughter loves you, too. Oh, this is so thrilling!"

They both signed the piece of paper she proffered, and then Nick took Lauren's shopping bags and said, "Let's go, we're getting out of here. Walk swiftly and don't make eye contact."

She giggled. "You sound like the CIA."

He took her hand and she found herself beginning to melt.

The valet had his car waiting outside. Nick slid him a twenty.

"Get in, fasten your seatbelt – we're gonna talk whether you like it or not."

"I told you," she protested, knowing it was useless. "I have a plane to catch."

"I'll see that you do."

She got into the passenger seat of his red Ferrari. "I thought a Cadillac was the car of your dreams," she said, remembering how he used to talk about it all the time.

"It was – the dream turned into a nightmare."

"Oh, not so patriotic any more?"

"You could say that." He revved the engine and zoomed off down the street.

"Where are we going?" she asked.

"To the beach. I have a house there."

"Of course you do," she said, dryly.

They didn't talk in the car. He pushed in a Van Morrison tape and concentrated on his driving. She stared straight ahead as they sped down Wilshire on their way to the Pacific Coast Highway.

It took twenty minutes before he made a dangerous left turn

505

into a winding driveway, pulling up outside a shuttered house. "This is my retreat," he said. "The only place I get any privacy."

"How do you know your wife's not here?"

"'Cause she doesn't know about this house. I bought it without her. I needed somewhere that's all mine. A place that's not filled with servants, ringing telephones and people driving me crazy."

"You don't sound too happy," she said, as he helped her from the car.

"Hey – I got a lotta demands in my life, don't you?"

"Yes, but I love every one of them."

He walked her to the front door. "That's because you've turned into a workaholic. Can't pick up a magazine without seeing you."

"Can't go to the movies without seeing you."

They both began to laugh, breaking the tension.

He pulled out a key, opened the massive door and she entered paradise. The house was located on top of a bluff with full-length glass windows overlooking the ocean. Perched on the edge of the grounds was an infinity swimming pool – creating the optical illusion of disappearing into the sea, even though it was hundreds of feet above it.

"This is absolutely breathtaking," she said, as they strolled outside.

He turned her towards him, placing his hands on her shoulders. "You never called me in New York. I sat in that fucking hotel room for five days waiting."

"I would have, if I'd thought we could be together," she found herself saying.

"Why *can't* we be together?" he said, urgently. "Let's cut out the shit. You know as well as I do it's what we both want."

"Nick, be serious. I'm still married, and now you're married too."

"Are you happy, Lauren?" he asked, staring at her.

"No," she replied, getting lost in his green eyes. "But what's that got to do with anything?"

"How about this for a plan," he said. "We could both get divorced."

She shook her head. "You make it sound so simple. Life isn't like that."

"Life's what you make it, Lauren. We've both worked hard, why *can't* we be together?"

"Are you suggesting I go home, say, 'Hey, Oliver, I went

to LA, met this old friend of mine and I've decided to divorce you.' You think he'll accept that? And what about you? What'll you say to your wife? 'Hey – Lauren's back – goodbye.' She's the mother of your child, Nick. You have responsibilities."

He refused to take no for an answer. "If we really wanted to we could work it out."

She shook her head again, trying desperately to stay cool. "I don't know if I want to, Nick. What kind of a life would we have together? You're this big movie star, and I work all the time. We'd never see each other."

"Hey – why are you making it so difficult?"

"I'm not. We're two different people. This isn't Bosewell; we're not kids."

He kissed her, taking her by surprise.

She didn't fight it. They stood quietly on the terrace entwined in each other's arms, their lips pressed closely together.

"I love you," he said very quietly, drawing back. "I always have and I always will. Nothing's gonna change that."

She felt weak. "Don't say it, Nick."

"I have to, because it's the truth."

They began to kiss again. Feebly she attempted to pull away. "I must get back, my plane . . ."

"I don't give a shit about your plane. You're staying here tonight. We'll have a night together neither of us will ever forget."

Oh, yes, that's what I want. That's what I really want. "Nick . . . you don't understand. I can't . . ."

"Hey, Lauren – this is the way it's gonna be," he said, forcefully.

She continued to fight it. "I don't know . . ."

He still wasn't taking no for an answer. "Yeah . . . well . . . I do."

His lips were on hers again and all was lost.

She'd promised herself that after the pregnancy scare with Lorenzo she'd never cheat on Oliver again. But this was her life and she had to live it. Damn the consequences. Nick was right. They deserved one magical night together.

Chapter 77

Nick awoke first. Rolling over he stared at Lauren asleep beside him. Jesus! She was the most perfect, beautiful woman in the world – everything he remembered and more.

He got out of bed, moving quietly so as not to disturb her. He'd known when he'd purchased this house it would come in useful one day. The only person who knew about it was Freddie – he'd arranged the deal and paid for it with money Annie was unaware of.

Christ! Annie. He hadn't phoned her – she'd be freaking out. She'd probably called the police by now and reported him as a missing person. He could just imagine the headlines. *Nick Angel vanishes. Wife inherits everything*. Oh, yes, Annie would love that. She'd finally be the centre of attention. Maybe it would even kick-start her acting career.

He knew he wasn't being fair; it wasn't Annie's fault that she was a pain in the ass. It was just that the guilt of what they'd done in Vegas weighed heavily on all of them.

He padded barefoot and naked into the kitchen. There was nothing in the fridge except champagne and 7-Up. He opened the cupboard and found a can of orange juice. Then he picked up the phone and called home.

Annie answered with a terse, "Yes?"

"It's me."

"Where are you?"

"I'm at a friend's."

Icily, "And what friend is that?"

"Don't question me, Annie," he warned.

"Then don't treat me like a fool. You're with a woman, aren't you?"

"Hey – wherever I am and whoever I'm with, I'm letting

you know I'm okay and I'll be home later."

"Maybe you shouldn't bother coming home."

"Is that a threat, Annie?"

"I don't appreciate being treated like nothing."

"We gotta talk," he said.

"Maybe *I* should have talked a few years ago."

He knew exactly what she meant and it was time they got it out in the open, but not now, not on the telephone. "I'll be home later," he said.

She slammed the phone down.

He took a deep breath. There was no way she was going to ruin his day. Swigging orange juice from the can he realized it was the first morning in a long time he hadn't wanted to add vodka to it.

Back in the bedroom Lauren was still asleep. He sat on the bed and stared at her. She was naked, covered only by a thin silk sheet. Her skin was smooth and white and very soft. He ran his fingers across the tips of her breasts. She sighed and made little groaning noises. Slowly she opened her eyes. "I thought this was all a dream," she murmured, stretching luxuriously.

"We actually got to spend the night together," he said. "First time we did that."

She sat up, hugging the sheet to her bosom, "Oh, God! I missed my plane."

"I love you," he said, stroking her arm.

She tried to sound firm. "Nick, this is hopeless."

"What's hopeless? I'll speak to Annie, you'll talk to Oliver. We'll work this out, Lauren, after all we've waited long enough."

She sighed. "You make it all sound so easy."

"It *can* be easy, if it's what we both want."

"I'm not so sure."

"You're wrong."

"It's more complicated than you think, Nick. We're not two unknown people. The press will be after us, watching our every move. Everything we do will be public knowledge."

"Hey – so what else is new?"

"It's not just you – now you have a child to consider. What about her?"

"Believe me, Lauren, we'll work it out."

She sighed again, completely hooked – he had some kind of hypnotic power over her. She was too weak to resist, and what's

509

more, she didn't want to. His love embraced her and she wanted more.

"If you say so," she murmured.

"I say so," he said, cradling her in his arms and kissing her very, very slowly. "I want you to know that last night was the most incredible night of my life. And you are the most incredible woman."

"Last night I should have been on a plane," she said, ruefully.

"But you weren't. You were in bed with me where you belong – and you have to admit it was the greatest."

Why was it that every time she was with him her heart started to race and her body tingled? Yes, he was right, it was the greatest and she couldn't deny it. Together they had something very special.

They continued to kiss, slowly at first, but more heatedly as his hands began to explore her body.

She craved his touch. He electrified her. Sex with Lorenzo had been pleasurable. Sex with Nick was beyond anything she'd ever known. He took her to new heights and then back again.

Eventually they made love fast and passionately. He teased her – taking her almost there and then making her wait until she begged for more.

"Tell me what I want to hear," he said, urgently. "Tell me – I want to hear you say it."

She couldn't stop herself. "I love you, Nick – I always have."

It was noon before they even thought about getting dressed.

"I've got to go," she said, reaching for her clothes.

"Why?"

"Because I have to get back."

"Do you want to?"

She touched his chin. "Silly question."

Before he could convince her not to she called the airline and booked another flight.

"We'll stop by your hotel, pick up your bags and I'll drive you to the airport," he said. "Maybe I should come with you."

"Oh – you'll sit there while I tell Oliver? That'll be very helpful."

"You're right," he agreed. "I'll take care of things here, and we'll talk tomorrow. It won't be like last time."

"No?"

"We're going to be together."

"Do you think so?"

He bent to kiss her again. "I *know* so."

She flew back to New York filled with confusion. The last forty-eight hours seemed like a dream. She'd come out to California so full of confidence, knowing she could handle any situation, especially Nick Angel.

But no, it was not to be. Once she was with him all her resolve failed, and having spent the night in his arms she knew there was no going back. It was time to tell Oliver their marriage was over. And when she was free, if Nick was able to extract himself from his marriage, they would be together. It was truly their destiny.

Halfway to New York she realized she hadn't called anyone to tell them she was arriving a day late. Knowing Oliver he was too busy to notice, but Lorenzo was probably furious she'd missed their meeting. She'd called her driver from L.A.X. and told him to be at the airport. Her plan was to go straight to the office, reschedule her meeting with Lorenzo and then tell Oliver they had to talk.

It was raining in New York, the skies were black and heavy with thunder.

"Pia Liberty would like you to phone her as soon as you arrive," her driver informed her.

She picked up the car phone. "Hi, Pia, I'm back."

Pia sounded distraught. "Oh, Lauren, thank God! I've been trying to reach you."

"What's the matter?" she asked, anxiously.

"It's Oliver. Last night he had a massive heart attack."

"Oh, no!"

"Come straight to the hospital, Lauren. Come quickly."

"As far as I'm concerned," Freddie Leon said, "she's got the part. You want her, don't you?"

"Ask a stupid question," said Nick.

"The studio people ran her test early this morning – they love her. In fact they're ready to make an offer." He paused. "And guess what?"

"What?"

Freddie looked pleased with himself. "I'll negotiate her deal."

Nick reached for a cigarette. "I've never seen you so interested in a woman."

"Me? Interested?" Freddie said casually. "I'm a happily married man."

"Yeah, yeah, just like all the rest of 'em."

"What is it between you and her, Nick?" Freddie asked, curiously. "I sense there's more to this."

"I told you," Nick replied, speaking slowly. "We're old friends."

"So if I *was* interested . . ."

"Forget it," he said, sharply.

Freddie nodded knowingly. "That's what I thought."

Nick had stopped by to see Freddie on his way home because he wasn't that anxious to face Annie. He had a feeling he should talk to his lawyer first, fill him in on all the facts. But no, surely Annie wasn't going to come up with the same old threat? And if she did – would they ever find the body in the desert? It must have decomposed by now, nobody would be able to identify the man. And how could they pin it on him anyway?

When he finally got back to the house the housekeeper handed him a note from Annie.

"Mrs Angel and Lissa have gone away for a few days," the woman informed him.

"Where to?" he asked, aggravated.

"Mrs Angel didn't say," the housekeeper replied.

He was pissed. Annie had known he wanted to talk to her, she'd done this purposely. And how dare she take Lissa without telling him where they were going.

Angrily he walked into his study, threw himself into the leather chair behind his desk and ripped open her letter.

Dear Nick,

I refuse to be humiliated in this fashion. It is common knowledge in Hollywood that you sleep with whores. I do not intend to be made a laughing stock. If your behaviour continues, I will take Lissa and you will never see your child again.

You should also remember the information I have. Information that has been a burden for me to keep all these years and would be a great relief for me to reveal to the authorities.

I like being Mrs Angel and I plan to remain Mrs Angel, so I suggest that if you continue to whore around you are more discreet. Remember what is at stake.

Your loving wife,
Annie

He read the letter twice and couldn't believe it. Bitch! Blackmailing bitch! She wasn't going to quit until they were both dead.

He picked up the phone and called his lawyer. "Kirk, I need to see you. Can you drop by the house this afternoon?"

Kirk Hillson – along with Freddie Leon – was one of the Hollywood power elite. As a top lawyer he had plenty of clout and knew all of the right people in all the right places. Nick had a feeling Annie was not going to be easy to get rid of – and he needed Kirk's full support – which meant there could be no secrets. It was about time he got the Vegas thing off his mind – all he'd done was bury a body – he hadn't murdered anyone for Christ's sake. The way Annie carried on you'd have thought he'd pulled the fucking trigger.

He didn't mind paying Annie a bundle – after all, he could certainly afford it. But there was no way he was allowing her to give him a hard time when it came to seeing Lissa. His daughter, along with Lauren, was one of the most precious things in his life; he'd fight for her all the way.

When Kirk arrived he told him the whole story – omitting Cyndra's name. It wasn't fair to involve her until he checked it with her first.

Kirk, a sleek, well-preserved man with startling horse teeth, was non-committal. "It makes you an accessory," he remarked, sipping a glass of unchilled Evian.

"I know," Nick agreed. "Why do you think I've stuck with Annie all these years?"

"On the other hand, maybe she imagined the whole thing," Kirk said, getting up and walking to the window.

"What do you mean?"

"Well – what's she going to prove? Does she know where you buried the body? Do *you* know?"

"I kinda remember," Nick said, hesitantly. "I think I know where I drove to – I'm not sure."

"By this time the evidence will be gone, believe me."

"Yeah, but is it worth taking a risk?"

Kirk glanced at his Rolex – he was late for a golf game. "It's one of those things. You're Nick Angel – they won't dare touch you."

"Then I want out," Nick said, firmly.

"Have you met someone else?" Kirk enquired.

"There is someone else," Nick explained. "She's been in my

life a long time – it's just that we've never gotten together before now."

"Is she worth it?"

"She's worth anything it'll cost me."

"It would be better if there wasn't somebody else," Kirk said, admiring his manicure. "You know what they say about a woman scorned?"

"Annie won't be scorned. She doesn't give a shit about me, anyway. All she cares about is the money and status. She's pissed my career took off the way it did and she never made it."

"I've heard that story a hundred times," said Kirk. "But whatever you say she'll try to hurt you."

"I want out," Nick repeated. "It's time."

"Does she have a lawyer?" Kirk asked.

"You're her lawyer."

"I can't represent both of you. Perhaps I should recommend someone. By the way, have you told Freddie?"

"Not yet."

"You should bring him in on this."

"You mean tell him about Vegas?"

"Not at this stage. But he should know you're planning to divorce Annie."

"I'll tell him."

"Excellent." Kirk headed for the door. "I don't foresee any problems. If you're prepared to give her ninety-nine per cent of your money we'll be fine."

Nick laughed. "Jeez, lawyer's humour – just what I need."

Kirk smiled. "It'll cost you, so I hope your freedom's worth it."

"You know something, Kirk? I'd pay her every dime I had if I could be free tomorrow."

And he meant it. Being with Lauren was the most important thing in his life. He couldn't wait.

Chapter 78

Aretha Mae had been bedridden for several weeks. Cyndra had nurses there day and night to look after her. The doctor had recently informed her that Aretha Mae was suffering from bronchial pneumonia and should really be in the hospital.

"No hospitals," she said, firmly. "I want her at home where I can watch her."

"She'd get better care in the hospital," the doctor pointed out.

"No," Cyndra replied, remembering what had happened to Luke. "My mother stays here."

Marik tried to persuade her. "C'mon, baby, let them take her to the hospital."

"No," Cyndra said, flatly. "Those places kill people."

"She's dying anyway," Marik said.

"Oh, that's encouraging."

But she knew he spoke the truth. Aretha Mae did not have long to go.

Every evening at six o'clock she went into her mother's room and sat with her. She held her hand, the frail little hand that had once cooked greasy fries and bacon, slapped her kids, brought them up and allowed them to survive.

"How you doin', Mama?" she whispered, leaning in close.

Aretha Mae stared at her. "I soon be with Luke," she said. "Soon be happy."

"Mama – I have something to ask you," Cyndra said, speaking softly.

"Yes?"

"You have to be very truthful with me. You must promise."

"Tell me, girl, what is it?"

"Who's my real father?"

Aretha Mae looked up at her with sunken eyes and was silent

515

for a long while. "Benjamin Browning – he be your father," she said at last.

Cyndra nodded. She'd known it was true the first time Aretha Mae had told her, but she'd needed to hear it again. "Is there any proof?" she asked.

Aretha Mae nodded, weakly. "There's a letter in the bank in Bosewell. You'll get it when I die."

"You're not gonna die, Mama."

"I don't mind dying, girl. I be with Jesus, an' my sweet baby Luke."

"No, Mama, you are *not* going to die," Cyndra repeated fiercely.

Aretha Mae smiled mysteriously. "I always knew you'd survive, girl. I was always sure."

Later that night Cyndra sat with Marik and talked about her past in a way she never had before. He listened quietly while she told him about Benjamin Browning, the rape, the abortion, and all the other bad things that had happened to her.

"Oh, baby, baby, I had no idea," he said, holding her tight.

"Why should you?" she replied. "It's my pain – I can handle it."

"That Benjamin Browning must be one bad son-of-a-bitch,' Marik said. "We could have somebody sent down there who'd fix him good."

"No," she said, sharply. "Benjamin will pay for his sins, just like Mama would want him to. But it'll be my way."

The next day she signed a contract to star in her own television show. She took the contract home and proudly waved it in front of Aretha Mae. "You see, Mama, you see? I'm gonna be on television all over the country. Everybody will watch me. Everybody in Bosewell. What do you think of that?"

Aretha Mae smiled a sad little smile and managed to nod her head. "You be a star, girl, you did real good."

And then she shut her eyes and died peacefully.

Cyndra threw herself on her mother's body and started sobbing. The nurse called for Marik. He rushed to the room, took Cyndra in his arms and comforted her.

"I want you to be my wife, baby," he crooned. "It's time you had somebody looking after you."

"We'll see," she said, between sobs. "We'll see."

Nick couldn't believe she was doing it to him again. Lauren had been gone for two days, and although he'd left countless messages on her private answering machine she still had not returned his calls. What was it with her? She'd done the same thing to him in New York when he'd sat in his hotel room waiting for five days. This time he wasn't going to stand for it.

He contacted a girl who worked at I.A.A. in New York and told her to go to Lauren's office.

"Make sure she calls me immediately," he said. "And don't leave until you see her. I'll be waiting by the phone."

The girl did as he asked and then called him in Los Angeles. "I'm sorry, Mr Angel, Ms Roberts is at the hospital."

"What's wrong?" he asked, panicking.

"Her husband had a heart attack."

"A heart attack?" he repeated, blankly.

"Yes, I spoke to her personal assistant and she said she'd try to get a message to Ms Roberts that you're trying to reach her."

He put the phone down and shook his head. Had Lauren told her husband and then he'd promptly had a heart attack? Was it Oliver's way of hanging on? Jesus, this was not good.

Freddie called and said, "You're not going to believe this."

"What?"

"Lauren Roberts turned us down. According to Samm, her New York agent, she doesn't want to do the part."

"Why not?"

"Her husband's in hospital."

"He's going to be all right, isn't he?" Nick asked, flatly.

"Nobody knows. Apparently she's at his bedside day and night."

It was bizarre. Fate brought them together every so often, and fate split them apart. If he knew anything about Lauren at all, he was certain she would not leave Oliver while he was sick.

"Any suggestions?" Freddie asked.

"About what?"

"Your leading lady."

"Give it to Carlysle. She wants it."

"I don't think the studio'll go for Carlysle Mann – she's old news."

"She's not even thirty for crissakes – she's right for the part. Tell 'em I want her, that should do it."

"Are you sure?"

"Very sure."

And he was. Carlysle Mann was exactly what he needed to

get him through the next few months. Because Lauren was not going to be around. Of that he was sure.

Oliver smiled, weakly. "Somebody should have told me I was overdoing it."

"They did. Constantly," Lauren replied, fussing around his hospital bed.

"They did?" Oliver asked, innocently.

"Yes. *I* told you, Howard, Pia. We all did. Non-stop work and no play makes Oliver a candidate for a very big heart attack."

"It wasn't that big."

"With a pacemaker anything's big."

A nurse entered the room carrying more flowers. The room already resembled a flower shop.

"I'll slow down. I promise."

Lauren nodded. "If you wish to stay around I suggest you do."

He held out his hand. "Come over here, my beautiful neglected wife."

Inexplicably her eyes filled with tears. She was so relieved he was alive. According to Pia, if their butler hadn't been working late when Oliver collapsed, he would not have survived.

While your husband was almost dying, Roberts, you were in LA in bed with Nick Angel. Proud of yourself?

I didn't want this to happen.

Well, it did, and you're lucky he's still here.

Every time she cheated on him something bad happened. First the false pregnancy – now this. It was a sign. She and Nick were not meant to be.

He squeezed her hand and gazed helplessly into her eyes. "I'm making plans," he said. "We'll go to Rome and Venice. We'll travel together. I don't know what I'd do without you, my darling. I'd be lost."

He was her husband and she was fond of him, but if she were to tell the truth he was more like a father figure than a husband. He'd never made love to her. In fact, for the last four years they'd had no physical contact at all.

Oliver was almost seventy. She was thirty. Oh God! She was totally and absolutely trapped.

"Don't worry, Oliver," she said. "I'm here. I always will be."

Later that night she called Nick.

"I heard," he said.

"I don't know what to say."

"You don't have to say anything, I understand."

"I can't tell him now – not while he's sick. Maybe in a few months when he gets better."

"Lauren, you don't have to explain to me."

"But I do. This time I didn't want to leave you hanging."

"I'll always be hanging."

"Don't make me cry, Nick."

"Look, you must do what you have to do. I'm divorcing Annie whatever happens. I don't intend to stay in a meaningless relationship."

"Yes, well, your wife's not lying in a hospital bed."

"Can we at least speak?"

"It's not a good idea."

"You're killing me, Lauren, you really are. You come into my life every so often, screw me up, and vanish. You're fucking killing me."

"Nick, if it means anything at all, I love you. I truly love you, but I can't leave this man, not now."

"When you're free, call me," he said. "I hope I'll still be waiting."

Nick attended Aretha Mae's funeral with Cyndra. She was buried at Forest Lawn, and there was a good turn-out of people showing their respect for Cyndra.

"Actually, Nick," she told him, "they're showing their respect for my stardom, but what do I care?"

"Are you sure she wants to be buried here?" he asked. "Wouldn't you be better off sending her body back to Bosewell?"

"I thought about it," she said. "But then I remembered she had nothing but bad times there. She'll rest in peace here."

A few weeks later she informed him she was going to visit Bosewell.

"What do you want to do that for?" he argued.

"Marik's coming with me," she said. "I have people to confront before I can be at peace with myself."

"Are you crazy?" he said, trying to talk her out of it. "You're a big star now. If the tabloids get hold of your story you'll be sorry."

"I don't care," she said, stubbornly. "It's something I have to do."

He realized her intentions. "You're after Browning, aren't you?"

She nodded.

"How does Marik feel about this?"

"He'll go along with me."

"And Gordon? Have you told him?"

"No," she said, irritably. "I don't have to tell him. He's not my father confessor."

"Maybe you should listen to his advice."

"I know what his advice will be. He'll tell me not to go, just like you. But some things are unavoidable."

"Well, lots of luck, Cyndra. You know I mean it."

"Want to come with me, Nick?"

"You've *gotta* be kidding. I wouldn't go back there for all the money in the world."

That afternoon Annie arrived home. Lissa rushed into the house first, raced up to him and threw herself into his arms.

"Daddy! Daddy! I missed you *sooo* much!"

"I missed you, too, little kid," he said, hugging her tightly.

"Gotta go pee!" she giggled, wriggling out of his arms and running off.

Annie marched in with a sour face.

"Where the fuck have you been?" he demanded.

"With friends," she said coldly, going to the bar and pouring herself a drink.

He followed her. "What friends?"

"The same friends you were with. How do you like it when *I* vanish?"

"Don't ever take off with my kid," he said, sharply. "Don't ever do that to me, Annie, because you'll regret it."

She arched her eyebrows. "*I'll* regret it?"

"I want a divorce," he said.

"No," she replied, sipping straight gin.

"It's too late. I've already talked to my lawyer. I want out of this marriage. Neither of us are happy. It's not good for Lissa – all she ever sees us do is fight."

"Didn't you read my note, Nick? I *like* being Mrs Angel. There's no way I'm letting you go."

"You have no choice, Annie."

"Oh, but I do. You seem to forget what I know."

"I'm not forgetting anything. Kirk will recommend a lawyer for you. I'll be fair with you, but it's over."

"Oh, yes," she said, spitefully. "It'll *really* be over when I tell everything I know."

"You know something, Annie?" he said, wearily. "You've held

this over me for too many years now – I don't give a shit what you do or who you tell. I'm through – get it into your fucking head. I'm through."

"You'll regret it. I'll take Lissa and you'll never see her again," she said, playing her trump card.

"Oh no, that's where you're wrong," he said, curtly.

"Your career will be over, Nick."

"You can't touch me, Annie."

She smiled, contemptuously. "We'll see who's right."

Chapter 79

Oliver's recovery was slow, but true to his word he began to take it much easier. This affected Lauren because she was used to getting on with her own career and not worrying about Oliver being lonely or wondering where she was. Now he demanded her attention.

She informed Lorenzo she did not wish to proceed with the cosmetic line at this particular time.

Lorenzo was upset. "What will you do? Stay at home and look after an old man?"

"I don't think it's any of your business."

"You cannot waste your life like this, Lauren," he said, genuinely concerned. "You are at the peak of your career, you can achieve anything."

"I'm taking some time," she said, quietly. "I have to look after Oliver. He needs me."

Samm was equally outraged. "You fly to Hollywood, test for a role in a Nick Angel movie, get the part – and then tell me you can't do it. I don't believe this!"

"Samm, sometimes life comes before fantasy. Making a movie is fantasy, being with my husband is real life. I'm looking after him until he's better."

Samm shook her head, too perplexed to argue.

"And another thing," Lauren added. "No more modelling assignments until I feel Oliver is back on his feet."

"You have your commitment to Marcella," Samm pointed out.

"I'll keep that commitment. Right now put everything else on hold."

As soon as Oliver was out of the hospital she accompanied him to their house in the Hamptons where they spent several weeks sitting around doing nothing. She bought him piles of magazines and books, classical tapes and videos.

"You know, I rather like doing nothing," Oliver confessed. "Especially with you beside me."

She smiled, wanly. "I thought you might."

"We've spent so little time together over the last few years. I'm going to make it up to you, Lauren, you'll see."

She tried not to think about Nick. It was quite obvious their relationship was not to be, and Oliver's heart attack was God's way of warning her. She'd been very blessed. Having Nick was not part of the deal.

When Oliver was feeling better she booked them on a long cruise and they took off for several months.

She'd thought about phoning Nick before she left, but then decided against it. They both had their lives to lead. They had to do it separately.

"C'mon, stud – fuck me!" Carlysle urged, in a feverish voice. "C'mon, Nick, fuck me good."

She was unbelievable. What the hell did she *think* he was doing?

"Hey – we're already rocking the trailer back and forth," he pointed out.

She laughed hysterically. "What do you care? You think the crew don't know what we do in here all the time? You and me, Nick Angel, we're a pair – right?"

"Yeah, right," he said, giving it to her just the way she liked.

She caught her breath. "Mmm . . . that's nice. We should've gotten together a long time ago."

"We did get together a long time ago," he panted.

"No, I mean permanently. Like married."

He started to laugh, only Carlysle managed to fuck and carry on a conversation at the same time. "You want to get married?"

"I've tried it twice," she gasped. "You could be third time lucky."

Oh God, he was almost there. "Did you say lucky?"

"Hmm . . ." She let out a deep groan. "Don't forget I knew you when, and I *screwed* you when. All these little girls running after you now – they want you because you're Nick Angel. I had you when you were nothing. Remember?"

"Yeah, I remember," he said, thinking about the apartment in New York and the way she'd greeted him in nothing but a bath towel.

"Think about it, Nick," she said, speaking very fast. "You're getting divorced – we'd be good together. And we wouldn't have to worry about that whole boring faithful thing. I could bring girls home for you whenever you wanted. You know how you love threesomes."

He groped for a nearby bottle of vodka taking a healthy swig.

"Shouldn't drink when you're working," Carlysle admonished. "Especially when you're fucking."

She was right and he knew it.

One final thrust and he climaxed.

Carlysle joined him, letting out a blood-curdling scream.

Someone hammered on the trailer door.

"God!" exclaimed Carlysle, struggling into a sitting position. "You'd think they'd be used to us by now." Giggling, she yelled out, "Who is it?"

"You're wanted on the set, Ms Mann. Is Mr Angel there?"

"Haven't seen him," she yelled back, pulling on her panties. "Try his trailer."

He got up and zipped up his pants. Carlysle made him feel like a teenager. Dirty sex on the floor. Getting it on anywhere they could. Getting it on anywhere that would make him forget Lauren.

He took another swig of vodka from the bottle. Carlysle wagged a finger at him.

"Don't sweat it," he said. "It works for the part."

"Okay, okay."

He left her trailer and returned to his.

"Your lawyer called," said his personal assistant.

"Anything interesting?" he asked.

"Yes, he left a message for you to call him. Something about Las Vegas."

Las Vegas. So Annie was finally making her play. They'd been separated for a couple of months. He'd become a weekend father, seeing Lissa on Saturdays and Sundays, taking her on jaunts to Universal, Disneyland and the movies – always accompanied by his bodyguards. He didn't like it.

At least Annie hadn't gone through with her threat to keep Lissa from him. But still . . . being a weekend father did not cut it.

Grabbing the portable phone, he waved his assistant out of the trailer and called Kirk. "What's going on?" he asked.

"I don't want to discuss it on the phone," Kirk replied. "How about a drink later?"

"Come by the set. I don't know what time we'll be through tonight. Could be shooting late."

Kirk sighed. "I don't do sets, Nick."

"For me you'll do it," he said, persuasively.

"All right, have your secretary call my secretary with the address. And I hope the location is in Beverly Hills because my Rolls doesn't leave the vicinity."

"C'mon, Kirk, you're such an old pussy. We're shooting downtown – risk it."

"No, Nick, call me when you get back to your house. I don't do downtown."

"I'll be tired when I get home."

"Do you want to hear what Annie is planning or don't you?"

"Okay, okay, I'll call you."

He didn't need to hear what she had planned. He already knew. She was going to screw him, and she was going to screw him good.

Cyndra arrived in Bosewell in a blaze of glory. She did it the way she'd always wanted to – in a huge limo, followed by two back-up limos containing her entourage. She wore a red fox coat, wild extensions in her long dark hair, and a glamorous gown. The town of Bosewell wished to present her with the keys to the city at a special luncheon ceremony. The prodigal daughter was returning a huge star.

A TV crew followed her, recording her visit to be made into a television special. Small-town girl made good. Big, big star. What could be better?

Returning with Nick seven years earlier had been a small happening. Now she was coming back as a mega-star.

Marik was by her side – along with two publicity people from the record company, a producer from her new television show, her personal make-up artist, her hairdresser, and her clothes co-ordinator. Plus the television crew.

They all stayed in the big Hilton in Ripley and made the cavalcade limousine journey to Bosewell on Saturday morning.

They were escorted into town by the Bosewell police and taken straight to the Town Hall for a reception in her honour.

The town turned out in force. Cyndra looked around as she was led inside and recognized many of the faces. Nobody had given two cents about her welfare when she'd lived in Bosewell. Now they were fawning all over her – touching and grabbing – telling her how wonderful she was and how they were so proud of her and how they'd always known she could do it. Well, fuck 'em. Let 'em weep.

A dark woman wearing too much eye make-up and a tight orange dress grabbed her arm. "Hi, Cyndra, remember me?"

"Dawn," she said, remembering immediately.

Dawn Kovak beamed. "What a memory! We were at school together."

"We sure were," Cyndra said, recalling that Dawn had been one of the few people who'd talked to her. "Still here, huh? I thought you'd have gotten out long ago."

Dawn waved her hand, flashing a sizeable diamond ring. "I stayed," she said. "And last year I married Benjamin Browning." She beamed, triumphantly. "His wife died a few years ago, so now *I'm* Mrs Browning. Ain't that a kick? Now everyone really has to kiss my ass."

"*You're* Mrs Browning?" Cyndra said, barely concealing her surprise. "*You* married Benjamin?"

"Yeah," Dawn nodded, happily. "You can imagine the scandal. Not much goes on here, but when I bagged him, boy, was there an uproar! Stock went nuts – couldn't accept it. Ben and me – we hadda throw him an' his wife outta the house. She's such a pain anyway."

The crowds were pushing and shoving. Marik attempted to hustle her along.

"I'm sorry, Dawn, I can't talk now," she said.

"I'll see you later," Dawn said, moving off into the crowd.

There were so many people and they all wanted a piece of her. One by one they came up to her saying things like – "You remember me?" "What fun we had in school." "It's *so* good to see you again!"

Some phoney group. If she wasn't Cyndra, big singing star, they wouldn't even remember her name.

So Dawn Kovak, the school tramp, had bagged the richest man in town. In fact, Dawn had bagged her daddy. Well, they were all in for a big shock.

She saw Stock fighting his way through the crowds to get near her. Stock, once the handsome football hero, was now thirty pounds overweight with heavy jowls and a puffy red face. An overweight Meg clung to his side.

The TV crew captured every moment as they finally fought their way over to her.

"I always knew you'd be a star," Meg breathed, excitedly. "When you visited a few years back I said to Stock – 'She's going to be such a big star.' I love your records. You know, we were planning on coming out to Los Angeles with the children for a vacation. What do you think? We'd adore to see your house."

Stock eyeballed her with lecherous eyes. He'd been one of the worst offenders at school, calling her dark meat and other offensive names. She wondered how he was going to take the fact that she was his half-sister.

"Is your daddy around?" she asked him.

"You heard the news?" Stock said, scowling. "He married Dawn. He's damn senile."

"It's shocking," Meg added, in a hoarse whisper. "She only married him for his money. But we're seeing a lawyer. We're not going to let him change his Will. Stock's entitled to everything."

Cyndra smiled. *That's what you think.*

"How long we gotta stay here, baby?" Marik asked. "I'm getting depressed."

"Just long enough for me to attend the lunch," she assured him. "Then they'll hand me the keys to the city, an' we're on our way."

"I still don't understand why you wanted to do this," he grumbled. "This town treated you badly. Why *did* you want to come back?"

"You'll see," she said, smiling sweetly.

She had not revealed her plans to Marik, but they were all in place. She knew exactly what she was going to do.

They were finally seated. The lunch was long and boring. People got up and made little speeches about what an excellent student she'd been, how they'd all known she would do so well, even the school principal spoke glowingly of her.

Eventually it was time for the presentation. The Chief of Police stood up, made a short speech and handed her the keys to Bosewell. A round of applause rippled around the room.

She smiled and got to her feet.

"A long time ago this town was my home," she said, speaking clearly. "I lived in the trailer park. Nobody took much notice of any of us then, but we just about survived. My mother worked as a maid. In fact she worked for the illustrious Browning family who I'm sure you all know." She shot a vindictive glance at Benjamin, sitting with his new wife. "Oh, the Browning family was very good to my mother. They used to give her their cast off clothes and stale food."

A buzz echoed around the room.

"And when I was a little girl," Cyndra continued, "my mother took me with her to their house. It was always fun at their house. Well, let me put it this way – I was too little to understand what fun was all about – but I think Mr Browning had a good time. He used to come into that back room when I was a little girl and pat me on my cute ass, and run his hand up my panties, and sometimes he even lifted my dress so he could *really* get a good feel."

A murmur of consternation from the crowd.

Cyndra checked to see that the TV cameras were recording everything. They were.

"Yes," she continued. "That filthy bastard abused me good when I was a child. And then when I was a young girl, he raped me." She paused for effect. "I was sixteen and a virgin. His wife was out shopping at the time, and his spoilt bigoted son was at school, screwing all the girls. Mr Browning raped me, and called me every foul name he could think of. I had to go to Kansas to get an abortion. Before my mother died she told me the truth. When she first went to work for the Brownings she was a young, innocent girl. Benjamin Browning raped her too. And you want to hear the twist to this lovely American folk story? I'm his daughter. *I'm* Benjamin Browning's daughter. And I have a letter to prove it."

The room erupted.

"Oh, baby, baby, when you do it, you really do it," muttered Marik. "Let's get the hell outta here, and fast."

Cyndra refused to be stopped; she kept right on going. "I've come back to town," she said, in a loud clear voice, "because I know there's nothing you all love better than a good old American success story. And I thought you'd enjoy hearing the truth."

Cyndra's story made every TV news programme in America, and she was thrilled. "I *had* to bring it out into the open," she explained to Marik. "I needed to. It was my life and he tried to ruin it. Now I've ruined his. I'm a survivor, but there's lots of kids out there who'll never survive – because their fathers or uncles or somebody else is abusing them every day. This is something we shouldn't hide. I refuse to be ashamed any more."

"Right on, baby," Marik said. "I'm with you all the way."

Marik had supported her royally. On the way back to LA she'd made him stop in Ripley and, with her two security guards, they'd searched for Harlan and kidnapped him just as she'd sworn to do. They'd found him in a bar dressed in tattered clothes and drugged out of his mind. He hadn't recognized her at first, but when he had he'd broken down in tears and allowed himself to be taken without a fight. He was such a pathetic sight. She'd vowed there and then that she'd look after him and help him make a decent life for himself. He was her brother and she loved him.

Back in LA, she'd put him into a private clinic to break him of his habit, visiting him every few days.

Three weeks after getting back she and Marik were married in a lavish ceremony in Beverly Hills.

She'd long forgotten about Reece Webster. As far as she was concerned he was dead.

Chapter 80

"She wants five million dollars in a bank in Switzerland. This demand is separate from the divorce settlement."

"Shit!" Nick exclaimed.

"I know," Kirk agreed. "Apparently it's the price of her silence." He paused. "Is it worth it or do you wish to take a risk?"

"I don't know," Nick said, pacing up and down. "You tell me."

"You're a big star. You'll make a lot more movies. In the long run five million dollars won't mean that much to you. My advice is to pay it."

"Jesus – she's getting half my money as it is, and she wants another five million bucks on top of it. How greedy can you get?"

"I've seen worse," Kirk said. "In Hollywood it's often this way. When the husband is famous and the wife isn't, there's always resentment. Usually the wife came to Hollywood to be an actress. Instead she marries a famous man, and has the compensation of being a wife with clout. When that clout is taken away she wants revenge – usually the revenge is financial."

"And what about Lissa?" Nick said. "Can I spend as much time as I like with her? I don't want to have to ask permission to see her. I refuse to be a weekend father. Oh, yeah – and when I'm not working I'd like her to be able to come and live with me."

"If you're amicable to the agreement I'm sure we can work it out."

"Do I have the money?"

"I've spoken to your business manager; right now it's tied up in bonds, but he can make arrangements. Yes, you have it, Nick. You're doing pretty damn good."

"Okay," he said. "If this is what it takes to get my freedom."

"Good," Kirk said. "I'll have the papers drawn up."

"Fast, Kirk, fast."

As soon as Kirk left he called Carlysle. "I'm lonely," he said.

"Naughty boy, I just left you. We did it three times today in the trailer – what more do you want?"

"Come over. Bring a friend."

She pretended to be insulted. "I'm not a hooker, you know."

"What's the matter, Carlysle, you getting old?"

These were the dreaded words for any actress. "I'll be there," she said. "Who do you fancy?"

"Remember that Indonesian friend of yours? Is she still around?"

"No, she's in New York. But there's this girl I met on the set the other day – she's an extra. Great bod. I'll see if I can contact her."

She turned up an hour later with Honey, a seventeen-year-old nymphet. Honey had huge eyes, a delectable mouth, an unbelievable body and she was a fan.

"I can't believe I'm here with Nick Angel," she sighed, gazing around his house in awe.

"You won't be unless you shut up," Carlysle said, sharply. "Don't talk, enjoy. That's the way he likes it."

He got through half a bottle of Scotch and still managed to make love to them both. Honey was one of the most obliging girls he'd ever come across. Anything he wanted she did.

In the end Carlysle got jealous; she could see he was really getting off on Honey and she didn't like it.

"Don't forget your promise," she whispered, as they left.

"What promise?" he slurred, squinting at her.

"After your divorce – you and me – we'll be together."

He might be drunk, but he wasn't that far gone. "I never said that."

"Oh, yes, you did."

"Oh, no, I didn't."

When they finally left he staggered up to bed and got two hours sleep before his early call.

He got through the week, and on Friday night he stayed sober, preparing for his Saturday visit with Lissa.

He picked her up early in the morning.

"Where are we going today, Daddy?" she asked.

"Wherever you want, sweetheart."

He took her to the toy store and out to lunch. But even with his ever watchful bodyguards it was impossible. Everywhere he went people stopped him, requesting autographs, wanting to take his photograph, telling him how much they loved him. There was no privacy.

Lissa was upset. "I don't like it, Daddy," she said, beginning to cry. "Why can't people leave you alone?"

"Hey, kid – my sentiments exactly."

Eventually they went back to his house and Lissa settled in front of the television watching a video of *The Sound of Music* for the hundredth time. "I like this movie, Daddy," she said, cheering up. "It's nice."

He didn't take Lissa home when he was supposed to.

A furious Annie called up. "Where is she?"

"She wants to stay here tonight," he said.

"She can't," Annie replied.

"What are you going to do about it?"

"I'll get a court order."

"You won't get a court order until Monday."

"You'd better send her home, Nick. I'm warning you."

"Stop threatening me, Annie. It's over."

He went into the kitchen and told the cook to make Lissa a hamburger and a milkshake. Then he sat beside her and watched the film.

An hour later a furious Annie was at his door. She barged into the house. "Lissa, come with me," she said, her tone brooking no argument.

"No, my Daddy says I can stay here tonight," Lissa said defiantly, curling up on the couch.

"You see," Nick shrugged. "She *wants* to stay here. There's nothing you can do."

Annie turned on him. "You son-of-a-bitch."

He stood up. "Don't use language like that in front of Lissa. And don't let's fight in front her either."

Annie's lip curled. "I can't imagine why I ever married you. You're nothing but a piece of shit."

"Oh, and I suppose you're Mother Theresa."

Annie went up to Lissa and grabbed her by the arm, yanking her off the couch. "You're coming home with me."

Lissa's eyes filled with tears. "Daddy! Daddy! You said I could stay."

Annie was in a rage. "You're coming with me, you little bitch!"

Nick tried to stop her. "Don't talk to her like that, Annie."

"I'll do what the fuck I want. I don't have to listen to you, I *hate* you." She pulled the reluctant child towards the door.

Lissa began screaming and crying.

"Don't do this, Annie," he said, going after them. "Can't you see she doesn't want to go?"

"I'll do what I damn well please."

He wanted to slap her down, but he couldn't do it in front of his daughter – this scene was traumatic enough for Lissa to deal with.

He followed them outside. Christ! Money, fame, none of it mattered when it came to Lissa.

Annie shoved the child into her car. "Don't you ever pull this stunt again, Nick, or you won't see her at all."

"Quit threatening me, Annie, 'cause I'm through taking your crap. I'm talking to Kirk about this."

She jumped into the car. "Your high-priced Beverly Hills lawyers can't help you get Lissa," she sneered. "I'm her mother; she'll always stay with me." She started the car and roared off down the driveway.

"Don't bet on it," he yelled after her, filled with an impotent fury.

It was the last he saw of either of them. Their car was in a head-on collision. Neither Lissa nor Annie survived.

BOOK FOUR
December 1992

Chapter 81

Two over-ripe teenagers in short, black knit dresses with black hose and "fuck me" shoes boogeyed the night away beneath the midnight tent, where lights sparkled like mini stars and an assortment of predatory deadbeats circled the dance floor on the lookout for a score of some kind or the other.

Honey Virginia, bleached blonde hair pulled demurely back, finely tuned body clad in strapless lace, sat on Nick's knee, purring sweet sexual promises into his ear.

Diana Leon, sitting across the table next to her husband, watched from the corner of a jaundiced eye. Nick Angel never failed to amaze her. His capacity for everything was overwhelming. Honey entered his life on and off, and in between Nick covered the waterfront.

Diana often urged Freddie to talk to him. "Does he practise safe sex? Does he understand about AIDS?"

Freddie always placated her. "I'm his agent, not his sex therapist."

"But he's so . . . irresponsible. You *should* talk to him. You're his friend."

Freddie knew better than to discuss women with Nick Angel. Nick was a legend, having steadily laid every fuckable woman in Hollywood since he'd first arrived in town. It was surprising he could still get it up. But then little Honey could raise the dead if the mood took her, and Nick was by no means dead – just a touch jaded. And at age thirty-four showing definite signs of wear and tear. Freddie decided that maybe he *would* have a talk with him. Nick was getting out of control – it was becoming increasingly obvious. It had been a steady build-up since Lissa's death in the car crash with Annie. At first Nick had been inconsolable, he'd gone off to a retreat and stayed there for several months. When he'd returned it was like nothing had ever happened. He refused to discuss the accident. But Freddie knew he was breaking up inside. Nick had always been a drinker, and as the months turned into years his habit escalated.

"You should get into one of those twelve step programmes," Freddie had suggested one day. "I think you've got a problem."

Nick had turned on him, green eyes full of a deep hidden anger. "You think it's time I started looking for a new agent, Freddie?" he'd asked.

Freddie knew when to back off. It was one of his strengths.

"Can we go?" Diana whispered in his ear. She hated parties and had only attended this one because the woman for whom the party was being given was Freddie's latest client – a blonde video superstar called Venus Maria.

"Five minutes," Freddie promised, "and we're out of here."

Honey removed herself from Nick's knee, stood up and stretched. Every man at the party craned his neck to get a better look at her spectacular body.

Nick had been with her for four years on and off. In between he screwed all his leading ladies and anybody else he fancied. He was playing a dangerous game – AIDS was not selective.

Diana was getting restless. She rose from the table. "Good night, Nick. Good night, Honey, dear," she said, politely.

Nick leant back. "Are you two going?"

"Past my bedtime," Diana said, with a stretched smile.

"See ya," Nick said. He'd always considered Diana Leon a tight-assed broad. The older she got the more tight-assed she became.

Honey decided to join the two over-ripe teenagers on the dance floor. She put them to shame with moves even strippers hadn't thought of.

Nick watched her. The next morning they were leaving for New York. He had a birthday coming up and he didn't care to celebrate it in Los Angeles. Not that there was any cause for celebration; getting older was a pisser.

Two years ago he'd purchased a New York apartment. He liked having a place in the same city as Lauren, although they hadn't seen each other in four years. She'd called him when the news of the accident hit the headlines.

"Is there anything I can do?" she'd asked, full of concern.

Yes, be here with me, he'd wanted to say. But he knew she wasn't going to leave Oliver.

He decided it was time to get the hell out. Honey was still busy on the dance floor. He walked over and pulled her by the arm. "C'mon, we're going."

"I don't wanna . . ."

"I *said* we're going."

She followed him dutifully. Twenty-one years old and an idiot with the best body in town. That was all right – he wasn't interested in conversation. Meaningless sex. His life.

"Why did we have to leave so early?" Honey complained in the car on the way home.

"'Cause I might feel like flying the plane tomorrow. If I do I want to be able to see where I'm going."

He'd been taking flying lessons for a couple of years; it was the one thing he did where he tried to remain sober.

Back at the mansion Honey did a slow striptease for his benefit.

She was undeniably luscious.

He watched her for a few minutes, then passed out.

She might be luscious but he'd seen it all before.

"You look tired, *bellissima*," Lorenzo said, full of concern.

"Thank you," Lauren replied, crisply. "That's just what I want to hear when I'm about to go before the camera."

"The camera loves you. You will always look beautiful. Me – I know you too well, and you do look tired."

"I *am* tired," she confessed. "I had so much more energy when I was working all the time. Every morning was a challenge – I'd get up and there was always something new to do. Now that Oliver's retired I do nothing but sit around at home."

"Why?"

"Because he likes me there. It makes him feel secure."

"You don't have to do this, Lauren."

"Yes, I do," she said, defensively. "I'm his wife."

"You don't love him."

"What's love got to do with it?"

"When I married my wife I loved her. When I fell out of love we got a divorce."

"Well, Lorenzo, you do things in a much more simple fashion than I do. I believe in loyalty and sticking with somebody through bad times."

"Oliver is perfectly healthy now."

"I know, but he got used to not working. He liked it so much he decided to retire."

"That doesn't mean *you* have to waste your life."

"I'm doing the new Marcella campaign," she said. "What more do you want?"

"Yes, but that's all you're doing. Before you were so vital – everything excited you."

"I guess I'm not excited any more, Lorenzo. This is the last year I'll do the Marcella campaign. As you know, we're moving to the south of France."

"Lauren, you're making a mistake – shutting yourself away from the world."

"It's not a world I particularly want to be in any more. Anyway, the south of France is beautiful. And Oliver's found this wonderful old farmhouse way up in the hills – miles from anywhere."

Lorenzo shook his head. He simply didn't understand her.

It was Sunday afternoon and Cyndra was entertaining. She paused at the top of the stone stairs leading to her patio. She paused just long enough for people to notice she was making an entrance.

Smiling at her guests she watched Marik leap to his feet. He was always so attentive and concerned about her welfare. He was also a consistently good lover. It was a shame he wasn't more attractive.

Don't think that way, she scolded herself. *Marik is the best thing that ever happened to me. He's kind and caring, and he genuinely loves me. Apart from that he's a wonderful producer, and he made me a star.*

Behind her, Patsy, their plump English nanny, carried their little girl, Topaz. Topaz was the pride of her life. Three years old and adorable. Cyndra would do anything for her child – so would Marik; he worshipped their daughter.

"Hi," Cyndra greeted her guests graciously, going from table to table, smiling and chatting warmly.

Marik crept up behind her hugging her tightly. "You look fantastic, woman," he said, nibbling her ear. "Every year you get better looking."

"Thank you, dear."

Out of the corner of her eye she noticed Gordon and Odile

arriving. Gordon was still her best friend. She confided in him, went to him for advice, discussed most things with him – including the incident in Vegas – which he'd told her to forget about.

She went over to greet them. "Hi, Gordon."

"Hi, beautiful." Gordon said, kissing her on both cheeks.

"Hello, Odile," she said, with a smile.

"You're looking hot, Cyndra."

"Thank you. From you that's a compliment."

Over the years she'd actually gotten to like Odile. Yes, she was beautiful and, yes, she was Gordon's wife. But she was also an extremely nice woman.

Gordon and Odile were Topaz's godparents, along with Nick, who was godfather number one. She was upset Nick hadn't been able to come. He'd flown off to New York complaining he was depressed.

"Why don't you stay here for your birthday?" she'd asked.

"I don't feel like it," he'd said.

She wished he'd dump Honey. The girl made dumb look intelligent. But Nick was on some sort of self-destruct course; he didn't seem to care about the company he kept. Ever since the accident he hadn't been the same man. Unfortunately he blamed himself.

"It wasn't your fault," Cyndra repeatedly assured him.

"If I hadn't been fighting with Annie, it would never have happened."

"No, Nick, you mustn't think that way."

But he did, and she knew there was nothing she could do about it.

Maybe Nick would have a good time in New York. At least he'd be away from the pressures of Hollywood, and there was always Harlan to keep him company.

Ah, Harlan . . . What a character he'd turned out to be. After kidnapping him and getting him off drugs she'd moved him in with her. He'd quite taken to Hollywood, and met an older man whom he'd decided to go work for as his valet. When the man died of AIDS two years later Harlan had not wanted to stay around. Cyndra had arranged for him to work for Nick in New York. He loved it.

Marik took her arm and led her over to sit down. She was surrounded by friends and loving family. Little Topaz created a furore wherever she went, running from table to table, giggling and cute.

Cyndra surveyed her guests, her family and her beautiful home. *I'm so lucky*, she thought to herself. *I have everything*.

Only sometimes, late at night, the thought occurred to her that maybe she was too lucky. Then she shuddered and hugged herself and prayed to God that her good luck would last. For family meant everything to her and she didn't want to lose it.

Chapter 82

Reece Webster had not had a good time in prison. For once in his life his looks had not worked in his favour. In jail they were particularly fond of snake-hipped white guys with blond hair and nice looks, and he'd had two choices – give it up or get the crap beaten out of him.

Reece soon learnt which way to turn. Not that he was a faggot. No way. But taking it up the butt from one big black brother, as opposed to watching his ass every move he made, seemed to be the better deal.

Eleven years. Eleven fucking years of his life and now he was out.

He lingered outside the jail in North Carolina trying to decide what to do first. He wanted a woman bad, but he also wanted a fat juicy steak. An inmate had given him the name of a whorehouse that served up the best women, and food, too. What more could he ask for?

He tilted his rather beat-up stetson and took the bus into town. He didn't have much money. Fuck! He didn't have much of anything. But he sure as hell knew how he was going to get plenty. He'd studied up on that. In eleven years a man could do a lot of studying.

The whorehouse served him a dried-up steak and a dried-up hooker who'd seen better days. It was not a first-class operation. But any woman was better than none at all.

He wore a condom supplied by the house. He didn't argue because he'd heard it was pretty dangerous out on the streets now. Sex was not the carefree pastime it once was.

He fucked the whore three times.

"You bin in jail, dear?" she asked, not particularly impressed by his stellar performance.

"Howdja know?"

"I can tell. You convicts are always the horniest."

Yeah. He'd been in jail all right. Sixteen years was the sentence he'd been handed, and he was out in eleven for good behaviour. Sixteen lousy years for something he'd never done.

When he'd split Vegas he'd travelled all the way to Florida, where he'd met a nightclub hostess who took a shine to him and let him move in with her. He hadn't been living with the bitch two weeks when Max, her old boyfriend, returned. She'd omitted to tell him that Max was a convicted felon who specialized in robbing banks. Since Max was with his latest girlfriend – a ditsy redhead – there seemed no need for him to move on, so the four of them had palled up.

"People who work legitimate make me sick," Max told him one day. "Me – I kin take any bank I fancy. I jest walk in, show 'em my gun, scoop out the money an' I'm on easy street."

"What if you get caught?" Reece enquired, thinking it sounded simple enough, but there was always a downside.

Max chortled. "You realize how many people git busted? Outta a hundred hits mebbe five people git themselves caught. I bin doin' this goin' on twenny years."

"But you were in jail once."

"Only short time – it weren't nothin'."

They went on a car ride through several states, and Max showed Reece exactly how easy it was. On their ninth job Max blew away the security guard.

They were caught, arrested and charged with armed robbery and murder. The sentence was not light.

Screw it. He hadn't pulled the trigger, but nobody took that into account – he was sentenced along with the rest of them.

Now he was out and he was bitter as hell. If Cyndra hadn't gotten him into that mess in Vegas, he'd never have met the nightclub hostess in Florida, and he'd never have spent eleven years of his precious life in jail.

Fuck little Cyndra. While he was away she'd become a big star and so had Nick Angel. He'd watched their rise carefully – oh yeah, he was no fool.

Now he was out and he knew exactly where to go and what to do. Little Cyndra must be worth millions, and he was going to get himself some of that great big score.

Yes. Reece Webster had a plan.

California, here I come . . .

Chapter 83

The new Marcella photos were done and Lauren had nothing left to keep her in New York. Oliver was anxious to leave. For some time he'd been severing his ties in America, selling the East Hampton house, putting the New York apartment on the market and preparing for their move to France. At first Lauren had been unsure. It was a radical move, but, on the other hand, what was the point in sitting around New York when Oliver wasn't working. In France he would have his garden, the view, the tranquil surroundings.

Christ! You're beginning to sound like an old lady, Roberts.

It's my life – I have to accept it.

Pia came by with Rosemarie, a particularly bright little girl, and watched her pack. "Are you sure you're making the right move?" Pia asked, wandering around the room.

"Yes, I'm sure," Lauren said, although she wasn't sure at all.

"It's just that everything's so different for you now," Pia remarked. "I mean, you went through a period where you really loved your life, it showed on your face. Now you're kind of like . . ."

"Are you calling me a zombie, Pia?" Lauren asked, gathering together a pile of sweaters.

"You said it, not me."

Lauren placed the sweaters in a suitcase. "I'll do things in the south of France. Maybe even start an interior design business."

"Oh, that sounds very challenging. Decorate houses for senile old millionaires who've moved there to retire."

"Can I come visit, Auntie Lauren?" Rosemarie asked, a polite little girl with a sweet smile.

"Of course you can, darling, any time you want."

She packed several pairs of Charles Jourdan shoes and wondered why she was taking them anyway. Where was she going to wear them? Even in New York they never went out any more.

"How's Howard?" she asked.

"Howard has turned into Oliver," Pia said. "He works day and night, never gets back from the office before nine, then goes straight to his study where he spends the rest of the evening on the phone. I told him the other day if this goes on I'm not standing for it."

Lauren laughed. "You know you love it."

"Love what?"

"Being Mrs Howard Liberty. It's a lot of fun when your husband's the head of a big important company."

"I'm not so sure I do," Pia said, thoughtfully. "It was all right for you when you had your high-powered career – but I don't enjoy being the little wife. Half of the parties we go to I'm ignored. He's the big gorilla."

"Pia, I'm sure you're never ignored."

"You'd be surprised."

Lauren shut the suitcase. "Why don't you and Rosemarie stay for dinner tonight?"

"We'd like that. I'll call Howard and tell him if he gets through early enough he can join us."

At dinner Oliver was particularly animated. He was looking forward to the move and it showed.

In the middle of dinner Lauren had a phone call from Lorenzo.

"I have unfortunate news," he said, sounding upset.

"What is it, Lorenzo?" she asked.

"There was an accident in the lab – the negatives of the new photographs are ruined."

"You're kidding me?"

"No, this is a freak thing. It's never happened before. You must stay and shoot again."

"I can't do that. You know we're leaving tomorrow."

"Oliver will have to leave without you. You'll join him a few days later. I'll organize everything as quickly as possible."

"Lorenzo," she said, crossly. "This is most inconvenient."

He was more than apologetic. "I know, my darling, for me too."

"What's the matter?" Pia asked, when she hung up.

Lauren sighed. "The Marcella photographs are ruined. Lorenzo wants me to do the shoot again."

"But you're leaving tomorrow."

"That's exactly what I told him."

"Don't worry, my dear," Oliver said, perfectly calm. "I'll go ahead without you."

"You can't fly all that way by yourself."

"I'm not an invalid, Lauren," he said, rather snappily. "Our travel agent has perfectly good people on both ends to meet me and take care of the luggage. I'll settle in and you'll be there when you can. No problem."

"Are you sure?"

"Yes, I'm very sure."

She went into the bedroom and called Lorenzo back. "This better not be one of your crazy scams."

"Lauren, I can assure you."

"Okay, I'll stay. Tell me tomorrow what time we're going to do the photos."

"My darling," he said happily, "you are a princess."

"And you are a prince – the prince of bullshit."

"I'm so glad our relationship gets closer every year."

The next morning she was up early helping Oliver with last minute packing.

"How about if you postpone the trip?" she said. "Then I can come with you."

"It's all arranged, my dear. You worry too much."

"I'm coming to the airport," she said.

"You don't have to – the traffic . . ."

"I'm coming to the airport."

She sat next to him in the limo and saw him safely on the plane. Then she rode back to New York, alone and thoughtful. Soon she would be leaving the city and her life would change. She'd come a long way from Bosewell and the little girl she once was.

Nick . . . Every so often he lingered in her thoughts. She wondered how he was, how he was doing. She missed him. She always missed him.

"What do you want for your birthday?" Honey demanded.

Peace. "No celebrations," he said, sternly.

"Why not? I get off on birthdays," she said, toying with a strand of her long hair.

He hoped she wasn't planning anything – at twenty-one it was easy to love birthdays, but he was not in the mood.

"I'm telling you, I don't want anything. No surprises," he repeated, hoping she'd get the message.

She pouted. "I'll think of something."

"Don't," he said.

Had he made a mistake bringing Honey with him? He wasn't sure. Sometimes it was nice to have a warm body lying next to him in the middle of the night when he woke up and thought about Lauren. And he thought about her often. Over the years he'd grown to accept the fact that she was an obsession. Only the drinking made her go away.

In the New York apartment there was a stack of scripts waiting for him to read. Word was out that he wanted to make his next movie in New York, and every producer in town seemed to know it. There was a pile of faxes, a ton of mail and a list of phone calls waiting for him.

"Teresa, you deal with this shit," he said, calling upon his assistant.

Teresa had worked with him for a year now. She was the best assistant he'd ever had. He figured she was gay because she'd never come on to him, and that suited him just fine. Before her he'd had a series of assistants who'd looked at him with mournful eyes day and night, and eventually confessed undying love. Who needed that?

Teresa was all business. A black belt karate champion who could also type. The perfect combination.

"I'm taking the week off," he told her. "Don't bother me with anything – you deal with whatever comes up, okay?"

Teresa nodded. She looked like a man. He wondered if she had a girlfriend; he hadn't noticed any lurking about.

Tomorrow he was going to be thirty-five. It was a milestone. Ever since he'd started acting it had always been young Nick Angel. He'd always played the rebel, the kid without a cause. Now he was moving into a different age group. He was going to have to start playing responsible roles, and he wasn't sure if he was ready for it. He still felt like a kid at heart, sometimes a very weary kid, but always young.

He shut himself in his den and put his favourite Van Morrison on the CD player. Honey tried to come in and annoy him, but he waved her away.

Closing his eyes he let the music sweep over him.

He wasn't happy, but he hadn't quite figured out what he could do about it.

Chapter 84

It wasn't difficult finding out where Cyndra lived. Reece purchased a map to the stars' homes from a street vendor and thumbed through it. Sure enough, there was Cyndra's address printed clearly for all to see.

He chuckled to himself. Sweet little Cyndra. Sweet little bigamist.

Who did she think she was fooling? He reached for the latest copy of *People Magazine*. There was a big story on her and he read it for the sixth time. Sitting in his rented car he studied the pictures. Cyndra in her fancy bathroom. Cyndra by her fancy pool. And Cyndra with her cute little girl, Topaz, sitting on her daddy's lap.

Cyndra had gone and married one of her own kind. A producer they called him. Marik Lee – he was no Billy Dee Williams. But the two of them together seemed like they had it all their own way – and nobody was worried about Reece Webster.

He'd spent eleven years in jail and they didn't give a damn. Motherfuckers! They'd soon find out he was back.

He pulled the car up to a hot-dog stand and bought himself a greasy dog with plenty of relish and onions. Life's small pleasures, how he'd missed them in jail.

Later he drove down Melrose, stopped at a store and bought himself a new stetson, and some sharp looking leather boots. He handed the sales clerk a cheque that would bounce, but he'd be long gone by the time they discovered it was no good.

He admired himself in a full-length mirror. Still looked good. Still had that lean body and handsome face. Nobody would guess where he'd been for the last eleven years. He could do with a suntan. Didn't have time to wait to get one. Shame.

By three o'clock in the afternoon he was ready to start the

action. He knew exactly where Cyndra's house was. He drove up into the hills, through the winding streets, until he reached her security gates. Then he leaned out of his car window and pressed the entry buzzer.

A man's voice said, "Yes?"

"Cyndra?"

"No, she's not here. Who is this?"

"I'm here to see Cyndra," he said.

"I just told you, mister, she's not home."

"Then I'll wait."

"Who are you?"

Should he spoil the surprise? Tell this moron that he was her husband?

No, it was better to confront her face to face.

"I'm a relative," he said. "What time will she be back?"

"I can't reveal that information. Leave a note in the mailbox and I'll see she gets it."

What kind of garbage was this? He was leaving no note. He drove the car half a block away, turned it around and sat in it waiting and watching.

After a while a fancy white limousine drove down the street and turned into the gates.

Reece started his car, and as soon as the gates opened he followed the limo in, thinking to himself how stupid these people in Hollywood were if they actually thought a pair of fancy gates were enough to keep anybody out.

He followed the limousine up a long driveway until they reached the grand entrance to an imposing mansion.

A driver got out of the limo, noticed Reece's car behind him and rushed over.

"Can I help you?" the driver said.

The back door to the limo opened and a man that Reece recognized as Cyndra's supposed husband got out. "Hey, Clyde, what's going on?" the man called.

"I'm looking into it," Clyde replied, embarrassed because he was at fault for not noticing the car before.

Reece got out of his rented car. "I'm here to see Cyndra," he said.

"I'm sure you are," Clyde replied, very hostile. "A lot of people would like to see her. If it's an autograph you want, leave your address and we'll see you get one."

"You don't understand," Reece said. "I'm a relative."

Marik walked over. "What's going on here?" he said.

"I want to see Cyndra," Reece said.

"You shouldn't follow people into private property. We're going to have to call the police."

"I don't think you'll want to do that," Reece said.

"Look, man," Marik said, patiently. "I know you're a fan – and you love her. A lot of people love Cyndra – but you cannot follow her into her private home. Get it? Now I suggest you get back in your car, turn around, go away and we'll forget about this."

"You don't recognize me, do you?" Reece said.

"No," Marik said. "I don't."

"Think back," Reece said. "And fuckin' weep. I'm Cyndra's husband."

Cyndra had been crying on and off for hours. In the back of her mind she'd known the good life would not last. One moment she had everything she'd ever wanted, and the next Reece Webster came back like a ghost from the past to ruin it all.

At first she'd tried to deny she knew him. She'd gotten out of the limo, stared him in the face and said, "I don't know this man. I've never seen him before."

"Hey, bitch," Reece had taunted. "Would you sooner I went to the newspapers with this? I'm giving you the courtesy of coming here first."

They went into the house and the story began to unfold. How she'd married him. How he'd used her. And then Vegas. "She shot a guy," Reece said. "Shot him stone cold dead."

"I didn't do it – you did it," she said, accusingly.

Marik looked from one to the other and shook his head. Then he stared at Cyndra with hurt eyes. "Why didn't you tell me, baby?"

Her world was crumbling. "'Cause I never thought Reece would come back."

"Here I am," said Reece. "Would've been here sooner – but I got myself put in jail on a false charge. That's where I've been."

"What do you want?" Marik asked.

"Why, I would imagine that's pretty obvious," Reece said, taking in the luxurious surroundings. "I want my wife back."

"Let's talk straight here," Marik said, grimly. "What do you *really* want?"

"Well," Reece said, tilting his stetson at a rakish angle. "If I can't have the little lady, then I guess I'll have to be compensated for my loss."

"Yes," Marik said. "I understand you want money. And Cyndra wants her freedom. We'll pay. And the money will buy a quiet divorce."

One thing about this Marik guy – he certainly wasn't stupid. "How much you got in mind?" Reece said.

Marik glanced at Cyndra. She was too upset to look at him. "We have to discuss it," he said. "In private. I'll talk to my lawyer and we'll come back to you with an offer."

"It better be a big offer," Reece said. "Oh, and by the way, I thought I might pay me a visit to Nick Angel."

"What's Nick got to do with this?" Cyndra snapped.

"He helped you out, didn't he, sweetheart?" Reece said, slyly. "I saw what happened that night. You thought I left, but I didn't – I stuck around, followed you. So y'see, I know exactly what went on. You took that good old boy out into the desert and buried him. You're all as guilty as hell. I think Nick Angel will want to contribute to my future well-being, don't you?"

"Leave him out of this, Reece. We'll make a deal, but leave Nick out."

"Now, now, don't go getting upset."

Cyndra's mouth twitched dangerously. If she had a gun she'd blow his head off. All her life she'd been a victim, and now, just when she'd thought she was through with being victimized, this creep had to come back to haunt her with his threats.

"Calm down, Cyndra, we'll settle this," Marik said, taking charge.

"We're not talking pennies here," Reece said, warningly.

"I understand," Marik replied.

"When will I hear from you people?" Reece asked.

"Tomorrow," Marik said. "Where are you staying?"

"Give me a thousand bucks cash for now, an' I'll contact you tomorrow."

"I don't have that much cash."

"What *do* you have?"

"Five hundred."

"It'll do."

As Marik was escorting Reece to the front door, Topaz came running out of her room. "Mommy! Mommy! Look at my new dress. Isn't it pretty?"

Reece stopped. "Yeah, sugar, that's *real* pretty. You're the image of your mama."

"Stay away from her," Cyndra turned on him, her dark eyes stormy. "Get out of my house and stay away from my family."

He shrugged. "Trouble with you, Cyndra, is you got no appreciation. Who gave you singing lessons, taught you how to dress an' fix your hair? You were nothing when I found you hanging out in New York. Now you're a big star. I expect plenty of compensation for all I did."

"You'll get it. I told you that," said Marik, leading him to the front door.

Cyndra rushed over to Topaz and picked her up. "Come here, sweetie."

"Bye, little girl," said Reece, waving. "See you around."

She ran upstairs with Topaz and tried to call Nick in New York. He was out. She left a message with Harlan for him to call her back. Then she went to her closet and searched behind her clothes for the secret compartment where she kept her most valuable possessions. There, alongside her diamond necklace and ear-rings, was a small pearl-handled gun. One of her security guards had given it to her as a gift. He'd told her how to use it, too.

"Never hurts for a lady to have a gun," he'd said. "Especially a famous lady like yourself."

She'd never told anybody about the present, otherwise the guard would have gotten fired. But she'd always appreciated it.

Soon she had a feeling she might be forced to use it.

Chapter 85

Lauren called Oliver in the south of France to make sure he'd arrived safely and was settled in.

"I'm perfectly fine," he said. "In fact, last night Peggy invited me over for dinner."

Vaguely Lauren remembered Peggy – a titled English widow who'd sold Oliver the farmhouse.

"That's nice," she said. "I'll be there soon."

"You don't have to rush," he said. "It's beautiful here, so peaceful and quiet. I'm very content."

Oh, God! Should she bring her knitting?

Oliver seemed perfectly satisfied with the tranquil life, but she wasn't so sure it was for her. Maybe she was making a mistake after all. She wished she had the courage to tell him. No. It was impossible. This was her life.

Lorenzo called bright and early to inform her that the photo session was on for the next day.

"No more fuck-ups, Lorenzo," she said, sternly. "I have to get out of here."

He was hurt. "Please, Lauren, do not insult me."

She got dressed and wandered around the apartment she'd grown to love. It was on the market and every day people came to see it. She hated showing them around and tried to stay out of the way, leaving the tour in the hands of their realtor. It had been her home for almost twelve years and she was certainly going to miss it.

She sipped her morning coffee sitting at a table on the outside terrace overlooking Manhattan. It was a chilly December day, but clear. She loved looking out at the bustling city laid out below her.

The maid brought her the newspapers. She glanced through

them quickly, stopping at an item in *USA Today*. She scanned it once, then read it more slowly a second time.

> *Today millions of fans across the world celebrate the*
> *thirty-fifth birthday of cult superstar, Nick Angel, and*
> *the opening of his latest movie,* Killer Blue. *A statement*
> *issued by Panther Studios disclosed that Nick will not*
> *be present at the Los Angeles premier of* Killer Blue *as*
> *expected.*
>
> *A personal spokesman for Angel reported that the*
> *actor will spend his birthday in New York.*

Nick Angel . . . he was in New York and it was his birthday . . . Was she ever going to forget him?

I can call him if it's his birthday.

No, you can't.

Why not?

Because he'll want to see you and you're leaving for a new life with Oliver in France.

She shut her eyes for a moment, saw his face, and wanted to be with him more than anything else in the world.

So why are you punishing yourself, Roberts?

I'm not punishing myself.

Yes, you are. If you want to be with him you should.

I murdered his father.

Maybe. Maybe not.

I murdered his baby.

You had no choice.

She reached for the phone. Her hand hovered over the receiver for a few minutes. Then she shook her head. No, it wasn't right. She'd be tempting fate again – just forget it.

Honey took the second phone call from Cyndra. "He left here early," she said. "I think he's taken his plane up."

"But I need to speak to him," Cyndra said.

"He'll be back later. I'm having a surprise party for him."

"Nick doesn't like surprises."

Honey giggled. "He'll like this one."

"Let me talk to Harlan," Cyndra said.

Harlan got on the phone sounding swishier than usual. Since his move to New York he'd become extremely caustic. "Sister, dearest – and *what* can I do for you?"

"I need to talk to Nick. Is there any way I can reach him?"

"He's *not* in the best of moods," Harlan said. "Raced outta here like he had a ferret playing tag up his ass."

"Tell him to call me as soon as he gets back."

"Will do."

He'd got out of his apartment, left them all standing there, and now he was completely alone.

Behind the wheel of his small plane Nick felt a glorious freedom. There was something about being alone, totally un-surrounded by .people – a rarity for him. Oh, sure, he had his retreats, but one by one they got discovered. The *National Enquirer* had the number of his beach house. Every fan in town knew where he lived. Most of his business acquaintances had somehow or other gotten hold of his private phone number.

Now he was totally cut off from everything and everyone, and it was a wonderful feeling.

Flying was something he'd never imagined himself doing. He'd taken it up because of some macho bet with an old actor who'd appeared in one of his movies. Now he enjoyed it better than anything.

Colour me dead.

It was a tempting thought. He could fly this little mother right into the fucking ocean and vanish forever. The ultimate thrill. No more hassles. No more fame. Because the fame was suffocating the life out of him. And there was nothing that made him happy any more . . . except Lauren . . .

And what had he done about that situation?

He'd let her get away again. Hadn't even bothered to pursue her.

"Call me when you're free," he'd said. And four years had passed.

She was never going to leave Oliver. She'd stay with him until he dropped.

Well, shit, he couldn't take it any more.

On a sudden impulse he turned his plane around and headed back to base.

Reece thought about Cyndra, he thought about her a lot. Damn, she looked hot – a real juicy piece. He'd been right about her all along. Cyndra was a star – and only because he'd had the foresight to pay for her singing lessons and the rest. The truth was that he'd discovered her before anyone. He was the one that deserved all the credit. Goddamn it! He'd even introduced her to Reno Records. They owed him plenty, too. They should all be sucking his dick.

He was bored in his hotel room, there was no way he was sitting there waiting to hear from Marik. He had five hundred dollars. The idea was to go out and spend it.

He got in his car and drove down Sunset, cutting up La Brea to Hollywood Boulevard. A sign caught his eye. *Naked Live Beauties. Topless, Bottomless, Big Bare Babes.*

He parked his car, went inside and got himself a seat at the bar where he watched a long-legged dyed blonde bump and grind as she removed strips of black leather from her sinewy person.

He beckoned her over with a twenty dollar bill.

"Come here, doll. Get that sexy ass over here."

She edged closer to the side of the bar – which doubled as the stage.

He folded the bill into a thin strip.

She squatted down, and he inserted the money into her G-string, grabbing a quick feel at the same time.

"Later," she hissed. "It'll cost you more than twenty."

He was insulted. He'd only ever paid for it once, and that was the day he got out of jail. But still, paying for it wasn't such a bad thing. At least you knew where you were.

He winked at her. She winked back. As far as he was concerned they had an agreement.

After coffee on her terrace Lauren went inside and finished off packing. Lorenzo had wanted to come round, but she'd put him off.

"What are you doing tonight?" he'd asked.

"Staying home."

He'd sighed. "Lauren, Lauren – one more night on the town before you fade into retirement, please, I beg you."

"Well . . . maybe."

Going to dinner with Lorenzo was a temptation she didn't need. She'd accustomed herself to the life she had now. No sex.

What are you, a nun, Roberts?

No, but I have the strength of character not to play around on my husband.

Oh, get off your soapbox.

At two o'clock her phone rang again. If it was Lorenzo she decided to tell him that she wouldn't have dinner with him after all. Why tempt fate?

"Hey, Lauren."

She held her breath for a moment. "Who's this?" she asked, although of course she knew immediately who it was.

"Nick."

"Nick," she repeated, dumbly.

"It's been a long time. How are you?"

"I'm leaving in a couple of days," she said, quickly. "Oliver and I are moving to France."

"I want to see you."

"It's not possible."

"Lauren, it's my birthday. Remember old times? You always looked after me on my birthday."

"You know what happens every time we see each other, Nick," she said, weakly.

"Five minutes of your time, that's all I need."

"For what?"

"You can't spare me five minutes on my birthday?"

"Oh, Nick, come on, this is ridiculous."

"Be downstairs in half an hour; I'm on my way."

Before she could say anything he hung up.

She paced around the apartment undecided about what to do. Then she realized that since there was obviously no stopping him she'd better see him.

You don't have to.

Oh yes I do!

She felt totally wired as she ran into her bedroom, stripping off the boring silk shirt and skirt she had on, and reaching for her favourite faded jeans and a familiar sweatshirt – it wouldn't do to look like she'd tried. Then she brushed her hair, added soft shadow around her eyes and a blusher to her cheeks. She stared quickly at her reflection. Talk about glowing. She looked alive for the first time in a long while.

Here we go again.

She put on tennis shoes, grabbed her Oliver Peoples shades and ran downstairs.

"Do you need a cab, Mrs Liberty?" the doorman asked.

"No, no, that's okay," she said.

"It's cold out," he said.

"It's not that cold. The sun's shining."

"If you're going for a walk you'll need a coat."

"I'm not walking, Dave, somebody's picking me up. I'll only be out for five minutes."

What was she explaining herself to the doorman for?

"Oh, by the way, Mrs Liberty," he said, handing her an envelope. "I was supposed to give you this letter today. Mr Liberty left it for you. I was about to bring it up to your apartment when you came down. Saved me a trip."

She glanced at the envelope and recognized Oliver's handwriting. Quickly she opened the letter and read it.

My dear Lauren,

I have known for some time now that you are not completely happy. The truth is – neither am I. I feel that both of us are compromising our true feelings, and that we would be better off apart. I have never wished to be treated as a burden, and whether you know it or not, that's what our relationship has become. Over the last few months I have become quite close to Peggy during the course of our negotiations on the farmhouse. She is a wonderful woman – nearer to me in age, and quite ready for a settled life. You, my dear, are not. So I arranged with Lorenzo to keep you in New York. It's where you belong.

I am releasing you, Lauren, because I love you, and we will have better lives apart.

Of course, I quite understand –

The letter continued on in the same vein, and she read it filled with mixed emotions. Oliver wanted out! *He* was releasing her!

Oh God!

Free at last!

Free to do whatever she wanted!

The timing was unbelievable. And the best thing was, she didn't have to feel guilty, because he'd found someone else. Pocketing the letter she peered through the glass doors, impatiently waiting, pacing up and down until eventually she saw the Ferrari approaching – red of course.

She rushed outside. It had been four years since she'd seen him, and her heart was in overdrive. He looked a little ragged, but it was still her Nick.

He leapt out of the car. "Hey –"

"You're crazy, you know that?" she said, speaking too fast.

He took her hand. "Get in the car."

"Five minutes," she said, her heart beating wildly.

"Yeah, yeah."

Dave was standing at the entrance staring. He'd suddenly realized it was Nick Angel she was with. Before he could recover she jumped in the car and Nick took off.

"Happy birthday," she said, looking at him sideways.

"You're my present," he said.

"I am, huh?"

"I need to tell you something."

"What?"

"I've waited for you ever since I left Bosewell, and I'm not waiting any longer."

She sighed. "Nick, don't do this to us again."

"Why?"

"Because . . ."

"Listen, Lauren – I love you and you love me. You can't fight it any longer."

For a moment she thought how simple it would be to agree with him, because that's what she really wanted to do. But there was too much he didn't know about her. He didn't know she'd killed his father. He didn't know she'd killed his baby. And if he knew those things he wouldn't want to be with her anyway.

She glanced at her watch. "Your five minutes is up."

"What five minutes?" he said, steering the Ferrari on to the freeway.

"You said five minutes."

"I lied."

"Oh, God, Nick, don't start."

"I'm taking you for a ride in my plane."

"I'm not going in your plane."

"Oh yes you are."

"No way."

"Will you shut up? Just shut up for once."

Why did I let him talk me into this?

Because you wanted him to.

So do like he says – shut up and enjoy it.

She leaned back in her seat and didn't say another word.

Forty-five minutes later they were at the private airstrip. "Come on," he said. "Out."

"I told you, I'm not going in a plane with you."

"Maybe I should knock you out and carry you over my shoulder. What do you think?"

"You're crazy, Nick Angel."

He grinned, so happy to see her. "Yeah, yeah, you told me that before. Shouldn't come as a shock to you."

She knew she should back out, but she was already drawn into the game. She got out of the car and walked with him over to the plane.

"Five minutes," she said, sternly.

"Sure," he said.

She shook her head. "This is the last time I'm going anywhere with you, Nick."

"Hey – never say never."

"Why not?"

"'Cause you could live to regret it."

He took her hand and helped her aboard.

"Five minutes," she repeated.

"Hey – whatever you say."

Chapter 86

"How much do you think he wants?" Cyndra asked.

"It's not the money," Marik responded. "It's what he can do to us."

"What do you mean?" she said, fearfully.

"Think about it," Marik said, sounding calmer than he felt. "Over the last few years you've had massive national publicity. You've been on all the shows talking about pride and strength and women not allowing themselves to be abused. How do you think it'll look if Reece spills his guts?"

"Where's he staying?" she said, thinking about how she could put a stop to Reece Webster once and for all.

"Our driver followed him. He's at the Hyatt on Sunset." Marik peered at her, suspiciously. "Why'd you want to know?"

"Why not?" she said, flatly.

"You're not to try and talk to him," Marik said, warningly. "You're to leave this to me and Gordon."

"What's Gordon got to do with it?"

"We'll need his help," Marik said. "I've already called him, he's coming right over."

"Damn!" she said.

"What?"

"I don't want him involved."

"Cyndra, baby," Marik said, patiently. "This is big-time stuff. We gotta work it out carefully. A pay-off has gotta mean just that. A one time score – no coming back for more. We need Gordon's brain in on this."

"All right," she said, reluctantly. "But I don't want to see him – it's too humiliating. I'm going to bed."

He came over and kissed her. "Don't worry, baby, it'll all be taken care of."

You bet it will, she thought to herself. *By tomorrow morning Reece Webster will be history.*

The sinewy blonde took him back to her apartment, fucked him, then demanded three hundred dollars.

He laughed in her face.

"Pay up, bastard," she said, "or I'll set my boyfriend on you."

"I'm Reece Webster," he said, disdainfully. "That's who I am. Not some dumb john off the street."

"I don't give a cocksucking crap *who* you are," the blonde replied, showing her true vulgarity. "You're payin' an' ain't that the truth."

Reece zipped up his pants, pulled on his boots and reached for his stetson. He'd been threatened by bigger and better than this dumb cooze. "You ain't worth three bucks, let alone three hundred," he sneered.

"I hate cheap cocksuckers," she said.

"And I hate cheap whores," he responded, walking through her front door.

She picked up a heavy glass ashtray and hurled it after him. The jagged edge of the ashtray hit him on the side of the head, making a deep gash in his temple and knocking his stetson to the ground.

"Bitch!" he started to say, reaching up and feeling sticky blood pumping from the cut.

She ran over and slammed the door shut, leaving him out in the hallway.

At least he hadn't paid the whore.

He stooped to pick up his hat and felt dizzy. For a moment he slumped against the wall, his hand holding the wound. Soon his hand was covered with slippery blood.

Better get out before her boyfriend arrives, he thought, feeling quite unsteady on his feet. The goddamn bitch had hurt him. She'd pay for this.

He staggered downstairs, blood dripping on to his jacket, soaking through the material.

Out on the street a woman walking past took one look at him and quickly shrank away.

Christ! What was going on? He hardly had the strength to walk.

He blinked once, twice, tried to clear his head and remember where he'd parked his car.

The street light reflected an eerie shadow. He sat down on the kerb, putting his head in his blood-soaked hands. Nausea overcame him and he threw up.

Goddamn it, better get to his car and get out of here.

Cyndra crept into Topaz's room and watched her baby sleeping. The little girl was so cute. She had a snub nose, wide eyes and Marik's tight curly hair.

Carefully Cyndra extracted her thumb from her mouth. "No buck teeth, Topaz," she whispered, softly. "Gotta think beautiful."

Back in her own bedroom she went to her closet and changed into a black track suit. Then she pulled her hair severely back, covering it with a squashy Garbo type hat. Large sunglasses completed her disguise. Unrecognizable, she thought. As Cyndra, her public image was cascades of long dark hair, shimmering gowns and provocative make-up.

Reece Webster was threatening her future. Marik thought money would solve the problem. Cyndra knew it wouldn't.

She reached for her purse, checked that the small pearl handled revolver was loaded and in place, and slipped quietly down the back stairway into the garage.

Reece slumped behind the wheel of his car. He was lucky to have made it. He had a headache from hell and blood was still pumping from his wound. Ripping off his jacket he held it to his head and started the engine.

One hand on the wheel and one hand holding his head, he set off towards his hotel.

Cyndra took the nanny's station wagon – best not to call attention to herself with her Rolls or Marik's Jaguar. She locked the doors – second nature for a woman driving alone in LA – and drove down the hill.

The car was weaving. Reece felt it swaying this way and that – he couldn't seem to control it. All he had to do was get back to the hotel, put a dressing on his head and lie down. He'd be fine after a rest.

It occurred to him that maybe he needed to go to the Emergency Room – but those places were always filled with the lowest of the low – gunshot wounds, stabbings, heart attacks and worse. Who needed it? Besides, he should be at the hotel in case Marik phoned. Didn't want to miss the deal of the century.

Three million bucks. That's what he'd decided to ask for. And cheap at the price.

The sound of a blaring horn almost made him swerve off the road. Bastards! Why didn't people concentrate on their driving instead of hassling him?

He saw the hotel in the distance and slowed down.

More blaring horns.

Goddamn it, people didn't know how to behave any more.

Cyndra decided against valet parking. She found a space on the street and left the station wagon, locking the doors with a remote control.

Bump! Big bump!

Fuck, someone hit him. What did he care, it wasn't his car, only a rental.

Christ, his head was getting ready to explode. Was he at the hotel yet? Must be. He could hear noise, confusion. Leaning on the steering wheel he closed his eyes while blood dripped steadily on to his new cowboy boots.

There was something going on outside the hotel. Cyndra hurried along the street glancing over as she approached the entrance. A car had crossed over to the wrong lane and smashed into two other cars. The hotel doorman was running over to investigate.

A figure in the offending car was slumped over the driving wheel, his weight on the horn which let out an incessant noise.

She covered her ears and was just about to detour by when she realized the yellow car – a Chevrolet – looked awfully familiar. In fact it was the same car Reece Webster had been driving when he'd followed her limo up her driveway.

She stopped, watching – while the doorman – assisted by two other people – opened up the door and extracted the driver.

"He's dead," she heard one of them say. "Looks like he bled to death."

She edged closer for a better look as they laid the figure on the ground. No mistaking those cowboy boots. Reece Webster was certainly dead.

"Thank you, God," she whispered, and quietly made her way back to her car.

Chapter 87

"I didn't know you could fly a plane."

He put it on auto pilot and raised his arms. "Look, Ma, no hands!"

"Very funny," she said, sternly.

"Hey –" he caught her with a green-eyed stare. "Have I told you lately that I love you?"

"Nick –"

"Yeah?"

"Please stop," she begged.

"What? Stop loving you? I'm sorry, but I can't seem to do that."

"I think you can."

"How's that?"

She lowered her eyes. "There's things I've never told you."

"What things?" he asked.

She turned away from him, staring out of the window at the clear blue sky, determined to be truthful so there could finally be an end to this.

"Nick," she said, hesitantly. "When you left Bosewell, I was . . . I was pregnant with our baby."

"Oh Jesus, Lauren, I had no idea –"

"I know you didn't." She hesitated before carrying on. "I went to the trailer park to tell you – I guess it was the day after you left. Your father was there –"

"Yes?" He had a feeling he wasn't going to like what he was about to hear.

"He . . . he tried to attack me," she continued. "I stabbed him – then the tornado came and I don't remember anything else. When I woke up I was on the grass and the trailer was gone. The town was in chaos – my parents were both victims. I was sent to live in Philadelphia with relatives. Shortly after I arrived they made me have an abortion." Her eyes filled with tears. "Nick – they made me kill our child."

It was the first time she'd spoken of any of this and the relief was overwhelming. Suddenly it wasn't her secret any more – the burden was not hers alone.

"I didn't know," he said. "If I'd known I'd never have left. We would have worked it out somehow – Jesus, Lauren – I don't know what to say except that I love you. I always have and I always will. I'm sorry for what happened. I'm sorry I wasn't there with you, and for everything you had to go through without me."

All these years she'd expected him to be angry, to blame her for what had happened. Now he was the one that was sorry.

"I murdered our baby, Nick," she cried out, in case he hadn't understood.

"Come here, sweetheart," he said, taking her in his arms. "You had no choice. You were a kid – we both were. You did what you had to do – so stop blaming yourself."

It felt so good in his arms. She was at peace. It was as if she belonged there.

"As for Primo," he said, holding her tight. "You didn't kill him – he died of head injuries. It's public record".

"It is?"

"Yup. I had it checked out."

"All these years I thought I'd killed him."

"Why didn't you tell me this before?"

"Because . . ."

"Because what?"

"I don't know."

"You're crazy. And I love you."

"Nick," she said hesitantly, feeling like a kid again.

"Yes?"

"I love you, too."

He grinned. "So what are we going to do about it?"

"We're going to be together."

"We are?"

"Yes," she said, filled with a sudden strength and determination. "Forever."

"Fasten your seatbelt," he said, relinquishing his hold and concentrating on piloting the plane. "We're preparing to land."

"Where are we?" she asked.

"Canada."

"*Canada?*"

"I figured I had to take you somewhere remote – where nobody can bother us – not unless we want them to. There's this little log cabin –"

"How did you arrange it? And how did you know I'd come with you?"

"Hey – it's my birthday."

She smiled, softly. "Happy birthday, Nick."

"Thank you, Lauren."

They stared into each other's eyes and smiled.

The dream was finally coming true.

They were together and they both knew without a doubt that this time nothing would ever split them apart again.

Thrill!

*For all my friends and family, who
are always there for me.*

*Also, all my friends at Simon & Schuster
and Macmillan – two great teams, who are
a pleasure to work with.*

*Mort Janklow and Anne Sibbald – who
give great agenting.*

Andrew Nurnberg and the gang.

*And a big thank you to Marvin Davis
for his caring counsel and warm friendship.*

*A special thought for Felipe Santo Domingo,
whose smiling face I shall never forget.*

*For Vida – who patiently deciphers my writing
and gets it on the word processor in time!*

*And Melody and Yvonne and Jacqui – who force
me out there at 5:00 a.m. to do satellite
TV, amongst other tortures!*

And, of course, to Frank – my own very special hero.

PROLOGUE

HERE'S THE truth of it – I can fuck any woman I want any time I want – no problem. Every one of them is ripe and ready, waiting to hear the magic words that'll persuade them to do anything. Married, single, older, younger, desperate, widowed, frigid, horny – point 'em out, and they're mine.

You see, I know what to say, I discovered the key, and believe me it opens the lock every single time.

My mother was a hot-looking natural blond from Memphis who got herself murdered when I was seven. She was beaten up and strangled, then thrown from a moving car. For a while the cops suspected my old man, they even took him into custody for a day or two. But he had an airtight alibi, he was in bed with his mistress at the time – a pie-faced redhead with the biggest tits I'd ever seen.

My dad had the face and attitude of a handsome gangster. He was an extremely snappy dresser – only the best for him. He wore the finest Egyptian cotton shirts, silk ties, hand-tailored suits, gold cuff links and a Rolex watch – all the trimmings. He could have any woman he wanted, and did. I remember when I was growing up I used to watch him operate. He owned a fancy restaurant, and cock-walked the room flirting with all the female customers. Women were his for the taking, and from an early age I got an education observing him in action. He always had plenty of pussy, but after my mom died there were more women than ever. They felt sorry for him – and he ate it up.

He drank, though, and I was smart enough not to want to end up like him. He started off the evening looking like dynamite, halfway through the night he was a wreck, and by the time his restaurant closed he was falling-down drunk.

We lived in an apartment and had a maid come in twice a week. He was screwing the maid, too. He didn't give a toss what the women he bedded looked like, in fact, he used to say, 'Get an ugly one between your legs, an' she'll really show you what it's all about. They're cock-hungry and very grateful.'

My dad didn't have much time for me, so I became a loner. Instead of having other kids over, I joined a gang at school and began getting into trouble. Running the streets stealing cars and knocking off liquor stores was more of a kick than sitting in an empty apartment waiting for my dad to stagger in whenever he felt like it.

I started following in his footsteps. Fuck 'em and leave 'em was his motto. Why shouldn't it be mine, too?

By the time I hit fifteen and he was fifty, the restaurant was long gone and so were his looks. His handsome face was puffy and bloated. He had a big beer gut and rotten teeth – too chicken-shit to visit a dentist, he simply let 'em fall out.

One memorable day I asked him something I'd wanted to for years. I demanded to know if he'd killed my mother.

He whacked me so hard he split my lip, still got the tiny scar to prove it. 'Leave my fucking house,' he screamed, his bloodshot eyes bulging with fury. 'I don't ever wanna see your ugly face again.'

Fine with me. I had two steady girlfriends and plenty of contenders.

I chose to move in with Lulu, a twenty-year-old stripper who was happy to have me. Of course, she had no idea I was only fifteen on account of the fact I looked about nineteen and pretended to be twenty.

The nice thing about Lulu was that she didn't care I had no job, she was happy to indulge me. When she wasn't working we spent all our time at the movies – both getting off on the fantasy. Hollywood – the ultimate dreamland. 'You're so talented,' she was forever telling me. 'You should be a movie star.'

Brilliant idea! As far as I could tell, movie stars didn't have to do much, except stand around looking macho – women worshipped them, and from what I read in Lulu's fan magazines, they made plenty of big bucks.

Lulu found out about an acting class, and even sprung for the bucks for me to go. Nobody could ever accuse her of not being a sport.

After we'd been together a year, I came home early one day, and caught her in bed with another guy. My dad had warned me not to trust women. I figured he was wrong on that score, but then I'd never imagined they'd screw around on me.

Big surprise. There was Lulu with her legs in the air moaning and groaning. Horny little bitch.

I pulled the guy off her and he ran, shaking, from the apartment, because I looked mad enough to beat the crap out of him.

Lulu lay there, thighs spread, naked and scared, begging my forgiveness.

I knew then I had the power. I didn't even slap her, although she deserved it. Instead I packed my things and made a fast exit. No woman was ever going to get one off on me again. Next time I'd make sure I did it first.

An unclothed Lulu chased me down the hallway yelling her guts out. 'It was a mistake! You can't go! Please! Don't leave me!'

Too late. By that time I'd figured out what I wanted, and it wasn't some cheating whore who didn't know how to be faithful.

I wanted to be a movie star and own the whole fucking world.

I was sixteen, what did I know?

Chapter One

LARA IVORY stepped carefully toward the camera, managing to appear cool and collected under the crushing weight of a heavy crinoline gown, her slender waist cinched into an impossible seventeen-inch span, lush cleavage spilling forth.

Lara's fellow actor in the shot, Harry Solitaire, a young Englishman with tousled hair and droopy bedroom eyes, walked beside her, delivering his lines with an enthusiasm that belied the fact that this was their seventh take.

It was eighty-four degrees in the South of France garden setting, and the entire crew stood silently on the sidelines, sweating, as they waited impatiently for Richard Barry, the veteran director, to call cut, so they could break for lunch.

Lara Ivory was, at thirty-two, an incandescent beauty with catlike green eyes, a small straight nose, full luscious lips, cut-glass cheekbones and honey-blond hair – right now curled to within an inch of disaster. She had been a movie star at the top of her profession for nine years, and miraculously the fame and glory had never changed her, she was still as likeable and sweet as the devastatingly pretty girl who'd arrived in Hollywood at the age of twenty and been discovered by the director, Miles Kieffer, who'd spotted her when she'd come in to audition for a minor role in his new film. Miles had taken one look and decided she was the actress he had to have to play the lead. Gorgeous and fresh, she'd portrayed a naive hooker in a *Pretty Woman* style movie – beguiling everyone from the critics to the public.

From that first film, Lara's star had risen fast. It only took one special movie. Sandra Bullock was a prime example with *Speed*. Michelle Pfeiffer had gotten her break in *Scarface*. Sharon Stone with a spectacular performance – not to mention flashing her pussy – in *Basic Instinct*.

The public never forgot a star entrance. The trick was keeping up there.

Lara Ivory had managed it admirably.

At last Richard Barry called out the words everyone was waiting to hear. 'Cut! Print it! That's the one.' Lara sighed with relief.

Richard had been a successful director for nearly thirty years. He was a tall, well-built man in his late fifties, with even features, a well-trimmed beard, longish brown hair flecked with grey at the temples, and crinkly blue eyes. He also had dry humour and a sardonic smile. Women found him extremely attractive.

'Phew!' Lara repeated her sigh, her smooth cheeks flushed. 'Someone get me out of this dress!'

'I'll do it!' Harry Solitaire volunteered with a lascivious leer, flirting as usual.

'That's OK,' Lara retorted, smiling because she liked Harry, and if he wasn't married he might have been a contender. She considered married men strictly off-limits, and refused to break her rule for anyone – even though she hadn't had a date in six months, ever since she'd broken up with Lee Randolph, a first assistant director, who, after a year of togetherness, had been unable to take the pressure of being with so famous a woman. The sad truth was that what man enjoyed being background material? Relegated to second

8

place? Attacked by crazed stalkers and fans? Referred to as Mr Ivory by waiters and limo drivers?

It took an exceptionally strong man to cope with that kind of deal – a man like Richard Barry, who'd handled it admirably for the four years he and Lara had been married.

She and Richard had gotten divorced three years ago, and along with Richard's new wife, Nikki – a costume designer with whom he'd hooked up while shooting a movie on location in Chicago – they were now good friends.

Nikki was dark-haired, feisty and extremely pretty in a gamine-like way. She also knew how to bring out the best in Richard. Early on in their relationship she discovered that like most men he was a lot of work. Before she entered his life he'd been a smoker, a philanderer and a heavy drinker, plus he expected to get his own way at all times, and when he didn't, he sulked. Nikki had taken stock of his strengths and weaknesses and decided he was worth the effort. Somehow she'd calmed him down, fulfilled all his needs, and now his biggest vice appeared to be work. He was a bankable director, much in demand, whose movies always made money, and in Hollywood that's all that counts.

Lara considered Nikki her closest girlfriend. Right now they were all enjoying working together on *French Summer* – a beautifully scripted period film that Richard was passionate about. The three of them were sharing a rented villa on the six-week location. Lara hadn't wanted to intrude, but Nikki had insisted, which secretly relieved Lara, because the loneliness of being by herself was sometimes hard to cope with.

'That last take was magical,' Richard said, coming to her side and squeezing her hand. '*Definitely* worth waiting for.'

Lara frowned; she was her own sternest critic. 'Do you think so?' she asked, worrying that she could have done better.

9

'Sweetheart,' Richard assured her, anticipating her concerns because he knew her so well, 'seventh take perfect. Nothing to improve.'

'You're just being kind,' she said, her frown deepening.

'Not kind – truthful,' he replied sincerely.

Her disarmingly honest green eyes met his. 'Really?' she asked.

Richard regarded his exquisite ex-wife and found himself wondering if her painful insecurity had contributed to the demise of their marriage.

Maybe. Although catching the make-up girl giving him head in his trailer had been the final nail in the coffin of his infidelities – that was one he hadn't been able to talk himself out of.

For a year after their somewhat public and acrimonious divorce they hadn't spoken. Then Richard met Nikki, and she'd insisted in her usual no-nonsense way that it was crazy they couldn't all be friends. As usual, she was right. The three of them had gotten together for dinner and never regretted it.

Nikki strode over, looking enviably cool in baggy linen pants and a yellow cotton shirt knotted under her breasts, exposing her well-toned midriff. She was in her early thirties, shorter than Lara, with a lithe, worked-out body, cropped dark hair worn with long bangs, direct hazel eyes and an overly ripe mouth. Nobody would guess that she had a fifteen-year-old daughter.

Richard enjoyed the fact that Nikki was smart and sassy, and most of all that she wasn't an actress. After losing Lara he'd considered never getting involved again, because there'd never be another woman who could live up to her. Nikki and her upbeat ways had changed his mind.

'Get me out of this dress!' Lara implored. 'It's cutting me in half. Worse torture than being married to Richard!'

'*Nothing* can be worse than that!' Nikki joked, rolling her expressive eyes.

'Wasn't Lara great in that last take?' Richard interrupted, putting an arm around his current wife, trailing his fingers up and down her bare skin.

'He's just being kind,' Lara said with one of her trademark deep sighs.

'I know the feeling,' Nikki responded crisply. 'That's exactly what he says when he praises my cooking.'

Lara widened her eyes. 'Don't tell me you cook for him?' she exclaimed. 'I never did.'

Nikki pulled a face. 'He forces me, you know how persuasive he can be.'

'Oh, yes,' Lara agreed. They laughed conspiratorially.

Richard frowned, pretending to be annoyed. 'It's really irritating that you two are such good friends,' he said. 'I hate it!' Truth was he loved having both women in his life.

'No, you don't,' Nikki retorted, looking at him with the kind of expression a woman gets when she's totally secure of her man. 'You get off on it.'

With an amused shake of his head, he walked away. Nikki signalled one of her wardrobe assistants to follow them to Lara's trailer. 'For a grown man, Richard can be such a baby,' she remarked.

'That's why our marriage didn't work,' Lara said lightly. 'Two giant egos fighting for the best camera angle!'

'And one of them screwing around like Charlie Sheen on a bad day.'

'You cured him of *that*.'

'I hope so!' Nikki said forcefully. 'The moment he points his dick in another direction, I'm gone.'

'You'd leave him?'

'Immediately,' Nikki said without hesitation.

'I bet you would,' Lara said, wishing she had the inner strength her friend possessed.

'Hey, listen,' Nikki said, wrinkling her freckled nose. 'I'd expect him to dump me if I screwed around, so why shouldn't the same rule apply?'

Lara nodded. 'You're absolutely right.'

Why didn't I do it? she thought. *Why didn't I tell him to take a hike the first time I suspected he was being unfaithful?*

Because you're a pushover.

No. I simply believe in second chances.

And third ones and fourth ones . . . Richard hadn't known when to quit.

They'd met when he'd directed her in her third movie. Although by that time she was a star, she was still impressed at meeting the great Richard Barry – a man with quite a reputation. He moved in on her like a carnivorous snake. She was twenty-four and by Hollywood standards a total innocent. He was forty-six and difficult. Their wedding at her agent's house in Malibu made headline news, with helicopters hovering overhead and paparazzi lurking in the trees. It was a media circus, which pleased neither of them. The divorce had been even worse.

'We're going to Tetou tonight,' Nikki announced. 'I hear the bouillabaisse is to die for.'

Lara shook her head. 'I can't do it. I have lines to learn and sleep to get, otherwise I'll resemble an old hag in the morning.'

Nikki raised a disbelieving eyebrow. The irritating thing was that Lara acted as if she looked like any other mere mortal, even though she was certainly the most beautiful woman Nikki had ever seen – a woman who never acknowledged her powerful physical beauty. 'You're coming,' Nikki said determinedly. 'I've already checked – you have a late call tomorrow. It's about time you forgot about this damn movie and had some fun.'

'Fun – what's that?' Lara said innocently.

'Exactly how long *is* it since you've gotten laid?' Nikki asked, cocking her head to one side.

'Too long,' Lara muttered.

'It doesn't have to be a big thing, y'know,' Nikki offered. 'How about a one-nighter? There's some hot-looking guys on the crew.'

'Not my style,' Lara said softly.

'You gotta have a man's mentality,' Nikki said, with a knowing wink. 'Fuck and run. I used to – before I married again.'

Richard was Nikki's second husband. Her first was Sheldon Weston, whom she'd wed when she was sixteen and he was thirty-eight. 'I was searching for a father figure,' she often joked. 'And I got stuck with an uptight shrink.' Their daughter, Summer, lived in Chicago with her dad.

'You're different,' Lara said. 'You can do that and get away with it. I can't. It has to be a committed relationship or I'm not interested.'

'Whatever,' Nikki replied vaguely, not understanding at all. 'But you're definitely coming tonight.'

Chapter Two

 JOEY LORENZO burst into Madelaine Francis' Madison Avenue office as if he had every right to be there, even though he didn't have an appointment and hadn't seen her in six years.

A harassed secretary chased after him. She was a round-faced girl with ample hips encased in a too-short mini.

'What the hell is going on—' Madelaine began to say. Then her bleak eyes, hidden beneath tinted prescription glasses, recognized Joey, and she quickly waved her secretary away. 'It's all right, Stella,' she said with a weary sigh. 'I'll handle this.'

'But, Miss Francis,' Stella said, full of piss and outrage, 'he told me to—' she hesitated for a moment, two bright-red blobs colouring her chubby cheeks, 'the F-word off.'

'Thank you, Stella,' Madelaine said, dismissing her. 'You're excused.'

Still glaring at Joey, Stella backed out of the well-appointed office, while he threw himself into a leather chair opposite Madelaine's large antique desk, draping his long jean-clad legs over the side of the expensive chair.

'I'm back,' he said, with an insolent grin.

'So I see,' said Madelaine, shifting uncomfortably, wondering what wrong deed she'd committed to have Joey Lorenzo reappear in her well-ordered life.

Six years ago they'd been living together – the forty-eight-year-old agent and the twenty-four-year-old actor. An unlikely combination, but for eight months it had worked. Then one night she'd arrived home to find Joey gone, along with seven thousand dollars in cash she'd kept in her safe.

Now she was fifty-four and he was thirty and the bastard was back.

'What do you want?' she asked, her voice a tight coil of buried anger.

'You're pissed, aren't you?' Joey said nonchalantly, as if he'd merely popped out for cigarettes and a beer. '*Really* pissed.'

'Yes, Joey, I am,' she said, removing her tortoiseshell-framed glasses and staring at him bitterly. 'Wouldn't *you* be?'

'Guess you musta wondered what happened t'me,' he mumbled.

'Yes, I wondered – about you *and* about my money.'

'Oh yeah, your money,' he said, groping in the pocket of his weathered leather jacket and producing a packet of hundred-dollar bills neatly tied with a rubber band. 'Here's three thou. I'll get the rest to you in a coupla weeks.'

She couldn't believe he was returning her money. Not all of it, but three thousand dollars was a start. She continued staring at him. Six years had done him nothing but favours – he was more handsome than ever. His hair touched the back of his collar, thick and black – too long, but it didn't matter. His body was nicely muscled with a washboard stomach. He had grown into a man, with knowing eyes, full sensual lips and a smile that would melt stronger women than she. She remembered that smile. She also remembered his cock, even though she tried not to. Perfect. Like the rest of him.

Pity he was a thieving sonofabitch.

'What do you want?' she repeated, keeping her voice on the hard side, knowing time had not been as good to her as it had to him. Her reddish hair was flecked with grey. Lines and wrinkles abounded. And she'd put on fifteen pounds of disgusting fat.

'Here's the thing,' Joey said, fixing her with his intense eyes, seeing right through her. 'Before I took off, you'd gotten me two movie roles.'

'That's right,' she said coldly. 'Your career was just about to happen. You ran out on that, too.'

'Somethin' went down that was outta my control,' he said restlessly.

She refused to give him the satisfaction of begging for an explanation. 'I don't care, Joey,' she said, shuffling a stack of papers on her messy desk. 'If you return the rest of my money, we'll leave it at that.' She paused a moment, remembering the first time he'd walked into her office – a cocky kid from the Midwest, with way too much attitude. She'd seen the potential and decided to help him. Eight months of craziness and great sex. Eight months she'd never forget.

'I didn't go to the police,' she said slowly, 'even though it's what I should've done.'

He nodded, face sincere, faint stubble on his chin adding to his look. 'Y'know, Maddy,' he said. 'I wouldn't've taken your cash unless it was an emergency.'

She was silent. How many times could she ask him what he wanted from her now? Obviously it wasn't money.

He broke the silence, placing his hands on her desk. Long artistic fingers, pianist's fingers. She noticed his nails were manicured – which surprised her, considering Joey had always favoured the macho look. 'I need to get back into the business,' he said. 'An' you're the person who can do it for me.'

She raised a disbelieving eyebrow.

'Here's what I'd like,' he continued. 'Another movie. Not

16

TV. I'm not into TV. Fuck that *ER* shit. I gotta be back on the big screen.'

Well, nobody ever said he didn't have nerve. But surely he didn't expect her to resurrect a career he'd run out on?

'Joey,' she said, deliberately pacing her words, watching his face as she spoke, 'you blew your career, such as it was. You had your shot and you ran.'

'No fuckin' way!' he shouted, banging his fists on her desk. 'Don't you get it? If you did it for me once, you can do it again.'

A moment of pure satisfaction. 'I have a reputation to uphold,' Madelaine said. 'And I am not about to ruin it by sending you up for anything.'

'That's bullshit,' he muttered.

'You're unreliable,' she continued, quite enjoying putting him down. 'And worse than that – you're a thief. No, Joey,' she continued, shaking her head, 'I'm afraid I can't recommend you to anyone, so do yourself a big favour and get out.'

She waited for his anger to deepen, remembering his sometimes violent temper. But this time she wasn't frightened, he wouldn't dare lay a hand on her in her office.

Instead of more anger he went the other way. Little boy lost. So handsome and alone. She'd never been able to resist that stance and he knew it. Joey could turn it on like nobody else.

'OK, I get it,' he said, pushing his hand through his thick hair. 'I'm like yesterday's news. Nobody'll hire me. Guess I may as well go back to drivin' a cab.' He got up and went to the door, pausing with his hand on the knob. 'Can I buy you dinner? Try to explain what happened. I owe you that.' His intense eyes tracked her from across the room. 'Can I, Maddy?'

She was well aware that if she accepted, she'd look like a pathetic old fool . . .

It didn't matter, because there was no way she could resist.

☆ ☆ ☆

Joey knew exactly what he was doing, every move thought out way ahead. Dinner at a small Italian restaurant; a bottle of house red wine – three-quarters of it drunk by Madelaine, who didn't realize he wasn't keeping up. Intimate conversation – mostly about how much he'd missed her, and how great he thought she looked.

Lies, lies, but what did she care? By the time they took a cab back to her apartment on 66th Street, she was feeling sexy and womanly and very horny. Joey had fed her some story about a sick aunt in Montana and a family business he'd had to single-handedly save. She didn't believe him, but so what? He was paying her more attention than she'd had in six years and she desperately wanted him to make love to her.

Joey didn't disappoint. His lovemaking was even better than she remembered. Prolonged foreplay; leisurely oral sex; and then long, steady penetration until she cried out in a torrent of ecstasy.

She didn't feel over fifty and fifteen pounds overweight. Joey made her feel like a beautiful, desirable woman.

He stayed overnight, making love to her again in the morning, his hard body pressing her flesh in the most incredibly exciting way. She knew she was hooked again. One night of lust made up for six years of anger.

'Why didn't you call me? At least let me know where you were?' she asked plaintively, her fingers trailing up and down his smoothly muscled back.

'I'm here now,' he responded. 'Isn't it enough that I came

18

back?' And his lips pressed down on hers, weakening her crumbling resistance until it ceased to exist.

Two days later he moved back in. A few days after that she asked him to drop by her office.

'I'm sending you up for a small role you could be right for,' she told him. 'If you get it, that'll be a start in the right direction.'

'You're the best, Maddy,' he said, smiling the irresistible Joey smile.

And she knew she was probably being used, but somehow – once again – it didn't matter.

Chapter Three

 TETOU WAS a famous fish restaurant perched above the sandy beach between Eden Roc and Juan Les Pins. Popular for many years, it was an expensive hang-out for rich locals and affluent tourists – nothing in the South of France was cheap.

Nikki had also invited Harry Solitaire and Pierre Perez to join them. Pierre was a French actor with brooding eyes and a dreamy smile – he'd flown in from Paris that morning and was due to start work on the movie in two days.

'Pierre's not married,' Nikki whispered as they sat down. 'Not even engaged. Use a condom and go for it.'

'Will you stop!' Lara said crossly.

Pierre was as charming as Harry was persistent. Richard glared at them both disapprovingly. He was extremely protective of his ex-wife; she might be a famous movie star, but she was fragile and needed nurturing, only *he* knew how much.

'Why did you invite these two assholes?' he muttered to Nikki, as Lara parried the attention.

'To piss you off,' Nikki muttered back, grabbing his crotch under the long tablecloth.

'Quit that!' he said sternly.

She grinned. 'Why? You know you love it.'

'There's a time and a place.'

'The time is now,' she said, attempting to unzip his fly.

He couldn't help smiling as he shifted her hand. Nikki never gave him time to think about other women, she was always up to something.

When dinner was over and they were lingering over coffee, Harry leaped to his feet. He lived for locations, a legitimate separation from his wife was one of the perks of being an actor. 'Let's go dancing,' he suggested enthusiastically. 'I know a terrific place in Monte Carlo.'

'Count me out,' Lara said quickly.

'Why?' Harry persisted, his eyes saying: *You like me, don't you? You're attracted to me – so come on, let's get down and dirty.*

'I have lines to go over,' she demurred.

'Perhaps five minutes in the Casino?' Pierre suggested.

She glanced at Richard for help. He rallied immediately – now that he wasn't her husband he was for ever her knight in slightly tarnished armour. 'As Lara's director,' he said, sounding a tad pompous, 'we're taking her home.'

'Christ!' Nikki muttered under her breath. '*Why?*'

'What?' Richard said irritably.

'Let her go,' Nikki insisted, glaring at him.

He returned her glare with one of his own. 'Lara's free to do as she likes. She *wants* to come home with us.'

'Don't talk about me as if I'm not here,' Lara interrupted, sensing tension.

'You have an early call,' Richard said possessively. 'You should come home.'

'Maybe, maybe not,' Lara retorted, a glint of annoyance suddenly surfacing.

Harry got the picture and quickly helped her up, gallantly escorting her to the door. 'Your ex still has a hard-on for you,' he said in a half amused, half pissed-off voice.

'Excuse me?' she said coolly.

'It's obvious,' he said as they stood outside the restaurant, the warm Mediterranean air ruffling her honey coloured hair, now freed from the excruciating curls of earlier.

She shook her head. 'You're wrong.'

'Oh, no, I'm not,' he said, grabbing her hand and running her across the busy coast road to the parking lot.

'I am *not* going dancing, Harry,' she said firmly.

'Don't be foolish, Lara,' he said, still flirting. 'I give you my word as an Englishman that I will not attack you.'

'I'm *so* relieved,' she replied with a sarcastic edge. They held a long steady look, then the others joined them.

'Come along, sweetheart,' Richard said, taking her arm and hustling her toward his car.

Lara didn't like his proprietary attitude, and she noticed Nikki was not thrilled either.

'You know what,' she said, loosening Richard's grip, 'I'm taking Pierre up on the Casino idea. Not that I gamble, but I'd enjoy seeing the inside of a French casino. Is it like Vegas?'

Pierre smiled his dreamy smile. Harry scowled. Richard began to object, but Nikki stopped him. 'Have a good time,' she said with an encouraging wink, giving Lara a little shove toward Pierre's car. 'And don't worry, we won't wait up!'

☆　☆　☆

The casino in Monte Carlo was not like Vegas at all, it was an imposing building located in a busy square close to the sea. Accompanied by Pierre and Harry, who'd insisted on coming too, Lara walked around, watching the avid players intent on losing their money. Old women in beaded evening gowns, bedecked with expensive jewels, played next to obvious rogues busy piling stacks of chips on their lucky numbers as the roulette wheel turned; steely-eyed card-sharps sat next to stone-faced blonds at the blackjack tables; craps, chemin de fer and other games abounded.

'It's so . . . unbelievably grand,' Lara said, groping for the right description. 'Almost from another era.'

'Rather decadent,' Harry said with a jolly laugh. 'I like it!'

An alert floor manager with boot-black hair and a matching dinner jacket swooped down, landing on Lara with an ingratiating smile. 'Mademoiselle Ivory, it is a pleasure to welcome you to our casino,' he said in velvety tones. 'Would you and your friends care for a drink?'

'No, thank you,' she said, introducing Harry and Pierre.

The manager's whiter than white smile was in overdrive. 'Anything at all we can get for you, please do not hesitate to ask.'

She smiled back.

'You are a wonderful actress, Mademoiselle Ivory,' the manager added, his English impeccable.

Lara dazzled him with another smile. 'Thank you.'

He was on a roll. 'And may I say that in person you are even more beautiful.'

Excessive compliments bothered her. Even after all this time she still felt a deep flush of embarrassment when people singled her out. They had no idea who she really was. Nobody knew the true story – not even Richard, and he'd gotten closer to her than anybody.

'She certainly is,' Harry said, hanging in because only *he* knew the way to her villa, so goodbye Pierre.

'Will you be playing tonight?' the casino manager asked. Finished with her beauty and talent, he now wanted her money.

She smiled sweetly. 'Perhaps another time.' The manager drifted away. She turned to Pierre. 'Shall we go?'

Pierre took her arm. Harry moved protectively in on her other side. Together they escorted her to the door.

Lurking on the steps outside the casino were several

paparazzi. They sprung into action, yelling her name, flash-bulbs bursting into light all around her.

Automatically she shielded her eyes, as Harry quickly distanced himself, making it appear that she and Pierre were a couple.

Great, Lara thought, *now I'll be all over the tabloids*. She hated being linked to someone she hardly knew. Last month she'd been in the same restaurant as Kevin Costner, and the supermarket rags had written they were planning marriage!

The paparazzi chased them all the way to their cars. Harry was furious, it meant he couldn't make his move without being photographed – his wife was a jealous woman who wouldn't appreciate late-night photos of him and the delec-table Ms Ivory getting into a car together while she sat at home in Fulham with two under-five children and his seventy-six-year-old mother. He had no choice but to allow Lara to go with Pierre.

However, all was not lost – he had a plan. Jumping in his rented Renault, he stuck close behind Pierre's car as they moved off into traffic.

As soon as he was sure they were not being followed, he began honking his horn and flashing his lights, forcing Pierre to pull over.

'What's the matter?' Lara asked, as Harry leaned in the window.

'Richard insisted I drive you home,' he said. 'I promised I would.'

'Why?'

'Because Pierre will never find the house.'

'Of course he will.'

'Do you have the address?'

'No . . .' she said, hesitating for a moment. 'But it's in St-Paul-de-Vence. I'm sure I can direct him.'

'There's a hundred twists and turns up there. You'll have

to come with me, otherwise you'll be driving around all night.'

'Harry—'

He shrugged as if he didn't care. 'Listen, luv, whatever you want.'

What she didn't want was to be lost in the hills with a French actor she hardly knew. 'You're right,' she said, reluctantly getting out of Pierre's car and into Harry's.

Pierre was not upset. It was late and he was tired – too tired to try scoring with an exquisite American movie star who would probably reject him. Besides, his real preference was men – a secret he'd managed to keep to himself on account of the fact it would ruin his blossoming career as a leading man.

Lara waved goodbye to Pierre, settling back in the passenger seat of Harry's Renault. She closed her eyes, and decided she must have been crazy leaving the security of Nikki and Richard to run around Monte Carlo with a couple of actors. Why did she always manage to do the wrong thing?

For a moment her mind drifted and she thought about Lee – her former boyfriend. Lee was a genuinely nice guy, admittedly not the most exciting man in the world – but he'd satisfied her needs.

What *were* her needs?

Someone to cuddle up with. A warm body in the middle of the night. Occasional sex. Companionship.

Christ, Lara, you sound as if you're seventy-five!

She frowned.

Harry glanced over at her. 'Don't look so happy,' he chided.

'I was thinking.'

'What about?'

'My ex-lover, if you must know.'

'Did you dump him?'

'He dumped me, actually.'

Harry laughed disbelievingly. 'That's impossible.'

'Told me he couldn't take the heat.'

'You have to be joking.'

A long deep sigh. 'I'm not.'

Harry considered the possibilities of a red-blooded male actually dumping Lara Ivory. It seemed highly unlikely. 'Why would he do a thing like that?' he asked at last. 'Was the fool brain-dead?'

'Too much attention,' Lara said wryly. 'And all directed at me.'

'You need to be with a fellow actor,' Harry said confidently. 'We *know* how to share.'

Sure, Lara thought. *The only thing actors know how to share is a scene, and then they'll kill for the close-ups.*

She'd met enough megalomaniac actors in her time.

The movie star with the polished pecs and the wry humour. He was addicted to steroids and only slept with models.

The macho action hero with the slit eyes and thin smile. He got off beating up on women and sexually abusing them – but only if they were below the line and couldn't fight back.

The popular black star who only considered busty blonds candidates for his extremely large waterbed.

The charismatic king of comedy with the enormous dick who was currently screwing his children's nanny.

And the 'serious' New York actor who could only get it up for transvestites.

Ah yes, movie stars, a charming, well-adjusted bunch.

While she was busy with her thoughts, Harry seized his opportunity. Swerving the car to the side of the road, he leaned over, pressing his warm lips down on hers.

'Harry!' she exclaimed, managing to push him away. 'What *do* you think you're doing?'

Words tumbled from his mouth in a senseless torrent as his hands went for her breasts. 'You're so fucking beautiful, Lara ... so gorgeous ... the first time I saw you ... my wife's a cold fish ... we never sleep together ... maybe a couple of times in the last year ... my cock burns for you ...'

She slapped him hard across the face – a theatrical gesture, but one that seemed to work.

'Good God!' he exclaimed, stopping his extended grope.

'Harry,' she said, sounding more calm than she felt. 'Get control of yourself. I do not get involved with married men, so kindly start the car and take me home.' He slumped away from her like a rejected fool. 'It's not that I don't find you attractive,' she continued, her voice softening. 'But everyone has to stick to their principles.'

Her smooth words soothed him. 'Sorry, Lara,' he muttered, quite abashed. 'It won't happen again.'

You bet it won't, she thought. *'Cause this is the one and only time I'll find myself alone in a car with you.*

'I'll forget if you will,' she said quietly, saving his damaged pride.

'Thanks,' he mumbled, and drove her to the villa where Richard waited at the front gate – standing outside like a protective father.

'Wasn't sure you had your keys,' Richard said, glaring at Harry.

Lara marched into the villa without a word to either of them.

Men! If only she could find one worth keeping, then maybe she'd be happy.

Or would she?

Could anyone make her forget the dark memories of her past?

Could anyone make everything all right?

27

Chapter Four

 ALISON SEWELL was never the pretty girl – always the outcast, a loner with no friends. By the time she was fourteen, she already weighed over a hundred and sixty pounds. Hefty and round-faced, the kids at school taunted her, calling her all sorts of names. 'Sewer' was a favourite, 'the Dump' and 'Big Boy' two others. Just because her mother made her cut her hair in a manly crop, it wasn't fair to call her Big Boy – that was downright mean. But Alison didn't care, she knew she was smarter than all of them, even though she managed to flunk out in most subjects.

'You're an idiot,' her father often said to her.

Then one day he fell off a ladder, hitting his head and suffering an untimely death. Who was the idiot now?

Shortly after her father passed away, Alison and her mother, Rita, a small sparrow of a woman who worked as a laundress at a downtown hotel, moved in with Rita's brother, Cyril. He lived in a small ramshackle house a short walk from the seediest part of Hollywood Boulevard. He was divorced and childless, and since he'd recently broken his leg while 'on the job', he needed help.

On the job for Cyril was photographing celebrities – usually when they didn't care to be photographed. He hung around outside popular restaurants and clubs, camera at the ready – grabbing any shots he could. His big claim to fame was catching Madonna and Sean Penn in a steamy embrace before anyone knew they were a couple. Pure luck, really. But he made plenty of money from those particular photos, and garnered a modicum of respect from the other freelancers, who couldn't believe Cyril had finally scored.

Alison was fascinated by Uncle Cyril, to her he was a celebrity himself. As soon as he recovered from his broken leg, she began following him around, watching in awe as he went about his job. Since Cyril had no children of his own, he didn't mind Alison trailing him, especially as she was strong enough to carry his equipment, and big enough to shove other photographers out of his way – a task she seemed to relish.

By the time she reached the age of twenty, Alison was taking pictures too. She knew where to go to catch the famous faces, and she didn't care what she had to do to get the shot. She proved to be more tenacious than Uncle Cyril, chasing her famous subjects aggressively into their cars and limos if they failed to cooperate – taunting them with insults – getting away with it because she was a female. Not an attractive one by any means – overweight, surly, pushy and rude. But because she was a woman they didn't dare fight back.

Uncle Cyril said she was a natural, but the other photographers loathed her. They nicknamed her 'the Hun' and steered clear.

Over the years Alison made some good scores. Whitney Houston screaming at Bobby Brown outside The Peninsula. Charlie Sheen screaming at *her* as she chased him and his sexy date to his limo. A dishevelled Nicholson exiting a club. A drunken Charlie Dollar falling down a flight of stairs. An abashed Hugh Grant outside the police station after being arrested for dallying with a prostitute. And Kim and Alec with their baby – a rare sighting.

And then, one day, into her life came Lara Ivory, and everything changed.

Obsession wasn't the word for it.

Chapter Five

 FRENCH SUMMER was almost finished and Lara felt the usual sadness that another film coming to an end always brought. Making a movie – especially on location – was like becoming part of an extended family – the family she didn't have. The nice thing was that everyone looked out for her – from the hair and make-up people to the teamsters and grips. She was a special favourite with film crews, because even though she was an enormous star, she wasn't a prima donna, and knew how to treat everyone with fairness and respect. Most of the male members of the crew usually fell in love with her. And why not? She was exquisitely beautiful with a gorgeous body, and as if that wasn't enough, she was smart, friendly, *and* a good sport.

Nikki had organized a lavish wrap party to take place at the rented villa. There were huge tables of food set up in the garden, and plenty of beer, wine and spirits to accommodate the mostly English crew. The tennis court had been transformed into a flashy disco complete with a dreadlocked disc jockey who was into sixties soul.

'Everything looks wonderful,' Lara exclaimed, emerging from her room, dressed in a filmy white sleeveless dress and flat sandals, skin glowing, her shoulder-length hair freshly washed.

'Enough with the wonderful shit,' Nikki responded, hands on black leather clad hips. 'I worked my butt off to make damn sure it's the wrap of the year. I want everyone to know that when they work on a Richard Barry movie, they *know* they're appreciated.'

'I hope Richard appreciates *you*,' Lara remarked.

'He'd better,' Nikki said with a grin.

'You've been so good for him,' Lara continued. 'He's a much nicer person.'

'Want him back?' Nikki asked jokingly.

Lara laughed. 'No, thank you.'

'That's good,' Nikki said, with another wide grin. ''Cause he's totally unavailable.'

As if he sensed he was the subject of discussion, Richard appeared, strolling out to the garden wearing beige linen pants and a casual silk shirt.

'Hmm . . .' Lara remarked. 'He even dresses better now.'

'Of course,' Nikki said. 'I drag him to Neiman's twice a year and make him spend all his money!'

'Are you two talking about me again?' he asked, as usual pretending not to enjoy the attention.

'You know, Richard,' Lara said, lightly touching his arm, 'you're incredibly lucky to have found a woman who cares so much about you.'

'Hey—' Richard objected. 'What about her? She got me!'

'Ah . . . the ego gets bigger and bigger,' Lara murmured.

'And that's not all,' Nikki said with a lewd wink, flinging her arms around Richard's waist and hugging him.

'Seriously, though,' Lara said. 'I couldn't be happier for the two of you.'

'Now all we have to do is find the right guy for you,' Nikki said, ever the matchmaker.

'I keep on telling you,' Lara said patiently, 'I'm perfectly content by myself.'

'Bull*shit*!' snorted Nikki. 'Everyone needs somebody.'

'I'm sure Lara is quite capable of finding him on her own,' Richard said, aggravated that Nikki was so intent on setting Lara up.

Lara wished they'd both leave her in peace. She was happy by herself – most of the time. 'I'm going to miss you guys,' she said wistfully. 'It won't be the same without you.'

'You'll be slaving so hard on *The Dreamer* you won't even notice we're missing,' Nikki said, referring to Lara's next movie, which started principal photography in the Hamptons in a week.

'I want to work with you two again,' Lara said. 'This was a memorable experience.'

'Tell your agent,' Nikki said crisply. 'According to him, you're booked for the next three years.'

'Nonsense!'

'Richard,' Nikki nudged her husband, excitement lighting her face, 'shall I tell Lara about the book I took an option on?'

'What book?' Lara asked curiously. 'And why are you mentioning it now when I'm practically out of here?'

'It's called *Revenge*,' Nikki said, her eyes sparkling with enthusiasm. 'A true story about a schoolteacher who gets gang-raped – nearly dies – then recovers and exacts her own form of punishment.'

'Sounds exciting.'

'I'm producing,' Nikki announced proudly. 'My first attempt.'

'That's great!'

'Richard's promised to help – which means he'll be keeping a steely eye on everything I do. I'm going for a hot young director. Unfortunately, it's a depressingly low budget. But the lead's a fantastic role for an actress.'

'I don't get it,' Lara said. 'Why didn't you *tell* me?'

Nikki shot a baleful glare at Richard. '*He* said I shouldn't bug you.'

'Which is exactly what you're doing now,' Richard interrupted, with a *What am I going to do with you?* look. 'I've told you, Nikki, this is not the kind of movie Lara would be interested in.'

'Do you have a script yet?' Lara asked.

'Nothing I'm satisfied with.'

'I'd love to read it.'

'Just for fun?' Nikki asked hopefully.

'I'm curious to see what you're letting yourself in for.'

'She has no idea,' Richard said drily. 'Try stopping her – *I* can't.'

'Isn't that what life's all about,' Lara said gently. 'Helping other people achieve their dreams?'

'Right on!' agreed Nikki, squeezing Richard's arm. 'And when I'm a big fat mega-rich producer with an out-of-control coke habit, a live-in stud and a majorly inflated budget, the *first* person I'll hire will be Richard Barry – who by that time will be an ancient out-of-shape drunk, living in Santa Barbara with nothing but his memories and a couple of senile fart-filled dogs.'

'Thanks, darling,' Richard said ruefully. 'You sure know how to make a person feel good about himself.'

'Only joking.'

'Like I didn't know that?'

'Don't get uptight.'

'Who's uptight?'

'You two,' Lara said, shaking her head and laughing. 'You're acting like a roadshow version of Virginia Woolf!'

'Let's go get a drink,' said Richard. 'We may as well be first.'

☆ ☆ ☆

Much later in the evening Harry Solitaire grabbed Lara on the dance floor. He was sweating through his red polo shirt, his hands clammy as he placed them clumsily on her shoulders. His wife, a pleasant-looking English girl who'd arrived in time to spend the last weekend with her husband, sat in a corner conversing with the first AD. Lara felt sorry for the poor girl. After Harry's aborted attempt at making it with her, he'd had a series of one-nighters with her stand-in, the continuity woman, and two extras. There was no such thing as a secret fuck on location, everyone knew the moment it happened.

'I want to thank you for not saying anything about the other night,' he said, shooting a furtive glance at his wife, feverishly hoping the first AD was not saying anything he shouldn't.

'Why don't you try being a gentleman and stop cheating on your wife?' Lara suggested. 'What would you do if she carried on the same way?'

'She wouldn't,' Harry said gruffly.

'Maybe she should,' Lara retorted crisply. 'See how you'd like it.'

'My wife's not that kind of woman,' he said, sweat beading his upper lip.

'What makes you so sure?'

'It's different for men,' he said, as if she should understand. 'Everyone knows that.'

'No,' Lara said unwaveringly, 'that's where you're wrong.'

Harry was not about to argue. He had the delectable Lara Ivory in his arms, and this was his last chance to score. He pulled her so close she could feel his erection pressing against her thigh. Before she could move away, he managed a sly – 'I'd give my left ball to make love to you. You know that, don't you?'

'Oh, for God's sake, grow up, Harry,' she said, pushing him away and leaving the dance floor.

Wrap parties. Sometimes they were too much of a good thing.

☆ ☆ ☆

The next morning Lara departed early for the airport. Nikki and Richard came to the door of the villa to see her off – both clad in terry-cloth bathrobes, bleary-eyed with monster hangovers.

'Can't believe it's over,' Nikki said, stretching her arms high above her head.

'I know what you mean,' Lara agreed. 'I feel the same way.'

'Be sure to look after yourself, sweetheart,' Richard said, squeezing her hand. 'Anything you need – call me. You know I'm always here for you. Day or night.'

'I hate goodbyes,' Lara said, giving them both a quick hug and jumping in the car, her luggage already loaded. She didn't look back as the car left the driveway.

Her loyal assistant, Cassie, met her at Nice airport. Cassie was an overweight woman in her mid-thirties who bore a fleeting resemblance to Elizabeth Taylor in her Larry Fortensky years. She'd worked for Lara for six years and made sure everything went smoothly. Today she was anxious to get Lara on the plane to Paris, where they would make a connection to New York.

'I'm tired,' Lara said, yawning.

'You don't look it.'

A man from the airline fell all over himself to help them aboard. Another airline representative met them in Paris and escorted them to their Air France flight to New York. Lara settled into her first-class window seat. Cassie handed her the script of *The Dreamer*, and a large plastic bottle of Evian water.

'Thanks,' she said, taking an unladylike swig. 'If I fall asleep, don't wake me.'

'Not even for food?'

'No, Cassie, especially not for food!'

A businessman across the aisle was stretching his neck to get a better look at her. Finally he couldn't stand it any longer and came over. 'Lara Ivory,' he said, his middle-aged voice filled with a mixture of awe and admiration.

'That's me,' she said brightly, knowing exactly what he would say next.

She was right. 'You're far more beautiful in the flesh,' he managed.

She smiled, dazzling him – even though it was still morning and she had on casual clothes and hardly any make-up. 'Thank you,' she murmured.

Cassie ran interference, placing her considerable bulk between Lara and her admiring fan.

He took the hint and returned to his seat.

'Civilians!' Cassie muttered.

Lara wondered what it would be like to go out with a civilian. The only men she came in contact with were connected to movies – actors, producers, directors, the crew. She'd met Lee while working on a film – Richard had set up their first date. Lee had been painfully shy – a condition not helped by being thrust into the limelight as her boyfriend. They'd spent most of their year together at her house in LA. She'd known two months before the break-up that it was coming. There was no passion left in their relationship, and Lee wasn't happy living in her shadow. Plus she was being tracked by an obsessed stalker which made him crazy. Eventually they'd agreed to part amicably, and she hadn't heard from him since.

'The steward wondered if he could get your autograph,' Cassie said.

'Sure,' she replied. 'Tell him to come over.'

A few minutes later, the steward – a gay guy with impossibly long eyelashes and gentle eyes – knelt beside her seat. 'I'm *so* sorry to disturb you, Ms Ivory,' he said in reverent tones, 'only my friend would hang and quarter me if I *dared* to come home without your signature. Is it a terrible imposition if I ask you to sign his book?'

'Of course not,' she replied, with a faint smile. 'Do you have a pen?'

'Right here,' he said, fumbling in his pocket.

'What's your friend's name?' she asked, taking the blue leather book from him.

'Put "To Sam, the man of my dreams".'

Graciously she did as he requested. Some stars wouldn't sign autographs at all, others made their fans pay for it. Lara felt privileged that she even got asked. Being a movie star was a big responsibility – people looked up to her. She remembered seeing Demi Moore on *David Letterman* once, stripping off to an almost non-existent bikini. At the time Demi was the highest-paid female star in the world, and it seemed so dumb that she would get up and blow her image in front of millions of viewers – becoming just another babe with a body. Of course, she'd redeemed herself with a stellar performance in *GI Jane*, but was that enough?

Lara slept most of the journey, waking half an hour before their arrival in New York. She'd hoped to spend a few days at her house in LA, but there wasn't time. Three frantic days of costume fittings and interviews in New York, and then she had to leave for the house the studio had rented for her in the Hamptons. Cassie had flown in several weeks earlier to check the place out. 'It's absolutely your style,' Cassie had assured her. 'Very Martha Stewart – comfortable, with a pretty garden and beach access. Oh yes, and you'll love this – extremely private.'

Cassie knew her well, when she wasn't working she loved seclusion. Parties and the night life were not for her.

A limo took her straight to the St Regis Hotel, where she was booked into the Oriental Suite, courtesy of Orpheus Studios, who were in charge of her for the next seven weeks while she shot *The Dreamer* – a light comedy about two divorced people who meet, fall in love, fall out of love, and finally get together for good. It was a contemporary piece – a welcome change from Richard's film, where day after day she'd been locked into excruciatingly uncomfortable period gowns. She'd loved making the movie – hated wearing the clothes.

Her co-star in *The Dreamer* was Kyle Carson – a bankable star who'd recently separated from his wife of seventeen years. Lara had met Kyle briefly at several industry events and he'd seemed attractive and charming – she hoped his recent separation hadn't changed him. The director was Miles Kieffer, an old friend, who'd directed her in her first movie.

The hotel staff greeted her with welcoming smiles, remembering her last visit. She was gracious to everyone, it wasn't in her nature to be otherwise.

The manager personally ushered her upstairs to the sumptuous suite, making sure she had everything she required.

She often reflected on the strangeness of her life. Limos and rented houses, first-class travel, everybody ready to grant her slightest whim. It was understandable that movie stars grew to believe their own publicity and importance. They were so protected and cosseted that reality ceased to exist.

She'd been thinking about Nikki's project, and wanted to read the book. She called out to Cassie, who was in the bedroom, busily unpacking for her. 'Do me a favour, Cass,' she said, wandering into the room. 'Call Barnes & Noble and have them send over a copy of *Revenge*.'

'It's done,' Cassie said, heading for the phone.

The book arrived within the hour. After eating a light room-service dinner, she sat down to read.

She read way into the night, finally falling asleep with the book in her lap. She awoke early, and at nine a.m. New York time called her agent in LA.

'Quinn,' she said, 'is it true I'm booked for the next three years?'

'You're as busy as you want to be, Lara,' Quinn replied, struggling to wake up. 'I could have you working steadily for three, four, five years – take your pick.'

'What if I felt like making a small low-budget movie?'

That *really* woke him. 'Why would you even consider such a thing?' he asked, alarmed.

'*Could* I do it?' she persisted.

'It's possible.' A pause. 'Is there something I should know about?'

'Not right now.'

'Good,' he said, relieved. 'Can I go back to sleep?'

'You certainly can.' Thoughtfully she replaced the receiver. Quinn was an excellent agent, but like most agents his prime interest was making money. She pictured his face if she told him she wished to do Nikki's film.

And if the script turned out to be as powerful as the book, there was a strong possibility.

Chapter Six

 THEY FORMED a group in the corner of the room – two casting women, the male director and a female producer. Joey concentrated on the women. One by one he gave them powerful eye contact – penetrating looks that signalled *If this was another time – another place – I'd like to fuck you until you screamed for mercy. Until your hot little pussies couldn't stand it any more. Until you came ten times.* Women read into his silent looks, it worked every time.

The female producer – pretty in an older bimbo kind of way – cleared her throat. Joey knew she must have humped some poor schmuck to get this gig – maybe she was even married to the geezer.

The two casting women were opposites. One young, one old. One fair, one dark. One short, the other tall. They were both unattractive. He gave them the treatment anyway.

The director was a straight white male, married with a shiny gold wedding ring to prove it.

'Are you prepared to read?' the female producer asked.

Joey nodded, glancing briefly at the pages he'd been studying in the waiting room. Then he placed the typed sides on a table, and performed the scene from memory, with the younger casting woman reading the other role. He gave it his best and when he was finished he knew that he'd managed to impress them.

The older casting woman lowered her spectacles, staring directly at him. 'Weren't you in *Solid*?' she asked.

''S right,' he responded, pleased she remembered.

'That was—'

'Six years ago,' he interrupted, saying it first so it didn't seem as if he had anything to hide.

'What have you done since then?' asked the director, twisting his wedding ring as if he wanted to wrench it off his finger.

'My mother got sick,' Joey said, turning on the sincerity full voltage. 'Hadda go home and look after the family.'

'I'm *so* sorry,' gushed the female producer, playing with a strand of stringy blond hair. 'I do hope she's better now.'

'No,' Joey replied in his best Little Boy Lost voice. 'She, uh . . . died. I stayed to see my little sister through school.'

'That's so *caring* you would do that,' exclaimed the younger casting woman, hungry eyes coming on to him.

'Well . . .' he said modestly. 'Now I'm back, an' I gotta get my career goin' again.'

'This is a very small role,' warned the director.

'Can't expect the lead every time,' Joey quipped.

'Nice reading,' said the female producer.

'Thanks for coming in,' said the director.

'We'll be in touch with your agent,' said the older casting woman.

Joey knew dismissal when it was staring him in the face. But that didn't mean he wouldn't get hired. They liked him, he could tell.

He exited the office with a jaunty swagger. Outside, in the waiting room, were a dozen young actors sweating their turn. 'Don't bother,' he informed them, cracking his knuckles. 'I nailed it.'

Nothing like making them feel insecure.

Four days later he got the part.

'It's decent money,' Madelaine informed him. 'Three days' work spread out over two weeks' location in the Hamptons – they'll pay for your hotel and a reasonable per diem. Don't let me down, Joey.'

'Would I do that, Maddy?' he asked innocently.

That night he satisfied her in bed, sending her to sleep with a smile on her face. He'd slipped a Halcion into her decaf cappuccino, causing her to sleep so soundly that she was unaware when he left the apartment.

He roamed the streets restlessly, finally going into a strip club and paying a cheap-looking girl with large silicon-enhanced breasts to perform a private lap dance. She did nothing for him. She was a whore. He hated her. Why did he keep on punishing himself with fast cheap sex that meant nothing?

He took a cab back to Madelaine's apartment and eased into bed beside her. He'd never had a relationship that meant a damn thing. Never. In this life you had to use or get used. Sex was power. That's all.

He lay on his back, eyes wide open, unable to sleep.

Sometimes the screaming in his head was so loud it was impossible to live with.

☆ ☆ ☆

Madelaine took out insurance and paid for Joey to go to an acting coach. Even though he'd let her down once, she was so pathetically grateful to have him back she convinced herself he would never leave her again. Somehow she managed to ignore the nagging voice of her subconscious that kept assuring her he would.

Patsy Boon, his acting coach, was a big brassy Australian

blond, who favoured billowy kaftans and addressed him as 'sweetie'. 'Do it this way, sweetie.' '*Never* slouch, sweetie.' 'Pitch is everything, sweetie.'

Patsy chain-drank tea and spent half her time in the bathroom, but she gave him confidence. He hadn't acted in six years and he needed the reassurance that he could still do it.

Of course he immediately charmed Patsy, and she soon offered extra coaching for free.

By the time he set off on location, he felt pretty secure he was ready to deliver a worthy performance – one that might get him noticed and back on track. Fuck it. He had no time to waste.

As soon as he arrived in the Hamptons, Madelaine called. 'What's the hotel like?' she asked.

'Small, nothin' fancy.'

'I thought I might come down for the weekend – spend a couple of days.'

'That'd be great, Maddy.'

No. It wouldn't. Didn't want the cast and crew knowing he was schtupping the old bag. Even worse – an agent old bag. They'd all think she'd gotten him the part. Truth was she hadn't. His *talent* had gotten him the part. His *presence*.

He was smart enough not to put her off. At the last minute he'd think of something to keep her safely in New York.

He was supposed to go straight to the wardrobe trailer and get fitted for his clothes. Instead he took a stroll around, getting his bearings. Parked behind the hotel were the huge mobile movie trailers, lined up like a long circus procession. Clothes, make-up, camera equipment, props, lighting, the stars' trailers, and a scattering of trucks and cars driven by union men who sat around swapping dirty jokes and playing cards. Joey checked out the names on the stars' trailers. Kyle Carson and Lara Ivory. One of these days maybe his name would be on the side of a trailer. *Joey Lorenzo*. That would be a day to make him proud.

After exploring, he went back to his room and took a shot of vodka from the minibar. It wasn't like he had a drinking problem, he simply wanted to be as relaxed and charming as possible when he hit the set.

The truth was he wanted everyone to love him.

Chapter Seven

 'I WANT to read the script before anyone else,' Lara said, holding the phone away from her ear as Roxy, her hair person, attempted to streak her hair, folding thin strands of honey-blond locks into skinny strips of tinfoil.

'You loved the book *that* much?' Nikki exclaimed excitedly.

'Couldn't put it down. I was up all night reading. I look like Quasimodo today.'

'Yeah, sure,' muttered Roxy. 'In a freakin' pig's ear.' Roxy was a Brooklyn girl with razor-cut bright-red hair, a skinny body, and several fierce-looking body piercings. She'd done Lara's hair on three movies and they had a congenial working relationship.

'I should have something I'm happy with soon,' Nikki said. 'Maybe I'll deliver it myself, spend a day or two.'

'Will Richard allow you to do that?'

'*Allow* me!' Nikki said, laughing. 'Are you *serious*? Besides, when we get back to LA he'll be shut in the editing rooms eighteen hours a day – you know what he's like when he's finishing a movie.'

'Yes, I remember,' Lara said, recalling many long and lonely nights.

'I'm completely psyched you like the book!' Nikki said.

46

'It's very empowering.'

'True story. I met the woman it happened to, she's a real survivor.'

'Get me a script as soon as possible,' Lara said. 'If it's as strong as the book, we're in business.'

'Oh, wow! This is crazy.'

'Why?'

''Cause there's no way we can afford you.'

'How about scale and a piece of the action?'

'Quinn would *never* let you do that.'

'I spoke to him this morning.'

'You *did*?'

'He may *think* he controls my career – the truth is, I'm in charge.'

'Tell me about it,' Nikki said knowingly. 'Everybody imagines you're this delicate little flower, but underneath the sweetness lies a heart of stone, right?'

Lara chuckled. 'Right.'

'And talking of your stony heart, you'd better find someone to date on this movie. You're definitely in need of thawing out.'

'How many times must I tell you?' Lara sighed. 'I'm perfectly happy on my own.'

'In that case I'm buying you a vibrator for your birthday.'

'You're vulgar, you know that?'

'What's vulgar about a vibrator? It's better than a man any day, and vibrators don't give you any shit. They're reliable, always on time, and you don't have to look your best.'

Lara laughed and hung up.

'Did I hear the word vibrator?' Roxy asked, skilfully folding tinfoil.

'My friend Nikki,' Lara replied. 'All she's interested in is fixing me up.'

'Nikki ... Nikki ... isn't she the costume designer who *married* your ex-husband?'

'That's her.'

'Jeez – you're understanding,' Roxy said, rolling her eyes. 'I got two exes, an' if I see either of 'em walkin' down the street, I cross over to avoid 'em. They're both bastards. One of 'em was screwin' my sister – an' the other one I caught wearin' *my* best black dress along with *my* gold evening shoes. How's *that* for balls of steel?'

'I'm sure you handled it perfectly.'

'You bet! I raced into Bloomingdale's, charged five thousand bucks' worth of designer clothes on his credit card, then divorced the cross-dressing sonofabitch.' She shrieked with laughter. 'I wasn't around to see his face when he got the bill – gotta hunch he's *still* payin' it off.'

Lara smiled, for as long as she'd known Roxy there were always tales of dastardly men who'd done her wrong. Yoko, her regular make-up person, also had man problems, as did Angie, her stand-in. It was nice that on this movie she'd be surrounded by familiar faces – women she'd worked with before, and enjoyed having around.

'Did you run into Mr Carson yet?' Roxy asked, standing back to admire her work.

'Not yet.'

'Major babe,' Roxy said, sucking in her cheeks.

'What's his reputation?' Lara asked, knowing that Roxy always had the inside story.

Roxy spoke and worked at the same time. 'His wife threw him out on account of the fact she found him playin' you show me yours I'll show you mine with some bimbo TV anchor. *I* should be so lucky. A week later she ran off with her trainer. Word is, Kyle wants wifey-pie back, 'cause she's goin' for half his fortune. An' since he's made like a jillion movies in the last ten years, she could score big.'

'*Very* big.'

'You know what surprises me about guys?' Roxy said, raising her thinly pencilled eyebrows.

'What?' Lara asked, amused.

'They're always ready to give up their pissy little dicks, but when it comes to money, they hang on like we're nailin' their precious balls to the hood of a 1965 Cadillac!'

'You're so eloquent,' Lara said, still smiling.

'Yeah, that's what my date said the other night – right after I told him to screw off on account of the fact he came all over my new Anne Klein skirt.'

'Roxy!'

'Well, he did,' she said indignantly. 'What was I *supposed* to do? Kiss him? I don't think so.'

As Roxy finished twisting the last strip of tinfoil there was a knock on the trailer door.

'Who is it?' Roxy yelled out.

The door opened a few inches and Kyle Carson stuck his head in. He was good-looking in a laid-back way – kind of a latter day Gary Cooper. He had an easygoing smile and fine brown hair that seemed to be thinning in the front, although a cunning hairpiece hid this fact from his adoring fans.

'Hello,' he said. 'Is Lara Ivory around?'

Lara twisted in her chair. 'You've caught me in my tinfoil,' she said, pulling a rueful face.

'Will it embarrass you if I come in?'

'Not at all.'

'Hi,' he said, ambling inside. 'I've heard nothing but good things about working with you. I'm delighted we're finally doing it.'

'So am I,' she said, as he moved over to shake her hand. 'And meet Roxy, she's the hair genius who always makes me look good.'

49

'Oh, yeah,' Roxy muttered. 'It takes a lot of geniuses to make *you* look good.'

'Thought I should come find you,' Kyle said. 'Since we're starting work tomorrow.' He was staring at her beauty – very evident in spite of her tinfoiled hair. 'Uh . . . if there's anything I can do for you – if you'd like to run lines before we get together in front of the camera, that's fine with me. Maybe dinner at the hotel tonight?'

'I'm not staying at the hotel,' Lara replied. 'The studio's rented me a house.'

'That's what they were going to do for me,' he said. 'Only I figured since I recently separated from my wife, I wouldn't enjoy being stuck alone in a house. Thought a hotel might make things easier.'

'I'm sure you're right,' she agreed.

'You *do* know I'm separated?' he asked, making sure she was aware he was semi-available.

'I heard.'

'About tonight – I could drop by *your* house if that makes it easier for you.'

'You know, Kyle, I just got back from Europe and I'm still jet-lagged. Would you mind if we rehearsed on the set tomorrow?'

'Hey,' he shrugged. 'Simply trying to accommodate you.'

'That's very sweet, I appreciate it.'

He gave her another easygoing smile before exiting the trailer.

'Oh, boy,' Roxy said. 'Has he got a hot nut for you!'

'He's being polite,' Lara said.

'Polite my ass – he was drooling all over you.' Roxy sighed wistfully. 'But then, they all do, don't they? You ever get sick of it?'

'It's the image they drool over,' Lara replied thoughtfully.

'As an actress I create characters on the screen people fall in love with.'

'*You* call it love – *I* call it lust!' Roxy said with a dirty laugh. 'I gotta tell you, there's not a guy I know that doesn't wanna screw you.'

'Thanks, Roxy,' Lara said drily. 'That's exactly what I wanted to hear.'

'Honey, the truth is the truth. Wake up and smell the hard-on.'

A few minutes later, Miles, the director, appeared. He was a tall man in his early fifties with a mane of longish silver hair, steel-rimmed glasses and an animated expression.

'I guess this is my day for getting caught with my hair in a mess,' Lara said as he bent down, kissing her on the cheek.

'You're always exquisite, my dear. I'll never forget the first time you walked into my office.'

'I'll never forget it either, Miles. You started me on this road.'

'And you've travelled it well, my sweet.'

'Thanks,' she said, indicating her hair. 'I thought the lighter blond streaks would work for the character.'

He squinted at her hair. 'You were right.'

'It's Roxy's idea – she's doing a great job.'

'I can see.' He perched on the edge of the counter, facing her. 'So, how was it, working with Richard now that you're divorced?'

'Absolutely a great experience. I love him *and* Nikki.'

'That's a healthy attitude.'

'Being married to him was a nightmare. Having him as a friend is a whole other deal.'

Miles nodded as if he totally understood. 'I hear good things about the movie.'

'Yes?'

'The word is excellent.'

'Richard's a marvellous director. He knows exactly what he's doing.'

'So do you.'

'I'm looking forward to working with *you* again, Miles.'

'We'll have a splendid time.'

'How's Ginny?'

'Still into her charity thing in LA. I'm sure she'll try and visit. Oh, and she sends you her love.'

'Send mine back.'

'How about dinner tonight?'

'Do you mind if I pass? I'm planning on getting a good night's sleep so I'll be bright and camera ready in the morning.'

'Then I'll see you tomorrow.' He blew her a kiss and left the trailer.

'Another one with a crush on you,' Roxy remarked.

'You think everybody has got a crush on me,' Lara said, exasperated. 'Miles is a married man.'

'The worst kind,' Roxy said with a knowing wink. 'Show me a married man and I'll show you a hard-on in full bloom, only it ain't directed in the wife's direction.'

'You're such a cynic.'

Roxy laughed. 'You got that right.'

Later, back at her rented house, Cassie had arranged for the Filipino cook to fix them a light salad. They sat out on the back deck overlooking a stretch of white sand and the sea. There were wooden steps leading down to the beach, edged with a profusion of evergreens and colourful wild flowers.

Lara took a deep breath. 'I know I'm going to love it here,' she said, gazing out at the ocean. 'You picked a winner, Cass.'

'I'll do my best to keep out of your way,' Cassie said. 'All you have to do is yell when you want me around.'

'Hey – I *asked* you to stay here with me, I'd be nervous on my own.'

'Not much crime here,' Cassie remarked.

'It's not crime I'm worried about,' Lara retorted. 'Ever since I was stalked by that crazy woman last year, I feel more comfortable not being by myself.'

'At least *your* stalker's in jail.'

'She'll be out,' Lara said, her beautiful face grim for once.

'That's stardom,' Cassie said with a flippant laugh. 'Your own personal stalker!'

'Something I can *definitely* do without,' Lara said, thinking briefly of the obnoxious and frightening woman who'd followed her everywhere for several scary months, taking photographs, sending numerous letters and gifts – and worst of all – turning up at her front door on countless occasions.

'The good news is,' Cassie said, 'that we've got a guard every night. He'll be sitting in his car at the front of the house – probably asleep on the job, but we can buzz him any time we want.'

'I hate having to live like this,' Lara fretted.

'The studio's paying,' Cassie said, practical as ever. 'What does it matter?'

Cassie didn't get it, but that was OK. Being stalked was a living nightmare. 'I think I'll take a walk along the beach,' she said. 'Care to join me?'

'Much as I fancy the idea,' Cassie said, shifting her comfortable bulk, 'I'd sooner have a piece of chocolate cake and a carton of ice cream.'

Lara raised a disapproving eyebrow. 'What happened to your diet?'

'I left it in LA along with all those hard bodies.'

'Hmm . . .' Lara said. 'When we get back I'm buying you a year's membership at a health club.'

'I'd sooner have a Porsche!'

'Very funny,' Lara said, laughing. 'I'm going to walk before it's dark. Be sure I get a wake-up call at five thirty.'

'It's done,' Cassie said, her favourite expression.

The beach was windswept and deserted. Lara strolled by the seashore, kicking off her sandals and walking barefoot, loving the feel of the damp sand on her feet.

She thought about Nikki's book, and the role of Rebecca – the rape victim who takes her own revenge. She wanted to play the part; it was a challenge, and life *should* be a challenge sometimes.

Of course, it wasn't a star vehicle, but if the script was good, she was definitely interested. She had all the success she could ever possibly want – why not take on something risky? Something that would stretch her as an actress? Something that could maybe help her avenge her past?

Lara Ivory – beautiful movie star. If people knew the real truth . . .

If they only knew . . .

Chapter Eight

 AFTER BEING away from LA for almost three months Nikki had a thousand things to do. Her fifteen-year-old daughter, Summer, was arriving any moment, so her main concern was opening up the Malibu house and getting everything organized. Summer sometimes spent vacation time with Nikki, but mostly she stayed with her father in Chicago.

Nikki often reflected on her former life and wondered how she'd ever been that person. Mrs Sheldon Weston – respectable wife and mother – locked into a loveless marriage simply because she'd gotten herself pregnant at the age of sixteen during an adventurous six-week fling with an older man. Sheldon had done the right thing and married her. Well, he'd had to, he was twenty-two years older than her and a respected psychiatrist – he couldn't risk tarnishing his spotless reputation. Plus her uptight parents had insisted he marry her. If it wasn't for them she might not have been such a wild child, but since sex was never allowed so much as a mention in their house, she'd had to go out and find out for herself. So, even though she'd balked at going through with it, neither Sheldon nor her parents had given her a choice. She'd been sixteen – what did she know?

Apart from being an extremely successful psychiatrist,

Sheldon was a very controlling man – similar to her father in a way. Once they were married, Nikki found he expected her to obey his every whim, and while at first she enjoyed playing the obedient little wife, it soon grew to be a burden – especially after Summer was born.

By that time Nikki was seventeen and craved fun.

Sheldon was thirty-nine and expected her to always be at home waiting for him.

After a couple of years she had a hunch he played around. She knew that many a society woman flopped down on his couch and told him everything, and while they were there, she suspected he did a lot more than listen. It took her years to catch him – and when she did, she had no firm evidence to take to court.

Divorcing Sheldon had not been easy. He hadn't relished letting her go, in fact, he'd threatened that if she left him, she'd never see Summer again.

His threats had not worked. She'd hired a canny female lawyer and fought back, ending up with shared custody.

Summer was eight when they split, and extremely verbal about spending the majority of her time with her father at his rambling house in the suburbs of Chicago where she could ride horses and keep her pet rabbits. She hated her mother's small apartment, so Nikki gave up – allowing her to stay with Sheldon.

It was a mistake. Summer bonded with her father and began treating Nikki like a slightly crazy older sister.

Nikki was hurt, but over the years she'd grown to accept it. Instead of parenting, she'd concentrated on getting together a career, starting as an assistant and eventually becoming a much in demand costume designer on movies – much to Sheldon's chagrin.

When Richard Barry had arrived in town to shoot a film,

he'd requested Nikki as clothes designer. She'd been flattered and intrigued.

Their first meeting was classic Richard, he'd shot orders at her as if she was still an assistant, which infuriated her. After a while she'd taken him to one side and set him straight. 'I know you're this big Hollywood director,' she'd told him, 'but I have a reputation of my own, so please don't tell me how to do my job – and I won't tell you how to direct your movie.'

Two nights later they were in bed together, and to her surprise and delight it was pretty sensational sex.

By the time the movie was finished, Richard had asked her to marry him and she'd accepted – even though he was another older man.

Now they had been married two years, and although Richard didn't approve, she'd decided she wanted to become a producer and was trying to get *Revenge* together.

Since she'd married a famous film director and moved to Los Angeles, Summer was a lot warmer toward Nikki. Now she actually seemed to look forward to spending vacation time with them. Of course, the fact that they had a beach house in Malibu helped.

Summer was extremely pretty, tall and coltish, with long white-blond hair – natural of course – and a Lolita-type demeanour. Richard had nicknamed her jailbait, and whenever they were together they giggled a lot. It occurred to Nikki that Summer got along much better with men than women.

Recently Sheldon had married again. Nikki had thought Summer would hate Rachel, Sheldon's new bride, considering she was only three years older than Summer. But quite the contrary, the two girls had become quite close; in fact, Summer had even asked if she could bring Rachel with her for a few days.

'Absolutely not,' Nikki had said, horrified at the thought.

Nikki ran around the house making sure everything was right. She was thrilled Lara had asked to see the script, what a coup if she agreed to make the movie!

Today the writer was delivering his final draft. She hoped it arrived before Summer, because all she really wanted to do was sit quietly in a corner and read.

☆ ☆ ☆

Summer Weston checked out the young limo driver holding up a white card with her name printed on it in big bold letters. He was cute in a goofy way, with sticking-up carrot-colour hair and a cheeky expression. He stared at her bug-eyed, and couldn't believe his luck when she headed straight for him.

'Hi,' she said, casually. 'You're meeting me.'

'I am?'

'Yup,' she said, thrusting her carry-on bag at him.

He took the bag and said, 'Uh . . . shall I bring the car around, or d'you want to come with me to the lot?'

'I've got like luggage.'

'A lot?'

'Six bags.'

'You're here to stay, then?'

'Maybe,' she said, flirting.

'Whyn't I take you to the luggage carousel, then I'll go get the limo.'

'Cool,' she said, excited that Nikki had sent a limo to meet her.

They began the long walk. 'You an actress?' he asked, throwing her a sideways glance.

She giggled, flinging back her long blond hair. 'What do you think?' she responded, pleased that he thought she was.

He squinted at her. 'You look like that girl in *Clueless* – y'know, Alicia something.'

'Well, I'm not.'

''S OK,' he said casually. 'You're prettier.'

'Honestly?'

A laconic— 'Yeah.'

This was an excellent start to her trip. A sure sign LA was the place for her to be. Her father had wanted her to go to the Bahamas with him and his teenage wife, but much to his annoyance, she'd refused. The less time she had to spend with him the better.

They arrived at the luggage carousel and waited for her bags to appear. 'I'm Jed,' her driver said, edging close to her. 'Doing this job to make the rent – in real life I'm an actor.'

'You must meet a lot of cool people.'

'Yeah,' he laughed. 'Like you. Only you can't score me a job.'

'My stepfather's a famous director,' she boasted.

'No shit? What's his name?'

'Richard Barry.'

His eyes bugged. 'I'm impressed.'

Later, sitting in the back of a long silver limo heading for Malibu, she reached in her purse and lit up a joint. She'd been smoking grass for two years, it helped her get through all the things she had to put up with. Without it she didn't know what she would've done.

Jed caught on immediately – sniffing the air – eyeing her in his rear-view mirror. 'You're gonna stink up the car,' he remarked.

'So,' she said haughtily. '*I'm* paying.'

'Right,' he said, snickering. 'You an' your rich daddy.'

'Want a drag?' she offered. 'It's free.'

He hesitated for a moment, then said, 'Why not?'

She moved over to the glass partition, passing him the joint. He dragged deeply. A veteran.

'I could get canned for this,' he said, not sounding too upset at the prospect.

'Yes, but think how amazing you'll feel for the rest of the day,' she said with a giggle.

'You got that right,' he responded, with a crooked smirk.

By the time the limo reached Malibu he'd given her his phone number and the name of a club where he hung out when he wasn't working. 'Come on by,' he said, hot for this girl with the long blond hair and the primo grass.

'Maybe I will,' she said, still flirting.

'Maybe you should,' he replied, thinking that he'd finally found a live one.

☆ ☆ ☆

Nikki heard the limo pull up and hurried to the door, throwing it open.

'Hi, Mom,' Summer said, emerging from the car, slightly stoned but hiding it well. 'Where's Richard?'

'Editing,' Nikki replied, hurt that the first words out of Summer's mouth were, *Where's Richard?* 'Don't I get a hug and a kiss?'

'Whatever,' Summer said casually, giving her mother a perfunctory hug.

Nikki wasn't sure, but for a moment she thought she smelled the strong aroma of pot.

The young driver was busily unloading suitcases from the trunk. Nikki directed him to Summer's room.

'LA's awesome,' Summer announced, wandering through the house. 'Chicago's like *soo* hot and muggy. Ugh! *Disgusto* weather!'

60

'It *is* beautiful here,' Nikki agreed, following her. 'I guess I never take the time to appreciate it.'

'Course, I could've gone with Daddy and Rachel to the Bahamas,' Summer continued. 'Thing is I've already been there twice and it's way boring. Besides, I wanted to see Richard – and you, of course.'

'That's terrific,' Nikki said, checking out her daughter's outfit, shades of early Madonna crossed with Courtney Love – a look that did not suit Summer's fresh prettiness. 'Let's go shopping tomorrow,' she suggested. 'We'll explore Melrose, there's plenty of new stores I'm sure you'll love.'

Summer groaned, as if it was the worst idea she'd ever heard. 'C'mon, Mom, y'know we don't have the same taste.'

'I'm hardly an old fuddy-duddy,' Nikki replied, resenting Summer's comment. 'In fact, I am one of the most successful clothes designers in movies.' *I'm also younger than Madonna*, she thought. *So don't treat me like some decrepit old fart.*

'Yeah, Mom. Thing is – you like *so* don't get me.'

Great! She didn't get her own daughter.

'I'm starving,' Summer said, racing into the kitchen. 'Is there anything to eat?'

There was plenty to eat, but Summer had this infuriating habit of flinging open the fridge and saying, 'Yuck! Nothing edible!' She did it now. Then she threw open every cupboard in the kitchen, failing to close them.

Nikki tried to stay calm, her daughter's messy habits drove her totally insane.

'Bummer!' Summer exclaimed. 'Richard's not home and there's no food.'

'Tell me what you'd like, and I'll send the maid to the market.'

'Forget it, Mom. I'm gonna hit the beach. I plan on getting a way cool tan.'

61

So much for mother–daughter bonding, Nikki thought ruefully.

☆ ☆ ☆

The moment the messenger delivered the script, Nikki grabbed it and hurried onto the deck overlooking the beach. Summer was lying down below on the sand, topless. Since she was almost flat-chested it didn't really matter, except that it *was* inappropriate – especially as this was a public beach where you were not supposed to do that kind of thing.

She contemplated calling down and telling her to put on a top, but what was the good? Summer would do so for two minutes, and as soon as Nikki turned around she'd take it off again.

Clutching the script under her arm, she curled up in a comfortable wicker chair and began reading.

For an hour and a half she was completely absorbed. It was a brilliant final draft – the writer she'd hired had done an excellent job incorporating all her notes. Placing the script on a table, she shivered with excitement. Lara had to see it immediately.

It crossed her mind she could deliver it personally. Then she remembered that Summer was staying, and it wouldn't be fair to leave her alone with Richard. Maybe she'd Fed Ex Lara the script, give her a chance to read it, and then get on a plane. Yes, she decided, that was the way to handle it.

She called Richard in the editing rooms. 'The script's here,' she said. 'I just finished reading, it's exactly on target.'

'Don't get too excited,' he warned. 'The money people have to take a look, and they *always* have comments.'

'Who cares?' she said recklessly. 'I think it's good enough to send to the directors I have in mind, get their reactions.'

'Well . . . they're all waiting to see it,' he mused. 'Only

remember I'm tied up for the next few weeks, I won't be much help.'

'I can handle it,' she said confidently. 'This is *my* project, and although I appreciate your input, I'm OK on my own.'

'You're sure you want to do this?'

'Absolutely.'

She was about to call Federal Express and package the script off to Lara when she remembered Summer, who'd definitely been out on the beach too long. She went over to the edge of the deck and peered down. Summer was sprawled on the sand – still topless. A muscled boy was crouched down next to her, talking nonstop. *Hmm*, Nikki thought, *it hasn't taken her long to find some local action.*

She realized she shouldn't be so critical, but she didn't want the same fate happening to her daughter that had befallen her. Pregnant at sixteen, married at seventeen, divorced at twenty-five. A little voice murmured in her head, *It's not your problem, it's Sheldon's. He's in charge.*

She called out Summer's name.

Her nearly naked daughter swung her head around, looking up at her as if she was a total stranger. 'Yeah?'

'Shouldn't you come in now? You don't want to get too much sun on your first day.'

Summer whispered something to the boy. They both shrieked with laughter.

Somehow Nikki knew she was the butt of their joke, but she pretended not to mind and hurried back into the house. She called Federal Express and dashed off a short note to Lara. After that she sat down at her desk and began calling the directors she planned on sending the script to, alerting them it was on its way.

☆ ☆ ☆

Summer knew there was one thing she could do without any effort: attract boys – or men, it didn't matter as long as they were male. Five minutes on the beach and this big burly surfer came along and started chatting to her. She took off her top, told him everyone in Europe sunbathed topless, and while his eyes bugged out of his head, she asked him where she could score some grass. He informed her he could get her anything she wanted, invited her to a party and fell in love.

Men! Summer thought disdainfully. *They're all so easy!*

Later, she wandered into the house barefoot and sandy, a thin shirt barely covering her bikini. 'Gotta go out,' she told her mother. 'Can I borrow a car?'

'You're too young to drive,' Nikki pointed out. 'You have to be sixteen, remember?'

'I drive Daddy's car all the time,' she said, pouting.

'Maybe Daddy's prepared to take the risk,' Nikki answered crisply. 'We can't do that.'

'I'm a way cool driver, Mom.'

'I'm sure you are, but you're not allowed to drive here. It's the law.'

'I won't get caught.'

'I said no.'

'You're such a downer,' Summer mumbled, thinking that her mother was not going to be as easy to manipulate as Daddy Dearest.

'Where are you off to, anyway?' Nikki asked. 'I thought we'd all have dinner tonight.'

'Can't,' Summer said. 'Going to a party.'

'Already?'

'You wouldn't want me sitting home, would you?'

'Does your father give you a curfew?'

'A curfew? *Me?* Huh!'

64

'Don't get smart, Summer. What time do you have to be home in Chicago?'

'Any time I like,' she replied boldly. *Or,* she thought, *any time he says.* Because Sheldon always liked to know she was there when he wanted her to be.

'The rules are different here,' Nikki said, tapping her watch. 'Back by midnight.'

'Midnight!' Summer squealed. 'Parties don't even get *started* until then!'

'How do you know?'

'I've got friends here.'

'You have? Who?'

'Nobody you know.'

Oh God! Summer had reached the difficult age. Nikki gritted her teeth. She was going to need Richard's help, and at the moment he was totally unavailable. 'I'll give you cab money,' she said at last, not wanting to come down too hard. 'And be home by twelve. Deal?'

'Whatever,' Summer muttered, stomping off to her room, thinking what an uncool drag her mother was.

☆　☆　☆

Richard didn't arrive home until past ten. He was elated. 'The movie's looking incredible,' he said, fixing himself a hefty drink. 'The South of France locations are exquisite, and Lara's performance is luminous. The way she's grown as an actress is quite remarkable.'

'How long before it's all together?' Nikki asked.

'I should have a rough cut in about six weeks.'

'That's exciting. Do the clothes look good?'

'Come over tomorrow and see for yourself. You'll be pleased.'

'I will?' she said, putting her arms around him.

'Yes, my dear, you will.'

'I love you, Richard,' she said, nuzzling her face against his chest.

'Love you too, sweetheart,' he responded, not really concentrating. 'Where's Summer? Wasn't she supposed to be here today?'

'She arrived, caused her usual chaos and went out.'

'Left you here by yourself?'

'She's not exactly my companion, Richard. I said it was OK for her to go out. Told her she had to be home by twelve. We don't have to wait up, I've decided to trust her.'

'Good for you.'

'You've been neglecting me,' Nikki said, wishing he would pay her more attention. 'Who comes first – the film or me?'

'You know it's always the movie,' he said, teasing her.

'You're such a bastard,' she said, standing on tiptoes and kissing him. 'I don't know why I love you.'

He wrapped her in his arms, almost sweeping her off her feet.

'Carry me in the bedroom and ravish me!' she joked. 'Take advantage while I'm in the mood.'

'I'm hungry,' he said. 'All I've had is coffee and doughnuts.'

She put on her best sexy voice. 'I'll give you something to eat you'll *really* like.'

'Yes?'

Now she had his full attention. 'Oh, yes, Mr Barry. You'll like it plenty.'

Laughing, they retired to the bedroom.

SO THERE I was, sixteen years old and out on my own again. I wasn't about to stay with Lulu, the cheating little whore.

I had a couple of options. One of them was Avis Delamore, the old bag who ran the acting class I'd been attending. Avis claimed she was a famous stage actress from England. I wasn't so sure, because every time she got excited, I noticed a touch of the Bronx in her accent.

When I got to know her better I discovered I was right. She'd lived in England for a couple of years with some loser bit-player she'd picked up in a bar. That was the extent of her English heritage.

Avis had a big crush on me, so when I rang her bell and told her I had no place to stay, she immediately said, 'You'd better sleep on my couch.'

Yeah – sure. That night the couch turned into her bed and I was in with a vengeance. Like I said before, if I really concentrate I can get any woman I want.

Unfortunately Avis wasn't Lulu, with her tight stripper's body and perky tits. Avis was a big woman with floppy breasts and heavy thighs.

I soon learned what it was like to fuck a woman who hadn't been getting it in a while. My old man was right. Grateful was good. Grateful meant they'd give you anything you wanted. And she did. All I had to do was ask.

I never thought about my dad or what he was doing. As far as I was concerned, he was yesterday's news. I'd moved on and didn't give a shit.

Of course, like Lulu, Avis had no idea I was only sixteen. Told her I was twenty, an' she bought it.

She got me to do jobs around her crumbling old house – informing everyone I was her assistant. For this I got to screw her and pocket fifty bucks a week. Trouble was she wanted it every night, and I wasn't inclined to give it up on such a regular basis.

I compromised by making sure she gave me plenty of head. I like getting head – it means I can lie back and not get involved. Avis on her knees, and me fantasizing about movies and all that Hollywood shit. It doesn't matter what they look like as long as they give a decent blow job.

The one good thing about being with Avis was that I got to study acting every day. And the class was hot – there were always different girls coming and going – so naturally I took full advantage of the situation.

Avis was my bread and butter. The girls were my delectable desserts.

Of course, I made damn sure Avis didn't know – didn't even have a suspicion. I was smart enough to realize she wouldn't take kindly to me putting it about.

Everything went smoothly, until one day Avis's daughter, Betty, returned from California, where she'd been visiting her dad – Avis's estranged husband. By this time I was seventeen and quite settled into my new life, so when Betty appeared I wasn't expecting problems.

Betty was the same age as me, and not at all pleased to find me in residence. I heard her arguing with her mom the first night she was there. 'What the hell is he doing here? It's disgusting – he's young enough to be your son.'

Avis didn't like confrontations, which was one of the reasons her husband had run off in the first place. 'It's my life,' she said, defending her position. 'We're very happy.'

'Well, I'm not happy,' Betty yelled back. 'And I'm not living here with him.'

Betty and I hated each other for three weeks. On the fourth week we had unbelievable sex on her mother's bed, then things got really complicated.

Betty was a bad girl, the kind I'd always been attracted to. She loathed her mother, and couldn't believe I was sleeping with her. 'How can you do it with such an old bag?' she sneered. 'You're really a low life.'

I didn't appreciate her calling me names.

One night she came to me with a plan. 'I know where my mom keeps her jewellery – let's take it an' run. We can stay with my dad and his girlfriend in LA.'

'You mean steal her stuff?' I said, sounding like jerk of the year.

'No, we'll ask her for it,' Betty said with her best sneer. 'What d'you think I mean, dummy?'

Avis had been good to me, but then I'd been good to her, too.

On the other hand Betty offered excitement and adventure. She was young, pretty and totally wild. I had nothing to lose and a shitload of adventure to gain.

So we grabbed all of Avis's jewellery from the safe deposit box she kept under her bed, and took off for California.

I was finally on my way to Hollywood.

Chapter Nine

 JOEY PROWLED restlessly around the hotel. He'd explored the town, checked out the beach and now he was bored. Two weeks' location and only three days' work spread out over fourteen days – he'd go crazy if he didn't think of something to keep him occupied.

He considered visiting the set – they were shooting at a beachside restaurant. But hanging around sets when not working was hardly smart. Besides, it was boring.

Yesterday he'd finally gone to the wardrobe trailer – manned by Eric, a gay guy with a muscular body and white crew-cut, and Trinee, a young Hispanic girl with glossy jet hair hanging below her waist. They'd fitted him in a black silk T-shirt, and a white Armani suit. He got off on the look, it was straight out of *GQ*.

Now – since he had nothing else to do – he decided to return to the trailer. He left the hotel and slowly strolled over.

Trinee was the only one there. She was busy organizing racks of clothes, while quietly humming a Gloria Estefan song under her breath.

Joey leaned against the door watching her for a few seconds. 'Where's Eric?' he asked, like he cared.

She barely glanced up. 'On the set with Kyle Carson.'

'How come *you're* not there?'

'I'm in charge of the trailer today,' she replied, a touch pleased with herself.

Joey took a closer look. She was very pretty with bold eyes, a crushed rosebud mouth, and small inviting breasts. Unfortunately she was short, and diminutive girls failed to turn him on.

'Can I try on my stuff again?' he asked.

'Everything fit, didn't it?'

'Putting on the clothes helps me get in character.'

'OK,' she said, reaching along the rack for a hanger with a cardboard tag bearing his name. He noticed she had a small pearl ring on her engagement finger – which probably accounted for the fact she wasn't falling all over him.

'I see you're engaged,' he remarked.

A pleased smile spread across her pretty face. 'Two weeks,' she said proudly, holding up her ring hand and waving it in his face.

'I'm engaged, too,' he lied, deciding that it wasn't a bad idea to pretend he was. Trinee would spread the word and it would give him more substance – plus it would keep the women on the movie at bay. He had a rule he tried to keep – never fuck where you work.

'Really?' Trinee said, cheering up considerably. '*My* fiancé is a boxer. What does yours do?'

Joey considered his reply. He wanted to make himself look good – no models or actresses need apply. 'A lawyer,' he said at last. 'She's the youngest lawyer at her firm.'

'Wow!' Trinee responded. 'Cool!'

'Very,' Joey agreed.

He tried on his outfit again.

'You look hot,' Trinee said admiringly.

He stared at himself in the full-length mirror, wishing that his role in the movie was bigger. He was capable of anything and ready to fly, nothing was going to hold him back – not after where he'd been. 'Do I get to keep the clothes?' he asked.

'That's up to the producer,' Trinee replied. 'It's not usual unless you're the star.'

'One of these days I'll *be* the star,' Joey said confidently. 'You can bet on that.'

'Well . . . you're sure handsome enough,' she agreed with a light laugh. 'Y'know, I'm surprised they hired you.'

'How come?'

'Kyle Carson's gonna shit when he sees you're better looking than him.'

He smoothed back his dark hair, still gazing at his reflection. 'You think I am?'

Now that they were both safely engaged she indulged in a little light flirtation. 'Oh, c'mon, man, you *know* you are.'

'The director liked me,' he mused. 'So did the producer – what's her name?'

'Barbara Westerberg.'

'She liked me a lot.'

'I'm totally in shock you slipped by Kyle.'

'What does *that* mean?'

'I worked on his last movie,' she said with a knowing nod. 'Oh boy! Every actor had to be older and less handsome than him.' She lowered her voice to a confidential whisper. 'He's losing his hair, you know.'

'That's gotta make him real insecure.'

'Not really,' she replied. 'He still tries to jump everything that moves.'

'Yeah?'

'Only females, though,' Trinee said with a giggle. '*You're* safe.'

'Gee, thanks,' he said drily.

'When do you work?'

'Tomorrow. The bar scene.'

'I'm sure you'll be great,' she said. 'You'd better take the clothes off now. Those pants have to be pressed.'

☆ ☆ ☆

Lara hit the set surrounded by her all-female entourage. There was Roxy, dressed up for the first day's action in a lime green micro-mini and ankle-clinging white go-go boots, her red hair a blaze of glory. There was Yoko, her make-up girl – Japanese and pretty, with flat black cropped hair and a wide face. There was Angie, her stand-in – a poor man's version of Lara, with a tired look about her, due to the fact that she was married to a stuntman who continually gave her a hard time. And then there was Cassie, trailing behind, cellular phone in hand, plus yellow legal pad and poised pen ready to make notes.

Lara recognized several of the crew she'd worked with before. She greeted them by name, adding a warm handshake and sincere enquiries about their families. They all loved her for remembering.

Kyle was already on the set lounging in his canvas director's chair, long legs stretched out before him. He got up as Lara approached. 'Morning, beautiful,' he said in a deep rich voice. 'You get a good night's sleep?'

'I certainly did,' she replied.

Miles came over. 'You look particularly gorgeous,' he said, kissing her on both cheeks. 'That hair thing really works.'

Instinctively her hand reached up, touching her newly streaked hair. 'Thanks,' she said modestly. 'It's all due to Roxy here.'

Miles didn't acknowledge the hairdresser, she wasn't important to him. 'Let's do an immediate walk-through,' he said, ready to set the scene.

73

Roxy pulled a face behind his back.

Cassie handed Lara her script.

'How come,' Lara said to Miles, 'that the first scene on the first day is always a kissing scene?'

He laughed. 'Can you come up with a better way to get the two of you hot for each other? Raw sex, honey, it works every time.'

She ignored his crassness and quietly stated her case. 'Surely you understand that if you arranged it for later in the schedule, the actors performing the scene would have more chemistry together.'

'Don't worry, hon,' Miles said, in a patronizing tone. 'You and Kyle are set to burn up the screen.' He winked at Kyle, who winked back. All boys together.

Lara remained silent. She'd learned that as a successful woman in the movie industry it wasn't worth getting into an argument over small things. Better to save her power for when it was really needed.

Miles blocked the action, showing them exactly what he wanted them to do. When he was finished, they started to rehearse, running through the page and a half of dialogue several times.

Soon it was time for the kiss. Lara turned to Miles and said, 'Do you mind if we wait until we're actually shooting? It'll be more spontaneous that way.' She wanted to add *no tongue*, but decided to wait and see if Kyle was a gentleman. Fortunately, this was a fully clothed kiss. Later in the script there was a nude scene. Her contract stated she did not do nude scenes, but she *had* agreed they could hire a body double.

Kyle obviously didn't know this, because when he pulled her close, readying himself for the first kiss, he whispered, 'Don't worry about a thing, Lara, when we shoot the sex scene, I'll be right there to protect you.'

He was talking to her like she was a novice. She'd made nine highly successful movies, she knew exactly what she was doing.

After a few more rehearsals Angie moved in front of the camera while the scene was lit. Lara took a break, sitting in her chair while Roxy fussed with her hair and Yoko touched up her lipstick. Fifteen minutes later they were ready to shoot.

Lara loved the silence that descended after the first assistant yelled, 'Settle down, everybody, we're going for a take.' She enjoyed acting, becoming someone else, creating fantasy. It was her life – the only life that made her feel secure.

They would have gotten the scene in one if Kyle hadn't fumbled his lines. 'Sorry, babe,' he muttered.

She noticed little beads of sweat on his forehead and wondered if he was nervous. His make-up person, a statuesque black girl, strolled over and powdered him down, followed by his hair person, a short gay guy, who squinted at his hairpiece making sure it was securely in place.

'OK, let's go again,' Miles shouted. 'We're ready for another take.'

This time it was second take perfect, right up to the kiss. Lara kept her lips firmly clenched together when Kyle bent to kiss her, but he had other ideas as he pushed against her soft lips, managing to insert his slippery thick tongue.

She immediately jerked back, uncomfortable at this sudden intimacy.

'Cut!' Miles called. 'Is there a problem?'

'I feel like she's shoving me away,' Kyle grumbled. 'We're supposed to be falling in love. Shouldn't she be more into it?'

Lara threw him a look. There was nothing worse than a leading man who tried to insert a little tongue action when shooting a love scene. It wasn't necessary, the camera couldn't see. And why was he talking to Miles as if she didn't exist?

Sensing tension, Miles quickly drew her to one side. 'What's the matter, hon?' he asked in his *I care about actors* voice. 'Something bothering you?'

'He's coming on too strong, Miles,' she complained. 'There's no reason for him to put his tongue down my throat.'

'You want me to talk to him?' Miles asked soothingly.

'Yes, do that,' she said, walking over to her chair.

Roxy approached. 'Hmm . . .' she remarked knowingly, tugging at her too-short skirt, which kept riding up over her skinny thighs. 'The old tongue trick, huh?'

'Right,' Lara agreed.

'You can't blame the guy for trying,' Yoko said.

'It's unprofessional,' Lara said.

'It's a man thing,' Roxy responded. 'They see a mouth – they want in!'

Yoko nodded in agreement as she went to work on Lara's lips, outlining them with a steady hand.

Miles obviously spoke to Kyle, because he came over a few minutes later, and said a contrite, 'Sorry if I offended you, Lara. Only doing what comes naturally.'

'You didn't offend me, Kyle,' she replied coolly. 'It's simply not necessary for you to French kiss me.'

'Most actresses love it,' he boasted, going for the macho swagger.

'Well,' she said, as sweetly as she could manage, 'I'm not most actresses.'

The line was drawn. Kyle was on his side of the fence, she was on hers.

At lunchtime they both sat with their people at different tables. Roxy began carrying on about Yoko's boyfriend back in LA giving her a hard time and how she should dump him. Yoko retaliated by saying that Roxy only dated weirdos and perverts and was obviously jealous. Angie announced that her husband was working with a mega action star who was notorious for beating up his three ex-wives and had gotten more plastic surgery than any woman. And Cassie listened to it all, finally saying, 'Give me food over a guy any day!'

Lara was glad she had none of their problems. She didn't need a man, she was perfectly happy on her own. Or so she kept trying to convince herself.

☆ ☆ ☆

Later Joey returned to the hotel and lay on top of his bed watching an old Clint Eastwood movie on television. He was relaxed and feeling good. At least he was back in action.

Madelaine called. 'How's it going?' she asked.

'Nothing much happenin' yet,' he said, aiming an imaginary gun at Clint. 'Think I work tomorrow.'

'Well, Joey, do your best,' Madelaine said, sounding like his seventh-grade teacher. 'Don't let me down.'

He wished she'd stop saying that, it was getting on his nerves. He'd baled on her once, but he was back and at least he'd started paying her the money he'd taken. She had no idea what he'd gone through, how tough things had been. 'Hey, listen,' he said, with a slight edge. 'When did I ever let you down?'

'Let's not get into that,' Madelaine said, her voice sharp. 'I'll definitely be there this weekend.'

Fuck! He had to think of a reason for her not to come.

'Great,' he lied. 'I could use the company.'

☆ ☆ ☆

At the end of the day Lara was tired. Much as she loved it, making movies drained her energy, there was so much down time doing nothing. That's why she liked her group around her – Roxy, Yoko, Angie and Cassie. They amused her with their raunchy dialogue, kept her from getting bored. Besides, they were her family, her only real friends.

After the kissing incident, the atmosphere between her and Kyle had definitely cooled. Between takes they stayed away from each other, although on camera they still generated enough heat for her to know the scenes were working.

Back at the house she studied her script, preparing for the next day. In the upcoming scene, Kyle's character picks a fight with her in a restaurant and walks out. Then a guy at the bar begins flirting with her, comes over, they have a conversation, and just as she's about to dance with him, Kyle reappears. The scene ends with Kyle punching the guy out.

Hmm, Lara thought, *Kyle's probably into all that macho stuff men get off on.* Most leading actors loved playing the hero. In fact, many of them had it written into their contract that they couldn't play anything else on account of the fact they felt the public had to see them in a shining light at all times.

She checked the call sheet to see who was playing Jeff, the guy at the bar. Joey Lorenzo – an actor she'd never heard of.

Cassie had gone to the movies with Angie, so since she had nothing else to do, she went to bed early and was asleep by nine o'clock.

In the morning she was up long before her wake-up call. Throwing on a tracksuit, she jogged along the deserted beach. She was lucky, she could eat anything and not put on weight, which meant she didn't have to slave away in the gym getting the hard body that was a requisite for most young actresses today. Jogging was different, it cleared her head and gave her energy.

When she got back to the house, Cassie was sitting in the kitchen eating a substantial breakfast. 'You were up early,' Cassie remarked, her mouth full of cereal.

78

'There's not much to do around here except sleep,' Lara said. 'I'm making the most of it.'

'Miles left a message last night. They're showing dailies at lunch-time, and he wondered if you'd like to forgo lunch and take a look.'

'Absolutely,' Lara said, although seeing herself on screen was always a painful experience.

When she arrived at the location she found Yoko and Roxy indulging in their usual banter. They were sitting at one of the long trestle tables set up by the catering truck, facing each other. Roxy had a plate piled high with scrambled eggs, toast and bacon, while Yoko chewed on a granola bar.

'You're early,' Roxy said, scooping up eggs.

'Who wants me first?'

'I do,' Roxy said, mouth full. 'I'll put your hair in rollers, then you're all Yoko's.'

Lara stood by the table a moment. 'I'll be in my trailer,' she said. 'Send somebody to fetch me when you're ready.'

'I'm ready now,' Roxy said, stuffing a piece of bacon into her mouth.

'There's no rush. Finish your breakfast.'

'I need my strength,' Roxy giggled. 'Had a heavy night.'

'Yeah,' Yoko said, rolling her eyes. 'She dated one of the drivers. The fat charmer that sits around reading porno magazines all day.'

'He's *not* fat,' Roxy objected. 'He's big-boned. Besides, I like something I can hang on to in the middle of the night.'

'Oh, yeah, and I bet you did *plenty* of *that*,' Yoko sneered.

Lara left them to it and went to her trailer. It amazed her that in this day of AIDS both Roxy and Yoko were so casual about sex. Didn't they realize how dangerous it was out there?

She'd never been like that, for her it was always a relationship or nothing.

Maybe she was wrong. Maybe one-night stands were the way to go.

No. It wouldn't work for her. Eventually someone worthwhile would come along. And if he didn't . . . well, she had her career, her house in LA, her dogs and horses and her friends . . .

Deep down she knew it wasn't enough.

Chapter Ten

 JOEY WAS having fun on the set. Females were everywhere, and they all wanted to make sure he was a happy camper.

He was happy all right. The cute little Japanese thing who'd done his make-up was sweet as candy. And when her red-headed hairdresser friend came in, she was all over him too. It was some smart move telling Trinee he was engaged. Naturally she'd informed the world. They could look, but not touch.

Trinee had elected to leave the wardrobe trailer today to make sure his clothes were OK. 'I've got to watch out for you in the fight scene,' she'd explained. 'We've got another pair of pants – no more jackets, so try not to get too messed up.'

'I'll do my best,' he said, grinning.

'You do that,' she responded, grinning back.

They both knew why she was there.

☆ ☆ ☆

Lara leaned back in the make-up chair while Yoko attended to her face – working fast with a light touch.

'Can you believe Roxy?' Yoko said, shaking her head in disgust. 'That girl is one loco woman!'

'What happened now?'

81

'Well,' Yoko shrugged, 'she picks up this dude on the set yesterday, and last night she's rolling around in bed with him. The guy's gonna tell everyone. Her reputation's shot.'

'I hope she used a condom.'

'Ha!' Yoko said. 'Probably not. Roxy's under the impression she's immortal.'

'Perhaps you should mention it to her,' Lara suggested. 'I mean, using a condom is merely common sense.'

'You tell her,' Yoko said pointedly. 'She never listens to me.'

'Maybe I will.'

Jane, the second AD, entered the trailer. She was a tall, lanky woman with a long horse face. 'Yoko,' she said pleadingly. 'Do me a big one and make up the actor playing Jeff.'

'I'm only supposed to work on Lara,' Yoko said with a stubborn expression.

'I know,' Jane said. 'But there's a problem with one of the other make-up people, and I need this favour. Lara, you don't mind, do you?'

'Doesn't bother me,' Lara said. 'I'm nearly finished.'

'What about Kyle's guy?' Yoko said, standing her ground. 'Can't *he* do it?'

'Kyle takes longer in make-up than Lara,' said Jane. 'It'll hold everyone up.'

'OK.' Yoko said, with a put upon sigh. 'Send him in. What's his name?'

'Joey Lorenzo. And wait till you get a look at him.'

Lara got up from the chair. 'Am I finished?'

'Can't improve on the original,' Yoko said, stepping back and admiring her work in the mirror. 'I merely enhance the rose.'

Lara leaned close to the mirror. 'This lipstick is a good colour,' she said. 'I'll let you know how it comes across in dailies.'

'Maybe I can go with you,' Yoko said hopefully.

Lara shook her head. 'Miles is very particular about who watches.'

'That's dumb. Everyone connected with the movie should be allowed to see 'em.'

'He gets uptight.'

'Directors!' Yoko muttered.

Lara made her way to the hair trailer. Roxy greeted her at the door clad in a tight leopardprint sweater, black leather micro-skirt, and faux tigerskin shoes. 'Shit!' she said excitedly. 'You gotten an eyeful of the actor playing Jeff?'

'No,' Lara said.

'We're talkin' a twenty,' Roxy enthused. 'Trinee says he's engaged. But you know *me* – makes me want him even more!'

'What's he been in before?' Lara asked, more interested in his track record than his looks.

'According to what I heard, he had a promising career going, then he had to go take care of his sick family or something. Sounds like a *real* nice guy.'

'Did you see him this morning?'

'He dropped by my trailer, an' I directed him to the other hairdresser.' She rolled her eyes. 'I must be gettin' soft in the head – the man's a freakin' stud!'

'Really?' Lara said. Actors didn't do anything for her, they were too self-involved and needy, always concerned about themselves first.

'Kyle's gonna shit a brick when he sees him,' Roxy said with a manic giggle. 'Shit a *freakin'* brick!'

'He's *supposed* to be attractive,' Lara explained, sitting down. 'Why would my character let him pick her up if he wasn't?'

'There's attractive, then there's major babe,' Roxy said knowingly, licking her glossy lips. 'This one's m.b. I'm tellin' you, Kyle ain't gonna like it.'

Half an hour later Lara strolled over to the set where Miles greeted her with a kiss on each cheek. 'Gorgeous as ever, my darling.'

She looked around. Kyle was nowhere in sight.

'Our other star is on his way,' Miles said, reading her thoughts. 'He's having a slight hair problem today. As soon as he arrives, we'll rehearse.'

'Where's the actor playing Jeff?'

'Under that swarm of women over there.'

Lara glanced across the set. 'Everyone's talking about him. Who is he?'

'Didn't think he'd cause *this* much of a commotion,' Miles said, clicking his fingers at Jane. 'Bring Joey over. Miss Ivory would like to meet him.'

☆ ☆ ☆

When Jane tapped him on the shoulder and told him the director wanted to see him, Joey was on his feet in a flash.

Lara watched as he approached. For a second she felt a jolt of pure sexual hunger – the kind of feeling she hadn't experienced in a long time. Roxy was right, this was one good-looking guy.

Cassie, hovering somewhere behind her chair, muttered an awed, 'Oh, my! Time to go on a diet!'

Lara remained cool, checking him out as he drew nearer.

Joey took one look at Lara Ivory and was overcome by her startling beauty. She was exquisite – from her honey-blond hair falling softly around her smooth shoulders, to her beautiful face and incredible body. He was immediately aroused, something that never happened to him unless he wanted it to.

Miles stepped between them. 'Joey, say hello to Lara Ivory. I'm sure you've seen her in many movies.'

Lara stood up and extended her hand. He took it in his.

84

An electric shock went right through him as he stared into her direct green eyes. 'It . . . it's a privilege to be workin' with you today,' he managed.

She smiled, a soft, generous smile capable of driving a man totally crazy. 'Thank you,' she said.

'While we're waiting for Kyle to put in an appearance,' Miles said, oblivious to the sexual tension steaming up the set, 'let's run your dialogue.'

'Good idea,' Lara agreed.

Joey continued to stare, unable to take his eyes off her – she was mesmerizing.

In the scene he was sitting at the bar while she and Kyle were at a table exchanging insults which culminated in Kyle's abrupt exit.

Joey began to read from his script – even though he'd learned his dialogue and was word-perfect.

'I've been watching you,' he said, in character as Jeff. A pause. 'Was that your husband who walked out?'

'He's not my husband,' Lara replied, suitably flippant.

'Then . . . I guess you're free to dance with me.'

A coquettish tilt of her head. 'Why would I do that?'

''Cause I think it's what you want to do.'

At that point in the script she was supposed to get up and head for the dance floor with him. It was a short scene, but their chemistry together was undeniable.

They read the scene through twice, and were about to do it a third time, when Kyle appeared, striding onto the set like the movie star he was.

Miles said, 'Kyle, meet Joey Lorenzo – he's playing Jeff.'

Kyle nodded curtly, barely acknowledging him. 'Let's go,' he said to Miles, cracking his knuckles. 'I'm ready to rock 'n' roll.'

'Fine with me,' Miles said. 'We'll start with you and Lara at the table. Joey, for the master you'll be at the bar.'

They all moved in front of the camera, Lara and Kyle in the foreground, Joey at the bar.

'OK, everyone,' the first AD shouted, 'we're going for a rehearsal. Let's have some quiet.'

Kyle and Lara rehearsed their scene several times before Miles was satisfied. Then the make-up and hair people ran in, powdering and primping the two stars. Finally they were ready to shoot.

Kyle was not one-take Charlie. They went through nine takes before Miles was satisfied and yelled a terse, 'Cut! OK, print it!'

Joey had nothing to do except sit at the bar watching them. He was hot and pissed off, with a hard-on against Kyle Carson, who'd treated him like he was a lowly extra. Big movie star asshole. Who exactly did he think he was?

Lara Ivory had his attention full-time. Ms Ivory, he decided, was too fucking beautiful for her own good.

At the lunch break Trinee commandeered him. 'Let's go,' she said cheerfully. 'I'm accompanying you to the lunch truck, protectin' you from the women.'

'What're you talkin' about?' he asked, like he hadn't noticed that every female on the set was trying to get close to him.

'I'm with you, man,' Trinee announced, appointing herself best friend. 'We engaged people gotta stick together.'

He grinned and kept watching Lara as Miles took her arm and they left the set together.

Was she sleeping with the director?

No, she had too much class for that.

'Where's Barbara Westerberg?' he asked Trinee, thinking it was about time he put his charm to good use. 'Haven't seen her around.'

'She doesn't get to the set until the afternoon,' Trinee said. 'Stays about an hour – then leaves. That's what producers do, unless they're the line producer – then they're on your ass the whole time.'

'How long you been in this business?'

'Two years,' Trinee answered proudly. 'I'm learning. One of these days I'm gonna be a producer.'

'Can you do that?'

'Why not? It's about time. How many Hispanic female producers you see around? Anyway – my fiancé says I can.' She giggled. '*I'll* be a producer, and *he'll* be world heavy-weight champion. What you think?'

'Sounds good to me.'

'We'd better put an old T-shirt on you,' she said. 'Just in case you ruin your clothes over lunch.'

He followed her to the wardrobe trailer where Eric was stretched out on the floor engaging in vigorous push-ups. 'Oh!' Eric exclaimed. 'It's the engaged couple!'

'*Veree* funny,' Trinee said, stepping over him.

'Is there a gym around here?' Joey asked. He needed to work out, keep himself in prime physical shape.

'Yes, and it's Kyle's,' Eric said. 'Mr Carson has his own personal gym trailer. I'm sure he'll let you use it. *Not!*'

'He seems like a nice enough guy,' Joey said carefully.

'Just you wait,' Eric said, pursing his lips. 'Mr Americana is a snake in the ass.'

'What's *that* mean?'

'How many lines do you have?' Eric asked, getting up off the floor.

'Not that many.'

'You'll end up with one line and a knockout punch,' Eric said knowingly. 'That's if you're lucky.'

Joey's stomach knotted up, it was shit being nobody. *He* should be the star. *He* should have everything Kyle Carson had.

'Hey,' he said easily. 'Doesn't bother me.'

Trinee tossed him an old denim shirt. He took off his jacket and shirt and put it on.

She hung his movie clothes on a hanger. 'You coming for lunch, Eric?' she asked.

'Wouldn't miss the maddening crowds,' Eric said, reaching for a pink sweater to throw over his Hawaiian shorts.

☆ ☆ ☆

They watched the dailies in Barbara Westerberg's trailer. Lara studied her performance, noting every move. The streaks in her hair worked perfectly, she made a mental note to congratulate Roxy.

Kyle had genuine screen magic, and they were definitely a hot couple, which pleased her. This would be an easy shoot, and the result was sure to equal excellent box office. She needed a light frothy comedy to counterbalance the more serious roles she'd been playing lately.

'*I'm* happy,' Miles said, as Barbara clicked off the VCR. 'Everyone else satisfied?'

'No criticism,' Barbara said. 'Nice hair, Lara.'

'How about me?' Kyle said, glaring a little.

'Kyle, you *know* you're the best-looking man on the screen today,' Barbara said, feeding his ferocious ego. 'You put Kevin Costner and Michael Douglas to shame.'

'Michael Douglas!' Kyle exploded. 'He's fifteen years older than me.'

'And *looks* it,' Barbara assured him.

'I'm off to grab a quick bite of lunch,' Lara said, anxious to get out of Kyle's way.

'I'll come with you,' Miles said, taking her arm.

They left the trailer together. 'I know you think Kyle's an asshole,' Miles said. 'But you have to admit the two of you are pretty damn hot together.'

88

'Ah . . . movie magic,' Lara said, laughing softly. 'Fools 'em every time.'

'*You've* always had movie magic,' Miles said admiringly. 'Even in our first film together. You were so young and innocent and—'

'And playing a hooker,' she interrupted matter-of-factly. 'Every healthy American male's fantasy. The sweet little whore who stops turning tricks for the right man.'

'It worked for you, babe,' Miles said, with a quick laugh. 'Made you a star. Did the same for Julia Roberts in *Pretty Woman*.'

'There's nothing like a good hooker role to jump-start a career,' Lara said drily.

'That or a spread in *Playboy*,' Miles added. 'Which, of course, you never did.'

'No, Miles. Taking off my clothes for a bunch of horny guys to jerk off over is not my idea of a good time.'

Cassie appeared as they approached the catering truck. 'Can I get you anything, Lara?'

'I'm fine,' she replied, noticing Joey Lorenzo sitting at a table surrounded by women.

Miles said, 'I'll have a bite in my trailer. Work calls.'

Lara turned back to Cassie. 'Same for me. Something light, maybe a salad.'

'It's done.'

She took another look at Joey and his female entourage. He glanced up. Their eyes met for a few seconds. She smiled, that cool little smile she used to such good advantage. Then she turned and walked to her trailer.

He was an engaged man. A flirtation was out of the question.

Chapter Eleven

 JOEY CAUGHT her looking at him a few times, but that was about as near as he got to the delectable Ms Ivory. He kept his distance, well aware she must be so used to men going apeshit over her that the only way he had a chance was to make her realize he was different.

He sat at the bar playing background all day, waiting for them to reach his scene – which they never did on account of the fact that Kyle Carson was the slowest actor on two legs and seemed incapable of getting anything right.

Trinee kept him company between shots, giving him a running commentary on everyone involved with the film. She'd warmed up considerably since he'd revealed that he too was engaged.

'Tell me about Lara Ivory,' he asked casually. 'What's she really like?'

'Oh, everyone loves Lara,' Trinee replied. 'She's very popular. No big-star trips with that lady.' She shot him a quick glance. 'Gorgeous, isn't she?'

Joey nodded. 'Who's she sleeping with?'

'How would I know?'

'C'mon, Trinee, if she's in bed with someone it must be all over the set.'

'Word is she doesn't do it with just anyone.'

'How come?'

'She's particular.' Trinee yawned, bored with talking about Lara. 'So,' she said. 'Your fiancée gonna visit us?'

'She might,' Joey answered vaguely. 'How about yours?'

'Marek's coming for the weekend,' Trinee said, with a huge grin. 'An', man, this girl can't wait!'

☆ ☆ ☆

That night Lara had a long phone conversation with Nikki. They spoke about Richard and his satisfaction with her performance and the way the editing was going on *French Summer*. Then they discussed *The Dreamer*, and Lara began telling Kyle Carson tales.

Nikki started to laugh – she couldn't get enough. 'He sounds like the definitive Mr Big Star,' she said. 'A true pain in the ass.'

'You've got that right,' Lara responded. 'And slow. The crew are calling him Ten-take Kyle!' They both giggled. 'How's Summer doing?'

'I can't control her,' Nikki said. 'All she cares about is parties, parties and more parties!'

'It's her age,' Lara assured her. 'She fails to see you as a mother figure. After all, you're only seventeen years older than her, she's probably a little jealous.'

'Nonsense,' Nikki said firmly. 'Why would Summer be jealous of *me*? She's gorgeous.'

'So are you – with personality, a great career, and a well-known and respected husband.'

'No,' Nikki said. 'It's not the jealousy thing. Girls of Summer's age think everyone's a raving idiot, and that they're the smartest person on the planet. I know I was like that, weren't you?'

'I don't remember,' Lara said quickly.

Nikki knew Lara didn't like talking about her childhood, it obviously hadn't been very happy. All she knew was that Lara's parents had been killed in a car crash when she was very young, and that she'd been raised by various relatives. Once she'd asked Richard. 'Lara doesn't get into her past,' he'd said. 'Leave it alone.' So she had.

'Anyway,' Lara continued. 'Don't worry about Summer, she'll come around.'

'I sure hope so,' Nikki said glumly. 'I'm beginning to feel like nag of the year.'

'I'll read the script as soon as it gets here,' Lara promised.

'Then call me at once. Can't wait to get your reaction.'

Lara put the phone down and wandered out onto the back deck, staring out into the darkness. She wanted to walk along the beach, but not by herself, the dark was too scary.

Sometimes everything was too scary . . . Especially when the memories came back to haunt her. The nightmare memories . . .

☆ ☆ ☆

'Scaredy cat!' Andy, her older brother, yelled in her face. 'Skinny little scaredy cat!'

'I'm not! I'm not!' Lara Ann responded.

'Yes you are,' said Andy. He was eight and very handsome. When they weren't fighting Lara Ann worshipped him.

'Mommy, Mommy – can I have another piece of chicken?' Lara Ann asked.

'What, honey?' Ellen, her mother, seemed distracted as she moved around the kitchen.

'More chicken, Mommy, it's sooo yummy.'

'Sorry, honey, I have to save some for your daddy.'

'Why must we wait for him?' demanded Andy. 'He's always late.'

''Cause Mama says we have to,' Lara Ann said, primly.

'You shut up,' Andy said, sticking out his tongue behind his mother's back.

'No, you *shut up*,' Lara Ann retorted, red in the face. 'Mama's always right – aren't you, Mama?'

'Hush, both of you,' Ellen said, brushing back a loose strand of hair. She was an exquisitely pretty woman, with wide-set hazel eyes and natural blond hair that fell in soft waves below her shoulders.

Lara Ann gazed up at her mother and sighed wistfully. 'I wanna be just like you one day, Mommy. You're sooo pretty.'

'Thank you, darling,' Ellen said, removing a carton of chocolate ice cream from the freezer. 'You're pretty too.'

'No, she's not,' taunted Andy. 'She's a stupid dumb girl.'

'Can I be a famous artist when I grow up, Mama?' Lara Ann asked, ignoring him. She'd been thinking about school and all the fun she'd had in painting class. 'Can I?'

'You can be whatever you want, my sweet,' Ellen answered, gently touching her daughter's cheek.

'I know what you can be,' sneered Andy. 'You can be the ugliest girl on the block.'

'I've told you once, Andy,' Ellen said crossly, 'and I'm not telling you again. Do not be mean to your little sister.'

'I'm not mean,' Lara Ann said proudly. 'I'm nice.'

'You're mean, too,' Andy retorted. 'Mean! Mean! Mean!'

'No I'm not.'

'Yes you are.'

'Will you two behave yourselves,' Ellen exclaimed. 'I'm not in the mood today.'

'Can I watch Charlie's Angels, please, Mama?' Lara Ann asked.

'No, I wanna see Dukes of Hazzard,' Andy interrupted.

'It's Lara Ann's turn to choose,' Ellen said. 'Tonight you'll both watch Charlie's Angels.'

'Piss!' Andy said.

Ellen frowned. 'What did you say?'

'Piss! Piss! Piss!'

'When your father gets home he'll wash your mouth out with soap, young man.'

'Don' care.'

'You will when he hears what you've been saying.'

'Mama,' Lara Ann asked, her pretty little face completely innocent, 'what's a cocksucker?'

'What? What did you say?' Andy began to snigger. 'Where did you hear a word like that?' Ellen asked, her cheeks flushing red.

'Daddy said it one day about Mr Dunn.'

'Your daddy does not use language like that.'

'He does! He does! I heard him.'

'No, he doesn't. And don' ever say that word again. It's a very bad word.'

'What's it mean, Mama?'

'I know what it means,' Andy said, smirking. 'It's when a man puts his dickie in a stupid girl's mouth.'

Ellen turned on him angrily. 'Stop it, Andy. Stop it right now!'

At that moment the door opened and Lara Ann's father, Dan, walked in. He was a big, blustery man – handsome, although heavy around the jowls, with a gut that was growing every day.

'Daddy, Daddy!' Lara Ann squealed, running over to him, throwing herself into his arms. Dan swept up his little daughter, hugging and kissing her. She smelled liquor on his breath, but she was used to it. Her father owned a liquor store, and every Saturday morning he took her there, and sometimes, when it *wasn't busy, they'd sit in the back and he'd let her drink as many Coca-Colas as she could manage, while he'd swig Scotch from the bottle and warn her not to tell.*

'Can I have half your chicken, Daddy?' she asked, cuddling up to him.

'You're late,' Ellen said, moving over to the stove, sounding grumpy.

'Glad you noticed,' Dan replied, putting Lara Ann down.

'What's that supposed to mean?' Ellen asked.

'You know what it means,' he said, swaying slightly.

'No, I don't.'

Dan pulled out a chair at the kitchen table, sat down, and told the two children to go in the other room and watch TV.

'I wanna stay with you, Daddy,' Lara Ann objected, clinging onto his hand.

'No, pumpkin,' he said, giving her a little shove. 'I'll see you after I've had my dinner.'

'C'mon, scaredy cat,' Andy said, pulling her arm.

Ellen wagged a warning finger at her handsome son. 'Don't forget – Charlie's Angels.'

Lara Ann sat quietly in front of the television staring at Farrah Fawcett and her glorious mane of golden curls. Andy picked up a toy car and began zooming it around the living room floor making loud car noises. 'Be quiet, Andy,' she said.

'No!' he said, sticking out his tongue again. 'You're a stupid girl. Girls gotta shut up.'

'No they don't.'

'Yes they do.'

'No they don't.'

They were so busy arguing that at first they didn't hear the raised voices coming from the kitchen.

Then Andy said, 'They're fighting again – shush!'

'Bitch!' they heard Dan shout. 'Cheating bitch!'

Then Ellen's voice. 'How dare you accuse me.'

I'll accuse you of what I want. Everybody in town's talking about you and that dentist! It's not just your teeth he's filling, Ellen . . . it's not just your fucking teeth.'

'Elliott Dunn is nothing more than a friend.'

'Yeah, a friend who screws your ass off.'

The raised voices frightened Lara Ann. 'What are they talking about?' she whispered.

'Dunno,' Andy said.

'I refuse to be the laughing stock of this town,' Dan yelled. 'Oh, no – not me. Not Dan Leonard.'

'People like to gossip, there's nothing going on.'

'Says you.'

'It's the truth.' A moment of silence – then— 'Dan . . . Oh my . . . what are you doing? What are you doing?'

'Defending my fucking manhood. Something I should've done a long time ago.'

'Don't be silly, Dan.' Ellen's voice rose in panic. 'This . . . isn't . . . sane. PLEASE DON'T . . . DON'T . . . NOOO!'

There was a terrifically loud explosion. Lara Ann jumped, and covered her ears. She knew something bad had happened.

Andy leaped up.

'Don't go,' Lara Ann whimpered, clinging to his arm. 'I'm frightened, Andy. Stay here with me.'

'I gotta go see,' he said, pulling away and running into the kitchen.

Lara Ann cowered on the couch. She heard her father bellow something, then the sound of a short struggle, and after that another loud explosion.

She stayed exactly where she was, still covering her ears.

Suddenly her father ran into the room with a wild look in his eyes. 'C'mon, pumpkin,' he said, pulling her up.

His eyes were all bloodshot and scary, but she loved her father more than anything in the world, so she didn't argue.

'Where are we going, Daddy?' she asked meekly.

'Away from here,' he muttered, scooping her into his arms and carrying her through the kitchen.

Sprawled on the kitchen floor was her mother, a thin spiral of smoke snaking out of a gaping hole in her chest.

Slumped by the door was her brother, his head blown half away. There was blood everywhere.

'Daddy! Daddy! Daddy!' Lara Ann began to scream. 'Mommy's been hurt. Mommy's bleeding. So's Andy.'

He wasn't listening. He carried her out the door and almost threw her in the back of his car. Then he jumped in the driving seat and roared away from the house.

'Daddy, Daddy,' she whimpered, so frightened she could scarcely breathe. 'What happened? Why's my mommy on the floor? Why's Andy all bloody?'

'Nothing,' he muttered, picking up a bottle of Scotch from the seat next to him and taking a swig. 'They'll be fine.'

She squeezed her eyes tightly shut, bringing her knees up to her chest. 'Daddy, something bad happened! Who did that to Mommy and Andy? Who did it?'

'Your mother got what she deserved,' he muttered. 'Cheating bitch!'

Lara Ann began to cry, big gulping sobs that shook her entire body.

Dan drove to a motel, stopped at the desk and got a key. Next he parked outside a room and carried her inside. She was still crying, a river of silent tears running down her face. She loved her father, and yet she knew in her heart he'd done something terribly bad.

'Sit down and watch the TV,' he ordered gruffly.

'I wanna go home,' she whimpered.

'Do as I say. Switch on the TV, and don' start whining like your mother.'

He slumped into a chair, taking another swig from the bottle of Scotch, which was now almost empty.

Her daddy had never spoken to her so harshly, but she knew his anger had something to do with the bottle in his hand. Andy had told her that when people drank stuff like that they got drunk. And when they were drunk they got sick and talked in a funny way. Her daddy was sick.

As the evening wore on, she grew more and more exhausted. Her father went out to the car and came back with another full bottle of Scotch. She peeked at him as he drank the whole bottle, muttering to himself.

Later that night she heard the sound of police sirens in the distance. Her father heard it, too, because he sat up very straight and stared right at her. 'Y' look jus' like your mother,' he said, slurring his words. 'You're pretty, but inside you're a slut, like your mother. An ... ugly ... little ... slut. Thass' what all women are. Unnerstan' me?'

Her eyes filled with more tears and rolled down her cheeks. Her father had never said such horrible things to her before. She'd always been his favourite, he'd always loved her.

Her world was crumbling and there was nothing she could do. 'I want Andy,' she cried out. 'And I want my mommy.'

Dan took a gun from his pocket.

Lara Ann stared at the harsh glint of metal. He was going to shoot her, just like she'd seen people get shot on Charlie's Angels, *just like he'd shot Mama and Andy. She wouldn't even have a chance to grow up.*

'Daddy—' she started to say, her little face puckering.

'Doncha ever forget,' he mumbled, his mouth twitching. 'Inside you're an ugly slut, jus' like your cheatin' mother.'

Then he put the gun in his mouth and blew his brains out.

Blood and hair and pieces of flesh splattered all over her.

She was five years old.

☆ ☆ ☆

After a while Lara went back inside, contemplating another long lonely night.

It was OK, she was used to being by herself. She'd manage. She always had.

Chapter Twelve

 ALISON SEWELL first spotted Lara Ivory at a film premiere. At the time Alison was trapped behind a pack of stinking sweaty men, all of them blocking her way.

Alison was not popular with her fellow photographers, so any time they could keep her from getting the shot, they did. Truth was they hated her.

Alison didn't care, she had ways to outsmart them – her ways. A swift kick in the shins. A lethal knitting needle thrust into a vulnerable body part. A feigned fainting fit. Oh yes, Alison had tricks that could get her anything she wanted. After all, she was a woman – so the pigs thought twice about fighting back.

One guy tried. He tripped her up, following this move with a vicious punch. She promptly sued him. They came to an arrangement out of court, giving her a six-thousand-dollar settlement. It was a warning to all of them. Don't mess with Alison Sewell or you'll regret it.

She'd been in the business for eight years, taking over from Uncle Cyril when he succumbed to throat cancer. She made a reasonable living catching celebrities and politicians doing things they never wanted to be seen doing. Once a month she flew to New York. Three times a year she covered Washington. Every night she was out on the streets staking

100

the openings, fancy premieres and parties. She had photos of OJ during the famous freeway chase; she was outside the house when he was arrested; she'd caught Johnny Romano with a hooker; Madonna in Miami with a new toy boy; Venus Maria topless by her swimming pool.

Yes, Alison Sewell got the gritty pictures the tabloids craved. And for that, several photo editors paid her handsomely, although none of them particularly liked her.

Alison didn't give a damn; she had no personal life. Men didn't attract her, nor did women. Sex was the cause of all evil, and Alison Sewell simply wasn't interested.

She lived with her mother – now bedridden – in Uncle Cyril's house, which he'd left to them in his will. Most days she slept, hitting the streets at night clad in her uniform of army combat pants, sturdy hiking boots, brown T-shirt and a flak jacket with numerous pockets in which she stored her precious film.

Alison worked alone. She didn't need anyone slowing her down.

In all her travels she'd never actually seen Lara Ivory in the flesh. And the first time she did, it was a striking revelation. Pure innocent beauty. A face so perfect Alison almost cried out.

She automatically raised her camera above her head, popping off as many shots as she could. Then she went home and developed the film in the shed Uncle Cyril had converted into a dark room at the back of the house.

When the finished images came to life, Alison was stunned by Lara's incomparable freshness and staggering beauty. Hers was the most special face she'd ever photographed, and she immediately wanted more.

After that she didn't look back. Lara Ivory became her major obsession.

Like a ravenous lion tracking its prey, Alison set about

finding out everything she could concerning the famous star. She changed her working habits to include any event Lara might attend and was always up front, kicking anyone who got in her way.

Soon Lara began to recognize her, favouring her with a smile, a friendly wave. Alison saw this as a sign. She began writing notes and printing up photos for her idol and handing them to her – or trying to. Usually some unwanted publicity flack or bodyguard came between them, blocking her line of communication. This infuriated her, because surely – without interference – they could become friends.

Alison had never had a friend, somebody to talk to and confide in. All she had was her mother, who did nothing but whine and complain as she lay in bed withering away, her frail body riddled with cancer.

'*That'll* teach you to smoke,' Alison scolded almost every day, the same thing she'd said to Uncle Cyril when he was dying.

Alison didn't smoke. Instead she ate chocolate bars – sometimes seven or eight a day. They might make her fat, but she wasn't stupid enough to smoke like her two closest relatives. Look where it had gotten *them*.

One day Alison decided to pay Lara a visit. She'd located her address in a 'map of the stars' book, and kept it beside her bed for two weeks before getting up early on a Saturday morning, and setting off in her beat-up old station wagon for the long drive to Hidden Valley Road – which, according to the star book, was located somewhere off Sunset.

Alison was excited. It was a bold thing to do, but she knew in her heart that Lara would welcome her. She took with her a scrapbook she'd put together – a pictorial record of Lara's comings and goings for the last three months. There were some wonderful photos, but the only one the tabloids had chosen to run was Lara and her current boyfriend, a man called Lee Randolph, having an obvious fight in public.

Alison did not like this Lee Randolph character. He was not good enough for her Lara, she deserved better. Although why Lara needed a man was beyond Alison's comprehension. Men were pigs. They farted and swore and spat and fought. They were liars and cheats and philanderers and Alison hated them all.

When she reached the house she was surprised to find it unprotected. No high hedges or big iron gates. Just a driveway leading up to the simple-looking – although quite large – ranch house.

She rang the doorbell and waited. Just her luck – Lee Randolph came to the door.

'Yes?' he said. 'Can I help you?'

'Uh . . . I've got something for Lara.'

'I'll take it.'

'No! I need to see her personally.'

He gave her a funny look and told her to wait. Then he closed the door in her face, and ten minutes later the police were there asking what she wanted.

That bastard! If Lara only knew what he was doing. He wasn't protecting her, he was isolating her from her real friends.

She informed the cops she was a loyal friend of Lara Ivory's, but the sonsofbitches didn't believe her, and she was forced to leave, mission unaccomplished.

After that she started writing Lara letters – one or two a day – rambling on about how unworthy Lee Randolph was – what a moron her publicist was – how if only people would get out of their way they could be friends.

And then she started going back to Lara's house – sometimes seeing the housekeeper or Lara's assistant or Lee.

Each time she was there someone called the police, until eventually the cops told her that if she came back again they'd arrest her for stalking.

Stalking! Who did they think she was – John Hinckley? What a bunch of dummies. She was Lara's friend, that's all. She didn't mean her any harm.

But Alison didn't want trouble, so she stopped visiting the house and instead continued sending letters and photographing Lara whenever she could.

After a while she started noticing that the people around Lara – her so-called protectors – began instructing their star not to look in her direction or go near her at premieres and big functions.

At first she thought it was her imagination. But no, it was actually happening. Lara no longer smiled and waved. The intimate looks stopped. And Alison began to get furious. Truly furious.

She had to do something to regain Lara's trust and attention.

Something that nobody would forget.

Chapter Thirteen

BEFORE JOEY knew it, Friday arrived, and they still hadn't gotten to his scene. For three days he'd been stuck on a bar stool observing Kyle Mr Big Star Carson blow take after take, while Lara sat there serene and lovely – never once complaining.

Kyle was a major dick – he refused to acknowledge him, acting as if he didn't exist, which pissed Joey off as he wasn't used to being ignored. The women on the set made up for it. In spite of the fact they thought he was engaged, he was getting more invitations than he could handle. Truth was he could've nailed any one of them, including Trinee. But he didn't. There was a time and a place, and this wasn't it. Besides, since setting eyes on Lara, he had no desire to do so. Instead he concentrated on charming them all, weaving tales about his lawyer fiancée and how smart she was.

They ate it up. Women loved a man they thought they couldn't get.

Every day Lara seemed to go out of her way to greet him with a friendly wave and a smile. They'd never had a conversation, but he knew she was aware of his presence. Of course, it would be hard for her not to be, since he was always in the background of her scene, watching her.

He'd made it his business to find out more about her. Trinee was right, she *wasn't* in bed with the director, she *didn't* have a current boyfriend. She was staying in a rented house on the beach with her assistant and a guard, and everyone seemed to love her.

In spite of her friendly demeanour it appeared to Joey she was a loner – exactly like him. His kind of woman. But for once in his life he was too edgy to go for it.

Joey Lorenzo. Stud supreme. There was no way he'd risk a turn-down.

Madelaine had threatened to arrive that evening, so his immediate problem was figuring out a way to stop her. He borrowed a cellphone from one of the crew and called her. 'You're not gonna believe this,' he said in a husky voice.

'What?' Madelaine asked suspiciously.

'I got a bitch of a sore throat. It's so freakin' bad I can barely speak. Only good thing is they'll never get to my scene today. I gotta be OK by Monday, so I'm gonna spend the weekend in bed drinkin' hot tea an' missin' you.'

'Wouldn't hear of it,' Madelaine said briskly. 'I'll come look after you.'

'No, honey, no,' he said. 'I'm serious about this. I have to rest up.'

'But, Joey,' she said, hating herself for sounding needy, 'I was looking forward to seeing you.'

'Jeez, Madelaine,' he snapped. 'Don't make me feel guilty about bein' sick. It's my big scene on Monday – you understand, don't you?'

'Yes,' she said reluctantly. 'I suppose you're right.'

'Doesn't mean I won't miss you,' he said, turning on the charm again.

'Are you sure?'

Now the full seduction voice came into play. 'C'mon, baby, you *know* I will.'

That taken care of, he headed back to the set.

☆ ☆ ☆

Lara had read through the script of *Revenge* three times, and although it was a tough read on account of the language, honesty and violence, she'd recognized that it was a powerful piece – and with the right director it could be an amazing film.

Placing the script in her purse, she left her trailer and headed for the set, literally bumping into Joey Lorenzo on the way.

'Sorry!' he said, stepping back.

'No, *I'm* sorry it's taking so long to get to our scene,' she said, and for some unknown reason she felt her heart fluttering. 'You must be going nuts watching us flub lines.'

Once again, up close and personal, he marvelled at her dazzling beauty. ''S OK,' he said, managing to sound casual. 'I'm gettin' used to sittin' on a bar stool – takes me back to my juvenile delinquent days.'

'Oh, yes?' she said, with a beauteous smile, thinking that he was quite incredibly handsome and funny too. 'Was that so long ago?'

'A while.'

'Shy about your age,' she teased.

'I'm thirty – how old are you?'

She was not used to being asked such a direct question. 'Actually, I'm thirty-two,' she said, answering him anyway. 'My publicist keeps on urging me to say I'm twenty-nine. But since every magazine knows the truth, I keep on telling him it's somewhat pointless.'

They both laughed.

'It can't be easy being as famous as you,' he said, unable to stop himself from staring.

'It's not,' she replied, meeting his gaze. 'Although it does have compensations.'

'Yeah,' he grinned. 'I bet.'

Jane barged between them. 'Both of you are needed on the set,' she said officiously.

'Thank you, Jane,' Lara said, dismissing her in a nice way. She began walking towards the action. Joey fell into step beside her.

'I hear you're engaged to a lawyer,' she said. 'That must be an interesting profession.'

'Yeah,' he said. 'When the OJ case was goin' on I had my own runnin' commentary. *She* should've been up there instead of Marcia Clark – she'd've done a better job.'

'Have you been engaged long?'

'A year,' he lied. 'It's kinda like a commitment without being the final closed door, y'know what I mean?'

She laughed softly. 'I'm sure your fiancée would love to hear *that*.'

'Hey—' he said quickly, lest she thought less of him. 'I didn't mean it in a bad way. It's just that – well, y'know, marriage is important to me. When I get married, it's gonna last for ever.' He looked at her intently. 'Isn't that how you feel?'

'My track record's somewhat blurred,' she said, thinking that was exactly how she'd felt when she'd married Richard. 'I'm divorced.'

'Didn't know that.'

'Hmm . . . I guess you don't read *People* magazine,' she said lightly. 'My divorce was rather public.'

'Who was the lucky guy?'

'Richard Barry, the director,' she replied as they arrived back on the set.

'How long were you married?'

'Long enough to realize it was a mistake. The good news is we're friends now.'

'That's nice.'

'Time to work,' she said crisply. 'And if Kyle stops tripping over his lines, maybe we'll get to your scene this afternoon.'

'That'd be a surprise.'

They held a long, steady look. He was making her nervous, the way his eyes seemed to penetrate right through her. 'Uh . . . I'm glad we finally got to talk,' she said.

'Yeah,' he said, still watching her closely.

'Is your fiancée visiting you this weekend?' she asked. *Oh, God, Lara, what a stupid question!*

'No, she's workin' a case. Why?'

'Oh,' she said, groping for a reason. 'I . . . uh . . . was going to invite the two of you to a party at my house tomorrow night.'

'Yeah?'

She couldn't believe the words coming out of her mouth. Was she insane? She had no party planned. 'It'll be fun,' she continued. 'Yoko and Roxy are coming, and most of the crew.'

His black eyes continued to draw her in. 'OK if I drop by alone?'

'Of course,' she replied, slightly breathless.

'Then I'll be there.'

'Good. Oh, and if your fiancée *should* arrive, please bring her.' She made a quick escape, hurrying over to Miles, who waited impatiently. *I'm having a party*, she thought. *Better get Cassie on the case immediately. She'll be thrilled.*

Joey watched her go. She was certainly something else.

Knockout beautiful, incredibly nice and friendly. Not like any woman *he'd* ever known.

Lara Ivory was the real thing and he desperately wanted her.

Joey Lorenzo had never met the real thing before.

Chapter Fourteen

 NIKKI SAT on the American Airlines plane on her way to New York. She'd told Richard a couple of days ago that she planned to visit Lara.

'Why?' he'd asked irritably.

'Because it's important. I need to get her reaction to the script.'

'*Revenge* is not a project for Lara to be involved in,' he'd said in his *I know best* voice. 'She's a big movie star, you're making a small film.'

'I know. But she is considering it. Think what a coup it would be if I got her!'

'You can't go asking favours.'

'It'll be entirely her decision.'

'She won't do it, Nikki.'

'Wasn't it you who said that one of the most important things a producer can do is follow their instincts? Well, that's what I'm doing.'

'If you have to – then go.'

'And you'll take care of Summer?'

'She'll be fine with me.'

Later, she'd spoken to Summer, telling her that Richard had promised to watch out for her.

'Excellent!' Summer had said. 'Richard's the greatest.'

'I'll be back in two days. You'll have a nice time together.'

'I'm having a good time anyway,' Summer had said. 'LA's amazing. Wish I could stay here for ever.'

'Do you?' Nikki had said, quite surprised. She could just imagine Sheldon's face if she told him his daughter wanted to live permanently in California. He'd be furious. Summer was his precious prize – there was no way he'd let her go.

'We'll discuss it when I get back,' she'd promised.

Now she was on her way, ready to talk Lara into the role of her life.

She slept most of the flight, trying to avoid conversation with the German businessman sitting beside her whose reading material consisted of *Penthouse*, *Playboy* and the *Wall Street Journal*. He ignored the *Journal*, and studied the centrefolds at least twenty times, grunting to himself.

'You need to get laid,' she muttered, as they disembarked.

The man frowned, small raisin eyes under monstrous bushy eyebrows. 'Excuse me?'

'I said the stewardess needs to get paid – for the headphones.'

His frown deepened. American women were very strange.

Lara had sent a limo to the airport. Nikki got in and settled back, enjoying the ride to the Hamptons.

By the time she arrived it was past seven and Lara was home from her day's work.

'What a house!' Nikki exclaimed, walking around. 'It's so charming.'

'I'm considering making an offer,' Lara said.

'You're not contemplating moving?'

'No. I'd use it as a retreat, somewhere nobody could find me.'

'That's right – become even more reclusive!'

'I'm not reclusive.'

'Says you.'

Later they had dinner on the back deck.

'Well?' Nikki asked, unable to wait any longer. 'What's your opinion of the script?'

'Truth?' Lara said, teasing her.

'Of *course* the truth.'

Lara smiled. 'I love it!'

Nikki sat up straight. 'You do?'

'It's everything I wanted it to be.'

'Am I pleased to hear that!' A beat. 'Now the really important question – will you do it?'

'Well . . .'

Nikki leaned across the table, her excitement palpable.

'Yes!' Lara said. 'I will!'

'Thank you, God,' Nikki said fervently, clasping her hands in front of her. 'I promise I'll be good for the rest of the year!'

☆ ☆ ☆

With Nikki safely out of the way, Summer planned on having an even better time. She called Richard in the editing rooms and begged off dinner – saying she had to attend a friend's birthday party.

Richard was quite agreeable. 'Don't be home too late,' he said. 'And for God's sake don't tell your mother I didn't take you to dinner.'

'Is it OK if I invite a few friends over on Sunday?' she asked, figuring she'd strike while he was in an amiable mood.

'Fine,' he said. 'I'm working all weekend.'

Goodbye, Richard, she thought gleefully. Much as she liked him, she preferred total freedom.

Jumping out of bed, she tried to decide what to do today. If only she could drive. Well, the truth was she *could* drive, but if she got busted behind the wheel of either Richard or Nikki's car she'd be in deep shit on account of the fact that she wasn't yet sixteen, and she didn't think that either of them would appreciate a visit to the police station to bail her out. Cabs were eating up all her cash, even though she was getting money from Richard, Nikki, *and* her father. She'd sent Daddy Dearest a frantic letter informing him that Nikki hardly gave her anything, and in return he'd mailed her five hundred dollars without so much as questioning what she needed it for.

She'd already made up her mind that the best thing would be to stay in LA, have Daddy Dearest send her money, and eventually move into a place of her own. After all, she'd be sixteen in a couple of months – she'd be able to drive legally. How radical would *that* be!

Of course, she thought sourly, Sheldon wouldn't appreciate her staying in California, he'd hate her being so far away. But if he put up a fight she could always blackmail him. She had stuff on Mr Big Shot Famous Psychiatrist that he wouldn't want anyone knowing – not even his precious Rachel, who in spite of being nice was a bit dense.

Oh, yes, if she wanted, she could blow his happy little deal in a second. *And* blow everyone's mind in the process. Especially Nikki's.

Hmm . . . if Daddy Dearest *didn't* cooperate, maybe she'd do just that.

She called Jed, who offered to pick her up and take her on a club spree. Jed had turned out to be the perfect contact, he seemed to know everybody – introducing her around as Richard Barry's daughter – which got her plenty of attention. She'd already been out with him a couple of times, and met all kinds of people – including Tina, an amazing-looking girl of eighteen, who, she'd decided, would be her new best friend. At school she always hung out with the older girls – fifteen-year-olds were too immature to bother with.

Jed had tried to make out with her the second night she was in town. She'd shoved him away – having already made her decision. If she was going to do it with anyone, it had to be a movie star. Still . . . Jed was a useful guy to keep hanging.

The club scene was way different from Chicago. There were all sorts of temptations – booze, coke, a variety of pills. Summer didn't go for any of it; an occasional joint was her only vice.

Back home guys were always trying to get her drunk, but she was too smart for them. Besides, her father watched over her with an unhealthy zeal – always waiting when she came home at night, checking to see if she'd been drinking or drugging; asking questions; grilling her to find out what she did with boys.

It was a big drag.

He was a big drag.

She couldn't wait to finally cut loose.

Jed was driving the limo when he arrived at the house. 'Got an airport pick-up later,' he explained.

'When?' she said, frowning.

'One a.m. Which gives us plenty of time,' he said, making a clumsy attempt to grab her.

She eluded his clammy grasp with a light giggle, shooting out the door to the sleek elongated limo.

'You'd better sit in the back,' he said, chasing after her. 'That way – if I run into any of the other drivers, they'll think I'm still on a job.'

'OK,' she said cheekily. 'I'll be your rich client giving you orders.'

'Like hell you will,' he said, leaning into the back seat, trying to grab a quick feel.

Summer had learned at an early age that all members of the male sex were easy, all she had to do was bat her big baby blues, show a little leg, and they were hers. In Chicago the boys came panting after her. In Hollywood it wasn't so different. Although when she looked around the clubs she realized the girls in LA were a lot prettier than the ones back

in Chicago – especially Tina, who was so cool and sophisticated with her long brown curls, vampy lips and sparkling
cat-eyes. Summer realized she could learn a lot from Tina.
And the sooner the better.

'Let's go, driver,' she said imperiously. 'I do not wish to
arrive late.'

'You're a tease, you know that?' Jed said, looking perplexed.

When was he going to realize he didn't have a chance?

☆ ☆ ☆

'Martini?' Richard offered.

'Why not?' Kimberly Trowbridge responded.

Kimberly was a tall, attractive woman in her late twenties,
with bobbed strawberry-blond hair and an understated way
of dressing. She was Richard's temporary assistant – hired to
replace his permanent assistant, who'd left to have a baby.

Kimberly was not only attractive, she anticipated his needs
and was extremely efficient. Since she obviously worshipped
him, he enjoyed having her around.

Tonight, when he'd finished editing, he'd asked her if she
wanted to grab a bite to eat. A perfectly innocent offer,
because since marrying Nikki and practically giving up drinking he'd been nothing but faithful. Dinner seemed an
innocent way of repaying Kimberly for all her hard work.

He'd taken her to Trader Vic's, where the exotic drinks
tasted innocuous – and packed a punch capable of felling a
mule! In his drinking days Richard could have downed three
Navy Grogs in a row – no problem. Tonight he wasn't sure if
he could manage one.

Kimberly was impressed by the restaurant. 'I've never been
here before,' she said, gazing around.

'Then you must have one of these.' And he ordered her a
Navy Grog, and a selection of appetizers.

She downed the exotic mixture as if it was lemonade, nibbled on a couple of spare ribs and an egg roll, and trotted off to the ladies' room.

When she returned he was already into his second drink, and there was another one waiting for her.

He noticed she'd undone a couple of buttons on her blouse, touched up her make-up, and sprayed herself with a musky scent. Talk about signals!

'You smell good,' he said.

'I thought you'd never notice,' she responded. And after that it was only a matter of time before he invited her back to his house.

☆ ☆ ☆

The first club Jed took her to was too crowded.

'Drag,' Jed said.

'Major,' Summer agreed.

They moved on to Pot, an outrageous dance club that operated out of different venues every weekend. Tina was there, and so were some of Jed's other friends. They all joined up.

Every time she ran into Tina, she was with a different guy. 'I get easily bored,' Tina confided with a giggle when Summer asked her why. 'Jed's OK, though. You should stick with him for a while – until you get to know your way around.'

'I will,' Summer agreed.

'I see you've been putting in time on your tan,' Tina said. 'Awesome! Maybe *I'll* do the same.'

Summer was flattered Tina wanted to copy her. Tina – who was so cool with her long dark curly hair and radical outfits.

'You can come out to my beach house any time,' Summer said, scrambling to jot down her phone number.

'Maybe I will,' Tina said.

Jed informed her that Tina worked as a model for a clothes manufacturer downtown.

'Wow!' Summer sighed enviously. 'I'd give *anything* to get into that kind of deal.'

'Ask her,' Jed said. 'Maybe there's an opening. And while you're at it, tell your stepfather to star me in one of his movies!'

'As if,' Summer snorted.

They both laughed, and Jed whirled her onto the crowded dance floor.

☆ ☆ ☆

Richard fixed two Martinis before walking Kimberly out onto the deck.

'This is *fantastic*!' she breathed, sipping her drink. 'A house – right on the beach – it's always been my dream!'

Richard put his Martini glass down on a ledge. He was mad at Nikki; how dare she desert him and go running after Lara, trying to persuade her to appear in her nothing little movie. Especially after he'd told her not to. Yes, he was mad, and now he was drunk, and it was all Nikki's fault. Ambition was a dangerous thing.

He reached for Kimberly and her musky scent. She melted into his arms as if she belonged there.

He put his hands in her hair, pushing it behind her ears. Then he went for the buttons on her blouse – undoing them one by one.

'Aren't you going to kiss me?' she asked.

Oh yes, of course I am.

He put his tongue in her mouth, wondered if he had a condom, hoped that she did because he had no need of them any more. Except now. To consummate this act of adultery.

God! If Nikki finds out she'll leave me.

There's no way she can find out.

He undressed Kimberly slowly. She had on lacy lingerie straight out of a Victoria's Secret catalogue – which really turned him on. First he undid her front-fastening bra – revealing nice tits with chewable nipples. Then he peeled off her thong panties – exposing her shaved bush. Finally he unclipped her garter belt and rolled off her stockings.

When she was naked he laid her across the outdoor glass table and fucked her quickly – pumping away for only a few minutes before coming.

The moment it was over he wanted her gone.

Get rid of her!

Get her out of here before Lara finds out.

Lara . . . he thought mournfully, *I never should've let you go. Why did I allow it to happen?*

Kimberly had other ideas – she was determined to experience the after-glow and nothing was going to stop her. Pulling him down on a lounger, she wrapped her long legs around his, trapping him in a tangle of damp luscious limbs. 'That was delicious,' she murmured, as if she had just consumed a dish of pasta and meatballs.

'Gotta call you a cab,' he mumbled, trying to disentangle himself. 'It's late.'

'I thought your wife was away,' she said accusingly. 'Why can't I stay?'

'My stepdaughter . . . she'll be home any minute.'

Risky business. What if Summer had walked in on them?

He finally managed to extract himself from Kimberly's clinging limbs and staggered to the phone, quickly ordering a cab. Then he gathered her clothes and gave her a little shove in the direction of the guest bathroom.

When she emerged a few minutes later she was dressed, but not happy. 'You didn't satisfy me,' she complained. 'I didn't come.'

What was wrong with women today? Wasn't it enough that she'd put a smile on *his* face? 'Next time,' he promised.

An awkward wait until he heard the cab drawing up. Then he stuffed a hundred bucks in loose bills into her hand and escorted her outside.

'What's this?' she said, staring disdainfully at the crumpled banknotes, almost ready to turn the money down.

'Cab fare,' he said.

'Oh,' she said, and kept the money.

Just as he was about to deposit her safely in the back of the cab, a limo drew up to the house, and out jumped Summer.

'Richard!' she exclaimed in surprise. 'Is Mom back?'

'Uh . . . no,' Richard said, completely thrown. 'My . . . uh . . . assistant and I were just finishing off some work.'

'That's right,' Kimberly said.

Summer chewed on her thumb. It was quite obvious he was up to something. Did he think she was a total dweeb?

Jed jumped out of the limo, determined to get introduced. 'Mr Barry . . . sir. I'm a big admirer of your work. You're one of the stalwarts of the industry.'

'Thank you,' Richard said stiffly. Did stalwart mean old? Who was this jerk anyway? And why was he bringing Summer home in a limo?

'Night,' Summer said, skipping inside the house, relieved she didn't have to fight Jed off.

Richard shoved Kimberly into the cab and followed Summer into the house, slamming the door behind him.

'Sleep tight, Richard,' Summer said, standing at the door of her room, looking cute, rumpled and very, very pretty.

'You, too,' he replied, completely unnerved.

The sooner Nikki came home, the better it would be for all concerned.

Chapter Fifteen

 THE PARTY at Lara's house – put together by a frantic Cassie at the last moment – was a raging success. Everyone was letting loose and having a good time.

Lara sat at one of the tables in the garden with Nikki. Seated with them were Miles and his Hollywood wife, Ginny; a solo Barbara Westerberg; and Kyle Carson, who'd flown in a date for the weekend – an anorexic English model who appeared to be no more than fourteen with her waif-like face and concentration camp body.

'If I'd realized you were planning a party,' Nikki said, sipping a Margarita, 'I'd have brought better clothes.'

'You always look great,' Lara said, smiling at her friend – a knockout in a short red Thierry Mugler dress.

'Thanks,' Nikki replied. 'And *you* always know the right thing to say.'

'Yes, like I'll do your movie. Right?'

'Right!' Nikki grinned, thrilled that Lara understood and loved the script.

'Is Richard OK by himself in LA?' Lara asked, remembering that he couldn't stand being left alone when they were married.

'He's got Summer to look after him,' Nikki replied, sipping a frozen Margarita. 'Crazy, isn't it? She loves my

121

husband – hates me. How did I become such a failure as a mother?'

'You're *not* a failure,' Lara said, choosing her words carefully. 'I told you – she's going through a phase.'

'I guess . . .' Nikki answered doubtfully. 'Anyway, I thought the two of them could bond even more. Eventually, if we have kids of our own, it'll be like we're all one big happy family.'

'Are you planning on having a baby?' Lara asked, surprised.

'*No*,' Nikki said quickly. 'Right now I'm *planning* on making a terrific movie, which – if everything falls into place – *you'll* star in. *Then* maybe I'll consider having another child – but only if Richard wants to.'

Ginny Kieffer – Miles's wife – leaned into their conversation. She was a well-preserved blond of indeterminate age, with carefully sculpted features – the pride of her plastic surgeon. 'Kids!' she muttered dourly, having swallowed several glasses of wine too many. 'Hate 'em. Lil' bastards don' appreciate anything you do for 'em. All they're after is your money.'

'That's not true, dear,' Miles interjected, surreptitiously moving her wineglass beyond her reach.

'How would *you* know?' Ginny said, throwing him a hateful glare. '*You're* never home.'

Nikki exchanged glances with Lara. The battling Kieffers were at it again.

'*I* wouldn't mind 'aving a baby,' piped up the anorexic model, who although she looked fourteen was actually twenty-two.

'Not with *me*, darling,' Kyle interrupted, loud enough for everyone to hear.

Two bright-red spots coloured her hollowed cheeks. 'I wasn't asking *you* to make me pregnant,' the girl said in a strong cockney accent. 'Got me a ton of guys in New York who'd *faint* at the privilege.'

Nikki decided the girl resembled a pretty young corpse. Someone should feed her. And soon, before it was too late.

'One cover on *Vogue* and they think they own the world,' Ginny mumbled, groping along the table for her wineglass.

'Lara, I marvel at how quickly you put this party together,' Barbara Westerberg said, twisting a strand of wispy hair around her finger. 'It's darling of you to invite the crew – they're *very* appreciative.'

'It seems silly to always wait for the wrap party at the end of the movie,' Lara said. 'I thought it would be fun to do one at the beginning.' She didn't add that her inspiration was Joey Lorenzo, who so far had not shown up.

Where was he, anyway? And why did it matter?

Hmm . . . wasn't she being foolish, considering he was engaged, and even if he wasn't, every female on the movie had eyes for him.

'*Such* a lovely idea,' Barbara enthused, always especially nice to her stars. 'Wish *I'd* thought of it.'

'Maybe you can pay for it,' Nikki said, *sotto voce.*

Barbara pretended not to hear. 'Oh,' she said, jumping up. 'There's Joey. Poor thing – he looks lost. Shall I invite him to join our table?'

'Who's Joey?' Nikki asked, chewing on a carrot stick.

'An actor,' Lara said vaguely, her heart starting to race, which infuriated her because he meant nothing to her.

'You mean that great-looking guy heading toward us?'

'That's him.'

'*Very* fuckable,' Nikki murmured. 'Why don't *you* lay claim before Barbara wets her panties?'

'Don't be ridiculous,' Lara said crossly. 'He's engaged.'

'Engaged means nothing,' Nikki said flippantly. '*Marriage* is the only condition that counts.'

Lara picked up her glass of non-alcoholic fruit punch. 'Actors don't interest me,' she said firmly, thinking – in spite of herself – that this one did.

'Haven't you ever heard the words "location fuck"?' Nikki said mischievously. 'It's a perk of the business. One great fling with a fantastic-looking guy, and at the end of the movie you both go your separate ways. Everyone does it.'

'Is that what you used to do before you met Richard?'

Nikki nodded enthusiastically. 'You bet your sweet ass.'

Roxy danced by, clad in a tigerprint jumpsuit. She was clinging tightly to her trucker, rubbing up against him as they rocked and rolled their way past.

Hmm . . . Lara thought, trying to get her mind off Joey, *Yoko's right – he* is *a fat one.*

Roxy was followed closely by Yoko with *her* boyfriend, a muscled hunk who looked like he belonged on the cover of *Playgirl*.

Right behind them came Trinee, accompanied by her fiancé – a solid tree-trunk of a man who favoured a kind of crazed Mike Tyson look, and towered over the diminutive Trinee.

Lara waved, happy to see everyone having a good time, forcing her thoughts away from Joey once and for all.

'Oh, boy,' Nikki said, sitting back and observing the passing couples. 'There'll be plenty of fucking on the beach tonight!'

☆ ☆ ☆

Joey circled the edge of the party, winked at Trinee on the dance floor, and decided not to go over to the above the line table where Lara was sitting. Kyle would probably treat him like shit, and he wasn't into being humiliated in front of Lara.

He noticed Barbara Westerberg heading in his direction with a determined look on her face. 'Hi, Joey,' she said, greeting him warmly.

'Barbara,' he replied, knowing he could have her any time he wanted. 'Knockout dress – *veree* sexy.'

She basked in his compliment. 'Thanks, Joey.'

Trinee had given him the scam on Ms Westerberg. She'd been married to a well-known producer who'd gotten her into the business. After a couple of years he'd run off with his accountant, leaving Barbara to manage his flourishing production company by herself. She'd kept working, divorced husband number one and married husband number two, a writer who never worked unless she got him the job. They both slept around.

Barbara grabbed his hand and squeezed it. 'You look lonely, Joey,' she said, giving him a *you can fuck me if you want* look. 'Couldn't your fiancée make it?'

'Uh . . . she was all set to fly in, then somethin' came up. She's workin' a real important case. We were on the phone – that's why I'm late.'

The truth was he was late because he'd sat in his room waiting for Madelaine's call. Sure enough, she'd phoned at nine o'clock, checking up on him. He'd wheezed and coughed over the phone, and as soon as he'd gotten rid of her, he'd left a message with the switchboard he was not to be disturbed and raced out.

'What a shame,' Barbara said, not sorry at all.

'Yeah,' Joey agreed. 'Hey – gotta let her do her thing, she's busy makin' a name for herself.'

'I insist you come and sit with us,' Barbara said.

'Gonna pass,' he said, shaking his head. 'Kyle doesn't like me.'

'Kyle doesn't like *any* man he considers competition.'

'Me? Competition?' Joey said, laughing derisively. 'Me? Who's got three lousy scenes?'

'I know,' Barbara agreed. 'Try to understand, Kyle's getting older, losing his hair,' she lowered her voice. 'Look what happened to Burt Reynolds. And to add to Kyle's humiliation, he's now dating children.'

'Huh?' Joey said, his eyes straining to watch Lara.

'The girl he's with tonight can't be more than seventeen.'

'What a loser!'

Barbara glanced around, making sure no one was listening. 'Try not to say that anywhere Kyle can hear you. And Joey, if you repeat any of the remarks I've made, I'll deny them.'

'You can trust me,' he said, trailing her to what was obviously the A table.

Lara rose to greet him. 'Hi, Joey,' she said graciously. 'So glad you made it.'

He stared at her incredible face. She was a Madonna for the nineties – breathtakingly pure and beautiful. He wanted to ravish her there and then, and yet he realized she was special – not just another conquest. 'Looks like a happenin' party,' he said easily. 'Thanks for invitin' me.'

She smiled, lighting up the night. 'It is.' Nikki gave her a sharp nudge. 'Uh . . . meet my friend, Nikki Barry,' she said, getting the hint.

Joey nodded at the pretty, dark woman, hardly noticing her – as far as he was concerned everyone paled in comparison to Lara.

'Well, hello,' Nikki said, sitting up straighter.

Barbara took his arm in a possessive fashion. 'Come sit over here, Joey,' she said, pulling him away.

'Excuse me,' he said politely, as Barbara steered him to the other side of the table.

'You're excused,' Lara responded with an amused smile –

just to let him know it didn't bother her that he was in demand.

'She's hot for him,' Nikki murmured, watching him go. 'And who can blame her?'

'They're *all* hot for him,' Lara replied calmly. 'I don't think he plays around.'

'*That* makes a nice change,' Nikki said archly. 'A guy who actually *doesn't* walk around with a permanent hard-on! Surely you jest?'

Lara smiled and wished she could stop her heart from pounding uncontrollably. 'His fiancée is a lawyer.'

'Older than him?'

'How should I know?'

'How old's he?'

'I've no idea,' she said coolly, although she did know. 'I told you – I'm not interested.'

'Oh, yes, you are,' Nikki said with a knowing wink.

'Why do you say that?'

'I can tell. As soon as he walked in, you got that itchy-pants look.'

'Bullshit!' Lara said, swearing – something she almost never did.

'Oh, bullshit, huh?' said Nikki, thoroughly amused. 'Now I *know* you're interested.'

Lara jumped up, sometimes Nikki could be the most annoying person in the world. 'You're such a fucking pain in the ass!' she exploded.

'*Two* swear words!' exclaimed Nikki, still laughing. 'I do believe you're in love.'

Lara took off, wandering around the party, furious at Nikki for making such a big deal out of nothing.

And why was Barbara Westerberg coming on to Joey, anyway? Wasn't she aware he was engaged?

Freddie, the focus puller, who'd indulged in one vodka

too many, grabbed her hand as she passed. 'Lara, Lara, Lara,' he said pleadingly. 'Dance with me?'

'Love to,' she said, on automatic-pilot response.

Freddie pulled her onto the dance floor, slippery palms gripping her slim waist. 'What a party!' he exclaimed. He had fuzzy ginger hair, out-of-control matching eyebrows, and a cheeky lopsided grin.

'It's fun, isn't it,' she responded.

'Never thought I'd get the courage to ask *you* to dance,' he said, bowled over at his own nerve.

She smiled, having learned over the years how to be friendly but not overly familiar. It worked every time. Nobody dared make a move unless she gave them a green light.

She glanced over at her table as Freddie whirled her past. Miles and Ginny were bickering as usual. Barbara Westerberg was leaning into Joey, speaking intently. Kyle had struck up a conversation with Nikki, while his date stared blankly into space.

She decided it was foolish to be mad at Nikki, who after all was right – she *did* find Joey attractive, although she'd never admit it because that would mean nonstop teasing.

'Thanks,' she said, deftly spinning out of Freddie's grasp. 'You're a delightful dancer.'

'I'll never wash my hands again,' he said, cheeky grin going full force.

Later that night, when the waiters were packing up and everyone had gone home, Nikki said a contrite, 'Sorry if I pissed you off.'

'You didn't,' Lara responded.

'It's just that I hate seeing you by yourself,' Nikki explained. 'I'd like nothing better than for you to be with a guy who'll be as good to you as you'll be to him.'

'Listen, Nik,' Lara said, her beautiful face quite serious. 'I know you mean well, but it's *my* problem, not yours. And you know what? It's not even a problem because I don't *need* a man. I'm very happy by myself. In fact, I'm a lot happier than I was when I was with Richard.'

'Ouch!' Nikki said.

'So do me a favour,' Lara continued. 'Stop pushing. Joey's an attractive guy – which every woman on the set will attest to – but *I* am *not* interested. So quit teasing me about him.'

'I get it, boss,' Nikki said, mock saluting.

'Why are you calling me boss?' Lara snapped.

''Cause you're going to star in my movie. *You'll* be the one with the clout.'

'No, Nik – learn this now – *you're* the producer, which makes *you* the boss. It has to be that way, otherwise everyone will step all over you.'

'Got it,' Nikki said.

Lara surveyed the waiters, still busy clearing up. 'I would say the party was a success.'

'Made *you* Miss Popular,' Nikki said, reaching for a chocolate and popping it in her mouth. 'Oh, did I tell you about Kyle?'

'What about him?'

'He invited me back to his hotel.'

'I thought he was with that skinny model.'

'Hmm . . . I think Mr Movie Star had a threesome in mind.' She giggled. 'Do I strike you as a swinger?'

'As a matter of fact—'

'Don't start,' Nikki said, tossing a napkin at her.

'Would you have?' Lara asked curiously. 'In your single days?'

'Let's just put it this way,' Nikki said. 'Why do you think I'm so nervous about Summer? When I was single, I'd have tried anything.'

Lara stood up, stifling a yawn. 'Let's go inside, it's bedtime.'

'Yes, and I've got to catch an early plane.'

'Wish you could stay longer,' Lara said wistfully.

'I have to get back. Can't leave them alone too long. You know Richard – he expects my full attention.'

'Tell me about it,' Lara murmured.

They entered the house where Cassie was busy supervising the caterers as they packed up.

Lara headed for her bedroom. 'Don't forget,' she called over her shoulder, 'when you're selling the movie – use my name, that should get you all the financing you need.'

'God, Lara, I *really* appreciate it,' Nikki said gratefully. 'Can't wait to tell Richard.'

'Oh, you'll return the favour one of these days.'

'Any time,' Nikki replied earnestly. 'You call, I'll be there.'

☆ ☆ ☆

Joey left the party early, Barbara Westerberg in hot pursuit. There was no point in staying when he couldn't get close to Lara – everyone wanted to be near her and he wasn't about to join the line. Now was not the time to make his move.

In the hotel lobby he extricated himself from Barbara, who was intent on luring him up to her room. 'Look,' he finally said, 'you're a very sexy woman, but I'm engaged. I can't do this and have a clear conscience.'

'Nobody will know,' Barbara assured him, licking her lips suggestively.

'Everyone will know,' he replied. 'Besides, you've got a husband.'

Barbara played her ace card. 'Y'know, Joey,' she said, circling him with words, 'I have three movies in development ... it's quite possible I can help you with your career.' A meaningful pause. 'We're talking big-time help.'

If Lara Ivory hadn't existed he might have been tempted.

Why not? If he could sleep with Madelaine Francis he could certainly sleep with Barbara Westerberg. But things had changed. Since meeting Lara he had no desire to do anything that might jeopardize his relationship with her. 'Sorry,' he said regretfully, trying to let her down easy. 'Can't do it.'

Her expression was flinty. 'Can't or won't?'

'It doesn't matter,' he said, making his escape, and going up to his room, where he lounged on the bed, staring at the television for a while.

There was a bottle of vodka on his dresser. He got up, demolished half of it, fell back on the bed and eventually drifted into a troubled sleep.

In the morning he made up his mind. He wanted Lara Ivory more than he'd ever wanted anyone in his life.

And somehow or other he was going to get her.

BETTY WAS out for adventure. Well, of course, I was not averse to a little adventure myself, so we made the perfect pair. There I was, seventeen, ready to rock and roll, and on my way to California.

I gotta tell you, though – Betty was the biggest pain in the ass a man could ever get stuck with. She nagged the shit out of me. The only time she was quiet was when I was jamming it to her – and that didn't last long.

We hitched most of the way. I lurked in the bushes while Betty stood at the side of the road in the shortest shorts known to man and an almost non-existent tank top – upright little tits on red alert. Every trucker screamed to a stop. As soon as they pulled up, I'd run out from my hiding place and we'd both climb aboard. They weren't happy, but tough shit – there was nothing they could do. A few of them came on to her anyway, and she winked at me and asked what they'd pay for a threesome.

I wasn't into that. To tell the truth, I didn't even know what a threesome was. Years of living in California and it was my speciality – me, two sexy girls, and three thousand bucks a show. Money for pleasure, we all got off.

But I'm getting ahead of my story.

Finally we arrived in LA. I had it in my head we were on our way to a fancy house with a big swimming pool just like I'd seen on the movies. But no, Betty dragged me down to Oxnard, a small seaside town halfway between LA and Santa Barbara where her dad and his girlfriend lived. Thing is, you gotta be where it's all happening. Oxnard was a stopgap. I knew we were going nowhere if we stayed there.

It wasn't a problem, because Betty's dad took one look at us and more or less told us to piss off. He wasn't into his daughter screwing up his life. So we hit the road again, hitching our way back to LA – where we lived on the streets around Hollywood Boulevard for a couple of months, even though we still had Avis's jewellery stashed in Betty's backpack.

Betty got off on living on the streets, she was into spending time with all the other kids who'd run away from home. It wasn't my scene, sleeping in abandoned houses with a bunch of misfits, scrounging food from the back of restaurants and hanging out on the Boulevard. I was used to comfort and a proper bed.

'We should sell your mom's jewellery and rent an apartment,' I informed her.

'Then we'll havta pay rent every month,' Betty complained. 'How're we gonna make enough bread t'do that?'

She had a point. Truth was I didn't know. I'd never had to make money, there was always a woman to take care of me.

In spite of Betty's objections we sold the jewellery and rented a one-room apartment. When the money ran out, Betty started hooking to pay the rent and buy her coke – a habit she'd gotten into in a big way.

Since Betty was the only one making money she thought I should get a job. We fought all the time. 'Shift your lazy ass and do something,' she'd yell at me.

Who made her ruler of my fucking planet?

I had my eye out for another deal, and one day, while walking down Sunset, I found it. Attractive woman in her late thirties; white convertible broken down; car phone out of action.

'Hey,' I said, zeroing in – 'cause I knew a good thing when it was staring me in the face. 'You look as if you need help.'

'My car died,' the woman said. 'Can you do me a favour and call AAA for me if I give you my card?'

I did better than that. I fixed her car myself, then I asked her to give me a lift to Fairfax. By the time we got there, I'd told her I was an out-of-work actor who'd recently broken up with his girlfriend and was looking for a place to crash.

'What the hell – you can stay in my pool house for a couple of nights,' she said, checking me out and liking what she saw.

That's all it took. Three days later I moved into the main house and into her bed with the fake-fur bedspread and smooth satin sheets.

Although she wasn't in the movie industry, she certainly had money. And after I showed her a good time in bed, she wasn't averse to passing some of it my way.

I didn't tell Betty I was moving on, because I knew she'd make a scene. I simply never went back.

So here I was, two days before my nineteenth birthday, living with a hot babe in a house in the Hollywood Hills, feeling like I'd definitely arrived. Trouble was, I still didn't have any money.

Soon after moving in I discovered my new lady love was a high-class call-girl, which didn't bother me at all.

'You should do what I do,' she told me one day, lounging on satin sheets wearing nothing but stiletto heels and an enigmatic smile. 'The women in this town are desperate. The men too. You can take your pick.'

And so I started a new career. It wasn't the one I'd had in mind, but it would do. For now.

Becoming a movie star would have to wait.

Chapter Sixteen

 WHEN NIKKI arrived home from New York the next afternoon, she found Summer entertaining. The house was full of young people lounging around in their shorts and swimsuits acting as if they owned the place.

She stood in the hallway perplexed. What the hell was she supposed to do now?

'Have you seen my daughter?' she asked a long-haired surfer, who gazed at her blankly with glassy eyes and a dazed smile. 'Summer,' she repeated, 'my daughter.'

'Oh, yeah, Summer,' the guy said, scratching his chin. 'She's like on the deck.'

Seething, Nikki made her way out to the deck, where she discovered a dozen other bikini-clad babes and long-haired dudes lolling around. She spotted Summer over in the corner necking with a bare-chested boy in tightly fitting chinos sitting dangerously low on his skinny hips. Marching over she said a sharp, 'Excuse me.'

The boy had his thumbs in the top of Summer's bikini pants. He barely turned his head. 'Get lost,' he mumbled.

'No,' Nikki responded. '*You* get lost. This is *my* house, and that's *my* daughter you're slobbering all over.'

Summer pushed him away and sat up. 'Oh, hi, Mom,' she said, casual as can be. The boy took off.

'I don't remember you asking if you could throw a party,' Nikki said, quietly furious.

'Well, you were away, an' Richard said it was no biggie,' Summer said, little Miss Innocent.

'You're sure about that?'

'Yeah, I mentioned I was like having a couple of friends over, and he said I should go for it.'

'Summer, there are at least fifty people trashing my house. That's not exactly a couple of friends.'

'You know how it is, Mom, word gets on the street, an' it's Sunday and people have nothing to do, so it kinda turned into a crowd. 'S not my fault.'

'Who's fault is it? Mine?' *Oh, God!* Nikki thought. *I'm beginning to sound like my own mother!*

'Hey,' Summer's pretty face clouded over, 'like what do you *expect* me to do – throw them out?'

'Yes,' Nikki said. 'That's exactly what I expect you to do. Get everyone out of my house. And do it now.'

'Gee, Mom,' Summer said, curling her lip in disgust. 'You're sounding so *old*.'

'Five minutes,' Nikki said through clenched teeth. 'Do you hear me, Summer?' She turned and marched back into the house, going straight to her bedroom.

There was a naked couple making out on her bed. The girl couldn't have been more than fifteen, the boy maybe a year or two older. 'Are you aware you're in a private home?' she said angrily. 'And this is my bedroom.'

The girl grabbed her panties, the boy grabbed a joint, smouldering in an ashtray on the floor next to the bed. She couldn't help noticing he was well hung and very muscular. They grew them big these days.

'Listen,' she said wearily, 'I'll look away while you get dressed, then kindly get the hell out of here.'

She turned around and listened to them scrambling for

their clothes littered all over the floor. A few moments later they ran past her out of the room.

Locking the door, she picked up the phone and called Richard in the editing rooms. A woman answered.

'Who's this?' Nikki asked.

'Kimberly. Who's *this*?'

An assistant with attitude, just what she needed. '*This* is Mrs Barry. Get me my husband.'

After a few moments Richard came on the line. 'Hi, sweetheart, you're back,' he said.

'Yes, I'm back, and our house is full of sex-crazed teenagers,' she said sharply. 'Did you tell Summer she could have a party?'

'Excuse me?' he said, sounding completely uninterested.

She knew why. He was sitting in front of the editing machines with his team of editors, completely absorbed. He couldn't care less if Summer was entertaining the Dallas Cowboys.

'Summer said *you* told her it was OK if she had people to the house,' she said accusingly.

'You can't begrudge her that on a Sunday afternoon. The kid had nothing to do, so I told her it was all right to have a few friends over.'

'The few friends turned into fifty people. When I went into our bedroom there was a couple of under-age sex addicts making out on our bed!'

'Aw, Jesus!' he groaned.

'Weren't you supposed to give her some kind of supervision while I was away? Obviously, she's running wild.'

'Then *obviously* you shouldn't have left her with me,' he said sourly, like *she* was the one in the wrong.

Nikki took a deep breath, striving to stay in control. 'I don't want to fight over this.'

'*You're* the one making it into a fight.'

'I am not,' she said indignantly, furious he was taking Summer's side.

'Look,' he said abruptly, 'I'm working. I can't handle this kind of pressure.'

'Thanks a lot!' she said, slamming down the phone. She couldn't believe that with all the good things about to happen in her future, she had to deal with this shit. And Richard was no help, all he thought about was his precious movie.

She waited a good fifteen minutes before emerging from her bedroom. The house was clear.

'Summer,' she called out. No response. She hurried into the guest room – Summer's temporary quarters. It looked like a disaster area. 'Summer,' she yelled again.

Still no answer.

She went back into the living room and out onto the deck. Summer had taken her party down the beach. They were camped in front of somebody else's house like a raggedy band of gypsies – a portable CD player blasting loud rap music.

She went back into the house, it was a shambles. They'd broken into the liquor cabinet, spilled drinks on the carpet, ashtrays were overflowing, boxes of half-eaten pizza everywhere. They'd even invaded Richard's study, although they hadn't touched his desk. Thank God for that. Or maybe it would have been a good thing if they had – *finally* he'd wake up to what a devious little madam Summer really was.

'*I'm* not clearing up,' she muttered to herself, picking up the phone and trying to reach Sheldon in Chicago.

'Mr Weston, he away,' a heavily accented maid informed her.

'When is he coming back?'

'Don' know. He in Bahamas.'

Trust Sheldon – he'd gotten rid of Summer and gone off on a fabulous vacation. Typical. The kid was with her and he didn't give a damn. At least he could have warned her what a prize pain in the ass their daughter had turned into.

No. That wasn't Sheldon's style. He'd wanted her to find out for herself.

☆ ☆ ☆

'Rad party!' Tina remarked. 'Shame your mom had to ruin it.'

'I know,' Summer agreed, swigging from a can of beer as they sprawled on the sand watching the party disintegrate around them. 'She's a real downer.'

'Wouldn't've thought it – her being so young and all.'

Summer picked up a handful of sand and let it trickle through her fingers. 'She left me when I was a kid. Took off.'

'Who looked after you?'

'My dad. He's a big-deal shrink.'

Tina nodded, like she understood. 'I bet he spoils the shit outta you.'

No, that's not what he does, Summer thought, wishing she had the courage to confide in Tina. *He comes into my room late at night, slobbers all over me, then shoves his thing inside me. He's been doing it since I was ten. Now that he's married to Rachel it's not so often, but he still does it when he thinks there's nobody around to discover his dirty little secret.*

'My dad's in Chicago,' she said flatly. 'I'm staying here with my mom and her new husband.'

'Oooh, stepfathers!' Tina said, with a fake shudder. 'They creep me out! I've had three, and the pervs all came on to me. That's why I split when I was sixteen – I so couldn't take the hassle. I mean it's *embarrassing* – some old dude with a hard-on chasing you around the room while your mom's out cruising Saks.'

Summer wished *she* could put things into perspective the way Tina did. 'Your mom ever find out?' she asked.

Tina shrugged. 'Who knows? Who cares?' She jumped up. 'I'm getting another beer. Want one?'

Summer shook her head as Tina took off. The party was going on all around her, but she didn't feel like joining in. The mere thought of her father was enough to bring back the old familiar sickness in the pit of her stomach that had been such a part of growing up.

The first time he came to her room was bad enough, but after that he'd visited her once a week, and there was absolutely nothing she could do. She was ten years old and petrified. Besides, he'd sworn her to silence, threatening all kinds of terrible things if she talked.

After a while she'd learned to tolerate his abuse. She was too ashamed to tell, because whoever she confided in would think she'd condoned it. So, as painful as it was, she'd kept the terrifying secret to herself.

Maybe if she told Tina it would make things better.

Maybe.

Maybe not.

☆ ☆ ☆

'Your wife sounds like a real bitch,' Kimberly whispered in Richard's ear.

He glanced over at his two editors to see if they'd heard. They were too intent on the Avid machine to notice.

Kimberly's hand rested on his crotch. 'She obviously doesn't understand you,' she whispered.

Wasn't that supposed to be *his* line?

'Richard,' Jim, his chief editor said, turning around, 'take a look at this – see if it's what you meant.'

He moved away from Kimberly to view the sequence of

film they'd put together at his request. 'We need the close-up on Lara,' he said brusquely. 'My mistake. Put it back in.'

Kimberly was right, ever since Nikki had gotten it into her head she could be a producer, she had turned into a bitch. Treating him like the goddamn babysitter. Phoning up and complaining when she knew he was working. Where the hell was she coming from?

Jim put the close-up of Lara back in. Richard viewed the film and was satisfied. It had been a long week, but they were getting there, the assembled footage looked great.

'Thanks, guys,' he said, standing up and stretching. 'See you early Monday. Go home to your families, they've probably forgotten what you look like!'

Kimberly hung around, waiting until the two men left. Richard was busy entering notes into his laptop.

'Don't you have a boyfriend?' he asked, when he finally realized she was still there.

'I do now,' she said in a sexy voice.

He was just about to say, 'Oh, no you don't!' when she stepped out of her dress, and there were those chewable nipples staring him in the face, and he hadn't eaten all day . . .

Sometimes temptation was just that.

☆ ☆ ☆

Summer wandered back into the house at sunset. 'Sorry, Mom,' she mumbled, like it was no big deal. 'The party kinda got outta hand.'

'Out of hand!' Nikki exclaimed, to her horror sounding more and more like her mother every minute. 'They've trashed my house. Who's clearing it up?'

'The maid'll do it,' Summer said, slouching into the kitchen and opening the fridge.

'The maid will *not* do it,' Nikki said, flushed with anger as she followed her daughter into the kitchen. '*You*, young lady, will take care of it yourself.'

Summer almost laughed in her face. 'Not me,' she said. ''S not *my* mess.'

For a few seconds Nikki was completely at a loss for words. This damn kid was pissing all over her, and she wasn't going to take it any more. 'Summer,' she said, attempting not to lose it completely, 'get something straight. You might do what you want when you're with your father. However, when you're here, I call the shots, and if you don't like it, you'll be on the next plane back to Chicago. Get it?'

Summer got it. By the time Richard arrived home the house was clean, and Summer – clad in an innocent-girl long paisley dress, her white-blond hair pulled back in a ponytail – greeted him with a kiss and a hug.

'Thanks for looking after me while Mom was gone,' she said, her expression angelic. 'You're the best!'

Richard glanced at Nikki as if to say – *What are you complaining about? This kid is perfect.*

Nikki wanted to say – *It's an act, Richard, get with the programme.*

But she didn't, and the three of them went out to dinner at Granita, and Summer behaved perfectly all night.

During dinner Nikki told Richard that Lara had agreed to be in *Revenge*. He didn't say a word.

'Isn't it great?' she pressed.

'No,' he responded, grim-faced. 'You're in for nothing but trouble.'

She wasn't about to get into it in front of Summer. In fact, she didn't want to get into it at all. He had his opinion, she had hers.

Later, in bed, when she wanted to make love, he demurred. 'I'm tired,' he said. 'I've been working all day.'

'And *I've* been on a plane,' she said. 'But I'm not too tired.'

'Tomorrow,' he said, turning his back and going to sleep.

She realized it was weeks since they'd made love, and decided she'd better do something about it. Maybe a weekend in Carmel or San Francisco, somewhere romantic, where they could be alone with no outside disturbances.

In the morning when she awoke, Richard was gone and so was Summer. He'd left a note on the kitchen table.

TAKEN SUMMER TO SEE HOW IT'S DONE. WILL CALL YOU LATER.

She felt a small pang of jealousy. Why wasn't he inviting her?

Don't be ridiculous, she told herself. *He's being helpful. Taking Summer off my hands before she drives me totally nuts.*

Besides, he knew she was meeting with one of her potential directors today – and the truth was that right now her movie was more important than anything.

143

Chapter Seventeen

 IT WAS Monday morning and they were about to begin shooting at the same restaurant location. The make-up and hair trailers were buzzing with talk of Lara's party. 'Some insane blow-out!' Roxy exclaimed. 'You certainly know how to throw a party. Plenty of booze, amazing sounds, wild dancing. I had a blast, so did everybody else.'

'Thanks,' Lara said, smiling. 'I had a pretty good time myself.'

'Yeah, *I* saw you whirling around the dance floor with Freddie. He hasn't stopped creamin' about it ever since.'

'I'm glad everyone enjoyed themselves.'

'Show me someone who didn't, an' I'll show you a party pooper,' Roxy said, checking out her reflection in the mirror as she finished styling Lara's hair. 'Yesterday I had one *bitch* of a hangover – couldn't even function. Today I'm back to my usual wonderful self.'

'That's nice to know.'

'By the way,' Roxy added, in her best confidential *I've got a secret* tone. 'Did you hear about Joey and Barbara Westerberg?'

'What about them?' Lara asked, her stomach sinking.

'She tried to lure Joey up to her room after your party, and he turned her down. Miz Westerberg is not a happy camper.'

Why did she feel so relieved? *He's an engaged man, get over him*, she told herself sternly. Besides, she wasn't some man-hungry desperado like Barbara Westerberg.

'My heart goes out to her,' she murmured, uncharacteristically bitchy.

Yoko was equally enthusiastic about the party, as was Jane when she escorted her to the set.

As soon as Miles saw her, he grabbed her arm, manoeuvring her to one side. 'We have a big problem,' he said, chewing on a wooden toothpick. 'Kyle doesn't like the actor playing Jeff. He wants him out.'

'*Excuse* me?'

'I know, I know, it's crazy. He's been in the background of your scene for the last three days.'

'What will you do?'

'Keep the actor and ignore Kyle's shit. We don't have the time to reshoot three days' work. I'm warning you, 'cause he's bound to get on your case.'

'I can deal with Kyle.'

Miles laughed drily. 'I'm sure you can.'

'I hope you haven't mentioned this to Joey.'

'What do *you* think? We're shooting his scene this morning.'

'That's good,' she said. 'Because you know how sensitive we actors are.'

'Yeah, especially Kyle,' Miles said, with an ironic laugh. 'That guy's about as sensitive as a racoon's ass!'

Angie, her stand-in, was sitting in her place while they lit the scene. Joey was at the bar surrounded by women. Lara noticed that Trinee, the pretty wardrobe girl, was constantly by his side.

'Here's the plan,' Miles said. 'We'll shoot the scene. Once it's in the can there's nothing Kyle can do – except be totally pissed off. If he stirs up too much crap, I'll deal with it in editing.'

'I can't believe he's this insecure,' Lara said, shaking her head.

'Believe it – he's an actor.'

'Thanks a lot, Miles. Didn't I just tell you how sensitive we actors are?'

'Honey, you're not like other actresses I've worked with. You've got your shit together.'

Did having your shit together mean being by yourself? Always lonely? Always wondering why there was nobody there to take care of her, hold her and share her secrets?

'OK,' the first AD yelled out, 'we're going for a rehearsal. Everyone settle down.'

Lara moved to the table. Miles followed her. Joey came over.

'OK,' Miles said. 'Joey, you'll enter the scene from camera left.'

'Finally,' Joey said with a wide grin.

Lara smiled back at him, murmuring a succinct, 'Guess what? Mr Carson will *not* be on the set this morning, so if we're lucky, this'll fly.'

'Now *I'll* probably start blowing lines,' he said ruefully.

'No, you won't.'

'I haven't done this in a while.'

'You'll be fine.'

'With you, anybody would be fine.'

Was it her imagination, or did their eyes lock every time they looked at each other?

Miles blocked the scene, then told them to take a short break while his cinematographer lit it and the second AD placed his extras.

'Wanna get a coffee?' Joey asked.

'I don't drink coffee,' she replied. 'Maybe an Evian?'

'Let's go,' he said. 'Kraft service awaits.'

They walked together to the Kraft service stand set up

outside. Joey picked up a bottle of Evian and a plastic glass, handing them to her with a flourish.

Cassie came running over. 'You OK, Lara?' she asked protectively.

'I'm fine, Cass,' Lara replied calmly. 'I'll call you if I need anything.'

'OK,' Cassie said, shooting Joey a suspicious look.

'You've got people watchin' you all the time, huh?' he said.

'Not all the time,' she responded, marvelling at his impossibly long lashes, shadowing his brooding dark eyes.

'I hear Kyle wants me out.'

'Where did you hear that?'

'I got an antenna for trouble. Only they can't do it on account of the fact I'm in all the background shots.'

'Exactly.'

'So what's Miles gonna do?'

She took a sip of Evian from the plastic glass. 'He's certainly not firing you. And if he dared to do so, *I'd* have something to say about it.'

He looked at her quizzically. 'You would?'

'It's not fair.'

'Nobody said leadin' men had to be fair.'

'I'm a leading lady and *I'm* fair.'

He broke into a big smile. 'Well, yeah, everyone knows – you're the fairest of them all.'

Was he coming on to her, or merely being friendly? She was so confused. 'I hear Barbara Westerberg gave you a hard time,' she said, deciding he was being friendly.

'News travels around here.'

'With Roxy and Yoko there are no secrets.'

He paused a moment before answering. 'Barbara's a nice lady,' he finally said. 'Guess she didn't realize I'm taken.'

'You really are an old-fashioned gentleman, aren't you?' she said, regarding him quizzically. 'You refuse to say anything bad about anyone. I like that about you, Joey.'

He fixed her with an intense look. 'You want me to list the things I like about you?'

She was wrong – he was definitely being more than friendly. 'You wouldn't be flirting with me, would you?' she said lightly.

He laughed. 'Wouldn't dare.'

'No?'

'No way.'

'How did your fiancée's case go?' she asked, figuring it was safer to move on.

'She's workin' it.'

'What did you say her name was?'

His mind went completely blank. Shit! He'd invented a fiancée who had no name. 'Uh . . . Phillipa,' he blurted, and wished he hadn't because it sounded like such an uptight name.

Jane appeared behind them, all business. 'Lara, Joey – you're both wanted on the set.'

He took the plastic glass from her, causing their hands to touch for a moment.

His touch weakened her. Abruptly she turned away and hurried to the set. *Admit it, Lara. Nikki's right, you are interested, and there's nothing you can do about it.*

Their scene together went smoothly. First Miles shot his master, then several close-ups of Lara, and a couple of tight shots on Joey. Nobody blew any lines and they were finished before noon.

'Wow!' Lara said, fanning herself with a newspaper. 'This makes a nice change.'

'Good going,' Miles said. 'For once we're ahead of schedule. We'll shoot the fight scene next.'

'Guess that means I've got the rest of the day off,' Lara said jokingly.

'Not you,' Miles said. 'You're *watching* the fight scene, remember? You're the damsel in distress.'

'Actually,' Roxy said, hovering over Lara's hair with a brush and a can of hairspray, 'she's the bitch who caused all the trouble in the first place!'

They all laughed.

Jane rushed over, urgently whispering in Miles's ear.

'OK, we're taking an early lunch break,' he said, sounding annoyed.

'How come?' Lara asked.

'Kyle's not ready,' Miles said grimly. 'Apparently he's having trouble with his fucking hair.'

Joey realized that if he was going to do something about Lara, he'd better do it soon, before it was too late. Once they shot the fight scene, his work on the movie was over.

He grabbed his opportunity before she vanished into her trailer. 'Dunno about you,' he said quickly, 'but I've had it with the food off the catering truck. Wanna sneak off to this burger place I found down the beach?'

She regarded him for a long silent moment. Cool green eyes and the most beautiful face he'd ever seen. 'Yes,' she said at last, thinking that the sooner she got over this mild crush, the better. 'I'd like that.'

Chapter Eighteen

 NIKKI MET with three directors, the last of them being Mick Stefan – a rat-faced twenty-nine-year-old, with gap teeth, long, wild-man hair and oversized, heavily magnified glasses. A brown herbal cigarette dangled from the corner of his thin lips and he couldn't seem to keep still.

'I wanna shoot your script,' Mick said, fidgeting uncontrollably. 'I wanna make something fuckin' ferocious.'

'Ferocious?' Nikki responded.

'Yeah – you got the heroine chick-babe in deep shit, and here's the item turns me on – she's a chick-babe with balls. I dig that. The way I'm gonna shoot it, we'll *touch* her rage. We'll make it clear to every motherfuckin' member of the audience that this is one angry pissed off outta her head chick-babe.'

Nikki was delighted he liked the script. Mick Stefan was a comer who'd already directed two small, highly acclaimed films, both of which had won several prestigious awards. Now he was hot and the studios were after him.

'I have good news,' she said.

Mick chewed on the end of his herbal cigarette while peering at her through his alarmingly large glasses. 'Give it up.'

'Lara Ivory has agreed to play Rebecca.'

'Ya *gotta* be shittin' me,' he said, kind of disgusted like.

'Do you have a problem with that?'

'Yeah, I got a problem. Lara Ivory's a fancy fuckin' movie star. I wanna make this movie with no names.'

'I don't understand,' Nikki said, hoping he wasn't going to be difficult. 'How do you expect me to complete financing with no names? You should be jumping up and down that Lara Ivory has agreed to play a role like this.'

'Jesus!' he said, pointed nose twitching. 'She's one of those glamour chick-babes – can't act for shit.'

'Oh, yes, she can,' Nikki said, defending her friend. 'Lara's a very talented actress.'

'Yeah, in all those big fuckin' over the top sixty-million-dollar movies.'

'Mick,' Nikki said earnestly, 'surely you understand that with Lara Ivory we'll have a real chance of getting this film off the ground? Without her it could get lost.'

'You think somethin' *I* do is gonna get ignored?' he said sharply.

She was beginning to think that his ego was so big it was going to trip everybody up. Wait until he met Richard – they'd surely butt heads. *You're the producer*, a little voice screamed in her head. *Assert yourself.*

'You know,' she said quietly. 'If I was forced to make a choice – you or Lara Ivory – who do *you* think I'd choose?'

Mick removed his glasses and threw her a gap-toothed grin, brown cigarette sticking to his lower lip. 'Me?' he said, attempting to be cute and lovable. It didn't work.

Nikki shook her head. 'Wrong. Not only is Lara a fine actress, she's also a friend of mine, *and* she's agreed to work for scale. So Mick, if you're *not* interested, let me know now and we'll stop wasting each other's time.'

'Oh, a tough chick-babe, huh?' Mick said, screwing up his eyes. 'I get off on tough chick-babes.'

Ignoring his sexist tone, she spoke seriously. 'This is my first movie as a producer, and I want it to happen on all levels. I'd love to hire you if you can be part of a team. If you can't, say so now.'

'She gonna do the rape scene?' he demanded, small eyes blinking rapidly.

'Yes.'

'None of that body double shit?'

'No,' Nikki said, although the truth was she hadn't discussed with Lara how far she was prepared to go.

''Cause if she's gonna play prima donna – I'm out. But if she's into it all the way – I'm in.'

After Mick left, Nikki paced around the house. Out of all the directors she'd met, he was the one she wanted. He had the passion and the enthusiasm. Plus she loved his work – his movies were edgy with a real nineties style.

She glanced at the clock. It was just before six. Where the hell was Richard? He and Summer had been gone all day and he hadn't even bothered to call. Right now she needed his counsel and advice before making a decision to hire Mick. It was important that she spoke to Lara, too. Nothing could go wrong, and it was up to her to make sure of that.

☆ ☆ ☆

After sitting around watching Richard edit his movie, Summer got bored and called Jed, who happened to be home. He took her surfing – or at least she got to watch him do it. Jed had settled into a respectful crush, because she'd made it very clear she wasn't interested. 'Platonic,' she'd warned. 'Or nothing.'

He'd settled for platonic.

Later in the afternoon she met up with Tina, who took her to the showroom downtown where she occasionally worked, modelling lingerie and swimsuits for out-of-town buyers. The owner of the place was a round-faced Greek man who followed her around with a lecherous leer – that is until his fat wife appeared, then his smirk was quickly replaced with a sour expression.

'His old lady's swallowed his nuts,' Tina said, with a tough little giggle. 'I'm surprised she lets him employ me. Course,' she added thoughtfully, 'the buyers love to ogle my fine young bod – especially in all the see-through shit.'

'How long have you worked here?' Summer asked, wondering if she too could get a job.

'Long enough,' Tina replied, pulling a face.

'Is it fun?'

'Dunno,' Tina said, not sounding as sure of herself as usual. 'Sometimes, when I see all these old cockers with their eyes bulging like they've never seen a *female* before, *then* it's fun.'

'Oh,' said Summer. And suddenly she was glad it wasn't her up there with a lot of horny old men eyeballing her body.

Tina drove her back to town in her red sports car, dropping her outside Century City. 'Call you later,' she said. 'Maybe we'll do something.'

Summer nodded. She knew that whatever they got up to, it would certainly be more fun than Chicago.

Chapter Nineteen

 'So, HERE we are,' Joey said. 'And me feelin' like I've kidnapped the golden princess.'

Lara regarded him seriously. 'What does that mean?'

'Did you see Cassie's face when you said you were takin' off for lunch?'

'She's . . . protective.'

'Gotta feelin' everyone's talkin' about us.'

'Why would they? I mean, my God, if two people can't have lunch together . . .'

'Hey, I'm with *you*.'

'Anyway, you're right,' she said, sipping a glass of water. She'd changed out of her film clothes into faded jeans and a baggy white T-shirt. She still looked sensational. 'I couldn't face another of the caterer's chicken à la king dishes. A burger is exactly right.'

Joey had a million sure-fire lines he could use, but he abandoned all of them. She was too good to listen to his bullshit.

'C'mon, Lara,' he said, fixing her with his penetrating eyes, 'tell me somethin' about you I'm not gonna read in a magazine. I've told you about my love life, so it's only fair.'

She laughed easily. 'I don't *have* a love life.'

'Cut me a break,' he said disbelievingly.

'Well ... I did. I was with someone for a year ... we broke up six months ago.' She sighed deeply. 'It's not easy being with me.'

'Why's that?'

'Isn't it obvious? Whenever I go to a movie premiere or an opening, photographers jump all over me. The man I'm with is merely the escort who'll make the tabloids because he's new in my life. It does nothing for a man's ego. How would you like it?'

'Hey – my ego's pretty secure.'

She couldn't help smiling. 'So I noticed.'

He grinned back. 'Yeah?'

'I've been watching you on the set – all these women flocking around you. You're not famous yet, but it's definitely in your future. How will you handle it then?'

'Same as I do now.'

'No, you don't understand,' she said, her eyes clouding over for a moment. 'Everything changes when you're famous. You find yourself surrounded by people who'll do anything for you.'

'You're wrong, Lara, people do anything for *you* 'cause you're nice.'

'How can you say that?' she said, staring at him. 'You hardly know me.'

'I've been doing nothin' but watchin' you for the last three days.'

'That's because you had to,' she said lightly. 'Stuck forever in the background of our scene.'

'I do know,' he said, sincerely, 'that you're the most beautiful woman I've ever seen.'

'Genes,' she murmured, laughing uncomfortably. 'It's all on account of my ... parents.'

'You don't like compliments, do you?'

'They embarrass me.'

'Why?'

'How do I know?' she said, biting into her hamburger and wondering for the twentieth time what she was doing with him. He was taken. She was free. Not a good mix.

'Whaddya do every night?' he asked, watching her eat.

'Oh,' she said flippantly, 'throw wild parties, hang out on the beach. And you?'

'Sit in my hotel room.'

'And speak to your fiancée?'

'She's too busy,' he said, dismissing the fictional Phillipa as quickly as possible. 'Always workin' – never stops.'

'And you accept that?'

'I dunno,' he said. 'As a matter of fact . . .' he hesitated. 'Naw, I'm not burdenin' you with my problems.'

'Go ahead, burden me. I've a few of my own I can discuss.'

He laughed. 'Yeah – sure. Tell me and I'll sell 'em to the tabloids.'

'I bet you would.'

'Anythin' to make a buck.' They grinned at each other. 'It's funny,' he said, suddenly serious. 'How many people do you meet where you get to feel an instant connection? Y'know, a kinda brother–sister thing.'

'I could be your big sister,' she said good-naturedly.

'Hey, don't get carried away – you're only two years older than me.'

'I feel like I'm playing hooky from school,' she confessed. 'I never leave the set when I'm working. This is fun.'

'Like I said, they're probably all talking about us.'

'Little do they know how innocent it is.'

'Maybe we should give them somethin' to talk about,' he said casually.

'Like what?' she asked, equally casual.

'Like how about I take you to dinner tonight?' he said,

leaning across the table. 'There's this little fish restaurant I discovered.'

She took a long deep breath. 'Uh . . . Joey, I should warn you, if we're spotted anywhere in public, there's likely to be paparazzi leaping out the bushes. Lunch is one thing – but I've a strong hunch Phillipa wouldn't appreciate photographs of us dining out in all the tabloids.'

'She's not jealous,' he said flatly. *She doesn't even exist.*

'I would be,' she said quietly.

'No,' he said. 'I can't see you being jealous.'

'You'd be surprised. I can be a bitch.'

'Oh no,' he said, shaking his head. 'Not you.'

And then his dark eyes met hers again, and she felt an intense connection that made her very nervous indeed. 'Uh . . . we should be getting back,' she said, glancing at her watch.

'Yeah,' he said. 'I gotta rehearse with Kyle and the stunt coordinator. Should be interesting.'

She stood up. 'I'm sure Kyle will make it *very* interesting. Just remember – everyone's on your side.'

They walked outside to her car and driver.

Joey opened the door and she slid onto the back seat. 'Dinner?' he asked. 'We doin' it or not?'

She felt a flutter in her stomach. This was absolutely ridiculous . . . and yet – why not? 'Yes,' she said breathlessly. 'Let's live dangerously.'

He nodded as if he'd known she'd agree. 'Pick you up at seven.'

☆ ☆ ☆

Lara sat in the make-up trailer having her lips touched up. For some unknown reason she couldn't stop thinking about Joey – his dark brooding eyes, long hair, sensational smile.

'Hmm . . .' Roxy remarked, busy with a pot of pale lip gloss and a thin brush. 'He's quite a hunk.'

'Who?' Lara asked, snapping back to reality.

'The Pope,' Roxy answered good-humouredly. 'Who do you *think*? Joey Lorenzo, of course.'

'Oh yes, Joey. He seems like a nice enough guy,' Lara said, keeping her tone noncommittal.

'*Ha!*' Roxy exclaimed. 'And how was your lunch?'

'Actually, Roxy,' Lara said sweetly, 'it's none of your business.'

Roxy knew when to keep her mouth shut.

☆ ☆ ☆

Joey was working with the stunt coordinator when Kyle finally put in an appearance, striding over to the stuntman, once again failing to acknowledge Joey's presence. 'Give me the moves,' Kyle said curtly. 'Let's get this over with.'

Screw you, Joey thought. *You and your phony hairpiece and phony smile. Big fucking movie star. Who gives a shit?*

The stuntman began explaining the way the scene should go – telling Kyle exactly how to throw a punch without actually striking Joey.

'I know, I know,' Kyle said impatiently, cracking his knuckles. 'Done it a thousand times.'

In rehearsals all went well, but as soon as Miles called for a take, Kyle hauled off, hitting Joey for real, landing a crunching blow to his jaw.

It was so unexpected that Joey fell like a stone.

He was professional enough to stay down until Miles yelled, 'Cut!' When he got up he was ready to kill.

Miles stepped between them and said to Kyle, 'What the hell happened here?'

'Guess my hand must've slipped,' Kyle said, a sneer in his voice. 'Better do it again.'

Miles edged Kyle to one side. 'Stop the punch when you're supposed to,' he ordered tersely.

'Yeah, yeah,' Kyle said, as if he gave a shit.

There was silence on the set as they shot the scene again. This time Kyle behaved himself and pulled his punch.

'OK, once more,' Miles shouted, still not satisfied.

Roxy nudged Yoko. 'Watch him cold-cock the poor bastard,' she whispered.

'Settle down, everybody,' yelled the first AD.

Kyle hit Joey so hard he thought the sonofabitch had broken his jaw, and although it dredged up a lot of bad memories, he managed to stay down until Miles shouted, 'Cut! Print it, that's a take!'

As soon as he knew the camera had stopped rolling, he was on his feet, chasing after Kyle, spinning him around, hauling back and punching him on the chin.

For a moment Kyle couldn't believe he was under attack. Then he responded with a left hook of his own, and before anyone could stop them, the two actors were embroiled in a serious fist fight.

'Told you!' Roxy said.

Several of the crew stepped in to separate them, but not before Joey had managed to bloody Kyle's nose.

'You fucking prick!' Kyle screamed, eyes bulging, hairpiece slipping. 'I'll make sure you never work again, you dumb fucking asshole!'

Rubbing his knuckles, Joey walked away.

Lara came after him as he left the set.

'The jerk asked for it,' he muttered.

'You were provoked,' she said. 'Everyone saw what happened.'

'Yeah, but I should've taken it out on him later,' he said, furious at himself for losing control. 'Not here, in front of everyone.'

'Joey, he deserved it.'

'That's what I like about you,' he said ruefully. 'You always support the underdog.'

She placed her hand lightly on his arm. 'I'd hardly call you an underdog.'

He looked at her intently. 'We still havin' dinner tonight?'

'Of course,' she said, clear green eyes gazing into his. 'Wouldn't miss it.'

And he knew that it wasn't long before he'd make her his.

Chapter Twenty

THE INCIDENT had happened on a hot June night. Alison Sewell was not in the best of moods. Her mother was infuriating her with her constant whining and complaining – so much so, that Alison had paid the neighbour's kid – a fourteen-year-old freak who needed money for her heroin habit – to sit with her while she was out. The teenager had green hair and a ring through her nose and God knew where else. This did not sit well with Mother, who told Alison she'd sooner be dead than subjected to this kind of company.

OK with me, Alison thought. *Then perhaps I can get some sleep around here.*

She'd taken off at six to land a good position outside the Directors' Guild for a screening Lara Ivory was due to attend. Alison obtained celebrity attendees lists from an acquaintance. Of course she had to pay him, but nothing in life was free – including the new hiking shoes she'd recently purchased which were squeezing her feet, making her even more bad-tempered.

She stood at the back, wondering who Lara's escort would be tonight. According to *Hard Copy*, Alison's favourite TV show, she'd recently gotten rid of the Lee Randolph creep – he was history. So now Lara was free again. Alison hoped she didn't start dating just anybody. If Lara made bad choices she'd be forced to warn her – 'cause Alison knew plenty about all of them. She knew who cheated on their wives; who was in the closet; who liked transvestites; who was into hookers.

So much for Hollywood's so-called Macho Men. A bunch of perverts with dicks.

The reason Lara had dumped Lee was probably because she'd taken heed of all the warnings Alison had written her. Sometimes she'd sent her three or four letters a day, just to make sure she knew that Alison Sewell was on her side, rooting for her. She'd been thinking that now Lee Randolph was gone, she might resume her visits to Lara's house. Only today she'd written her a long letter telling her idol they could now spend plenty of time together since the loser was history. The loser being Mr Lee Randolph himself, who, if she had her way, would have gotten a bullet in his brain because it was his fault she wasn't living in Lara's house and hanging out like real girlfriends did.

And when that happened – *Bye-bye, Mother. You can whine yourself to death all by yourself, 'cause your little Alison has moved on to bigger and better things.*

'Here comes the Hun,' she heard one of the other photographers say as she elbowed her way to the front. 'Must be our lucky night.'

'Fuck your mother in the butt,' she muttered, shouldering her way to a good position, right behind the rope that separated the photographers from the stars.

'Something stinks around here,' one of the guys said, directing his rude comment at her.

'Yeah, your breath when you talk,' she snapped back.

Personal hygiene had never been a big priority with Alison. She took a bath every couple of weeks when the smell got so bad even *she* couldn't stand it.

'Lara! Lara! Lara!' The cry of the crowds swelled like a mantra of adulation. Alison stood to attention as Lara swept into view wearing a green strapless dress that matched her startling eyes.

As soon as she saw what she was wearing, Alison scowled. The dress was too low cut for her liking. Lara wasn't some raunchy starlet desperate to show off the goods to get attention. She was Lara Ivory, the queen of Hollywood.

Somebody wasn't advising her right, and this made Alison mad.

'Take a look at the tits on Lara tonight,' one of the photographers remarked. 'Wouldn't mind suckin' on those juicy little cuties.'

Alison turned on him. 'Shut your filthy mouth,' she hissed.

'Get lost, freako,' he muttered.

Her temper flared and she kicked him in the calf.

'Crazy cunt!' he yelled, hopping on one leg. 'I'll fuckin' sue your fat ass.'

Lara glanced over, her attention attracted by the commotion.

She wants me to be with her, Alison thought. *Not trapped back here with these uncouth pigs.*

Without really thinking about it, she lunged forward, ducked under the rope, raced over to Lara and embraced her.

Everything seemed to happen in slow motion after that. Lara's publicist leaped forward, trying to shove Alison away. But she was too quick for him, she swung her right arm, hitting him hard across the face.

A woman moved in, attempting to pull her off Lara. Alison whacked her too.

Lara was completely stunned.

'I've come to save you,' Alison reassured her. 'I'm the only one who cares. I *am* your saviour.'

Before she could say or do anything else, two burly security guards descended on her, grabbing her under the arms, hauling her away from Lara. A cop rushed over, and she managed to kick him in the groin – even though the security guards had a firm grip on her.

Then she was struggling with all three of them, until she was hurled into the back of a police van, but not before she'd managed to kick and scratch and attack as many people as she could.

Alison Sewell was a very angry woman indeed.

Chapter Twenty-one

 THE FISH restaurant by the beach was candlelit and romantic. Lara couldn't remember when she'd had such a good time just talking – casual stuff, gossip about people on the set and their idiosyncrasies, more serious talk about acting. Since she and Joey were not involved in a relationship there was none of that intense *where are we going?* stuff. Instead they discussed movies, books, TV shows – it was delightfully relaxing, and yet while she was busy speaking, her inner voice was sending out all kinds of messages.

He's gorgeous. You like him. He's funny. He's sexy. Even better – he's nice. What are you planning to do about it?

Nothing, she told herself sternly. *Because most of all, he's taken.*

'Kyle's threatening to sue me,' Joey said, not sounding too upset. 'I told him to contact my lawyer – I could use the publicity.'

They both laughed. She sipped her wine and wondered when he was going to make a move. If he did, she'd have to say no – much as she didn't want to.

The waiter brought over the dessert menu.

'Not for me,' she said, shaking her head regretfully. 'Can't do it.'

'Tonight you're indulging yourself,' he said, taking charge.

'I am?' she said wryly.

'You am.'

At his insistence she ordered chocolate cake while he went for pecan pie. They shared each other's desserts, savouring every decadent bite.

'I'm outta here tomorrow,' Joey said, gulping down a cappuccino. 'There's nothin' else for me to do.'

She pushed a piece of chocolate cake around her plate with a fork. 'Where are you going?' she asked.

'Back to New York.'

She knew it wasn't her business, but she couldn't help herself. 'Do you and Phillipa share an apartment?'

'Right now we do,' he lied.

'That's good,' she said, nodding. 'It's always best to get to know someone before you marry them.'

'You an' Richard live together before you made it legal?'

'No. We should have.' She paused for a moment before continuing. 'Richard turned out to be a very complex and needy man. Now that he's married to my friend, Nikki – you met her at the party the other night – he's calmed down a lot.'

'Let me see . . . needy . . . needy . . . What exactly did he need? Other women?'

'You're very perceptive,' she said, her beautiful face serious. 'I caught him several times before it finally occurred to me that he had no intention of stopping.'

'Jesus! It's tough to believe any guy would screw around on you.'

She smiled wanly. 'I'm not that special, Joey.'

He stared at her, his dark eyes burning into hers. 'Don't ever let me hear you say that.'

She looked away, confused, and then began speaking again, much too fast. 'I'd like to meet Phillipa sometime. Maybe if the two of you come to LA you'll visit me. I have a small ranch off Old Oak Road. That's where I keep my horses and dogs.'

'An animal lover, huh?'

'I've always found animals more reliable than people.'

'Sometimes I think about gettin' a dog. Then I realize there's no way I can keep one locked up in an apartment all day.'

'No,' she said softly. 'That would be cruel.'

'Phillipa doesn't like animals anyway.'

'She doesn't?'

'Naw – she's a city girl.'

'You should try and convert her. Buy her a small dog.'

'And have her leave it alone all day? I don't think so.'

'Send it to me for vacations,' Lara joked. 'I'll take care of it.'

'Hey,' he said, looking at his watch, 'I promised I wouldn't keep you out late. You're working tomorrow.'

'That's OK,' she said quickly, not wanting the evening to end.

'No,' he said. 'I refuse to be responsible for bags under those beautiful eyes.'

Was it possible he *wasn't* going to make a move? This was a first. She was more than intrigued.

He snapped his fingers for the check, paid the bill in cash and helped her up.

Outside the restaurant they walked for a few minutes before Joey hailed a cab and gave the driver her address. She'd offered to bring her car and driver, but Joey had said it wasn't a good idea – too much gossiping would take place. And she'd agreed.

'Would you like to come in for coffee?' she asked tentatively, when the cab pulled up outside her house.

Before he could answer, her guard appeared. 'Evening, Miss Ivory.'

Was there no privacy?

Joey shook his head. 'You gotta get your beauty sleep.'

'You are coming by the set tomorrow to say goodbye to everyone, aren't you?' she asked, thinking she sounded a touch needy.

'*Not* a good idea,' he said, dutifully escorting her to the front door. 'You wouldn't want me and Kyle gettin' into it again.'

Her guard was hovering behind them. 'Thank you, Max,' she said crisply. He got the message and promptly retreated. 'Sorry about that,' she said, hoping he was at least going to kiss her good night.

'Don't worry about it. I like the fact you got people watchin' out for you. Wouldn't want to think of you bein' alone.'

'Are you sure about the coffee?'

God! How much more open could she be?

'Quite sure,' he said. 'Oh, an' by the way – if you ever get to New York, me and Philly would love to take you out.'

'She won't mind us having dinner tonight?'

'She knows she can trust me,' he said, leaning forward and kissing her chastely on the cheek. 'Thanks, Lara – for everythin'.' Then he turned around and strolled back to the cab.

Lara was shocked. Was this it? Was he simply going to walk out of her life and she'd never see him again?

Yes, Lara, this is it.

She hurried into the house, hands trembling. She'd wanted him to come in so much, and yet, he obviously had principles – a quality she was forced to admire.

Why couldn't *she* meet a man like Joey Lorenzo? Handsome, charming, and most of all incorruptible.

She got undressed, slid between the sheets, closed her eyes and attempted to sleep.

After a few minutes the phone rang. She grabbed it, foolishly hoping it was Joey. 'Hi,' she murmured, husky-voiced.

'Well, hi to you, too,' Nikki said. 'Hope I'm not waking you.'

'No, no, I . . . I only just got in.'

'Hmm . . . out on a hot date, I hope.'

'Actually, I was having dinner with Joey Lorenzo.'

'You're *kidding*?'

'Don't start getting the wrong idea, Nik, it's purely a friendship thing.'

'Oh, a guy who looks like that, and it's purely a friendship thing. Yeah, yeah, I believe you.'

'How many times do I have to tell you he's engaged?' Lara said, exasperated. 'In fact, if you want the truth, I asked him in for coffee and he turned me down.'

'You *are* joking?'

'No, I am not. He's nice and I like him, but he's *definitely* not available.'

'Wow! That's really something.'

'Yes, isn't it?'

'Anyway, I called to fill you in on Mick Stefan. I met with him today.'

'How did it go?'

'He's kind of over the top – quirky – with a touch of the Quentin Tarantinos. I'm crazy about his work, and I'm sure he'll do an amazing job.'

'That's good news, isn't it?'

'Look, before I hire him, I need to get your take on something.'

'Yes?'

'He started asking how you felt about the rape scene. I told him you always use a body double, but he feels the scene is pivotal to the movie, and that you have to be completely into it.'

Lara considered her reply. 'If Mick does the movie, and he's as good as you say, then I guess I'm in his hands.'

'That's all I needed to hear,' Nikki said, sighing with relief.

Lara put the phone down. She couldn't sleep, and much to her annoyance she couldn't stop thinking about Joey.

Reaching for the TV remote, she tuned into a Sylvester Stallone, Sharon Stone movie, and tried to concentrate on the two actors as they writhed on the screen in a heated love scene, their perfect bodies naked and glistening with sweat.

Just what she needed. A steamy sex scene. She clicked the TV off. Try as she might, she couldn't get Joey out of her head.

One thing she knew for sure. Phillipa was a very lucky girl.

☆ ☆ ☆

Joey made it back to the hotel. He was revved, Lara had given him an opening and he hadn't taken it. The only sure way to score with a woman who could have any guy she wanted was to play hard to get. Right now she was sitting at home thinking that she couldn't have him, and that's exactly how he *wanted* her to feel.

A bunch of people from the movie were hanging out in the bar as he passed – Roxy, Yoko, and several members of the crew. Roxy waved, beckoning him to join them.

'I'm out of it,' he said, making a quick excuse. 'Gotta get some sleep.'

'We wanna buy you a drink,' said Freddie, the ginger-haired focus puller who'd danced with Lara at her party. 'You're our hero, man. Punching out Kyle Carson. That's good stuff.'

Everybody cheered.

'Yeah, well, I was only doing a public service,' he said modestly.

'C'mon,' Roxy said, smoothing down her clinging sweater, hard nipples thrusting through the flimsy fabric. 'We don't bite – not unless you request it! Have a drink with us.'

'Yes,' said Yoko, 'you can sit next to me.'

He wasn't even tempted to score with any of these women. They were nothing and Lara was everything.

'Gotta make some calls,' he said, excusing himself. 'I'll catch up with you guys in the mornin'.'

He went upstairs and stared at the phone, forcing himself not to call Lara. Had to make her wait. Had to make her yearn for him as he yearned for her.

He'd already decided that as soon as he got back to New York, he'd take the money he'd made from the movie, pay Madelaine back and move out. That way he'd be under no obligation, and she couldn't go around saying he was a thief.

Of course, that meant he'd be broke again, but so what? He'd survive. He always had.

For a moment he almost gave in and picked up the phone, stopping himself just in time.

He knew *exactly* how to make Lara want more.

She was his future, and he couldn't afford to screw it up.

Chapter Twenty-two

 'THAT'S NO way to behave,' Madelaine said, her pinched face tense with anger.

'What?' said Joey, not really listening as he idly switched TV channels. Why did he always get caught in these traps with women he didn't want to be with? Madelaine had been good to him, but now that he'd found Lara, he had to get out for both their sakes. It wasn't fair to string Madelaine along.

'What kind of a name will you get in the business if you go around punching people on the set?' Madelaine demanded, all steely-eyed and pissed off. 'Kyle Carson's a big star – you can't afford to have people like that mad at you. And let me assure you, Joey, word soon spreads if you're difficult. Then the work stops.'

'We had a fight scene,' he explained, clicking off the remote. 'Kyle Mr Fucking Big Star Carson was supposed to pull his punch. Instead he knocked me flat on my ass.'

'Kyle Carson is the star of the picture,' Madelaine stormed, dismissing his explanation. 'You should have accepted it.'

'Is that what you think I should've done?' he said sarcastically. 'Well, Jeez, Mad, guess what? I'm not in this business to get punched out – an' I don't give a crap *who's* doin' the punching.'

'You won't be in this business at all if you carry on like this.'

She'd been irritable ever since he'd gotten back. He knew it was because he'd refused to have sex with her. Of course he'd come up with a credible excuse, told her he might have herpes.

'What?' she'd asked, astounded.

'I've got this ridge on my dick – dunno *what* it is,' he'd lied. 'I'm worried about it. The girl I went with before you had kind of a dubious history.'

'I can't believe this!' Madelaine had exclaimed, the colour draining from her face. 'What if I've caught something?'

'Don't worry,' he'd said. 'I'm sure it's nothin', only I wouldn't wanna put you at risk. Here, take a look,' he'd added, unzipping his pants.

'No.' She'd shrunk back, horrified. 'Tomorrow you must see a doctor.'

The next day he told her he'd been to a doctor who'd informed him it was merely an abrasion, and that he should refrain from sex for a couple of weeks.

So now they were living in the same apartment and not having sex, and this did not please Madelaine one bit, since as far as she was concerned sex was his main attraction.

The third night he was home he waited until she was asleep, and then took off. He did not do his usual prowl around the mean streets, instead he went straight to a bar, found a pay phone and called Lara in the Hamptons.

She answered the phone herself. 'Remember me?' he said.

'Joey,' she responded, sounding pleased to hear from him.

'Thought I'd check in – see how it's goin' on the movie,' he said casually.

'Everything's great, thanks. Nice of you to think of us.'

'Kyle's gotta miss me like crazy,' he joked. 'Anythin' happen after I left?'

'He mumbled about you a lot, told Miles to be sure to cut you out of the movie . . .'

173

'Will he?'

'Not if I have anything to say about it. Our scene together is in the script I accepted. I fully expect to see it on the screen.'

He laughed. 'I like a woman with clout.'

She laughed back. 'You don't know the half of it.'

A short silence – then— 'Hey, Lara, it was really good spendin' time with you.'

'I enjoyed it, too,' she said softly.

'When are you off to LA?'

'Three weeks.'

'Bet you're lookin' forward to some down time.'

'Me? Down time?' she said ruefully. 'I'm making the most of it while I can, before I turn into an old hag.'

'Yeah, thirty-two's really gettin' up there.'

'Actually, my next project is Nikki's movie.'

'Nikki?'

'You met her at my party. She's producing her first film. In fact, she's signed Mick Stefan to direct.'

'Interesting choice. Although I heard somewhere he's a maniac.'

'It's a different type of role for me – something that will stretch me as an actress.' She paused for a moment, then added thoughtfully, 'You know, Joey, they're not going with stars – maybe there's something in it for you. Shall I ask Nikki if they'll see you?'

'That'd be great.'

'Problem is they're all on the West Coast.'

'I can fly to LA.'

'What about Phillipa?'

'Too busy, as usual.'

'I'll speak to Nikki – see what she says.'

'I'd appreciate it.'

'Consider it done.'

'Uh . . . Lara?'

'Yes?'

A long beat. 'Nothin' . . . I'll call again in a coupla days – don't wanna keep you up.'

'No, no,' she said quickly. 'I was watching television.'

'Well . . . it was good talkin' to you.'

'You too, Joey.'

He put the phone down, strolled over to the bar and had a beer.

Things were looking up. Lara Ivory *and* a role in her new movie – what could be a better combination?

☆ ☆ ☆

Lara hung up. She had to admit she was ridiculously pleased to hear from Joey. The truth was she couldn't get him out of her mind.

She called Nikki and asked her if there might be something for Joey in the film.

'Mick has very set ideas,' Nikki said. 'That's not to say I can't get him to meet with Joey as a favour to you. Is he coming to LA soon?'

'If there's a chance for him to see Mick Stefan, he'll be on the next plane.'

'Hmm . . .' Nikki murmured thoughtfully. 'Am I reading something into this? Let me see – the guy is engaged, you had dinner with him, invited him in for a coffee – he didn't go for it. Now you're trying to get him a part in *Revenge*. Could be you're taking a shot?'

'No way,' Lara said indignantly. 'We're just friends.'

'You're just friends 'cause *he* chooses to have it that way,' Nikki said knowingly.

'You think I couldn't get him?' Lara responded boldly.

'You're too nice to go after another girl's guy. It's not your MO.'

'Don't be so sure. You don't know *everything* about me.'

She put the phone down. Nikki could be so infuriating.

☆ ☆ ☆

'I think Lara's finally found herself a man,' Nikki said matter-of-factly.

Richard placed the copy of *Variety* he was reading on the bedside table, removed his glasses and looked up. 'What did you say?'

They were sitting comfortably in bed, propped up by pillows, surrounded by newspapers, magazines and the daily trades.

'I *said*,' Nikki repeated slowly, 'that Lara has found herself a guy.'

'What makes you think that?'

'She met an actor on her movie. He's supposedly engaged, but there seems to be something going on between them. She wants me to see him for *Revenge*. He's prepared to fly out. Now, would she go to all that trouble if she wasn't interested?'

'Have you met him?'

'I saw him when I was in the Hamptons. He's a looker – macho, dark. I don't know how talented he is, but hey – if it's what she wants, I may as well read him.'

'Why would she get involved with an actor?'

'It's really none of our business who she gets involved with.'

'Yes, it is,' he said irritably. 'I look out for Lara and her interests, she *needs* looking after.'

'She's your *ex*-wife, Richard,' Nikki reminded him. 'You don't have to watch out for her any more.'

'I thought she was your friend.'

'She *is* my friend and I love her. I'd like nothing better than for her to get laid – it's been almost a year.'

'God, you're vulgar!'

She moved closer to her husband, gently touching his thigh, her hand moving slowly up. 'Isn't that what you like about me?'

He picked up his copy of *Variety* again. 'I'm not in the mood,' he said, pushing her hand away.

'You always used to be,' she said, adding jokingly, 'in fact, for an old man you're extremely horny.'

'And I'm not old either,' he said, failing to see any humour in her crack.

'OK, OK,' she said, backing off because she realized he was age-sensitive. 'I stand corrected – middle-aged.'

'I hate that phrase,' he muttered.

'Well, that's what you are,' she said, continuing to needle him.

'Where's Summer tonight?' he asked, changing the subject.

'I've given up tracking her. The only person she'll listen to is you.'

'That's because *you* treat her like a baby. Give her more space, let her know you trust her.'

'I *don't* trust her, Richard. Every time I see her she's with a boy – kissing, groping . . . God knows what else.'

'Isn't that what you used to do when you were her age?'

'Yes, but not in front of my mother.'

'Ease up – then maybe you'll have a better relationship.'

Nikki realized that since Summer had arrived their sex life had definitely taken a dive. Usually when she made the first move, he was ready, willing and able. Not tonight. In fact, not for the last month.

She tried it again, deftly plucking *Variety* out of his hands, running her fingers lightly across his bare chest.

He reached over, switching off the bedside lamp. 'I'm tired,' he said.

She continued to work on him, her fingers travelling downwards, stroking his skin in little circles the way she knew he liked.

'Don't pressure me, Nikki,' he said, moving her hand again.

'Pressure you?' she repeated, amazed. 'I thought you *loved* me taking the initiative.'

He stretched out with his back toward her.

She moved up behind him, nuzzling against his comforting warmth. 'Tomorrow night,' she murmured, yawning. 'Let's go to bed early, then neither of us will be tired.'

'OK,' he said. 'Oh, and Nikki—'

'Yes?'

'Don't push Lara into anything.'

'*Me?*'

'Yes, *you*. You have a habit of forcing things. She's fine by herself.'

Nikki shifted away from him. He wanted Lara to be alone. He didn't like the idea of her being with a man. In some sick way he felt he still had a hold over her.

For a moment she was hurt and angry. Then she thought, *This is silly – he loves me, not Lara.*

And she closed her eyes and fell into a deep sleep.

☆ ☆ ☆

The next morning Lara realized she didn't have a number to contact Joey, so she sent Cassie into the production office to collect a cast and crew list. Sure enough he was listed, with a Manhattan address.

She took his number home with her that night and sat on her bed, contemplating whether to phone him or not. Finally she decided to do so, after all, she had a perfectly legitimate reason.

She dialled his number in New York. A woman answered. It had to be Phillipa. Panicked, she hung up.

Oh, great, she thought. *You really do like him, because if you didn't, you'd talk to his fiancée and explain why you're calling.*

To make matters worse, that night she had an erotic dream about him, awakening in the early hours of the morning flushed and aroused.

Nikki was right. It was time she got herself a man.

Chapter Twenty-three

 'YOUR FEELINGS are showing up in dailies,' Miles said over a catering truck breakfast.

'Excuse me?' Lara responded, pushing two poached eggs around her plate because she wasn't hungry and the Swedish caterer – who harboured a big crush on her – had insisted on fixing her an enormous plate of food.

'We're making a love story,' Miles pointed out, removing his glasses and staring at her with faded blue eyes. 'And the chemistry between you and Kyle is fast running out.'

She pulled a face. 'Is it about the kissing scene yesterday?'

'You got it.'

'I'm sorry, Miles,' she said. 'Kyle had garlic for lunch and his breath stunk, plus he's *always* trying to shove his tongue down my throat.'

'I know he's a pain in the ass,' Miles agreed, nodding his shaggy mane of silver hair, 'only we're making a movie here, and on screen you two are supposed to be hopelessly in love. I have to see it, otherwise we're stone cold at the box office.'

'I'm trying.'

'Try harder. Weave your special magic, Lara, pretend he's someone else.'

Pretend he's Joey. The thought popped into her head completely unexpectedly. *Pretend he's Joey Lorenzo whom I haven't heard from in two and a half weeks even though I promised to get him an audition for* Revenge, *so shouldn't he be calling daily?*

'OK, Miles. I promise I'll do something about it,' she said, getting up from the table and heading for the make-up trailer.

Today they were shooting the big love scene, which meant she'd have to summon all her acting skills and try her best to get into it.

As far as she was concerned, Kyle Carson was the worst kind of phony. He presented one image to the world – that of the poor hard-done-by movie star whose wife had abandoned him, while in true life he was an out and out womanizer who couldn't keep it zipped. Over the last few weeks his supply of females had accelerated – a new one arriving every other day. Roxy commented he was having a fuckathon – an apt description of his activities. Roxy also observed that he had a saggy butt and should hire a butt double – a pronouncement that broke everyone up.

Lara sighed – not only did she dislike kissing him, she was also nervous she could contact some dreaded disease. Thank God she had a body double replacing her for the more intimate moments of the love scene. It was sad that females on the screen were forced to show it all, whereas their male counterparts modestly got away with a brief flash of butt. Demi Moore was probably the only movie star who actually seemed to enjoy revealing everything.

The previous week three actresses had arrived from LA to audition for her body double. There was much ribald laughter and nudging on the set as the girls paraded into Miles' trailer for their interviews. Miles had asked her to sit in on the auditions. 'After all,' he'd said, 'it's *your* boobs that'll be up there. You want 'em to look good, don't you?'

'I'm sure you'll pick the best pair,' she'd replied wryly,

wondering what it must be like to parade in front of a bunch of strangers exhibiting your breasts.

Barbara Westerberg stood in for her, and they'd finally hired Wilson Patterson, a veteran who'd doubled various body parts for Michelle Pfeiffer, Julia Roberts and Geena Davis. She wasn't knockout beautiful, but she did have a spectacular body and was not shy about showing it.

Today Wilson stood naked at the other end of the make-up trailer, having body make-up applied to every finely toned inch.

'Hello,' Lara said, as she entered the trailer.

'Hi,' Wilson replied, completely unembarrassed. 'Hope I'm gonna do you justice.'

'I'm sure you will,' Lara said, sitting in the make-up chair – deciding that in her next contract she would not allow a body double, it was cheating of the worst kind.

'Have you seen the wig?' Yoko asked, cleansing Lara's face with a moist pad of cotton.

'What wig?'

'Roxy came up with this fantastic wig. From behind Wilson looks *exactly* like you.'

'I don't know why they have to do this,' Lara complained. 'It's embarrassing.'

'How come you allow it?' Yoko asked, patting a fine moisturizing cream onto her skin.

'Because they're paying me megabucks, therefore I'm expected to make concessions. And if I refuse to do it myself . . .' She trailed off. 'This is the last time.'

'I like Roxy's idea,' Yoko said, giggling slyly. 'A butt double for Kyle. How about a front double, too? You know, if an actor has a tiny dick, bring in a stuntman with a huge one – that'd be good for their egos, huh?'

'You're beginning to sound more like Roxy every day,' Lara said, laughing.

'God, no!' Yoko objected.

Lara closed her eyes, allowing Yoko's soothing hands to work on her face. As she lay back, her thoughts drifted once more to Joey. Nikki had called yesterday and said, 'Where is he? The movie's practically cast. I thought you wanted me to see him.'

'I've no idea,' she'd confessed a trifle sheepishly. 'I haven't been able to reach him.'

'Gee,' Nikki had said sarcastically. 'He must be really anxious to make a career for himself.'

She couldn't understand it, why *hadn't* he called? Maybe he and Phillipa had run off and gotten married. The thought disturbed her more than she cared to admit.

Kyle was waiting on the set with minty breath and an overly friendly smile. 'Ready for our big love scene, Princess?' he greeted.

'Do me a favour, Kyle,' she said vehemently. 'No more garlic for lunch.'

'Sorry about yesterday,' he said, not sorry at all. 'Did my breath offend you?'

'*I* wouldn't do it to you, so kindly return the favour.'

'Ah . . . Lara, Lara,' he said, shaking his head. 'You're so perfect. Don't you ever get wild? Let it all hang out? What d'you do for *fun*?'

'I work,' she replied, stony-faced.

'Work ain't fun. Getting down is fun.'

'From what I hear, you've been getting down every night.'

He gave a brittle laugh. 'What's a guy supposed to do when his wife walks? I was married for ever. Now it's getting out of jail time.'

'Aren't you worried about catching something?'

He regarded her as if she was crazy. 'Me? Worried? No way. All I have to do is look at a girl, and I can tell if they're clean.'

'That's kind of dumb, Kyle.'

'Are you calling me dumb?' he said, bristling.

'Not at all,' she said, realizing it wasn't worth a fight.

An hour later they were embroiled in a heavy love scene. She hated every minute of it, but she was an actress, so she closed her eyes and made believe he was somebody she yearned for. It worked. Their kisses took on a new intensity. *Now* Miles would be happy.

In the middle of the second take she felt Kyle's erection against the side of her thigh and tried to ignore it.

'Oh, baby, am I hot for you,' he muttered, right after Miles called cut.

Coldly she replied— 'Let's see if we can act like professionals, shall we, Kyle?'

'What are you – frigid?' he taunted, furious he couldn't get to her. 'Don't like guys?'

Why was it when a movie star couldn't score there always had to be something wrong with the woman?

'That's right,' she said, deliberately needling him. 'I'm lesbian of the year, didn't you know?'

By the time her body double took over, she was desperate to get out of there. Wilson sauntered into place wearing nothing but body make-up and a pleased smile. The entire crew went into a state of schoolboy excitement. Kyle immediately began making tit jokes.

Lara walked off the set, she had no desire to hang around watching all the guys ogle Wilson. It didn't take much to reduce grown men into horny little boys. They all acted like they'd never seen a pair before.

Her designated driver was sitting in the car outside. He could hardly wait to drop her off at her house and race back so that he could get an eyeful too.

She had the afternoon free, so she put on shorts and a T-shirt, took a towel and her script of *Revenge*, then set off down the beach. Finding a shady spot, she spread the towel out, lay on her stomach and began studying Rebecca's lines. *Revenge* was definitely the movie she'd been looking for – certainly the meatiest role she'd ever had.

She stayed on the deserted beach for a while, enjoying the solitude. When she returned to the house, Cassie greeted her on the back steps looking agitated. 'That actor's here,' Cassie said.

She frowned, hoping it wasn't Kyle and his erection paying a house call. 'What actor?'

'You *know*, the good-looking one. Joey something or other.'

'Joey's here?' she said, experiencing a small shiver of excitement.

'I know I should've sent him away,' Cassie wailed. 'Only he was very insistent, assured me you'd want to see him. He's sitting in his car.'

'You made him wait outside?'

'You didn't tell me he was coming. Were you expecting him?'

'Yes,' she said, hating that Cassie felt she had to know everything. 'I must have forgotten to tell you.'

'Oh,' Cassie said, not pleased to be left out of the loop.

'Invite him in,' Lara said, hurrying into the guest bathroom. She stared at her reflection, picked up a brush, ran it through her hair, then quickly dabbed gloss on her lips. All of a sudden her heart was pounding.

Trying to compose herself, she went out to the deck, sat in a chair and picked up a magazine.

When Joey walked out she was cool and collected.

'Hey,' he said, grinning at her. 'Don't you look cute in shorts.'

'Hey,' she replied, putting down the magazine and smiling up at him.

Cassie stood in the doorway, observing the two of them, wondering what was going on.

'Would you like a drink? Tea, coffee ... something stronger?' Lara asked, her voice sounding husky.

'I could use a beer,' he said, cracking his knuckles.

'Cassie – one beer, and I'll have a 7-Up.'

'Coming right up,' Cassie said, reluctantly going back into the house.

'So, Joey, this is a surprise,' she said, putting down the magazine. 'Have a seat.'

He flopped into a chair, long legs stretched out in front of him. He had on scuffed combat boots with ripped jeans, and a white T-shirt that defined the muscles in his arms.

'Guess you're wondering what I'm doing here,' he said.

'Weren't you supposed to call me?' she asked, trying to sound as if it didn't matter. 'I set up an interview for you in LA.'

'Had other things on my mind,' he said, taking a long beat. 'It's been a tough coupla weeks.'

'Really?' she said, once again admiring the darkness of his eyes, the faint stubble around his chin and the thrust of his finely etched jawline. Oh, God! What was going on here?

'Yeah,' he said, grimacing. 'Then today everything blew up. Hadda talk to someone – an' you always seem to understand me.' He threw her a long, penetrating stare, thinking she was even more beautiful than he remembered. 'You're not pissed I drove down to see you?'

'You came all this way just to see *me*?'

He nodded. 'Phillipa an' I finally broke up. We, uh ... couldn't work out our differences. She gave me back the ring an' here I am.' He laughed ruefully. 'Hey – *now* I can go to LA.'

'Is that what you were fighting about? Going to LA?'

'Naw,' he said, clearing his throat. 'She was so into her

career, she didn't have time for me.' A long pause, another penetrating stare. 'I need somebody who's gonna put *me* first.'

'Of course you do,' Lara murmured sympathetically.

'I kinda figured that as we got deeper into our relationship, things would change,' he continued, drumming his fingers on the coffee table. 'Then I started realizin' her career came before me, an' that's no way to build a future – not when two people can't communicate.'

'Joey,' she said, understandingly, 'I know you're upset now, but if that's how things were, then you've probably made the right decision.'

Cassie returned carrying a tray with a bottle of beer, a can of 7-Up, two glasses and a dish of chocolate cookies. She placed the tray on a table in front of them, and hovered, dying to find out what was going on.

'Thanks,' Lara said, dismissing her.

Cassie had no choice but to go back inside.

Joey picked up the bottle of beer, flipping the top open with his teeth. 'You know what's so crazy about all of this?'

'Tell me,' she said softly.

His eyes met hers. 'How come I'm *here*?'

'I . . . I don't know . . .' she answered, feeling uncomfortably warm.

He took a couple of swigs from the bottle. 'It was like I *hadda* come,' he said intently. 'Like you're the only person I can talk to without feelin' I'm bein' judged.'

'I'm flattered,' she said, reaching for a cookie, even though she knew that right now she was incapable of swallowing.

'Hey, listen,' he said, rubbing his chin. 'I know you're a big movie star and all, but somehow I feel you're my friend.' Another long pause. 'Does that make me crazy, Lara?'

'No, Joey,' she said quietly. 'I am your friend.'

He jumped up, striding over to the edge of the wooden

deck, staring out to sea, his back to her. 'I never screwed around on Philly,' he said flatly. 'Although believe me, I had plenty of opportunities. *Plenty*.'

'I'm sure you did,' she murmured.

'Y'see, I believed we were gettin' married. Now I can do what I like.'

'And what *do* you like?'

He spun around and their eyes met again for a long silent moment. 'I'd like t'fly to LA an' meet Mick Stefan. Whaddaya think – am I too late?'

'I'm not sure,' she said truthfully. 'I'll be returning to LA in a few days, the studio's sending a plane. If you want, you can hitch a ride with me and we'll see.'

'Sounds like a plan.'

'Where can I contact you?'

'Dunno,' he said with a vague shrug. 'Can't go back to our apartment, it's hers now.'

'So you have nowhere to live?'

He took another swig of beer. 'I rented a car an' stashed my two suitcases in the trunk. It's my new home.'

'Where will you stay until we leave?'

'I was thinkin' I'd check into the same hotel I was at before.'

'No,' she said quickly. 'Don't do that. Everyone will wonder why you're here.'

'Hey—' he said with a bitter laugh. 'Even I'm wondering why I'm here.'

She fixed him with her cool, green eyes. 'You told me why, Joey. I'm your friend.'

He grinned, marvelling once again at her outstanding beauty. 'OK, *friend*, you wanna have dinner tonight? I know a great little lobster place on the beach.'

She began to laugh. 'The same place you took me to before?'

'We had fun, didn't we?'

'Joey . . .' she said impulsively. 'Why don't you stay here? I'll have the maid set up the guest room, then you can fly to LA with me on Saturday.'

'C'mon, Lara, people will talk.'

'I'm over twenty-one, you know. And you said you needed a friend.' A beat. 'So . . . *will* you stay?'

'Well . . .'

They exchanged warm smiles.

'Good,' Lara said, and the butterflies in her stomach refused to calm down.

Chapter Twenty-four

 RICHARD REALIZED he'd made a mistake sleeping with his assistant. Once sex entered the picture everything changed, and now Kimberly was after him with a vengeance, forever asking when they could get together again. He regretted bringing her back to his house and making love to her. He especially regretted Summer almost catching them together. She hadn't said anything, but she was a bright girl – she knew. He wanted to ask her not to tell Nikki he'd had Kimberly at the house – but if he did, it would be as good as admitting guilt. He simply had to hope she wouldn't open her mouth.

She caught him at breakfast one morning. 'Richard,' she said guilelessly. 'Will you talk to Mom for me?'

'About what?' he asked guardedly.

'Well . . . here's the thing. I uh . . . want to stay in LA. Don't want to go back to Chicago.'

'Tell her yourself.'

'She won't listen to me – we always get in a fight.' She gave him a winning smile. 'But if *you* do it . . .'

'OK,' he agreed, albeit reluctantly.

'Thanks, Richard,' she said, favouring him with a little hug. 'You're the best!'

And he knew she had his number.

Actors trekked in and out of Mick Stefan's office at a lightning pace. He was not a patient man, and if someone started to read and he wasn't immediately sure they were getting it, he leaped to his feet, waved his gangly arms in the air, and yelled, '*Sayonara*,' before they could finish. There were a lot of pissed-off performers marching out of his office.

Nikki was in shock. He did not work like other directors – he certainly didn't work like Richard. Speed was his mantra – *get it done and get it done now!* And he didn't care whose feelings he hurt.

As a favour to her, Richard came to one casting session and left after twenty minutes, shaking his head in disgust. 'You can't treat people the way he does and live,' he said. 'The man's insane. One of these days he'll find an actor waiting in the parking lot with a loaded .45!'

Nikki felt she had to support Mick, this was her movie and it was absolutely necessary that she was in synch with the director, otherwise the film would run away from her. 'It's his way,' she informed Richard. 'Everyone has a different work method.'

She was worried about Lara's reaction to Mick. He was definitely an acquired taste, and once he and Lara got together she might balk at working with him. Even though Lara had verbally agreed to make the movie, she still hadn't signed a contract. Her agent was stalling. Nikki called him daily, but he always had an excuse. It was obvious that he didn't want his most important client starring in a small, low-budget movie – especially since his client had made the decision without consulting him.

Nikki was sure that once Lara got to LA Quinn planned on talking her out of it. *That's* why there was no signed contract on her desk.

Oh God! What a nightmare if Lara backed out.

She spoke to Mick. 'Listen,' she said. 'I'm not saying

Lara's on a star trip or anything, only it's imperative that you treat her with respect.'

'Respect – what's that?' Mick said, smirking, the eternal cigarette dangling from his lower lip.

'For starters she hates cigarette smoke,' Nikki said briskly. 'And she won't appreciate you smoking on the set.'

'Don't do it when I'm working,' he said, crinkling his eyes. 'Freakin' problem solved.'

'Also, your language. Can you clean it up for her?'

'Are you out of your mothafuckin' mind?' he said, baiting Nikki because he got off on putting her on. 'I'm gonna treat her like I treat any other actor.'

'Great,' Nikki groaned. 'That'll go down really well.'

Richard couldn't wait to inform her that she'd hired the wrong director. 'He's a loose cannon,' he said ominously. 'I've checked him out.'

'You've also seen his work, so you know he's very talented.'

'*I'm* very talented,' Richard replied immodestly. 'And I don't run around screaming at people and acting like a maniac.'

'Let's give him a chance,' she said. 'I can always fire him.'

'That's a great attitude,' he answered with a derisive snort. 'Do you *know* how much it costs firing a director once you've started shooting? *Revenge* is a low-budget movie, and it's *your* job to keep it that way. If you want my opinion – you've made a *big* mistake talking Lara into doing this.'

'I didn't *talk* her into it,' she said defensively.

'I think you'll find that when she and your precious little genius director get together, it won't be a walk in the park.'

Richard was voicing her worst fears. 'Everything will work out,' she said, standing firm. 'You'll see.'

'I hope so,' he said grimly. 'For your sake.'

Mick persuaded her to hire Aiden Sean for the lead villain.

Aiden was an edgy and dangerous actor – not conventionally good-looking, he had a certain sinister style that worked perfectly for the role of the main rapist. The problem was he'd been in and out of drug rehab so many times, he was almost uninsurable. Coke had been his pleasure, heroin his pain – supposedly he was now straight. The fact that he was an extraordinary actor was his only saving grace.

'Can you control him?' she asked Mick, before agreeing to hire him.

'*Me?*' Mick said innocently. 'I can control an army of ants parading up your cute little chick-babe ass!'

'We're on such a tight budget,' she worried, ignoring his sexist remark. 'We can't afford to be a second over.'

'You tell me every day,' Mick replied, with a wide-mouthed yawn.

'I tell you every day so that hopefully it'll sink in.'

'Y'know, I like you,' Mick said as if he'd just made up his mind. 'You're a tough chick-babe – but sexy with it. How'd you get into this business?'

'Don't worry about that,' she said sternly. 'All *you've* got to worry about is getting *Revenge* finished on time and on budget.'

☆ ☆ ☆

The next morning Summer got up early for once, catching Nikki on her way out. 'How's your movie going, Mom?' she asked, cute and pretty in rumpled cotton pyjamas.

Nikki had taken Richard's advice and eased up on her daughter. It wasn't like she was responsible. Summer lived in Chicago, and would soon be on a plane home. Still . . . she couldn't help regretting that they weren't closer.

'It's going great,' she replied, surprised, since this was the first glimmer of interest Summer had shown in her project.

'Like I'm kinda psyched,' Summer said. 'It's such a way cool thing to do.'

'Yes, it is,' Nikki said, pleased that her daughter was finally paying attention.

'Uh . . . Richard told me you signed Aiden Sean,' Summer added, trailing her to the door.

'That's right,' Nikki said, groping in her purse for her car keys. 'Do you approve?'

'Like he's totally bitchen!' Summer exclaimed, rolling her eyes. 'I'd give *anything* to meet him.'

So *that's* what this new-found interest was all about. *Hmm* . . . Nikki thought, remembering her own hero-worship days. She'd loved Robert Redford. Had a huge crush on Al Pacino. Been destroyed when John Lennon got assassinated.

'We don't start shooting for a while,' she said. 'But when we do, maybe you'll visit the set.'

'That'd be awesome!'

'I have to go now,' she said, checking in her purse to make sure she had her Filofax. 'What are your plans today?'

'The usual,' Summer answered vaguely.

'What's the usual?'

'Shopping, sunbathing. I met this girl – Tina – we hang out together.'

'Sounds fun to me.'

'It is!' Summer said with a big smile. 'Thanks, Mom.'

'For what?'

'Oh, I dunno. It's kinda way cool being here.'

Nikki left with a good feeling. When Summer wanted to, she could be adorable.

☆ ☆ ☆

That night Nikki and Richard had a quiet dinner at a small Italian restaurant in Malibu. Richard was still in a lecturing mood – carrying on about the do's and don'ts of movie making.

'Contrary to what you think, I *do* know what I'm doing,' Nikki said, fed up with his constant criticism.

'You've got a crazed director, a drugged-out leading man, and Lara for a leading lady,' he nagged. 'This is destined to be some fucked-up shoot.'

'Thanks, Richard,' she said flatly. 'I appreciate your words of encouragement.'

Later, they lay in bed, both keeping to their own sides. David Letterman was chatting with Sandra Bernhard on television – neither of them watched.

This movie is not good for my marriage, Nikki thought. *It's separating us. Driving us apart.*

Unfortunately there was nothing she could do. She had to proceed, there was no choice.

☆ ☆ ☆

And while Richard and Nikki were safely in bed, Summer was cruising the clubs on the Strip. Her vacation had turned out to be a total blast. It was so cool the way Richard kept on telling her mother to lay off – giving her the freedom she deserved. Things were way too complicated back in Chicago – what with her father and all. If only she could move to LA permanently.

At the Viper Room, Johnny Depp's club on Sunset, she sat in a corner with Jed, Tina, and a few other friends – most of them stoned or drunk.

'OhmiGod!' she suddenly exclaimed. 'Take a look at who just came in.'

'Who?' Tina asked, stretching her neck to see.

'Aiden Sean and Mick Stefan,' Summer said, her eyes swivelling to follow the emaciated-looking actor and the gawky director as they walked up to the bar accompanied by a drugged-out redhead in a black rubber tube dress and purple ankle boots. 'They're both so out there!' she said, flushed with excitement. 'I'm going over.'

'You can't do that,' Jed said, frowning. 'You don't even know 'em.'

'Who cares?' Summer said recklessly. 'Aiden's going to be in my mother's movie, and Mick's directing it – so it's *almost* like I know them.' Her blue eyes gleamed. 'C'mon, Tina, go with me.'

'No,' Tina said haughtily. 'I don't pick up men – *they* come to *me*.'

'That's right!' Jed muttered, not pleased Summer was chasing other guys.

'Well, *I'm* going over,' Summer said, jumping to her feet and sashaying across the room before anyone could stop her.

She went straight up to Aiden Sean. 'Hi,' she said, staring directly at him. He ignored her.

'Get lost, blondie,' said the drugged-out redhead.

'Hello, gorgeous!' Mick responded, lowering his glasses to gaze at this innocent teenage vision with the pouty lips and big blue eyes. 'How about a drink?'

She was carrying a fake ID Jed had given her, so why not?

'Martini,' she said, aware that it was a cool drink.

'One Martini comin' up,' Mick said, licking his rubbery lips.

'Uh . . . thanks,' she said, still staring at Aiden, who was taking absolutely no notice of her. A real bummer because she considered him killer. It was him she wanted, not the geek-faced director.

Three Martinis later she was feeling delightfully dizzy. Jed came over and said they had to go.

'I'll take her home,' Mick said.

'No way, man,' Jed replied.

''S OK,' she managed, even though the room was starting to spin. 'Mick'll look after me.'

Reluctantly Jed left.

'I'm gonna have a big hangover tomorrow,' she giggled. 'Big, big hangover.'

'I got a magic cure for hangovers,' Mick said with a knowing wink.

'What's that?' she asked boldly.

'Come outside to my limo an' I'll show you,' he offered.

Should she? Shouldn't she?

Why not? If she went with Mick, maybe Aiden would notice she existed.

'OK,' she said, suppressing a hiccup.

'OK!' Mick repeated with a wild cackle. And off they went.

By THE time I was twenty-one I had a reputation for being a guy who could deliver the goods. And there were plenty of rich women in Hollywood who were into regular sex with a man who could actually get it up.

I had my own apartment, a new Corvette, and a slew of regular appointments. In a way I was living the good life, although I didn't have what I really craved, which was to be a movie star.

I was definitely leading a double life. I had a closet full of expensive clothes – most of them bought for me by grateful clients; and a separate closet filled with jeans and T-shirts.

On one hand I was the big stud. On the other – a guy who still went to acting class, mixing with people who were pumping gas and parking cars.

I even had a legitimate girlfriend, Margie – a sweet girl who didn't know shit about what I did on the side. She was under the mistaken impression I came from a rich family.

I liked Margie because of her innocence. Most of the girls I'd encountered in Hollywood were hard-nuts who'd gotten where they were by winning a beauty contest or some such shit, after which they'd high-tailed it out to Hollywood, done time at the Playboy mansion, fucked every sleazeball playboy in town, and ended up stoned out of their minds.

Margie was different. She lived in the Valley with her

family. A former child star, she'd starred in a series until she was fifteen, when suddenly her career came to a sharp stop.

Now she was nineteen and trying to get back in the business.

Margie and I had fun together. It was the first time I'd had fun with a girl who wasn't handing me money.

I had one particular client, Ellie von Steuben, who I had a hunch could do me some good. Ellie was married to Maxwell von Steuben, a big-shot producer. Ellie and I met twice a week in a fancy penthouse on Wilshire Boulevard. I had no idea whose apartment it was, but I suspected it wasn't Ellie's since there was never anything personal around.

'This your place?' I asked her once.

'No,' she replied, refusing to reveal any more information.

Ellie was probably a real looker in her time, and even in her fifties she could still turn heads. She told me her husband hadn't touched her in years. 'He's too kinky for me anyway,' she confided, scratching my back with long talonlike nails. 'He prefers call-girls, so why shouldn't I have my own pleasure?'

No reason, sweetheart. Especially when you're paying me five hundred bucks a time.

Ellie was very businesslike. She made sure the money was always on the bedside table – five crisp hundred-dollar bills. And she wasn't into conversation, all she required was sex – and plenty of it.

I could do that. I could do it better than anyone she'd ever had before.

After a while she started recommending me to friends, which was how I built up such an exclusive clientele. The Hollywood women who weren't gettin' any – they were all mine. The big director's wife. The ex-wife of a superstar. The horniest old agent in town.

One day I asked Ellie if she'd help me with my career.

'I already have,' she replied coolly. 'I've given you more clients than you can handle.'

'That's not the career I'm talking about,' I replied.

She cupped my balls with a perfectly manicured hand and said, 'You don't want to be an actor, darling. Actors are jerk-offs – everybody treats them like garbage. You're king in your field. Stay a king.'

I was angry that she took my ambition so lightly. That night in acting class I got up and performed a scene with Margie. We kicked ass. The whole fuckin' class stood up and applauded.

Our acting teacher, an older man with flowing white hair and yellow skin, took me aside. 'It's time you got yourself an agent,' he said. 'You're ready.'

It was the first encouragement I'd ever gotten. He was telling me I was good enough to be a professional! He was saying I could do it. And fuck it – I could.

I made a decision. I was going to give up hustling and go for it. But first I had to get myself a stash of money. I'd already opened a bank account and taken out a safe deposit box, in which I had a few thousand cash. Now I had to concentrate on really piling it up.

I decided to spend six more months servicing women, then I'd say goodbye to that business. Maybe I'd even marry Margie, buy a little house in the Valley, have a couple of kids – live a normal life.

I started asking Ellie about agents. She started telling me to shut the fuck up and do what I had to do. She wasn't a nice woman.

One night I was doing what I had to do, when Maxwell von Steuben walked in on us. 'Jesus Christ!' he screamed, taking in the scene – Ellie with her legs clasped around my neck and me with my ass in the air. 'Jesus Christ! What kind of a whore am I married to?'

'What kind of a whore are you married to?' she retorted, wriggling out from under me. 'You're the worst whoremonger in this city, and you have the gall to criticize me?'

While they were screaming at each other I began scrambling for my clothes, not forgetting to scoop up the money sitting in its usual place.

Maxwell von Steuben ignored Ellie for a moment, turning his anger on me. 'Who are you?' he yelled, red in the face. 'Who the fuck are you?'

Oh, yeah, like I was gonna tell him.

'You'd better get your filthy ass out of this town. I never want to set eyes on you again.'

I grabbed my clothes and ran.

Ellie usually called me every Monday to set up our weekly appointments. The following Monday she did not call, nor did any of her friends.

The truth dawned. Ellie had been caught, and I was blacklisted.

Fuck!

I decided it was a sign – I'd go straight.

So I sold my expensive suits, moved out of my costly apart-ment, rented a small place, and with my savings managed to keep it together while I did the rounds of agents, and spent more time with Margie – who, although she was very sweet, had begun to bore me.

I finally got me an agent who liked me as much as I liked myself. A woman, naturally. Had to fuck her, of course, but then she started sending me on auditions, and that was a real kick. I actually landed a couple of small parts in TV shows. And I was good. One thing led to another, and one day I was sent out on an audition for a big action movie.

The day of my interview I sat in an outer office in Hollywood with seven other guys, all of us nervously sweating until it was our turn to go in.

Eventually I was called. I sauntered into the casting room determined to impress.

Sitting around were the usual casting people, a well-known director, and – wouldn't you know it – Maxwell von Steuben himself.

What kind of a lucky break was this?

Our eyes met. It took him a couple of seconds, but he recognized me. The old man leaped to his feet, waving his arms in a blind fury. 'Get him out of here!' he screamed. 'Get him the fuck out! You're finished in this town. Finished! Do you hear me, punk?'

The entire town heard him.

So once again my career as a movie star was put on hold.

Chapter Twenty-five

 DINNER WITH Joey was another memorable experience. Lara felt so comfortable with him – it was as if they'd known each other for years and were in perfect synch. Halfway through the evening he reached for her hand across the table and said, 'Something's happenin' here, Lara, an' I'm not sure what.'

'We're falling in like,' she said, smiling nervously – she who was usually so in control.

He smiled back. 'So *that's* what it is.'

'Maybe.'

They exchanged a long, intimate look.

She held her breath, lost in the moment. Kyle Carson chose that exact moment to enter the restaurant with his date for the night – an almost fully clothed Wilson, in a short orange tank dress that barely covered her ass, and pointy-toed stiletto heels. On her head was the Lara wig.

'Oh, no!' Lara groaned, spotting them and quickly sliding down in her chair.

'What?'

'It's Kyle – with my body double.'

Joey glanced over to where Kyle and Wilson were being seated at a nearby table. 'They seen us?' he asked, squinting across the room.

'I'm not sure,' she replied, dismayed they'd chosen the same restaurant.

'Somehow I got a feelin' you don't want them to.'

'Guess again.'

'Let's split, then. You slide off to the john, I'll grab the check. We'll meet outside.'

'Can we get away with it?' she asked hopefully.

'Yeah – if you go now, before they see you.'

She eased out of her seat and hurried to the ladies' room, hoping Kyle wouldn't spot her.

Safely inside, she leaned against the mirrored vanity unit studying her reflection. Joey had said it first: 'Something's happening here, I'm not sure what.'

Then she'd given him her flip reply. Nikki would be proud of her – she was coming up with lines!

Once again, her heart was racing. This was definitely the start of something, it was only a matter of time. Reaching in her purse, she removed her compact and began to powder her nose.

'Lara!' Wilson's reflection appeared in the mirror behind her. 'What are *you* doing here?'

'Oh, hi,' she said, furious at getting caught.

'Gotta say the scene went great,' Wilson boasted, tugging at her short dress. 'Boy! He's some sexy guy.'

'Who?' Lara asked quickly, hoping she wasn't referring to Joey.

'Kyle, of course,' Wilson said, fishing in her purse for a pot of jammy red lip gloss and a thick brush. She moved up beside Lara in the mirror and began applying the goo to her overly full lips. 'Do you happen to know what his situation is now? Somebody told me he's getting back with his wife. *I* don't think so. Let me tell you – he's *hot* to macarena – an' honey, I'm *into* dancin'!'

'I'm sure,' Lara murmured.

'Who're *you* with?' Wilson asked, dabbing on too much gloss.

'Friends,' Lara replied vaguely. 'We're on our way out.'

'Shame,' Wilson said. 'We could've all joined up.'

'Wouldn't that cramp your hot to macarena action?'

Wilson laughed. 'Right!'

Lara began edging toward the exit.

'See ya,' Wilson called out, heading into one of the stalls.

'Uh . . . thanks for doing a good job,' Lara said.

'Honey,' Wilson joked, 'your nipples never looked so good!'

Lara hurried outside to where Joey was waiting. 'I got cornered in the ladies' room,' she said.

'What're you worried about?'

'I don't want the whole set talking about us. Everyone knows you're engaged, I'd be perceived as some kind of . . . you know . . . fiancé stealer.'

'Fiancé stealer?' he said, laughing at her.

She couldn't help joining in.

'C'mon,' he said, 'I'm taking the fiancé stealer home.'

'I have a better idea,' she said impulsively. 'Let's go for a walk along the beach. It's something I've been dying to do.'

'So how come you haven't done it?'

She laughed self-consciously. 'I'm scared.'

He regarded her quizzically. 'What of?'

She shrugged. 'I don't know, the dark, the unknown . . . There are times I don't feel . . . safe.'

'Lara,' he said, his handsome face serious, 'when I'm around, you need never be scared.'

She nodded, not sure how to respond.

'Anyhow,' he said, 'tonight I'm takin' you straight home. You've got an early call tomorrow.'

'What about our walk?' she asked, disappointed.

'Another time.'

'Promise?'

'We'll see.'

☆ ☆ ☆

'I got to fuck you last night,' Kyle said in a low-down dirty voice. It was early in the morning and he'd sidled up behind Lara's chair, taking her by surprise.

'Excuse me?' she said, not quite sure she'd heard correctly.

'And it was *goood*,' he said, making a smacking noise with his lips. 'Finger-lickin' *goood*!'

She gave him a cold look. 'Are you losing it, Kyle?'

'If you can't get the real thing, go for the substitute,' he said, laughing rudely. 'I put my hand over Wilson's face, and what with the wig and the body, I could've sworn I was fucking you.'

'You're disgusting,' she said contemptuously.

'No,' he replied, not at all put out. '*I'm* honest.' A short pause. 'By the way, I hear we were at the same restaurant last night. Who was *your* hot date?'

'I have to work with you, Kyle,' she said icily. 'I sure as hell don't have to talk to you.'

Roxy walked over. 'What's up?' she asked, noticing Lara was upset.

Kyle slouched away and began talking to Miles.

'The man's a pig,' Lara said vehemently.

'They all are,' Roxy sighed, like it was no big surprise.

'Kyle's the worst.'

'What'd he do now?'

'Believe me,' Lara said, shaking her head, 'you don't want to know.'

'Oh, yes I do!' Roxy replied, always up for juicy gossip.

'How come Wilson got to leave the set last night with the wig?' Lara asked.

'That bitch!' Roxy said, narrowing her eyes. 'I *told* her to come straight to the hair trailer with it, and she never showed up. This morning I found it stuffed in a bag outside my hotel room – and a fine mess it's in, too. God knows what she did with it!'

'Forget God, try Kyle,' Lara murmured.

'Oh, *really*?' Roxy said. 'And why should I be surprised, he's dicked everything else that has a pulse!'

Miles came over. 'Ready, my sweet?'

'Yes, Miles.' And she thought— *Only three more days and I never have to see Kyle Carson again.*

Forgetting about her personal feelings, she threw herself into the first scene of the day, hoping to get by with as few takes as possible.

Of course, Kyle blew it as usual, fluffing his lines and worrying about his hair.

At the lunch break she had one of the drivers take her to her house. Cassie was on the phone in the living room, surrounded by boxes, organizing everything for their imminent departure.

'What are *you* doing here?' Cassie asked, putting the phone on hold.

'Had to take a break, too much testosterone flying around the set,' Lara said, adding a casual— 'Uh . . . where's Joey?'

'Out,' Cassie said.

'Did he say where he was going?'

'Nope.'

Lara went into her bedroom, wondering why she felt so disappointed. She'd run home like a schoolgirl with a crush, and now he wasn't even here. Hmm . . . Never expect anything in life and you'll never get disappointed.

A few minutes later Cassie knocked on her bedroom door.

'Lara,' she said, hovering in the doorway, 'is it OK if I say something out of line?'

'*Nooo*,' Lara replied, smiling faintly because she knew Cassie would say it anyway.

'This Joey guy—' Cassie said, a frown creasing her brow. 'What do you know about him?'

'As much as I need to.'

'Granted he's great-looking,' Cassie continued. 'But so are a lot of other guys.'

'Your point?'

'Are you sure it's wise letting him stay here?'

'It's only for a couple of days,' Lara said defensively. 'He's hardly an axe murderer. Don't worry, Cass, I know what I'm doing.'

'If you say so,' Cassie said, nodding unsurely. If she had her way Lara would get back together with Richard.

'I'd better return to the set,' Lara said. 'When Joey returns, tell him I'll be home later. Oh, and have the cook fix pasta tonight, we'll be eating outside.'

'It's done,' Cassie said.

☆ ☆ ☆

Shortly after Lara left for the studio, Joey had gotten in his rented car and taken a ride. He had to get out of the house, Cassie had her eye on him, and he was aware he hadn't won her over. She was suspicious, couldn't quite figure him out. Staying around was dangerous.

He drove aimlessly, stopping at the drug store to pick up a pack of cigarettes.

Madelaine had not been pleased when he'd announced he was moving on. 'Why are you leaving this time?' she'd demanded. 'I got you a job, gave you a place to live, what more do you want?'

'I can't make you happy, Maddy,' he'd said – the oldest line in the world, but it worked every time because there *was* no answer.

'You can try,' Madelaine had said, near tears of frustration.

'No,' he'd replied. 'I'll only make you miserable, and that's not good for either of us. I'm flyin' to LA – takin' a shot.'

'What about my money?' she'd asked, forgetting her tears for a moment.

'I'll pay it back.'

'When?'

'Keep my cheque for the movie when it comes in.'

'Don't imagine you can get around me again, Joey,' she'd warned. 'If you go this time – that's it.'

Yeah. Sure. I can walk into your life any time I want and you'll always take me back.

'I understand,' he'd said.

And so it was over and he'd hired a car, and driven out to see Lara.

He wasn't surprised that she'd asked him to stay. Some things were meant to be.

Chapter Twenty-six

 EARLY EVERY morning Nikki left the Malibu house and drove to the *Revenge* production offices in the Valley. She had her own private office next to Mick's. He'd surrounded himself with a team of alarmingly young production people, while she'd brought in several thirtysomethings who knew what they were doing, and a very capable line producer. Hopefully, together, they'd make a cohesive group.

Everything was a go situation. The advantage of having Lara in the lead role was that they didn't require any other star names. Apart from Aiden Sean, the movie was cast with a group of talented unknowns; the financing was in place, and principal photography began in two weeks. Being a producer was very different from merely designing the clothes. Now she was in a boss situation, and it felt good when everyone came to her for answers.

Only another two days and Lara would arrive from New York, then she could meet with Mick. *Oh, God!* Nikki thought. *They're either going to hate each other or it will be a love fest.* She prayed it was the latter.

If only Richard would lighten up. She'd expected him to be proud of her for what she was doing, instead he did nothing but put her down.

So far she hadn't met Aiden Sean, although Mick kept

insisting the three of them should get together, so today they were having lunch.

'I'm depending on you to keep him in line,' she reminded Mick sternly. 'Aiden's your responsibility. If he screws up, it's all your fault.'

'I got it, I got it,' Mick said, snapping his fingers in the air.

'Any trouble at all and he's out. I hope you've told him that.'

'Don't havta tell him. He knows.'

When Aiden turned up an hour late, Nikki was shocked at how pale and gaunt he was. White, almost translucent skin stretched across the fine bones of his haunted face, bleak ice-grey eyes, dusty brown hair pulled back in a scruffy ponytail, and a painfully skinny body decorated with various tattoos. In spite of being a scary presence, he was still attractive in an offbeat, drugged-out way. Like a world-weary rock star – he had the look.

He shook Nikki's hand, burnt out eyes staring right through her. She noticed that his nicotine-stained fingers trembled when he went to light a cigarette immediately after their introduction.

Mick had assured her that Aiden was straight now – in all kinds of programmes – a guaranteed reformed addict.

No true drug addict is ever reformed, she thought – *they're merely taking a long pause before their next fix.*

If Aiden had not been an out-and-out junkie for so many years, he could have had a big career. As it was, he'd only managed to survive in the business because he was fiercely talented and always gave an amazing performance – in spite of being half crazy on drugs most of the time. Directors liked to employ him because he always delivered. Producers didn't because he was a major risk.

The three of them went to an Italian restaurant on

Ventura. Aiden slid into the padded leather booth, immediately ordering a double Jack Daniel's on the rocks. Nikki observed that he smoked three cigarettes before the salad, even though the waitress – a pretty girl who was a fan – kept informing him there was no smoking in the restaurant.

'Fuck it,' Aiden said, his voice like cracked tar over gravel. 'A guy's gotta have *some* outlet.' Ice-grey eyes carefully checked her out. 'I gave it all up, Nikki,' he said mournfully. 'No coke, no speed, no fucking anything. I'm havin' a drink – don't let it bother you – I give up drinking when I'm working.'

'I'm *sooo* looking forward to being on the set with you two,' Nikki drawled. 'Mick doesn't smoke when he's working, *you* don't drink. Wow – this is going to be a blast watching the two of you control your addictions.'

Aiden smiled – a small, thin smile. 'You produced anything before, Nikki?'

'No,' she said, immediately on the defensive. 'However, I've worked in movies for the last six years. I've had plenty of experience.'

'Doing what?'

'Costume designer,' she replied, determined not to let him intimidate her. 'And of course, my husband's Richard Barry, so I've certainly had an education in all aspects of making movies.'

Now why had she told him *that*? He was supposed to be impressing *her*, she didn't have to give him her résumé.

'How old're you?' he asked, sucking on an ice cube.

'That's an extremely rude question to ask a woman.'

He expelled the ice cube back into his glass. 'You ashamed of your age? What are you – thirty-five – forty?'

'Thanks a lot,' she said indignantly. 'Thirty-two.'

He chuckled – a chuckle with a mean streak. 'Knew I could get it out of you.'

'Why?' she couldn't resist asking. 'Do I look older?'

'Just f-in' with you, darlin',' he said casually.

Shouldn't he be kissing her ass? This was the first job he'd had in eighteen months and, with his track record, he was lucky to get it.

'How old are *you*?' she demanded, not happy with his attitude.

'Thirty-four goin' on dead,' he said blankly.

'You're both old,' Mick said with a crazed cackle. 'Now me, I still got it goin'. Last week I had a babe who couldn't've been more than fifteen givin' me head in the back of my limo.'

'And you're *proud* of that?' Nikki asked, amazed.

Mick sniggered. 'It's a guy thing,' he said with a superior smirk.

'Yeah – probably a guy who can't get it up,' Nikki muttered.

'Now, now – don't go getting jealous,' Aiden said, mocking her.

Oh, God, she'd been worried about Lara meeting Mick, when this one was ten times worse.

She didn't want to think about the rape scene. Richard had warned her to be absolutely sure about the people she hired – especially the actors – and she hadn't listened. Now he'd spend the next seven weeks saying, 'I told you so.'

She decided getting too friendly with these two misfits was not a good thing. Distance was good. A cool attitude would let them know who was boss.

As soon as she'd finished eating she consulted her watch, said a quick— 'I hate to eat and run, but I have an appointment.'

'Somethin' I should be at?' Mick asked, mouth twitching.

'No. It's uh . . . personal,' she said, sliding out of the booth.

'See ya on the set,' Aiden said, looking her over in a way that made her uncomfortable.

She hurried from the restaurant, stood outside on the sidewalk waiting for her car, and took a big gulp of fresh air.

There was something about Aiden Sean that spelled trouble.

Nothing she could do about it now – his contract was signed, he was part of the team.

And yet . . . in spite of everything, he did have a certain charisma – working with him would definitely not be dull.

Her car arrived and she jumped in, tipping the valet much too generously.

She had work to do. Time to concentrate.

☆ ☆ ☆

'I haven't called Mick and I don't intend to,' Summer said defiantly. ''Cause I didn't even like him. Aiden Sean's the hot one.'

'Then why'd you do stuff with Mick in the back of his limo?' Tina asked, ever practical.

'I *didn't*,' Summer answered indignantly. 'One sloppy kiss, and then he made me try to suck his you know what.'

'Did you?'

'No way. I thought going outside with him would get Aiden to notice me. I was into a stupid fit,' Summer admitted. 'Don't you ever do anything that even when you're *doing* it you know is dumb?'

They were sitting on the beach wearing minuscule bikinis with thong bottoms, smoking a joint and working on their tans.

'Yes,' Tina agreed. 'When I was a hokey little kid.'

'You're not so old.'

'I've been around.'

'So have I,' Summer said, throwing back her head to catch the sun.

A fiftyish man, jogging along the beach, double-taked both girls and almost stopped.

'Married. Three kids. Cushy job,' Tina said, eyeing him up and down. 'I could have him any time I wanted.'

'Men!' Summer said.

'Pricks for brains,' Tina said.

'You've got it!' Summer agreed.

And they both rolled on the beach in fits of giggles.

Chapter Twenty-seven

 LARA AND Joey walked along the seashore hand in hand, barefoot and completely at ease with each other. They'd eaten dinner on the back deck – light pasta and a green salad accompanied by a bottle of red wine. After they were finished, Joey had said, 'C'mon, we're takin' that walk along the beach you were on about.'

'Great,' Lara had replied, her mouth dry with anticipation.

Now they were together, strolling along the damp sand, and she couldn't stop thinking about what would happen next. It was inevitable that he'd make a move, unless she was reading something into their friendship that didn't exist.

This was ridiculous, merely holding his hand was having a major effect. Talk about chemistry!

Halfway back to the house, he stopped and sat on the sand, pulling her down next to him. 'Take a look at the moon,' he said. 'Somethin', huh?'

'Beautiful!' she sighed.

'Like you.'

'Thanks,' she murmured, wondering why her pulse was racing and she felt so lightheaded.

'Hey, Lara,' he said, jumping up. 'Let's take a swim.'

'Don't be ridiculous,' she replied nervously. 'It's dark and cold. You won't see a thing.'

He laughed, stripping off his shirt. 'You think the fish care?' he said. 'You think they give a rat's ass whether it's dark or light?' He unzipped his pants, stepping out of them.

'You're crazy,' she said, shaking her head. 'You don't even have a towel.'

'Miss Practical,' he said, teasing her.

'Well, it's true,' she said, hating herself for sounding like the school prude.

'C'mon,' he said, pulling her up. 'There's nothin' like the ocean at night. It's like bein' in a big, dark, think tank.'

'I don't have a swimsuit,' she said primly.

'Your underwear will do,' he said, standing next to her in his jockey shorts, his clothes in a pile by his feet.

'What makes you think I wear any?' she asked boldly.

'Oh, *you* do,' he said, laughing at her. 'I'd bet a thousand big ones you do.'

'Why's that?'

''Cause all good girls wear panties.' She couldn't help laughing. 'Let's do it,' he urged. 'You gotta live dangerously some of the time.'

'I . . . I can't afford to catch cold.'

'Not into adventure?'

Her heart began racing. Joey had such an incredible effect on her, and she had no idea how to handle her feelings.

'OK, so *don't* do it,' he said, 'but I'm outta here,' and before she could stop him, he raced into the sea, plunging head-first into the breaking waves.

She stood on the moonlit beach, shivering. *Join him*, her inner voice urged. *If you want something to happen, then do it*.

She stepped out of her dress, tentatively approaching the cold water until the sea was lapping around her ankles. 'Joey,' she called, staring into darkness. 'Joey!' she shouted, edging further into the surf.

She was almost up to her waist in water when he pounced. 'Gotcha!' he yelled, grabbing her from behind.

'OhmiGod!' she shrieked, shivering uncontrollably. 'You startled me!'

'Follow me,' he said, taking her hand in his.

They waded out until the water was above her shoulders. 'Now start swimming,' he commanded.

'Not too far,' she said nervously. 'I . . . I can't see anything.'

'Don't sweat it,' he assured her. 'I'm right beside you.'

She wasn't the strongest swimmer in the world, but she trusted him, and he was right – this was an adventure. And why shouldn't she have fun instead of doing nothing but work?

They swam out in the dark ocean. They could feel the waves swelling around them, before lazily making their way inland and crashing on the shore. 'Uh . . . Joey . . . I want to go back,' Lara shouted, starting to get nervous.

'OK,' he yelled. 'Turn around an' follow me.'

She did as he said, and they began swimming toward the beach, struggling against a sudden undercurrent.

Lara swam strongly, but she soon found herself lagging behind.

'C'mon!' Joey yelled over the noise of the sea.

She was out of breath and on the edge of panic as she struggled to keep up. Oh, God! Tomorrow her hair would be full of salt water, her eyes red and bloodshot from the cold. She'd look a mess, and Yoko and Roxy would have to work hard to put her together. That's if she ever made it to shore.

Something brushed against her leg. She let out a startled scream, her eyes wide with fear. 'Are there sharks here?' she gasped.

'Sharks?' he yelled over his shoulder. 'Yeah. Tons of 'em!'

She began doing a frantic crawl, trying desperately to catch up with him.

'Hey – stop freakin' out,' he said, treading water until she drew alongside. 'Guess what? You can stand here.'

Her feet touched the bottom and she calmed down.

'C'mon,' he said, taking her hand again. 'We'd better get you outta here before a shark eats you up!'

'Very funny,' she said crossly, gasping for breath as they staggered out of the water onto the damp sand.

'How are we going to dry off?' she asked, once again shivering uncontrollably.

'Body warmth,' he said, wrapping his arms around her and hugging her close. 'It'll do it every time.'

It was then she realized that somewhere between going in and coming out he'd lost his jockey shorts.

She felt his hardness pressing insistently against her leg. 'Joey . . .' she began, 'I . . .'

He brought his lips down on hers, and all rational thought deserted her as he began exploring her mouth with his tongue.

It was finally happening, and she was powerless to stop it. What's more, she had no desire to do so.

They kissed for a long time, kisses the like of which she'd never experienced. One moment his lips were tender, the next – strong and assertive, his tongue slowly caressing her teeth, making her shudder with the anticipation of what was to come next.

He didn't rush things, he took his time, until she was silently begging him to touch her in other places.

Her nipples were erect, straining against the wet silkiness of her bra. She longed for him to undo the clip and touch her breasts. She'd reached the point of no return – a moment she'd been building toward for weeks.

He continued kissing her – long, sensual kisses that were beginning to drive her a little bit crazy.

Weak with desire, she moaned, reaching down to caress him.

He removed her hand as if to say – *Be patient. I'll tell you when.*

Although the wind was bitter, she didn't notice. Every inch of her was on fire, all she could think about was Joey being inside her.

He treated her with extreme care. Lara wasn't like other women – she was a beautiful Princess who made him feel like a Prince. *Her* Prince.

From the day he'd set eyes on her he'd given up casual sex, saving himself for her.

Her mouth was so sweet – she tasted of all things good and fresh.

Ignoring the urge to throw her down on the sand and make hard passionate love to her, he held back, curbing his appetite – because he knew he had to make this night extraordinary.

Very slowly he began touching her breasts.

She moaned again, thrusting toward him, silently urging him to release her from the confines of her bra.

He didn't. Instead he began teasing her nipples through the flimsy material, stroking them ever so lightly.

'Take . . . it . . . off,' she mumbled, unable to stop herself from begging, frightened that she'd come before him, because she couldn't recall when she'd ever been this aroused. '*Please!*'

He lightly brushed the tips of her nipples with his fingertips.

Feverishly she reached up, unclipping the front fastening on her bra.

Slowly he peeled her bra open, revealing her breasts. Beautiful, just like the rest of her. He cupped them in his hands. Then, pushing her to her knees, he began rubbing his cock against her erect nipples, moving back and forth between them, faster and faster.

'Joey!' she gasped his name, totally unaware of the cold wind and the gritty wet sand digging into her knees.

'What?' he asked. 'Tell me exactly what you'd like.'

'You!' she said, her breath catching in her throat. 'I . . . want . . . you!'

He put his hands under her arms, picked her up and began kissing her again – long, torturous kisses – more pleasurable than anything she'd ever known.

Next he raised her hands above her head, while he bent his mouth to her left breast and drew in the nipple as if he was suckling milk.

'Ohhh . . .' Before she could help herself, she came with a series of shuddering convulsions that shook her body from tip to toe. And he hadn't even touched her where she craved to be touched.

He released her hands, pulling her to him. She snuggled against his chest, her body tingling with a deep warm satisfaction.

'Was that good for you, baby?' he asked, stroking her hair. 'Was it special?'

'God, yes!'

'Tomorrow it'll be even better.'

'Forget about tomorrow,' she murmured, inhaling his salty masculine smell and loving it. 'Let's go home to bed.'

'No,' he said, firmly. 'You've gotta work tomorrow. Sleep comes first.'

'But, Joey . . .'

He placed a finger on her lips— 'Quiet,' he commanded. 'Let's get dressed before we freeze.'

They groped on the sand for their clothes, hurriedly dressed, and raced back to the house. She was expecting him to come to her bedroom, but he didn't. He kissed her chastely on the lips and bid her a fast goodnight.

She was completely stunned that he would leave her, and

yet she knew he was right, she *did* have an early call, and if he'd come into her bed neither of them would have gotten any sleep.

She lay in bed, thinking about his face, his hair, his smell, the way he smiled.

Joey Lorenzo. Was he her destiny? Had she finally found the man capable of making her forget her past?

☆ ☆ ☆

Joey went to his room, restlessly paced around, and lit up a cigarette. So *this* is what he'd heard about all these years. *This* was love.

It didn't seem possible that it had happened to him. He'd never wanted it, never expected it. Women were women and getting laid was getting laid.

Now this. Christ! What was he supposed to do?

He waited until she'd left in the morning, and then took off.

It was the only way.

☆ ☆ ☆

Lara's alarm woke her at five a.m. She was so tired she could barely stagger out of bed. She immediately began sneezing and didn't dare look in the mirror.

At work Roxy greeted her with a caustic— 'What in *hell* happened to your hair?'

'I . . . I went swimming in the sea . . .'

'Shit, Lara,' Roxy said, running a hand through her own spiky locks, 'we're gonna havta shampoo.'

She sneezed twice in quick succession. 'OK.'

'Don't tell me you caught a cold?'

'Seems like it.'

'Great!' Roxy grumbled. 'Now we'll all get sick.'

'I promise not to breathe in your direction.'

'Yeah, yeah.'

Yoko was not much kinder; just as Lara had suspected, her eyes were bloodshot from the salt water. Yoko noticed immediately and complained loudly, then she made her lie on a couch with cucumber slices over her eyes for fifteen minutes, and after that she smeared a thick mud treatment all over her face.

By the time Roxy and Yoko were finished with her, she looked her usual gorgeous self. Unfortunately she was an hour late hitting the set.

Kyle was in a sulk, while Miles paced up and down, mumbling ominously under his breath.

'Glad you could make it,' Miles said sarcastically.

'Yeah, Lara, nice of you to honour us with your presence,' Kyle added.

'This is the first time I've been late,' she pointed out, thinking that all she wanted to do was complete the day's scenes and hurry home to Joey. They needed to talk, discuss what was going on between them.

How had it happened so quickly? One moment they were casual friends – the next they were naked on the beach, and she'd wanted him so much she would have done anything he'd asked.

Oh, God – even thinking about him now she felt herself becoming aroused. The way he'd made her come . . . it was like he'd hardly touched her and she was ready.

Was she that desperate for a man?

No. She could have any man she wanted. It just so happened Joey was the one.

She thought about his muscled body, knowing eyes, and the way he looked at her with such direct intensity . . .

'What are you smiling about?' Kyle demanded, startling her back to reality. 'This is supposed to be a serious scene.'

'Uh . . . sorry . . . I was just uh . . . remembering something funny.'

'Didja get it on last night, Lara?' he asked slyly, nudging her.

She flushed. Was it written all over her face for the world to see? 'Excuse me?' she said, freezing him out.

'Guess not,' he sneered. 'The Ice Princess doesn't do it, does she?'

At lunch break she borrowed Jane's cellphone and called home. Cassie answered.

'Get me Joey,' she said, drumming her fingers impatiently on the side of the phone.

'He's gone,' Cassie said.

'Gone,' she repeated blankly.

'Told me he had an emergency in the city. He'll call you tomorrow.'

'*What* emergency?'

'Don't know.'

'Did he leave a number?'

'Nope.'

'Well, why didn't you get one?' She heard herself shouting and abruptly stopped. She shouldn't take it out on Cassie, it wasn't her fault.

'Sorry,' Cassie said, sounding hurt. 'I didn't realize it was that important.'

'It's not,' she said, and clicked off the phone.

'Something wrong?' asked Yoko, who was standing nearby.

'Nothing,' she said, wondering how she was going to get through the night without him. 'Nothing at all.'

Chapter Twenty-eight

 AFTER THE incident outside the Directors' Guild, Alison Sewell appeared in court, and was sentenced to eighteen months in jail for stalking, aggravated assault and attacking a policeman.

Alison considered the whole thing grossly unfair. She wasn't stalking Lara. She was her friend. Didn't the morons get it? SHE WAS HER FUCKING FRIEND.

Why weren't the dumb cops out arresting real villains? Murderers and rapists, child molesters and thieves?

Some stupid private investigator, hired by Lara's business manager, had produced all the letters she'd written to Lara. Those letters were private, and were for Lara's eyes only. But the stupid investigator stood up in court and read extracts aloud for all to hear. Alison was furious.

Then Lara herself had gotten up and claimed that she, Alison Sewell, had been bothering her for months, turning up at her house uninvited, making over a hundred unwanted phone calls, trying to gain access to wherever she was working.

What bullshit nonsense. All Alison had done was try to be her friend, and look where it had gotten her. Prison. Locked up with actual criminals.

She shared a cell with some loony who'd poisoned all the

cats in her neighbourhood – a nice old lady with white hair and a pleasant demeanour. Until one night, when Alison was dozing, the old cow had tried to strangle her.

Her new cell mate was a bottle-blond hooker who'd stabbed one of her johns and now refused to speak.

This suited Alison fine. She had a lot of thinking to do.

Because when she got out – Lara Ivory was going to pay.

Chapter Twenty-nine

 THE PHONE refused to ring. For two nights Lara stared at it feeling like a lovesick fool, until she realized that of course – there must be something wrong with the line.

She picked up the receiver. Perfectly normal dial tone. Slamming it down, she grabbed a book and attempted to concentrate.

Impossible. All the while a little voice kept chanting in her head – *Joey ... Joey ... Joey ...* And she kept reliving their evening together in her head – fast-forwarding to the beach – the two of them running out of the ocean ... falling into each other's arms . . . the way he'd touched her . . . the intensity of her orgasm . . .

Oh, God! All she had to do was think about him and she was completely finished. She'd never felt this way with Richard. And as for Lee – he'd merely been a comfortable interlude.

As far as she was concerned it had been magical. What was *his* problem?

Phillipa. That had to be his problem.

Phillipa. Could he have gone back to her?

She felt like an idiot. Joey Lorenzo entered her life and five minutes later she'd invited him into her house and practically begged him to make love to her on the beach.

Now he was gone without a word of explanation. Joey Lorenzo. *Where the hell are you?*

The movie was finished. Cassie had packed up everything, tonight was the wrap party and tomorrow morning she'd be on a plane home to LA.

Without Joey Lorenzo thank you very much. And you'd better get used to it, he's definitely history.

She was Lara Ivory – movie star. And in spite of the adulation and vast rewards she was lonely. Achingly lonely. Haunted by her past and unable to forget. Somehow she'd thought Joey would change all that.

But no, he'd seen beneath the façade. He'd seen the ugly little slut . . .

Oh, God. How could she ever forget her father's harsh words. And his blood . . . splashing over her . . . the chunks of charred flesh . . .

Abruptly she put her book down and forced herself to start getting dressed for the party.

The phone rang. She reached for it.

'How's everything?' Nikki asked.

'Great!' she replied, falsely cheerful.

'Can't wait till you're here,' Nikki said. 'Mick's dying to meet you.'

'You're getting along?'

'Don't believe one word you hear about him. He's a touch eccentric, but that goes with the talent.'

They chatted for a few more minutes. Lara was tempted to confide about Joey, then decided she had nothing to gain from revealing her schoolgirl crush.

As soon as she put the phone down she began thinking about *Revenge* and the gruelling weeks of work ahead. Quinn was right – she should never have agreed to make the movie, the shooting schedule was a killer, and having just completed two major films back to back what she needed was a long vacation.

If it was anyone else but Nikki . . .

No. She refused to let her best friend down, it wouldn't be fair. Besides, making *Revenge* would take her mind off Joey.

She finished dressing for the party in a simple turquoise dress and strappy sandals. There would be dancing on the beach and all the guys from the crew would expect to have their picture taken with her.

She brushed her hair, then added gold hoop earrings and a wide gold bracelet Richard had given her shortly after their marriage. Satisfied with her appearance, she went downstairs.

Joey was standing in the living room talking to Cassie.

For a moment she was filled with confusion. Joey was back. Her Joey.

He's not your Joey. Get your head together and stop fantasizing.

She stood very still.

'Look who's here,' Cassie said, like it wasn't painfully obvious.

Time to return to her movie star roots. Chill him out. Nobody played Ice Princess better than Lara Ivory.

'Joey,' she said lightly. 'What are you doing here?'

'I'll go see if the car's outside,' Cassie said, hurriedly heading for the door.

'Don't!' Lara said sharply.

Cassie paused, unsure what to do.

'Uh . . . I'd kinda like to speak to you alone,' Joey ventured, giving her one of his intense stares.

'I'm sorry,' she replied, green eyes freezing him out. 'We're late for the wrap party. Maybe another time.'

He edged closer, speaking in a low voice. 'You're pissed, huh? Not interested in hearin' why I had to split.'

For a moment she weakened. Then her strong side took over and she thought, *To hell with him – he's stringing me along like some nothing little bimbo.*

'No, Joey, I'm not angry,' she said evenly. 'Why should I be?' And as she spoke, she moved toward the door, adding an off-handed— 'Right now you'll have to excuse us.'

'Phillipa tried to kill herself,' he muttered flatly. 'OD'd on pills.'

She stopped abruptly. 'Oh, God!'

'Don't you understand?' he continued. 'I *had* to leave.'

'Wait in the car,' she said to Cassie, who quickly left. 'Why didn't you call me?' she asked, turning on him accusingly. 'Why did you take off without a word?'

'Had to get my head straight,' he explained, running a hand through his thick dark hair. 'You've no idea what it was like – the guilt – sittin' in the hospital . . . knowin' that all I wanted was to be with you.'

'Oh,' she said, completely confused.

'Soon as she was strong enough, I told her there was someone else, an' came right back.' He moved closer, taking her hand in his. 'Didn't mean to let you down.'

A feeling of relief swept over her. Perhaps there was a future for them after all. 'It can't have been easy,' she said quietly.

'Hey—' he said, squeezing her hand. 'It wasn't.' And he knew, as he gazed into her eyes, that his plan had worked – she was all his. 'If it's OK with you, this time I'm stayin'.'

She felt the sheer physical thrill of having him close again, and her anger and disappointment slowly began to dissolve. 'Yes, Joey,' she said, with a little sigh. 'It's perfectly all right with me.'

☆　☆　☆

'Holy shit!' Roxy shrieked. 'Will ya get an eyeful of who Lara's comin' in with.'

'Who?' Yoko asked, craning to see.

'Joey whatever his name is. And Lordy, Miss Y – they are holdin' hands!'

'No!'

'See for yourself.'

'Thought he was engaged.'

'One sniff around our Lara, an' his engagement musta taken a dive.'

Roxy and Yoko weren't the only two observing Lara's entrance – the buzz was everywhere. Kyle, who'd flown in his estranged wife, Jean, for the party, noticed immediately. '*What* is Lara doing with *that* deadbeat?' he demanded of Jean – a pretty woman with curled brown hair and a long-suffering expression.

'What's wrong with him?' Jean asked, wondering if her un-faithful dog of a husband had slept with the exquisite actress.

'He's an extra, for Chrissakes,' Kyle said grumpily, non-plussed that Lara would show up with such a loser when she could've had him. 'Jesus Christ!' he added, conveniently forgetting about his own many indiscretions. 'Doesn't she get it? Hollywood Rule number one – *never* screw below the line.'

☆ ☆ ☆

'I got a hunch we're causin' a commotion,' Joey remarked.

'What?' Lara asked, clasping his hand.

'I'm tellin' you – we're exhibit number one. Everyone's starin'.'

'Really?' she said, completely unabashed. Let them stare, let them all stare. She was with Joey, and she didn't care who knew it.

'Your hairdresser's eyes are out on stalks!' he added, laughing.

'Hmm . . .' she said, with the trace of a smile, 'I've a feeling you were starring in a few of Roxy's fantasies.'

'I was?' he asked innocently.

'Come on, Joey,' she chided. 'You must know how women feel about you – they consider you prey.'

'You say the cutest things!'

'It's true,' she said, smiling broadly. 'I'm sure you're aware of your lethal effect.'

'I'm not interested in *women*,' he stated. 'Only you.'

'How gallant,' she said, shivering with anticipation, because tonight they'd surely consummate their relationship.

'Cold?' he asked, concerned.

'No. *Veree, veree* hot,' she murmured, teasingly.

'Hey,' he said, grinning, 'you're tellin' me? I'm the lucky guy who was on the beach with you – remember?'

Their eyes met, fusing a connection that blew her away. 'I . . . I've got to mingle,' she said, catching her breath. 'Y'know, take pictures with the crew, play nice.'

'Are we goin' to LA in the mornin'?' he asked casually.

'You're coming?'

He grinned again. 'Think I'd let you go without me?'

Chapter Thirty

 'WHAT IN hell's going on?' Roxy asked Trinee, raising her painted eyebrows.

'How would I know?' Trinee replied, irritated because she didn't.

'You were tight with the guy. You should be able to give us the scam.'

Trinee shrugged. 'Soon as he unglues himself from her side, I'll ask him.'

'Do that,' Roxy said. ''Cause I know men, and this one's a player.'

'Why do you say that?' Yoko interrupted. 'We never saw him screw around, and he sure had plenty of opportunities.'

'I got a hunch about him,' Roxy said, nodding knowingly. 'He's not for Lara.'

'You've got a hunch 'cause you wanted him for yourself,' Yoko said. 'Now our star has him and you're green, baby.'

'Not true,' Roxy objected. 'I'm *glad* Lara's landed herself a guy. I only hope he's the right one.'

'Tall, dark and handsome, something wrong with that?'

'Lara's not street-smart like us,' Roxy responded. 'She hasn't been around the block three hundred times.'

'Speak for yourself,' Yoko said crisply. 'Personally, I'm a one-man woman.'

'Yeah,' Roxy muttered. 'One man at a time.'

☆ ☆ ☆

Joey found a corner and settled back in a chair. Lara had fallen into position – no problem. Keep 'em wanting more and they'll always be there.

It occurred to him that maybe he hadn't needed to play games, but it had certainly been a smart move.

After taking off, he'd checked into a nearby motel and holed up for a couple of days doing nothing except stare at the TV. It had taken all his self-control not to call her. Now, as he watched her flit around doing her movie star thing – posing with the guys, smiling nicely and making conversation, he knew that she was his.

Every so often their eyes met and the connection between them was on fire. Tonight he'd make love to her. She was more than ready – although anticipation always added to the event.

'So,' Trinee said, flopping down in a chair opposite him, interrupting his flow of thought. 'I thought you were this engaged person – same as me. Now you're here with Lara. What's goin' on, man?'

He regarded Trinee through narrowed eyes. She had a nerve, coming over and pestering him with personal questions. Didn't she get it? Things were different now. 'It's like this, Trinee,' he said, feeding her the information he wished her to pass around. 'Do you believe in fate?'

'Fate?' she repeated blankly.

'That's what happened between Lara an' me.'

'Yeah?'

'Unavoidable.'

234

'What about your fiancée? Man, she must be pissed!'

'She'll get over it,' he said calmly. Across the room he caught Barbara Westerberg glaring at him. He avoided eye contact.

'You're somethin' else,' Trinee said.

'What I am is honest.'

Trinee flounced off.

Eventually Lara came back, face flushed. She was clutching a gardenia one of the grips had presented her with. 'Duty done,' she said breathlessly. 'We can go now.'

'Good. The natives are not exactly friendly.'

'Who's not friendly?'

'Barbara Westerberg's been throwin' me the cold-fish eye all night.'

'She wanted you,' Lara said lightly. 'They all wanted you.'

'And look who won the prize.'

'You know what they say about prizes?'

'Tell me.'

She laughed softly. 'They're to take home and play with.'

'Lara!' he said, pretending to be shocked. 'An' I thought you were a nice girl.'

'No, Joey, I'm not the perfect little prude everyone imagines.'

'Let's split,' he said. 'We got better things to do.'

She found Cassie and told her they were leaving.

'You sure you're OK?' Cassie asked, frowning slightly. This thing with the actor was beginning to worry her.

'OK?' Lara said, glowing. 'I feel absolutely wonderful.'

'If you say so,' Cassie said, thinking she'd never seen Lara so out of control.

'Oh, c'mon, Cass . . . how long is it since I've been this happy?'

'I want it to be good for you, Lara,' Cassie said earnestly. 'If you think Joey's the right guy . . .'

She laughed. 'I'm not *marrying* him, Cass, I'm merely having fun. Oh, and by the way, you'd better let the pilot know that Joey's coming with us in the morning.'

Now Cassie was really confused. 'To LA?'

'That's right,' she said, running over and kissing Miles. 'See you in LA, my darling.'

'Lara, you're the best,' he said, beaming. 'You make my job easy.'

'The same applies, Miles. We'll do it again.'

She nodded at Kyle and his wife, feeling sorry for the poor woman. 'Jean, nice to see you again. Kyle, I'm sure we'll meet in the dubbing rooms.'

'Be careful, Lara,' Kyle said, standing up.

'Excuse me?'

He leaned close to her ear so his wife couldn't hear. 'You got no idea where he's been, honey. Make sure you get him tested for AIDS.'

She drew away, flushed with annoyance. 'One rule for you, Kyle, another for me,' she said in a low voice. 'You give chauvinist pigs a bad name.'

Joey was waiting outside in the car. She slid into the back seat next to him. He took her hand and they rode in silence until they reached the house.

Once inside, he stopped her from switching on the lights by grabbing both her wrists, holding them above her head and roughly kissing her, bruising her lips. 'I've been wanting to do that all night,' he said, releasing her at last.

'And I've been wanting you to,' she whispered back.

'How long's Cassie stayin' at the party?'

'Does it matter?'

'Yeah, it matters. We should be alone here.'

'She'll be a while.'

'Lock the front door.'

'Joey . . . shouldn't we talk?'

'Not now,' he said, and began kissing her again – long deep soul kisses until she didn't care about anything except him.

Soon he began peeling down the straps of her dress, easing it off her shoulders. Then he roughly unclipped her bra, tossing it across the room.

She was faint with excitement. Trembling slightly, her hands grabbed the zipper on his pants, boldly pulling it down, reaching in to explore.

He yanked the rest of her dress down over her slender hips, taking her bikini panties along with it.

'Lie on the floor,' he commanded.

As if in a trance she did as he asked, watching as he stripped off the rest of his clothes.

She'd never wanted a man so badly in her life. With Richard things had always taken place in the bedroom; with Lee they'd been a little more adventurous; here with Joey, lying on the floor of her rented house in the living room, she was wild with passion.

Then he was on top of her – no foreplay this time, she didn't need any as he moved smoothly inside her, causing her to moan deeply in the back of her throat.

Soon they were in perfect rhythm, riding a giant wave, balancing precariously on the edge . . .

In the distance she could hear someone screaming. Vaguely she realized it was her.

They reached the peak together, climaxing with a frenzy of moans. And it was all she'd ever hoped for and more.

When they were finished he remained spreadeagled on top of her, neither of them moving. She was hot and sticky and totally ecstatic. 'Joey,' she murmured contentedly. 'Oh, God, Joey.'

'Was it good for you, baby?' he asked lazily, rolling off and throwing his arm across her.

'The best,' she whispered happily. 'The absolute best.'

'Tell me,' he urged.

'Tell you what?'

'Tell me that there'll never be anyone else for you. That I'm it. I'm your whole fuckin' world.'

'Joey . . .'

A week. All he needed was a week and she'd tell him anything he wanted.

Chapter Thirty-one

'I WANT you to see a rough assemblage tonight,' Richard said. 'Meet me here at six, and we'll drive to the screening room together.'

'Can't wait,' Nikki responded, hoping she'd be able to get away from the production office early enough to accommodate him.

'You won't believe Lara's performance,' he raved. 'She's sensational.'

'I'm hardly surprised,' Nikki said, wishing that he wouldn't carry on about Lara quite so much. Besides, didn't he remember that it was *she* who'd designed every stitch of clothing that covered Lara's gorgeous body in the movie, making her a big part of the movie's success. It was a costume picture, after all.

They were eating breakfast out on the deck. Normally she would have left by this time, but as she was on her way out Richard had announced he had something important to talk about, so she'd delayed her early start, even though she was anxious to get to the office.

Impatiently she glanced at her watch. So far he hadn't come up with a subject that merited her staying any longer. 'Lara flies back today,' she said, making conversation. 'I thought we'd have her over for dinner tomorrow, and Mick, too, if that's OK with you.'

'Why *that* asshole?'

'It seems a good plan for them to meet socially. Kind of a get to know each other before the movie starts.'

'Lara will hate him,' Richard said flatly. 'She sees right through assholes.'

'She won't hate him.'

'Trust me, she will.'

'Richard,' Nikki said, feeling defensive, 'when I started this project you were very supportive – now, every day, you seem to get less so.'

'Because you're making the wrong choices,' he said, his voice a monotonous nag. 'You refuse to listen. You should *never* have cast Lara, nor hired Mick Stefan.'

'Why not? He's brilliant.'

'He might be brilliant, but he needs a producer who can control him. You've had no experience, Nikki. You *need* experience.'

'Oh, gee, thanks. I appreciate your confidence,' she said, checking her watch again. 'I have to get going, Richard. Was there anything else?'

'I promised Summer I'd talk to you.'

'What about?' she asked, annoyed, because if Summer had something to say, she should come out with it herself.

'She said that every time she tries to talk to you, the two of you end up getting in a fight.'

'Not so.'

'*She* seems to think it is.'

Nikki sighed. 'So what is it?'

He pressed his fingers together, staring directly at her. 'She wants to come and live with us.'

'Excuse me?' Nikki said, not sure she'd heard correctly.

'She doesn't want to go back to Chicago. She'd sooner go

240

to school here.' There was a long silence. 'You should be thrilled,' he added. 'She *is* your daughter.'

'Yes, my daughter, whom I've had hardly anything to do with since she was eight. Quite frankly, I'm not sure if I can take on the responsibility now.'

'You're not being very understanding,' he chided, annoying her even more.

'You know, Richard,' she said, beginning a slow burn, 'I resent the fact that she asked *you* to speak to me.'

'I'm merely the messenger,' he said, sipping his coffee. 'You should sit down with her.'

'I will – when I've got time. Right now I'm late for the office.' Grabbing her car keys from the table, she set off, seething. How *dare* Summer run to Richard and persuade him to plead her case!

For a moment she was tempted to go back to the house and roust her lazy daughter out of bed. According to the maid, Summer slept in every day until noon, then got up, met friends, and wasn't to be seen again until it was to put on a different outfit. Then Nikki changed her mind, suddenly overcome with guilt – after all, as Richard had so succinctly pointed out, she *was* Summer's mother. She decided the fair thing to do was discuss Summer's wish to move to LA with Sheldon.

When she arrived at the office, Mick was in the middle of a big production meeting. He'd started without her, which pissed her off even more.

She sat down next to him. He threw her a vague wave. She'd known making movies was hard work, but being involved on the production side was completely time consuming, there were so many decisions to make. Each department had questions, and it was imperative that every detail was in place before the start of principal photography.

As soon as they took a break, she instructed her assistant

to send Lara flowers with a note welcoming her back and inviting her to dinner the following night.

Mick grabbed her at lunchtime. 'Aiden's nutto about you,' he said, sucking on his lower lip. 'You charmed the crap outta him.'

'How nice,' she replied, noncommittal.

'Yeah, he thinks you're a real cool chick-babe.'

'As long as he behaves himself I couldn't care less what he thinks.'

'How many times I gotta tell you?' Mick said, beaming. 'Aiden's a pussy.'

'Don't forget,' she reminded him, 'tomorrow night at my house. I know you and Lara will get along.'

He cackled. 'Yeah, well, we gotta, haven't we?'

'Try to remember, Mick, she's a star, treat her with respect.'

'Enough already – I'm getting the message. I'll even wear a tie – I got one, y'know.'

'You don't have to do that.'

'Yeah, yeah – kinda a respect move.'

She made it home before seven. Richard and Summer were sitting out on the deck playing a game of Scrabble. She felt like an intruder as she walked past them.

'Oh hi, Mom,' Summer said, sweet as apple candy. 'Did you have a good day?'

How come when Richard was around, Summer played the perfect daughter?

'I'm exhausted,' she said, flopping into a chair.

'Ha!' Richard said. 'If you think you're tired now, wait until you start shooting.'

Summer jumped up. She wore minuscule shorts and a cropped top. *Too much flesh*, Nikki thought. 'Gotta get changed,' Summer announced. 'I'm off to a party.'

'*Another* one?' Nikki said.

''S OK, Mom – Richard said I should enjoy myself while I'm young.'

'Did he?' Nikki said, throwing him a look.

'I'm having such an amazing vacation,' Summer said enthusiastically, throwing her arms around Nikki's neck. 'Thanks, Mom.' Then she ran over and kissed Richard, too, before vanishing into the house.

'Why do you always complain about her?' Richard asked, pushing the Scrabble board away. 'She's a lovely girl.'

'You only see the good side,' Nikki replied ominously.

An hour later they were settled in a small screening room watching a rough cut of *French Summer*.

Nikki forgot about *Revenge* and concentrated on the exquisite images playing on the screen before her. The cinematographer was a master, the period clothes she'd designed were perfect, and Richard was right – Lara's performance was incandescent; plus Harry Solitaire and Pierre Perez both gave charming performances.

When the lights came up Richard had a big smile on his face.

'You've excelled yourself!' she exclaimed. 'I love everything!'

'Couldn't have done it without Lara,' he said. 'She was the perfect leading lady.'

Great, Nikki thought, *what about me?*

They stopped at Dan Tana's on the way home, ordered steaks and salads, and Nikki listened while Richard talked endlessly about his movie. He really was obsessed. She tried to bring up *Revenge*, but he wasn't interested.

After dinner they drove to the beach.

'Let's go straight to bed,' she suggested as soon as they entered the house.

'What's your hurry?'

Maybe I'm feeling horny, she wanted to say, but she didn't.

243

Instead she followed Richard into the bedroom, locking the door behind them.

'Why are you doing that?' he asked, pulling off his sweater and dropping his pants.

'For privacy.'

'Summer's out. And even if she was home, she wouldn't come in here unannounced,' he said, clicking on the television.

'Who can tell with Summer?' she said, going into the bathroom, emerging a few minutes later clad in a sexy black nightgown.

Richard was now lying under the covers staring at the television, mesmerized.

'Why is it,' she said, climbing into bed beside him, 'that I get the distinct feeling you're more into *Nightline* than me?'

'Don't be ridiculous,' he said, holding tightly on to the remote lest she try to grab it from him.

'We haven't made love in weeks,' she pointed out.

'That's because we've both been so busy,' he replied, seemingly unconcerned.

'When did that ever stop you?' she asked, reaching over and expertly stroking him until he became aroused.

After a few moments he moved on top of her, and without a word began pumping away until he was satisfied. Then he rolled off, closed his eyes and immediately fell into a deep sleep.

Nikki was outraged. Whatever happened to romance? Not to mention foreplay. One thing about Richard, he'd always been a considerate lover – now this. And the biggest insult of all was that he'd kept the television on.

She turned away from his snoring presence, burying her head in the pillow, hurt and angry.

When *Revenge* was completed, they were due to have a long talk, and not a moment too soon.

Chapter Thirty-two

 'I COULDN'T get in last night,' Cassie said, tight-mouthed.

'Sorry,' Lara replied guiltily. 'I must've locked the door out of . . . habit.'

'I had to break a window,' Cassie continued accusingly. 'We're responsible for a replacement, I've made a note of the damage.'

'Of course.'

'Everything OK?'

Lara smiled a beauteous smile. 'Yes, Cassie, everything's wonderful.'

Cassie handed her a folder. 'I've put together an LA schedule for you,' she said. 'It's tight, but as long as you don't come down with the flu or anything, you'll manage.'

Lara glanced at the hourly schedule and groaned. 'This is impossible,' she said. 'It barely gives me time to breathe.'

'You wanted to make *Revenge*. Quinn warned you.'

Lara frowned as she studied the crammed schedule. 'I'm sure we can cancel some of the things on here.'

'Not really,' Cassie said. 'It's all important. There's publicity for your last two movies. Dubbing on *French Summer*. TV commitments. Your charity work. Doctor and dentist appointments. PR stills. Magazine covers—'

'OK, OK, I'll go over it on the plane.'

Cassie nodded and left the room. Lara glanced out of the window. Her limo was outside the house, the luggage stacked beside it. Their driver was busy loading the trunk. Ten more minutes and they should be on their way.

She went back into the bedroom. Joey was in the bathroom, naked, staring at himself in the mirror.

She moved up beside him, dressed and ready for their flight. 'We've got to go,' she said, thinking how much she liked his body. He was muscular without it being too much. His shoulders were broad, his stomach washboard flat, and his legs long and athletic. On his chest was a smattering of black hair – exactly the right amount. He had the best butt in the world.

'I know,' he said, still studying his reflection.

She slapped him lightly on his ass. 'You'd better stop admiring yourself and hurry up, Mr Handsome.'

He turned around, leaning his bare butt against the sink.

She noticed he was hard and automatically her legs began to weaken. How had they gotten this intimate so quickly? She couldn't believe he was standing around naked in her bathroom as if they were an old married couple. She, who was usually so careful, had fallen into something like lightning. And she didn't care. She was enjoying every irresponsible exciting moment.

'Why don't you get down on your knees?' he suggested matter-of-factly. 'Why don't you do it *now*?'

'Why don't *you* get dressed?' she responded.

He smiled at her. 'See something you like?'

She smiled back. 'Yes, and I'm sure it'll still be there when we get to LA.'

He laughed. 'OK, OK – I'll get dressed.'

'Five minutes. The plane will be waiting.'

'It's a private plane, isn't it?' he said, reaching for his underwear.

'That doesn't make any difference. They have a flight schedule to keep to.'

'Yes, *ma'am*,' he said mockingly, pulling on his shorts.

She ran into the kitchen, alive and glowing. Through the window she saw Cassie standing by the limo chatting to their driver. She couldn't wait to confide in Nikki – shout out the news that she was in love – well maybe not love – but certainly lust.

She'd never fallen into bed with anyone so quickly. Richard had waited months before she'd slept with him; and she'd kept Lee hanging for six weeks. Now Joey. And it was instant. And the sex had never been so exciting and passionate. Nikki would understand totally.

Remembering last night, she shivered with pleasure, hugging her secret to herself.

Joey emerged a few minutes later. He'd put on worn jeans and a faded denim work shirt, his dark hair was ruffled and untidy.

'I'm taking you shopping when we get to LA,' she announced. 'You could use some Armani jackets and pants, socks and ties, and—'

'Wait a minute,' he interrupted, his expression hardening. 'If I was into that kind of shit – which I'm not – I'd buy it for myself. I don't need *you* to pay my bills.'

'I didn't mean I was going to buy you clothes because you *needed* them,' she said, flustered. 'I wanted to get you stuff simply because . . .' she trailed off. Why had she made such a stupid suggestion? She was acting as if he didn't have any money. Of course he was insulted, any man would be.

He stared at her. She looked so radiant with her luminescent skin and sparkling green eyes – how could he possibly be mad at her? 'C'mere,' he said, his tone softening. 'Have I told you lately you're the most beautiful woman I've ever seen?'

'And *you're* the most beautiful man,' she replied, happy again.

They walked out to the limo hand in hand.

The chauffeur opened the door for them. They sat in the back. Cassie chose to sit up front with the driver. Throughout the ride to the airport they only had eyes for each other.

Nikki will not *believe this*, Lara thought. *It's all happened so fast I can hardly believe it myself.*

The Gulfstream jet was waiting at the airport. The pilot greeted Lara personally, honoured to be flying her. An attentive steward escorted them aboard.

The plane was comfortably equipped with four armchairs placed around an oblong table, and several other luxurious seating areas. In the back of the plane there was a bedroom and a shower.

'Do we get to use the bedroom?' Joey whispered.

'I'm a star, I can do what I like,' Lara joked. 'However,' she added, more seriously, 'here's what I *think* we should do.'

'What?'

'Talk . . . take the time to get to know each other. I want to find out all about you – where you're from – your family – what kind of cereal you like in the morning . . . everything . . .'

'How's this for a fantasy?' he interrupted. 'Our lives begin now, forget about the past.'

'I can go with that.'

'Then good – no talkin' – we'll spend all our time in the bedroom.'

'Joey!' she chided, laughter in her eyes. 'Are you a sex maniac?'

'C'mon,' he said persuasively. 'You know you want to.'

Yes, she wanted to. But the truth was she should be studying her script, preparing for her first meeting with Mick

Stefan. Principal photography on *Revenge* was due to start in less than two weeks and there was much to do. She hadn't been home for nearly four months, and the last thing she'd planned on was an involvement.

Joey took her hand, placing it casually atop his growing erection.

She quickly pulled it away, motioning toward Cassie, whose face was hidden behind a copy of *USA Today*.

'There's enough for her, too,' he whispered.

'You're incorrigible!' she said, laughing softly.

The steward came by to take their drink orders. Joey requested a beer, and Lara went for a 7-Up. 'I need the sugar,' she said with a wry grin. 'You've sapped all my energy.'

'Yeah?' he said, pleased. 'An' we haven't even started yet.'

She smiled, thinking about the previous evening, once again shivering with pleasure.

'So,' Joey said. 'When do I get to meet Mick Stefan?'

'I think the movie's cast.'

'You're the star,' he said casually. 'Fire somebody.'

She laughed, sure he was joking. 'I can't fire anyone. I haven't even met Mick.'

'Hey,' he said, turning on the little boy charm. 'Surely if you want your boyfriend to have a part . . .'

She tilted her head to one side, regarding him quizzically. 'Is that what you are, Joey? My boyfriend?'

'How about lover? It sounds sexier.'

'Works for me,' she said, still smiling. 'My . . . lover.' She paused for a moment. 'Oh, God! Wait till the tabloids find out.'

He leaned over, placing his hands behind her neck and pulling her close. 'Come here, you,' he said, running his tongue slowly over her lips. 'I got an idea,' he said in a low voice. 'Throw Cassie off the plane. Tell her to fly commercial—'

'I can't do that.'

'Yes, you can.'

'Joey – I can't,' she repeated, thinking he couldn't possibly be serious.

'OK, just a suggestion,' he said lightly. 'I always had an urge to run around naked on a plane. Can't do it with her on board.'

'You're crazy,' she said, smiling indulgently.

'Never said I wasn't.'

'That's true.'

'Let's see now,' he said, squinting at her. 'According to you I'm a sex maniac, crazy an' incorrigible. Anythin' else you wanna throw at me?'

'Not that I can think of.'

'Good.'

'Are you fond of dogs?' she asked curiously.

'Love 'em – from a distance. Why? You gonna set 'em on me?'

'I have three.'

'Big or small?'

'Mixed.'

'What else d'you have I should know about?'

'Horses. And a couple of cats.'

'You sure there's room for me?'

'Uh . . .' She didn't know what to say, they hadn't discussed where he was going to stay. Now it was obvious he assumed he was staying with her.

He caught her confusion. 'Don't sweat it,' he said quickly. 'I plan on checkin' into a hotel for a coupla weeks. Then if I decide to settle in LA, I'll rent an apartment.'

'Joey,' she said impulsively – thinking, *My God, it isn't as if we're strangers* – 'I'd like you to stay at my house for a few days until you find a place.'

'Naw,' he said, shaking his head. 'Wouldn't want to impose.'

'It's not an imposition, you'll be very comfortable,' she said, fastening her seatbelt as the plane began taxiing down the runway.

'Hey,' he said, breaking out another grin, 'as long as I'm with you, nothin' matters.'

And that was the truth, because he'd finally found the woman he could be with for ever.

Lara smiled. Yes, it was happening fast, but the good thing was that it all seemed so right. And best of all, it was great to be with someone who cared.

Chapter Thirty-three

 NIKKI DECIDED to cook; it wasn't often she spent time in the kitchen, but because Lara had been away for so long, she suspected a home-cooked meal would be appreciated. She was fixing roast chicken, creamed potatoes, broccoli, peas and English bread sauce – all of Lara's favourites.

Richard arrived home early for a change, and headed straight into the kitchen where Nikki was busying herself slicing avocado for the salad. He kissed her on the back of her neck.

'Guess what?' she said brightly, knowing he'd be pissed, but after his performance the night before she couldn't help needling him.

'What?' he said, picking up a slice of avocado.

'Lara's bringing someone.'

His eyebrows shot up. 'She is?'

'Yeah – remember I told you about that guy she was kind of interested in, the actor I met, Joey Lorenzo? Well, apparently she's more than interested.'

'How do you know?'

'I haven't had a chance to talk to her, but Cassie called to say she wants to bring him tonight. Naturally I said it was OK.'

'Didn't you mention to me that he was engaged?'

'Looks like he's disengaged now.'

'I don't get it,' Richard said, sourly. 'Why would she hook up with some unknown actor?'

'Why not? Who else does she meet?'

'And she's bringing him here tonight?' He shook his head. 'Who'd believe *this*.'

'Believe it, honey. Your ex is venturing out on her own again.'

Richard opened the fridge and took out a bottle of white wine. 'I'll talk to her,' he said.

Nikki snorted derisively. 'And tell her *what*? That she can't get laid without your permission?'

He threw her a steely glare and marched out of the kitchen carrying the wine just as Summer entered, wide-eyed and smiling. 'Mom!' she exclaimed, deliciously pretty in a pale pink sundress. 'Something smells way good!'

'Thanks,' Nikki said, wondering what Summer wanted. A car? The house? Richard?

You're not being very nice, she thought. *Lighten up and try getting through to her.*

'Nikki!' Richard yelled from the other room. 'Pick up the phone – it's Mick.'

Oh, God! Don't tell me he's cancelling, she thought, grabbing the phone.

'I got a big one to ask,' Mick mumbled. 'A bigeroonie.'

'Go ahead.'

'It's real important to me.'

'What is it?' she asked impatiently.

'Aiden's goin' through a bad time. He's livin' in a rented dump – got no friends.'

'Are you asking if you can bring him?' she said with an exasperated sigh, knowing she'd regret it.

'That's the deal.'

'Eight o'clock. Casual.' She slammed down the phone. 'Wanda!' she yelled. 'Set another place.'

'Is it OK if I stay for dinner?' Summer asked, bright blue eyes shining as she danced around the kitchen. She'd overheard the conversation and couldn't believe her luck.

Nikki couldn't help herself. 'How come you're not going out?'

'What – and miss your yummy cooking?' Summer replied, dipping her fingers into the salad and plucking out a small red tomato.

What could she say to her daughter? *I'm expecting guests – you can't stay.* 'It's actually a business dinner,' she said lamely.

'Richard said Lara's coming. I like love Lara – haven't seen her in ages.'

'It's not only Lara,' Nikki said quickly. 'We're also having my director, Mick Stefan. There'll be a lot of shop talk. You'll be bored.'

'Don't you *want* me to stay home, Mom?' Summer asked accusingly.

No. This was the one dinner she didn't want Summer to attend. 'Of course I do,' she said, feeling the old familiar guilt. Turning to the maid she said a brusque, 'Wanda, set one more place, we're growing by the minute.'

'Thanks, Mom!' Summer exclaimed, racing out of the kitchen.

Nikki made a mental note to check with Sheldon as soon as possible. If Summer was serious about staying, then maybe she'd give her a chance. Perhaps there was hope for them after all.

☆ ☆ ☆

Summer rushed into her room. Mick Stefan coming to the house was the best! She'd never told him who she was. He'd

254

freak when he spotted her! But the big news was Aiden Sean.
The babe himself. She couldn't be more excited.

What to wear, that was the problem. Something so sexy
he'd be unable to resist her. Yeah! Tonight was the night!

☆ ☆ ☆

Lara sat in front of her dressing table adding the finishing
touches to her make-up, thinking how good it was to be
home.

Yesterday, as soon as they'd arrived at the house, she'd
instructed Mr and Mrs Crenshaw, the elderly Scottish couple
who worked for her, to set up the guest room for Joey. Mrs
Crenshaw had nodded, slyly checking Joey out, which made
Lara smile. The Crenshaws – like everyone else – were very
protective of her.

Once Joey was settled, he'd begun exploring her house.
'Jeez! This is some place,' he'd exclaimed, roaming around.
'I didn't realize you lived like this.'

'It's where I spend all my time when I'm not working,'
she'd explained. 'I've tried to make it as comfortable as
possible.'

'You sure did a good job.'

He was like a kid let loose in Disneyland, fiddling with the
stereo system, checking out the many televisions, playing ball
with the dogs, and when he discovered she had a gym he was
in heaven.

In the evening they'd had a quiet dinner together outside
in the garden. Later she'd waited for him to make a move.
Disappointingly, he hadn't. He'd kissed her chastely on the
cheek, remarked that they were both exhausted, and vanished
into the guest room.

She was confused. One moment he was her lover, the next
merely a house guest.

She'd lain in bed, unable to sleep, thinking about him. But he hadn't come to her, and she was too proud to go to him. One thing about Joey, he certainly didn't believe in pushing it.

They'd both gotten up early and met in the kitchen. After breakfast she'd taken him down to the stables to see her horses. 'Can you ride?' she'd asked.

'I can try,' he'd said.

Mr Wicker, the man who ran her stables, had chosen a horse for Joey to take out. He'd mounted it without faltering and they'd set off. He was a natural.

'Unbelievable!' she'd exclaimed. 'I've been riding for years, and you simply climb on a horse and get it immediately.'

'I can do anythin' I set my mind to,' he'd boasted, grinning. 'Anythin'.'

They'd lunched around the swimming pool and spent a relaxing day, thanks to Joey, who'd insisted she cancel all her appointments. 'C'mon, Lara,' he'd said. 'You deserve one day to yourself.'

Cassie was not pleased as she sat in her small office attempting to rearrange the already overcrowded schedule.

Now Lara was getting ready for dinner at Richard and Nikki's.

She wondered what Richard's reaction would be to Joey. Sometimes her ex-husband was too possessive – it would do him good to see her with another man.

Joey knocked and wandered into the room, looking very handsome in a black silk T-shirt, Armani jacket and black pants, a thin lizard-skin belt enclosing his narrow waist. He'd taken his outfit from the film – too bad if they didn't want him to have it.

'I'm glad you're meeting Mick this way,' she said, adding

a touch of blush to her high cheekbones. 'Better than going in for an interview. I promise I'll ask him if there's anything in the movie for you.'

'Don't *ask* – *tell*,' he said, picking up a Lalique perfume bottle and sniffing the scent.

'I can't force them to do anything,' she said, standing up and reaching for her purse.

'They can't force you, either,' he reminded her, unexpectedly plunging his hand down the front of her dress, enclosing her left breast, tweaking her nipple.

She gasped, taken by surprise.

'We'd better go,' he said, removing his hand.

All she really wanted to do was stay home and make love. Instead she followed Joey from the room.

Outside in the garage, he walked around inspecting her cars. She had a grey Range Rover, a sleek gold Jaguar XKJ, and a black Mercedes with dark tinted windows.

'Three cars?' he said, grinning. 'Lady – I like your style.'

'Which one shall we take tonight?' she asked.

'The Jag,' he answered quickly. 'I'll drive.'

He opened the door for her, and she got into the passenger seat. 'Do you have a car, Joey?'

'In New York? No way. Soon as I know what I'm doin', I'll lease somethin' here.'

It occurred to her that if he didn't get a part in *Revenge* he might have to go back to New York, and then when would she see him?

Stop it, she told herself sternly. *This is no big romance, it's a fling. Short and sweet.*

Or is it?

Maybe Joey's the man I've been waiting for. The man who's going to make a difference in my life.

No more lonely nights.

No more sickening nightmares.
She could only wish.

☆ ☆ ☆

So now her cosy little dinner for three was seven. *Great!*
Nikki thought.

Two actors – who would probably hate each other; two
directors – who couldn't be more different; a beautiful movie
star; a difficult teenager; and herself. What a group! And on
top of everything else, Richard had started drinking too much
again – which wasn't a problem unless he took it too far. And
from the look in his eyes she knew that tonight he'd definitely
take it too far. He'd already consumed half a bottle of wine,
and was now on to Martinis.

She put the CD player on shuffle – a selection of Sting,
Jamiroquai and Jewel. Then she sampled one of Juan's lethal
Margaritas. She'd sent for Juan at the last minute to help out
at the bar; one quick inspection and she wished she hadn't.
Juan – who was Wanda's son – had the look of a juvenile
Antonio Banderas with his slicked-back jet hair, bedroom
eyes and cocky attitude. Last time she'd seen him he'd been
a boy – now he was eighteen and she shuddered to think
what would happen when he set his horny eyes on Summer.

'Your son's certainly grown up in a short time,' she
remarked to Wanda as they stood in the kitchen.

'Juan's a good boy,' Wanda said, beaming proudly. 'He
no get involved with gangs. He wanna be singer.'

'A singer, huh?' Nikki said, checking on the chickens
roasting away in the oven.

'Big talent,' Wanda said. 'Mebbe you and the Mister
wanna hear?'

'Another time,' Nikki said quickly. Right now she had an
evening to get through.

RUNNING INTO *Maxwell von Steuben did not help my career one bit. In fact, true to his word, the sonofabitch tried to have me blacklisted.*

Here's what he didn't think of. He didn't think I could change my name, and that's exactly what I did. All of a sudden I was a new guy in town, and as long as I avoided going on any auditions where Maxwell might be, I was safe. The dumb shit was blacklisting someone who didn't exist any more.

Soon after the incident with Maxwell I dumped Margie. Had to. She gave boring a whole new meaning. My dreams of a little house in the Valley with a couple of kids vanished. Who gave a damn? There were too many women out there who needed my attention. Too many babes who had the money to pay for it.

Changing my name was an ace move. As far as my career was concerned, it changed my luck, too. After a few months, I landed the lead in a late-night TV action show. Kind of low-core porno on syndication, but it sure made me feel like a king. All of a sudden people were bowing and scraping, running to take care of my every command. There's nothing like being the star of a show, however bad the show. And I even got to direct a couple of episodes – a real kick.

My co-star was a nervous blond who'd done time around the track several times and then some. Once she'd been a contender, only she'd never quite got to the top. Now she was doing shit shows like mine, and lucky to get the job because she'd never see thirty-five again. And for a woman over thirty in Hollywood – unless you've already made it – it's finito.

Her name was Hadley. She had long legs and a voracious sexual appetite. I wouldn't fuck her, didn't want to mix business with pleasure. This drove her totally crazy, causing her to do everything in her power to turn me on. She came to my trailer wearing nothing but a mink coat bought for her by her gangster boyfriend; paraded around the make-up room in stiletto heels and Frederick's of Hollywood lingerie; and sent me outrageous gifts from a sex shop she frequented.

I didn't fall for her act. I was finally getting smart. But one day she pushed my buttons. We were shooting a night scene in Culver City, and she picked up one of the extras – an outrageously sexy black girl – and one thing led to another, and the three of us ended up in Hadley's trailer, bombed out of our skulls on straight tequila and very fine Mexican grass.

From what I can remember I must have fucked her, and not gone back for more, because shortly after she managed to get me fired. Bitch!

What the hell – I found myself a new agent and started doing the rounds again. An Australian company was making a series of low-budget action movies for Asia. They wanted an American actor, and they discovered me. I was into a little kick boxing, and with the help of a coach I soon honed the skill.

All of a sudden, I was a half-assed star in Asia. Big fucking deal. I went there for a promo trip, and spent the majority of time getting laid and drugged out of my head. Asian drugs, man, they are something else!

By the time I got back to the States I had myself a habit that wouldn't quit.

Truth was I was well and truly hooked.

Chapter Thirty-four

 LARA AND Joey arrived first. Nikki took one look at her glowing countenance and didn't have to ask – they were definitely in bed together. And who could blame her? Joey Lorenzo was one of the best-looking men around.

She hugged Lara, said a cordial hello to Joey, then led them out to the deck where – much to Nikki's annoyance – Richard was on his third vodka Martini.

He immediately jumped to his feet when he saw Lara, enveloping her in a loving embrace. 'I've missed you, sweetheart,' he said warmly. 'I've *really* missed you.'

'You, too, Richard,' she said, extracting herself from his arms. She hesitated a moment, not quite sure how to introduce Joey. 'Say hello to my, uh . . . friend . . . Joey Lorenzo.'

Joey stepped forward, anxious to check out the ex-husband. 'Mr Barry, it's a real pleasure, sir.'

The 'sir' hung in the air like a dirty word. Nikki stifled a nervous giggle, Richard's annoyance was palpable. 'Let's not be so formal,' she said, hurriedly taking Joey's arm and steering him over to the small bar. 'I'm Nikki, he's Richard. What would you like to drink?'

'A beer'll do it,' Joey said, remembering that apart from being Lara's best friend, she was also the producer of *Revenge*, therefore he'd best be nice to her.

'One beer,' Nikki instructed Juan. 'And Lara – what can we get you?'

'Champagne,' Lara replied, completely incapable of wiping the dreamy smile off her face.

'Mick's on his way,' Nikki explained. 'He's bringing Aiden Sean, so you get to meet them both at once.' She noticed Joey reach for Lara's hand. This was love all right, she'd never seen Lara in such a trancelike state.

'So, you're an actor,' Richard boomed, joining them at the bar. 'What have you done?'

Lara laughed lightly. 'Now, now, Richard, Joey doesn't travel armed with his résumé.'

'Maybe he should,' Richard said nastily.

'Yeah, why's that?' Joey asked, challenging the older man with a long hard look. He wasn't about to take shit from anyone.

Fortunately Mick chose that moment to make his entrance. True to his word, he'd worn a tie – decorated with a nude Marilyn Monroe. He also wore an ill-fitting sixties style white tuxedo, baggy pants, a frayed shirt and a goofy grin.

Aiden Sean shuffled in behind him – low-key in khakis and sinister impenetrable shades.

'Welcome to our home,' Nikki said graciously. 'I'm glad you could make it.'

'I bet you are!' muttered Aiden.

She pretended she hadn't heard as she effected introductions.

Joey checked out Mick and Aiden. A couple of big-time losers who'd struck it lucky. Shit! Why wasn't he directing movies and starring in them? He probably had more talent in his dick than these two had between them. And Lara – *his* Lara – was putting herself in their hands, it didn't make sense. He nudged her. '*This* is the boy wonder?' he whispered rudely. 'What a jerk!'

'Be nice,' she whispered back. 'Don't judge him on his appearance.'

Why the fuck not? he wanted to say. But he remained silent. He'd learned at an early age that the smart thing was to find out everyone's deal and then speak up.

'Lara,' Mick said, gulping down a frozen Margarita as if it was lemonade, 'gotta tell ya – I'm totally psyched you're doing my movie.'

Nikki caught the 'my movie' and didn't like it one bit. Since when was it *his* movie?

'Nikki's developed an excellent script,' Lara replied, dazzling him with a smile. 'How could I resist?'

'I got a lotta new ideas,' Mick said enthusiastically. 'Lotta bigeroonies.'

'Great,' she replied, 'I'm always open to suggestions – if they're good.'

That put Mr Big Shot Stefan in his place. Joey was proud of her, she knew how to handle herself around jerks. Not that he'd ever doubted her.

Aiden Sean hadn't said a word. After ordering a Jack Daniel's on the rocks, he'd slumped down on a lounge chair as far away from everyone as he could get.

Nikki contemplated going over, playing the polite hostess. Then she thought, *Why should I? He's the uninvited guest, let him put himself out.*

Summer timed her entrance five minutes before dinner. She sauntered outside, barefoot, in sprayed-on denim cut-offs, and a midriff-baring top. Her long white-blond hair was freshly washed, framing her pretty face. 'Hi, everyone,' she said, innocence personified. 'Gee, Mom – dinner smells good enough to eat!'

'Holy shit!' Mick exclaimed, his voice cracking.

'Meet my daughter,' Nikki said, hoping he wasn't into teenagers. 'Everyone – this is Summer.'

'Your daughter?' Mick croaked, arms flailing wildly.

'Yes,' Nikki said, noticing that Juan was standing to attention, completely mesmerized by Summer.

Fortunately she hadn't spotted him yet. With a little luck it would stay that way.

Ignoring Mick, Summer spotted Lara and ran over. 'Lara!' she squealed.

'*You've* certainly grown up,' Lara said, hugging her. 'And so pretty. Say hi to Joey Lorenzo.'

'Hello, Joey,' Summer said, checking him out.

'Hello,' he replied, staring jailbait in the face. If Nikki was smart she'd lock this one up and swallow the key until she was eighteen.

Summer edged her way over to Aiden Sean. He looked at her blankly. 'I'm a major fan,' she said, determined to get his attention. 'Seen all your movies like ten times! You're way, way the most genius actor around.'

No reaction from Aiden, who seemed more interested in nursing his glass of Jack Daniel's.

'Don't you *remember* me?' Summer demanded, lowering her voice so nobody else could hear.

He barely moved his head. 'Nope.'

'The Viper Club.'

'Sorry, kid,' he said, yawning in her face.

She glared at him. He'd pay for calling her kid.

☆ ☆ ☆

Across the deck Joey didn't miss a thing. 'How old's the nymphet?' he whispered to Lara.

'Fifteen. Frightening, isn't it?'

'She's sure made Mick's evening. Take a look – his eyes are buggin' out.'

'Don't be disgusting, she's a child.'

'This one grew up a long time ago.'

'What makes you think that?'

'I can tell.'

☆ ☆ ☆

Mick grabbed Summer's attention on the way into dinner.

'Whyn't you tell me who your mother was?' he demanded, mouth twitching.

'You didn't ask,' she retorted flippantly.

'And how come you didn't call me?'

''Cause I knew you'd be mad when you found out my mom was Nikki Barry.'

He looked perplexed. This little Lolita was confusing him.

Before he could say anything else, she'd moved away, and he found himself seated between Lara Ivory and Aiden.

☆ ☆ ☆

The conversation around the dinner table was dominated by Mick, who decided the only way to get Summer's attention was to spew forth his opinions on everything from politics to crime. 'We gotta bring back public hangin',' he said, distractedly circling Marilyn's left tit with his index finger, while managing to keep a keen watch on Summer, who so far had refused to look at him. 'Hang 'em up by the balls an' watch 'em squirm. *I'd* pay.'

'That's obscene,' Richard said, his face clouding over. 'We may as well all run around in loincloths carrying spears.'

'The law of the jungle – fuck 'em before they fuck you,' Mick said, winking at Summer, who immediately looked away.

Joey observed the scene. Someone should tell the kid that directors were the ones with all the power, not actors – the little tease hadn't taken her baby blues off Aiden all night. He placed his hand on Lara's leg under the table, slowly moving it up her thigh.

'Are you aware of how many people are executed by mistake?' Richard demanded, banging his fist on the table.

'Hardly any,' Mick responded. 'An' y'know why? 'Cause bleedin' heart liberals like you wanna end the death penalty altogether.'

'The death penalty is *not* a deterrent,' Richard announced sternly, wishing everyone would get the hell out of his house.

'Bullshit!' shouted Mick, turning to Lara. 'What do *you* think?'

'It depends on the crime,' she said, determined not to get trapped in the middle of their fight.

Aiden stood up from the table. He had not removed his dark glasses all night and barely spoken a word. 'Where's the head?' he muttered.

'In the front hall,' Nikki replied.

'I'll show you,' Summer said, leaping to her feet and accompanying him from the room.

She led him all the way to the guest bathroom, and when they arrived she attempted to enter with him.

'What the fuck are you playing at?' he asked, blocking her at the door.

'Nothing,' she answered innocently. 'I had no idea you were in my mom's movie.'

'And I suppose you didn't know Mick was her director,' he said, as if he didn't believe her.

Ah, so he *did* remember her. 'Honestly, I didn't,' she said, trying to edge into the bathroom with him – aware that if she wrapped her long blond hair around *it*, and enclosed *it* with her sweet young lips, she could send a man to heaven. Mick had been susceptible, but it was Aiden she really wanted.

'Go away, little girl,' he said, slamming the door in her face.

Reluctantly she returned to the dinner table. Aiden Sean hadn't heard the last of her, she'd show *him*.

☆ ☆ ☆

Lara and Joey left shortly before eleven.

'Some night!' Lara exclaimed in the car going home. 'I must say – Mick's quite a character. And as for Aiden Sean . . .'

'Your ex has a major crush on you,' Joey remarked.

'Not really,' she said quickly.

'How come he let you get away?'

'I told you, he was unfaithful,' she said with a deep sigh. 'I finally realized I'd had enough.'

'Bet he regrets it now.'

'He and Nikki are very happy.'

'Don't be so sure.'

'They are,' she insisted.

'C'mon, honey,' Joey teased, 'you don't think he doesn't dream about you in bed? Your incredible skin? Your soft arms? Your long legs wrapped around his neck . . . ?' He took one hand off the steering wheel, and cupped her left breast. 'Take off your bra,' he ordered.

'What?' she replied breathlessly.

'You heard. Slip it out from under your top.'

'Joey,' she laughed nervously, 'can't you wait until we get home?'

'No,' he said insistently. 'I've been wantin' to touch you all night. Now do it.'

Her throat was suddenly dry with anticipation. This man was insatiable, and she loved it.

Reaching under her blouse, she unclipped her bra and slipped it off.

Immediately his hand snaked under her blouse, pressing her nipple roughly between his fingers.

She moaned, flooded with desire. He had such an amazing effect on her, she couldn't think straight when he touched her.

'Unzip my pants,' he instructed, staring at the road ahead. 'Take it out.'

'Joey,' she objected, 'we're on a public highway. People will see . . .'

'What people? We're in a moving vehicle. Do it!'

'Joey . . .' But in spite of her protests she found herself obeying. It was almost as if he had her under a spell and she was powerless to say no. The truth was she had no desire to refuse him anything. Releasing him from his pants, she caressed him, wishing they were home so he could make love to her properly.

'Suck it!' he commanded, pushing his hand firmly against the back of her head.

Oh, God! All he had to do was ask . . .

She bent her head, tasting him, enclosing him. And when he came, they were racing along the Pacific Coast Highway at seventy miles an hour, and the kick was so potent that she felt herself climaxing too.

'You belong to me, baby,' he said, his eyes fixed on the road. 'Don't ever forget it. You're mine, all mine. Right, baby. *Right?*'

And she nodded dreamily and leaned back in the seat and couldn't wait until they were home in bed together.

☆ ☆ ☆

As soon as Aiden Sean and Mick Stefan left her mother's stupid dinner party, Summer called a cab. Aiden wasn't treating her nicely, even though he now knew who she was.

God! Mick's face when she'd walked in and Nikki had announced she was her daughter. Talk about sudden panic! She'd almost laughed out loud. Mick had taken her for some little nymphet fan the night she'd met him at the Viper Club – nothing more than a teenage blow job. Big shock for him!

She didn't care about him anyway, he was too geeky. It was Aiden Sean she liked, and when Summer wanted something she was determined.

Before the party she'd called the production office and told them her mother needed Aiden's home address. Smart thinking, because as soon as he left she'd informed Nikki she had a party to go to, and now she was sitting in a cab on her way to his place.

He lived in a ratty little apartment in North Hollywood on a narrow dusty street. She paid off the cab and rang the doorbell.

Aiden came to the door stark naked, except for dark shades covering his eyes, and a pair of knitted slippers on his long callused feet. 'Aw, Jesus!' he groaned. 'You followed me home.'

'You're not very nice to me,' she said, pushing past him into his apartment. The television was blaring and there was a half-empty bottle of Jack Daniel's on the table. She remembered all the things she'd read about him in the tabloids and shivered with excitement. 'Are you *really* a drug addict?' she asked, wide-eyed.

'Are you *really* a fucking moron?' he responded, quickly pulling on a pair of pants. 'Where does Mommy think you are now?'

'Told her I had to go to a party. She doesn't care, she's too busy with her movie and Richard.'

'That old fart,' Aiden growled, taking a gulp of booze from the bottle.

'Richard's OK,' Summer said. 'I can get anything I want out of him, and he's like an *amazing* director – better than your friend Mick.'

Aiden lowered his shades and regarded her for a moment. 'What are you after, kid?' he asked, flopping down on a worn out couch. ''Cause whatever it is, you're not getting it from me.'

'I'm into experiencing life,' she said ingenuously.

'You're treading a dangerous line. Fortunately for you, I'm not a bastard.'

She giggled disbelievingly. 'You're *not*?'

'Some people would've screwed the ass off you an' not given a shit. But I got principles.'

'Anyway,' she said matter-of-factly, 'that's why I'm here. I want you to . . . uh . . . do it to me.'

'Not me, kid – I got enough problems.'

'If you won't, I'll tell my dad you did, and the police'll arrest you 'cause I'm under-age.'

He stared at her for a long silent moment. 'You'd do that, wouldn't you?'

'My dad's a big-time shrink in Chicago,' she boasted. 'He's got real pull. He knows the Mayor.'

Aiden shook his head in disbelief. 'Get the fuck outta here or your mom's gonna hear about this.'

'She won't believe you, and you'll like get dumped from her movie.'

'You think I give a fast shit?' he said, hustling her to the door. 'Go home, little girl, an' don't come back.'

'You'll be sorry,' she said, shocked that he was rejecting her.

'So I'll be sorry. Big fucking deal.'

Chapter Thirty-five

 LARA AND Nikki sat in the Chinese restaurant across the street from the production offices enjoying a sumptuous feast of wild rice, sweet and sour shrimp, egg rolls and won tons.

'I've never seen you like this, you're positively glowing,' Nikki said, reaching for an egg roll. 'And if you don't wipe that annoying smile off your face, I'll be forced to smack it off!'

'Isn't he great?' Lara said dreamily. 'And it's not only his looks – God knows I've passed up dozens of handsome guys.'

'Silly you,' Nikki murmured.

'You've got to understand,' Lara said, her green eyes burning bright, 'Joey is different. He's gentle and strong, smart and undemanding . . . and *soo* sexy.'

'Oh,' Nikki said, nodding wisely, 'now I get it. It's a sex thing.'

'No,' Lara objected quickly, 'honestly, Nikki, it's not just sex.'

'Yeah, yeah,' Nikki said disbelievingly. 'He's got you hooked sexually. And how is he in that department?'

Ignoring her friend, Lara continued, 'It's as if we belong together. Like we were out there alone and . . . somehow . . . we found each other.'

Nikki plucked a won ton off her plate and popped it in her mouth. 'Does he have money?'

Lara frowned. 'What does money have to do with anything?'

'Don't be so naive. Let us not forget you're a rich woman.'

'He's not asking for anything.'

'He doesn't have to. Not yet, anyway.'

Lara took a sip of black tea, attempting to remain calm. 'Why are you being so nasty?' she asked at last. 'You're the one who kept on begging me to sleep with someone.'

Nikki ran a hand through her short dark hair. 'I'm merely playing devil's advocate. A great fuck is one thing – but if you're falling in love, you need to know more about him. Like who he is would be a good start.'

'I know plenty.'

'Like what?'

'Like right now he's the perfect man for me.'

'I give up!' Nikki said, throwing her hands in the air. 'This is exactly what happens after a long dry spell.'

'Excuse me?'

'Getting laid again. Screws up your head quicker than anything.'

'Can't you be happy for me?'

'I am. It's just that this guy came out of nowhere. Dumped his fiancée and moved in on you big-time.'

'He didn't move in on me. I *invited* him to stay.'

'OK, OK, as long as you know what you're doing.'

They ate in silence for a few minutes, both busy with their own thoughts. Sometimes Lara resented Nikki's way of saying exactly what was on her mind. It was none of her business what she did or who she did it with.

'By the way, I need a favour,' she said, breaking the silence.

'Speak now.'

'I want Joey in the movie.'

Nikki groaned and stopped eating. 'You've *got* to be kidding.'

'We talked about it before.'

'That was weeks ago. Every role is cast.'

'You're the producer,' she said sharply. 'Find him something, he's an excellent actor.'

'I'm sure he is. But the truth is, you've left it too late.'

'Too late for what?'

'For Mick. He's meticulous about his casting. Every character is set.'

'Y'know,' Lara said, speaking in measured tones to be sure Nikki got the message, 'I'm doing this movie as a favour to you. A *big* favour.'

Nikki was shocked, this was not the Lara she knew and loved. 'So?' she said belligerently.

'So,' Lara responded, allowing her words to hang in the air. 'I'm requesting something back.'

'You're asking for something I can't do anything about,' Nikki said, furious at being put in such an awkward position.

'Yes, you can,' Lara countered. 'Be realistic.'

'I'll talk to Mick,' Nikki said resentfully.

'I'd appreciate it.'

They finished lunch barely speaking.

☆ ☆ ☆

Summer awoke in her own bed, late. She yawned and stretched, allowing her mind to wander over the events of the previous night. First the dinner party. Boring. Then her nocturnal visit to Aiden Sean. What a big fat disappointment he'd turned out to be. Just because her mother was Nikki Barry he hadn't wanted anything to do with her, he'd practically thrown her out – which really sucked.

Still . . . Aiden Sean was a movie star, and that had to

count for something – especially in Chicago where she could impress everyone – including her dad's new wife, who thought she was such a hot number. Well, not hot enough – because *Rachel* hadn't almost made out with a movie star.

What would happen if she told Rachel the truth about the man she was married to?

The Monster Man.

My Daddy.

Suddenly Summer's eyes filled with tears as the truth came crashing back. She could never tell anyone. She was too ashamed.

Get over it, her inner voice screamed inside her head. *GET OVER IT!*

But it wasn't that easy.

☆   ☆   ☆

Back at the production offices, Mick stopped by to say hello to Lara, staring at her through his strange, magnified glasses. 'Lookin' forward to tomorrow,' he said, rubbing the tips of his long bony fingers together. 'The read-through's gonna be a happenin'.'

'I'm looking forward to it, too,' she replied, wondering what working with him would be like.

Later, after Lara had gone off to meet with the wardrobe people, Nikki cornered Mick in his office. He was on the phone having a conversation in which he appeared to be begging some woman to forgive him for a past indiscretion. 'C'mon, sweetie baby-love,' he wheedled. 'We'll have dinner, sex, a few laughs. You know you get off on me.'

Apparently the woman didn't, because Nikki could hear the loud dial tone on the other end of the phone as she hung up on him.

Mick pretended she was still on the line, mumbled a phony

'Goodbye,' put the phone down and turned to Nikki. 'What's up?' he asked, slumping back in his chair. She began pacing up and down in front of his desk, apprehensive about broaching such a delicate subject. 'Uh . . . this is the deal, Mick,' she said, dreading his reaction.

'Yeah?' he mumbled, checking out her legs.

'The truth is we're lucky to have Lara in our movie, on account of her being such a big star and all.'

'What're you telling me?' Mick asked irritably. 'She met me, doesn't like me, an' wants to walk? Is that it?'

'No, she thought you were charming,' Nikki said. Actually they'd been so busy discussing Joey, they'd barely mentioned him.

'Bull's-eye,' Mick sneered. 'I score charming award of the year.' He snickered wildly. 'That's before she's worked with me, right?'

Nikki sighed. 'She wants us to give her boyfriend a part.'

'Aw, shit!' he said, sitting up straight.

'I *told* her everything was cast.'

'You mean that creep she was with last night?'

'He's not a creep,' Nikki said patiently. 'He's her current boyfriend, and she wants him in the movie.'

'Who does he expect him to play? One of the freakin' rapists, for Chrissakes?'

'Maybe a detective?' Nikki suggested in her best *please do this for me* voice. 'Perhaps you can write another one in.'

'When didja ever see a detective that looked like him?' Mick grumbled. 'He's freakin' Mel Gibson twenty years ago – an' taller, too. Bastard!'

'That doesn't necessarily make him a bad guy,' Nikki murmured.

'It don't make him a good actor either.'

'The thing is, we'd like to have a happy star, wouldn't we?' She trailed off, hoping he got it.

'This is some fuckin' drag,' he mumbled. 'I never hadda compromise before.'

Well, you've only been in the business five minutes, she was tempted to say. But she didn't, knowing it wouldn't help matters.

'Will you think about it, Mick? For me? After all, I did you a favour with Aiden last night, who, I might add – wasn't exactly the life and soul of the party.'

'Do I at least get to read the boyfriend?' Mick asked, curling his lip.

'Of course.'

'Have him here at seven in the mornin' before the read-through. For you I'll check him out.'

'Thanks, Mick,' she said gratefully. 'I owe you one.'

'A blow job'll pay me back,' he said with an insane cackle.

'I'll tell Richard, he'll be flattered someone else wants me.'

'Not *you*,' Mick said scornfully. 'Your daughter.'

She gave him a long cold look. 'I take it you're joking.'

He laughed hysterically. 'Never joke about pussy.'

'Then I'll make believe I didn't hear you,' Nikki said, thinking that sometimes his pathetic attempt at humour was way out of whack.

'Whatever gets you through the night,' he said, with a manic shrug.

Yeah, she thought, *whatever gets me through the night. Richard's turning into a cold fish, Lara's in the throes of a love affair, Mick wants to get it on with my teenage daughter, and I'm left out in the cold trying to keep it all together.*

She went into her office, closing the door behind her, and immediately began thinking about the previous night's dinner party.

By the time everyone had left, Richard was completely plastered. He'd staggered into their bedroom, flopped on the bed, and she'd been forced to listen to his ranting and raving about *Revenge*, and Mick, and what a mistake Lara was making, before he'd fallen into a drunken stupor.

She had no respect for him when he drank too much – being loud and belligerent didn't suit him. What was it with these old guys she married? First Sheldon, now Richard. Was this marriage starting to crumble, too?

In the morning she'd left before he got up. And now she was at the office trying to get Lara's boyfriend a job. Producing a movie was not going to be as easy as she'd thought. Everybody had an angle – including Lara.

☆ ☆ ☆

When Lara arrived home, she found Joey in the den, watching sports on TV, looking perfectly content.

'Hi, beautiful,' he said, barely glancing up.

'I've got you an appointment with Mick tomorrow morning at seven,' she announced triumphantly. 'You cannot be late.'

'Seven!' he groaned. 'That's kinda early.'

She picked up the remote, clicking off the TV. 'I did as you asked, Joey,' she said quietly. 'I compromised myself.'

He stood up. 'How'd you do that?'

'I almost threatened Nikki I'd walk off the movie, which wasn't very nice of me.'

'Well, yeah, but we've both discovered you're not as nice as everyone thinks,' he said, putting his arms around her waist, pulling her close and running his hands over her body. 'You give out this aura of goodness, but underneath you're nothin' but a bad little sexpot!'

'Is that what you think?' she asked, shivering.

'C'mere, beautiful,' he said, bending her back and kissing her passionately on the mouth. 'Gotta tell you – I missed you all day.'

'You did?' she said, luxuriating in his kisses.

'Every second.'

'What did you do?'

'Worked out, swam. Mrs C. cooked me eggs, an' I took a look at your CD collection. You do know it's in need of serious work.'

'As if I have time to go to Tower and browse.'

'Hey – let's go together.'

'I get recognized in public places.'

'How 'bout we disguise you? Like Michael Jackson.'

'Michael Jackson is recognized everywhere he goes. And if I put on a white surgical mask and gloves, I'd be recognized too.'

'We'll get you a short black wig an' big shades. Or maybe we'll dress you up as a little boy.'

'A *little* boy?' she asked, laughing.

'Naw, a teenager. You could pass for a teenager, you're kinda flat-chested.'

'So now I'm flat-chested, am I?' she said, pretending to be exasperated.

'Not exactly.' He laughed, tweaking her nipples. 'They're big enough for me.'

She picked up a magazine, slamming him on the head.

He held up his hands, protecting himself. They both collapsed laughing on the couch.

He enfolded her in his arms, holding her close against him. He'd never had a relationship like this with anyone, and he liked it. Not only was Lara staggeringly beautiful and famous, she was genuinely nice. And warm and caring and sexy and fun. How had he finally gotten so lucky?

She snuggled into his chest, totally content. 'I usually get home from a day like this dead to the world,' she murmured. 'Now you're bringing out somebody in me I didn't know still existed.'

He looked at her with a quizzical expression. 'You tellin' me you'd forgotten how to have fun?'

'My past relationships were very staid. Richard's much older than me.'

'I noticed.'

'Lee was sweet.'

'Sweet don't cut it, babe,' he said, enclosing her breasts with his hands, working on her nipples. 'I bet he couldn't excite you the way I do, huh?'

She struggled to sit up. 'Joey – this is crazy. We've been together such a short time, and yet . . . sometimes I feel I've been with you all my life.'

'It's called soulmates,' he said, suddenly serious.

She stood up. 'Oh, that's what it's called, is it?'

He got up, too. 'What did Nikki say? Yes, I'll put Joey in the movie, I'll fire Aiden Sean and give him *that* role.'

'Oh, sure, I *really* want you playing the rapist.'

He walked over to the bar, opened the fridge and extracted a can of beer. 'I was readin' through the script today,' he said, flipping open the can. 'It's pretty heavy stuff.'

'I know.'

'Do you trust this Mick Stefan guy? He may be a hot director, but is he for you? You're playin' against your image big-time.'

'I know that, too.'

'You gotta consider your fans,' he said, swigging from the can. 'Why d'you think they go see you?'

'Because I'm a good actress?' she said flippantly.

'They go see you 'cause you send out this aura, this image.'

'I do?'

'You got it all, babe. You're beautiful an' nice. You're what every guy dreams about – the sexy good girl.'

'I'm glad you added sexy,' she said with a soft smile.

'Let's analyse it,' he said. 'Why was I so attracted to you? 'Cause – truth is – I've had a lot of women.'

'Before you were engaged, I presume,' she said archly.

'No question,' he replied seriously. 'I'm a big believer in fidelity – aren't you?'

'Yes,' she said, equally serious. 'I absolutely believe in it, Joey. After my experience with Richard, I vowed no man will ever cheat on me again.'

'What would you do,' he asked teasingly, 'if you'd come home today and found me in bed with a girl?'

'That's not a good question.'

'No, c'mon, tell me,' he urged. 'Would you have blown my head off? Kicked me out? Screamed at me? At *her*? What *would* you have done?'

'I'd have walked away,' she said calmly. 'Simply walked away.'

'Oh, no, baby,' he said confidently. 'There's no way you could walk away from me.'

For a moment her green eyes darkened. 'Don't bet on it, Joey. Don't ever bet on it. I'm stronger than you think.'

☆ ☆ ☆

By the time Nikki arrived at the Malibu house Richard was drunk again.

'This is getting to be a habit,' she said coldly. 'I thought your drinking days were behind you.'

'What's the matter?' he asked belligerently. 'Aren't I allowed to relax?'

Oh, God! Not another fight. 'You still working on post?' she asked, walking into the kitchen.

'Everything's done,' he said, following her.

'Where's Summer?'

'Out,' he replied, still bad-tempered.

'Listen, Richard,' she said, determined to clear things up, 'it was you who encouraged me to get involved in producing. I thought you wanted me to make this film.'

'I didn't tell you to drag Lara into it, put her together with a piece-of-shit director and ruin her career,' he said curtly. 'You're using your connections, and I don't like it.'

'Lara *wants* to do my film,' she said, opening the fridge and removing two steaks neatly enclosed in Saran-wrap.

'She's only doing it because of me,' he said, sourly.

'If that's what you think,' she said, placing the steaks on the grill.

'You wouldn't even *know* Lara if it wasn't for me.'

'What kind of remark is that?'

'The truth.'

'I'm sorry you feel this way,' she said flatly, not ready to get into another fight. 'Can we discuss it later? Right now I'm fixing dinner.'

Later, he was too drunk, and they went to bed not speaking.

☆ ☆ ☆

Summer and Tina went back to Club Pot, where they danced all night, sometimes with each other, sometimes with a selection of different guys. They finally sat down, their hard tanned young bodies glistening with sweat.

'Last night Mick Stefan and Aiden Sean were at my mom's house,' Summer confided. 'Can you *imagine*? Mick almost crapped! While stupid Aiden pretended he so didn't know me.'

'*That* dick!' Tina said scornfully.

'And you know what I did?'

'What?'

'Took a cab to his stinky old apartment and told him what a phoney he was.'

Tina raised an eyebrow. 'You did that?'

'Well . . .' Summer giggled. 'Actually, I went there to get him to sleep with me. But he wouldn't do it. I think he must be gay.'

'Really?'

'I don't see why else he wouldn't.'

'Y'know, Summer,' Tina said thoughtfully, 'if it's a movie star you want, *I* can get you plenty.'

'No way,' Summer said.

'Way,' Tina boasted. '*And* – here's the kicker – they'll pay you to do stuff. Big big bucks!'

'Wow!' Summer responded, thinking that getting paid for anything at all was a really wild idea.

'If you're serious, I'll arrange it,' Tina said casually. 'Only if I do – you can't fink out on me.'

'Go ahead,' Summer said boldly. 'I'm up for anything.'

'Are you sure?' Tina asked. ''Cause I'm not playing games. This is the real thing, and if I bring you in, there's no way you can let me down.'

'I wouldn't do that.'

'OK. I'll set it up. Call me in the morning.'

Another adventure. Summer couldn't wait.

Chapter Thirty-six

 UNFAIRLY INCARCERATED for stalking and attacking her best friend, Alison Sewell spent most of her time in jail plotting and planning the revenge she would wreak when she got out. Her eighteen-month sentence was automatically reduced to half. Nine months inside. Pregnant with hate for the woman who'd put her there.

Lara Ivory. Bitch. Whore. She wasn't a friend after all, she was the enemy, exactly like the rest of the morons Alison had to deal with.

Lara Ivory had fooled everyone with her beautiful face. But Alison realized the face was merely a cover for the evil woman who lurked within.

As soon as she got out, Alison knew she had to do something about the bad seed that was Lara Ivory.

Yes, she'd wipe the sweet smile off Lara's ugly face for ever.

Meanwhile she had prison to deal with, and no camera to hide behind. And as each day passed, her thirst for revenge grew.

Chapter Thirty-seven

 'WHERE'D YOU study?' Mick asked, swinging back in the chair behind his desk, legs splayed in front of him, beady eyes behind his heavy glasses crinkled in a deep squint.

'Does it matter?' Joey asked, trying to figure out a way to get through to this asshole. He knew the guy hated him, had to hate him. He was too good-looking for most men, especially someone like Mick, with his wild hair, pointed face and geeky clothes. However, Joey knew there had to be a way to connect, there always was.

'LA, New York, where?' Mick pressed.

'I, uh . . . I kinda studied around New York,' Joey said, purposely keeping it vague. 'Actin' class, workshops, things like that. Then I got a break in *Solid*.'

'Thought I'd seen you somewhere before,' Mick said, squinting even more ferociously. 'How come nothin' happened after that?'

'Family problems took me back home for a while,' Joey mumbled. 'Soon as I hit New York again, I scored the role in *The Dreamer*.'

'An' that's where you met Lara, huh?' Mick said, wriggling his ankles. 'She's a real cool babe-chick. Some freakin' looker.'

'She sure is,' Joey agreed.

Mick leered. 'Pretty nice when you get 'em great looking *an'* they wanna get you a job.'

All of a sudden Joey got it, he knew exactly how to bond with this cretin. 'I'm fucking her, why shouldn't I be in her movie?' he said calmly.

This was the kind of talk Mick understood. 'Got it!' he said, a huge beam covering his pointed face. 'Hey – I can bump somebody if I gotta. There's like this older detective with a younger partner. I was into the younger guy being black, no reason it couldn't be you.' He tossed a script across the desk, burping loudly. 'Course, I'll havta dump the black actor, which means the NAACP'll cream my ass, but who gives a shit? Page fifty-two – wanna read?'

Joey held the script. 'Who'm I readin' with?'

'Me,' Mick said, getting up and walking around the desk. 'I'll play the older detective. Used t'be an actor, y'know.'

'Yeah?'

'You don't have much to say, but you'll be there, keepin' watch on your girlfriend.' He snickered. 'She's gotta be something in the sack, huh? Wild legs. Those classy ones got it all goin'.'

'You could say that,' Joey replied, searching for the right page.

Mick winked, happy with Joey's reply. 'Maybe when we're workin' together – hanging out – we can get down to details. Whaddaya think?'

'I think,' Joey said slowly, 'when I'm doing the movie, you and I can hang out as much as you want.'

Mick cackled again. 'OK, let's read the motherfucker.'

☆ ☆ ☆

'Richard?' Lara said, cradling the phone under her chin. 'Has Nikki left yet?'

'What's the matter?' Richard said. 'Don't want to speak to me?'

'You're always so busy.'

'Never too busy for you, sweetheart.'

'That's nice,' she said, wishing he'd put Nikki on the line.

'Wait till you see the movie, Lara,' he said enthusiastically. 'Your performance is impeccable.'

She remembered what Joey had said about Richard still having a crush on her, and knew in her heart that it was true. She wasn't flattered. The only reason Richard wanted her was because he couldn't have her any more.

'I'm excited about seeing it.'

'I'll arrange a screening.'

'Is Nikki there?'

'I was thinking,' Richard said, with no intention of getting off the phone, 'you and I should have lunch.'

'Sounds good, only right now my schedule's frantic.'

'Nobody understands that better than me. But think about it, Lara – how many people *really* care about you? You have no family.'

She'd told Richard the same story she'd told everyone else. Her family were all wiped out in a car crash. She'd been raised by a distant relative – now deceased. It was safer never to reveal the truth.

'I'm worried about you, Lara,' Richard continued. 'That guy you brought with you the other night – that actor – who is he?'

She was not in the mood for a question and answer session. 'Why does everyone keep on asking me who he is?' she said, exasperated. 'What am I *supposed* to do – get a Dunn and Bradstreet on every man I go out with?'

'For almost the last year you haven't been out with anyone. Before that it was Lee.'

'Keeping a score card?' she asked, annoyed that he was questioning her.

'Now Lee was an OK guy,' he continued, ignoring her acid comment. 'He'd been in the business for years and knew his way around. Nobody knows anything about this Joey guy. Where's he from? What's his story?'

'Richard,' she said, trying to keep her aggravation in check, 'I'm a grown-up. I don't need anyone watching out for me.'

'This isn't like you, sweetheart. We must sit down and talk face to face, just the two of us.'

'How about Nikki?'

'She won't mind,' he said, clearing his throat. 'We can do it tomorrow. Lunch. You and me, the Bistro Gardens in the Valley. It's important to me, Lara, don't let me down.'

'Well, all right,' she found herself saying. 'But no third degree, because I'm very happy. In fact, I'm happier than I've ever been.'

'I only want the best for you, sweetheart.'

'*Now* can I speak to Nikki?' she asked patiently.

'Hang on a moment.' He went off to fetch her.

After a few moments Nikki got on the line.

'What time are you leaving?' Lara asked.

'Soon. Why?'

'And the read-through is ten o'clock?'

'You're up for it, aren't you?'

'Of course.'

'Then *what*?'

'I'm anxious to know the outcome of Joey's meeting with Mick, so maybe you'll call me when you get there.'

'Listen,' Nikki said evenly, not sounding like her usual warm self, 'you gave me an ultimatum. I passed it on to Mick. He'll hire Joey, he has to.'

'Really?'

'You're the star, Lara, you made that very clear.'

'I didn't mean I'd walk if he wasn't hired.'

'Yes, you did,' Nikki sighed. 'But I understand.'

Nikki was pissed – too bad. She couldn't please everybody all the time.

She thought about Joey and smiled. Joey Lorenzo. He treated her like a woman, not a movie star – and she loved it. Joey. The man who excited the hell out of her. For the last two nights he'd slept in her bed, and they'd indulged in hot, exciting, incredibly intense sex. She hadn't realized that making love could be so inventive and different every time. Joey gave new meaning to passion.

She hadn't thought she'd ever find this kind of relationship, and now that she had – all everyone wanted to do was criticize him. What did she care about his background or where he was from? Although she had to admit she was a tiny bit curious about his ex-fiancée, Phillipa, whom he never mentioned, even when she'd tried to question him once.

But the truth was, keeping secrets was OK. She had her own, and those weren't to be shared either.

When she was almost dressed she found herself going into his room. His two suitcases were on the floor – stacked one on top of the other. She felt guilty invading his privacy, but somehow she couldn't help herself.

Opening the closet, she peered inside. He didn't have many clothes – not even a suit. She was prepared to buy him anything he desired – a car, clothes, it didn't matter to her. As far as she was concerned their future was together.

The thought never occurred to her that he might be with her because she was rich. Without false modesty she was well aware she could have almost any man she wanted, and not just because she was a movie star. No, her fame wasn't the main attraction. It was her beauty that made men desire her with such a longing.

Sometimes she called it her cursed beauty.

When she recalled her youth . . . the far-off dark days . . . the nightmare times nobody knew about . . .

Her face clouded over. No! She wasn't getting into *that* today.

She couldn't find anything personal in the room. No photos, papers, nothing. Her face flushed with guilt at what she was doing, she opened the top suitcase, coming across a jumble of dirty socks, T-shirts and underwear. The other suitcase was locked.

She looked around, but couldn't find a key. Hating herself for snooping, she quickly left the room, bumping into Mrs Crenshaw in the corridor outside.

'Everything all right, Miss Lara?' Mrs Crenshaw asked.

'Yes, thank you,' she replied, escaping to her bedroom.

She'd told Joey to call as soon as he got through with Mick. He hadn't done so yet. Hopefully things were going well.

She dressed hurriedly and left the house, arriving at the production offices early. When she walked into the main room she found Joey sitting at a table with Mick and a couple of crew members. They were laughing, drinking coffee and eating doughnuts. She presumed from his attitude that everything had worked out.

'Hi, baby,' he said, standing up and grinning.

'Hi, Joey,' she replied, a touch cool because he hadn't called her.

He grabbed her in an intimate hug, kissing her full on the mouth, letting everyone know she was his.

Mick lurched to his feet, a knowing leer all over his pointed face. 'Hiya, Lara,' he said, absent-mindedly rubbing his crotch. 'You're early.'

'Yes, I am,' she said with a tight smile. 'Joey, can we go downstairs for breakfast?'

'Sure, baby,' he said, winking at the guys. 'See ya.'

Why did she have this uncomfortable feeling that they'd been talking about her?

'You were supposed to call me,' she said, as soon as they were in the elevator.

'I couldn't get away from Mick,' he explained. 'After he gave me the part of detective number two, he kept on talkin'. What could I do?'

'So he hired you?'

'Course he did. An' the good news is it'll mean I'll be there to keep a watch on you.'

'I don't need anyone watching over me, Joey,' she said. 'When I'm working I'm *very* focused.'

'I bet you are, but you still need somebody around to protect you.'

'Cassie follows me everywhere,' she said, as they stepped out of the elevator. 'She's enough protection for anyone.'

'No, no, baby,' he said insistently. 'On this movie you're gonna need *me* around.'

'Well, anyway, I'm delighted it all worked out,' she said, squeezing his hand. 'You'd better call your agent, have him make a deal.'

Somehow he didn't think Madelaine Francis would appreciate his phone call. 'Don't wanna use the one I had in New York,' he said.

'Then go to mine. I'll have Cassie arrange an appointment.'

'Whyn't you call him yourself?'

'If that's what you'd like.'

They left the building, crossing the street to the coffee shop. Several cars nearly ran into the back of each other when the drivers spotted Lara. She didn't appear to notice.

As soon as they were seated, she took out her cellphone, contacting Quinn at his office. 'I have a new client for you,' she said crisply. 'Joey Lorenzo, a very good friend of mine. He needs you to negotiate a deal for him on *Revenge*.' She paused for a moment, tapping the side of the phone. 'Yes, Quinn, I *know* there's no money on this movie. Do the best you can.' She covered the mouthpiece. 'Joey, can you see him tomorrow morning?' He nodded. 'OK, he'll be there around ten. Thanks, Quinn.' She clicked off the phone. 'Done,' she said, pleased with herself.

Joey leaned across the table, fixing her with one of his looks. 'How come you're so good to me?' he asked.

'Because you're good to me, too,' she replied softly. 'It's a two-way street.'

'I try.'

'You're succeeding.'

The waitress came over, pad poised. Lara ordered an egg-white omelette and herbal tea. Joey went for coffee and a Danish.

'Did you see Nikki this morning?' she asked.

He shook his head. 'Naw. Why?'

'She's not very pleased with me – thinks I pressured her to get you in the film. But I *know* you won't let me down.'

'Now Mick knows it too,' he said confidently. 'I gave a pretty good reading.'

'I'm sure,' she murmured.

He reached across the table and took her hand. They smiled intimately at each other.

It was a physical thing. They couldn't keep their hands off each other.

Chapter Thirty-eight

 ONCE AGAIN Summer awoke late, it was getting to be a habit, and why not? She didn't have school to go to or people nagging her to get up. Daddy's housekeeper, Mrs Stern, was just that – an ornery old witch who, if she ever knew what was going on under her pointed old nose, would drop on the spot.

It was so amazing being away from them all – living her life without the threat of her father molesting her . . . the image of his face looming over her in the middle of the night.

She shuddered at the thought. Ah . . . freedom . . . She couldn't wait to get out permanently.

Last night she'd staggered home at four a.m., encountering Richard in the kitchen getting a glass of water – which is exactly what she'd planned on doing to counteract the major hangover heading her way. She'd had three or four potent drinks called Gangbusters – a mixture of vodka, fruit juice and rum – and she'd felt like she was about to throw up.

'Just getting in?' Richard had asked, crinkling his eyes.

Oh, no! Not a lecture. Please!

'I was staying at my girlfriend's,' she'd explained. 'Then there was like a huge fire in the kitchen, and everywhere filled with smoke, so I came home.'

Richard had laughed. 'Very inventive, dear. Save those kind of stories for your mother.'

She'd giggled. Richard never gave her a hard time. He was the best. She couldn't understand why he and Lara had gotten divorced, it seemed crazy. Lara was so sweet and beautiful, how could any man give her up?

She turned over in bed, then remembered she'd promised to call Tina – who'd said something about meeting stars and making money. How radical would *that* be?

If she could only make enough money, she'd *never* have to go home.

☆ ☆ ☆

The actors gathered together at ten for the reading, which was taking place in a large conference room beneath the production offices. Lara was secretly thrilled Joey was now part of the production; the truth was she *did* feel more secure having him next to her.

Most of the actors were hanging around the coffee machine getting to know each other. Lara didn't recognize anyone, but she made eye contact and smiled, well aware that it was up to her as the star to create a friendly atmosphere.

Now that he was in the movie, Joey decided it might be a smart move to charm Nikki. He went over to her. 'I owe you a big thank you,' he said. 'I know you had a lot t'do with gettin' me this gig.'

'Thank Lara, not me,' she replied, a touch snippy.

'Oh, I will.'

'Make sure you do,' she said, heading for the coffee maker.

He fell into step behind her. 'You two are good friends, huh?'

'We certainly are.'

'That's great. Friendships are important.'

Nikki stopped, regarding him for a long silent moment. What did he want? Her approval? Obviously. 'A lot of people love Lara very much, including me and Richard,' she said at last. 'So, Joey, you should know that if you ever hurt her—'

'Hey,' he interrupted, 'I may be new in her life, but I love and respect Lara, I always will.'

Nikki nodded and walked away.

She wasn't easy, but Joey figured he'd better persevere – as Lara's best friend he needed her on his side.

Lara took her place at the head of the big conference table, motioning Joey to sit beside her. He did so.

Mick stood up, waving his gangly arms in the air. He then made an impassioned speech.

Nikki was impressed. A good director had to be a powerful leader, and with all his foibles Mick seemed to be just that.

Aiden Sean arrived late, clad in grungy jeans, a wrinkled T-shirt, and a black baseball cap emblazoned with a scarlet *Eat my sorrow*. Dark shades covered his eyes.

'Glad you could make it,' Nikki said coolly as he passed her chair.

He lowered his shades, peering at her over the top. 'Don't worry 'bout me,' he mumbled. 'You got problems closer to home.'

She frowned. Could he possibly know that she and Richard weren't getting along? 'What do you mean by *that*?'

'Forget it,' he said, slouching over to a chair at the end of the table.

The reading began.

Joey got off on the way Lara handled herself. As she read Rebecca, the schoolteacher, so she became the character. It was almost as if her glowing beauty slipped away and she *was* the plain, timid woman.

Twenty pages into the script came the rape scene. Lara

handled it like the true professional she was. And Joey did well with the few scenes he had.

The script was extremely powerful – a real tour de force for Lara. At the end of the reading she was emotionally drained.

Mick rushed over, kissing her full on the mouth. 'You're the greatest,' he said, beaming and twitching. 'Never thought you could make it work this good, but lady – you're fanfuckingtastic!'

She was happy that she'd done the words justice. 'Thanks, Mick,' she said shyly, thinking how she couldn't wait to go home and be with Joey, snuggled in the safety of his arms.

Nikki hugged her, unable to stay mad. 'I'm so happy,' she said excitedly. 'You're so much more than just a movie star, and it's about time people realized it. This movie will finally bring you the recognition you deserve.'

'I'll do my best,' Lara said modestly.

'Your best is amazing!' Nikki replied, laughing.

They hugged each other again. 'I'm sorry if I've been on your case,' Nikki continued. 'I realize that if you like Joey, he *must* be an OK guy. And he did fine today. He's actually very good.'

'I didn't mean to force you to hire him,' Lara said. 'It's only that how often does someone come along who's special? And if Joey wasn't working, he'd have to go back to New York, then you'd be stuck with one miserable actress.'

'It all worked out,' Nikki said cheerfully. 'Now – the big question. Are you comfortable with Mick?'

'He's no Richard, but I'm sure we'll get along.'

'I feel so much better about everything today,' Nikki exclaimed. 'Even Aiden's cutting it.'

'Richard asked me to lunch tomorrow. Will you come?'

'I can't, too busy.'

'You don't mind?'

Nikki laughed. 'You and Richard having lunch? Oh yeah, I'm *really* bent out of shape. Although it would've been nice if he'd invited me too.'

'He's *your* husband.'

'Yeah, lucky me,' Nikki said, grinning ruefully.

'Is everything OK?' Lara asked, picking up bad vibrations.

'Sure,' Nikki replied, determined not to throw her troubles in Lara's lap. 'Why wouldn't it be?'

'If you want to talk . . .'

'Yeah, yeah, I know – you've been there, done that. Thanks, anyway.'

Lara glanced around, searching for Joey. He was over the other side of the room talking to a young production assistant with long curly hair and a spectacular body. She felt a tingle of jealousy. Ridiculous! She'd never been jealous before. Joey had her emotions completely out of control.

'How's it working out with Summer?' she asked, forcing herself to turn back to Nikki.

'Considering I hardly ever see her, I guess it's fine,' Nikki said. 'I decided rather than nag her to death, I'd allow her plenty of freedom. She wants to move here.'

'Is that such a good idea?' Lara asked gently. 'This is a tough town for a teenager to be loose in.'

'I know,' Nikki said with a deep sigh. 'But right now I haven't got time to play mother.'

'Perhaps you should send her back to Chicago until you finish the movie.'

'You're right, that's exactly what I should do. I'll call Sheldon tomorrow.'

'She shouldn't be running around by herself.'

Nikki frowned. 'Did Summer tell you something I should hear about?'

'No, it's just that I remember when I first came to LA I was only nineteen, and believe me – I know how the sleazy guys in this town hit on young girls.'

'Ah yes,' Nikki said, with a smile. 'But I'm sure you handled it with your usual indomitable style.'

Lara's eyes clouded over. *If Nikki only knew*, she thought.

She glanced in Joey's direction again. He was on his way toward her. Grabbing her arm, he smiled broadly. 'Isn't she the greatest?' he said to Nikki. 'This woman is amazin'!'

'*I've* always thought so.'

He drew Lara close to him, his hand creeping down and squeezing her ass. 'My star. My baby. You're the best!'

Hmm, Nikki thought. *He wants everyone to know he has power of ownership.*

Lara didn't seem to mind; in fact, from the way she gazed up at him, Joey could do whatever he wanted and get away with it.

'Why don't we leave one of the cars here and go home together?' he suggested. 'Send Mr and Mrs C. to pick it up.'

'I can't make them drive all the way to the Valley,' Lara objected.

'Why not? They work for you.'

'Yes, but . . .'

'OK, settled. We're takin' the Jag.'

'I guess you're taking the Jag,' Nikki said drily.

'I guess we are,' Lara replied, perfectly happy to let Joey take charge.

In the parking structure, Lara got into the passenger seat of the Jaguar, while Joey sat behind the wheel. He leaned over and kissed her. 'I'm so proud of you,' he said. 'Whenever I look at you, an' realize you're mine, I can hardly believe it.'

'How about you?' she said, smiling. 'I'm proud too. You were great.'

'C'mon, I've hardly got anythin' to do.'

'What you did have was very impressive.'

'Flattery will get you the key to my dick!'

'I'll have it gold-plated,' she deadpanned.

'Show off!'

They both laughed as he steered the car out into the street.

'Y'know, I was thinking,' he said. 'After this movie's finished, we should take off – go to Bali, Tahiti, somewhere exotic.'

'I'm always too busy working.'

'I bet you've been everywhere, huh?'

'The only places I get to see are locations.'

'You wanna do it, then?'

'I'll check my schedule.'

'Lara,' he said, looking at her quizzically, 'tell the truth – before me, didja do *everythin'* by schedule?'

'As a matter of fact, yes,' she admitted sheepishly.

'Then as soon as you finish the movie, we're tearin' up your schedule, 'cause from now on it's a whole new life.'

She smiled contentedly. 'Whatever you say, Joey.'

☆ ☆ ☆

Summer met Tina at an outdoor restaurant on Sunset Plaza Drive. Tina was sitting with an attractive older woman who Summer reckoned was about the same age as her mother.

'Meet Darlene,' Tina said, introducing them. 'Darlene's cool. She organizes things.'

'Hi, Summer,' Darlene said with a pleasant smile. Her hair was dark blond and upswept, and her teeth white and even. She was expensively dressed in Chanel, and real diamonds glittered on her ears and fingers.

'Hi,' Summer responded, quite impressed with this woman's obvious sophistication.

298

'Sit down, dear,' Darlene said.

She sat in a chair next to Tina, noticing Darlene's perfect manicure and blood-red inch-long nails.

'Well, Summer,' Darlene said, 'I understand you might be interested in working for me.'

Summer glanced at Tina, who nodded reassuringly. 'It's what we talked about,' Tina reminded her. 'Y'know – the movie star thing.'

'Oh,' Summer said. 'Uh . . . yes.'

'It so happens,' Darlene said smoothly, 'that there's an extremely handsome young movie star who'd love to meet you.'

Talk about things moving fast! 'There is?'

'Are you interested?'

She had absolutely nothing to lose, and money and freedom to gain. 'Sure,' she said quickly.

Darlene licked her generous lips. 'How does five hundred dollars in cash sound to you?'

Summer couldn't believe this was happening to her. 'Uh . . . amazing,' she managed.

'Just one thing,' Darlene said. 'You're not a virgin, are you? You do know how to look after yourself?'

No, I am not a virgin on account of the fact that my dear daddy has been screwing me since I was ten.

'Yes, I know how to look after myself,' she said, thinking that a condom and a joint would get her through any tricky situation.

'Tomorrow night,' Darlene said, getting up from the table. 'I'll set it up. Tina will give you the details.' She nodded approvingly at Tina. 'You were right, dear. Summer's quite lovely.' And with that she walked over to a chauffeured Mercedes waiting kerbside, got inside, and the car slid off.

'Wow!' Summer exclaimed. 'Who is she?'

'Isn't she great?' Tina said admiringly. 'I want to be her one day. You should see her house!'

'Where did you meet her?' Summer asked, swiping a slice of pizza from Tina's plate.

'Around,' Tina said vaguely. 'I was doing a modelling job and one of the other models introduced us. Darlene's primo. I've made tons of money with her. You can, too, only whatever you do, *don't* tell her you're only fifteen – I said you're seventeen. Remember that.'

'I *know*,' she said. What kind of idiot did Tina take her for?

'And keep this to yourself,' Tina warned. 'No telling Jed or any of the others. This is our secret.'

'I'm good at keeping secrets.'

'Knew I could trust you.'

And Summer beckoned the waiter and ordered a whole pizza for herself, because soon she was going to be rich.

Chapter Thirty-nine

 RICHARD SNAPPED his fingers at the wine waiter and requested a bottle of Chardonnay.

'I'm not drinking,' Lara said, already wishing she hadn't agreed to lunch with him.

'Come on, sweetheart,' he said persuasively. 'For old times' sake.'

'Old times' sake?' she said, irritated. 'I thought the purpose of this lunch was that you wanted to talk to me about Joey.'

'Yes, but that doesn't mean we can't enjoy ourselves while we're doing it,' he said smoothly, turning on the charm. 'A glass of wine with your ex-husband – is that such a terrible thing?'

'I have to be truthful with you, Richard,' she said, glancing across the room, 'I'd be a lot more comfortable if Nikki was here.'

'How can you say that?' he complained, giving her a hurt look. 'I was *married* to you, for Chrissakes. It's not as if we're having a secret assignation.'

'I suppose you're right,' she said, gazing blankly around the restaurant. So far she'd had a busy day. She'd taped several TV interviews for Australia, followed by an hour with a reporter from *Premiere* magazine. And now lunch with Richard. Later she'd agreed to do even more print interviews at her publicist's office, something she hated, even though she'd done so many of them it was like being on automatic pilot.

She was half tempted to excuse herself from the table, go to the phone and cancel, but then she realized she'd be letting everyone down, and publicity was important, especially as she had three upcoming movies to promote.

The truth was she had no desire to spend a couple more precious hours sitting in her publicist's office when she could be with Joey.

Ah, Joey . . . Was she thinking about him too much? Was she getting in too deep too fast?

Who knew? Who cared? She was content for the first time in ages, and that's all that mattered.

'Are you happy?' Richard asked, as if delving into her thoughts.

'Very,' she replied firmly. 'Joey's allowing me the freedom to be myself.'

He stared at her, wondering how he could ever have let this woman go. 'That's an interesting statement,' he said. 'What exactly does it mean?'

'Oh, I don't know . . .' she said vaguely. 'Shedding my inhibitions, becoming totally free.'

His eyes gleamed. 'Sexually?'

'That's really none of your business.'

'Well,' he said, leaning back in his chair. 'Since we're being so truthful, that *was* one of the reasons I found myself seeking out other women.'

'*Excuse* me?' she said, frowning.

'Don't get me wrong,' he said, afraid he'd overstepped her tolerance level. 'But, sweetheart, you have to admit – you were never exactly adventurous in the bedroom. There are times a man needs more . . . . spice.'

She glared at him, her green eyes suddenly cold. What

gave her ex-husband the right to talk to her this way? If their sex life was so lousy it certainly wasn't *her* fault, *she* hadn't been the one out there screwing around. 'Y'know, Richard,' she said, her tone cool, 'I may not have been as adventurous as you might have liked, but did you ever consider that you seemed to prefer watching TV?'

Now it was his turn to do a slow burn. This was the second time he'd been told he preferred television to sex. First Nikki. Now Lara. Shit! He'd had more sex than they'd had hot dinners. 'If you want to get into reasons—' he began.

'I don't,' she interrupted, realizing the smart thing would be to make a move before they became embroiled in a real fight. 'This lunch was a mistake,' she continued, standing up. 'In fact, I'm leaving while we're still talking.'

'You can't do that,' he said, standing too.

'You tricked me into coming so you could talk about our past. You know what, Richard? I think you're jealous because I've found somebody I'm in synch with.'

'That's ridiculous!' he objected.

'Joey's young and good-looking,' she said heatedly. 'We're having a great time together, and it's sticking in your gut. So don't start telling *me* I was a dud in the bedroom. Let me tell *you* something – when a woman's not good in bed, it's because the man doesn't inspire her. So . . . no more cosy little lunches for two. Let's stay friends and out of each other's business, OK, Richard?'

And before he had a chance to reply, she was on her way to the door.

She stood outside trying to compose herself. How dare he criticize her performance in bed. Joey certainly had no complaints.

A hovering photographer began taking shots, which always made her nervous. As soon as the valet brought her car, she took off, realizing that she now had an hour to waste before going to her publicist's office. Not enough time to go home, so, after driving over the hill, she stopped at Neiman Marcus, indulging in some mindless shopping.

The attention she received from customers and sales people alike was stifling – one of the drawbacks of having a famous face. She smiled politely and signed a few autographs before reclaiming her car and heading over to her publicist's early, startling several assistants who couldn't do enough for her.

Linden, her publicist, a handsome black man in his early forties, was delighted to see her. 'How's my favourite client?' he asked, kissing her on both cheeks.

'Tired,' she replied, suppressing a yawn.

'You sure don't look it,' he said cheerfully.

Linden was a former stuntman who'd lost an arm in a stunt gone wrong on one of Lara's early movies. She'd helped him make the best of a bad situation by investing in the publicity firm he put together, and becoming his first client. Now, six years later, he was extremely successful and well liked in the business. He often told her he owed it all to her. She laughed, and refused to take credit.

'You're always so sweet, Linden,' she said.

'I try to please my clients at all times,' he replied with a smile.

'You certainly do that.'

Linden settled her in a private office and she called home. Mrs Crenshaw informed her Joey was out.

She didn't want him to be out. She wanted to talk to him, tell him she missed him and couldn't wait to be in his arms.

Last night he'd made love to her in the games room – bent her over the pool table, lifted her skirt and taken her just like that. It had been incredibly erotic.

Joey was never predictable sexually. Sometimes he made

her feel like a whore and sometimes the perfect lady. The combination was dangerously addictive.

Merely thinking about him caused her a shudder of excitement.

She smiled. Joey always put a smile on her face, and that's exactly the way she liked it.

☆　☆　☆

'Thanks for seein' me, I appreciate it,' Joey said.

As if I had a choice, Quinn Lattimore thought sourly, running a hand through his dyed hair as he regarded Joey through suspicious eyes and asked too many questions.

Joey kept it vague as Quinn pressed for more information. 'I'm startin' fresh,' he explained.

I bet you are, Quinn thought, trying to figure out what was going on with Lara lately. First she'd insisted on making this cheapo movie *Revenge*. Now she'd gotten her boyfriend a part in it, and the capper was she expected *him*, Quinn Lattimore, to represent this unknown actor, even though she knew he was obsessively fussy about the people he took on, turning down good-looking actors every day. And Joey was a cagey one, refusing to reveal anything about his past, including what agent had represented him in New York. Quinn found this highly suspect.

He sat back, checking Joey out. He had to admit that the young man *was* extremely handsome, but who knew if he had talent?

'You'll need to get some new head shots,' he said, tapping his stubby fingers on the desk. 'I suggest you go to Greg Gorman – he's the best photographer around for men. Not cheap, but definitely worth the investment.'

'How much is not cheap?' Joey asked casually.

'Have Lara call him,' Quinn said. 'Greg loves her. Maybe she can cut you a deal.'

Who doesn't love Lara? Joey thought. 'Listen, Mr Lattimore,' he said slowly. 'You should know I'm very fond of Lara.'

'I'm sure you are,' Quinn said.

'I'm plannin' on lookin' after her,' Joey added, staring at him intently.

'Does she *need* looking after?' Quinn asked, raising a cynical eyebrow.

'*I* believe so,' Joey said, wondering how much commission this fat cat had made out of her. 'Sometimes people are inclined to take advantage of a woman on her own – 'specially a famous woman.'

'*I* advised her not to do *Revenge*,' Quinn said pompously. 'I insisted she take a well-deserved break, but you know Lara – she's stubborn, wouldn't listen.'

'She's pushin' herself too hard,' Joey said. 'If I'd been with her I wouldn't have allowed her to do it. It's too tough a role. Plus it goes against her image big-time.'

Quinn decided it might be prudent to get Joey on his side. Better to be friends with the man who was in bed with his most successful client rather than enemies. 'Joey,' he said, warming up considerably, 'I'll get you what I can for *Revenge*, only I should warn you – they have a non-existent budget.'

'Yeah,' Joey said, standing up. 'Lara mentioned it.'

'Good. Because I wouldn't want to disappoint you.'

Joey nodded, at least Quinn was a straight shooter. 'I'll look into those head shots you mentioned.'

'The sooner the better,' Quinn said.

Joey left the office on Sunset Boulevard, and walked around the corner to Lara's car. A group of musicians were unloading their equipment outside a rock club. An outstandingly pretty girl in a skimpy outfit sat on one of the speakers, casually filing her nails. She glanced up as Joey passed, smiling invitingly. 'Hi,' she said.

'How ya doin'?' he responded, hardly noticing her.

'Wouldn't mind a coffee,' she said, all stoned eyes and exposed pink flesh.

Once he would have taken her up on her invitation, but now he had no intention of doing so. He'd finally discovered the woman he'd been searching for all his life, and no way was he screwing it up.

☆ ☆ ☆

Nikki sat behind her desk trying to get her head straight. Richard was behaving like a horse's ass, and she didn't know what to do. He was a big success, he had his own movie coming out – *French Summer*, which was going to garner nothing but great reviews and mega attention – and yet he seemed to be jealous of her modest film.

It didn't make sense. Last night they'd barely spoken again. Truth was he resented Lara appearing in *Revenge*. Well, too bad, she hadn't *forced* her to say yes. Lara was free to make her own choices, including Joey – whom Richard hated.

It startled Nikki that he was so concerned. She wanted to remind him that Lara was his ex-wife, and it was about time he let go.

A production assistant stopped by with a stack of memos. Nikki riffled through them, placed them on her desk, then picked up the phone and called Sheldon in Chicago, a task she'd been putting off.

'How are you, Nikki?' Sheldon asked in that supercilious tone she remembered so well and loathed so much.

'Fine,' she replied, waiting to see if he mentioned Summer first. He didn't. 'Nice vacation?' she asked, merely being polite.

'Pleasant,' he replied.

A short silence. Nikki broke it. 'Uh . . . Sheldon,' she said, plunging in, 'I'm calling to discuss Summer.'

'What about her?'

'She wants to go to school in LA.'

'Why?' he asked sharply.

'She likes it here.'

'I certainly hope you haven't been allowing her to run riot,' he said sternly.

'You know your daughter, she's hardly the easiest girl in the world to keep tabs on. Besides, she told me you never gave her a curfew.'

'Surely you didn't fall for that?'

How she hated speaking to Sheldon, it brought back every bad memory from her past. 'So – what do you think?' she asked breezily. 'Is it a good idea or not?'

There was a long silence while Sheldon thought it over. 'Are you available to spend plenty of time with her?' he asked at last.

'Actually, right now I'm producing a movie,' she said, wondering how he'd take *that* piece of news.

He snorted derisively. '*You're* producing?'

'Is that so strange?' she said, immediately defensive.

'What experience do *you* have?'

'Enough, thank you.'

'No,' he said, abruptly. 'It's not a good idea. I want her home as soon as possible.'

'I'll tell her that's how you feel.'

'Do that.'

'She'll be disappointed.'

'I don't particularly care.'

No. Of course he didn't. Sheldon was as cold as a dead shark, with about as much personality.

'OK,' Nikki said slowly. 'Maybe when the time comes for her to go to college, we can consider her moving here then. She could attend UCLA or USC, both excellent choices.'

'That decision is *mine*, Nikki.'

'No,' she said heatedly, 'it's mine, too. We're both her parents.'

'You gave up that right when you left her with me.'

Fuck you, Sheldon. Who do you think you're talking to? The naive little girl you married? I'm a big girl now. I can stand up for myself.

'If you remember,' Nikki said, her voice a flat monotone, 'you *insisted* she stay with you. And you made her feel so guilty that she told me it's what she wanted.'

A cold laugh. 'Ah . . . Nikki, Nikki, you always were adept at making excuses.'

The old familiar anger began to overwhelm her. 'How's your child bride?' she asked bitchily.

'That's right,' he said calmly. 'Try and get at me that way.' A brief pause. 'The truth is, my dear, it won't work. I've told you before – you're damaged, you need help.'

'Oh, screw you!' she shouted, suddenly snapping. 'You're *still* an asshole!' And she slammed down the phone, furious she'd allowed him to goad her.

Now she was stuck with the job of telling Summer she couldn't stay. Of course, if she was truthful, she knew it was for the best, considering she had neither the time nor the inclination to watch over her. Summer was better off with her father – even if he *was* major prick of the year.

For a brief moment she was tempted to call him back and tell him that. Sheldon, with his shock of thick white hair of which he was so proud; his smug expression; his perfectly capped teeth; and his small dick.

She couldn't help a vindictive smile when she recalled his tiny member. Sheldon was a big man everywhere except in the one place it really mattered. A psychiatrist with a small dick problem. Not the perfect combination. It forever pissed him off, which is why he went for young inexperienced girls who had nothing to compare it with.

She sighed. Sheldon and his small dick were part of her past, she'd moved on long ago. So why did he still bug her?

There was a tap on her office door and Aiden Sean wandered in looking like he'd just staggered out of bed – which he probably had.

'What's up?' she asked.

'You've got that tense face on,' he said, flexing a skinny arm.

'Me, tense?' she said lightly. 'Why would you say that?'

'I got a feelin' for emotions.'

'Can I help you?' she asked, determined not to fall into his *let's get intimate* trap, because she instinctively knew he wanted to get closer.

'Yeah. I need a coupla changes in the script. Wanna talk t'you about it before I go t'Mick. He can be an uptight bitch 'bout changin' stuff.'

'In other words, you'd like me on your side?'

'Why not? You're the boss.'

She grinned, forgetting about Sheldon and Richard and all her problems. 'Flattery will garner you my full attention.'

He nodded, like he'd known that all along. 'Let's get a drink,' he said. 'You look like you could use one.'

'I do?'

'Yes, boss-lady.'

She looked at him sceptically. 'How come you always treat me like I'm a hundred and two?'

He shrugged. 'Maybe I like t'bug you.'

'Why?'

''Cause you're so easy.'

She shook her head ruefully. 'Thanks.'

'OK, Nikki. Are we goin' for a drink or not?'

'You sure you're supposed to drink?'

He laughed drily. 'I was a druggie, not an alcoholic.'

'Well . . . I guess I could use a glass of wine.'

'Big boozer, huh?'

She ignored his remark and picked up her purse. It was past six, she should be heading home – but for what? To have another fight with Richard? She needed his support, not his constant criticism.

Besides, if Aiden wished to discuss the script it was her duty as the producer to be there for him.

Chapter Forty

 JOEY WAS lying on the couch in the den, watching sports on TV, when Lara arrived home. Laid out on the coffee table in front of him was a bowl of caramel popcorn and a plate of freshly baked cookies.

'I see Mrs Crenshaw is looking after you,' she said, pleased that he seemed to be settling in so comfortably.

He barely looked up. 'I got her under my voodoo spell,' he said, casually tossing a handful of popcorn into his mouth.

'They're all under your spell,' she replied, lightly touching his cheek. 'Women adore you, and you love it.'

'Whatever you say,' he said, eyes fixed firmly on the TV.

She wished he'd shut off the television and pay her some attention, she wasn't used to being treated in such a cavalier fashion. 'So,' she said, perching on the edge of the couch. 'Tell me what happened with you and Quinn.'

'Nothin' much,' he answered vaguely.

'Will he negotiate for you?'

'You told him to, didn't you?'

'Yes.'

'Well,' he said, a slight edge to his tone, 'when Miz Ivory tells people to do things – they do 'em. Right?'

She paused for a moment before saying— 'Aren't you pleased?'

'I dunno,' he said moodily. 'Sometimes I think I shouldn't be askin' you t'do stuff for me. You got me *Revenge*, then you got me your agent . . .'

'Joey,' she said softly, 'I can only open the door. Once you're in, you have to prove yourself.'

'Yeah,' he said, laughing sardonically. 'Like they're gonna fire me if I don't deliver. There's no way they'd risk pissin' you off.'

'I didn't get you *The Dreamer*,' she pointed out. 'You did that by yourself.'

'Yeah, clever me,' he mumbled.

'Is something the matter?' she asked, treading carefully around his bad mood.

'I'm feelin' kinda down tonight,' he admitted, finally giving her his full attention, even though he didn't bother lowering the sound on the TV.

'Why?'

''Cause you deserted me today.'

'Joey,' she explained, sure he must be joking, 'I had to do publicity. I've got two movies coming out soon.'

'I know, I know . . .' A long beat. 'Truth is I'm feelin' kinda homesick.'

'Homesick?' she said, frowning.

'I miss the New York street action. I don't know anybody in LA.'

'I can introduce you to people.'

He gave an ironic laugh. 'Oh, yeah – like the people you'd introduce me to are gonna be interested in meetin' me.'

She decided this conversation was not taking a good turn. 'What do you want to do tonight?' she asked, changing the subject. 'We could go out, stay in – whatever you like.'

'What do *you* wanna do?' he said, turning the question around so that it was she who had to make the decision.

'I don't mind,' she replied.

'Then maybe I'll watch the end of the ball game,' he said, turning back to the television.

Was he dismissing her? She couldn't believe that she'd been thinking about him all day, and now that she was home, he was behaving this way toward her. 'Are you saying you want to be alone?' she said, trying not to sound upset.

'Is that OK with you?'

'Fine,' she said, 'I'll see you later.'

She hurried upstairs to her bedroom. They'd hardly been together ten minutes and all of a sudden he was pulling this moody stuff on her. Was it something she'd done? Had she offended him in some way?

How *could* she have offended him? As he'd pointed out, she'd gotten him an interview with her agent, a job in her movie. What else was she supposed to do?

Maybe it hadn't been such a good idea suggesting he stay at her house, a hotel might have been better.

For a moment her eyes filled with tears. She'd so wanted this to turn out to be something good, now she wasn't so sure.

She went into her bathroom, stopping in front of the mirror and staring at her reflection. Lara Ivory. Beautiful movie star. The woman who could have anyone. Yeah. Sure.

And the real truth is – Lara Ann Miller – you know who she is – the kid who watched her father butcher her mother and brother – then sat back while he blew his brains out.

Some nice little girl.

Some ugly little slut.

Dammit! She wasn't about to start feeling sorry for herself.

She went back into the bedroom, buzzed the kitchen and reached Mrs Crenshaw. 'Where are the dogs?' she asked.

'Mr Joey said they'd be better off spending more time outside in the dog run,' Mrs Crenshaw replied.

'Oh, he did, did he? Well, kindly let them back into the house right now.'

'Certainly, Miss Ivory.'

He'd told her he loved dogs, now he was banishing them outside the house. What was going on?

She was tempted to go down and confront him. But what if he split? What if he said, 'OK, this isn't working out, goodbye.' Was she ready for that?

No. She wasn't prepared to give up on this relationship. Not yet anyway. They were still getting to know each other – she had to give it time.

☆ ☆ ☆

Nikki and Aiden drove to the Chateau Marmont in her car. Aiden shut his eyes and slept all the way. *Hmm*, Nikki thought, *he's certainly not into being polite*. 'Wakey, wakey,' she said drily when they arrived.

'I'm beat,' he said, rubbing his eyes. 'Takes a crap-load of energy doin' nothing. Can't wait to start work.'

They sat at a small table. Aiden ordered his usual Jack Daniel's. She went for a glass of red wine. He lit up a cigarette, blowing a stream of smoke into her face. She coughed, clearing the air with her hands.

'Sorry,' he mumbled, not looking sorry at all.

'So,' she said, all business. 'What's your problem with the script?'

'It sucks.'

'Excuse me?'

'I wanna change my dialogue – do a rewrite, an' get compensated.'

'I presume you're joking.'

He dragged on his cigarette. 'Deadly serious.'

315

'Not possible, Aiden. We start shooting in a few days, no time for rewrites. Plus, everyone else is perfectly happy with the script.'

'It's corny shit.'

Now he was starting to aggravate her; *Revenge* was a great script. 'Then why did you accept the part?' she asked coldly.

He gave a mirthless laugh. 'Only game goin' on. I'm trouble – didn'tcha know?'

Fortunately she was used to dealing with actors, they were all insecure – this one more than most. 'Listen to me,' she said, as calmly as she could manage. 'Mick hired you. He promised me you were in good shape, now you're coming to me with this.'

'I'm fuckin' bored,' Aiden said, ice-grey eyes restlessly scanning the room. 'I'm fuckin' bored with everyone tellin' me what I can do an' what I can't. Right now I wanna get laid. You into fast sex?'

Why had she agreed to have a drink with him? Rule one for producers – stay away from actors. 'You're nuts,' she said, shaking her head.

'Bin told that many times. Wanna fuck or not?'

'Not,' she said, briskly rising from the table. 'I have to get home.'

'Hubby waitin' patiently?'

'What's it to you?'

'You're too young to set up house with such an old cocker.'

'Why don't you concentrate on getting your act together and leave me alone?'

''Cause I like you.'

'Really,' she said, feigning uninterest, although if she was truthful, she had to admit he did intrigue her.

'Somethin' about you,' he added, with a sly grin.

'It's not reciprocal,' she said sternly.

'Big word.'

She sighed. 'Go home, Aiden. That's what I'm doing.'

'What's it like living with someone twenty years older than you?' he asked, not finished with her yet.

What made him think he had the right to get into her business?

'No accounting for taste,' she said tartly. 'Didn't you tell me you had a fifteen-year-old giving you head the other day? Let me see – you're thirty-four – that would make her nineteen years younger than you. She's probably never heard of Bruce Springsteen. Doesn't that make you feel *ancient*?'

He laughed bitterly. 'You've got it wrong. Mick was the guy with the fifteen-year-old. Not me. I'm not into juveniles.'

'Of course not,' she said disbelievingly.

He took another gulp of Jack Daniel's. 'Then I guess you're not gonna help me do somethin' about the script?'

'Take it up with Mick. He's the creative genius.'

'I'd still like to fuck you.'

'Wow – Aiden, you're such a romantic! Your girlfriends must faint with pleasure.'

'What girlfriends?' he said sourly. 'I don't have any.'

'How about the fifteen-year-old?'

'Aren't you *listening* to me?' he said, burnt-out eyes watching her closely. 'It was *Mick*. 'Sides, she's major trouble.'

'Not to mention under-age,' Nikki said crisply. 'Aren't you *embarrassed*?'

'Aren't you?' he snapped back.

'Excuse me?'

'She's *your* daughter.' The words were out before he could stop himself.

There was a moment of deathly silence. The colour

drained from Nikki's face and she sat down abruptly. 'What?' she said blankly, thinking that there was no way he could be telling the truth.

'Shit! I shouldn't've told you,' he muttered, taking another swig of his drink. 'Mick had no clue she was your kid. He told me she came on like a seasoned groupie – you know, the kind you trip over in this town. When he saw her at your house, he had a shit fit.'

'Oh, God!' Nikki said, suddenly feeling sick.

'Later she turns up at my apartment, an' starts tellin' me that if I don't screw her, she'll go to her dad and he'll have me arrested 'cause of her being under-age an' all. This is bad for my karma, Nikki. I'm tryin' to keep it together, which ain't easy – so do everyone a big favour an' warn her off.'

'Did you . . . sleep with her?' Nikki asked, her mouth dry with the anticipation of his reply.

'Who, me?' he said indignantly. 'No way. She's a fucked-up kid who's way out of her league. You'd better do something about her.'

For once Nikki wished that Sheldon was there to share this enormous problem.

'I don't understand,' she said wearily. 'Why are you telling me this?'

'Didn't mean to. 'Sides, if I was gonna fuck anyone in your family – it'd be you.'

'You're disgusting!' she said angrily.

'No – *I'm* honest,' he said, watching her closely. 'How about you?'

Her heart was beating fast. Stress, stress, stress. She was too young to feel like this. What should she do?

She stood up, determined to gain control of the situation. 'Consider it taken care of, Aiden,' she said, as coolly as she could manage. 'And I'd appreciate it if you didn't mention this to anyone. Including Mick. I'll deal with it in my own way.'

'You got it,' he said, draining his glass.

She hurried from the hotel and waited impatiently for the valet to bring her car around.

Who could she turn to? Sheldon or Richard? Or maybe it was best to leave them both out of it and handle it herself.

Yes, she decided, that's what she'd do, deal with it herself.

☆ ☆ ☆

Lara was asleep, tossing restlessly, dreaming of the sea enveloping her, flooding her house, taking away everything. She cried out in her sleep, waking abruptly, covered in a thin film of sweat.

She lay very still for a moment, the heavy darkness wrapped around her. Her breathing was heavy – too heavy. With a sudden start she realized she was not alone. Seated in a chair next to the bed was Joey. She sat up, clutching the sheet to her chest. 'God!' she exclaimed. 'You scared me.'

'Maybe you should lock your door,' he said.

'Maybe *you* shouldn't sneak around,' she retorted, trying to take a peek at the clock on her bedside table.

'It's two a.m.,' he said obligingly.

For a moment she was afraid, perhaps Richard and Nikki were right to be concerned about Joey. What *did* she know about him? Exactly nothing. They'd had great sex for a few weeks, but tonight she'd encountered a stranger sitting in front of her TV, casually ignoring her. And now that stranger was in her bedroom and he was making her very nervous.

'What do you want, Joey?' she asked, keeping her tone even and noncommittal.

'We gotta talk.'

'Now?'

'I can't do this, Lara,' he said, speaking fast and low. 'Can't go for any kind of commitment. You're too nice for me . . . I wanna be here for you, but I'm not sure I can make you happy.'

'Joey, you *are* making me happy.'

'I could blow it at any time. That's me. I'm selfish, want my own way – I'm not into this relationship thing, it's too tough.'

'Are you saying you want to leave?'

'Dunno,' he muttered.

'Joey,' she murmured softly, understanding that he was frightened of commitment and not afraid to voice his fears. After all, he was coming out of a broken relationship and what had happened between them had taken place so fast – a lightning connection that was enough to frighten anyone. 'I understand, I really do. We're *both* confused by what's happened between us.'

'It's not like I don't *wanna* be here for you,' he said. 'Trouble is there's nothin' I can give you that you don't already have.'

'Yes, there is,' she whispered.

'What?'

'You. I want you.'

'You got me. You got me all the way,' he said, burying his head on her shoulder, snuggling against her like a little kid seeking solace.

She stroked his thick dark hair, holding him close, and it was at that moment she realized she loved him. Not a sexual moment. Not a having fun moment. Just a pure connection that made her melt inside.

'Get into bed,' she said serenely, quite sure they belonged together.

'You sure you *want* me to stay?'

320

This was a different Joey, vulnerable and insecure. 'Yes,' she said, loving him all the more.

And he got into bed, and they held each other, and after a while they fell asleep in each other's arms, perfectly content.

Lara knew she'd finally found the happiness she'd been searching for all her life.

I CALL them the drug days. Although truth is I should call them the drug years, because time passed so quickly and I had no idea what was going on.

Drugs took over my life. Drugs were the only reason to get up in the morning. Drugs ruled.

I bought myself a shack on Zuma with the money I'd made from the action movies, and moved to the beach. Since I'd stopped working, the money didn't last long, so I hooked up with Christel, a beautiful swimsuit model who was also into the drug scene, and was not averse to performing a little extra money action on the side.

My life had gone around in a circle. But I didn't care. I didn't care about anything.

After a while the usual happened, Christel got fed up with supporting me and told me that I had to throw some money into the pot or she was gone. I was bloated and out of shape, couldn't get a job acting. Didn't want to anyway – who needed to work? Somehow I'd lost all ambition to be a movie star. The dream was gone.

One of my dealers sold me a gun. 'You need protection, man,' he told me. 'These are dangerous times.'

I liked the gun. It was my faithful companion when nobody else cared. It never answered back, and was always there when I needed comfort. I slept with it under my pillow, fully loaded.

This totally freaked Christel, who imagined it might go off one night and pierce one of her very expensive silicon breasts. She got on my case so often that I used to take it out and point it at her simply to piss her off.

Hey – when you're stoned out of your head you do strange things.

Eventually, Christel left me. Bitch! When you get right down to it, they're all bitches.

So there I was, a drugged-out beach-bum with no money, and boy, I needed money badly because I couldn't get through the day without a little help from my pharmaceutical friends.

Then I remembered Hadley. She owed me, because she was the cunt who'd gotten me fired.

Hadley lived in a mansion at the top of Angelo Drive, bought for her by her gangster boyfriend who resided in New York with his plump Sicilian wife.

I drove up there one night with good intentions. All I wanted was to borrow a couple of thousand until I got it together again.

There was nobody home except Hadley. Her boyfriend wouldn't let her have live-in servants on account of the fact that he didn't want anybody proving he stayed there when he was in town.

She answered the door herself, staring at me like she was seeing a ghost.

'Yeah, I know,' I said. 'It's been a coupla years. I don't look so hot, right?'

'You look like dog shit,' she said flatly. 'What do you want?'

'Missed you, too,' I said, not pleased with her snotty attitude.

'You're stoned,' she said in a disgusted voice.

'Does that mean you won't lend me money?'

'Get the fuck out of here,' she snapped.

A woman telling me to get the fuck out. Me! I couldn't believe it. Usually they were begging me to stay.

'Do you wanna repeat that?' I said belligerently.

'You heard me,' she said.

Enough was enough. I took out my gun, pointing it straight at her.

She went very pale and stepped back into the house, reaching for a conveniently placed panic button.

Not convenient enough. Quick as a flash I slapped her arm away and burst into the house.

She began to kick and struggle, somehow or other jogging my trigger finger. Anyway, I think that's what happened. The gun went off, blowing a gaping hole in her chest that seemed bigger than China. She fell like a fucking stone.

Jesus! Whatever else happens to me I'll never forget that moment. I was totally high, but even through the fog – I realized what I'd done.

I turned and ran from the house like a maniac – sweat pouring down my face.

Halfway along the driveway I remembered I'd touched the door handle, so I raced back, taking off my shirt and wiping off the handle – the only thing I could recall touching. Then I made it to my car and somehow or other drove to the beach.

Hadley's murder made the second page of the LA Times. Even in death she wasn't a star.

There was nothing to connect me to her, but just in case, I took off for Mexico where I spent the next couple of years drying out. It was the start of a new beginning.

Chapter Forty-one

 KIMBERLY HAD to go. She was becoming a total whiner, and Richard didn't care to be reminded of his cheating nature every time he glanced in her direction. He'd slept with her no more than four or five times, now she wanted more. 'When are you telling Nikki?' she kept on nagging.

Telling Nikki? Was she insane!

Why did women have to place so much importance on sex? Casual sex was exactly that, and they should get with the programme and understand.

But how to get rid of her without a sexual harassment suit? Kimberly was the type who wouldn't think twice about trying to ruin a man's career.

The truth was he should have stayed married to Lara. She was beautiful, undemanding, and most of all, truly nice. But no, he'd had to screw that up too – systematically fucking his way through each year of marriage with a variety of different women.

What a jerk he'd been. He would never forget the look on Lara's face when she'd caught the make-up girl giving him head in his trailer. Her face had turned to stone. 'I want a divorce,' she'd said, and after that there was no going back.

With Nikki he'd managed to stay faithful for almost two

years. Now Kimberly and her chewable nipples were giving him a hard time.

'I'd love to visit your house again,' Kimberly said, sneaking up behind him as he stood by the window in his office. 'Can I?'

'It's not possible,' he said, furious she would even ask. 'Nikki's in town.'

'When are you telling her?' Kimberly demanded, like she had a right to know.

'I'll get around to it,' he lied.

And so the dance continued.

As Nikki drew up outside the house in Malibu, she noticed that Richard's Mercedes was not in his parking space, even though it was nearly nine. He'd probably gotten fed up with waiting for her and popped out for something to eat. She knew she should've called, but, quite frankly, he was the last person on her mind.

All the way home she'd been thinking about Aiden and the things he'd said. It didn't seem possible Summer could behave in such a way, and yet, why not? *She's my daughter,* Nikki thought, *and I was just as adventurous at her age. In fact, I married Sheldon at sixteen because he knocked me up.*

Like mother like daughter.

Oh, God! What was she going to do?

Send her back to Chicago, that's what. But first – even though she was dreading it, she had to accept her responsibility and talk to her. A mother–daughter talk was way overdue.

Summer was due to rendezvous with Tina at the same open-air restaurant on Sunset Plaza they'd met at before. Earlier in the day they'd gone shopping on Melrose, and Tina had loaned her the money to buy a short purple tank dress – very sexy – and some high wedgie sandals. After their shopping jaunt she'd rushed back to the beach to work on her tan.

Things were looking up, as long as she could avoid going back to Chicago and the all-encompassing arms of her father, she'd be happy.

Just before she left to meet Tina again, Richard arrived home. 'Where are *you* going, all dressed up?' he asked with an indulgent smile.

'Another party,' she replied, surreptitiously tugging at her short dress, which barely covered the tops of her golden thighs.

'I thought you'd be partied out by now,' he remarked, fixing himself a vodka on the rocks.

'Oh, Richard,' she said, gazing at him wistfully, big blue eyes drawing him in. 'I wish I could stay here for ever. You promised to talk Mom into letting me stay. *Please* do it, Richard. *Please.*'

'I'm trying,' he said, digging into his pants pocket and handing her fifty dollars. 'You'll need this for cabs.'

'Thanks!' she said gratefully.

Richard was so easy, especially now she had something on him. Of course, she didn't blame him for making out with his assistant while Nikki was away. She'd often wondered what he saw in her stupid mother anyway. OK, so Nikki was pretty, but she was also dumb. She *must've* been dumb to have left her with Sheldon in Chicago. Didn't she realize what a sicko pervert he was?

Whenever Summer thought about her mother she conveniently forgot the screaming fits she'd thrown – insisting she was happier with her father and would kill herself if Nikki didn't let her live with him. Those were distant memories she didn't care to revisit.

At the restaurant, Tina was already sitting at a table looking pleased with herself. 'Park your butt,' she said, patting the chair next to her. 'I've a shitload of stuff to tell you.'

'What?' Summer asked, adjusting her Guess sunglasses, which she'd purchased that afternoon.

'Darlene told me this movie star dude wants to meet *both* of us,' Tina said excitedly. 'How way out is that?'

'*Both* of us?' Summer questioned.

'You know,' Tina said, giggling knowingly. 'For fun. We're on our way to making megabucks, sister!'

The waiter came over. Summer couldn't help checking him out. He was typical LA, with long blond hair and a surfer's body. Another out of work actor waiting to be discovered, she thought. LA was full of them. That's what made it such an awesome place!

She ordered pizza and a milkshake, because she hadn't eaten all day and felt quite light-headed, while Tina went for an iced coffee.

'Will he take us out?' she asked, imagining a night at the Viper Room or some other happening club.

Tina screwed up her nose. 'You're a bit naive, aren't you?'

'I'm not naive,' she said flatly. 'I've done things you so wouldn't even dream about.'

'Then there's no problem,' Tina said, waving at a guy in a passing Ferrari. 'It'll be the two of us and him.'

Summer frowned. 'I don't get it.'

'Oh, *c'mon*,' said Tina, a touch scornful. 'Haven't you ever done it with a girl before? That's what all these guys are into – watching two girls together. Especially two *young* innocents like us. Ha! If they only knew!'

'You mean like . . . sex?' Summer asked hesitantly.

'Why are you even thinking about it?' Tina said irritably.

'You would've done it for nothing with that sleazy dog Aiden Sean, so what's the big deal?'

'At least I knew *him*.'

'So you'll know this other guy soon.'

'Who is he anyway?'

'Dunno, but Darlene said he's a major babe. And trust me, she knows major babes.'

The waiter delivered their order.

'The guys are gonna *love* us!' Tina said, giggling again. 'And it's not like you'll be doing anything you wouldn't do with a date. 'Cept this way you get paid, and you get a lot more respect.'

'How come?' Summer asked, slurping her milkshake.

''Cause they're *paying* for it, dummy. They know you're a pro.'

For a moment Summer thought about the road she was about to embark on. Sex with a stranger for money. Wouldn't that make her a prostitute?

No. Prostitutes cruised Sunset giving blow jobs to people like Hugh Grant in the back of cars. Prostitutes were cheap bimbos in vinyl boots and fake leopardskin miniskirts with bad hair.

'What time are we meeting him?' she asked, feeling excited and apprehensive all at the same time.

'Chill,' Tina said, sipping her iced coffee. 'We don't have to be at his hotel until nine. I'm psyched, aren't you?'

'You bet!' said Summer, not quite sure *how* she felt.

☆　☆　☆

No Richard to aggravate her. No Summer to drive her crazy. Neither of them were home.

Nikki didn't know what to do. Should she call Sheldon? It was past midnight in Chicago and he probably wouldn't appreciate a late-night phone call. Anyway, she could just imagine the conversation. *Hi, Sheldon. I'm sorry to tell you that your little golden girl has been going around giving out blow jobs. What shall we do about it?*

Of course Sheldon would blame her. *Why do you think I never allowed her to live with you*? he'd say. *It's your bad influence, Nikki. She learns from you.*

No, telling him would only complicate matters.

Why did this have to happen just as she was about to commence the biggest career move of her life? Producing a movie was not an easy job, she'd need every ounce of concentration she could muster to make sure it didn't get away from her – especially with a wild card like Mick Stefan directing, and an even wilder card like Aiden Sean starring.

Another thought occurred to her. Should she fire Mick before it was too late? Because once they started shooting it would be impossible.

No. Firing him now would create problems too big to contemplate. Much as she dreaded facing him – the movie had to go on. After all, it wasn't as if he'd *known* Summer was her daughter.

Oh, God! Decisions, decisions – maybe she should dump the whole thing on Richard and see what solution he came up with.

But Richard wasn't around. He hadn't even left a note saying where he'd gone.

She thought about calling Lara, then changed her mind. Now that Lara was with Joey, she wasn't as available as she used to be. Anyway, it wasn't fair to burden her with this.

Making her way into Summer's room, she stood in the doorway observing chaos. Obviously the maid had given up, because all she could see was a messy jumble of clothes, CDs, spilled make-up, magazines, 7-Up cans, dirty dishes, and several dried-up slices of pizza. What a mess!

She realized it was probably her fault. She'd been sixteen when she'd given birth to Summer, and never quite reconciled herself to the fact that she had the responsibility of a young child to raise. The truth was, she'd been happy to leave Summer with Sheldon in Chicago, enabling her to go off and have a life.

And yet, deep down she'd always wanted to be there for her daughter.

Unfortunately Sheldon had never given her the opportunity.

She found a yellow legal pad and wrote on it in large bold letters with a felt-tip pen.

MEET ME IN THE KITCHEN AT 8:00 A.M.
DO NOT LEAVE THE HOUSE UNTIL WE TALK.

Then she placed the pad on the centre of Summer's unmade bed, went into the living room and fixed herself a well-needed drink.

☆ ☆ ☆

Two hours later Richard arrived home.

'Hi,' Nikki said, now on her third vodka.

'Hi,' he replied, brushing off her hug.

'Everything OK?' she said, following him into the bedroom.

'Why wouldn't it be?' he said, removing his jacket and throwing it on the bed.

'Where did you go?' she asked.

He gave her an uptight look. 'Would you care for a written report?'

'No,' she said, holding her temper. 'That won't be necessary. I merely wondered if you'd eaten.'

'Yes,' he said, leaving the bedroom and going to his study. He'd taken Kimberly to a quiet restaurant further along the beach, and she'd blown him in the car. Now he felt guilty.

Nikki trailed behind him. He'd been drinking, she could smell it all over him. She could also make out the scent of another woman's perfume.

Suddenly she knew why he was being so distant. The sonofabitch was back to his old habits – he was screwing around on her!

This was all she needed. Goddamn it! Why hadn't she seen it coming? Why had she been so blindly self-confident that she'd thought he wouldn't do to *her* what he'd done to Lara?

She waited until he was settled at his computer, then she went back into the bedroom and did something she'd sworn she'd never do – rifled through his jacket pockets.

Bingo! A packet of condoms – one missing.

Bingo! A credit card receipt – dinner for two at The Ivy.

Bingo! A handkerchief with lipstick on – not her colour.

How could she have been so stupid?

Overcome with fury, she marched back into his study. 'I want you to pack up and get out,' she said, angrily.

He looked at her like she was totally insane. 'What?'

'Bad enough that you're drinking again,' she continued, her voice rising. 'But other women? Oh, no, I don't think so.'

'Are you crazy?' he said irritably.

Her heart was pounding like a sledgehammer. 'Yes, I'm crazy,' she said vehemently. 'Crazy to have imagined you'd ever change.'

'Calm down.'

'Fuck you, Richard,' she said, waving the packet of condoms in his face. 'Fuck you for reverting to your cheating self.' And she threw the dinner receipt on his desk, hurled the incriminating handkerchief on the floor and marched to the door. 'Get out, Richard. It's over. And don't come back.'

332

Chapter Forty-two

 NORMAN BARTON opened the door of his hotel suite with a rakish grin, holding a glass of champagne in one hand and clutching a joint in the other.

Norman was puppy dog handsome, with big brown eyes, a cowlick of muddy brown hair, and a wide toothy grin. He was in his mid-twenties and not very tall.

'Evening, ladies,' he said with exaggerated politeness, and a sweeping if somewhat drunken bow. 'Enter the land of good times.'

Summer recognized him immediately. He'd starred in a family TV series, then made it big in movies. He was constantly being written about in the tabloids and fan magazines. He'd been engaged three times, and when Heidi Fleiss got busted he was one of the famous names mentioned in her little black book.

Tina nudged her. 'Told you!' she whispered triumphantly.

Inside the hotel suite stood a small, skinny Hispanic man, somewhat older than Norman. Clinging to his arm was an exceptionally tall, sour-faced brunette, clad in slinky black leather.

'Park your butts, girls,' said Norman, indicating the couch. 'And tell me your pleasure? A joint? Champagne? Or how about a little nose candy?'

'I'll take a joint,' Summer said boldly.

Norman grabbed her hand. 'Now *that's* my kind of girl,' he said, with a boyish grin. 'And pretty, too. *Veree* pretty – just the way I like 'em.'

Summer breathed a little easier. She could get through this if all she had to do was be nice to this guy. He was cuter than Aiden Sean any day, although Aiden had that dangerous edge she hankered after.

She sat down on the couch next to Tina. The Hispanic man ignored them, so did his girlfriend.

'Listen, Norman,' the Hispanic man said in a low growly voice, 'I gotta get outta here. You have my money?'

'What's your hurry?' Norman grumbled. 'You're always in such a freakin' hurry. Whyn't you stay an' join the party?'

'He don' wanna join no party,' his girlfriend said, scowling. 'We have places to go. Give him what you owe, an' let's get the fuck outta here.'

'OK, OK,' Norman said, throwing up his hands. 'Don't get in a blue funk.' He winked at Tina and Summer. 'You two sit tight while I go take care of business.' He beckoned the Hispanic man and his bad-tempered girlfriend, and the three of them vanished into the bedroom, closing the door.

'Darlene told me we've got to get paid up front,' Tina said, speaking fast. 'The guy has a house account, but Darlene says he's way behind. And after what I just heard, we'd better make *sure* we get the cash first.'

'Well, we can't just like . . . *ask* for it,' Summer said.

'Why not? Those people did.'

'Who are they?'

'How do I know?' Tina said, pulling a face. 'Probably his drug dealers or something.'

'He has drug dealers to score pot?'

'Where do *you* get it?'

'Boys on the beach. They're always so ready to give me anything I want.'

'Oh, you're such a little princess,' Tina giggled. 'It's all that blond hair, and those perky tits!'

'I've been meaning to ask,' Summer said. 'When you left home – how could you afford to?'

Tina grinned. 'Scammed five thousand bucks from my stepfather's safe. Figured he deserved to give me *something* for all the trouble he put me through. Then I took off.'

'What about your mother?'

'She didn't give a shit. She's an actress.'

'Famous?' Summer asked, surprised because Tina had never mentioned her mother before.

'Who cares,' Tina said, defiantly tossing back her curly brown hair. 'I rented an apartment, and started doing a few modelling gigs. Then I met Darlene and everything changed.'

'Didn't your mom send people looking for you?'

'Ha! The old bag was thrilled I beat it. No more competition. Besides, I was sixteen and legal.'

'Wow!' Summer exclaimed, wishing she could do the same.

'When will *you* be sixteen?' Tina asked, scooping up a handful of nuts from a dish on the table and cramming them in her mouth.

'In a couple of months,' Summer said.

'Then do it,' Tina said matter-of-factly, taking out a mirrored compact and studying her pretty face. 'In fact, you can stay with me. We'll work as a team. Guys *really* get off on baby pussy.'

'If only I could,' Summer sighed, knowing that if she vanished her father would have the whole of Chicago searching for her.

Norman re-entered the room, trailed by the Hispanic man

and his sulky girlfriend. They headed for the door. 'Next time don' make us wait,' the woman warned, slamming the door behind them.

'Bye,' Norman said, with a jaunty wave at the closed door. 'Sorry you don't wanna stay and party.'

Once they were gone, he focused his attention on the girls. 'OK, ladies,' he crowed, grabbing the champagne bottle. 'Everybody naked and in the bedroom, it's *way* past gettin' it on time!'

'Now?' Summer asked innocently.

'Yes, *now*!' Tina said, jumping up.

'We hardly know him,' Summer whispered, finally coming to the conclusion that maybe this wasn't such a good idea.

'He's over twenty-one, famous and rich,' Tina said, ever practical. 'That's all we need to know. Come on,' she added impatiently. 'Let's go do it!'

Reluctantly Summer trailed her into the bedroom.

Chapter Forty-three

 SUMMER WAS confused. Sex was supposed to be getting one over on someone else, and yet Norman was treating her so nicely. After the debasing experiences with her father, she'd always regarded sex as dirty – something you used to get your own way. But Norman wasn't like that. Norman wanted to laugh and have fun and make her feel good. Not to mention plying her with champagne.

By the time she and Tina had to do some sex stuff, she was completely giggly and drunk. And it wasn't so bad. Although being naked with another girl was kind of icky.

Norman didn't join in. He sat in a chair and watched, as if he were viewing a particularly engrossing movie.

Tina kissed her all over, which made her want to giggle even more. And then she had to do the same to Tina, which kind of grossed her out.

When it was all over she couldn't wait to wriggle back into her clothes. Then Norman took her to one side, handed her a piece of paper with his phone number on, and said, 'Call me. We can do private business. No reason we gotta go through Darlene. Right, cutie?'

'It . . . it's not for me to say,' she stammered, staring at his familiar face that she'd seen on the cover of countless magazines.

He favoured her with his famous puppy dog smile. 'You're a very sweet girl,' he said. 'Kinda special.'

'Thank you,' she said demurely.

'Make sure you call me soon,' he said.

'Oh, I will,' she said, eyes shining.

Then he ordered two cabs, and sent them both home.

She sat in the back of the cab thinking about how wonderful he was, and what a perfect life they could have together.

He was a movie star and rich. He'd be able to keep her father away from her permanently.

When she crept into the Malibu house, she spotted Nikki, asleep on a couch in the living room. Trying hard not to wake her, she tiptoed into her room, shut the door, and fell into bed with all her clothes on.

Yes, she could be Mrs Norman Barton. That would suit her nicely.

☆ ☆ ☆

Lara awoke first and rolled over into Joey's arms. He groaned in his sleep. She nuzzled against his neck, inhaling his seductive masculine smell. God! She really did love him.

He opened one eye. 'Wa's goin' on?' he muttered sleepily. 'There a fire?'

'A fire?'

'Yeah . . . got caught in one once.'

'When?'

'Oh, years ago in a . . . hotel.'

'Guess you escaped.'

'Guess I did.'

'Lucky me.'

'Lucky you.'

They both started laughing. He threw open his arms and she snuggled into them.

'Where *are* you from, Joey?' she asked, lightly stroking his chest. 'I was thinking . . . I hardly know anything about you.'

'Florida,' he answered casually. 'Parents dead. No other family. Your turn.'

'The Midwest,' she replied, revealing as little as he did. 'Parents dead. No other family.'

'Jesus!' he exclaimed. 'We really are soulmates.'

She snuggled closer. 'Joey?'

'Yes?'

'Let's make love. Let's make wild passionate love.'

'*Now?*' he said, surprised at her unexpected boldness.

'No, next week,' she deadpanned.

'OK, OK – sex maniac,' he laughed. 'Get me in the mood.'

'Not a problem,' she said – thinking that Joey was bringing out a whole new her.

'Got an idea,' he said. 'Pretend you're the maid.'

'Joey!'

'Not into role-playing, huh?' he teased.

'Well, I never . . .'

'Never *what*, Lara?' he asked, hands reaching for her breasts, tweaking her nipples, making her cry out with pleasure.

'I never did that kind of fantasy thing,' she said shyly. 'You know, role-playing and all of that. Richard wasn't into it.'

'How many men have you had?' he asked, curiously. 'Was Richard your first?'

'How many women have *you* had?' she responded.

'Let's see . . .' He pretended to think. 'Guess you must be number two thousand and one.'

'Ha!' she said, sitting up in bed, crossing her arms across her breasts. 'You *know* women love you. I see them watching you all the time.'

He rolled onto his back. 'Like guys don't watch you.'

'It's not the same.'

'You know something, beautiful? In my world there's only you.'

'Really?' she asked breathlessly.

'Yup. You're the only good thing that ever happened to me.'

'I am?'

'You am,' he said, pulling her down on top of him, then kissing her so hard she thought he'd split her lip.

She didn't care. When she was with Joey she didn't care about anything except him. He was her life, her love, and she would do anything for him.

☆ ☆ ☆

Nikki awoke at first light, feeling lousy. After throwing Richard out, she'd managed to get through half a bottle of vodka – not usually her style, but she'd been forced to do *something* to relieve the tension. And on top of everything, Summer had failed to come home.

She got up from the couch and went into Summer's room. Her daughter was buried under the covers, asleep. She marched straight over to the bed and shook her awake.

'Wa's goin' on?' Summer mumbled, flinging out her arms.

'What time did you get home last night?' Nikki demanded.

'Oh hi, Mom,' Summer said sleepily. 'Why're you waking me? Isn't it like *really* early?'

'Yes, it's *really* early,' Nikki said flatly. 'And you obviously got home *really* late. Where were you?'

'Oh, um . . . a party,' Summer said, attempting to gather her thoughts.

'Whose party?'

'Friend of mine.'

'And I thought you were with an enemy,' Nikki said sarcastically.

'Funny, Mom.'

'I don't intend to be funny,' Nikki said brusquely. 'I don't intend to be funny about anything.'

'S' what's up now?' Summer asked, sensing bad vibrations.

'Well . . .' Nikki said, struggling for the best way to put it. 'I've been told something extremely disturbing . . .'

'Like what?'

'Look, honey,' Nikki said, sitting on the edge of the bed. 'You're young and unsophisticated. People will try to take advantage of you – especially in this town. Don't live your life too fast.'

Oh, God! Her mother had found out about Norman Barton and now she was in big trouble.

'Summer,' Nikki said, taking a deep breath, 'I know what you did with Mick Stefan, and it's not right. First of all, it isn't the kind of . . . uh . . . thing you should do with anyone, unless you're . . . uh . . . married. There are diseases out there . . . not just AIDS, all kinds of other terrible things.' She paused; discussing sex with her daughter was excruciating. 'LA's a tough town,' she continued, quoting Lara. 'There's a lot of men here who are into using young girls. You're far too naive to be out on your own.'

Summer rolled her eyes. 'Mom, I'm nearly sixteen.'

'Didn't you hear what I just said? I *know* what you did with Mick Stefan.'

Summer was silent for a moment. Was getting in the back of Mick's limo *that* bad? It wasn't as if she'd done anything, but all the same she was obviously in deep trouble. 'Who told you?' she demanded, wishing she had a joint to lighten the lecture.

'It doesn't matter.'

'Was it Mick?'

'No. It wasn't.'

'Anyway, whatever he said, it's not true,' she muttered sulkily. 'Nothing happened.'

'I'd be happy if it wasn't,' Nikki said. 'But since I know it is – here's my decision. I've booked you on a noon flight home to Chicago.'

That woke Summer up in a hurry. 'No!' she shrieked, her blue eyes filling with tears of frustration. 'I can't go back there.'

'Yes, you can,' Nikki said firmly. 'And you will.'

'Why do I have to?' Summer yelled. '*Why*? Why? *Why*?'

'Because you're only fifteen, and you must finish school and do what your father tells you. Perhaps next time you visit, you'll behave in a more responsible fashion.'

'This isn't fair!' Summer shouted, jumping out of bed.

'Fair or not, that's my decision,' Nikki said, her expression grim.

Later that day, she drove Summer to the airport, personally putting her on a plane. In the evening she called Sheldon to make sure their daughter had arrived safely.

'What did you do to her while she was in LA?' Sheldon demanded, sounding pissed off. 'She looks dreadful.'

'I didn't do anything,' Nikki retorted, forcing her voice into neutral. 'You sent me a kid who was out of control.'

'Not when she left here she wasn't,' Sheldon thundered.

Nikki held her temper in check. '*I'm* not the parent figure here, Sheldon – *you* are. So it's up to you to do something about her.'

And that was that. Mission accomplished.

Her daughter was off her hands and now she could concentrate on work.

342

Chapter Forty-four

 THEY'D BEEN shooting *Revenge* for five weeks, and although Lara was tired, she was also exhilarated. It was the most exciting film she'd ever been involved with, even though Mick was insane – his manic energy dominating the set as he raced around encouraging his actors to fly – arms waving in the air, huge glasses falling off his nose. He was truly obsessed, his unbridled enthusiasm encouraging everyone to do better.

Her life was making the movie and Joey, who since the night they'd discussed commitment had been there for her all the way, a constant reassuring presence.

She loved him so much. He made everything easy, cushioning any problems, so that all she had to do was concentrate on her work.

The people who usually surrounded her were not pleased. Cassie was relegated to sitting in the office at home, unless Joey said it was OK for her to come to the set. Nikki was around, but always busy. So her only close contact was Joey.

The fact that he was in the movie was a big plus. They even had scenes together and she loved working with him. They rehearsed at home, running lines, critiquing each other, getting into it. He taught her how to handle a gun – which wasn't an easy thing for her to learn, because it dredged up so many bad memories. However, with his help she mastered it, which was good, it meant she'd be prepared for the upcoming scene where she got to shoot Aiden's character.

In return she taught him certain tricks to use in front of the camera, and all about lighting. They made love every night, and each time it got better.

Most evenings they sat up in bed, side by side, watching old movies or *Seinfeld*, sending out for food, never feeling the need to go anywhere, perfectly content. Sometimes Mrs Crenshaw cooked, and on those nights they ate outside on the patio. Other times they rode the horses along the beach, or played with the dogs.

As far as Lara was concerned, things couldn't be more idyllic. She was making a powerful movie that meant something to her, and she had a man beside her who was everything she'd ever wanted. The nightmares were becoming more and more distant. It was amazing that they'd found each other.

She awoke with a flutter in her stomach, because today they were shooting the rape scene. There was hardly any dialogue, mostly action. Mick had told her he planned on tracking the action with three cameras, so there'd be no mistakes. Still . . . she couldn't help dreading it.

Joey walked in from the bathroom in his new white terrycloth robe, his jet-black hair damp and slicked back. He sat on the edge of the bed and said, 'Maybe you should smoke a joint – take the edge off.'

'You know I don't do grass,' she admonished, thinking how handsome he looked.

'I know, babe, but trust me, you might need it today.'

'Rebecca wasn't stoned,' she said, shaking her head. 'So *I* can't be.'

He got up and went over to the window. 'I dunno if I should come to the set today,' he said moodily.

'I want you there,' she said. 'I need your support.'

'If I havta watch those assholes attackin' you, I'm liable to kill 'em,' he said, vehemently. 'Tear the fuckers to pieces.'

'Honey,' she said soothingly, 'you're so dramatic. After all, it's only acting.'

'Yeah, yeah,' he said, coming back to sit next to her. 'I still wish you didn't have to go through it.'

'That's very thoughtful,' she said quietly.

'I'm not thoughtful, but thanks anyway,' he said, holding out his arms. She fell into them, and they rolled around on the bed, lost in a tight embrace.

'There's somethin' I've been meanin' to tell you,' he mumbled, crushing her until she almost couldn't breathe. 'Somethin' important.'

'What?' she gasped, feeling so secure and content in his arms, wishing she could stay there for ever.

'You're gonna think I'm crazy.'

'I'll let you know.'

'It's somethin' I should've told you before.'

'*What?*' she asked, attempting to sit up.

'It'll sound stupid . . .'

'Will you *tell* me?' she said, exasperated.

He hesitated for a moment. 'Naw . . . can't.'

She struggled into a sitting position. 'Yes you can.'

He stared at her, dark eyes fusing with her brilliant green ones. 'OK . . . OK,' he said at last. 'Here's the deal.' A long beat. 'I guess I kinda like . . . love you.'

She caught her breath, taken by surprise. 'You kinda like *love* me?' she repeated, thrilled that he'd finally said it.

He frowned. 'Hey – I told you it'd sound stupid.'

'Joey,' she said, gently reaching up to touch his cheek, 'it's not stupid.'

'No?'

'No.'

'How come?'

345

'Because . . . since we're being truthful, I . . . I love you, too.' A long pause. 'In fact, Joey, I think I've loved you since we first met.'

He broke out in a big grin. 'No shit?'

'Joey! Please! This is supposed to be a romantic moment.'

'Hey – you wanna see romance,' he said, easing her nightgown off her shoulders, fondling her breasts until she began gasping with pleasure.

One touch and she was his.

Nikki was right, he did have her hooked sexually, only their relationship was much more than sex. It was caring and loving and being together.

They made love slowly in the traditional way, and when it was over, she stretched luxuriously, murmuring a satisfied—

'Umm . . . that was better than grass any day.'

'What would you know about grass?' he teased, tickling her stomach.

'Oh, you think I'm such a little goody-goody, don't you?' she said, half serious. 'Let me tell you – there was a time I was wild.'

'What?' he said mockingly. 'You smoked a joint once – *that* was wild?'

'Joey,' she responded quietly, 'you don't know *everything* about me.'

'Why – you got secrets?'

'Maybe . . .' she said mysteriously.

He grinned. 'I'll tell you mine if you tell me yours.'

She smiled, perfectly happy. 'Whatever you want.'

But they both knew that neither of them were prepared to share their secrets.

Not yet anyway.

☆ ☆ ☆

346

Nikki arrived at the street location in time for an early breakfast. Mick was already there, sitting at a table near the food truck, diligently working on his laptop while shovelling down a huge plate of ham and eggs.

Although she considered him a degenerate jerk, she couldn't help admiring his work ethic; he was always prepared, and totally passionate about the film.

They were both aware that today could be difficult. Yesterday she'd sent Lara flowers and a note of encouragement, because although Lara was doing a wonderful job, everyone knew today was the real test.

Nikki hadn't heard from Richard since she'd thrown him out. Something had died between them – which was probably the reason he'd reverted to his old ways. In her heart she knew it had to do with Lara and the unhealthy obsession he still harboured. It was blatantly obvious he couldn't stand his ex-wife being in a sexual relationship, so he'd turned to another woman. Ah, yes, Richard's big solution – screw your troubles away.

Ha! I should've been a shrink, she thought wryly. *Sheldon and I would finally have something in common.*

Summer was back in Chicago, which was a big relief. She'd called her a few times over the last few weeks, and they'd had several stilted conversations.

'Maybe you'll visit at Christmas,' she'd suggested.

'OK,' Summer had replied, sounding listless.

In a way Nikki was relieved to be by herself. No Richard to get in her way. No Summer to run wild. She was able to concentrate on *Revenge* and nothing else. As soon as the movie was finished she'd consider her next move. Divorce was on her mind.

'Morning, sexy,' Mick said, glancing up from his laptop. 'What's goin' on?'

'How do you feel about today?' she asked, flopping down beside him.

'Don't worry,' he said confidently. 'Lara's got it together. She'll be cool.'

'You'd better warn the actors to go easy on her,' Nikki said, frowning. 'Make sure they don't get carried away.'

'Right,' Mick replied, sarcastically. 'I'll tell 'em to make it a *gentle* freakin' rape. Is that what you'd like?'

'You know exactly what I mean,' she said irritably, hating it when Mick waxed facetious. 'I'm worried about Aiden.'

'Aiden's fuckin' ace,' Mick said, cracking his knuckles. 'Didn't I tell you he'd stay clean?'

'Yes, I must admit you did.'

'C'mon, chick-babe, lighten up. We're three-quarters through the shoot, an' not one scamoose. You should be singin' your socks off.'

'Don't tempt fate, Mick.'

'We're way ahead of schedule,' he said, letting out a crazed cackle. 'Get with the freakin' ball game an' relax.'

What an asshole!

However, he was *her* asshole. The asshole who was going to deliver one fine movie. And until that time came she had to stay on good terms with him, much as it pained her.

Producer's Rule Number One. The film comes first.

Nikki considered herself an excellent producer.

Chapter Forty-five

 THE DAY after Alison Sewell was released from jail she received a mysterious phone call. Mysterious because only the tabloid editors she'd dealt with in the past had her number. Mysterious because the man on the other end of the phone refused to identify himself.

'I have a proposition that I know will interest you,' he said.

She was lying in bed at the time, gorging on Snickers bars and watching Michelle Pfeiffer on the *Rosie O'Donnell Show*.

While she'd been locked up in jail her mother had passed away, so now she had the luxury of answering to no one. They'd let her out for the funeral. Two hours of guarded freedom. Big deal.

'Who is this?' she demanded.

'A friend,' the man replied. 'A friend who wants to do you a favour.'

Sad fact of life. She didn't have any friends. Only Lara Ivory, who'd turned out to be a Judas. And yes, Lara *would* be punished. And soon.

'What kind of favour?' she asked, reaching for the powerful whistle she kept in a bedside drawer, because if this was a dirty phone call, she'd blast this sicko's eardrum straight through his asshole.

'I know why you were in jail,' the man said. 'And in my eyes it was injustice.'

'How do you know anything about me?' she asked suspiciously.

'Let's just say we have a mutual interest.'

'What mutual interest?' she snapped.

'Are your cameras in working order?'

She lowered the sound on the TV. 'You from one of the tabs?'

'No. But I do have an assignment for you. Something you should relish.'

'What's that?'

'Let me explain . . .'

Chapter Forty-six

 HEART POUNDING wildly, Lara walked down the dimly lit street, dressed in a simple blouse and skirt, sensible shoes, hair pulled back in a ponytail. Clutching a bag of groceries to her chest, she hurried along the deserted street, leather purse slung casually over one shoulder.

She *was* Rebecca Fullerton, a schoolteacher who worked hard at a job she loved, and took care of her elderly mother with whom she lived.

The real Rebecca was on the set today. Watching. Observing. This made Lara even more nervous, painfully aware that every detail had to be right.

Suddenly she heard footsteps behind her.

Mindset Rebecca. Did she realize she was being followed? No. Was she frightened? No. The real Rebecca had said she was thinking about what she was going to cook for dinner.

Taking a deep breath, she concentrated on walking as if nothing was about to happen.

How would *she* react in a situation like this? Rebecca had fought back, fighting and clawing until her strength deserted her. Even after she'd stopped fighting, she'd been beaten repeatedly.

They'd blocked the scene out before shooting just to make sure every move was in place right up until the attack. After that Mick had told the actors they were on their own – he was going for total reality with no set dialogue. 'Improvise,' he'd informed them.

Earlier she'd sat with the real Rebecca, asking questions. 'I was fighting for survival,' Rebecca had told her quietly, her thin face impassive. 'It was surreal, almost like a dream happening in slow motion to someone else. I'll never forget it.'

Yes. Lara could understand that.

They were working on a dusty street in the seedy part of town. Beyond the lights and cameras, onlookers and fans were cordoned off behind police lines. Mick had wanted a closed set, but since they were shooting on a public street it was impossible. Nikki had suggested they film this scene in a studio, but their production manager had informed them that it upped the budget prohibitively. Besides, Mick wanted the authenticity of being out on a real street.

Lara kept walking, trying not to tense her body in preparation for the attack she knew was coming any second. *Act natural!* a voice screamed in her head. *Go with whatever takes place*.

Joey had said he wasn't coming to the set, but in the end he'd relented and she knew he was lurking somewhere behind the main camera. Now she regretted asking him to be there.

Suddenly she felt the presence of the three actors as they fell into step beside her.

'Hey, cooze – what's a fine piece a ass like you doin' out alone?' Aiden jeered, shoving his hand in her grocery bag. 'Whatcha got for big daddy? Somethin' hot an' juicy? 'Cause, honey, that's what big daddy's got for you.'

'Go away,' she said, repeating the words Rebecca had said on that fateful night. 'Go away and leave me alone.'

'Don' wanna share what you got with big daddy?' Aiden

mocked, circling her like a snake, while the other two men laughed and crowed.

She could smell him, he hadn't bathed for several days because Rebecca had mentioned how badly the men smelled. Aiden was nothing if not a method actor.

She quickened her step, trying to escape. But as she passed the opening to the alley, Aiden's character struck, putting his arm around her throat, spinning her off balance and dragging her into the alley.

The bag of groceries fell to the ground, vegetables and fruit rolling everywhere.

Rebecca was right – no time to scream. Concentrate on survival.

She kicked out, and as she did so she felt one of the actors run his hand up her skirt.

In the distance she heard the whirr of the camera. Everything was surreal – just as Rebecca had said – like she wasn't being watched by hundreds of eyes – like this was actually happening to her and there was no way she could think about anything except getting through it. *Just like real life*, she thought.

Aiden flung her up against the side of a building, hurting her back. His smell was all over her as he began clawing at her clothes.

Mick had promised to shoot in such a way that her body would be hidden from the cameras. 'But like you gotta be in the moment,' he'd said. 'We gotta feel your pain.'

He meant that when Aiden ripped the clothes from her body, she'd be totally naked, apart from the flesh-coloured G-string she wore under her panties. And that she shouldn't let nudity hamper her performance.

One take, she kept on thinking. *I only have to do this once and then it's over.*

Aiden tore off her blouse, tipping her breasts out of her bra before dragging it from her body until she was totally naked and exposed.

In a daze she wondered what the camera could see and what it couldn't. She didn't wonder for long, because she was too busy defending herself. The man on top of her wasn't Aiden Sean any more – he was scum from the streets, violating her body, hurting her, exposing every secret she possessed.

He faked a violent slap across her face, then his hands were moving under her skirt, and she was frantically struggling and screaming, while the two other actors spread her legs, held her down, and dragged her skirt off. Next they went for her panties, and she felt the G-string come off with them, but there was nothing she could do, because if she called 'Cut,' they'd have to start all over again, and she couldn't take it a second time.

Aiden was on top of her, simulating fucking. The camera was behind him. He was breathing hard, his stink enveloping her.

She recoiled in horror. Why had she asked Joey to come to the set? She didn't want him seeing her like this – degraded and used. This might be a movie, but she was still the victim – just like she'd been once before . . . an innocent victim caught up in a wild frenzy of unspeakable violence.

'Dumb cunt!' Aiden screamed, faking another hard slap across her face. 'Tell me you love it, bitch. Tell me you're gettin' off!'

Aiden wasn't acting any more. She felt his hard penis between her legs. If he dropped his pants she'd be forced to scream, 'Cut!'

The other actors were all over her, faking slaps and punches, yelling vile obscenities.

She began to struggle and scream in earnest. This was too much – she wanted out. Why had she agreed to make this movie? She should have listened to Quinn and Joey, they'd both warned her it was a mistake.

She continued screaming, but it wasn't doing her any good, they still kept at her, swarming over her like locusts.

And somewhere, three cameras were busy covering her humiliation and degradation.

She felt Rebecca's rage and pain burning through her like a firestorm. And she screamed – an explosive scream of fury and frustration.

Finally Mick stepped forward and shouted— 'Cut!' The pack of rats retreated.

Rebecca and Nikki moved in next to her, comforting her, while the wardrobe woman threw a silk robe across her shoulders, covering her nakedness.

'You OK?' Aiden asked, his long thin face nothing more than a vague blur.

She nodded, still in a daze.

Mick dashed over, arms going like windmills. 'Unbelievable!' he enthused. 'Freakin' unbelievable!'

Without any warning she suddenly bent forward and began to weep, unable to hold back the unexpected flood of tears.

And she couldn't stop sobbing until Joey was beside her, scooping her up in his arms, carrying her to her trailer and safety.

Finally her ordeal was over.

Chapter Forty-seven

'THAT'S IT,' Joey said, scowling darkly. 'They've got their scene. No close-ups – nothing. Your stand-in can do the rest. That's fucking *it*!'

'Joey,' she murmured, 'if Mick wants close-ups, I'll have to do them.'

'No,' he said ominously. 'I'm taking you home.'

'I can't leave. I must finish.'

'Why the fuck did I let you do this?' he exploded, black eyes full of rage. 'I *knew* they were out to exploit you.'

She couldn't believe he was mad at *her*. What had *she* done?

'Joey—' she began, but it was no good reasoning with him – he was on a roll.

'How fuckin' stupid can you get?' he raged. 'How fuckin' dumb? This'll blow your whole career.'

Nikki knocked on the trailer door, entering tentatively. 'Spectacular!' she exclaimed.

'Yeah,' Joey said, turning on her, 'spectacular for your fuckin' movie. What do you think this'll do for Lara?'

'It'll get her an Oscar nomination, that's what,' Nikki said tightly.

'Yeah, *sure*.'

'Don't be so negative, Joey,' Lara said, attempting to keep the peace. 'It's OK, really it is.'

He turned on her, still furious. 'Negative? *I'm* tryin' to protect you. Can't you see what these people are doin' to you?'

'What are we doing to her?' Nikki asked, ready for battle.

'Screwing her, that's what,' he yelled.

'And what do *you* think *you're* doing?' Nikki retorted angrily, pushing a hand through her short dark hair.

'You *asshole*!' he muttered. 'All *you* wanna do is make money.'

'What the hell do you mean by that?' she blazed.

'You're exploitin' the shit outta Lara in the name of friendship.'

'How dare you!'

'Stop it!' Lara shouted, shivering uncontrollably. 'Get out of here – both of you. I can't take this.'

'Are you talkin' to me?' he said, turning on her – his dark eyes cold and hard. 'Are you tellin' me to get out?'

'It was my choice to play this role,' she said weakly, 'so don't make a big deal of it.'

'Fuck you,' he said angrily. 'Fuck *you*.' And he marched from the trailer.

'What's *his* problem?' Nikki said, still angry.

'He's upset. I shouldn't have forced him to come to the set, it was selfish of me.'

Nikki was amazed. He'd just screamed at Lara for no reason, called her stupid and God knew what else, and she was *defending* him!

'Why are you putting *his* feelings first?' she asked, exasperated.

'I'd react in the same way if I had to watch *him* getting beat up.'

'You're too understanding for me to fathom,' Nikki said, shaking her head in disbelief. 'The guy's with *you*, for Chrissakes – he should be kissing your ass.'

'Don't criticize him,' Lara said, clutching her robe around her. 'He treats me wonderfully.'

'Yeah, well, *I* haven't seen it.'

'You know what?' Lara said, wishing Nikki would vanish. 'It's really none of your business.'

'I'm your friend,' Nikki said earnestly. 'How do you know Joey's not just another bum actor hanging around for the glory?'

'I suppose you got that little speech straight from Richard. It sounds exactly like him.'

'No,' Nikki snapped. 'Richard and I have split up. I didn't want to tell you before, in case it upset you.'

'So now I guess it's all right because I'm upset anyway?'

'No. I didn't mean—'

'This isn't the time to get into it,' Lara said wearily. 'If you don't mind, I need to be alone.'

'Fine,' Nikki said, and left the trailer, disappointed Lara wasn't more concerned about her news.

As soon as she was by herself, Lara began shivering uncontrollably. She was in shock that the people closest to her were acting like this. First Joey walking out. Then Nikki and her problems. Just when she needed tender loving care, they'd both seen fit to dump on her.

She felt shut off from everyone – alone and frightened. Exactly the way she'd felt when she was six years old and the tragedy had taken place . . .

She hated remembering, but sometimes – in moments of trauma – it was inevitable.

She buried her head in her hands, and before she could stop it – the memories came flooding back.

☆ ☆ ☆

'Lara Ann, you're going to live with your Aunt Lucy.'

The policewoman who spoke had ruddy cheeks and several hairy warts on her face. Lara Ann concentrated on the warts. If she stared at them hard enough, maybe all the bad things would go away.

For over a week she'd been kept in a child care facility while the authorities tried to track down a relative who would care for her. They'd finally come up with Aunt Lucy, her father's second cousin, who lived in Arizona.

Aunt Lucy didn't come to fetch Lara Ann herself, she sent Mac, her big strapping son. He drove a pick-up truck, chewed gum nonstop, and was quite ugly. He scooped up little Lara Ann, tossing her into the back of the truck as if she was a rag doll. She remained there for most of the long drive to Arizona.

Aunt Lucy, a dour widow woman with a long miserable face, owned a small motel, which she ran with the help of her son. Aunt Lucy was not at all affectionate, and certainly not pleased to be stuck with Lara Ann. She greeted the child with a curt nod, showed her to the tiny storeroom in back where she was to sleep, and the next morning packed her off to the local school.

Lara Ann was utterly traumatized. Nobody mentioned the tragedy to her. Nobody spoke to her about the loss of her family. It was like they'd ceased to exist and not one person cared to address it.

Aunt Lucy certainly didn't mention it. Neither did Mac. Although one day his best friend said to her— 'Are you batty? Mac says you are, 'cause your daddy killed your mom. So you gotta be a loony, too.'

Lara Ann was frightened and confused. She couldn't understand what had happened, only that her life was in shatters.

She soon realized that Aunt Lucy didn't want her, and even though she was very young, she also sensed that she didn't fit in

*at the motel. She withdrew into silence – the only safe place –
speaking only when spoken to. At school she kept to herself,
desperately trying to fade into the background. Unfortunately,
as she grew, it was not possible to stay unnoticed, for she was
incredibly pretty. By the time she was thirteen, boys were chasing
her, even though she gave them no encouragement.*

*After school and all during summer vacations she helped out
at the motel doing the work of a maid – cleaning rooms,
scrubbing floors, folding laundry. Mac's best friend worked as a
handyman at the motel. He had his eye on her, and even though
she was only thirteen and kept to herself, she knew he was
watching her.*

*One day he trapped her in the laundry room, pinned her up
against the wall and tried to kiss and grope her. He wanted to
do more, but when she started to scream he got nervous and
ran.*

*Aunt Lucy appeared at the door of the laundry room, her
long face livid. 'Why are you encouraging him?' she yelled.
'What are you? A tramp like your mother?'*

'My mama wasn't a tramp,' Lara Ann whispered.

*Aunt Lucy didn't listen. Stern-faced, she proceeded to give
her a lecture about how lucky she was that they'd taken her in,
even though they could ill afford to, and she was a terrible
burden.*

*A burden? She was doing a full-time job for no wages.
Fervently she vowed that one of these days she would get away
from Aunt Lucy, and never speak to her again, because she was
a hateful woman.*

*Sometimes Lara Ann felt like Cinderella. She had no
friends, nobody to love and cherish her, nobody who cared.
Many nights she'd sob herself to sleep in her little room. School
was not much better. She was too pretty to fit in, and they all let
her know it. The other girls hated her, and the boys wanted to
jump her. Her only solace was reading, and she haunted the*

school library, getting hold of every book she could. Reading took her to another place – another life. It proved to her that things could be better.

When she was fifteen a tenant shot himself in one of the rooms. Lara Ann discovered the body when she went in to clean, and became hysterical.

Aunt Lucy slapped her across the face and told her to shut up and pull herself together while she called the police.

Two hours later the police arrived, took photographs, hauled the body away, and when the task was completed, Aunt Lucy told her to go in and clean up the mess.

'No!' Lara Ann shrieked, horrified. 'I can't go in there. I can't!'

'Pretty little miss doesn't want to get blood on her hands?' Aunt Lucy sneered. 'You get in there and do as I say.'

That was the day Lara Ann knew she couldn't take it any more. Unfortunately, she had no choice – there was nowhere for her to run.

And then, one Friday afternoon, a man called Morgan Creedo checked into the motel. Morgan was a half-assed country singer, twenty-nine years old, thin as a whippet, with long blond hair and a weather-beaten, heavily tanned face.

To Lara Ann he was glamour personified. She hovered outside his room, listening to him sing and play his guitar.

'Is he a movie star?' she whispered to Mac.

'No, he's not a goddamn movie star,' Mac snapped. 'Why'd you think that?'

''Cause he's so . . . special,' Lara Ann replied.

'Oh, you're just a dumb kid, what do you know?' Mac sneered.

He was right. She was a dumb kid. An ugly little slut. She didn't know anything. Aunt Lucy was always telling her how stupid she was. Mac called her a retard and a loony. Even the kids at school steered clear of her because she wasn't like them.

Maybe I am crazy, *she thought to herself.* Maybe I'm crazy to have stayed with these people all these years. *Because when she remembered her beautiful mother, and her fun-loving brother, and all the cuddles and love she'd received from her father before that fateful night when everything had blown up in her face – she knew life could be good.*

Morgan Creedo was appearing in a concert nearby, and she wanted more than anything to go. 'It's not like he's the star,' Mac said. 'There's about ten other acts, and he's appearing first – which means he's a nobody.'

'I'm going to ask him if I can go,' Lara Ann said.

'Ask away. Lucy won't let you.'

But she had no intention of getting Aunt Lucy's permission.

Later that day when she delivered clean towels to Morgan Creedo's room, she found him lying on the bed watching a Western on television.

''Scuse me, sir,' she ventured.

He barely glanced up. 'Yeah – whaddaya want?'

'I was wondering if you had a spare ticket to your concert,' she said boldly.

He laughed. 'You wanna come see my concert, little girl?'

'Yes, I'd like that a lot.'

'Well, well, well.' He sat up with a broad smile on his face. 'Heard about how good I am, huh?'

'I hope it's not rude, but I've been standing outside your door listening to your singing. You sound real good to me.'

'Yeah, I'm pretty damn good, kid. Trouble is I'm the only person who appreciates me.' He got off the bed and stretched. 'I'll get you a ticket. You got a name?'

'Lara Ann.'

'Lara Ann, huh?' He looked at her like he was seeing her for the first time. 'How old're you?'

'Fifteen.'

He laughed. 'Old enough, huh?'

'Do you have to be a certain age to come to your concert?' she asked, her beautiful face completely innocent.

He laughed again. 'Not what I was talking about, kid. Tell you what – I'll leave you a ticket in the room. The concert's tomorrow night. Come backstage after, I'll buy you a lemonade.'

The next day she found the ticket he'd left for her on the dresser in his room. She stuffed it in her pocket, barely able to conceal her excitement.

That night, after dinner was finished and she'd washed the dishes, she left the kitchen as if she was going to bed as usual, and snuck out the back door, making her way by bus to the concert hall where Morgan Creedo was appearing, her precious ticket clutched tightly in her hand.

The theatre was vast, but Morgan had gotten her a seat right at the front. She was so excited she could barely breathe. Most of the audience had come to see the star act, a female country and western singer, but when Morgan hit the stage, Lara Ann felt butterflies in the pit of her stomach.

He sang two songs. The audience didn't seem too interested, but Lara Ann clapped until her hands hurt. As soon as he was finished she got up her courage and approached a guard standing at the side of the stage.

''Scuse me,' she said, 'can you tell me how I get back to see Mr Creedo?'

'Mr Who?' the guard said.

'He was just up there singing.'

'He was, huh? You got a backstage pass?'

'No, but he gave me my ticket, and told me to go backstage after.'

'OK,' he said with a dirty laugh. 'Guess there's nothin' wrong with another groupie gettin' it on. Go on back, sweetie.'

He didn't move, forcing her to squeeze past him. As she did so, he pinched her bottom.

Backstage there were dozens of people running around. She spotted the star of the show with her big lemon-coloured hair, sequined dress and toothy smile. She stopped a girl with magenta curls, carrying a hairbrush.

''Scuse me,' she said politely. 'I'm looking for Mr Creedo.'

'Oh, you mean Morgan? He's outta here already.'

'I was supposed to meet him. Do you know where he'd be?'

'You're a little young for Morgan, aren't you?' the girl said, looking her up and down.

'I'm a friend of his.'

'Sure you are. Guess he'd be in the bar next door, sweetie, but I wouldn't pursue it if I were you.'

'Excuse me?'

'What I mean is, why'n't you go on home. You're too young for a reptile like him.'

Lara Ann didn't appreciate the girl calling Morgan a reptile. She made her way out of the stage door, and hesitated on the street. There were two bars in sight, one across the street and one next to the theatre. She decided the one next to the theatre might be where he was.

Pushing the door open, she was swept into a crowd of beer-drinking, card-playing men. She looked around, finally spotting Morgan at the bar nursing a glass of tequila. She went over and tapped him on the shoulder.

'What the fuck you want?' he said, turning around and staring at her with bloodshot eyes.

'I'm from the motel, remember? You left me a ticket. Told me I could come see you tonight. My name's Lara Ann.'

'Ah Jesus, kid.'

'You were so wonderful,' she said, her green eyes shining.

'I was shit,' he replied bitterly. 'I'm always shit. Did you hear? Those bastards didn't even listen to me. They're not interested – they just wanna eyeball that fuckin' fat blond with the big tits.'

'I thought you were wonderful,' Lara Ann repeated.

He squinted at her. 'You're a pretty little thing,' he said. 'How old you say you were?'

'Fifteen. But I'll soon be sixteen.'

'Big enough and old enough, huh?'

'Beg your pardon?'

'Nothin', darlin' – come here.' She moved closer to him. 'You think I'm wonderful, huh?'

'Oh yes,' she muttered adoringly.

They were married three weeks later on her sixteenth birthday. Aunt Lucy did not attend.

It wasn't until after they were married that Lara Ann realized Morgan had no home, only the cramped trailer attached to the battered old Cadillac he drove around the country. 'It ain't luxury, honey, but you'll get used to it,' he informed her.

She didn't care. She finally had somebody who knew she existed and whom she could look after. She'd learned to cook by watching Aunt Lucy; her ironing was impeccable; and she knew how to sew, keep house and clean.

What she didn't know was anything about sex. But this didn't bother Morgan.

'I'm gonna teach you everything you need to know, honey,' he said. 'This is what you do. You get down on your knees and you suck my dick till I come. That's all there is to it.'

'That's all?' she said, thinking about all the things she'd read about kissing and cuddling and making love.

'Yeah, so get goin', honey – I'm gonna teach you how to do it like a pro.'

They never did make love in the proper fashion. Morgan told her people only did it that way when they wanted to have kids. She wasn't sure she believed him, but what could she do? He wasn't interested in anything other than her getting down on her knees.

Morgan Creedo was a sonofabitch. He made Lara Ann into his love slave. And because he wasn't a star, he let out all his frustrations on his young innocent bride. Lara Ann had no one except him, and he liked that. He kept her to himself, never allowing her to speak to anyone else.

As she grew older, so she became more beautiful – which Morgan considered an added bonus. When he hit her – and he did so often – he made sure he never touched her gorgeous face. In the back of his mind he thought that one day – when his career was over – he'd get her a job in porno movies. With her looks she could make enough money to keep them both in luxury.

'Ever thought about acting?' he asked one day.

She shook her head.

'You got what it takes, hon,' he said, unzipping his fly and pushing her to her knees.

The following week he started taking her to movies so she could study the famous actresses on the screen.

She fell in love with the moving images and the actors she observed. Meryl Streep and Robert Redford. Al Pacino and Jessica Lange. They were all so magical. They inspired her – making her realize that there was another life out there. Oh God, how she yearned for another life.

By the time she was nineteen, Morgan was fed up. She might be beautiful, but she was also boring. She never answered back; let him get away with anything; serviced him whenever he wanted. He needed fire in a woman, not docile obedience. Maybe if he put her on the road to porno stardom she'd become more exciting.

Lara Ann was also fed up – but for different reasons. She'd thought Morgan really cared for her, but as each day passed she understood that she was no more than his servant. The way he treated her, she might have been better off staying with Aunt Lucy.

One day he informed her they were going to Hollywood. 'I've got the number of a producer who's promised to give you a break.'

'A break at what?' she asked.

'To be a movie star, dummy. That's what you want, isn't it?'

'If you say so.'

They got in his old Cadillac and set off.

Halfway to Los Angeles, he stopped the car in a lay-by and told her to service him the way he liked.

'No,' she said.

'"No"?' he repeated, as if he couldn't believe she was turning him down. 'Do it, bitch. An' don't argue.'

'I don't want to.'

Once again he repeated her words. '"You don't want to."' Then he grabbed her by the hair with one hand, unzipped his fly with the other, and forced her head into his lap.

The novelty of her saying no made him come even faster than usual, and when he released her, she got in the back of the car and curled up on the seat, tears in her eyes, planning in her mind that when they reached LA she had to get away from Morgan and start afresh.

God made it easy for her.

Ten miles outside of Barstow, Morgan fell asleep at the wheel. Seconds later their car skidded under a huge truck parked illegally on the highway.

Lara Ann woke up in a hospital two days later.

'Where's Morgan?' she asked. 'Where's my husband?'

Morgan was dead. He'd been decapitated in the accident.

Once again she was by herself.

☆　☆　☆

'Are you all right, Lara, dear?' The English wardrobe woman stood in front of her, a concerned expression on her homely face.

She glanced up, leaving the vividly real memories behind. 'I'm fine,' she murmured.

'I was knocking on the door for ages.'

'Guess I must've fallen asleep.'

'Mick says you're finished for the day. Can I help you get dressed?'

'That's OK. Can you please make sure my driver's outside.'

'He's there, dear.'

'Thanks.'

She couldn't wait to get home to the safety of Joey's arms. He was the only one she could truly depend on.

Chapter Forty-eight

 JOEY PROWLED around a fashionably rundown pool hall on Sunset. Most of the guys were intent on the game, except a few who were checking out the eager girls sitting in a row at the bar, hoping to be picked up.

Joey was edgy – for the first time in his life he realized he cared about someone, and this completely threw him. How had it happened? The instant he'd seen Lara he'd known it was going to be a whole other trip.

And yet, he was using her – living in her house, going to her agent, allowing her to get him a part in *Revenge*. Before, when he'd been with a woman, he'd always had a reason. Now everything was different. Shit! He didn't *want* to use her in any way.

What was he going to do? Harden himself against her? Get it back to where it should be?

He eyed the female talent at the bar. There were some pretty girls, but none of them came close to Lara.

He zeroed in on the prettiest, a curly-haired brunette in a white micro-dress sipping a Margarita. She was very young – too young.

'Hi,' he said, approaching her.

She looked him over, liking what she saw. 'You'd better

not hit on me,' she warned, flirting anyway. 'I'm with my date, and he gets real mad.'

'Which one's your date?'

She pointed out a short balding guy across the room, intent on the game.

'I've seen competition,' Joey said with a dry laugh, 'an' I got a feelin' he ain't it.'

She giggled, fluttering her long eyelashes, getting off on the attention. 'I'm Tina. Who're you?'

'Bob,' he lied.

'Hi, Bob,' she said, small pink tongue snaking out to lick the rim of her Margarita glass in a suggestive fashion.

'Hi, Tina,' he replied, giving her intense eye contact.

Could this vampy little brunette persuade him to forget Lara? Could she make him fall out of love?

He sincerely doubted it. 'What's your phone number, Tina?' he asked, deciding he'd pursue it anyway.

'I can't give you that!' she said, shrieking with laughter. 'I told you, I'm with my date.'

'Yeah, but what if you break up with him tonight?' he said, giving her the full intense stare. 'Wouldn't you be sorry you hadn't given me your number?'

She thought that one over. 'Well . . . OK, but if he sees, he's gonna kill me. *And* you.' Furtively she scrawled her number on a packet of book matches and handed it to him.

Score one. He'd probably never call her. Who gave a shit?

He left the pool hall and drove to a strip club several blocks down the street, paying an exorbitant price at the door.

The strippers were ˙lacklustre, contemptuous of their patrons, undulating and gyrating with a distinct lack of energy. He concentrated on a sloe-eyed blond, lowering her quivering thighs up and down a steel pole wearing only a G-string and nippleless bra. She didn't do a thing for him.

'Take it off, honey-pot,' yelled a fat guy sitting to his right. 'Get naked so's I kin get a real good look at those big bouncy jimmy-jammies!'

The girl slithered across the floor to the man who was doing the shouting. 'A hundred bucks'll buy you a private dance,' she said, provocatively sliding her tongue across pouty lips.

'Honey-pot, I'm *buyin*'!' the fat man crowed, sweat beading his upper lip.

'Back room, ten minutes,' the stripper said, taking a long sideways look at Joey. Their eyes met for a moment. He saw the interest start to rise. 'How 'bout you, baby?' she crooned, with a slight lisp. 'Wanna visit paradise?'

He didn't bother replying. Strippers. They were all into each other, anyway. The ones he'd known harboured a deep hate for the guys who sat and ogled them, referring to them as losers and dorks – guys who couldn't get it up in normal life.

He wondered what Lara was doing now. She must have arrived home and found he was not there. He knew she'd be upset.

Why was he treating her this way? She was so good to him, she didn't deserve it.

Insurance. To make sure she stayed interested.

He got up and left, not even glancing at the sumptuous redhead with giant knockers who was doing unbelievable things to a steel-backed chair.

He sat in Lara's car for a moment before taking out the matchbook with Tina's number scribbled on the flap. Disgusted with himself – he threw it into the gutter.

Why sabotage something so perfect?

☆ ☆ ☆

Sitting in the back of her limo on the ride to her house, Lara attempted to calm down. Not only had she gone through the ordeal of the rape scene, but when the memories came flooding back, she'd felt a deep sense of sadness and desperation. Over the years she'd become adept at shutting out the nightmares – closing down the moment her mind went in a bad direction – a trick she'd learned to protect herself. Today it hadn't worked.

Enough! a voice screamed in her head. *Enough! I'm not thinking about any more of this today.*

She inspected her arms, both badly bruised from the mauling Aiden had given her. Maybe Joey was right. Maybe she shouldn't have agreed to appear in *Revenge*. Still . . . it was completely unfair of him to get mad at her.

The dogs greeted her when she arrived home, racing out of the house, barking and wagging their tails, jumping to lick her face, delighted to see her. She fussed them for a minute, thinking that you never had to worry about animals – they always loved you, no matter what.

Mrs Crenshaw came to the front door. 'Everything all right, Miss Lara?'

'Yes, thanks, Mrs C.'

'Will you be eating home tonight?'

'Yes. I'd like dinner served in the bedroom on trays. Is Mr Joey upstairs?'

'No, he's not home yet.'

'Oh,' she said, disappointed. 'Did he call?'

'Not that I know of.'

She was overwhelmed with a sudden feeling of emptiness. Why wasn't Joey here to say he was sorry for the way he'd behaved, and to tell her he loved her? She had no desire to spend the evening alone, she needed him beside her.

More than a little disturbed, she went upstairs into her bathroom and ran a tub, slowly pouring bubble bath under the running taps. Then she lit scented candles and put a Sade CD on the player. *Smooth Operator* serenaded her as she pinned her hair on top of her head and slid into the tub, allowing the warm water to soothe her aching body.

It had been some day.

☆ ☆ ☆

When Nikki walked into the house she found three irate messages from Richard on the answering machine, each one more angry than the last. The gist of his fury was that he'd heard how graphic the rape scene was, and how could she and her amateur director have put Lara through such an ordeal.

It was like he didn't get it. They weren't together, she was contemplating divorce, yet he acted as if this was merely a temporary separation and he could still tell her what to do.

She wasn't in the mood to call him back. In fact, until the movie was finished, she didn't care to do anything about him at all. Yes, it was lonely in the house without him around, but it was better than putting up with a man who couldn't stay faithful.

She was anxious to see the dailies, her job now was to protect Lara in the editing room, where she planned on looking over Mick's shoulder the entire time.

The phone rang. She reached for it.

'What the *fuck* is wrong with you?' Richard yelled, causing her to hold the phone away from her ear. 'Are you trying to ruin Lara's career?'

'What the *fuck* is wrong with *you*?' she responded heatedly. 'She'll get nominated for this role.'

'You're full of shit, Nikki. You have no idea what you're doing.'

'Don't talk down to me,' she answered coldly. 'You remind me of Sheldon.'

'Oh, I see. Every time I say something you don't like, I remind you of your ex.'

'I don't appreciate being told what to do. I make my own decisions.'

'Yes, you do. Decision number one: ruin Lara Ivory's career.'

'Why do you keep on saying that?'

'Because it's all over town that she's flashing her snatch in your crummy little movie.'

'Excuse me?'

'You don't think there wasn't some spy on the set with a hidden camera?' he taunted. 'The pictures will be front page on the tabloids next week. You think it'll do *my* movie any good? My beautiful, gentle romance, and let's take a look at Lara Ivory with her snatch in the air.'

'Bullshit.'

'For Chrissake, Nikki, wise up. This is Hollywood in the nineties, there are spies everywhere. Jesus Christ! Lara's supposed to be your friend. Why are you doing this to her?'

'I'm trying to make a movie, Richard. I'd appreciate it if you'd leave me alone.'

'You're so naive,' he said, completely disgusted. 'I was under the impression you knew what you were doing, but it turns out you're nothing but an amateur.'

'I don't have to listen to this.'

'Then *don't*.' And he slammed the phone down, which infuriated her even more.

A repeat performance, she thought. *The older man talking down to me. Exactly like Sheldon.*

Why did I marry two old guys, anyway?

Sheldon always said I was searching for Daddy – at least he made one correct call.

She was just about to phone Lara when the doorbell

buzzed. Could it be Richard in person, all set to berate her some more?

'Who's there?' she called out.

'Aiden.'

She flung open the door and Aiden Sean ambled in, looking gaunt and worn and quite attractive in a grungy rock star sort of way. Kind of a younger Mick Jagger morphed with Tommy Lee.

'Y'know,' he said irately, rubbing his unshaved chin, 'I was in that scene today, too.'

She wasn't in the mood for Aiden and his complaints. 'Huh?' she said vaguely.

His bleak eyes scanned her face. 'Everybody's all over Lara like she's the President's wife. *I'm* what makes that scene real. I give it the power. Don't I get any credit?'

Actors! She'd forgotten to praise him and he was pissed. 'You were great, Aiden,' she murmured soothingly. 'You make the perfect rapist.'

He laughed drily. 'Thanks.'

'What's that smell?' she asked, wrinkling her nose.

'Me,' he said, utterly unfazed. 'Haven't had time to go home. Thought I'd use your shower.'

She frowned. Boy, he sure was different. 'You drove all the way to Malibu to use my shower?'

'No, I drove all this way to see you.'

A moment of silence while she tried to figure out if this was his way of flirting. 'Was that so I could tell you how great your performance was?' she asked lightly.

'I *wanted* to see you – is that allowed?' he said, fixing her with his burnt-out eyes. She fell into them and found herself admitting to herself that, yes – she *was* attracted to him, even though she'd been trying to bury her feelings.

'Uh, Aiden,' she said, thrown by the realization, 'I don't know how to tell you this, but uh . . . I'm married.'

'Separated,' he said, still pinning her with his mesmerizing eyes. 'It's all over the set.'

'I guess nothing's private when you're making a movie,' she said ruefully.

'Nothing,' he said, yawning and stretching. 'I worked hard today, now I feel like a piece of shit. Can I use your shower or not?'

His behaviour was bizarre, and she knew she should say no, but she wasn't in the mood to throw him out. She was in the mood for excitement and adventure, two things he seemed to offer. 'One shower and you'll go home?' she questioned.

A thin smile. 'Whyn't you be a good girl and fix us a drink while I'm in there.'

'Why don't you be a good boy and fix us a drink when you get out.'

He laughed, peeling off his work shirt. 'Lead me to the bathroom, Nikki. I can't even stand my own stink any more.'

And she knew that whatever happened next was inevitable.

☆ ☆ ☆

Richard Barry paced furiously around his hotel suite. How come *he* always ended up in a hotel, while his wives stayed put in the house that *he'd* paid for? He should never have married Nikki, she was too headstrong – full of her own importance now that she considered herself a 'producer'. As far as he was concerned, she couldn't produce shit. It was *his* fault for encouraging her, he should have known she wouldn't be able to cut it.

He should have stayed married to Lara. Getting divorced from her was the biggest mistake of his life. Now she was wasting her time with Joey Lorenzo – a first-degree loser. And he, Richard Barry, was sitting alone in a hotel room.

Thinking of Joey reminded him of a phone call he had to make. He fumbled in his pocket for a piece of paper with the number written on it, picked up the phone and dialled.

A woman answered.

'Ms Francis? This is Richard Barry,' he said smoothly. 'I'm sorry to bother you at home. I believe my assistant alerted you I'd be calling.'

'It's no bother, Mr Barry,' Madelaine Francis replied, wondering what this was about. 'In fact, it's an honour to speak with you. How can I help?'

He cleared his throat. 'I understand you were the agent for Joey Lorenzo on *The Dreamer.*'

'That's right.' A slight pause. 'Of course, I'm not responsible for anything he did after that, because he left my agency.'

Richard sensed tension in her voice and knew exactly what to say next. 'Actors . . .' he said understandingly. 'One little break and they dump everyone who helped them get there. I've seen it happen a thousand times.'

'You've got that right,' Madelaine said, her tone bitter.

'Ah, well, that's the way it goes,' Richard said sympathetically. 'So . . . Ms Francis – what exactly can you tell me about Joey Lorenzo?'

'Are you interested in using him in one of your films?' Madelaine asked. 'Because I have other people I can recommend. In fact, I have tapes of several very talented young actors I'd appreciate you viewing.'

'Joey's working in LA at the moment,' Richard remarked.

'I didn't know that,' Madelaine replied, realizing that she mustn't sound too interested, even though she was anxious to know where the little shit had run off to this time. 'What's he working on?' she asked casually.

'A low-budget movie. Nothing important.'

'I see.'

'I have a suggestion, Ms Francis,' Richard said briskly. 'I'll pay for you to come out to the coast. Bring the tapes of your actors, and we'll sit down and discuss everything. I have several projects in development, I'm sure I can use a couple of your clients.'

'I . . . I'd like that,' she said, still trying to figure out why Richard Barry was so interested in Joey Lorenzo.

'The sooner the better,' Richard continued. 'One of my assistants will make the arrangements. My casting people are excellent, but occasionally I enjoy meeting with agents, especially New York agents, who have a knowledge of all the new young talent.'

'That's nice to hear, Mr Barry. Not many directors in your position feel that way.'

'I look forward to meeting you, Ms Francis.'

'Likewise, Mr Barry.'

He put the phone down and nodded to himself. It was about time he concentrated on finding out more about Mr Lorenzo.

MEXICO CITY *welcomed me with open arms – this murdering, drug-addicted, dumb American. I slept on the plane with the help of half a bottle of vodka and a couple of joints. The whole thing was surreal. A fucking slow-motion trip of disaster. I kept on seeing Hadley's face, her look of surprise when the gun went off. Had anyone seen me at the house? Were there any witnesses? Was I going to get caught?*

The first thing I did was change my name again. Then I took a job at a gas station in a small town outside of the city. I rented a room and proceeded to dry out. Cold turkey. For once I was by myself. No woman to hold my hand and pay my bills. I wanted it that way. I wanted my life back.

After a couple of months I began to feel like a human being. I was punishing myself for what I'd done. No drugs. No booze. No sex. Working a dumb shit job. Sleeping when I wasn't working.

It was my punishment.

It cleared my head.

I was twenty-eight years old and a total fucking failure.

I met a woman. An American tourist searching for adventure. We travelled to Acapulco together. I paid my own way. She missed her husband. It was two weeks of nothing much.

After that I went back to being on my own. And it was then that I started to take stock of my life, my sad and sorry life. And I vowed that everything was going to change. Everything.

When I finally returned to LA I planned on being a totally different person.

Chapter Forty-nine

 'HI,' JOEY said, slouching into the bedroom.

Lara was sitting up in bed, watching *The Larry Sanders Show* on HBO, hair piled on top of her head, face devoid of make-up.

'God, you look beautiful!' he said, flopping down beside her. She ignored him as he edged nearer. 'You pissed at me, honey?' he asked.

'Can you wait until this programme is over?' she said coolly, her eyes following the actors on TV.

Oh, she was giving him a hard time. Well, she was entitled.

'Sure,' he said, reaching over and taking her hand. 'I can do anythin' you want.'

She allowed her hand to be limp in his, determined not to forgive him too fast.

'I'm sorry, baby,' he said with a deep sigh. 'I got crazy. Couldn't help myself.'

'I really appreciated you walking out,' she said accusingly.

'Didn't mean to.'

'Whether you meant to or not, that's exactly what you did.'

'Guess sorry doesn't cut it.'

'You *knew* how difficult the rape scene was for me. How could you act like that?'

''Cause I couldn't stand seein' you with those assholes crawlin' all over you,' he muttered. 'I warned you I shouldn't be there, it was you that insisted.'

'So now it's *my* fault?'

'In a way.'

'You're funny,' she said, shaking her head.

'Yeah, I'm the funny guy who doesn't wanna see you hurt. Is that so bad?'

'You didn't have to take it out on me.'

'Jeez! How many times do I havta say I'm sorry?'

'It's Nikki you should be apologizing to.'

Christ! Now Nikki! Wasn't it enough that he was back? That he hadn't fucked up her head by screwing around on her?

'Your so-called friend is way too possessive of you,' he said. 'Did you know the reason she split with Richard is 'cause he's pissed you're in her movie?'

'I don't believe that.'

'Hey – I'm fillin' you in on the set gossip. Believe what you like.' He rolled toward her, his tone drawing her in. 'C'mon, baby, let's not fight. You've been on my mind all night.'

'I have?' she asked, unable to stay mad at him for long.

'It's the truth.'

She gave a deep sigh, there seemed no point in fighting. 'I'm glad you came home,' she said softly.

'So am I,' he said, removing the remote from her hand and clicking off the TV.

'I was watching that—' she objected, none too strenuously.

'Y'know,' he said, stroking her hair, 'while I was thinkin' about you, I came up with a great idea.'

'You did?'

'Yup.'

She snuggled closer to him. 'Are you going to tell me?'

'Dunno,' he said, teasing her. 'Haven't decided.'

'Well, while you're deciding, shall I get Mrs C. to bring up dinner?'

'Sounds good t'me.'

☆ ☆ ☆

Aiden emerged from the shower and padded into the kitchen with only a thin bath sheet knotted around his narrow waist.

Nikki gave a low mocking whistle. 'Sex . . . ee!' She was trying to play this real cool because she wasn't sure *how* she felt. And what kind of nerve did this guy have anyway – parading naked around her house?

'Where's my drink?' he asked, perfectly at home.

'Aiden,' she said, 'a joke is a joke, but can you please put your clothes on and go home.'

'Can't.'

'Why?'

'They stink. Thought you could throw 'em in the wash.'

Oh God, how had she gotten involved in *this*?

'You're too much,' she said, shaking her head.

Ice-grey eyes met hers. 'Not the first time I've bin told that.'

She stared back at him. He was so thin that she could make out the outline of his ribs, and on his left shoulder he had a snake tattoo wending its way down his upper arm. Something drew her to it – she couldn't resist reaching out to touch.

Wrong move. Or maybe the right one. He grabbed her wrist, pulling her forcefully toward him, pressing his lips down on hers.

She kissed him back. What the hell – if it was OK for Richard . . .

Aiden was extremely passionate, hardly giving her a

383

moment to think. So unlike Richard, who'd moved at a leisurely pace, an older man's pace.

'First time I saw your lips I couldn't wait to suck 'em,' Aiden said, breathing all over her. 'Fuckable lips . . . fuckable you . . .'

His hands were everywhere. Under her sweater, up her skirt, sneaking around the elastic of her panties. Long inquisitive fingers exploring new territory.

'Slow down,' she gasped.

'Fuck slowing down,' he responded. 'I've wanted to do this ever since that first lunch.' And then he began kissing her again, his tongue jamming deep into her mouth.

She found herself responding with a sexual zeal she hadn't felt in a long time. He tasted of cigarette smoke and booze and forbidden excitement and she wanted him desperately.

After a few feverish minutes, he ripped off her bra – breaking the clasp. Her breasts tumbled free as he pushed her up against the kitchen counter, raising her hips so that she was half sitting, tearing at her panties until they too were history. Her skirt was around her waist, her sweater around her neck, the rest of her exposed to his probing eyes.

With one hand he untied his towel, letting it drop to the floor. With the other he crushed her breasts together playing with her nipples.

Then he put his cock between her legs – pausing for a moment before plunging in.

She let out a scream of pleasurable pain. Aiden might be thin – but he made up for it in other places.

And finally they were into a wild ride that lasted for a very long time. And after that, sleep – a deeply satisfying sleep.

☆ ☆ ☆

'I can't remember ever being more content,' Lara said with a big smile. They sat in bed, trays in front of them – having recently finished a delicious dinner.

'Yeah,' Joey said. 'Mrs C.'s cookin' does it for me every time.'

'Will you stop!' she said, laughing. 'You know exactly what I mean. The two of us – here together – nobody to bother us. It's like being in our own little world.'

'You're right,' he said. 'Truth is – I've never been happier either. Who needs to go out?'

'We're so alike,' she said, sighing contentedly.

'Yeah, two loners wanderin' around lost – then we got lucky an' found each other. Right?'

'You said it, Joey.'

He grinned. 'An' now—'

'We're together.'

'Like you said – soulmates.' A long beat. 'In fact . . .'

'Yes, Joey?'

'You ready to hear my great idea?'

'What is it?' she asked with an indulgent smile. 'Dinner in bed for two?'

'No, smart-ass.'

'I'm waiting.'

'Well . . .' He paused before plunging ahead. 'I kinda had this crazy thought that when you finish the movie – we should take off . . . an', y'know, kinda get married.'

'*Married?*'

'Yeah, that's what people in love do, y'know.'

She regarded him for a long silent moment. 'They do?' she finally managed, filled with mixed emotions.

'You an' me, somewhere quiet, where no one can find us. What d'you say, baby?'

She hesitated for only a second, and then she realized how

right it all was. 'I say . . . whatever you want, Joey. Whatever makes you happy.'

'No,' he responded – staring at the most beautiful woman in the world, 'whatever makes you happy. I love you, Lara, an' I'm gonna make *you* happier than you ever imagined possible.'

And then they kissed – a long deep soul kiss. And Lara knew she was making the right decision. They truly belonged together, and they always would.

Chapter Fifty

 THE MYSTERY voice had delivered. Yes, Alison Sewell knew she finally had a friend, someone she could trust.

The voice had told her exactly where to go to get the pictures of Lara Ivory that nobody else would have. A seedy hotel room overlooking the alley where *Revenge* was shooting the next day. A hotel room booked and paid for in the name of Mrs Smith. All Alison had to do was to go there with her cameras and telephoto lenses and wait.

'If I get the pictures you say I will,' Alison had said, 'and I sell 'em to the tabs, what d'you get out of it?'

'Satisfaction,' the mystery voice had replied.

All had come to pass. Alison had done exactly as instructed, and sure enough she was centre stage for the rape scene, with an unobstructed view of the action.

God! She could hardly shoot fast enough as the scene progressed. *Snap snap* – as Lara was shoved to the ground; zoom in for close-up as Aiden Sean ripped off her bra; automatic reflex – five shots a second – as they spread her legs and ripped off her panties.

Alison was breathing hard. These were the pictures a photographer of her calibre dreamt about! Naked celebrities fetched top price – especially a celebrity who was supposed to be so sweet and nice. Lara Ivory. Miss Incorruptible.

Well, look at you now, bitch. That'll teach you to cross Alison Sewell.

By the time she was finished, Alison was drenched with sweat. She hurriedly packed up her equipment and raced home, anxious to see what treasures her camera had brought her.

When she viewed the results she was in heaven. The photographs were so raunchy, so bad, so sellable . . .

Lara Ivory exposed for everyone to see.

Revenge was sweet as pie.

And this was just the start.

Chapter Fifty-one

 WHEN LARA reported for work the next day, Mick started jumping all over her, spewing forth compliments. 'Couldn't've asked for more,' he said enthusiastically, pushing his heavy glasses back on his nose. 'That was some freakin' kick-ass performance.'

'I'm so glad it's over,' she said crisply. 'It was quite an ordeal, but I think we got it.'

'You bet we did,' he crowed. 'Thanks to you.'

'Do I get to shoot someone today?' she asked calmly, quite confident that when the gun was in her hands she could handle it.

'Lara!' Mick exclaimed. 'What happened to you?'

'Oh, I can be tough too,' she said with a wicked grin.

He grinned back. 'Oooh, baby, I get off when you're *bad*.'

'Then I'll try to be bad more often,' she said, still smiling.

'We brought in a weapons expert for the scene today,' Mick said. 'He'll show you how to handle a gun.'

'Joey already did that.'

'Nothin' like expert advice.'

'If you insist,' she said, heading for the make-up trailer, unable to stop thinking about Joey. Last night they'd decided that as soon as the movie was finished they'd take off and get married. He'd made her promise not to mention it to anyone

– which wasn't easy because she wanted to tell the world. But he'd convinced her it was the only way if they didn't want a circus.

She hugged the secret to herself and couldn't stop smiling.

☆ ☆ ☆

Mick was already setting up the first shot when Nikki arrived – later than usual. 'What happened to *you*?' he said cheerfully. 'You're usually the early chick-bird on set.'

'I, uh . . . had a restless night,' she replied, wondering if it was written all over her face that what she'd actually had was great sex with Aiden and then overslept. 'Uh . . . Mick, do you know anything about anyone shooting photos yesterday?'

'"No press allowed" rule. Remember?'

'I heard a rumour someone might have gotten shots of Lara.'

'No way.'

'Are you certain?'

'On my set?' Mick said, arms flailing wildly. 'They would've been spotted and shot on the spot.'

'I guess you're right,' she said unsurely. 'Is Lara here yet?'

'In make-up.'

She headed for the make-up trailer, expecting to find Lara in a bad mood. But to her surprise Lara was smiling and chatting to the make-up woman, looking amazing as usual, in spite of yesterday's ordeal.

'Hi,' Nikki said, not quite sure where they were at.

'Morning,' Lara responded amiably.

'You look great.'

'I *feel* sensational. Now that the rape scene's over I can relax. This was a tough shoot, Nik. But I'm sure it's all going to be worth it.'

'You bet.' A pause. 'Uh, is Joey around?'

'He'll be in at noon. Why?'

'I was out of line yesterday, thought I'd apologize.'

Lara nodded her agreement. 'Truth is, you *both* behaved badly,' she said.

'I know, I know,' Nikki admitted. 'And I'm sorry. It's just that it hasn't been easy, what with Richard obsessing over you, plus my problems with Summer – which I won't even get into.'

'More problems?'

Nikki glanced at the make-up woman diligently doing her job. 'Uh . . . I'll tell you later.'

'How about lunch?' Lara suggested, feeling that maybe she'd been neglecting their friendship.

'Just the two of us?'

'Yes.'

'I'd like that.'

'So would I,' Lara responded warmly. 'It seems we never get a chance to talk any more.'

Nikki leaned over, impulsively kissing her on the cheek. 'You're my best friend,' she said. 'We'll always stick together, huh?'

Lara nodded. 'Of *course* we will, Nik.' And she wished she could confide her secret.

☆ ☆ ☆

The weapons expert was a beefy ex-cop who turned to mush in Lara's presence. He had difficulty explaining what she had to do, because her closeness rendered him speechless. She was gentle with him – knowing the effect she had on most men. Mick thought it was hilarious.

'Don't you *dare* embarrass him,' she said sternly. 'He's so sweet.'

'Sweet my ass!' Mick guffawed. 'He's a big old hairy pisser who'd jump you soon as look at you!'

Gingerly she held the gun and didn't feel a thing. No bad memories today. Little Lara Ann was safely tucked away in the back of her mind. No visual images of blood and gore and torn flesh . . .

When Joey arrived they embraced, completely oblivious that everyone was watching them.

'I booked the airline tickets,' he said, close to her ear. 'Under assumed names. We leave the morning after you wrap.'

'Shouldn't we wait a couple of days?'

'For what? We gotta do it fast, babe.'

'Where are we going?'

'Tahiti. I heard about a place where nobody'll bother us.'

For a moment she felt a frisson of anxiety. 'You're sure we're not rushing into this?'

'Do you *feel* as if we're rushin'?'

'No.'

'Then why're you givin' me a hard time?'

She smiled softly. 'I *never* give you a hard time.' And she gazed into his eyes and knew it was the right thing to do.

'That's what I like about you,' he said. 'That and your sexy body.'

'Hmm . . . right back at you.'

They both laughed.

'You wait until I get you alone on a tropical island,' he said in a low voice, nuzzling her neck. 'I'm gonna make love to you like you've never been made love to before.'

'You are?' she said, her voice husky with desire.

'Bet on it.' A beat. 'In fact, if we go to your trailer right now . . .'

'Uh . . . Joey, I promised I'd have lunch with Nikki today. You don't mind, do you?'

'Don't wanna have sex with me, huh?' he teased. 'Takin' me for granted.'

'It's just that Nikki needs to talk.'

'As long as you don't plan on telling her.'

She put her arms around his neck and kissed him. 'As if I would.'

He was pissed, although he didn't show it. Nikki had too strong a hold over Lara. Now that he'd made the final commitment he wanted her all to himself with no outside influences.

Still, only a few more days of filming, then she'd be all his, and there'd be nobody around to get in their way.

☆ ☆ ☆

'I can't believe you threw Richard out,' Lara said, pushing her fork around a bowl of cottage cheese and fruit. 'The two of you seemed so happy.'

'I can't believe it either,' Nikki replied. 'But I always harboured the philosophy that if he screwed around on me, I'd do it back to him.'

Lara shook her head sadly. 'And I thought the three of us would always be such good friends.'

'I'll be honest,' Nikki said, picking at a salad. 'Maybe I could have dealt with his infidelity. The thing I *couldn't* deal with was his obsession with you.'

'He doesn't have an obsession with me,' Lara said, stubbornly refusing to admit what everyone else seemed to know.

'Oh, yes he does,' Nikki insisted. 'I truly believe that if I hadn't asked you to be in *Revenge*, he wouldn't have gotten like this.'

'Could be he's jealous,' Lara said sagely.

'Of *what*?' Nikki snorted.

'Well . . . Richard makes big expensive Hollywood movies.

393

Revenge is a small, low-budget film – something he'll never get an opportunity to do again. Perhaps, deep down, he'd welcome the chance.'

'Who, Richard?' Nikki said derisively. 'He loves the fame and glory. Big budgets are his life. Surely you know that?'

'I suppose so.'

'The only thing *he's* jealous of is your relationship with Joey.'

'Well . . . he'd better learn to accept it if he wants to stay friends.'

'I don't get it,' Nikki sighed. 'Men and their dicks. Is there no way they can keep them zipped up?'

'You *knew* Richard was a risk going in,' Lara said.

'True,' Nikki agreed. 'If he screwed around on you – what made me think *I* had a chance?' She laughed ruefully. 'Dumb me. I guess my ego told me I was different.'

'At least *you* didn't catch him in the act.'

'Small compensation,' she said, sipping a glass of apple juice. 'Anyway, the good news is I had fun with Aiden last night.'

'At last!' Lara exclaimed with a smile. 'Someone *not* old enough to be your father!'

'Yeah,' Nikki said wryly. 'Better I should be with a reformed druggie.'

'As long as he's reformed.'

'He *tells* me he is. Who knows? I'm not planning on sticking around long enough to find out.'

'So,' Lara said, reaching for her sunglasses. 'What's going on with Summer?'

'It's complicated,' Nikki said, not quite sure how much to reveal. 'Well . . .' She hesitated a moment before plunging ahead. 'Aiden told me he saw her in a club one night coming on to Mick. Obviously it was before Mick knew who she was.'

'Coming on in what way?'

'How can I put this? She wasn't just flirting. Apparently Mick told Aiden she gave him a blow job in the back of his limo.' Nikki sighed, as if she couldn't quite believe it herself. 'Isn't that nice? Fifteen-year-old girl and crazed director. *My* director.'

'Are you sure?'

'Aiden wouldn't lie. Mick must've gone into shock when he came to my house for dinner and discovered who she was.'

'Did you talk to her?' Lara asked.

'I sent her back to Chicago. Sheldon's in charge, it's not for me to get into.'

'Yes, it is,' Lara said forcefully, remembering her own miserable teenage years. 'If *you* can't talk to her, at least fill Sheldon in. She needs guidance.'

'He'd throw a fit.'

'Don't let it go, Nik. She's only fifteen.'

'I know, I know, I've got to deal with it. Actually – there's more.'

Lara sighed. 'What now?'

'Nothing happened – but she came on to Aiden, too.' A long beat. 'I thought I'd bring her back here at Christmas, spend time with her then.'

'How can you do that if you're with Aiden?' Lara asked, frowning. 'What if this is the start of something you don't want to stop? *That'll* make her feel really comfortable – knowing he's probably told you.'

Nikki shook her head. 'It's not going anywhere with Aiden.'

'How do you know?'

''Cause we're too different.'

'Could be a challenge.'

'I've had enough challenges to last a lifetime,' Nikki

sighed, pushing her plate away. 'Anyway,' she continued, 'enough about me. How's *your* big romance?'

Lara's face lit up. 'Joey's wonderful,' she said dreamily. 'He makes me feel secure. In fact . . . he makes me feel like I've never felt before.'

'Great sex'll do it every time!'

'Don't you ever think about anything else?'

'Not if I can help it!' Another long pause. 'Y'know, since Joey's obviously a keeper – isn't it time you found out more about him?'

'Why?' Lara said defensively. 'What he did before me has nothing to do with us.'

'I know that. But surely a person's background is important?'

'No,' Lara said firmly. 'The past is exactly that. I know everything I need to know about Joey.'

And Nikki knew it was time to shut up.

☆ ☆ ☆

Much to Summer's disgust, Chicago was caught in a cold spell. Every time she ventured outdoors she was assaulted by strong winds and sleeting rain. It was bad enough on schooldays – but weekends, too? *Not that I have anywhere to go*, she thought, staring glumly out of her bedroom window, watching the relentless rain dribbling down the window pane, wishing she was still in sunny LA.

She'd been home almost a month, and back in school a week – which was the drag of all time, because she didn't belong any more, she was way ahead of everyone. *I've almost had sex with a movie star*, she wanted to yell at the boys who came chasing after her. *Get lost, you retarded little dicks!*

The only good thing was that since she'd been back, her

father hadn't touched her. Rachel kept him so busy that he didn't have time for his nocturnal visits, or maybe he was backing off now that she was old enough to complain.

Not that she'd ever complained. Who would she tell? Her absentee mother, who obviously didn't care? Her stepmother, Rachel? No way.

Her sixteenth birthday was coming up and Rachel had offered to throw her a party. She wasn't sure if she wanted one. Who would she invite? The geeks from school? None of them would be Aiden Sean or Norman Barton – so what was the point?

The night with Norman and Tina remained vivid in her mind. Norman had been so sweet and full of fun. And on top of having a good time, she'd actually gotten paid!

God! How she'd love to tell her father. Let him know that what he took from her without permission, she was now charging for. It would drive him insane, his sweet little girl having sex for money. A fitting punishment for him.

Sometimes she daydreamed about Norman setting her up in her own apartment in LA, visiting once a week and paying all the bills. What an awesome trip that would be!

The fact that her mother had shipped her back to Chicago without giving her a chance to contact him wasn't fair. She'd spoken to Tina a few times. 'Get your butt back here,' Tina had said. 'There's money to be made and mucho babes *panting* to pay us.'

'I'm trying,' she'd said.

'Try harder,' Tina insisted.

Rachel knocked and poked her head around the door. She was pretty, but not in a Hollywood way – she had none of the dazzle and style of Tina or Darlene. Actually she resembled a very young Nikki.

'What are you doing?' Rachel asked.

'Nothing much,' Summer replied listlessly.

'Want to go shopping? Spend a little of your daddy's hard-earned cash?'

'I'm always up for that,' Summer said, trying to dredge up some enthusiasm.

'Let's go, then,' Rachel said. 'I'll meet you by the car in five minutes.'

Summer peered at herself in the mirror. Her tan was fading, which really pissed her off because she didn't look half as good without a tan. Would Norman still like her all pale-faced and miserable?

She thought about Tina and Jed and the group of friends she'd hung with at the beach. Most of all she thought about Norman, and his cute puppy dog smile. They made a perfect couple.

What a blast she'd had in California. Why did she have to be stuck in Chicago?

And the big question – what was she going to do if her father ever came near her again?

Chapter Fifty-two

 For several days Nikki managed to avoid having contact with Aiden, until one afternoon he cornered her on the set. She didn't know what to say, everything had happened so fast the other night, and when she'd awoken in the morning, he was gone.

'*Finally*,' he said, looking perplexed.

'Oh, hi,' she said, quite flustered.

He leaned close, speaking intimately in her ear. 'You were somethin' the other night. A real wild woman!'

'I don't regret it, Aiden,' she said quickly, backing away, 'only please – take it as a one-off.'

He regarded her through narrowed eyes. 'A one-off?'

'It's too difficult for me right now.'

'I'm not askin' you to *marry* me, Nikki,' he said, his mouth curving into a thin smile.

'Gee – thanks. What *are* you asking for?'

He gave a noncommittal shrug. 'Thought you'd drop by my place later – fix a hungry man dinner.'

Well, he certainly had nerve. 'You thought that, did you?' she said, irritated.

'Don't you wanna see how the other half lives? Not everyone has a beach house in Malibu.'

'And what would I cook for you?'

'Pasta, a steak, whatever you're into.'

'Tempting offer. I'm passing.'

'Didn't imagine you'd say yes.'

His tone of voice indicated she was predictable. 'What does *that* mean?' she asked, a little bit angry.

'Nothing,' he said vaguely.

'No,' she said heatedly, 'I want to know what you meant.'

'It's your vibe.'

'What *vibe*?'

'Like you're only into money.'

'That's the *last* thing I'm into,' she said indignantly. 'The very last thing.'

'You married two rich guys, didn't you? The shrink in Chicago must have big bucks, and Richard's not exactly hurting.'

'Money has nothing to do with any of my relationships,' she said stiffly.

'Then come spend the night with a bum actor. I won't invite you again.'

'Fine, I'll be there.' And as she said it, she realized he'd caught her in a trap.

☆ ☆ ☆

Lara decided to surprise Joey when they returned from their honeymoon. She knew how much he loved the ocean, and when they were married it seemed like a great idea for them to have a romantic hideaway to run to whenever they needed to be alone. A year ago she'd rented at the beach for the summer – an old-fashioned Cape Cod style house perched on the edge of a bluff overlooking the ocean, located past Point Dume, and quite remote. She'd loved it so much that she'd tried to buy it. At the time it wasn't for sale. Recently she'd heard it was on the market, and she'd instructed her business manager to make an offer. The offer had been accepted, and the house was now hers, but she wasn't going to tell Joey until they got back. It would be her wedding present to him.

The only two people who knew about it were her business manager and Cassie, and she'd sworn them both to secrecy.

Thank God nobody had any clue that she and Joey were planning on getting married. She could just imagine the furore if it became public knowledge. Her lawyer would insist on a prenuptial and everyone else would worry that Joey was after her money.

How could people enter into a marriage like that? This wasn't a monetary deal. This was two people getting married because they loved each other.

The wonderful thing about Joey's love was that it had nothing to do with her being a movie star and all the trappings. He wasn't interested in publicity or being seen with her, he preferred the simple pleasures of life. And great loving insane sex.

Every time she thought about the sex she became aroused. She'd never encountered a man who could turn her on the way Joey did, one glance and she was his. Richard was right about her not being exciting enough in bed – with him she probably hadn't been, because the magic hadn't existed. Joey had the magic. And as far as she was concerned, they'd be together for ever.

☆ ☆ ☆

Later, Nikki rode in Aiden's truck to his apartment, stopping at a supermarket on the way to pick up a couple of steaks and some salad.

They stood side by side at the checkout line. When it was time to pay she waited for Aiden to make a move. He made no attempt to do so. 'I don't know why I'm doing this,' she grumbled, fishing out her credit card.

'Yes, you do,' he said, picking up the grocery bag and carrying it to his truck. ''Cause you want to.'

'No, I don't,' she responded, trailing after him. 'I told you – what we had was a one-off.'

'Glad I made such an impression,' he said, throwing open the passenger door.

'I'll fix you a steak,' she said, climbing into his truck, 'then I have to go home. Richard's bugging me, I think it's time I spoke to my lawyer.'

'You're going for a divorce?'

'That's the plan.'

His apartment was a dump. She walked around in shock. 'How can you live like this?' she demanded.

'Wanna move me into the beach house?' he joked.

'Yeah, right,' she said, inspecting the tiny kitchen, noticing that the grill had not been cleaned in months. 'No maid service?'

'Doesn't cut it, does she?' he said, ruefully.

'*That's* the understatement of the year,' Nikki replied, going to work – cleaning the grill, washing the steaks and placing them on it.

While the meat was cooking she chopped up tomatoes, lettuce and cucumbers, tossing everything into a big wooden bowl. 'Where's your olive oil?'

'You think I cook?'

'How am I supposed to fix a salad dressing? You'd better run out and pick up a bottle.'

'Jeez! This is so friggin' domesticated,' he complained, but he went anyway.

As soon as he left she took a more thorough look around. Aiden was obviously not into possessions. His bed was a futon on the floor, his closet was almost empty, and the only personal things were stacks of scripts piled everywhere. What kind of man was he, anyway? Interesting for sure. Different. And a pretty sensational lover.

She couldn't help herself, she opened the top drawer of his dresser just out of curiosity. Tons of mismatched socks, all mixed up. And a gun.

She shut the drawer as quickly as she'd opened it. Dangerous territory. What was Aiden doing with a gun?

I am not getting involved, she told herself sternly. *No way.*

By the time he got back the steaks were nearly done. 'Clear some of those scripts off the table, and we'll eat,' she said, searching in a cupboard for a bottle of steak sauce. 'Then I'd appreciate it if you'd drive me back to my car.'

'You're really pissy for somebody who had great sex,' he remarked. 'One orgasm doesn't do it for you, huh?'

'I hate to burst your ego,' she said quickly. 'It didn't mean a thing.'

'No?'

'I can be exactly like a guy in that respect.'

'Fuck and run, huh?'

'I've always thought that anything a man can do, a woman can too. It was retribution – pure and simple.'

'Oh, I get it,' he said, a little bit pissed off. 'It was a revenge fuck. And the fact that you and I have this kind of electric thing between us had nothing to do with it – am I right?'

'What *are* you talking about?'

'I'm talking about hot . . . lustful . . . *sex.*'

And before she could stop him, he spun her around and grabbed her, pressing his lips down on hers, his hungry mouth devouring her, while the steaks burned on the grill and neither of them cared.

She made a feeble attempt to push him off.

It was useless. She was as into it as he was.

☆ ☆ ☆

Shopping with Rachel was fun, although not as much fun as cruising Melrose with Tina. Summer yearned for LA. It was like a sickness, being there was all she could think about as she trailed Rachel through Saks. Rachel spent Daddy Dearest's money at a pretty fast pace – throwing her credit card in Summer's direction whenever she needed it.

Idly Summer wondered what Rachel would do if she told her the truth. Freak out and cry. She didn't have much backbone.

When she got home she called Tina again and they had the same old conversation. 'When are you coming back?' Tina demanded.

'Maybe for Christmas. I'll be sixteen then. If things work out I can stay.'

'Darlene says you got rave reviews from Norman. He keeps asking where you are.'

'Wow!' she said. Norman Barton, an actual movie star, wondering where she was. This was too amazing!

A few days later Rachel came into her room crying. 'It's my mother,' Rachel sniffed. 'She's sick. I have to fly to Florida.'

'Want me to come with you?' Summer offered.

'No, I'll be all right.'

Summer didn't much care if Rachel would be all right or not, she dreaded being left alone in the house with her father. It had been over a year since he'd touched her, but what if he started again?

Rachel departed the next morning. Summer watched her

go from her bedroom window, fervently hoping she'd be back soon.

An hour later she set off for school, but before she could make a clean getaway her father strode out of his study, blocking her by the front door. 'You and I will dine together tonight,' he said. 'The two of us – it'll be like old times, sweet pea.'

'Uh . . . I already have a date, Daddy,' she stammered – the words 'like old times' striking fear within her.

Sheldon did not look pleased. 'Who's the lucky young man?' he demanded.

'A boy at school,' she lied.

Sheldon stared at her for a moment, his thin lips twitching. 'I would like to meet him,' he said. 'Make sure you bring him in when he collects you.'

Oh no! What was she going to do now?

As soon as she got to school she approached Stuart, the school geek, who had a mammoth crush on her. 'Wanna go to a movie tonight?' she asked, cornering him by the lockers.

Stuart swallowed three times, so impressed was he by the invitation. 'Y . . . yes,' he stammered.

'OK, pick me up at seven, and don't make me wait around.'

Stuart was right on time, washed and brushed and eager as a frisky race horse. Summer marched him in to meet her father.

Sheldon looked him over with a cold eye. 'Be sure to have my daughter home by ten. And no monkey business.'

Monkey business! Was her father under the impression they were living in 1960?

'Yes, sir!' Stuart said, standing ramrod straight.

Ass-kisser, Summer thought.

Stuart took her to an action adventure epic starring Jean-Claude Van Damme. Halfway through the movie he attempted to hold her hand.

She snatched it away. 'Like get a life, Stuart,' she said in disgust, crushing any hope he might have had.

After the movie, they stopped for a hamburger and milkshake. Summer wolfed her burger, sipped her milkshake and barely spoke to Stuart. When they were finished he drove her home in his secondhand Buick.

She got rid of him with a brusque, 'G'night,' and rushed inside.

Her father was waiting in the front hall – a bad sign.

'Did you have a nice evening, dear?' he asked, puffing on a big stinky cigar.

'I'm really tired,' she said, feigning a yawn.

'I want to talk to you,' he responded. 'Come into my study.'

She didn't want to talk to him. She didn't want to be alone in the house with him. She didn't want to ever see him again.

Unfortunately she had no choice, so she reluctantly trailed him into his study.

'We haven't had much opportunity to chat since you got back,' he said, reaching for a glass of brandy – a *really* bad sign. 'Sit down, dear, and relax.'

She balanced uncomfortably on the edge of one of his stiff leather chairs, while he settled behind his desk, slugging back big gulps of brandy. 'You know, Summer,' he said, 'since you returned from California, you haven't been the same.'

'Yes, I have,' she answered defiantly.

'There's something different about you. I sense an unrest.'

'No, there's not.'

'I'm a professional when it comes to human behaviour, dear, and I feel that being with your mother was not good for you. She's hardly a positive influence.' A long pause. 'You see, I care about you, Summer. I should have insisted you came to the Bahamas with Rachel and me, instead of running off to LA.'

Ha! If he cared about her so much, how come he'd done all those vile things to her while she was growing up?

He refilled his brandy glass, fixing her with a penetrating stare. 'Did you go out with boys in LA, Summer?'

'I . . . uh . . . I dated a bit,' she stammered, wondering where this was leading. 'I'm nearly sixteen. I can do that.'

'I *know* how old you are,' he said sonorously. 'You're my daughter.'

'I'm allowed to date, aren't I?' she said boldly. 'Everyone else does.'

'I don't care what everyone else does.' Another sip of brandy. 'Tell me, pumpkin. Do these boys you go out with try to get fresh with you?'

Wow, he really is living in the sixties. 'No,' she lied, saying what he wanted to hear. 'I never let them touch me.'

He puffed on his cigar. 'How about kissing?'

'No . . . I don't let them kiss me either.'

He nodded to himself, satisfied with her reply. 'You're a good girl, Summer,' he said. 'I always knew you were a good girl.'

She twisted restlessly in her chair, hating every minute of this stupid inquisition. 'Can I go to bed now, Daddy?' she asked, biting her nails. 'I'm really tired.'

He nodded again, and before he could stop her, she leaped up and ran upstairs without looking back.

There was a lock on her bedroom door, but no key. Where was the key? She searched frantically, but couldn't find it.

She was scared, for tonight he was bound to come to her room, she'd recognized that horrible look in his eyes. And yet – if he dared to do so, she was determined to repel him, because she didn't have to take it any more, there were laws against incest and sexual abuse. Besides, she was big enough to fight back.

She quickly put on her pyjamas and got into bed, pulling

the covers up around her neck, watching television until she fell into an uneasy sleep.

She didn't know how late it was when she heard the click of her door opening. By the time she was fully awake, he was sitting on the side of her bed stinking of expensive cigars and too much brandy. *He always has to have alcohol*, she thought, her heart sinking. Alcohol and abuse. The two had gone together for as long as she could remember.

'Wass it like, kitten,' he asked, slurring his words, 'when boys kiss you? Whyn't you show Daddy 'xactly how they do it?'

'Daddy,' she said, reverting to the frightened little girl she once was, 'please don't do this any more. *Please*, Daddy, you know it's not right.'

'*C'mon*, sweet pea,' he mumbled, 'tell me what boys do to you. Do they put their tongue in your mouth? Touch your breasts? Your vagina? All your private places.' His big clumsy hands began unbuttoning her pyjama top. 'You can tell Daddy. Daddy's entitled to know.'

'No!' she shrieked, shrinking away from him. 'I warned you – you can't do this to me any more!'

'Wassamatter?' he slurred, his big hands fondling her breasts. 'Aren't you Daddy's little angel any more?'

'No! No! No!' she yelled, shoving him away with all her strength.

'But Daddy loves you,' he said, brandy breath enveloping her. 'You're my baby. My own little baby girly.'

And as his hands started to fondle her again, she leaped from her bed, raced into the bathroom, slamming and locking the door in his face.

Then she slid to the floor and burst into tears.

Enough was enough. She had to get out.

Chapter Fifty-three

 ALISON SEWELL had more money than she'd ever dreamed of. Her photographs of Lara Ivory were making her a fortune – especially the more explicit ones, too detailed for a weekly tabloid. Although she didn't believe in sharing her new-found wealth, she'd gone to an agent who specialized in selling the more sensational type of photos. He'd cut a deal with one of the monthly men's magazines, and now she was about to become even richer.

How proud Uncle Cyril would be of her. She regretted his demise *and* the death of her mother, who'd always said she'd never do as well as Uncle Cyril. She'd shown both of them. Pity they were ten feet under.

Now that she had Lara Ivory back in her sights, she thirsted for more. Staking out her house from a distance – because it wouldn't do to get thrown back in jail – she'd soon observed there was a new man in residence.

Tramp! Did she have to sleep with everyone?

Alison soon found out who he was. Joey Lorenzo – some small-time actor. He was good-looking. Big deal. Alison hated him too.

She kept far enough away that they couldn't spot her, and took a series of pictures of them coming and going.

While she was waiting for *Truth and Fact* to run, she

discovered that if she climbed a nearby tree she could get a clear shot into Lara's bedroom. This so excited her that she nearly fell out of the tree, only saving herself by clinging to a protruding branch.

She called her new-found agent. 'What if I can get shots of Lara Ivory screwing her boyfriend?'

He promised her a hefty cheque and a Cadillac. Incredible! Uncle Cyril had never gotten a Cadillac.

The night before *Truth and Fact* hit the stands she almost got the shot. Lara and Joey were in the bedroom, talking; then Lara walked into the bathroom, and Joey pulled off his T-shirt.

Click. Click. This was shaping up nicely.

Joey began flexing his muscles. *Click click click.*

He walked toward the window. Even better.

He pulled down the shades.

Bastard! How could he do such a thing?

But she'd get 'em, no doubt about that. All she needed was patience.

If there was one thing Alison excelled at, it was waiting around.

Chapter Fifty-four

 EARLY FRIDAY morning, photos of Lara taken from the set during the rape scene were front page on *Truth and Fact* – a particularly down and dirty tabloid.

Lara Ivory – skirt up around her waist.

Lara Ivory – topless.

Lara Ivory – lying in the gutter almost totally naked.

Nikki was the first to see them, because when she woke up in Aiden's rumpled bed and checked with her answering machine at home, there were several messages from an angry Richard yelling and carrying on.

She immediately woke Aiden and asked him to run out and get her a copy of the paper. He pulled on his jeans and obliged.

When he came back and handed her the offending tabloid she stared at it in horror. For once Richard's information was right. Somebody had gotten extremely graphic photographs of Lara.

Aiden inspected the photos over her shoulder. 'Hey, we should've been paid for these,' he remarked, like it was no big deal. 'I don't show off my ass for free.'

'Lara will freak,' Nikki groaned, dismayed. 'I'd better call Mick, find out how this happened.'

'It doesn't matter,' Aiden said. 'The photos are out there now. Look at it as good publicity for the movie.'

'You don't understand,' Nikki said. '*I* feel responsible. I should've posted guards on the set.'

'Fuck it,' Aiden said. 'I never believe anything I read, you shouldn't either.'

'It's not a question of believing. The pictures are *there* for everyone to see,' she said, reaching for the phone. 'I have to tell her myself.'

Mrs Crenshaw answered, informing her that Lara had already left and was on her way to work.

'I've got to go,' Nikki said, frantically gathering up her clothes from the floor and quickly dressing.

'I'll drive you,' Aiden offered.

She nodded. 'Can you break speed records? I have to get to her first.'

'We're on our way,' he said. 'I'm gonna give you the second greatest thrill ride of your life!'

☆ ☆ ☆

'Come in, make yourself comfortable,' Richard Barry said, ushering Madelaine Francis into his bungalow at the Beverly Hills Hotel.

'This is quite lovely,' Madelaine said, inspecting every detail.

'They recently refurbished the hotel,' Richard said. 'I like hotel living. Takes a lot of the daily responsibility out of life.'

'I thought you were married,' Madelaine remarked, placing her Prada purse on a table.

'Separated,' Richard replied, heading for the phone. 'What can I get you?'

'A decaf cappuccino would be nice.'

'Two decaf cappuccinos,' Richard said into the receiver.

Madelaine sat down. There was something vaguely familiar about Richard Barry, she felt as if they'd met before. But she couldn't remember where or when, which irritated her, because she prided herself on a brilliant memory. Of course, he was a famous director, so maybe he struck her as familiar because she'd seen his photo and read about his movies over the years. Yes, she decided, that was it.

True to his word, he'd made all the arrangements to fly her to LA. She'd arrived yesterday from New York, and was staying at the Beverly Regent Hotel for three nights. Well aware that this free trip had something to do with Joey, she was most curious to find out what. Patting her briefcase she said, 'I've brought tapes of several young actors whose talent I'm sure you'll appreciate. And if you care to see any of them in person, I can arrange to fly them out. Shall we view the tapes now?'

'No,' Richard said, wasting no time. 'Put them on the table. I'll take a look with my people later.'

'They're for you to keep,' Madelaine said. 'I had copies made.'

'You're very organized.'

'I have to be in my business,' she replied, thinking how charming and attractive he was – not what she'd expected at all.

'So,' he said, getting right to it, 'tell me about Joey Lorenzo.'

'What is it you wish to know?' she asked carefully.

Richard fixed her with a purposeful gaze. 'Everything,' he said.

For one wild moment she wondered if he was gay, and *that's* why he wanted information on Joey.

No. At one time he'd been married to Lara Ivory, and was

now married to Nikki Barry, the costume designer, so he couldn't possibly be gay. Although you never knew in Hollywood, there were always surprises.

'Everything is a very all-encompassing word,' she said slowly.

'I'll be truthful with you, Ms Francis—' he began.

'Please call me Madelaine,' she interrupted.

'OK, Madelaine, allow me to be frank. I'm looking forward to seeing the tapes of your actors, and I'm sure that sometime in the future we'll do business together. But right now I have a problem with Joey Lorenzo, and I need information.'

'You do?' she said, wondering if Joey had stolen money from him, too. 'And what might that problem be?'

'Unfortunately he's attached himself to my wife,' Richard said, his face grim.

'Oh,' Madelaine said, quite surprised.

'Nobody seems to know anything about him,' Richard continued. 'And the truth is – I'm extremely concerned.'

And so you should be, Madelaine thought. *Joey Lorenzo is a thieving sonofabitch.* 'Did he meet Mrs Barry on a movie?' she asked politely.

'It's not Nikki he's with,' Richard answered impatiently. 'It's my ex-wife, Lara Ivory.'

For a moment Madelaine was completely speechless.

Joey with Lara Ivory? Impossible!

Then she thought about it and suddenly everything made sense. Joey was devastatingly handsome with charm to spare – not to mention sensational in bed. Women chased him wherever he went. Why *wouldn't* Lara Ivory want him?

'I . . . I don't know what to say,' she said, shaking her head. 'Joey's quite volatile. You're right to be apprehensive.'

Richard leaned toward her. 'Can I ask you an extremely personal question, Madelaine?'

'I suppose so,' she said, thinking it wasn't fair. How could she, Madelaine Francis, compete with one of the most beautiful women in the world? Not that she wanted him back, no way.

His voice was low and intent. 'Did you and Joey have an intimate relationship?'

She felt herself blushing. 'Look, Mr Barry, I realize Joey's quite a bit younger than me, but . . . sometimes, men of my age only want twenty-two-year-olds.' A long pause. 'Yes,' she admitted, refusing to make any more excuses. 'Joey was there, and very responsive. We lived together for a while.'

Right, Richard thought triumphantly. *He's the hustler I imagined he was. Living with an older agent to further his career. Madelaine Francis has to be at least twenty years his senior, and she's hardly Jane Fonda.*

The room service waiter knocked on the door and delivered two cappuccinos. Richard signed the check.

'Can I get you anything else, Mr Barry?' the waiter asked hopefully – really wanting to say— 'Will you read my screenplay? I act, too.'

'No,' Richard said curtly.

Reluctantly the waiter left the room. As soon as he was gone Richard turned back to Madelaine.

'Exactly how long were you and Joey together?' he asked, his voice tense.

She hesitated for a few seconds, then decided that she might as well tell him *something*, after all she had nothing to lose and everything to gain if she could win Richard Barry's friendship. 'Joey was twenty-four when we first met,' she began, remembering the moment only too well. 'He was a young actor trying to make it in New York and not getting very far.' She let out a long weary sigh. 'Believe me, I did plenty for him. Landed him a substantial role in *Solid*, a movie for which he received fabulous reviews. After that stellar beginning his career was all set to rise. Then he vanished.'

'What do you mean – vanished?' Richard asked, his interest aroused.

'He left town,' Madelaine said, sipping her cappuccino. 'Nobody heard from him. Nobody knew where he'd gone. Six years later he reappeared, told me he'd had family problems. Like a fool I took him back, and shortly after, I sent him up for the role in *The Dreamer*, where he obviously met your ex-wife. That's the last I saw of him.'

Richard drummed his fingers on the edge of his chair. 'Where was he for those six years?'

Madelaine shook her head. 'I have no idea.'

'What about his fiancée?'

'Fiancée?' she said, frowning. 'I know nothing of a fiancée.'

'He told everyone on *The Dreamer* he was engaged.'

'To whom?'

'A woman called Phillipa?'

'Knowing Joey – my guess is he probably made it up to make him appear more substantial.'

'He'd do something like that?'

She gave a bitter laugh. 'Joey would do anything.'

'Didn't you ever try to find him when he ran off?'

She shrugged. 'Not my style, Mr Barry. I'm hardly a detective.'

'Were you living with him when he made *The Dreamer*?'

She nodded, her anger building. Dumped twice. It wasn't fair. Joey Lorenzo was a cheating no-good bastard and she hated him for the way he'd played her.

She managed to hold her anger in check, it wouldn't do to let Richard Barry know how dumb she'd been. 'Perhaps, Mr Barry, you can do *me* a favour,' she said, fumbling in her purse for a cigarette, desperate for a nicotine fix.

'What would that be?'

'Give me Joey's address. There's a business matter I need to discuss with him.'

Richard leaned over and lit her cigarette, noting her trembling hands. He felt sorry for her, she was his age, but everyone knew it was different for men. Men could get away with going out with girls twenty or thirty years younger than them, and nobody said a word. However, if a woman did it, she was considered a pathetic old desperado.

'He's living with my ex-wife,' Richard said. 'He's also in the movie she's shooting – *Revenge* – a low-budget piece of crap. I'll give you her number. In fact,' he added, as if the thought had only just occurred to him, 'it might be helpful if you told her personally about you and Joey.'

'I can do that,' Madelaine offered, filling her lungs with soothing smoke. *I'd love to do that.*

'Lara knows nothing about him,' Richard continued. 'If she did, maybe she'd see things more clearly.'

'Perhaps you'd like to arrange a meeting between us,' Madelaine suggested helpfully. 'I'm available.'

Hmm, Richard thought, *nothing like a cooperative vengeful woman.* 'As a matter of fact,' he said, 'I'm visiting the set this morning. Would you have time to come with me?'

'I'm sure I can make time.'

'Good.'

Madelaine Francis understood exactly what Richard Barry wanted her to do. And, she decided, it would be her pleasure. Her own personal way of getting back at Joey.

Chapter Fifty-five

 LINDEN, LARA'S publicist, got to her before anyone else, handing her the offending tabloid in the privacy of her trailer. She stared at the two-page spread of revealing photographs and felt sick. Who'd allowed a photographer to capture the most intimate of scenes? Why wasn't anyone protecting her?

'I don't believe this!' she said, utterly dismayed. 'How can this have happened?'

'Somebody on the set with a hidden camera,' Linden replied. 'Mick or Nikki should've had everyone on alert. If they'd been aware – this couldn't've been done.'

'It's simply not fair,' she whispered, her voice breaking. 'I feel so, so . . . *violated*.'

'It's a scene from a movie, Lara,' Linden said, trying to reassure her. 'It's certainly not you.'

'Of course it's me,' she answered vehemently, eyes flashing danger. 'You'd need a magnifying glass to read the small print that says the photos are from a movie.'

'I'll get into damage control. We'll put a whole other spin on this story.'

'How do I know they didn't release these pictures to get publicity for *Revenge*?' she asked flatly.

'You think Nikki would do that?'

'I don't know *what* to think any more,' she replied, feeling totally betrayed. 'Richard was right, he said they were using me. So did Joey.'

'There's nothing you can do about it now,' Linden said, taking the tabloid out of her hands. 'The best thing is to ignore it.'

'Thanks a lot,' she said, indignantly. 'You try ignoring it if these pictures were of you.'

'I don't think anyone would pay to see me in the buff,' he deadpanned.

'It's not funny, Linden.'

'I know, I know. Honestly Lara, I understand how difficult it is for you.'

No, you don't, she wanted to respond. *You have no idea what it's like to be humiliated this way. Reduced to nothing more than tits and ass.*

'OK,' she said, dismissing him. 'Go do damage control.'

He nodded. 'I'll check with you later.'

When he was gone she sat down, wondering how she was going to explain it to Joey. He was at an all-day photo shoot, so hopefully no one would mention it to him. She'd tell him tonight when she'd calmed down.

Shortly after Linden left, Nikki arrived. Lara didn't take a beat. 'What in hell happened?' she demanded coldly. 'How did these pictures get out?'

'Oh, God!' Nikki groaned. 'You saw them.'

'*Saw* them? I've had Quinn on the phone doing his "I told you so" number. Thank God Joey hasn't seen them yet, he'll go ballistic when he does. Richard's on his way over.'

Nikki could barely contain her annoyance. 'Why?'

'Because he called and I asked him to,' Lara answered defiantly. 'He *cares* about what goes on in my life, unlike *some* people.'

'I'm so sorry,' Nikki apologized. 'I don't know how anybody could've gotten those shots.'

'When I agreed to make *Revenge*, I expected to be protected,' Lara said, her voice an icy blast. 'The studios always protect me. Why can't you?'

'Believe me,' Nikki said earnestly. 'It's not my fault.'

'*You're* the producer of *Revenge*, that makes the responsibility yours.'

'Can't argue with that,' Nikki said sheepishly.

'Quinn's furious. He says this could have a very negative effect on my career.'

'I'm sure he's overreacting.'

'I understand your ambition, Nikki,' Lara continued. 'But I didn't expect I was the one who'd end up getting used.'

'Now you're being unfair.'

'I'm too angry to be fair,' Lara responded. 'I mean, how would you like to be out there in the tabloids – naked for everyone to see? I've never done nude photographs in my life, and now I find myself in this position because of your damn movie.'

Richard arrived shortly after, just as Nikki was leaving the trailer. They exchanged abrupt hellos.

He hurried over to Lara, put his arms around her and held her close, breathing in her seductive scent. 'Wouldn't listen to me, would you?' he said, hugging her tightly.

She pulled away with a helpless shrug. 'What can I say? You were right.'

'If it had been my set, you can rest assured it would never have happened.'

'I know,' she said ruefully.

'This is what you get when you work with amateurs.'

'I guess so,' she replied, sitting down. 'Thanks for coming, Richard, it means a lot to me.'

'Sweetheart, I have only your best interests at heart.'

'I know.'

'You're on my mind all the time.' He paused, gauging her mood. 'I'm sure you know the main reason Nikki and I are no longer together is because you and I still have a very special connection? A connection that can never be broken.'

'Don't start, Richard—' she said, hoping he wasn't going to get too caught up in this.

'No,' he said sharply, 'hear me out, Lara. Screwing around on you was the biggest mistake of my life. And I want you to know that if you can ever forgive me, and think about us getting back together, then I'm always here for you.'

'That's very flattering,' she said, picking up a cold mug of tea and sipping it anyway. 'But, Richard, I'm with somebody now. I'm very involved.'

'How involved?'

'Well . . .' She hesitated for a moment. 'Joey and I are thinking of getting married, only please keep it to yourself. No one knows.'

He stared into her clear green eyes and wondered how someone so beautiful and nice could be so fucking naive. 'Are you serious?' he said disbelievingly.

She nodded. 'Very.'

'Listen to me carefully, Lara,' he said in measured tones. 'I warned you what would happen on this movie. Now I'm warning you what will happen if you marry Joey.'

Why did he always have to try and run her life? Why couldn't he just be her friend? 'Richard,' she said, attempting to remain calm, 'please don't tell me what to do, because it's really none of your business.'

He began pacing. 'Did Joey ever mention Madelaine Francis?'

She shook her head.

'He used to live with her – in fact, he was with her when he met you.' He checked out her reaction. She looked surprised. 'You should talk to Madelaine,' he added, striking fast.

'Why would I want to do that?' she asked, her eyes two stubborn pinpoints of light.

He kept going, knowing exactly how to get to her. 'Scared of what you might find out?' he challenged.

She stood up, wishing he'd leave. 'This is ridiculous,' she said impatiently.

'Do it for me, sweetheart,' he said, using his best powers of persuasion. 'Meet the woman, if only for a few minutes.'

'There's no reason—'

'For old times, Lara.'

'Oh, all right,' she said, agreeing reluctantly, her curiosity aroused. 'But I can assure you, it won't make any difference.'

He smiled to himself. *Wanna bet?* 'She's in my car,' he said. 'I'll go fetch her.'

Chapter Fifty-six

 GREG GORMAN was a master photographer with several coffee-table books full of photos of stars. Joey was impressed. And the good thing was that Greg liked him, encouraged him to shine. So there he was in Greg's Beverly Boulevard studio, centre stage, under the lights, the camera clicking away, and Toni Braxton belting out a sexy love song on the stereo.

Joey got off on being the centre of attention. Getting primped and fussed over was his idea of a good time. And the good news was he hadn't even had to pay for the session, because Lara had spoken to an executive at Orpheus Studios – the studio responsible for *The Dreamer* – and gotten them to pay for it.

Greg stopped to change film, and the make-up person, hairdresser and stylist all descended on Joey at once.

This is how it should be, he reflected. *Me – on a star trip. It's about time.*

He grinned and stretched. He had a career. He had a fantastic woman he planned to marry. After all the shit, things were finally turning his way.

☆ ☆ ☆

Richard ushered Madelaine into Lara's trailer. She was sitting on the banquette seating, tapping her fingers impatiently on a plastic table. 'Hi,' she said, a little cold and a little tense.

'Hi, honey,' Richard said warmly. 'Say hello to Madelaine Francis.'

Lara nodded brusquely.

Madelaine stared at the beautiful actress. She was even more gorgeous in the flesh than on the screen.

Richard edged toward the door. 'Why don't I leave you two alone,' he suggested.

'Fine,' Lara replied, wondering why she'd agreed to do this. Oh yes, she knew – Richard and his persuasive ways had struck again.

As soon as he was gone, she shifted uncomfortably. 'I feel most awkward about this,' she said.

'So do I,' Madelaine agreed.

'It's Richard's idea,' she added. 'And quite frankly, if you have anything to say about Joey, I think he should be here to listen.'

'Wouldn't bother me,' Madelaine said, sitting down. 'In fact, he *should* be here.'

'Richard doesn't like Joey,' Lara stated with a weary sigh. 'He's busy digging for dirt.'

'Perhaps he's trying to protect you.'

'From what?' she answered sharply, appalled at the woman's nerve.

'Just a thought,' Madelaine murmured.

'Anyway, how do *you* fit into this?' Lara asked, her tone abrupt. 'Did you know Joey's fiancée?'

'Why does everyone keep mentioning a fiancée?' Madelaine said, irritably. 'When I got him the part in *The Dreamer*, he was living with *me*.'

'You?' Lara said, hardly able to conceal her surprise. The woman was old enough to be his mother. 'When Joey and I met, he was engaged to a girl called Phillipa. Are you Phillipa?'

'No,' Madelaine said, adding a dry— 'And I'm not a girl, as you've probably noticed.'

'I didn't mean—'

'Look, Miss Ivory,' Madelaine said brusquely, 'Joey Lorenzo and I were lovers until he met you. After that, it appears I was no longer useful.'

Lara took a long deep breath. *Why is this happening to me?* she thought. *Why?*

Because you're an ugly little slut and you don't deserve any happiness.

Her father's words came back to haunt her. So harsh. So unforgettable.

'Did Richard put you up to this?' she asked at last.

'Not at all,' Madelaine said. 'I've been an agent for twenty-five years, I have an impeccable reputation. You can ask anyone about me.' She began searching in her purse for a cigarette. 'Mind if I smoke?'

'Go ahead,' Lara said flatly.

'Unfortunately, several years ago I foolishly got involved with Joey,' Madelaine said, lighting up. 'We were together almost a year, then he took off for six years. I have no idea where he went. When he returned, he moved back into my apartment.' She dragged deeply on her cigarette. 'And this is something I *didn't* tell your ex – when Joey left the first time, he stole seven thousand dollars of my money.'

Lara felt a queasy sensation in the pit of her stomach. Instinct told her this woman was speaking the truth. 'What about Phillipa?' she asked in a strained voice.

'There *is* no Phillipa,' Madelaine said, waving her cigarette in the air. 'He made her up. Joey has a very lively imagination.'

'Why . . . why would he do that?' Lara stammered.

'Who knows with Joey? I can only assume he didn't want to tell you about me.'

'He could have,' Lara said bravely. 'There's nothing wrong with living with an older woman—'

'Be realistic, dear,' Madelaine interrupted. 'He was with me for what I could do for him. The ungrateful bastard *stole* my money, and *I* let him get away with it. If you'd found that out, you might have regarded him differently.'

Lara got up and began wandering aimlessly around the trailer. 'What else do you know about him?' she asked.

'Not very much. Joey was always secretive about his background – didn't want me prying.'

Lara remembered the number she'd called in New York – Phillipa's number. If it was the same as Madelaine's that definitely meant she was telling the truth. She asked Madelaine for her home number, then buzzed Cassie and had her check it with the call sheet from *The Dreamer*.

It was the same number.

She turned back to Madelaine. 'Are you sure he stole your money?'

Madelaine nodded. 'No doubt about it. When he returned, he gave me back three thousand dollars. The rest I recovered from the cheque he got from his work on *The Dreamer*.'

Lara's mind was in turmoil. So Joey – *her* Joey – was nothing more than a cheap opportunist – a thief who used women for what he could get out of them. Her head was spinning. 'I . . . I don't know what to say, Ms Francis . . . this is information I'd sooner not have heard. But now that you've told me, I suppose I'll have to deal with it.'

'I understand,' Madelaine said, bobbing her head sympathetically. 'It's not easy. Joey's *very* charming, he has the knack. And of course he's also an extremely talented lover – as I'm sure you know. When Joey makes love to you, you feel as if you're the only woman in the world.' She chuckled wryly. 'And believe me – at my age, that's quite a feat.'

'I'm sure,' Lara murmured, while her idyllic world spun out of control, crashing around her in tiny fragmented pieces.

☆ ☆ ☆

Early in the morning Summer complained of a stomach ache, staying safely in bed until her father had departed for his office. As soon as she heard his car leave the garage, she leaped out of bed and raced downstairs.

Mrs Stern, their housekeeper, regarded her in surprise. 'I thought you weren't feeling well, missy,' she said accusingly.

'I'm much better now,' Summer said, all blond innocence. 'Gotta get to school. Major test today.'

'Shall I prepare your breakfast?'

'No, thanks, Mrs Stern.'

'If you're sure . . .'

'Absolutely.' A very brief pause, then— 'I think I left some of my school work in Daddy's study. I'd better go take a look.' She dashed into his private domain, slamming the door behind her. As soon as she was sure Mrs Stern wasn't about to follow her, she began searching his desk. Tina had the right idea, find money and run. And if she did find some, she planned on running all the way to LA because there was no way she was staying around for any more nocturnal visits.

One by one she frantically ransacked his desk drawers, until hidden under a pile of matching folders in the bottom left-hand drawer she discovered a large manila envelope containing a stack of pornographic pictures – most of them featuring young schoolgirls. What a stinking pervert! Why had Nikki left her with him? Why hadn't she cared enough to take her along?

On impulse she grabbed the envelope and ran upstairs,

where she went straight to his closet, rifling through the pockets of his suits, remembering that when she was a kid that's where he'd kept his money. Her eager hands dived in and out of various inside pockets, finally coming across two thousand dollars secured with a rubber band.

She couldn't believe her luck. That much money should easily buy her a cheap ticket to LA.

Not wishing to alert Mrs Stern, she hurried into her room, quickly putting on her school clothes. Then she stuffed as much as she could into a large duffel bag, which she managed to smuggle out of the house before Mrs Stern noticed.

She lugged the heavy duffel bag to the corner of the street, hopping a bus into the centre of town. From there she hailed a cab to the airport.

LA – here I come! she thought. *And not a moment too soon.*

☆　☆　☆

'So Lara was really pissed with you?' Aiden asked, scratching the light stubble on his chin.

'Yes,' Nikki replied ruefully, as they stood by the Kraft service stand picking at a bowl of fruit. 'Then Richard turned up.'

Aiden bit into an apple. 'What did *he* want?'

'I told you, he's obsessed with Lara,' Nikki said, shaking her head. 'I must've been crazy to marry him. I didn't even see it. Although I do remember that on the South of France location he was always worried about where she was and what she was doing. Silly me – I thought he was merely being nice – y'know, the concerned ex.'

'Fuck Richard. Who needs him?' Aiden said, leading her over to a couple of high-backed canvas director's chairs. 'Let's talk about us.'

'What about us?' she asked, slightly breathless.

'I was kinda wondering,' he said, scratching his chin again. 'What happens after the movie? You and I gonna hang out? Be friends? Lovers? What's the deal here, Nik?'

Even though she liked him a lot, she wasn't in the mood to be pressured, everything was happening too fast and she needed time to think. 'Uh . . . well . . . I'll be shut away in the editing rooms for the next six weeks, trying to put this movie together with Mick.'

'Sounds like an experience,' he said drily.

'I'm looking forward to it,' she said. 'If *Revenge* is successful, I hope I get a chance to do it again.'

'You're really into this whole producing deal.'

'It's exciting – in spite of the setbacks.'

'Guess it beats sittin' around.'

'Aiden, I've been meaning to thank you—'

'For what?'

'For giving such a brilliant performance.'

'Hey,' he smiled faintly, pleased with her praise, 'it's what I do. And y'know something – Lara was pretty good, too. Surprised everyone.'

'She did, didn't she?'

'This movie's gonna get a lot of attention.'

'Do you think so?'

'Two thumbs up everyone's ass.'

She laughed, suddenly realizing she was going to miss him. 'So,' she said tentatively, 'what are your future plans?'

He shrugged like it didn't much matter. 'If anybody'll insure me, there's a few independents who're willing to take a chance. Course, once you're a known druggie, it's a bitch gettin' work.'

She watched him carefully. 'Tell me the truth, Aiden. Are you really straight now?'

'I take it day to day,' he answered restlessly. 'Course, it ain't easy, on account of the fact temptation's in my face every single minute. There's a shitload of actors into heroin – an' coke is like Sweet 'n' Low – you want a little snort with your breakfast – no freakin' problem. It's everywhere I go.'

'That must be difficult.'

A cynical grin. 'You could say that.'

'I *do* want to see you,' she said shyly. 'But first I need time for myself.'

'Hey—' a sly smile – 'as long as I'm not taken by the time you're ready.'

She smiled back. 'You're much nicer than you want people to think.'

'That a compliment?' he asked flippantly.

'I'll leave you to decide.'

Lara passed by on her way to the set, her expression grim. *Richard probably hasn't made things any better*, Nikki thought. *He's getting off on the drama. Damn him!*

'Need anything?' she called as Lara rushed past.

'Yes – a new life,' Lara snapped.

Nikki started to follow her. 'You *are* coming to the wrap party tonight?' she asked, hopeful that Lara would say yes.

'I wouldn't count on me if I were you,' Lara replied, not stopping.

Nikki knew when to back off.

☆ ☆ ☆

Lara had no intention of attending the end of filming party. She went to the set, performed her scene, then got on her cellphone to Cassie. 'We're taking a trip,' she said, her mind still in turmoil. 'Pack me a couple of bags, and meet me at the studio as soon as possible. I'm not coming home. Whatever you do, *don't* mention anything to Joey.'

'I take it he won't be coming with us?'

'You've got that right.'

'Where are we going?' Cassie asked curiously.

'To the house at the beach. Not a word to anyone.'

'It's done,' Cassie said.

Yes, Lara thought. *It's done. My life with Joey is done, too. Over. Finished. History.*

And she was filled with an overwhelming sense of sadness and loss.

Chapter Fifty-seven

 'HOW DID it go?' Richard asked, when Madelaine returned to his hotel as he'd requested.

'I'm sure it went exactly as you planned,' she responded crisply as he ushered her inside. She was not stupid, she knew the result Richard was after. He wanted his exquisite ex-wife back, and who could blame him?

He was cradling a hefty vodka on the rocks. 'Want one?' he asked.

'No, thank you,' she replied, walking over to the couch and sitting down.

He joined her. 'Did you tell Lara everything?' he asked intently.

'Yes.'

He nodded to himself. 'Excellent.'

'I also told her about the seven thousand dollars Joey stole from me.'

Richard sat up straight. Seven thousand bucks! Jesus! This was better than he'd thought. 'What did she say?'

Madelaine shrugged. 'She didn't have to say anything. It was all in her eyes. Disappointment, betrayal . . .'

'Good,' he said, before he could stop himself.

Madelaine raised a cynical eyebrow. 'Good?' she questioned.

'Uh . . . I mean it's good she found out the truth before it's too late.'

'I suppose so.'

'They were planning on getting married, you know.'

'Really?' Madelaine wasn't surprised. What did Joey have to lose by marrying Lara Ivory? Exactly nothing.

'Yeah. I'm sure you've persuaded her to change her mind,' Richard said, taking a hefty swig of vodka. 'When she gets over being hurt she'll thank both of us.'

'I'm glad I could be of service,' Madelaine said.

He jumped up; she'd served her purpose, now he was ready to see her on her way.

It was at that moment Madelaine's memory nudged her into almost remembering where she knew Richard Barry from. The walk, the eyes, something about the voice . . . 'Tell me,' she asked curiously, 'were you ever an actor?'

'No,' he said quickly. 'Never.'

'There's something so familiar about you . . .'

He prodded her towards the door. 'Actors are treated like cattle,' he said abruptly. 'I prefer the other side of the camera.'

'Well . . .' she said, 'don't forget to take a look at my actors. I handle some good ones.'

'I'll view your tape tomorrow with my people.'

'I shall look forward to hearing from you.'

He closed the door on her before she had anything else to say. Why did women always want to talk? Jabber jabber jabber. Their gossipy little mouths going full tilt. Why couldn't they just shut the fuck up?

Were you ever an actor? Was she insane?

☆ ☆ ☆

I am Richard Barry, famous director. I have been Richard Barry for almost thirty years. I took the Richard from Mr

Burton, and the Barry from a storefront opposite a movie theatre playing Caesar and Cleopatra.

Richard Barry. When I came back to America from my two-year sojourn in Mexico, that's who I was. The name had stature, dignity. The name represented the kind of life I aspired to. No more fucking my way to the bottom. What with the accidental killing of Hadley and my out-of-control drug days, I knew I couldn't sink much lower.

It was 1970. I was thirty years old and determined to make my mark. Since being thrown out by my father at sixteen, I'd fucked around for fifteen years. Now the fucking around was over, and Richard Barry was born.

I re-entered the States with a totally new agenda, plus papers proving who I was, and an attitude geared toward success. I also looked different. Thinner, fitter, with a neat beard and short hair. I did not resemble the stoned hustler who'd fled to Mexico, scared shitless he'd be arrested for murder.

After my married friend returned to America, I stayed in Acapulco – got myself a job working bar in a small place down by the water. The bar was owned by a long-retired film director, Hector Gonzales. Hector was a friendly man who loved to talk – especially to Americans. He owned a fishing boat, and one day he invited me to go out with him. After that first time we'd go fishing every weekend, and during our long hours of idly sitting there, waiting for a fish to bite, he'd regale me with tales about his life. And what a life he'd had. Married five times – twice to beautiful movie stars. Fourteen children. Twenty-six grandchildren. The recipient of many awards. The director of thirty-four movies.

It wasn't long before Hector invited me to his house, where he showed me books of yellowing press clips and photographs from the movies he'd directed. It was fascinating stuff and he was a fascinating character. Although he'd worked in Mexico most of his life, he'd directed one American film, and the tales he had to tell about that experience were quite something.

Listening to Hector was totally absorbing. I told him about directing a couple of episodes of a TV show in Los Angeles, and how much I'd enjoyed it.

'That's clever,' Hector said, with a knowing laugh, followed by a hacking cough. 'Everyone wants to be an actor. Don't they understand? The director is the one with the power.'

I began picking his brain, thinking that maybe I'd been pursuing the wrong profession all these years. I loved film, knew a lot about it – why couldn't I direct? The two times I'd done it had been fulfilling experiences, and I was certainly smart enough.

Every night after work, I'd go over to Hector's and view some of the movies he'd directed, learning about every aspect of film-making from the old man. After we'd finished with his films, he made me watch the great movies of other directors. Billy Wilder, John Huston and the like. Hector supplied me with the education I'd never had. The education I found I craved.

When I finally returned to America I was ready. I knew exactly what I wanted to do.

Hector had given me a couple of names to call, and I used his connections immediately. I'd put together an interesting fake résumé on the work I'd done in England over the past five years, and the first person I showed it to believed every word. I got a job as an assistant editor.

Since I'd temporarily given up women, work became my passion. From assistant editor it took me only a year to rise to main editor. And then an acquaintance of mine who read scripts for one of the big agencies let me have dibs on his rejection pile. One day I read a script called Killer Eyes. It was way before its time, but I immediately knew that here was the vehicle *that would enable me to start my directing career. I hired a writer, and together we restructured the script. Then – with a little help from Hector's connections – I raised the money to make an extremely low-budget film. Killer Eyes became an underground hit. And I became a force to reckon with. After that I never looked back.*

By the time I married Lara Ivory I was as big as they could get, and nobody ever recognized me from my nefarious past. I'd successfully managed to kill off the man I once was – the murdering stud who lived off women, did drugs, sold his body. I was totally reborn.

So what the hell did Madelaine mean by asking me if I was ever an actor?

No, sweetheart, I was never an actor. That person ceased to exist long ago.

And anyone who tries to bring him back will be severely punished.

Chapter Fifty-eight

'Hi,' Summer said.

'Hi,' Tina responded.

Then they both burst into giggles before awkwardly hugging each other.

Summer had called from the airport and Tina had insisted that she come stay.

'Enter chaos,' Tina invited, flinging open the door of her perfectly tidy apartment. 'Good flight?'

'As if!' Summer exclaimed, with a fake shudder. 'I was squeezed in next to a gruesomely fat lady with two whiny little geeks and a brain-dead husband.'

'At least you're here. Wait till Norman Barton finds out – according to Darlene, he's been asking for you ever since our one night of dirty lust!'

'He has?' she said, perking up.

'Yeah, but I didn't tell Darlene you were on your way back,' Tina said. 'Thought we'd work a deal for ourselves – knock out the commission factor. Whaddaya think?'

'Excellent,' she responded, the realization hitting her that she'd *finally* made a break and now she was free – totally out on her own! No more Daddy Dearest's midnight visits or Nikki's nagging to put up with. It was frightening, but at the same time extremely exhilarating. 'I'm starving,' she gulped.

'So'm I,' Tina agreed, leading her into the spare bedroom. 'Dump your stuff an' we'll go get food, scope out the action.'

Summer looked around. The room was filled with stuffed animals and glassy-eyed porcelain dolls; on the wall were giant posters of Brad Pitt and Antonio Sabbato, Jr. 'Didn't know you got off on Antonio,' she remarked, squinting at the posters.

'Oooh ... those big sexy eyes!' Tina said, making a suggestive sucking noise with her lips. 'Maybe if I'm lucky I'll get to find out if he's got a great big zoomer to go with 'em!'

'Sex maniac!' Summer giggled.

'Course I am!' Tina agreed, cocking her head on one side. 'Who do *you* like?'

She didn't hesitate. 'Norman Barton.'

'*That's* convenient,' Tina said, rolling her eyes.

'OhmiGod, it's so amazing to be back in LA,' Summer sighed, flopping down on the bed. 'Just walking through the airport made me feel as if I was coming home.'

'How'd you manage the daring escape?' Tina asked, darting into the hall and dragging Summer's duffel bag into the room.

'I ran. Just like you. Discovered two thousand bucks hidden in one of my dad's suits and grabbed it.'

Tina wrinkled her pretty nose. 'D'you think he'll come looking for you?'

'Spect so,' Summer replied matter-of-factly. 'Unless he's nervous I'll tell.'

'Tell what?' Tina asked casually.

'You know,' Summer answered uneasily, not sure if she was ready to reveal her dirty little secret.

'*What?*' Tina demanded, her curiosity aroused.

'The sex stuff,' Summer muttered. There, now that she'd said it, she felt better.

'Sex stuff!' Tina exclaimed in surprise. 'I thought he was your *real* father.'

'He is.'

'Gruesome!' Tina shuddered. 'What a vile old perv. You could have him *arrested*.'

'I could?' Summer said, flashing on a mental picture of Sheldon being dragged off in handcuffs – a most satisfying image.

'Yes. That's incest – it's against the law.'

'Didn't you tell me your stepfather used to come on to you?'

'Stepfathers!' Tina spat. 'They're a whole other deal.'

'I hate my father,' Summer said, feeling a strange sense of euphoria at having finally revealed her secret.

'No shit?'

'I *really* hate him,' Summer added, hammering home the message.

'You told your mom what he's been doing to you?' Tina asked curiously.

'She'd say I was making it up. Like I mentioned before – my dad's this big-time shrink in Chicago, nobody would take my word against *his*.'

'*I* would,' Tina said staunchly.

'That's 'cause you don't know him. He's scary business. Like Mr Authority.'

'Yeah – Mr Authority with a big fat hard-on for his innocent little girl,' Tina sneered in disgust. 'What a retard! How long's he been doing it to you?'

'I don't want to talk about it any more,' Summer mumbled, clamming up.

'OK, OK,' Tina said, nodding understandingly. 'But you should've told your mom, then you wouldn't've had to go back to the old degenerate, you could've stayed here.'

Tina was right, she should have gone to Nikki when it first started. But she'd been ten years old, and totally confused, plus her father was all she had.

And then there were the threats . . . *If you ever tell anyone what we do, sweet pea, they'll take you away and lock you up in a home for bad girls . . . You wouldn't want that, pumpkin, would you?*

She wasn't a bad girl then. But now she'd show him exactly how bad she could be.

He deserved punishing. He deserved punishing big-time.

☆ ☆ ☆

The session with Greg Gorman lasted several hours, and after they were finished Joey was so elated that he hung around the studio for a while talking to Megan, the pretty stylist, Teddy Antolin, hairdresser supreme, and a couple of Greg's assistants before driving home. *Finally* it was happening for him. It had taken a while, but he was almost there.

Comfortably settled behind the wheel of Lara's Mercedes, he put his foot down as he cruised along Sunset, feeling surprisingly relaxed considering he was getting married any moment.

Joey Lorenzo and Lara Ivory. Fuck! He'd hit pay dirt and found the perfect woman. And their life together would be perfect, he'd make damn sure of that.

When he reached the house he spotted Cassie in the driveway getting into her car. Cassie was never very nice to him, although he'd certainly tried with her. If she didn't change her attitude, after they were married he'd persuade Lara to let her go and hire someone who showed him more respect.

'Where're you off to?' he asked, leaning out the car window.

Cassie jumped guiltily. 'What?' she said, squeezing behind the wheel of her Saab.

He got out of the Mercedes and strolled over. 'If you're headin' to the set, ask Lara if she wants me there early, or is she gonna come home before the wrap party?'

'Yes, Joey,' Cassie said, wondering what he'd done to make Lara so mad that she was planning on taking off without him.

'Oh, and tell her to put her cellphone on, I can't seem to get through.'

'Certainly.'

'See ya,' Joey said, turning and walking into the house.

Not likely, Cassie thought, quickly setting off for the studio, Lara's bags safely stashed in the trunk.

☆ ☆ ☆

The action at the restaurant on Sunset Plaza Drive was hot and heavy as Summer and Tina made their entrance – an entrance that did not go unnoticed. Two delectable, sexy young girls always caused men to stare. The open-air tables were jammed with rich young Italians, French and Iranians. It was like a dating fest – everybody checking everybody else out.

'Eurotrash city!' Tina exclaimed, grabbing an empty table. 'I'm psyched *I* don't have to date any of these guys. They're all creepos.'

'How come?' Summer asked.

'Take a look – they all drive the same expensive sports car Daddy bought them; they all have too much spending money; and they're all into getting their dicks sucked.'

'*What*?' Summer said with a nervous giggle.

'No, thank you!' Tina continued, wrinkling her nose. 'If *I'm* sucking dick, *I'm* getting paid big bucks.'

Summer hoped she wasn't as cynical as Tina by the time she was her age. 'Do you think getting paid for sex is wrong?' she asked innocently.

'Wrong!' Tina shrieked, causing several heads to turn. '*Shit*, no! Why do it for free if you can get major bucks? I'd feel bad if I screwed a guy and *didn't* get paid. Then he'd really be scoring off me.'

'Right,' Summer said hesitantly, wondering if her father had discovered her absence, and if so – what was he going to do about it? 'When do I get to see Norman?' she asked, anxious to close the deal.

'Mustn't seem antsy,' Tina replied, as if she'd been giving it a lot of thought. 'We gotta have a plan. I was thinking I'll call him myself and set up an appointment. I filched his number from Darlene's Rolodex.' A maniacal giggle of triumph. 'She'd have a shit-fit if she knew.'

'I bet she would,' Summer agreed.

'*I* could do what she does,' Tina mused, nodding to herself.

'Like what?'

'Set girls up,' Tina said airily. 'Send them out on dates and pocket a big chunk of commission.'

'Why don't you?'

'Oh, I dunno – too much trouble. Who needs paperwork? Not me.'

Summer pushed back her long blond hair. 'But like if you only go with guys who *pay* you,' she said, frowning, 'how do you ever get into a proper relationship?'

'Ha!' Tina said. 'Take a look around this town. There's *plenty* of women who started off getting paid, an' now they're big-deal hostesses. Married to hot-shit lawyers and studio guys – all that crap.'

'You mean some men don't mind if they have to pay for it?'

'What do they care? As long as they get what they want. And from what I hear, once they marry you they don't want it at all. So *then* you've got it made.'

'I believe in falling in love.'

'Get over it!' Tina said with a rude laugh. 'There's no such thing as love.'

Summer disagreed. She'd read about it enough times to know it did exist, and she'd decided she was *definitely* making Norman Barton fall in love with her.

A young Iranian with blue-black hair and a conceited smirk cruised by their table. 'You girls wanna hit the club circuit tonight?' he offered, flashing his gold Rolex.

'With *you*?' Tina said, her voice holding just the right amount of disdain.

'Me and my friend,' he replied, indicating a shorter version of himself hovering nearby.

'Are you *paying* for it, honey?' Tina enquired with a put-down smile. He backed off quickly. She shrieked with laughter. 'Do I know how to get rid of them or what?' she said triumphantly. 'No guy likes to think he *has* to pay. The *real* smart ones are the movie stars and the big businessmen. They know it's the only way to go.'

'Really?'

'Yeah, really. And don't you forget it. If I'm gonna train you – you'd better start listening to me.'

'Oh, I will,' Summer murmured. 'I want to learn – honestly I do.'

Anything was better than going home to her father. And if Tina was prepared to teach her, she'd be the best pupil ever.

Chapter Fifty-nine

 LARA KNEW what she had to do and she didn't falter. Everyone thought she was so sweet and nice, but when she made up her mind, there was very little anyone could do to change it. She'd been a doormat over half her life – filled with guilt over her family's death; serving Aunt Lucy like a maid; a slave to Morgan Creedo. Until finally she'd gathered her strength and found her vocation – pursuing it with a steely passion. Now today everything seemed to be falling to pieces. First the revealing pictures spread all over a cheap tabloid. Then Joey.

Nobody could take her success away from her. It was her achievement in spite of horrible odds. And nobody was ever going to use her again.

☆ ☆ ☆

'Your husband's dead,' the nurse said, her expression a mixture of fake sympathy and Why do I have to give people bad news when it's the doctor's responsibility?

Lara Ann nodded. Bad news was nothing new; besides, during the four years she'd been with Morgan, she'd grown to hate him. He was no knight in shining armour come to save her from the rigours of working for Aunt Lucy. He'd turned

444

out to be a shiftless, controlling bully – with minor talent – who'd never so much as kissed her.

They'd been married almost four years, and she was still a virgin, because Morgan only required her to service him with her lips. Once, when he was very drunk, he'd told her why. 'My mama warned me that puttin' it in a woman's pussy weakens a man,' he'd said with an embarrassed snigger. 'Makes him no better than a stallion servicing a mare. I come inside you – you got me trapped for ever.'

She hadn't argued with him. By that time it was the last thing she wanted him to do.

After the nurse informed her of Morgan's demise, the doctor appeared. He was young, hardly more than a student, and quite serious.

'You had a slight concussion,' he said, studying her chart. 'Nothing serious. In fact, I'm letting you go home.'

'I don't have a home,' she said in a low voice. 'My home was the trailer behind the car. It's gone.'

'I'm afraid so,' he said. 'You're lucky to have survived. If you hadn't been asleep on the back seat . . .'

My head would've come flying off along with Morgan's, she thought. Gallows humour. She was allowed.

'Do you have family?' the doctor asked.

'No,' she answered softly. 'I have no one.'

'No one,' he repeated, clearing his throat.

'That's right.'

He looked into her appealing green eyes, and before he could help himself he'd offered her the use of the couch in his small apartment for a few days, until she decided what she was going to do.

'I won't have sex with you,' she said.

'It never occurred to me,' he lied.

And so she moved into his place with only the clothes she'd been wearing at the time of the accident, and her purse, which *contained all of their savings – five hundred dollars – and the phone number of Elliott Goldenson, a producer Morgan had said was prepared to give her a job in the movies. She wasn't quite sure she trusted Morgan's judgement – he hadn't even met Elliott Goldenson – but she called anyway, and a male secretary gave her an address in Hollywood and told her to come right over because Mr Goldenson was auditioning.*

She decided this was a sign, and hurried to the address as fast as she could get there.

When she walked into the waiting room, she knew she was in the wrong place. A gaggle of blonds everywhere, yammering away at each other. They all had one thing in common – enormous breasts.

A young man with a bright red ponytail sat behind a large desk strewn with pictures.

She went over to him. 'I'm Lara Ann Creedo,' she said. 'I called and you told me to come over. Am I in the right place?'

He looked up at her. 'Honeybunch, you couldn't be more wrong.'

'This isn't the place?' she asked, dismayed.

'You're not the kind of girl he's looking for,' he said, pursing his lips. 'Why are you here?'

'Because you said Mr Goldenson was auditioning.'

'I know. But what fool gave you this number to call?'

'My husband.'

'Oh,' he nodded knowingly, 'one of those deals.'

'Can I ask you something?' she said, leaning across the desk.

'Ask away.'

'If I'm not right for this role, is there another one coming up?'

He spoke in hushed tones. 'Sweetie bunch, you're in the wrong place. Mr Goldenson makes porno movies. I don't think that's what you're looking for.'

She stepped back. 'Oh!' she said, startled. 'But . . . my husband . . . he had this number. He said I'd be perfect.'

'Hmm . . . I'd have a word with your husband if I was you. Anyway, don't look so disappointed, at least I didn't send you in there to strip off in front of a bunch of dirty old men.'

'I wouldn't do that anyway.'

'I take it you're new in town?'

'Yes.'

'Well, precious, this is *my* advice. Find yourself a legitimate agent, and start doing the rounds. You're certainly beautiful enough.'

'How do I find a legitimate agent?'

'Look in the yellow pages. Go to William Morris, ICM – one of the big ones.'

'Who's William Morris? Do you have his phone number?'

He threw up his hands in despair. 'The girl is a total novice. William Morris is a huge agency. Don't you know anything?'

'I guess not.'

'I suggest you go back to your husband and bite his butt for sending you here.'

'I can't do that.'

'Why not?'

'He's dead.'

'Oh, my God – it's a sob story! Please, whatever you do, don't make me feel sorry for you. I'm sorry enough for myself, having to do this shitty job. The only reason they employ me is because they know I'm not about to hit on the girls. Girls not being my style, if you know what I mean.'

'Are you . . . gay?'

'Honeybunch, do rabbits mate?'

And so a friendship was born. His name was Tommy, and two days later she moved out of the doctor's apartment and into Tommy's place above a restaurant on Sunset Boulevard.

He was mother, father and brother to her. He guided and protected her; sent her to acting class; introduced her to a proper agent; fed and clothed her; counselled her on all subjects; got her a job as a waitress while she was waiting for her first break; and made sure nobody took advantage of her innocence.

And in return she nursed him after he got sick with AIDS, and sobbed at his funeral when he died ten months later.

A week after his death she landed her first big movie. Tommy never got to see her become a star.

☆ ☆ ☆

Lara sighed deeply, remembering her friend Tommy, and all the fun they'd had. It wasn't fair he'd been taken from her, but it had made her all the more determined to succeed. Tommy had given her warmth and comfort and most of all – the right guidance on how to handle herself in Hollywood. He'd taught her well. He'd also taught her never to put up with any shit.

She recalled the day she'd left Richard – the day she'd actually *caught* him getting a blow job, and he'd *still* thought he could talk her out of leaving.

Richard and his charm. In that respect he was exactly like Joey, they both had the same kind of masculine power they thought made them irresistible to women.

Well, when it really mattered, she *could* resist. And even though she loved Joey – she did not wish to continue in a relationship with a man who was a fake. He'd *used* her. Invented a fiancée, and reeled her in like a fish. God! He probably thought she was so easy. Easy and desperate for a man. Poor little frustrated movie star. How he must have laughed behind her back.

Thank God she'd found out before marrying him. What a mistake *that* would have been.

And yet, she thought sadly, *what am I going to do without his strong arms to hold and protect me? His insistent lips that brought me such unbelievable pleasure?*

Was everything about him a lie? She'd never bothered to find out. It hadn't mattered. But now that she knew, it did.

Maybe you should listen to his side of the story, her inner voice suggested.

Why? So he can lie his way out of it exactly like Richard used to?

No. She was too wise to go down that street.

As soon as Cassie arrived, she was ready to go. She'd completed her final scene, promised the cast and crew she'd see them later at the party, and managed to avoid Nikki – whom she didn't feel like confiding in.

'I brought *my* car,' Cassie said, her cheeks flushed. 'Thought if I called the limo company, people could easily track us.'

'Good thinking, Cass,' Lara said, stuffing her golden hair beneath a Laker's baseball cap, and covering her eyes with Jackie Kennedy blacker-than-black shades.

Cassie was dying to ask what was going on, but she didn't, because she knew her boss well enough to understand that she'd explain the situation when she was ready and not before.

'What did you tell the Crenshaws?' Lara asked, getting into the passenger seat and fastening her seatbelt.

'Nothing,' Cassie replied, starting the engine. 'I figured if you wanted them to know anything you'd call them later.'

Lara nodded. At least she could always depend on Cassie.

Chapter Sixty

 JOEY DRESSED carefully in a black silk Armani shirt, black slacks and a classic Armani blazer. Lara liked him in black, plus it suited him dressing against his looks. Casual yet hot.

He stared at his reflection in the mirror and remembered what he'd been doing a year ago. It wasn't a good memory – caused him sleepless nights and hot sweats. Thank God it was behind him. One day he'd tell Lara. In fact, when they were married he'd tell her everything – finally cleanse his soul to the one person he knew he could trust.

She hadn't called, which meant she was expecting him to meet her at the studio. Cassie had obviously forgotten to mention he was trying to get through on her cellphone, because the damn thing was still turned off.

He missed her, which was pretty ridiculous considering they'd only been apart one day.

That morning he'd held her in his arms stroking her into a state of almost orgasmic ecstasy. 'I'll finish the job later,' he'd joked.

'Since when did it become a job?' she'd laughed, flushed and breathless.

'You're gonna have to wait,' he'd said, kissing her soft inviting lips. 'But trust me – the wait'll be worth it.'

She'd smiled. 'Oh, I know that.'

Then he'd lain on top of the bed, hands propped behind his head, watching her dress.

She was so goddamn beautiful. How did he ever turn his life around and get this lucky?

Lara Ivory. *His* Lara.

Plucking the car keys off the dresser, he headed for the studio, a happy man.

☆ ☆ ☆

It started raining lightly as Cassie drove down Sunset toward the Pacific Coast Highway. All day there'd been storm warnings on the radio, but this was the first sign of bad weather.

Lara closed her eyes, agonizing over whether she was doing the right thing. As she relived the progression of her romance with Joey, she realized it had all been based on lies. He'd made up a fiancée, never told her about the money he'd taken, hadn't told her about living with Madelaine, hadn't told her anything really.

But then . . . what had she told him? Exactly nothing.

So, they were even. It was great fun, but it was just one . . .

'Another half-hour and we're there,' Cassie said, after she'd been driving for a while. 'I hope this rain stops. People in LA don't know how to drive when it rains here.'

'I'd forgotten how far it is,' Lara remarked.

'You wanted isolated.'

Cassie was right. She enjoyed being away from everyone and everything. Especially now.

She leaned back, desperately trying to shut out the jumbled memories that in times of stress always came flooding back.

There was so much of her past she'd never revealed to anyone. So many secrets . . .

One day she'd hoped to share them with Joey. Now it was not to be.

And that thought made her very desolate.

☆ ☆ ☆

'Anyone seen Lara?' Nikki asked hopefully, although she knew it was highly unlikely Lara would show.

'Saw plenty of her in *Truth and Fact*,' one of the grips sniggered.

Nikki threw him a disgusted look. She spotted Linden, and stopped him as he walked past. 'Is Lara coming?'

Linden shrugged. 'Don't know, Nikki. Sorry.'

The cast and crew were gathered on Sound Stage Four. A rock and roll band blared fifties classics, while everyone tried not to look self-conscious in their fifties outfits and bouffant hairstyles. The fifties theme was Mick's idea – he was very into that period.

Clad in black stove-pipe jeans that made his skinny legs even skinnier, and a Marlon-in-his-thin-days white T-shirt, Mick made the rounds, dancing with everyone from the nineteen-year-old prop girl to the sixty-year-old accountant.

'I'm pissed at Lara,' he said, sweeping Nikki into a quick jive. 'She should be here.'

'She's upset about the photos,' Nikki explained, as he swung her in a wide circle. 'So am I.'

'Shit happens,' Mick said totally unconcerned. 'Tell her to move on, and get her fine movie star ass down here. The crew's disappointed.'

'Maybe I'll call her, see what I can do,' Nikki gasped, as he somehow or other lowered her between his legs, then pulled her up in an elaborate arc. She spotted Aiden watching her with an edgy grin. Fuck it! He was making fun of her. 'Bye, Mick,' she said, managing a quick escape. 'I'm not in a dancing mood.'

As she hurried toward Aiden, one of the production assistants came at her with a cellphone. 'It's a Mr Weston calling from Chicago. Says it's urgent.'

Like she didn't have enough problems. She grabbed the phone. 'Yes?'

Sheldon's voice sounded indistinct and panicky, unlike his usual in-control self. 'Is she with you?' he demanded.

'Is *who* with me?'

'Summer.'

'What are you talking about, Sheldon? She's in Chicago with you.'

'No, she's gone. Vanished. Please tell me she's with you.'

'No,' she said, her stomach dropping. 'She's not here, Sheldon. So where the hell is she?'

Chapter Sixty-one

 THE THRILL of the chase had always appealed to Alison Sewell. She'd followed movie stars home on many occasions, right up to the point where they shut their great big gates in her face. However, following someone who was unaware they were being tracked was even more of a kick. It was a cat and mouse game. Alison considered herself the big powerful cat and Lara the poor little mouse.

Alison had been trailing Lara all day. She'd followed her from her house in the morning, then sat in the parking lot near the location, watching as they shot the last day of *Revenge*. She'd had a perfect view of Lara's trailer – popping off roll after roll of film as Lara came and went.

Miz Ivory looked upset. And so she should. *Truth and Fact* had done Alison's pictures proud. Her photographs were on the cover, *and*, as if that wasn't enough, there was a double-page spread inside.

That would teach Lara Ivory to mess with Alison Sewell, spurn their friendship and haul her up in court like a common criminal. Who exactly did the bitch think she was?

Late in the day when Cassie arrived to pick Lara up, Alison was surprised. Usually the big movie star sat in the back of her chauffeur-driven car and was taken home that way. But not tonight. Tonight her driver was sitting across the street reading a Frederick Forsyth paperback behind the wheel of his car, unaware his star was leaving by other means.

Hmm . . . Alison thought. *Something's up.*

She drew out of her parking place and slid her station wagon behind Cassie's Saab as it left the location.

I would have been the perfect assistant for Lara, Alison thought. *I could have protected her better than anyone. Certainly better than that one-armed stupid publicist, or that dumb handsome boyfriend. All she needs is me.*

When Cassie's car hit Sunset, Alison was right on her tail. Earlier she'd managed to have a conversation with one of the grips, acting real casual, as if she was a fan. He'd let slip that tonight was the wrap party. Surely the party wasn't at the beach, which is where Cassie seemed to be heading?

Alison hummed softly under her breath. She got a charge following the car, sure that she was the only person who knew Lara Ivory was in it. There were no other photographers around to bother her. No stupid men to deal with.

Truth was she was smarter than all of them. And the proof was that she'd made a fortune in the last week. Now she was rich, and could do whatever she liked. She'd made more money than Uncle Cyril ever did.

She switched on her windshield wipers to clear the sudden rain, so unexpected in sunny California. Then she reached in the glove compartment for a Snickers bar.

Unfortunately she now had a criminal record, thanks to Miz Ivory.

It didn't matter. She was rich. And she planned on getting even richer.

How much would pictures of Lara Ivory *dead* be worth?

How much could she score for pictures of a beautiful corpse?

Chapter Sixty-two

 TINA AND Summer walked back from the restaurant, laughing about the guys who'd tried to come on to them.

'Bunch of pathetic dogs,' Tina sneered. 'Now do you see why it's so stupid to go out with somebody and not get paid? These dudes are only looking to get into your pants. The ones that pay are like *real* men.'

'Doesn't getting paid mean we're prostitutes?' Summer asked, trying not to yawn.

'Prostitutes?' Tina shrieked. 'What kind of an old-fashioned word is *that*? We're . . . service givers. Very *expensive* service givers. Being a prostitute is like grabbing a Big Mac. What we do is like dining out in the coolest restaurant in town. Get it?'

'I guess so,' Summer said, thinking how ready she was to crawl into bed and sleep.

Tina was in an ebullient mood. 'I'll tell you what we're gonna do,' she said, breaking into a jog as it began to lightly rain.

'What?' Summer asked, hoping it was bed time.

'We're gonna call Norman,' Tina said, as they reached her nearby apartment.

'*Now?*'

'Yeah, why wait till tomorrow?'

'I thought you said we shouldn't rush into anything.'

'Who's rushing? He doesn't even know you're here. It's definitely time we told him.'

'OK . . .' Summer said unsurely.

'I'm asking for *big* bucks,' Tina said excitedly, her eyes gleaming. 'I'm gonna tell him you don't put out any more. Only for special johns.'

'Can I listen in?' Summer asked, anxious to hear the sound of his voice.

'Yeah, pick up the second line,' Tina said, dialling his number. She got right through. 'Hi, Norman,' she said, putting on a low, sexy voice. 'Remember me? Tina? I was over at your place a few weeks ago with Summer, that gorgeous blond you were so wild about. Darlene sent us, remember?'

'Sure do,' Norman answered, sounding stoned.

'You were *really* into Summer,' Tina continued. 'Kept asking Darlene when she'd be back. But you know what? Bad news. Summer gave up the business, and she'll only do it for very special clients. Now the good news – *you* happen to be extra special.'

'Whyn't you come over,' Norman said. 'Both of you.'

'Well . . .' Tina said, pretending to hesitate, 'if we do, you'll have to pay us direct, and not mention a word to Darlene, 'cause like I told you – Summer's no longer in the business. So you'll be dealing directly with me. OK?'

'I can do that, cutie.'

'Oh, and it has to be cash. And it'll cost more—'cause, like I just said—'

'I know, I know—' he interrupted, with a jolly chuckle. 'Your friend's not in the business. So quit with the talking and get your cutie-pie asses over here.'

'We'll be right there,' Tina said, hanging up the phone with a triumphant grin. 'See? Easy pickings.'

'It's past ten,' Summer said, yawning again. 'I'm kinda beat, what with the flight and all.'

Tina was already at the mirror fluffing up her hair. 'Too beat to have fun with Norman?'

'I was like thinking maybe tomorrow.'

'Don't sweat it,' Tina said, picking up her shoulder bag, reaching inside and producing a small white pill. 'Take this. It'll rev you up.'

'What is it?'

'Nothing serious. See,' she said, reaching in her purse again, 'I'm taking one, too.'

Not wanting to look like a baby, Summer quickly swallowed the innocuous-looking pill.

'Good girl,' Tina said. 'It'll make you feel seriously better.'

'Uh . . . another thing,' Summer ventured.

'Yes?'

'Shouldn't it be Norman and me alone together?'

'I didn't notice him saying, "Just send the blond,"' Tina retorted huffily. 'Are you up for it or not?'

Summer nodded. She knew that once he saw her again, he'd realize how much he'd missed her, send Tina home, and from then on everything would work out just fine.

☆ ☆ ☆

The first thing Nikki did was have Aiden drive her to the Malibu house to check if Summer was there.

'Do you think she's in LA?' she kept asking him.

'I hardly know her,' he answered. 'But from what I've seen – she can look after herself.'

'She's fifteen, Aiden,' Nikki fretted. '*Fifteen.*'

'What can I tell you? She's *your* kid.'

'What if she's *not* here?'

'Could be she's staying with a girlfriend in Chicago. Your ex check into that?'

'Knowing Sheldon, he checked into everything. He's on a plane right now. You'll get to meet him, he's a real treat.'

'She leave a note?'

'No . . . the housekeeper told Sheldon she left late for school this morning, and that some of her clothes are gone. Oh, and apparently there's money missing.'

'Shit!' Aiden exclaimed, swerving to avoid another car that had skidded across the road.

Nikki put on her seatbelt. 'Please drive carefully. I *would* like to get there.'

'She have a boyfriend?' Aiden asked, slowing down.

'Not that I know of. Sheldon spoke to the boy who took her to a movie last night – Stuart something or other. He didn't know anything.' She let out a long, weary sigh. 'Oh, God, Aiden. I can only hope she's at the house.'

'I don't get it. If she *was* coming back here – why wouldn't she call first?'

'How do I know?' Nikki said irritably.

'Don't get pissed. You're gonna find her.'

'Maybe Richard knows something. They were kind of close when she was here.'

'Call him.'

She took out her cellphone and punched out his number. 'It's Nikki,' she said when he answered.

'How come you're not at the party?' Richard said. 'I'm going there now. Lara told me to drop by.'

'Why would she tell you to do that?' Nikki said, before she could help herself.

'Guess she wants to see me,' Richard replied, purposely needling her.

'You're out of luck, Richard, Lara's not there.'

'How do *you* know?'

'She's not, OK?'

'No need to get bitchy.'

She refused to let him get to her. Some other time, but not now. 'Sheldon called from Chicago,' she said brusquely. 'Summer's missing.'

'What do you mean, *missing*?'

'It's pretty clear, isn't it? She's taken off, run away.'

'So . . . what do you want from me?'

'Thanks for your concern, Richard.'

'No, I mean if there's anything I can do—'

'Do you have any idea where she might go?'

'No.'

'She hasn't called *you*?'

'If she does, I'll let you know.'

'I'm on my way to Malibu. She could be there.'

'Then I guess I won't see you later.'

'You won't see anybody later. I told you – Lara's not at the party.'

'Where is she?'

'How would I know? If you hear anything call me.' She cut the connection and began biting her nails – a bad habit she only reverted to in times of extreme stress. 'He's such a cold sonofabitch,' she said. 'All he cares about is seeing Lara.'

'Why'd you marry him, Nik? And why'd you marry Sheldon? They both seem like assholes.'

'Yes, I know,' she said sarcastically. 'I would have been better off with a druggie like you, right?'

'That's not very nice,' he said, shaking his head as if he couldn't believe she was being so nasty. 'I'm getting it back together. I was kind of hoping you'd help me.'

'I can't help anybody right now. I'm too upset.'

'Calm down,' he said soothingly. 'Summer's probably sitting at the house waiting for you.'

☆ ☆ ☆

Nikki's call annoyed Richard. He did not appreciate her attitude, telling him that he wasn't going to see Lara. Showed how much *she* knew. Not only was he going to see her, he was going to divorce Nikki, and get back together with Lara the way it should be.

He knew Lara better than anyone. With Joey out of the picture, she'd be lonely and vulnerable. And he, Richard Barry, would be right there to console her.

Before anyone knew it, they'd remarry.

Yes. That's exactly what was going to happen, whether Nikki liked it or not.

☆ ☆ ☆

'I hope he still *likes* me,' Summer said. She'd taken a quick shower and put on one of Tina's skimpy dresses. Now they were standing in the elevator taking them up to Norman Barton's hotel suite, where he resided permanently.

'Of *course* he'll still like you,' Tina said, adjusting her stretchy tank top to show even more cleavage. 'According to Darlene, he asks about you all the time.'

'At least that's good news,' Summer said, shivering slightly, not sure if it was from nerves, the air-conditioned elevator, or the stupid pill Tina had forced her to take. 'I'm totally psyched about seeing him again.'

'Little Miss Romantic,' Tina teased. 'It must be true love!'

'I think it is,' Summer giggled.

Norman did not open the door of his suite himself. This time a girl did – a stunning black girl with a provocative smile and sinewy body.

Tina quickly nudged Summer. 'OhmiGod!' she whispered. 'It's that big-time model, Cluny.'

'Hi, girls,' Cluny said with a shimmering smile. 'Come in, join the party.'

Summer had no intention of joining any party, she was only interested in seeing Norman.

'Absolutely!' Tina said. 'This is Summer – I'm Tina, and you're Cluny. I recognized you, you're so beautiful.'

Cluny had huge quivering lips and seductive cat eyes. 'Why thank you, darling,' she said, clutching Tina's arm. 'You can be my new best friend.'

They entered the room. There were girls everywhere and no Norman in sight.

'*Sir* is in the bedroom,' Cluny said with a throaty chuckle. 'He'll be out shortly. In the meantime, take off your clothes, get comfortable.'

Most of the girls lounging around on the couches and floor were half naked. Summer was horrified, this wasn't what she'd expected at all. 'What's going on?' she whispered to Tina.

'Looks like an orgy to me,' Tina said, not too put out.

'I thought he wanted to see *me*,' Summer said mournfully.

'Apparently along with dozens of others.'

'I'm going home,' Summer said, deeply disappointed.

'Don't be such a baby,' Tina scolded. 'What did you *think* he was doing while you were in Chicago – sitting around pining for you? We're here now, let's get with the action.'

'I'm not staying,' Summer said stubbornly.

'At least see what he has to say,' Tina said. 'We showed up, he's gotta pay us.'

'I'm not taking off *anything*,' Summer said, close to tears.

'You don't have to,' Tina answered, guiding her over to one of the couches where they squeezed on the end, next to a short, busty redhead who was snorting cocaine from the glass-topped coffee table. 'Want some?' the redhead asked with a friendly smile. 'It's free.'

'Sure,' Tina said agreeably.

'What are you *doing*?' Summer hissed, as Tina picked up a small straw and began imbibing the white powder.

'Takin' a little snort,' Tina whispered back. 'Why don't you do the same? You're so uptight.'

'I don't want to be here,' Summer moaned. 'I like *really* don't.'

'Oh, for God's sake – stop whining,' Tina snapped. 'You *said* you couldn't wait to see him.'

'Not this way.'

A few minutes later Norman emerged from the bedroom, clad in nothing but a pair of red candy-striped shorts. He had a big shit-eating grin on his face and a girl on each arm, both of them totally naked. 'Cluny!' he yelled. 'I need more money!'

'Honey,' Cluny replied, digging into her shoulder purse and pulling out a stack of hundred-dollar bills, 'you are *wailin'* tonight. No stoppin' *you*.'

Summer jumped to her feet. 'That's it,' she said. 'This sucks. I'm out of here.'

'Don't be such a pain,' Tina retorted.

'Give me the key.'

'*What* key?'

'To your apartment. I'm going home.'

'If you're baling on me – then you can forget about going to my place.'

'Thanks a *lot*.'

'Hey, Norman,' Cluny said, 'before you vanish again – take a peek at dessert. Two juicy little pieces of fresh. I bag me the baby blond. Can I have her? Please? Pretty please?'

'She's all yours, babe,' Norman said, not even glancing in Summer's direction, too stoned to concentrate on anything.

Summer stood up. 'I'm gone,' she said, furiously heading for the door.

'Then you're on your own,' Tina shouted after her.

'Fine,' Summer said, tears pricking her eyelids. 'I'll pick up my things tomorrow.'

She rushed from the room. To her chagrin, Norman didn't even notice.

Chapter Sixty-three

 THERE WAS a Marvin Gaye tribute on the radio. Joey listened to the veteran soul singer all the way to the studio. The music soothed him. Marvin Gaye sure had style – not to mention an incredible voice.

He recalled that when he was growing up, his mother had often played tapes of Otis Redding and Teddy Pendergrass. She was into soul. Ah yes, Adelaide was into a lot of things.

He flashed on his mother for a moment, picturing her dancing around their living room – so strikingly pretty with her black curly hair, dark eyes and startling wide smile. He'd inherited his looks from his mother. God, she'd been a beauty.

As he pulled into a parking place outside the sound stage, he could hear the music blaring away. 'Rock Around the Clock' by Bill Haley and the Comets. Oh, Jeez, he'd forgotten, it was a fifties party, and he was supposed to be in some kind of rock 'n' roll outfit. Well, what did it matter? They'd probably only stay a short time. Then he'd take Lara home, and tomorrow they'd be on their way to Tahiti and a whole new life.

He strolled into the sweaty noisy throng, stopping to greet a couple of sound guys, smiling at the hairdresser and make-up woman. Then he began looking around for Lara.

'Seen Lara?' he asked the continuity girl.

She shrugged. 'Haven't.'

He wandered over to one of the second assistants. 'Is Lara around?'

'Don't think she's here, Joey.'

'How about Nikki?'

'Saw her dancing with Mick a while back.'

'Thanks,' he said, edging around the dance floor, finally managing to attract Mick's attention as he staggered off the floor with his arm around a pretty props girl.

'Hey, it's the Joey man,' Mick said, swaying on his feet. 'How's it goin'? Where's the love of your unworthy life? You lucky bastard.'

'I was just about to ask you,' Joey said.

'Ain't spotted the lovely Lara,' Mick said, pushing up his glasses. 'Guess she's still freaked over the photos.'

'What photos?'

'Oh, man – you mean you haven't seen *Truth and Fact*? Everyone's favourite weekly tabloid. Lara's pissed city. Go ask Linden, he's by the bar.'

Joey went over to Linden. 'What's this about some photos?' he asked, frowning.

'You don't know?' Linden said.

'No, I don't fuckin' know,' Joey said, starting to get aggravated.

'Some . . . uh . . . unfortunate photographs of Lara turned up in *Truth and Fact*,' Linden said. 'Somebody sneaked 'em while they were shooting the rape scene. They're *very* explicit, and Lara's *very* upset.'

'Jesus!' Joey said. 'How'd it happen?'

'That's what everyone would like to know.'

'So she's gone home, right?'

'I would think so,' Linden said. 'I'm positive she won't show up here tonight.'

'Does Nikki know about this?'

'She's upset too.'

'No shit?'

'I'm sorry it happened.'

'I bet you are,' Joey muttered, hurrying back to the Mercedes, where he picked up the phone and tried the house. Mrs Crenshaw answered. 'Lara back yet?' he asked.

'No, Mr Joey.'

'When she gets there, tell her I'm on my way.'

☆   ☆   ☆

The rain was getting heavier as Cassie turned off the Pacific Coast Highway onto a deserted dirt road. 'We're almost there,' she announced. 'Do you have the key?'

'No, *you* do,' Lara replied, still in kind of a daze.

'No, *I* don't,' Cassie replied, slowing down.

'Why not?' Lara asked, exasperated.

'Because nobody ever gave me one. I assumed when you said we were coming here that *you* had it.'

'Shit!' Lara exclaimed.

Now Cassie knew she was *really* upset, because Lara rarely swore. 'Shall I turn around and go back?' she questioned.

'No,' Lara said sharply. 'We'll get in somehow. There's probably an unlocked door or window. After all, nobody's living there.'

'If you ask me, we should stay in a hotel overnight, and have the realtor drop off the keys tomorrow.'

'We're here now,' Lara said flatly. 'Not having a key is the least of my problems.'

'You're the boss,' Cassie sighed, spooked by the heavy rain, the unlit road and the empty house ahead. She was surprised Lara had bought the place. Even when Lara was renting she'd never thought much of it – the house was too remote and quite gloomy, with none of the charm of the Hamptons house.

The Saab hit a bump in the road. 'I can't see a thing,' Cassie complained, switching on her bright lights.

Lara wished Cassie would stop bitching. She wasn't in the frame of mind to put up with anyone's complaints. One of the advantages of being a star was that she didn't have to – if she said jump, that's what people were supposed to do. *So shut up, Cass, we're staying whether you like it or not.*

She wondered if Joey had realized she was missing. It would take a while before he understood she was not coming back. In a couple of days she'd have her lawyer call to tell him to move out of her house. And that would be that.

The big iron gate leading to the property was open. 'Nice,' Cassie said, making the turn, the wheels of her car crunching through pebbles and thick mud. 'They're *really* security conscious.'

'It's a good sign,' Lara said. 'Means we'll have no trouble getting in.'

'Very reassuring!' Cassie sighed, fielding off hunger pangs. 'Can't wait to spend the night.'

☆ ☆ ☆

Joey pulled the Mercedes up outside a 7-Eleven store and ran inside. He picked up a copy of *Truth and Fact*, and stared in disbelief at the revealing photographs on the cover. Jesus! What had they done to his beautiful Lara? He knew how private she was, how closely she guarded her good reputation – these sleazy pictures were enough to drive her crazy.

Slamming down money, he stormed back to the car. It was all Nikki's fault, she'd probably set it up to get publicity for her goddamn movie.

He started the engine and roared off. Why hadn't Lara called him? Too upset, of course.

The sooner he was with her the better.

Nobody knew more than he how soul-destroying it was to get set up.

☆ ☆ ☆

'I need money desperately, Joey.' So spoke the lovely Adelaide, his mother, always asking for something.

Adelaide was seventeen when she met Joey's father, Pete Lorenzo – a small-time wise guy who was sixty when he knocked up the pretty teenager. Two years later he'd finally married her. He was getting on in years, it was time to settle down with a woman who'd look after him.

Only Adelaide wasn't that woman. Adelaide had no intention of looking after anyone except herself. Once she'd hooked Pete she hired a sitter to watch Joey, and proceeded to accompany her husband wherever he went. His hang-outs were the racetrack, the fights, poker games and pool halls. Adelaide was by his side every step of the way.

One weekend they took three-year-old Joey with them to Vegas. He nearly drowned in the hotel swimming pool while they were busy playing craps. Another time, in Atlantic City, they left him in a hotel room where he nearly got trapped in a fire.

It was a hell of a childhood, neither parent had much time for him.

By the time he was ten, his father was seventy and tired; Adelaide was twenty-seven and sleeping with any good-looking jerk who came her way. When Pete complained, Adelaide laughed in his face. Pete Lorenzo had lost his power – he was too old to control her, and she was too wild to be controlled.

Joey, an introverted kid, watched it all. He adored his pretty mother, but he soon realized she was untrustworthy; therefore, he figured, all women were the same.

When he was eighteen, his dad suffered a massive heart attack at the racetrack and died on the spot. After that Adelaide went through a series of live-in boyfriends — each one worse than the last. She was into hoods and low-lifes. Con-men and hustlers. She'd also started drinking and gambling big-time.

Joey decided he'd better distance himself before he beat up one of her dumb boyfriends, so he moved out, trying a variety of jobs — busboy, waiter, car mechanic, limo driver. And a different girl every week. Girls went for him because he was so good-looking, but he never let them stay around long enough to get close.

After a while he took the big step and moved to New York, where he immediately got the acting bug. One day he walked into Madelaine Francis' office, and there she was — his big opportunity. An agent with clout.

She'd gotten him a couple of great movie roles, and every-thing was looking good until the phone call from his mother.

'I don't have any money, Ma,' he explained, feeling guilty anyway. 'I've only had two acting jobs. When I make more, I'll send you plenty.'

'You don't get it,' she replied, sounding drunk and none too friendly. 'This time it's different. This time it's life or death.'

'What about Danny?' he asked, mentioning her current boyfriend. 'Get him to help you.'

'Danny's a no-guts loser,' she spat. 'He can't help shit. And I need ten thousand, otherwise they'll kill me, Joey, they'll kill me.'

'You're crazy, Ma.'

'So help me, it's the truth.'

He didn't know what to do. He loved Adelaide, but she was a degenerate gambler who was never going to quit. Now she was coming to him to pay her debts.

Where the fuck was he supposed to come up with ten thousand bucks? He'd tried to distance himself, make a new life. So he was living with a woman almost thirty years older than him. He'd finally gotten smart and found himself someone who could do him some good. Madelaine was OK, she didn't hassle him about making a commitment – unlike his contemporaries who made him extremely nervous with their clinging ways and petty demands. Besides, none of them were ever as pretty as his mother – his gorgeous mother, who was such goddamn trouble.

He called her back the next day. 'Can't get my hands on any money right now,' he said.

'Then you can kiss your poor mama goodbye.'

'Don't snow me with that dramatic crap, Ma.'

'I told you,' she said, her voice hardening. 'Unless you come up with the money, I'm dead.'

He wrestled with the problem. Madelaine kept cash in the apartment. Could he ask her for a loan?

No, she wouldn't buy it.

So what if he just took it? Helped Adelaide out for the last time, then came back and explained everything to Madelaine.

Yeah, that was the way to do it. Madelaine would understand.

As soon as she left for the office the next day, he broke into her safe. He felt bad doing it, but what choice did he have?

He found seven thousand dollars stashed in her safe. It wasn't enough, but he took it all.

Adelaide had to quit with the gambling. This was positively the last time he was bailing her out.

☆ ☆ ☆

A car horn blared, making him jump. He realized he hadn't been concentrating, and quickly swerved the wheel, almost skidding, taking no notice as the other driver gave him the finger.

Lara needed him more than ever. He had to hurry home.

Chapter Sixty-four

 As SUMMER stood outside Norman Barton's hotel in the pouring rain, it occurred to her that she had absolutely nowhere to go. Tina, who she'd thought was such a good friend, had dumped on her big-time. Well, she didn't want to be friends with Tina anyway, not if she was into doing coke. Smoking grass was one thing, but getting into coke could lead to nothing but trouble.

She hovered outside the hotel entrance in her skimpy little dress, shivering.

'Can I get you a cab?' a young uniformed doorman asked.

'No, thanks,' she said, shaking her head.

'You one of those girls from the Norman Barton party?' he asked, edging nearer.

'Excuse me?' she said, freezing him out with a cold glare. 'I'm staying at the hotel with my *parents*.'

'Sorry, miss,' he said, backing off.

A limo slid kerbside and Summer watched in awe as Johnny Romano, the famous movie star, got out. Although he was with three girls he threw her a moody look and a slight wink. 'Hi, chickie,' he said as he slinked on by.

What was it with all these stupid movie stars? One girl didn't do it for them? Apparently not.

She tried to take a peek at the limo driver. If it was Jed

472

she'd be saved. But no, it wasn't Jed, it was some gnarled old black man. And the annoying thing was she couldn't remember Jed's number.

She sighed, feeling let down and disappointed – not to mention slightly giddy. God knew what was in the pill Tina had forced her to take. Norman had *told* her to call, he'd insisted he wanted to see her again, causing her to fantasize about them having a future together. Now he'd turned out to be nothing more than a coked-out bum. Well, it was good she'd found out before she'd gotten even more involved.

She shivered again and wrapped her arms across her chest. What was she going to do? She was alone in LA with nowhere to sleep and all her possessions – including her money – at Tina's.

'Where are your folks?' the young doorman asked, coming over again. 'Do they know you're out here?'

'Have you ever heard of minding your own business?' she said haughtily.

'Excuse *me* for talking to the princess,' he snapped back.

'I could report you,' she said indignantly.

'Go ahead – like losing this job would ruin my day.'

'If you *must* know,' she said, 'I had a fight with my parents.'

'You shouldn't wander around this town by yourself,' he said. 'Not a girl who looks like you. I get off in an hour. If you want to go to the coffee shop and wait, I'll drive you wherever you're going.'

'I don't have anywhere to go,' she admitted.

'You could stay at my place.'

'As if!' she said in disgust.

He laughed. 'Do I look like a crazed rapist?'

She took another look at him. He was not traditionally handsome. He had a Tom Cruise look, with a toothy grin and spiky hair. He wasn't Norman Barton, but what choice did she have. 'I suppose you're an out-of-work actor,' she sighed.

'Wrong,' he replied. 'I'm an artist, doing this to make my rent.'

'What kind of artist?' she asked, not quite believing him.

'I paint portraits. In fact, I'd quite like to paint you.'

'In the nude, I suppose.'

'You offering?'

'Get a life!' she said scornfully.

'You want to camp out at my place tonight or not?'

She didn't see any other alternative. 'OK.'

He nodded. 'I'll meet you in the coffee shop in an hour.'

☆ ☆ ☆

'Maybe Mick knows something,' Nikki said, close to tears. 'Where does he live?'

'Calm down,' Aiden said. 'Knowing Mick, he's left the party and gone clubbing. Leave a message on his machine.'

'I can't just sit here doing nothing. She's my child – out there on her own.'

'Hey, Nik, with all due respect, you're coming on like the concerned mother a little late, aren't you?'

'Are you saying I haven't been a good mother?'

'What's *your* take?'

'I know I could have given her more attention. But when she insisted on staying with Sheldon, I guess my feelings were hurt.'

'She's a kid – you abandoned her. Have you considered the fact she was angry?'

'Richard didn't give a rat's ass, he can be such a cold sonofabitch.'

'Hey – get with the programme, Richard has his own agenda.'

'She could have gone to Lara's.'

'Call her.'

'We're not exactly on good terms right now.'

'Call her anyway.'

'You're right,' she said, dialling Lara's house.

Mrs Crenshaw informed her nobody was home.

'Is Sheldon coming here from the airport?' Aiden asked.

'Yes, then we should call the police.'

'He hasn't done that?'

'Apparently you have to wait forty-eight hours before you can report a missing person.'

'Summer's a minor – doesn't that make a difference?'

'I don't know, I'll have to talk to Sheldon.'

'Hey.' He held open his long, thin arms. 'Come over here, you need a hug.'

'This isn't the time.'

'I said a hug, nothing else.'

She allowed him to embrace her. He was right – she was in dire need of love and affection. 'How come you're so understanding?' she sighed.

''Cause I've been everywhere and back,' he said with a wry laugh. 'If I was you, I'd probably be imbibing every drug known to man. There's no way I could handle this. You're doing great, Nik. Just hang in there, we'll find her.'

☆ ☆ ☆

'Before I go with you, you'd better tell me your name,' Summer said, staring at the young doorman who looked even cuter out of uniform. If she hadn't felt so sick and dizzy, she might be enjoying this new adventure.

'Sam,' he said. 'And you're—'

'Summer.'

'Summer and Sam. What a team!'

'You're *sure* I can trust you, Sam?'

He laughed and took her arm. 'What's your choice? Me or the streets, right? Guess you're gonna have to trust me.'

And with his words ringing in her ears she left the hotel with a total stranger.

Chapter Sixty-five

 ALISON SEWELL often dreamed about what it would be like to be famous. As she turned off the lights on her station wagon and followed Lara's car down the dirt road, she couldn't help reflecting on the excitement that world fame would bring. Charles Manson and his cohorts were as famous as any President; John Hinckley was a name everyone knew because of his attempt to assassinate the President; Robert Bardo had made world headlines by killing Rebecca Schaefer; and Mark Chapman had waited outside the Dakota in New York, and shot John Lennon dead.

Because of their actions, these men would go down in history. They'd become icons themselves – appearing on the covers of *Time* and *Newsweek*. They were written about constantly, interviewed from their jail cells, fêted and acclaimed. Everyone knew their names. They were as famous as any movie star.

It occurred to Alison that she, too, could be famous. And why not? Was she supposed to be a nobody for ever? Pushed around and treated like dirt? No. She could do something about it.

Uncle Cyril would be so proud of her if she did. And the other cretins she'd worked alongside all those years – well, they'd be *fighting* to take *her* picture.

A smile spread across her face at the thought. Alison Sewell on the cover of *Newsweek*. She'd have to do something pretty outrageous to get that kind of coverage.

Was killing Lara Ivory outrageous enough?

There is a very thin line between love and hate. Alison Sewell had crossed that line.

She'd loved Lara Ivory with an absolute passion. Now she hated her enough to kill.

Tonight Lara Ivory was going to pay.

Tonight Lara Ivory was going to die.

Chapter Sixty-six

 THE BIG old house was deserted, dark and cold. Cassie had gained access through an open kitchen window, and then let Lara in through the back door. 'There's no power,' she complained. 'Lara, if you don't mind me saying so, this is *not* a good idea.'

'We're here now,' Lara said stubbornly. 'All we're going to do is sleep.'

'Oh,' Cassie said, unable to hold back a twist of sarcasm, 'like eating went out of style, I suppose. Not to mention heating.'

'I can tell you never camped out,' Lara said. 'A little hardship is good for you.'

Screw hardship, Cassie wanted to say. *NYPD Blue is on TV and I want my dinner.* But she didn't, because Lara was in one of her weird moods. The photo-spread in *Truth and Fact* had obviously freaked her. But why was Joey being punished?

'I'll get the flashlight from my car,' she said.

'Good idea,' Lara answered, thinking that all she really wanted to do was get into bed and shut out the world. Joey Lorenzo had completely fooled her, making believe he cared, while all the time he was waiting to score off her and then who knows?

479

She'd never had much luck with men; foolishly she'd thought Joey was different, but it was not to be.

The house was freezing. Maybe Cassie was right – a hotel might be a better idea.

But no, if she checked into a hotel she'd be recognized, and before she knew it Joey would find her. She wanted complete anonymity. In a way she was punishing herself for having been such a lovesick idiot.

She thought wistfully of Tommy and his wise advice. He'd tell her the photographs were yesterday's news and to forget about them. And as for his take on Joey— 'All men are pigs,' he'd say. 'It depends on what degree of piggery you're prepared to put up with.'

If only Tommy had been straight, she thought with a wan smile, *we could have gotten married and lived happily ever after.* That's if he hadn't gotten sick and died on her.

Cassie came back with a flashlight and they began looking around. Although she'd bought the two-storey house furnished, everything was covered in dust sheets.

As they started upstairs, Cassie said, 'It just occurred to me – there'll be no linens, so I guess my hotel suggestion is the only way to go.'

'Will you *stop* carrying on about a hotel,' Lara said sharply. 'God, you're such a complainer.'

Unfortunately Cassie was right, there were no linens on the beds.

'You see,' Cassie said triumphantly.

'No, I do not see,' Lara said, throwing open the big linen closet in the hall. It was stocked with everything they needed. 'Sorry, Cass,' she said. 'It seems we're going to be making beds after all.'

'I can't spend the night here unless I get something to eat,' Cassie muttered.

'OK,' Lara said, 'here's the plan. You go find a supermarket and stock up, while I stay here and make our beds.'

Cassie raised an eyebrow. '*You're* going to make the beds?'

'I'm capable, Cass. Besides, I feel like it.'

Cassie had no idea she used to be a maid at Aunt Lucy's motel and could make a bed in record time. Anyway, she didn't mind, sometimes housework was therapeutic.

'OK,' Cassie said, 'if you're sure. I'll buy food, batteries, candles. Anything else?'

'Nope,' Lara said. 'Don't worry, we'll be perfectly comfortable here.'

'What can I get you for dinner?' Cassie asked. 'How about a couple of Big Macs?'

'Hmm,' Lara scolded, 'we're really going to have to do something about your eating habits.'

'I can't help having a healthy appetite,' Cassie said defensively, well aware she was fifty pounds overweight.

'Healthy is the wrong word if you're talking Big Macs.'

'It's oral satisfaction.'

'Don't get me started, Cass. You should look after yourself.'

'I will,' Cassie promised, knowing she wouldn't. 'But not tonight. Now, what would you like to eat?'

'I'm not hungry,' Lara said, feeling depressed and sad. 'You pick up whatever you want.'

'I'll be quick,' Cassie promised.

'No need to rush. Who needs television or lights? If it stops raining I might even take a walk along the beach.'

'Don't even *attempt* to go down those rickety stairs,' Cassie said sternly.

'You worry too much,' Lara answered lightly. 'I've got a new policy – I'm doing what I want whenever I want, and I refuse to worry about anything.'

'Can I ask you a question?' Cassie said curiously. 'Will Joey be joining us tomorrow?'

'Joey?' Lara looked at her blankly. 'Who's Joey?'

☆ ☆ ☆

The dogs greeted him before Mrs Crenshaw.

'Is she back yet?' he asked.

'Not yet, Mr Joey.'

'Jesus! Where is she?'

'I'm sure I don't know,' Mrs Crenshaw said, a touch officiously. 'I've prepared dinner if you're hungry . . .'

'No, thanks.' He stared at the old housekeeper. Was she telling him the truth? 'You're certain she didn't leave a message?'

'Quite certain.'

He went upstairs. The bedroom was empty. It was almost ten o'clock. He could understand Lara was upset about the pictures, but why hadn't she called?

He went back downstairs to the den and put on the TV. *NYPD Blue* was just starting. He watched moodily for a while. Jimmy Smits, smooth as silk; Dennis Franz, crotchety as usual; Kim Delaney, edgy and wild. It was one of the few programmes he enjoyed, in fact, he'd decided to talk to Quinn about maybe getting him a guest shot. Of course, he wasn't into doing TV, but appearing on a show as good as *NYPD Blue* wouldn't be a bad thing.

He had no intention of becoming Mr Lara Ivory simply because they were married. Oh no, Joey Lorenzo was planning on making a name for himself.

As far as he was concerned, he hadn't even started.

☆ ☆ ☆

Cassie drove away from the big house. If Lara wasn't so damn secretive, she could've called Linden and instructed him to get his ass out there, so that he, too, could babysit Lara and put up with the inconvenience of spending the night in an empty house with no power. It was dark, frightening and plain stupid.

The first market she came to was fifteen minutes away and did not have anything she wanted. Plus an oversize biker with yellowing teeth, stringy grey hair and multiple leather crosses and chains hanging around his neck was eyeballing her like he wouldn't mind having her for supper. Even Cassie, who was constantly on the lookout for a man, was not tempted.

Getting back in her car, she drove all the way to the big supermarket in Malibu, where she suddenly had a brilliant idea – Granita, one of Lara's favourite restaurants was right there. She could order something special for Lara – a Wolfgang Puck pizza being a much better deal than something she'd pick up in the market. Before parking and going into the restaurant she called her sister with whom she shared a small house.

'Where are you?' Maggie asked.

Cassie explained the situation, finishing off with— 'I hope you're taping *NYPD Blue*.'

'Of course!' Maggie said.

'Hopefully I'll see you in the morning.'

She left the car and entered Granita. As soon as Wolf heard she was there for Lara, he came over, greeting her personally, promising to fix Lara's favourite chicken dish. Then he insisted she sit at a table while she was waiting, and a few minutes later he sent over one of his delicious smoked salmon pizzas.

She tried Lara on her cellphone. Unfortunately it was out of range.

Oh, well – Lara had seemed perfectly happy alone in the

house. Cassie didn't think she'd mind if she took longer than expected.

☆ ☆ ☆

Lara explored the big old house with only Cassie's flashlight to guide her way. First she went upstairs to the master suite where there was a spectacular view of the ocean. Not that she could see much tonight, only the stormy sky and the ocean down below, everything a raging mass of darkness.

Next she returned to the living room with its vast terrace perilously overhanging the edge of the cliff. From the terrace there was a gate, leading to a rough wooden staircase that went all the way down to the beach. When she was renting the house she'd taken a walk along the beach every morning at six, and loved the freedom.

She ventured onto the terrace for a moment. Too wet, cold and windy. She hurried back inside.

Somehow being in the house alone fit her mood – she wasn't planning on feeling sorry for herself, but she liked the idea that nobody could reach her.

In the morning she'd start making decisions about her future. As everyone couldn't wait to tell her – she'd been working too hard – nonstop, in fact. Was that why she'd fallen into Joey's trap, instead of treading carefully as she usually did?

Nikki was right, he'd hooked her sexually, damn him. *Good old Nikki. She certainly knows her stuff. Sex does it every time*.

It occurred to her that she'd probably been too hard on Nikki, putting the full blame for the photographs on her. *Revenge* didn't need cheap publicity, it was a powerful movie that could stand on its own merits.

I haven't been much of a friend, she thought. *Nikki's going through a tough time and I should be there for her.*

Reaching into her purse, she took out her cellphone. Unfortunately the battery needed recharging and she couldn't get a signal.

Now she felt really isolated. But that was good, it gave her time to reflect, and most of all, to regain control of her life.

☆ ☆ ☆

Joey paced restlessly around the house. It was past eleven and he had a bad feeling that something must have happened to Lara. He had no idea where to start looking. The only person he could think of to call was Nikki, so he found Lara's book and looked up her number.

Aiden answered the phone. Recognizing his voice, Joey said, 'Hey, man – I need to talk to Nikki.'

'About Summer?'

'Summer?'

'She's missing. You didn't know?'

'No, I'm tryin' to find Lara. Is she there?'

'Sorry.'

'Maybe Nikki knows where she is.'

'I'll see if she can talk.'

Nikki came on the line a few moments later. 'I have no idea where Lara is, Joey.'

'Aiden told me about Summer. What happened?'

'She took off. We don't know where she's gone.'

'Could she be with Lara?'

'I don't see how. Didn't Lara leave you a message?'

'No, nothing. She wasn't at the party, they said she never showed.'

'I wish I could help you.'

485

'Yeah, well, I'm sorry about Summer.'

'Wait a minute,' Nikki said. 'I just thought of something. Richard was on the set this morning.'

'With Lara?'

'Yes – he was busy putting in his ten cents about the tabloid photos.'

'Are you sayin' she might be with him?'

'No . . . but he was up to something. He had an older woman with him – he took her into Lara's trailer and left them alone together for a while.'

'Who was the woman?'

'I don't know. She was in her fifties, smartly dressed, reddish hair.'

The description chilled him. Could it possibly be Madelaine Francis?

No. Inconceivable.

And yet . . . Richard hated him and still lusted after Lara. Maybe he'd found out about Madelaine. If that was the case he was in deep trouble.

'Thanks, Nikki,' he said, clicking off the phone.

If Madelaine Francis was in LA he'd find her. And if Richard Barry had put her in touch with Lara, he was going to pay.

Something was wrong. And he'd better find out what, before it was too late.

Chapter Sixty-seven

 IT WAS cold sitting in her car watching the big house, but Alison Sewell was fired with energy. She leaned over, reaching into the back seat of her station wagon and grabbing a warm parka which she kept for just such occasions – the occasions when she had to track stars and sit outside their houses all night.

However, tonight was different. Tonight she wasn't hanging around waiting for a photo opportunity. Tonight she was getting it for herself, and Lara and her dumb assistant were making it very easy. A house with no electricity, shrouded in darkness, and now Cassie driving off without her boss. What could be better?

As soon as she saw Cassie leave, Alison exited her car, carefully making her way through the open gate, approaching the house warily. Many times she'd been attacked by guard dogs, or some tiresome security guard with a gun had jumped out demanding to know what she wanted.

Just in case she always carried her own weapons: a large hunting knife – similar to the one used in the Nicole Simpson/Ron Goldman murders; a couple of sharp knitting needles: thick leather gloves to protect her hands; a screwdriver; and a special credit card that could get her through any door.

Once she'd been lying in wait for a particularly outrageous rock star when his vicious dog had come sniffing around her crotch. Before the mutt could make a sound she'd slit its throat with her hunting knife. She remembered the way the knife had sliced through the dog's jugular vein, and how its blood had spurted all over her. It hadn't upset her at all. In fact, it had given her a strange thrill.

What would Lara look like when that happened to her?

What expression would she have on that beautiful face?

Alison wondered if Lara Ivory realized how lucky she was to have been born with such a perfect face. Stardom had fallen upon her like a golden mantle, and because of that face she'd led a charmed life.

As if the bitch deserved it. She deserved nothing, because she didn't know how to give. She was a selfish self-obsessed movie star like all the rest of them.

Well, Alison planned to change that.

The night was dark and murky, the rain pounding down.

Alison didn't need light. The rain didn't bother her. She knew exactly where she was heading.

The cover of *Time* and *Newsweek*, that's where she was heading.

Chapter Sixty-eight

 THE MOMENT Nikki set eyes on Sheldon she was overcome with that old familiar sick feeling in the pit of her stomach. It was years since she'd seen him – years of freedom and being away from his overbearing, pompous, full-of-shit presence. Now he was back and to her annoyance he still affected her physically.

He did not look his usual pulled-together self. He seemed more shopworn and weary, clad in a rumpled sports coat, open-neck shirt and creased pants. His face was lined and old. His grey hair dry and too long for a man his age. His thin lips tighter than ever.

'Is she here?' were the first words out of his mouth.

'No,' Nikki said. 'She's not.'

'I need a drink,' he growled.

From the smell of him she could tell he'd had quite a few on the plane. 'Help yourself,' she said, gesturing toward the bar. 'Uh, Sheldon, this is Aiden Sean.'

Barely glancing in Aiden's direction, Sheldon mumbled a curt, 'Good evening.'

Aiden exchanged glances with Nikki. 'I told you,' she mouthed behind Sheldon's back. 'Total asshole.'

Sheldon fixed himself a large snifter of brandy.

'Well, Sheldon, what happened?' Nikki asked.

'She ran away, that's what happened.'

'She wouldn't go without a reason. Did you have a fight?'

'Summer and I never fight. We are extremely close.'

'Then what was it?'

'Ever since she came back from Los Angeles she's been a different girl. It obviously has something to do with *you*.'

'Why *me*?' Nikki said indignantly.

'Because it was you who allowed her to run wild, let her go out with boys, and God *knows* what else she got up to while she was in your care.'

'Hey, listen,' Aiden interrupted, 'it's not my plan to get in the middle here, but shouldn't you both be concentrating on finding your kid?'

Sheldon threw him a frosty look. 'Who are you?' he said rudely.

Nikki bristled. 'Aiden's the man in my life,' she said, adding a terse— 'Not that it's any of your business.'

'What happened to Richard?'

'We're getting divorced.'

'Oh, *he* couldn't put up with you either.'

'Screw you, Sheldon!' she said, unable to control herself.

'Is that all you have to say?' He gave her one of his supercilious smiles. 'I hoped you would have mastered a more intelligent vocabulary by now.'

'Fighting won't solve shit,' Aiden interrupted. 'One of you should contact the cops. You checked her friends here, Nik?'

'Right,' Nikki said, glaring at Sheldon. 'I'll go through the stuff she left here, see what I can find.'

☆ ☆ ☆

Sam rode a motorbike, not exactly a Harley, but it was kind of a fun ride. Summer sat behind him, her arms clasped firmly around his waist, pressing her body up against his back – not by choice, but because she didn't fancy falling off.

Thank goodness there's some nice guys left in the world, she thought, *guys who don't hit on you the second you look in their direction*. She leaned her head against his back, her eyes almost closing. She was so tired, it was a big effort to stay awake.

Sam drove too fast for the rainy streets. It didn't bother her, she liked speed, it was exciting. Every time they stopped at a red light he turned his head and asked if she was having fun.

'Oh, yes,' she replied drily. 'Never had a better time.'

'You're a sarcastic little bitch, aren't you?' he laughed.

'Not so little,' she mumbled.

Sam lived in the guest cottage of a sprawling house in the Valley. His cottage consisted of two big rooms; one was his bedroom/living room, and the other his studio, filled with many paintings – mostly portraits.

She did an obligatory walk around. 'You really got it going,' she said admiringly. 'Cool stuff.'

'I know,' he responded, Mr Modest. 'One day I'll make it. Then no more parking cars for me.'

'Thanks for rescuing me tonight, Sam,' she said. 'Guess I should confess – I was at the Norman Barton party, only I couldn't stay there with all these lame hookers. I had *no clue* it was going to be like that.'

'I kinda figured that's where you were,' he said. 'No parents, right?'

'Not at the hotel.'

'Where?'

'My dad's in Chicago, mom's here. They're divorced.'

'My parents did that when I was five.'

Yes, but I bet you didn't have a father who came into your room at night and molested you, she wanted to say. Only she kept her mouth shut, telling Tina was bad enough.

'I haven't got much in the way of food,' he said. 'Help yourself to what's there.'

She checked out his fridge. There was a half-eaten pizza and a rancid piece of cheese.

'I'm not hungry,' she said. 'Just tired. Is it OK if I like crash on the couch in the corner?'

'Take the bed,' he said generously. 'I've got work to finish – probably won't get any sleep tonight.'

'You're sure?' she said, too exhausted to argue.

'It's all yours,' he said generously.

'Wow – *thanks*.'

'The bathroom's over there,' he said, pointing. 'You'll find pyjamas behind the door.'

She hurried into the bathroom, slipped out of her dress and put on the pyjamas he'd mentioned. Even though they were several sizes too big, they were better than nothing. Then she got into bed, thinking that tomorrow she'd collect her bag from Tina, and maybe stay in a hotel for a couple of days before deciding her next move.

Whatever happened, she was *never* going back to Chicago.

☆ ☆ ☆

Leaving Sheldon and Aiden alone together was not a great idea, but Nikki did it anyway while she scoured the guest room, searching through the few things Summer had left behind.

After a few minutes she found the name Jed scribbled on a piece of paper, with two exclamation points next to his name.

She tried the number, getting an answering machine. 'Hi,

this is Jed. You need me, I need you, so leave a message at the sound of the you know what.'

She waited for the tone, then said, 'Uh ... my name's Nikki Barry. I'm calling about Summer. It's urgent that I talk to you as soon as possible. Please call me back.' She left her phone number, then tried Mick at home. He was there. 'Oh,' she said, 'I thought you'd still be at the party.'

'Nice of you to stay around,' he drawled sarcastically. 'Jesus, Nik – that's no way to make friends and influence your crew.'

'I had an emergency.'

'What? Like the big movie star throwin' a blue freakin' fit about those photos?'

'It's my daughter, Summer. She's run away from home.'

'Oh.'

There was a long pause. Nikki broke it. 'Mick, I *know* what happened between you and Summer.'

'Huh?' he blustered.

'I'm aware you made her commit a ... sexual act, even though you must have known she was a minor. So ... if you have any information about her whereabouts, you'd better tell me right now.'

'Jesus, Nik – I had no freakin' clue she was your daughter, or that she was only fifteen ...'

'So you haven't heard from her?' Nikki interrupted coldly.

'No. And the truth is we didn't do a damn thing.'

'That's not what you told Aiden.'

'Guys boast,' he said sheepishly. 'Guess I got carried away.'

Nikki wasn't sure whether to believe him or not. 'Anyway,' she said, 'her father's flown in from Chicago, and when he contacts the police, I wouldn't want him telling them what you made her do.'

'Are you *insane*?' Mick shrieked. 'You'd get me thrown in

jail for something I *didn't* do? Is that the kind of publicity you want for our movie?'

'This is not about the movie, Mick. It's about my daughter. And I want her back.'

'Listen, chickie-babe,' he said, rolling his eyes as he clung on to the phone. 'I swear on my life, *my mother's life, Quentin Tarantino's* life – and you know he's my idol – I never touched her and I haven't heard from her.'

'If you're sure.'

'Dead sure.'

She was unconvinced. What if Summer *had* contacted him? What if she was sitting in his house even as they spoke?

Back in the living room she took Aiden to one side. 'I've got a feeling about Mick,' she said. 'I have to make sure Summer's not there. Can we go over to his place? We'll leave Sheldon here.'

'*C'mon*, Nik,' Aiden said, shaking his head. 'You gotta control your paranoia.'

'If he has nothing to hide, he won't mind us dropping by.'

'Jesus! You're serious.'

'Sheldon,' she said, going over to her ex, 'Aiden and I have to go out. We'll be back as quickly as possible.' She watched as he poured himself another hefty brandy. 'Oh,' she added sarcastically, 'and do make yourself at home.'

☆ ☆ ☆

Summer was asleep in the middle of Sam's big bed dreaming about running on the beach with Norman Barton and seven naked hookers when she felt her father's hands on her.

'No!' she screamed, opening her eyes in horror. 'Get off me, Daddy! Get *off*!'

But it wasn't Daddy. It was Sam.

'Come *on*,' he said impatiently. 'Gimme a piece of what you gave Norman Barton. You know you want to.'

'Drop dead, you horrible pig!' she yelled, trying to wriggle out from under him. 'Pretending to be my friend. I *trusted* you!'

'Lesson number one,' he said, pinning her arms above her head. 'Never trust anyone.'

'You'd better leave me alone,' she warned, struggling ferociously, 'otherwise I'm screaming rape.'

'Scream away,' he said. 'Nobody'll hear you.'

'This sucks!' she shrieked.

'Didn't your mommy warn you? Never go home with a stranger,' he said, tearing at the buttons of her pyjama top. 'Why'd you come with me if you didn't want it? Pushing your little titties up against me on the bike. You *know* you want it.'

He had one hand on her left breast. She kneed him in the groin as hard as she could.

'*Jesus!*' he groaned. 'What the hell do you think you're doing?'

'Getting out of here – that's what!' she shouted, rolling off the bed, grabbing her dress and shoes from the floor, and racing for the door before he could do anything about it.

She made it outside, and began running down the muddy garden path toward the front of the house.

A dog started to bark, she didn't care – she kept running as fast as she could.

Oh God, this is like the nightmare day of all time, she thought, hiding behind a tree, trying to shelter from the rain as she shimmied into her dress.

In the distance Sam emerged from his house and began calling her name. She stayed silent. After a while he went back into his house, slamming the door behind him.

What a loser geek! Him with his Tom Cruise smile and spiky hair. Brad Pitt he wasn't.

She waited until she saw the light go out in his house. Then she crept back down there, picking up a sharp piece of glass on the way, puncturing the tyres on his precious motorbike. That would teach the moron not to mess with Summer Weston.

Now it was past midnight and she was freezing to death, starving hungry, wet, tired and miserable. Maybe leaving Chicago hadn't been such a good idea after all. Although anything was better than life with Daddy Dearest. Shivering, she set off down the street.

By the time she reached Ventura Boulevard, unexpected tears were rolling down her cheeks mingling with the rain. She'd thought she could handle being out on her own, only now she had no money, couldn't trust anybody, and had nowhere to go.

She hesitated on the corner of the street. A truck shrieked to a stop.

'Wanna ride?' a man said, leaning out his window, a big leer spread across his ruddy face.

'Come on,' his companion encouraged, 'We ain't gonna bite – jump in – we'll show ya the sights. Get ya outta the rain.'

'Yeah,' the first man sniggered. 'We'll even throw in ten bucks if you're a *real* good little girlie.'

She turned and ran in the other direction, not stopping until she reached an all-night deli.

'Is there a phone I can use?' she said to the Mexican parking valet.

'Over there,' he said.

'I, uh . . . don't have money,' she said. 'Can you lend me a quarter to make a call? I'll bring it back tomorrow. Promise.'

The valet shrugged. He felt sorry for the young girl. She

was soaked and miserable. 'Looks like you can use it more than me,' he said, handing her the change.

Gratefully she took the quarter and ran to the phone booth. She'd made a momentous decision. She was telling Nikki everything.

She dialled her mother's number, praying she was home.

Someone answered the phone. Unfortunately that someone was her father.

'Oh God no!' she gasped, slamming the phone down and bursting into tears.

What was she going to do now?

Chapter Sixty-nine

 IF MADELAINE Francis was in LA, Joey figured she had to be registered at a hotel.

He tried the Beverly Hills Hotel first, they'd never heard of her. Next the Hilton – same thing. Then the Beverly Regent. 'One moment, please,' the operator said, 'I'll connect you.'

Fuck Richard Barry. The prick wanted Lara back and he'd go to any lengths to get her, including tracking Madelaine Francis.

'Hello?' Madelaine's voice, sounding sleepy.

'Madelaine?' he said, hardly able to believe it.

'Who's this?'

'Joey.'

'Oh.' A long pause. 'What do *you* want?'

What the fuck did she think he wanted? 'Did you go with Richard Barry to see Lara Ivory this morning?'

She took her time before answering. 'Who told you that?' she said at last.

'*Did* you?'

'Yes,' she admitted, refusing to be intimidated. 'I was there.'

'Couldn't accept me being happy, huh?'

'Get real, Joey,' she snapped, suddenly losing it. 'I'm thrilled you're happy. Not so *thrilled* that you stole my money. What would you *like* me to do? Sit back and let you trample all over me twice? Oh no, young man, Lara Ivory deserves better than you.'

'You've got your money,' he said.

'I waited six years for the first payment,' she said curtly. 'And no thanks to you, I deducted the rest from your *Dreamer* cheque.'

'What did you tell Lara?'

'I simply made her aware of who you are. Good God, Joey, you certainly fed her a crock of shit. A fiancée indeed! Frightened to mention you were living with an old bag like me? Did I embarrass you that much?'

'Where's she gone?'

'I have no idea. But I'm delighted to hear that she *has* gone. At least she has sense.'

'I don't suppose it matters to you, Madelaine – but you've ruined my life.'

'Don't mention it, Joey. You've already ruined mine.'

And she slammed the phone down.

He stared into space for a moment. Richard Barry had screwed him, destroyed the only chance of happiness he'd ever had. And the slick sonofabitch was probably with Lara now, consoling her, telling her what a lousy no-good bastard Joey Lorenzo was.

Well, yeah, maybe he was a bastard. And yes, he should have paid Madelaine back long ago.

But what opportunity had he had when he was locked up in jail for a crime he didn't commit?

What fucking opportunity?

☆　☆　☆

The same day Joey took Madelaine's savings, he hopped a plane to St Louis, where he got a cab to Adelaide's apartment.

When she opened the door he was shocked. He hadn't seen her in three years. Her long dark hair was matted around her shoulders, her face puffy, with dark circles under her eyes, and orange lipstick smeared crookedly on swollen lips. She wore a stained pink peignoir, from which peeped a torn white bra. She also had a black eye and a chipped front tooth.

Who was this addled old woman? It certainly wasn't the beautiful mother he'd left behind.

'I knew you'd come, son,' she said. 'Knew you wouldn't let me down.'

Why was she calling him son? She'd never done so before.

'OK, what's the deal here?' he said.

'I . . . I got into trouble playing the ponies. Borrowed money at the track. You know what it's like when you're on a roll. You think it'll never end — then it all falls to pieces, and the people I borrowed from — they're not very nice . . . and these threats have been coming . . .'

There was something not quite honest about her story. She was stammering too much, eyes downcast, unable to look at him.

'Where'd you get the black eye, Ma?'

'I fell,' she stammered.

'Who are these people you owe money to?'

'A . . . a syndicate. You know — they send collectors. A couple of guys came to the door. I'm frightened, Joey.'

'What's Danny got to say about it?'

'Danny!' She called out her boyfriend's name.

Danny wandered in from the bedroom clad in the definitive gangster outfit. Black shirt, white tie and spiffy black suit. Like Pete Lorenzo, Danny was a petty hood, only instead of being forty years older than her, he was ten years younger. 'Hey, Joey,' he said. 'How's it goin'?'

'Not so great,' Joey replied. 'Not when I see my mother lookin' like this. What happened to her?'

Danny shrugged. 'Beats me.'

'You live with her. Aren't you supposed to be watchin' out for her?'

'The broad's a drunk – what can I tell you?'

'Don't call my mother a broad.'

Danny shrugged. 'Whatever y'say, Joey.'

'So tell me about the gamblin' debts?'

'All I know is she's gotta pay. You bring us the money?'

Joey resented the way he said 'us', since when was Danny involved?

'I saw you in Solid, son,' his mother ventured, lower lip quivering. 'I was so proud, watchin' you up there on the screen.'

'How come you didn't call?'

'I was going to, and then I was uh . . . busy.'

Oh, yeah. She wasn't too busy to call when she needed money.

'How'd you chip your tooth?' he asked. 'Another fall?'

Danny sniggered. 'Yeah, the cunt can't walk straight when she's drunk.'

Joey threw him a long hard look. 'What did you say?'

'I tell it like it is,' Danny said, picking his teeth with a matchbook. 'Don't sit well with you, Joey boy? Well, fuck you. You're not the one stuck here lookin' after the old broad.'

'You'd better watch your mouth,' Joey said.

Danny narrowed his eyes. 'The pretty actor boy's gonna tell me what t'do?'

'You're an asshole,' Joey said.

'Now, now, guys,' Adelaide interrupted, like she was Lana Turner in some old gangster movie. 'Don't want you fighting over me.'

Joey felt like crying. She didn't get it, did she? This pathetic old woman was his mother, his once beautiful Adelaide – the shining light of his life, who'd never given a shit about him. Now she was this drunken crone, with a boyfriend from hell.

501

'I'll tell you what I'm gonna do,' he said. *'I'll meet with the guys you owe. Make a deal with 'em. OK?'*

'Not OK,' Danny said quickly. *'We need cash now.'*

'Back off,' Joey said. *'You're not gettin' shit till I straighten this out.'*

'There's only one way to straighten it out,' Danny said. *'And that's t'hand me the money.'*

'Yes, Joey,' Adelaide said anxiously. *'Give Danny the money, then you can go home.'*

What did they take him for – a fucking bank? Give them the money and get the fuck out. What was going on here?

'You have it, don't you?' Adelaide asked.

'Some of it,' he answered cautiously.

'Hope you didn't leave nothin' at your hotel,' Danny said.

'I'm not at a hotel.'

'Then you got it on you?'

'Maybe.'

'Hand it over, Joey boy.'

'Do it,' Adelaide encouraged, wringing her hands.

'The only way you're gettin' the money is when I pay it to the people she owes.'

'Dumb prick!' Danny exploded. And before Joey knew what was happening, Danny had pulled a gun and was pointing it in his direction. *'Drop the wad on the table, sonny, and get out.'*

Adelaide said nothing. She watched.

'What kind of a set-up is this?' Joey demanded.

'I'm sorry,' Adelaide murmured.

Sorry didn't cut it. He was burning up. He certainly hadn't come back to St Louis to be told what to do by some broken-down hood. And the motherfucker was holding a gun on him. No way was this prick getting away with this crap. Besides, Danny was too much of a coward to use it, Joey could see the yellow in his eyes.

He kicked out like he'd seen in the movies. Danny fell, and the gun went flying out of his hand.

'Dumb punk,' Danny roared, scrambling across the floor for his weapon.

'I'm a punk, huh?' Joey said, kicking the gun away. 'Wanna show me what kinda punk I am?'

'Stop it,' Adelaide groaned. 'Please stop it.'

Danny staggered to his feet and threw a punch. Joey retaliated – catching him on the chin.

'Cocksucker!' Danny yelled. 'You got no idea who you're dealin' with.'

'Who gives a shit?' Joey responded, struggling with the man. 'I want you out of my mother's life.'

'You *call* her your mother,' Danny sneered. 'I call her a dumb hooker cunt.'

Now they were rolling on the floor, exchanging blows. And then Danny pinned Joey down, grabbed a bookend from a nearby shelf, and smashed the side of Joey's head with such force that he lost consciousness for a moment. In the distance he heard a shot and thought that was it – he was gone.

He managed to open his eyes. Danny was slumped on the floor – blood pumping from a hole in his neck. Adelaide was standing next to him, shaking from head to toe, holding the gun.

'Oh fuck, Ma,' Joey groaned, staggering to his feet. 'What've you done now? Oh, fuck!' He snatched the gun out of her hand and made her sit down. Then he ran into the kitchen for a bottle of brandy and forced her to take a couple of swigs.

Neighbours began hammering on the door. A rough male voice. 'Everything all right in there? What's goin' on? We've called the cops.'

Without really thinking about it, he grabbed a cloth from the kitchen and wiped the handle of the gun clean. Then he put *his own prints on it. 'You didn't do it, Ma,' he said, sweat mixing with the blood trickling down his face. 'Remember, you didn't do it – I did. I was defending you. OK?'*

'Yes, son,' she repeated in a quavery voice. 'I didn't do it. You did.'

'Take the money,' he said, pulling the wad from his jacket pocket. 'Somebody must've called the police. I'm not runnin'. I'll tell 'em it was self-defence.'

Self-defence – sure. He got eight years for manslaughter – out in six for good behaviour – and that's why Madelaine didn't get her money.

His mother never visited him in jail. When he got out he discovered she'd moved to Puerto Rico with a lounge singer and left no forwarding address.

He got on a plane and went back to New York.

☆ ☆ ☆

Six years of his life locked up for a crime he didn't commit. Six lost years of harsh punishment he had nightmares remembering.

And then Lara had entered his life, and everything changed. He had a chance at genuine happiness. A chance that Richard Barry had taken and ground underfoot.

Screw Richard Barry and everything he represented. Screw the jealous prick who'd trashed his future.

Determined to find Lara, he picked up the phone and called the sonofabitch.

'What do *you* want?' Richard asked, cold as a three-day-old corpse.

'Where is she?' he demanded

'Looking for Lara?' Richard taunted.

'Where the *fuck* is she?'

'Y'know, Joey, I'd love to tell you she's with me,' Richard said, continuing to taunt him. 'But unfortunately, I have no idea where she is.'

'You had to screw it up, didn't you?'

'Excuse me?'

'I made her happy. We were together like you and she never were. You couldn't stand it, could you?'

'Spare me the sob story,' Richard said. 'I know what's best for Lara. I always have. And when she comes back, it's *me* she'll be with, not a two-bit loser like you.'

Joey slammed the phone down, he'd heard enough. The important thing was to get to Lara before Richard poisoned her against him even more.

Where would she go? That was the question.

Cassie. Yes, Cassie would know.

He frantically scanned Lara's phone book until he found her home number.

A woman answered her phone. 'Cassie?' he said.

'No, I'm Maggie, her sister. Who's this?'

'Joey Lorenzo, Lara's uh . . . fiancé. Is Cassie around?'

'She won't be home tonight. She's spending the night with Lara. Didn't they tell you?'

'Yeah, I uh . . . forgot. Lara left me a note, guess it got thrown out. *Where* were they going again?'

'The house at the beach.'

'You mean Nikki's house at the beach?'

'No. The one Lara rented last year.'

'That's right. I'm supposed to meet them later. What's that address?'

'Let me see . . . You go to the first turning past Point Dume Road, and it's the big house at the end.'

'Is there a phone number?'

'No, but if Cassie calls, shall I tell her you're coming?'

'Don't bother, Maggie. Thought I'd surprise 'em.'

Within minutes he was in the Mercedes and on his way.

☆   ☆   ☆

Lara was getting restless sitting in the dark, waiting for Cassie to return. She remembered waiting once before – huddled in a chair in a motel room – waiting until her father shot himself to death.

Joey had helped her get over a lot of her fears, he'd opened up her life with his warmth and love.

She sighed, maybe it wasn't fair, running away without giving him a chance to explain.

But what if he touched her? What if he overcame her with his lethal charm? A charm she found so utterly irresistible.

No, it was too dangerous to put herself in that position.

She remembered his face explaining about his fictitious fiancée, and the story he'd come up with about her trying to commit suicide. How sincere he'd seemed, how genuine and concerned.

What a bunch of *bullshit*! And she'd fallen for it. Taken in every lying word. How could she have?

She needed to talk to Nikki – get it all out. Nikki would help her be strong, and right now she could use all the support she could get.

Outside the wind was howling, and in the distance she could hear thunder. On the weather report this morning the weather man had said a September storm was blowing in. El Niño was warming the waters around Malibu, causing a series of storms and bad weather. This was supposed to be the first of many.

Why had she acted so hastily? One call to the realtor and she could've gotten the electricity turned on and a fridge stocked with food. Lights and a telephone would be very welcome right now.

Cassie had left her suitcase in the hall. She rummaged through it, finding a warm tracksuit, thick socks and running shoes. She put on the outfit and felt better – certainly warmer.

And then she heard a noise which chilled her.

'Lara?' A woman's voice – loud and clear. 'Lara? Are you there? Are you waiting for me, Lara dear?' A long ominous pause. 'In case you're wondering, this is your good friend, Alison Sewell. Are you ready for a reunion? Because *I* certainly am.'

Chapter Seventy

 THEY WERE arguing furiously in the truck as the rain pounded down and Aiden drove too fast.

'You're making a mistake,' Aiden said, scratching his chin. 'Why would you wanna piss Mick off? He told you – he doesn't *know* where Summer is.'

'How can we be sure?' Nikki replied, the set of her jaw saying she wasn't going to give up on this. 'He's some kind of sick paedophile anyway.'

'Hey – you've been working with him for the last two months,' Aiden said sharply. 'If he *was* after Summer, I've gotta think you would've suspected something before now.'

'I have to make certain,' she said stubbornly.

Aiden shrugged. 'OK, OK,' he muttered. 'Dunno how I got involved with you. Drugs were a lot easier.'

'Nobody's asking you to stay,' she snapped. '*You* were the one who forced this relationship.'

'Oh, I forced it, huh?' he said cynically. 'I didn't notice you racing out of my apartment after we hit the sheets.'

Without warning, she buried her head in her hands. 'I'm sorry, Aiden,' she said, too upset to fight. 'I keep on thinking of Summer out there by herself. She's only a kid, and I feel it's all my fault. I was never there when she needed me, now I realize I should've been.'

'Hey,' he said, reaching over and squeezing her hand, 'it'll work out. You'll see.'

Mick was renting a large ultra-modern house at the top of Benedict Canyon. Aiden turned his truck into the driveway and pulled up outside the front door.

By now Nikki had firmly convinced herself she was going to find Summer. She got out of the truck and rang the doorbell, nervously tapping her fingers together. Aiden stood behind her, smoking a cigarette in the rain. She rang three times before there was any response.

By the time Mick's voice drifted down from an upstairs window they were both soaked. 'Who's there?' Mick called out.

'Nikki and Aiden. Can we come in?'

'What're you *doin'* here?'

'Can we come in?' she repeated, determined to get inside his house so she could check the place out for herself.

'Hold on,' he said. 'I'll be down.'

They waited five minutes before he appeared at the front door. *Long enough for him to hide Summer*, Nikki thought.

'Why are you here?' he asked, blocking the door, dishevelled and barefoot in a black and yellow striped towelling robe with nothing underneath.

Nikki pushed past him into the house. 'Where is she?'

'Oh, Christ!' Mick groaned, his wild-man hair standing on end. 'Don't you *listen*? I told you on the phone, I do *not* have your freakin' daughter.'

'I don't believe you.'

'Who gives a shit if you do or not.' He turned to Aiden. 'This is insane.'

'I know,' Aiden said, his long, thin face expressionless.

'You don't understand, Mick,' Nikki's tone was even and calm. 'I won't be mad at you, I just need to know she's safe.'

'Mick?' a girlish voice drifted down from upstairs. 'Mick –

what's going on?' And down the stairs came an exquisite Oriental girl in a short silk robe.

Mick grimaced. 'Say hello to Tin Lee,' he said. 'We're holding Summer captive under our bed. Whyn't you come up – take a look.'

Aiden pulled Nikki out of the house by her arm. 'Satisfied?' he said, bundling her into the truck.

'I . . . I had a feeling.'

'Go ahead – search the freakin' house,' Mick yelled after them. 'I make one freakin' mistake in life and I'm supposed to pay for it for ever.'

'I'm sorry,' Nikki said.

'So you should be,' Mick grumbled, slamming the front door.

☆　☆　☆

Cold, wet and frightened, with nowhere to go, and shocked because her father was in LA, Summer decided to head back to Tina's. The only problem was she didn't have any money to get there, although if she took a cab she could always pay the driver when they reached her destination, that's, of course, if Tina was home. Now all she had to do was find a cab, which was virtually impossible in the driving rain.

She ventured down the street, her skimpy dress clinging to her body like a second skin, her long blond hair plastered to her head, raindrops dripping off the tip of her nose.

Cars and trucks zoomed to a halt – a pretty girl on the street alone after midnight was fair game, even if she did resemble a drowned cat.

She kept walking until she reached the Sportman's Lodge, then she went inside and asked if they'd call her a cab.

She was tired, hungry and dispirited. Sometimes life didn't seem worth living.

☆ ☆ ☆

'Anyone phone?' Nikki asked, running into the house, shaking the rain out of her short hair.

'Two hang-ups,' Sheldon said. 'The police need Summer's picture. And someone named Jed phoned.'

'What did he say?'

'He wanted to speak to you.'

'Did you ask him if he'd heard from Summer?'

'No, I didn't,' Sheldon answered. 'If you hadn't rushed out of here with your tattooed boyfriend, maybe you would have been able to get more information.'

'Don't criticize Aiden. He's a better man than you any day.'

'You say the most ridiculous things.'

'Really?' She glared at him, how dare he talk down to her as if they were still married. 'Oh, by the way, Sheldon, how's your teenage wife? How old are you now? Fiftysomething? You must make *such* an adorable couple when you go out in public.'

'I'm not interested in petty fighting,' Sheldon said coldly. 'I'm only interested in finding my daughter and taking her back to Chicago.'

'I've been thinking,' Nikki said. 'Summer's obviously not happy with you – perhaps she should stay here with me.'

'No,' Sheldon said flatly. 'She's coming with me.'

'Don't tell me no,' Nikki answered heatedly. 'When we find her, we'll ask Summer what *she* wants to do, exactly like you did when she was a little girl.'

Aiden drew her to one side. 'I gotta get outta here,' he mumbled.

'What's the matter?'

'I can't take all this fighting crap – it's not good for my karma.'

'Is that all you're worried about?'

His burnt-out eyes were restless lasers. 'I gotta cut loose, Nik. Please understand.'

'What does *that* mean?'

'It means I'll call you later.'

'Thanks,' she said indignantly. 'Walk out just when I need you.'

'If I thought I could help, I'd stay. But this shit between you and your ex is getting to me, dredging up too many bad memories.'

She tried to focus on Aiden for a moment. He was right, there was nothing he could do. 'OK,' she said, 'I'll call you if there's any news.'

'It'll be all right,' he said, giving her a hug.

After Aiden left, she went into the bedroom and called Jed back. She told him who she was and that Summer was missing.

'Sorry to hear that, Mrs B.,' he said.

'Who were Summer's friends when she was here?'

'Guess I was closest to her,' he said. 'I introduced her to a lot of people.'

'Anyone in particular you can think of?'

'There was this one girl she kinda hung with – Tina.'

'Do you have her number?'

'Got it somewhere.'

'It's important, Jed. I know she could still be in Chicago, but my gut feeling tells me she's here.'

'When you find her, ask her to call me,' Jed said. 'It wasn't like I was her boyfriend, only she did introduce me to Mr Barry, said she'd talk to him about putting me in one of his movies. I'm an actor, y'know.'

Surprise, surprise. 'Now's not the time to discuss it, Jed,' she said impatiently. 'Just give me Tina's number.'

He did so, and Nikki immediately called.

'Ha! I knew you'd call!' Tina crowed, before Nikki had a chance to say a word. 'Get your cute little suburban ass back here, Summer. I got *big* news about Norman. Move it, girl!'

Nikki didn't need to hear any more, she quickly replaced the receiver without saying anything. Then she called Jed back. 'Sorry to bother you again, do you have Tina's address?'

'I got it written down somewhere, think she's in one of those high-rise buildings off Sunset. Oh, an' Mrs B., while I got your attention, can you talk to your husband about maybe like interviewing me?'

'If you give me Tina's address, I'll take care of it next week,' she promised.

He gave her the information and she ran back into the living room, where Sheldon was pouring himself yet another hefty brandy. 'Let's go,' she said urgently. 'I think I've found her.'

'Thank God!' Sheldon responded. 'And then I'm taking her straight back to Chicago where she belongs.'

We'll see about that, Nikki thought. *Because this time I'm not letting her go without a fight.*

Chapter Seventy-one

 ALISON SEWELL. The madwoman who'd
stalked her for almost a year – sending
letters, photos and gifts; turning up at her
door; insulting anyone who got in her way.

Oh, God! This couldn't possibly be happening, this had to
be some bizarre nightmare. Besides, Alison Sewell was in jail
– locked up and out of her life. Lara had actually been in the
court room when the judge had sentenced the crazy woman.
She'd never forgotten the look of hatred that spread across
Alison's face when their eyes had met for the briefest of
moments.

The old house was filled with the noise of the relentless
rain, howling wind, and the crashing of the surf as the big
storm began whipping the sea down below into a frenzy.

Had she imagined the sound of Alison Sewell's voice?
Maybe the storm was messing with her mind.

No. Impossible. She wasn't hearing things. The woman
was actually in her house.

Get a grip, she told herself. *If she is here, you can deal with
it. Ask her what she wants. Tell her she's trespassing and that
she has to leave immediately or you'll call the police.*

*Oh yes? With what? Your phone doesn't work. You're
trapped here, alone with an obsessed maniac. And nobody
except Cassie knows where you are.*

'Alison?' she called out, trying to keep her voice firm and strong. 'Alison Sewell. Where are you? Can we talk?'

☆ ☆ ☆

Cassie left Granita feeling a lot better after stuffing down the whole smoked-salmon pizza and finishing off a full glass of red wine.

'Better get home before the storm hits,' Wolf warned her.

Rain was now pounding down. She'd borrowed an umbrella from the front desk, and balancing the carton of food in one hand she managed to get into her car and stay comparatively dry. Lara would be wondering what had happened to her, but Cassie was sure she'd be pleased when she came back with supplies, including plenty of candles, a couple of extra flashlights and the special chicken dish from Granita.

Maybe when she got back, Lara would reveal to her what dastardly deed Joey had committed to be suddenly cast out in the cold.

She attempted to start the engine on the Saab. It coughed a few times and wouldn't turn over. 'Damn!' she muttered, trying again. Fourth time lucky – the car started. She switched on her windshield wipers, the rain was so heavy she could scarcely see a thing.

She moved slowly out of the parking lot and headed toward the stop light on the corner. Her car phone rang, startling her.

'Cassie, my dear.'

She immediately recognized Richard's voice.

'Richard!' she exclaimed, wondering what he was doing calling her in her car at this time of night.

'Where are you?' he asked.

'In my car, obviously,' she replied.

'I was speaking to Lara and we got cut off. I thought she said something about being with you.'

Now it became clear. Lara was thinking of getting back with Richard, and *that's* why Joey was yesterday's news. Of course! This was excellent, Cassie had always favoured Richard over Joey.

'I'm on my way back to Lara now,' she said. 'I'm sure she told you the house has no power, no food, nothing. I went to the market to stock up. Looks like it's turning into a bad storm.'

Richard thought fast. *What house was she talking about*? 'I trust you got everything you need,' he said.

'I hope so,' Cassie said.

'I was thinking,' he added smoothly, 'that because of the storm, maybe I should drive out to be with you and Lara.'

'Sounds like a great idea to me,' Cassie said cheerfully.

'Then you'd better remind me how to get there.'

'You came out with Nikki one day, when Lara was renting. You complained about how long it took to get there.'

'That's right,' he said, with a self-deprecating chuckle. 'And I *still* can't remember the way.'

'Stay on the Pacific Coast Highway for about half an hour until you reach Point Dume Road. Then you make the first turning on the left past that, and it's way down. There are no other houses – so you can't miss it – just look for the big gloomy house at the end. I can't imagine *why* Lara bought it.'

'Nor can I,' he murmured.

'Please come soon. I know *I'll* be glad to have a man in the house tonight.'

'Uh . . . Cassie, since I got cut off from Lara, I didn't get a chance to tell her I was coming, so why don't you leave the door open and I'll surprise her.'

'Can I ask you something?' Cassie said. 'I know this is very forward of me, but are you and Lara getting back together? Is that what this is all about?'

'You guessed it,' he said.

'I *knew* something was going on when you spent all that

time in her trailer this morning,' Cassie said, quite delighted. 'I'm *so* pleased. Of course,' she added, a touch guilty, 'I feel sorry for Nikki, she's a nice woman, but in my opinion you and Lara always belonged together.'

'You're very smart, Cassie.'

'Thanks, Richard. We'll see you soon.'

'Don't forget – it's a surprise, so not a word.'

'Got it,' Cassie said, grinning happily. Maybe, when Richard arrived, she could leave and go home to the comfort of her own bed. What a pleasure that would be.

The red light changed to green and Cassie proceeded across the intersection, making a left-hand turn onto the Pacific Coast Highway.

She did not see the Porsche careening out of control heading in her direction, she was too busy thinking about Richard and Lara and what would happen next.

The Porsche smashed into the side of the Saab with a sickening crunch, sending both cars out of control. The Saab began spinning in circles before somersaulting across the slick surface of the wet road and turning over with Cassie trapped inside.

When the first rescuers reached the car, they couldn't tell whether she was dead or alive.

☆ ☆ ☆

When it rains in LA it doesn't take long before everything falls to pieces. Mudslides slither down the hills and cliffs; rivers overflow; gutters stop up; roofs leak; cars crash; in fact, everything goes out of control.

By the time Joey turned off San Vicente and headed down toward the ocean there were flood warnings in operation and the sea was crashing its way toward the well-kept decks of Malibu houses. Police and fire teams were already out on the roads, turning cars back and trying to direct the rest of the traffic, which was now moving at an extremely slow pace.

This gave Joey plenty of time to think. Exactly what was he going to tell Lara when he finally arrived? The truth, that's what. The truth about his fucked-up life, his efforts to break away from his background and become an actor, and how he'd gone back to see his mother and gotten caught in a trap, taking the rap for a murder he didn't commit.

And how had his mother repaid him? She'd run off with another loser, without even leaving a forwarding address.

But he wasn't perfect either. He'd used Madelaine, just as he'd used most women for sex or whatever he wanted from them. Then Lara had come into his life, and she'd made him aware that it was possible to care for another person and to have no ulterior motive.

Yes. He would tell her the truth. That she made everything special. She *was* his life, his true love, his soulmate. He'd throw himself on her mercy and hope she could forgive him.

It wasn't like he wanted anything from her. All he wanted was to be there for her, by her side, ready to support and protect her in every way.

Traffic had slowed to a crawl. He attracted the attention of a cop standing in the middle of the road. 'What's happening?' he asked.

'Big accident up ahead,' the cop said. 'I don't advise you continuing on this road unless you live here.'

'I do,' he lied.

'OK, take it easy.'

'I'll do that.' He switched on the radio. Billie Holiday was singing the blues. 'Good Morning Heartache'. Very suitable.

He couldn't wait to reach his destination. His love. His future.

☆ ☆ ☆

Alison could hear the bitch calling out to her. Yes, Lara Ivory remembered her name. And so she should. She'd been her loyal friend, but that wasn't enough. No. Lara Ivory had seen fit to betray her.

Of course Lara remembered her name. Soon *everybody* would know her name.

She started thinking about what photographs she had of herself. Which one would they put on the cover of *Time*? There was that snap Uncle Cyril had taken of her and her mother when she was nineteen. She hated it, but if they cut her mother out it wasn't so bad. And she was younger then, prettier.

You were never pretty, a voice in her head taunted her. *You were always the ugly girl. Always the slob. Nobody liked you. Nobody wanted to spend time with you. Sewer . . . the Dump . . . Big Boy* —the hateful nicknames came back to haunt her.

People would think she was pretty when she was on the cover of *Time*. People would look at her in admiration when her picture adorned the front of *Newsweek*. TV would get into the act, too. *Hard Copy* would run stories on her. *Inside Edition* would speak about her. *Prime Time. Dateline.* Even *Sixty Minutes.*

She'd be more famous than anyone in the world. The media would cover her case for months.

Alison Sewell would be right up there, along with Charles Manson, Mark Chapman, and the rest of them.

Alison Sewell. The first woman to gain such a distinguished honour.

'Alison. Why don't you come here, we can talk.'

She heard the bitch's voice again. 'Don't worry, Lara,' she called out. 'I'm coming right now. I'm coming to slit your pretty little throat.'

Chapter Seventy-two

 THE CAB driver couldn't seem to keep quiet. 'Damn American weather,' he kept mumbling. 'Damn California. Damn riots. Damn fires.'

Summer huddled on the back seat. She didn't want conversation, all she wanted was to shiver her way into oblivion.

'What's wrong with you?' the driver demanded, twisting his head. 'In my country – girls – they no run at night by themselves. This no right.'

'Where are you from?' she forced herself to ask. Maybe if she got him talking about his country, she could tune out while he blathered on.

'Beirut,' he said proudly. 'Beautiful place, till the bombing. Those bastards took everything, a man's pride, his home, those bastards took it all. Damn terrorists!'

'How long have you been in America?'

'Too long.'

'Aren't we going the wrong way?' she asked, peering out the window. 'Shouldn't you have taken Coldwater Canyon?'

'I go Sepulveda. Weather bad for canyon. Big flooding.' He gave a hacking cough before continuing his litany of complaints. 'Everything in LA too much. Flooding, fires, riots, car-jackings. They put gun to my head one day. Those bastards!'

'That's awful,' she said, not really caring at all.

There was a red light ahead. Her cab stopped just in time as the car in front of them smashed into the back of a Cadillac standing at the stop light.

'You see, you see,' her cab driver shouted excitedly. 'American maniacs!'

The driver of the Cadillac got out of his car, screamed at the other driver, and ran up to the cab driver's window. 'You see that?' he yelled. 'You're my witness.'

'No see nothing,' her driver said, staring straight ahead. 'Nothing.' Then he manoeuvred his cab around the two cars and drove on.

'How long before we're at the address I gave you?' Summer asked.

'In this weather? With lousy American drivers? Don't know.'

'If you hate Americans so much, why'd you come here?' she asked, fed up with his complaining.

He let out a crafty laugh. 'Good thing about America – money – money – money!'

☆ ☆ ☆

'What's with the traffic?' Nikki said impatiently, stuck behind a line of cars on the Pacific Coast Highway.

'I don't know why you didn't let me drive,' Sheldon responded irritably.

'Because it's *my* car and I know where we're going.'

'You never *could* drive,' Sheldon said.

'According to *you*, I was incapable of doing anything,' Nikki replied. 'Maybe that's why you married me, so you could take a child and mould her. Is that why you married Rachel, too?'

'I refuse to listen to your garbage,' he said, staring straight ahead.

'I was such a baby, wasn't I? So malleable. *That's* why you were able to talk me into leaving Summer with you, when she should have come with me, and you know it.'

'Summer is a very well-adjusted girl. Or at least she was, until she stayed with you in LA. Examine the way you conduct your life. Richard seemed decent, now you're with someone who looks like he belongs in a rock and roll band.'

'Aiden's a very fine actor.'

'I always said you were damaged. Now you've proved me right.'

'I'm not getting involved in a fight,' Nikki said with a weary sigh. 'I've achieved so much since you and I were together. If you'd had *your* way, I'd still be locked in the house while you systematically screwed your way through all your patients. God! I cannot believe you're a psychiatrist. It seems criminal.'

A policeman with a flashlight slowly moved down the line of cars, talking to the drivers. He reached Nikki's window. 'Big accident up ahead, ma'am,' he said. 'There'll be a delay.'

'How long?' she asked, impatiently.

'We're trying to move it along as fast as possible. But unless you have to make the journey, I suggest you turn around and go home.'

'Thanks,' she said. 'We have to get into town.'

At least she had an idea where Summer was now. If she was with her friend, Tina, it wouldn't be long before she found her.

And when she did, she was never letting her go again.

☆ ☆ ☆

The cab finally pulled up in front of Tina's apartment building.

'You'll have to wait a minute,' Summer said. 'I've got to get my money – it's inside.'

'Oh no, no no,' the driver said, his face turning purple. 'I no wait. You run out back door, I know American girls.'

'If you don't trust me, come in with me,' Summer said impatiently.

'I no leave cab,' he answered sternly. 'Somebody steal.'

She sneezed. 'I'm going inside. Either you come with me, or wait here for your money. I really don't like *care*.' With that she flung open the cab door and ran into the apartment building, almost slipping on the front steps.

God, she hoped Tina was home. What was she going to do if she wasn't? The wacko cab driver would probably have her arrested if she didn't pay him.

She rang the doorbell of Tina's apartment and waited.

Seconds later Tina flung open the door. 'About time,' she exclaimed. 'OhmiGod, look at you! What did you do, go for a swim in the ocean?'

'I've come to collect my things,' Summer said frostily. 'Then I'll get out of your way.'

'Don't be so lame,' Tina said. 'You look like you've had a crummy night. Come in. Anyway, I told you on the phone, there's a whole new development, so you'd better get spiffed up.'

'What new development?'

'Well . . . fifteen minutes after you left, Norman came out of the bedroom, dumps the two babes he's with, and says, "Where's Summer?" How'd you like *that*?'

'He did?' Summer said, perking up.

'He certainly did. So I told him you weren't pleased with the situation and had gone home. That excited him no end. Seems he likes a girl who's hard to get.'

Now Summer was really interested. 'What happened then?' she asked.

'He said, "I'll get rid of everybody – bring her back." And *I* said, "Show me the money!"'

'What're you talking about?'

'I told him you weren't coming back for nothing, and if I had to go find you, we wanted to get paid for our time.' Tina grinned. 'You know what? He gave me a thousand bucks and said, "Go find her." We're rich!'

'I've had the most horrible night,' Summer complained. 'I nearly got raped. Then I was lost, and couldn't get a cab. Now I'm hungry and tired.' Inexplicably she burst into tears. 'I think I made a big mistake coming back to LA.'

'No way,' Tina said, putting her arm around Summer's shoulders. 'I told you – we're gonna make a fortune. We got off to a bad start, that's all. Now go take a shower, and wash your hair. I'll fix you some hot soup, then I'll call Norman and see if he wants us back tonight or tomorrow.'

'I'm not going anywhere tonight,' Summer said, vigorously shaking her head. 'I have to sleep.'

'If he wants us to, we gotta go. If we *don't*, then I think he'll like lose interest. You don't want to miss out, do you?'

'Oh, wow!' Summer said, suddenly remembering. 'There's an angry cab driver downstairs waiting for me to pay him.'

'I'll take care of it. You go shower. And Summer—'

'Yes?'

'Sorry I acted like a major bitch before. Didn't mean to. Sometimes coke makes me crazy.'

'OK,' Summer nodded, relieved they were friends again. 'All is forgiven.'

The two girls hugged.

'I'll go pay your cab driver,' Tina said. 'Be right back.'

☆ ☆ ☆

Finally they crawled past the accident on the highway. Nikki could see two cars, both of them overturned and in bad shape. She looked quickly to see if one of the accident vehicles was Aiden's truck, he drove like a madman. Fortunately he wasn't involved.

Sheldon had slumped into silence, which was a good thing because she didn't have anything to say to him. She did not care to be in his presence. She should have left him at the beach house and come to find Summer by herself. But then again, maybe she'd need his support.

Why had Summer run away? That was the question.

She turned down Sunset. The twisting street was like a river, a slick of rain water rushing down toward the inadequate drains. Lightning flashed, accompanied by loud rumbles of thunder. Keeping to the inside lane, she drove as fast as she could without endangering both of them. When they drew closer to Beverly Hills she said, 'I have to make a right on San Vicente, so watch out, I can barely see a thing.'

Ten minutes later Sheldon said, 'Make your turn at the next stop light.'

She reached the light, veered to the right, and as they were turning into the apartment building on the left, Sheldon urgently said, 'Look – isn't that her?'

She glanced over. Summer was getting into a red sports car. Before she could cross in front of oncoming traffic, the sports car roared off in the opposite direction.

Sheldon sat up very straight. 'That *is* her,' he said. 'Follow that car.'

Nikki didn't need asking twice.

Chapter Seventy-three

 SHE'D FACED danger before. Sitting in the next room while her father had shot her family to death. The endless hours in the motel room before he'd turned the gun on himself. It had been raining *that* night, too; and the night Morgan Creedo's car had smashed into the truck, decapitating him.

Oh, yes. Danger. Lara knew what that was about only too well. But all the same, her throat was dry, her hands shaking. She was trapped in a dark house in the middle of a storm with an obsessed stalker.

She backed across the living room, feeling her way around the furniture until she reached the glass doors that led outside to the terrace. Slipping the catch, she opened the door and eased herself outside into the driving rain. If she could reach the stairs and get down to the beach, then she'd make a run for it – hopefully get to another house for help.

But what if Cassie came back, and walked into the situation? What if Alison attacked *her*? Oh God! Now she was in a quandary. Did she run, or did she stay? She had no weapon, nothing to defend herself with. Plus she wouldn't be much help to Cassie if Alison Sewell carried out her threat and slit her throat. Then the two of them would be dead.

No, the best thing was to go for help and call the police. Get out, that was the smart thing to do.

526

Fortunately, Alison Sewell had no idea there were stairs leading down to the beach.

The ground was thick with mud and overgrown plants. Lara kept on tripping as she ran toward the gate at the top of the outside steps. Unfortunately, when she reached the gate and tried to open it, she realized it was padlocked.

Now what?

She glanced back at the house. A flash of lightning lit up the sky.

In the momentary glare she could see Alison Sewell standing by the glass doors she'd just escaped from. Alison was holding a knife. And on her face was an expression of pure hatred.

☆ ☆ ☆

Richard smiled to himself. Ever since he'd come back from Mexico, his nefarious past firmly behind him, there was nothing he couldn't do.

He wanted to direct successful movies. Done.

He wanted to marry Lara Ivory. Done.

Now he wanted her back, and nobody was going to stop him. And if they tried to . . .

Well, he'd killed once – there was nothing to stop him doing it again if it meant protecting Lara.

Who else would think of calling Cassie in her car? God, he was clever. He'd come a long way from the sixteen-year-old street-smart kid who'd run away from home. Not to mention the twenty-eight-year-old drugged-out loser who'd shot Hadley and thought that was it. Over. *Finito*.

Yes. He was a true survivor. He'd reinvented himself, become an upstanding member of the Hollywood community – admired and respected.

And yet . . . only Lara had made him truly happy, and look what he'd done to her.

He was determined to make up for his cheating ways. When he and Lara were back together he'd treat her like a queen. No more make-up girls or Kimberlys or actresses who begged him to fuck them so they'd get more than their share of close-ups. No. Once again he was reinventing himself just for her.

He called the front desk and told them to bring his car around. Then he put on his raincoat and set off.

Soon he would experience a reunion with the love of his life.

As far as he was concerned, it couldn't be soon enough.

☆　☆　☆

The bitch was attempting to run. But running was no good, because Alison Sewell could run faster than anyone. She'd chased more celebrities than she could remember. Tracked them down and caught them in her lens.

Outside the rain was coming down in fierce torrents. Lara Ivory couldn't get away from her, no sense in trying.

Alison pulled the hood of her parka over her head and resolutely headed for the spot where she'd last seen Lara standing.

Bitch! She wouldn't be the pretty girl when Alison got through with her. No – not Lara Ivory who'd represented all the pretty girls Alison had been forced to look at year after year. The actresses on film. The haughty supermodels strutting down the runways showing off their skinny bodies and fake tits, smiling at the camera as if *they* were the only pretty girls in the world. She hated them all!

Lara would be punished for every one of them. Michelle Pfeiffer's calm beauty; Naomi Campbell and her superior smile; Cindy Crawford with her cute little beauty mark; Winona Ryder's winsome charm.

Yes, Lara Ivory would pay the price. She'd pay the price for all of them.

☆   ☆   ☆

'Oh, fuck!' Joey exclaimed, as he approached the accident site and recognized the remains of Cassie's car. Abruptly he pulled the Mercedes over to the shoulder of the road and jumped out.

Oh Jesus, God. What if Lara was hurt? What if she was *dead*? He couldn't bear the thought.

He raced over to the wrecking crew who were busy untangling twisted metal. 'Where are the people who were in this car?' he asked urgently.

'They took 'em to the hospital,' one of the guys said.

'What hospital?'

'Dunno, it wasn't long ago.'

'Was anybody . . . killed?' he asked, barely able to get the words out.

'You'll have to ask that cop over there. He was here when the ambulance came.'

He ran over to the cop. 'That your car over there?' the cop said. 'Get it outta here. Can't you see what's going on?'

'I knew the people in the Saab. Are they OK?'

'Yeah, yeah – the woman's pretty cut up with some broken bones, but the ambulance guy said she'll be all right. The man in the Porsche bought it. Straight through the windshield – no seatbelt.'

'There were two women in the Saab. Are they *both* OK?'

'Only one in the car – the driver. Kind of a large lady. Got a feeling her bulk saved her.'

'Only one? You sure?'

'Yeah. They've taken her to St John's. Now do me a big one an' get your car outta here.'

'It wasn't Lara Ivory?'

The cop laughed. 'The movie star? Are you kiddin' me? If it'd been Lara Ivory, I'd've known about it.'

'Thanks,' Joey said.

'They're talking mudslides down the highway, and some flooding, so if you don't havta go there, I'd turn back.'

'I gotta get home.'

'You'd better hurry, 'cause we may be closin' the roads soon.'

'OK, thanks.'

He ran back to the Mercedes. Something didn't feel right. He was filled with the same kind of uneasiness he'd experienced when he'd visited his mother that fateful day, and she'd ended up shooting Danny.

A lot of cars were turning around and heading back to town, which meant the traffic ahead was easing up. But the road was becoming more hazardous. People were dashing across the highway lugging sandbags; small boulders were beginning to roll down from the sodden cliff.

He knew he'd better hurry and get there while he still could.

☆   ☆   ☆

One look at Alison's face was enough to convince Lara that she had to get away as quickly as possible. And how was she going to do that when she couldn't even reach the steps down to the beach?

She hid in the heavy shrubbery surrounding the terrace, holding her breath, desperately thinking what she could use as a weapon if Alison came at her.

Then she remembered, there was a small garden shed at the side of the property. She began scrambling toward it.

☆ ☆ ☆

Once past the accident, Joey made good time. He tried calling the hospital on the car phone. They informed him Cassie hadn't been admitted yet. Next he phoned her sister, told her what had happened, and to get over to the hospital as fast as possible.

All he could think was thank God Lara hadn't been in the car.

The rain was blinding, the condition of the road getting more hazardous by the minute, but he managed to make good time, slowing down when he came to Point Dume Road, searching for the turning past it, finding it and making a sharp left.

Now he found himself on nothing more than a dirt road, dark and deserted. The wheels of his car were spinning and sliding in the mud, and as far as he could see there didn't seem to be anything down here. He slowed the Mercedes. Maggie must have made a mistake and given him the wrong directions.

He was ready to turn back when he almost ran into a car parked by the side of big open gates that led to an isolated house.

Two thoughts crossed his mind. Whose car was it? And why were there no lights on in the house?

Keeping the bright lights on the Mercedes, he drove through the gates, and drew up outside the house.

☆ ☆ ☆

Lara moved silently through the thick shrubbery, her arms getting scratched and torn by rose thorns and jagged palms. She kept going, sure that there must be something in the shed she could use as a weapon – something she could use to fight back.

She refused to be a victim. She'd been a victim too many times in her life, and it was not going to happen again. She was Lara Ivory – survivor. She wasn't an actress playing a part – this was real life, and she was in a situation she was going to have to get out of herself.

Watching her father shoot himself, she'd had no control. Now she was in control, and nobody was going to destroy her.

She stumbled up to the shed, and was about to open the door, when a huge body leaped on her from behind.

'Got you!' Alison Sewell yelled, wrestling her to the ground, rolling in the thick mud. 'Got you, you pretty little bitch,' Alison crowed triumphantly.

'What do you want from me?' Lara shouted. 'What have I ever done to you?'

Alison put her hefty arms around her, holding her in a tight bear hug. 'All I wanted was to be your friend,' she yelled above the noise of the howling wind. 'But you didn't want a friend like me, did you? I wasn't good enough for the likes of you. I was too ugly, wasn't I?'

'What are you talking about?' Lara shouted, desperately struggling to escape.

'As if you don't know,' Alison yelled, straddling her, pinning her to the ground with her weight.

Then she raised the knife.

Lightning lit up the sky. Lara looked up, saw the knife, and let out a long anguished scream.

'Now we'll see who's the famous one,' Alison yelled, cackling wildly. 'Now we'll *really* see!'

Chapter Seventy-four

 SUMMER TOOK a shower, washed her hair and touched up her make-up. Tina was more than solicitous. She made her a hot cup of celery soup, apologized repeatedly, then told her that she'd spoken to Norman, and he'd insisted they come back that night, because he was leaving on location the next day. 'We gotta close the deal,' Tina said excitedly. 'If you play it right, maybe he'll invite you to visit the location. How cool would that be?'

Summer was tempted. The soup and the shower had made her feel better, and to tempt her further, Tina lent her a very hot Dolce & Gabana pants suit.

It was past one in the morning, and she decided that maybe Tina was right – she'd be wise to close the deal while she had the opportunity. Although deep down she wished she could just go to sleep.

'OK,' she said at last. 'If you think so, we'll go.'

'Excellent!' Tina exclaimed, and they set off.

☆ ☆ ☆

'For God's sake,' Sheldon said. 'You're losing them.'

'No, I'm not,' Nikki retorted. 'I can see the car ahead of me.'

'They only have to make one green light, and you're fucked.'

'Oh, Sheldon,' she mocked. 'Using four-letter words. What happened to *you*?'

'I don't like you, Nikki,' he said, staring straight ahead.

'You liked me when I was young.'

'Well, I certainly don't like the woman you've grown into.'

'Then shut up and leave me alone,' she snapped. 'The only reason we're together is to find our daughter.'

☆　☆　☆

As they drew closer to the hotel, Tina said, 'Listen, there's something I forgot to tell you.'

'What?' Summer asked.

'Cluny might still be there,' Tina said. 'But that's cool, 'cause she's so famous.'

'Why might she still be there?' Summer asked suspiciously.

'I think he kind of like, you *know*, hangs out with her. Nothing romantic, but um . . . she's sort of like his friend.'

'I don't get it,' Summer said.

'Look,' Tina said reassuringly. 'I'm sure it'll be you and him alone together. If she's there, I'll keep her busy in the other room.'

Summer shook her head. Somehow she felt as if she was being sucked into something she didn't want to do. And yet – Norman Barton and his puppy dog smile. If she could be Mrs Norman Barton, *nobody* could touch her. And now that her father was in LA, she had to find someone to protect her.

'OK,' she said, with a little sigh. 'I guess if you keep Cluny in the other room, it'll be all right.'

'*And*,' Tina said, lowering her voice, 'Norman has primo grass. I told him that's what you were into.'

'You did?' Summer said, thinking that the last thing she felt like doing was smoking a joint.

'Hey – we're here,' Tina said. 'You want me to report that scuzzbucket who tried to rape you?'

'No, no,' Summer said quickly. 'Absolutely not. It was my own fault. I shouldn't have gone to his house. It was a dumb move.'

'You can say that again,' Tina said. 'C'mon, let's go.'

She jumped out of the car, gave the keys to the parking valet and they entered the hotel.

☆ ☆ ☆

'Make the turn,' Sheldon ordered.

'I can't, there's traffic,' Nikki replied.

'Do it!' he commanded, pissing her off.

'Don't panic, Sheldon,' she said coolly. 'They went into the hotel. We're five minutes away from being with her.'

The traffic eased up and she crossed into the hotel driveway.

'Are you a guest?' the parking valet asked, as he opened her door.

'No, we'll be out shortly,' she said. 'Please keep my car somewhere close.'

They entered the lobby. No sign of Tina or Summer.

Nikki went up to the desk, closely followed by Sheldon. 'Excuse me,' she said. 'Two young girls just came in here. Can you tell me where they went?'

The woman behind the desk said, 'I'm sorry, we cannot divulge that kind of information.'

Sheldon hammered his fist on the desk. 'One of those girls is my daughter,' he said. 'She is fifteen years old. I suggest you tell me where they went, otherwise I'll summon the police, and you can tell *them*.'

'Just a moment, sir,' the woman said, startled. 'I'll get the manager.'

'Do what you want, but I'm not leaving this lobby until I have my daughter back.'

☆ ☆ ☆

'Hey.' It was Norman Barton himself.

Summer gazed into his puppy dog eyes and thought, *No, I haven't made a mistake. It's really him. And he's really cute.*

'What *happened* to you?' he said, grinning. 'Saw you for a second, then you were gone.'

'It seemed to me you were pretty busy,' she said.

'Never too busy for a honey rabbit like you,' he said, taking her hand and drawing her into the suite.

Cluny was stretched out on the couch, looking quite out of it. She waved vaguely in their direction. Summer noticed that there was still a small mound of white powder on the glass-topped table and her stomach dropped.

'Want a snort?' Norman said, indicating the supply.

'I don't do coke,' she replied disapprovingly. 'Nor does Tina,' she added, shooting Tina a warning look.

'But if you've got any grass . . .' Tina said quickly. 'Then we're talking!'

'Hey, cutie,' Norman said, pulling Summer into the bedroom, 'let's go see what I got for you.'

'Just me?' she said, staring straight at him.

'Just you,' he replied, chicklet teeth flashing in her direction.

☆ ☆ ☆

The manager of the hotel was Beverly Hills perfect, with crimped silver hair and a nut-brown suntan. 'What seems to be the problem?' he said, ignoring Nikki and giving Sheldon an *all guys together* look.

'There's no problem at the moment,' Sheldon replied stiffly, taking charge. 'I'm Dr Sheldon Weston. My under-age daughter is in this hotel, and I would like to know where she is.'

The manager didn't want any trouble. He glanced at the desk clerk. 'Do you know where this gentleman's daughter might be?'

'Uh . . . yes, Mr Bell. She and another young lady went up to Mr Barton's suite.'

'That would be the penthouse suite,' the manager said. 'I can escort you up there and we'll see if your daughter is there. I usually wouldn't dream of disturbing my guests at this late hour, but since you seem so certain—'

'Oh, I'm certain,' Sheldon said ominously.

'Yes, he's certain,' Nikki added. 'And she's my daughter, too, so let's go.'

☆ ☆ ☆

Norman handed Summer a joint and told her to sit on the bed. 'I'm watching this great Mel Gibson movie,' he said. 'But you know what? You're so cute and pretty, I thought it'd be nice to have you hang with me.'

It was exactly what she wanted to hear. Hang with him. Become Mrs Norman Barton. Escape from Chicago for ever.

'I . . . I thought about you a lot while I was at home,' she ventured shyly.

'Where's home?' he asked, jumping on the bed beside her.

'Chicago.'

'Yeah? Did a promo tour there once. Kind of a happening city.'

'Maybe if you take me with you next time,' she said boldly. 'I could show you around.'

'Honey, all they do is move me from limo to limo. I never get a chance to see the sights.'

'That's a shame.'

'They pay me good.'

'Sometimes,' she said wisely, 'money isn't everything.'

He looked at her like he couldn't quite believe she was so naive. 'You really don't know what this is all about, do you?' he said.

She summoned all the sophistication she could muster. 'I've been around.'

'Hey,' he said, his attention suddenly taken by the action on the screen. 'Take a look at Mel Gibson with that insane long hair. He's really a cool dude, huh?'

'I love Mel Gibson,' she said.

'Yeah.' Norman grinned. 'He make you cream your panties?'

'Excuse me?'

He laughed. 'Jeez! They sure make them innocent in Chicago.'

☆ ☆ ☆

The manager knocked on the door of Norman Barton's suite. Cluny strolled over to answer it. Everybody recognized her.

'Hi, guys,' she said, totally sanguine. 'What's going on?'

'I'm so sorry to disturb you,' the manager said, trying not to stare at her smooth brown breasts almost escaping from a skimpy little wrap dress. 'I was told two young ladies were visiting Mr Barton's suite. One of them has to go home with her father, he's here to collect her.'

'Are you kidding me?' Cluny said, hands on narrow hips.

'I want my daughter,' Sheldon thundered, pushing forward. 'And I want her *now*.'

'Hold it,' Cluny said, shutting the door on them.

Tina was in the john. Cluny called out her name. 'Some old dude who says he's your father is here.'

'*What?*' Tina said, emerging.

'He's outside with the manager. We'd better get the coke off the table in case they start barging in.'

'I . . . I don't *have* a father,' Tina said. 'My old man's long gone.'

'Then it must be the other kid's.'

Sheldon began hammering on the door.

'Shit!' Tina said. 'You're right. It must be Summer's dad. What're we gonna do?'

'Quick, get rid of the coke, then we'll tell 'em nobody's here,' Cluny said, quickly sweeping the coke into a plastic bag and shoving it in her purse. When that was done she went back to the door and opened it.

'Where's my daughter?' Sheldon demanded.

'Um . . . Tina's the only person here,' Cluny said.

'Tina?' Nikki questioned. 'Where is she?'

'I don't think Mr Barton would appreciate you coming up here to disturb us in the middle of the night,' Cluny said, suddenly getting very haughty in her best supermodel way.

The manager was embarrassed. He began to apologize, but he hadn't reckoned on Nikki, who suddenly shoved past him into the suite.

Tina stared at her, startled.

'Are you Tina?' Nikki asked.

'Uh . . . yes. Why?'

'Where's Summer?'

'Uh . . . she's not here,' Tina started to say.

'Bullshit!' Nikki replied. 'I saw her come in with you.' And before anyone could stop her, she marched over to the bedroom door and flung it open.

Summer dropped her joint and jumped off the bed. 'OhmiGod! What are you doing here, Mom?'

'*Mom?*' Norman Barton said.

'We're going home, Summer,' Nikki said, attempting to remain calm, although she was completely unthrilled to discover her daughter sitting on a bed in a hotel room with some half-assed actor. 'And we're going now.'

Reluctantly, Summer slouched to the door. She could see that her mother wasn't in the mood to argue. 'I . . . I . . . dunno know what to say . . .' she mumbled.

'I'm sure you'll find something,' Nikki said. 'Your father's here, too.'

Summer stopped in her tracks. 'Oh no!' she shrieked. 'I'm not going anywhere with him. It's over, Mom, *over*. I'm *never* going back to him.'

'Why not?'

'Make him go away or I'm staying here.'

Nikki frowned. 'What are you talking about?'

'Please, Mom,' Summer said frantically. 'I can't tell you now. Not in front of all these people.'

Sheldon appeared behind her at the door. 'Summer,' he said sternly. 'What do you call this behaviour?'

'What the *fuck* is going on?' Norman Barton exploded. 'Cluny,' he yelled. 'Get rid of all these people.'

The manager swept in and ushered them all out into the corridor, Tina too. By this time Summer was sobbing uncontrollably.

'What's the matter with her?' Sheldon said. 'Is she on drugs?'

Tina turned on him. 'No, she's not on drugs, you filthy old perv. She's freaked at seeing you.'

Sheldon went very pale. 'I suggest you hold your tongue, young lady.'

'And I suggest you keep your pants zipped up,' Tina retorted.

'Will someone explain to me what exactly is going on?' Nikki interrupted.

'I guess Summer hasn't told you,' Tina said, heatedly. 'And if she hasn't – it's about time somebody did.'

'Told me what?'

'Your ex-old man has been creeping into Summer's room ever since she was ten, doing all kinds of dirty things to her. Why do you think she's so screwed up? And how come *you* didn't do anything about it?'

Nikki felt the bottom drop out of her world. She looked at Sheldon. He stared at the ground, white-faced. 'Is it true, Sheldon?' she asked, her voice rising.

'This . . . this crazy girl doesn't know what she's talking about,' he blustered.

Nikki turned to Summer. 'Is it?'

Summer nodded, her cheeks streaked with tears. 'I . . . I wanted to tell you, Mom, but I couldn't. You were never there, and I didn't want to upset you, and . . . please, Mom, let me come home with you. *Please!* I never want to see him again.'

Nikki held open her arms. 'And you never have to. That's a promise.'

Chapter Seventy-five

 RICHARD REACHED Sunset just as they were closing the road. Police barricades were already in place.

He leaned out of his window. 'What's going on?' he asked a cop.

'Sorry, we're closing the highway. There's flooding and a threatening mudslide.'

'I have to get through,' Richard said.

'It's for your own safety,' the cop said.

'It might be for my own safety, but what about my pregnant wife alone in the house?'

'I don't know about that.'

'Look, I can't leave her there, she's already panicked.'

'I have my orders.'

'And I have my wife. I'm Richard Barry, the film director. My wife is Lara Ivory.'

The cop was immediately interested. 'I didn't know Miss Ivory was pregnant,' he said. 'I'm a big fan.'

'She is, and she's alone. So if you'll lift the barricade, I'll take my chances.'

'Well,' the cop looked around. 'As long as you're careful out there.'

'Of course,' Richard said, and waited while the man summoned another cop to help him raise the barricade.

☆ ☆ ☆

Lara could hardly breathe, she knew if she didn't do something quickly, she'd suffocate.

Alison was sitting astride her, grinding handfuls of mud into her face. The mud was in her mouth, her eyes, her nose.

While she was doing it, Alison kept taunting her. 'Bitch!' she yelled. 'Pretty . . . little . . . *bitch*! Where shall I cut you first? Where would you like it, *Miz* Ivory?' Then she'd grind another handful of mud onto Lara's face.

'What did I ever do to you?' Lara managed to gasp.

'You wouldn't be my friend,' Alison screamed, wild-eyed. 'You had me thrown in jail. And for that you're going to die. Do you hear me, bitch? YOU'RE GOING TO DIE!'

☆ ☆ ☆

Grabbing a flashlight from the Mercedes, Joey entered the dark house. He was sure Lara wasn't there, because what would she be doing alone in the pitch black? Cassie must have taken her somewhere and dropped her off. Maybe to Richard's. The thought filled him with rage.

He almost tripped over Lara's open suitcase in the front hall. At least that proved she'd been here.

With the flashlight guiding him, he made his way into what he presumed was the living room. Across the room a glass door banged back and forth in the wind. He moved over to close it. A jagged streak of lightning lit up the sky, and outside on the terrace, he saw Lara – his Lara – with someone on top of her, the two of them struggling on the ground.

He ran outside, frantically screaming her name. As he drew closer he could see she was being attacked by a large woman. Jesus! What the fuck was going on?

He reached them, and was about to drag the woman off Lara, when she turned and struck out with a lethal hunting knife, slashing him across the cheek. Blood began pouring from his wound. The pain was intense, but he hardly felt it. All he knew was that Lara was in danger and he had to save her.

He went for the woman once more, grabbing her shoulders, trying to haul her off Lara.

She roared with anger and slashed out with the knife again, this time cutting him across the left hand.

He smashed into her face with his elbow and she loosened her grip on Lara, who managed to roll out from under her.

'Run!' Joey yelled. 'Get the hell outta here!'

☆ ☆ ☆

Richard drove through the heavy storm. Once he reached the house, Lara would realize he was her saviour. She'd finally know for sure how much he loved her.

It had taken him a long time to understand what true happiness was, and now that he did, he had no intention of losing it again.

Up ahead he heard an ominous rumbling. It wasn't thunder, it was a different kind of noise, reminiscent of the big Northridge 1994 earthquake.

For a moment he almost pulled the car to the side of the road to see what it was, but the rain was so strong, and sea water was beginning to creep across the highway, so he figured the safest thing was to keep going.

He did so. And as the rocks came tumbling down, enveloping his car, his last thought was of Lara.

☆ ☆ ☆

Now Joey was fighting with the woman who'd cut him. She was as big as any man, and strong, but at least he'd gotten her off Lara.

'You ignorant scum – get out of here!' Alison screamed. 'Or I'll cut you like a stuffed pig. Out of my way, you fucker!'

He attempted to prise the knife out of her hands as they struggled. Grabbing the wrist of her knife hand, he bent it back until she yelped with pain. But still she held on.

They were on their feet now, rocking toward the side of the terrace.

He made a concentrated lunge to get the knife. They fell against the fence, and with that, the flimsy fence – badly in need of repair – gave way, and they both began falling down the side of the cliff toward the roaring ocean below.

Joey's life flashed before him. Somewhere Lara was screaming. Desperately he tried to hold on to something, somehow or other managing to grab the branch of a tree.

Alison Sewell wasn't so lucky. He could hear her blood-curdling screams as she smashed into the sea below.

In excruciating pain, he tried to haul himself up the side of the cliff. Below him he could hear the raging surf, waves beating against the bottom, hungry for another victim.

'Joey, Joey!' Somewhere Lara was desperately calling his name.

'Down here!' he yelled. 'Get a rope, a sheet, anything. Dunno if I can make it on my own.'

'Joey, you've got to make it. You have to. For me!' She

was screaming over the noise of the wind. The sound of her voice gave him hope.

Then he felt the branch start to give. Was this how it ended?

Oh, sweet Jesus. Was this it?

ONE YEAR LATER

THE BEST of Hollywood turned out for Richard Barry's memorial service. The two women he'd been married to arranged it, making sure every detail was exactly as he would have wanted. Both of them were dressed in black – a sign of respect for the man they missed. For when he was good he had been very very good. And when he was bad, he'd been a total asshole.

In April, Richard had won a posthumous Oscar for *French Summer*. Lara Ivory, the star of the film, had made the presentation. Nikki Barry, his widow, had accepted on his behalf. The added bonus was that Nikki also won for best costume designer. A double celebration.

Now they were honouring the man who at one time had meant so much to them. An Oscar-winning director killed in an unavoidable act of nature.

☆ ☆ ☆

Linden arrived with Cassie. Since her unfortunate car accident she'd lost forty pounds, and somehow or other an improbable romance had blossomed between her and Lara's publicist.

She'd left Lara's employ, and now worked as a partner in Linden's firm. They were very happy together.

Mick Stefan wandered in next. He'd handed over his new white Rolls Royce to a parking valet, and was now worried that the guy might scratch it. *Revenge* had opened to critical acclaim and excellent box office, and Mick was currently directing a sixty-million-dollar-budget action adventure movie starring Johnny Romano and Norman Barton as two mis-matched cops.

He had a seventeen-year-old French movie star girlfriend, and a new mansion in Bel Air.

Mick Stefan was on a roll.

Summer came with Reggie Coleman, a boy she'd met in high school. He was a year older than she, handsome and nice with no secondary agenda. He made her feel good about herself. In fact, he made her feel sixteen, and it was a nice feeling.

She lived at home with Nikki and planned to attend USC Film School when the time came.

Summer was finally enjoying being a teenager.

Aiden Sean made it to the ceremony late. He'd spent the last year in and out of drug rehab. He tried his best, but it wasn't easy.

Nikki remained his good friend, always there for him.

Their romance was dead – a mutual decision.

☆ ☆ ☆

Tina didn't make it at all. She'd been 'discovered' by Cluny, and whisked off to New York to be a model. So far she'd appeared on three magazine covers, and was currently shooting a spread for the *Sports Illustrated* swimsuit edition.

She and Cluny had become more than friends.

☆ ☆ ☆

Nikki watched her gorgeous daughter walk into the ceremony. It was amazing what a little love, attention and caring could do. She was so proud of Summer – what a transformation!

Sheldon had returned to Chicago a much chastened man. Summer had refused to take action against him, and in return for her silence, he'd promised never to see or contact her again. Nikki considered this far too lenient a punishment.

Since working with Mick on the post-production of *Revenge*, Nikki had the producing bug in a big way. She'd read countless scripts and books, but had not discovered anything that fired her imagination, until one day, while sorting through Richard's personal papers, she'd come upon a fascinating manuscript written in the first person. She'd started to read, and become totally hooked. It was the story of a young man who runs away from home at sixteen and then lives a wild and interesting life – becoming everything from a thief to a male hustler to a movie star in Asia. The opening lines of the manuscript had really grabbed her attention: *Here's the truth of it – I can fuck any woman I want any time I want – no problem.*

The manuscript ended with a brutal murder, after which the protagonist takes off for Mexico.

Had Richard written it? Since there was no author's name attached, she assumed that he had – which was really something, because the material was so raunchy and un-Richard-like. Still . . . it was a powerful read, and she was sure it would make a fantastic movie. She'd hired a writer, and was now busy developing the script. She even had an actor in mind for the lead. Joey Lorenzo. He would certainly do the role justice.

☆ ☆ ☆

And as for Lara and Joey, true love, soulmates – call it what you like – they'd recognized a certain sadness and need in each other, and although the sex was just as great as ever, it was the mutual need and understanding that had drawn them together. They were inseparable. Fate ruled.

Lara shuddered whenever she remembered the night of the storm. How she'd summoned the strength to drag Joey up from the side of the cliff she'd never know. God must have put his hand on her shoulder and helped her.

Nobody could help Alison Sewell. Her body washed up three miles down the coast, five days later. There was a brief investigation. Nobody cared. Only Lara, who paid for a proper burial.

Joey confessed everything about his past. He bared his soul with searing honesty and Lara believed him. In return, she'd told him about *her* demons, the nightmare stories she'd never revealed to anyone.

They were married quietly a month later in Santa Barbara. Six weeks after that Joey landed a key role in a movie starring

Charlie Dollar, following that with the lead in a low-budget thriller. He was good. He was very good.

☆ ☆ ☆

The memorial service was a fitting tribute to Richard Barry. Many people he'd worked with got up and spoke. There were tears and there was laughter. Summer made a particularly moving speech – calling Richard the father she'd never had.

As Lara and Joey walked away from the service, she reached out for his hand. 'Joey,' she murmured, thinking how handsome he was, and how much she loved him, 'there's something I've been meaning to remind you about.'

'What?' he asked, thinking she was just as beautiful inside as she was out, and that he was possibly the luckiest man in the world.

'You owe me a honeymoon,' she said softly.

He lifted her hand to his lips. 'I know. We leave for Tahiti tomorrow.'

'Joey!'

'Don't fight it. Look what happened last time we didn't go to Tahiti!'

She smiled, basking in the glow of his love. 'That's true.'

'Have I ever let you down?'

'No. Never.'

And as they reached their limo, the paparazzi pressed forward, multiple flashbulbs blinding them.

And Lara knew she would never be frightened of anything again because she had Joey beside her, and he was her world.